WAR STORM

WAR
STORM

VICTORIA AVEYARD

ORION

First published in Great Britain in 2018 by Orion Books,
an imprint of The Orion Publishing Group Ltd
Carmelite House, 50 Victoria Embankment,
London EC4Y 0DZ

An Hachette UK company

1 3 5 7 9 10 8 6 4 2

Copyright © Victoria Aveyard 2018

A CIP catalogue record for this book is
available from the British Library.

ISBN (Hardback) 978 1 4091 7598 8
ISBN (Trade Paperback) 978 1 4091 7880 4

Printed and bound by CPI Group (UK) Ltd, Croydon, CR0 4YY

MIX
Paper from
responsible sources
FSC® C104740

www.orionbooks.co.uk

to my parents, to my friends, to me, and to you

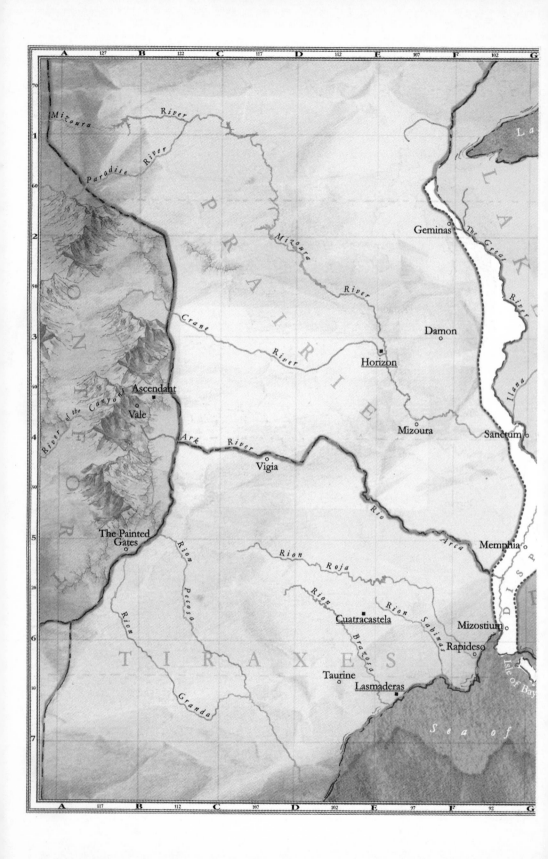

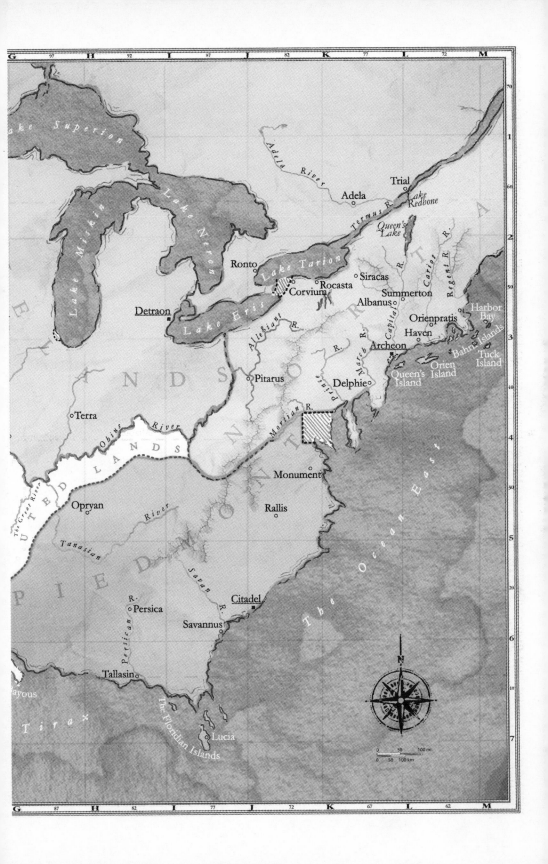

ONE
Mare

We drown in silence for a long moment.

Corvium yawns around us, full of people, but it feels empty.

Divide and conquer.

The implications are clear, the lines sharply drawn. Farley and Davidson regard me with equal intensity, and I stare back at them.

I suppose Cal has no idea, no inkling, that the Scarlet Guard and Montfort have absolutely no intention of letting him keep whatever throne he wins. I suppose he cares more about the crown than about whatever any Red thinks. And I suppose I shouldn't call him Cal anymore.

Tiberias Calore. King Tiberias. Tiberias the Seventh.

It's the name he was born with, the name he wore when I met him.

Thief, he called me then. That was my name.

I wish I could forget the last hour. Fall backward just a little bit. Falter. Stumble. Enjoy one more second of that strangely blissful place where the only thing I felt was the ache of tired muscles and repaired bones. The emptiness after battle's adrenaline. The certainty of his love and support. And even through the heartbreak, I can't find it in myself to hate him for his choice. The rage will come later.

Concern crosses Farley's face. It seems strange on her. I'm more accustomed to cold determination or red anger from Diana Farley. She notes my stare with a twitch of her scarred mouth.

"I'll relay Cal's decision to the rest of Command," she says, breaking the silent tension. Her words are low and measured. "*Just* Command. Ada will carry the message."

The Montfort premier ducks his chin in agreement. "Good. I think Generals Drummer and Swan may have an idea of these developments already. They've been keeping tabs on the Lerolan queen since she came into play."

"Anabel Lerolan was in Maven's court long enough, at least a few weeks," I reply. Somehow, my voice doesn't tremble. The words come out evenly, full of force. I have to look strong, even if I don't feel it right now. It's a lie, but a good lie. "She probably has more information than I ever gave you."

"Probably," Davidson says with a thoughtful bob of the head. He narrows his eyes on the ground. Not searching, but focusing. A plan spirals out in front of him. The road ahead won't be easy. A child would know that. "Which is why I have to get back up there," he adds, almost in apology. As if I could be angry with him for doing what he must. "Ears and eyes open, yeah?"

"Ears and eyes open," Farley and I respond in unison, surprising each other.

He steps away from us, backing out of the alleyway. The sun flashes in his glossy gray hair. He was careful to clean up after the battle, washing away the sweat and ash, replacing his bloodstained uniform with a fresh one. All to present his usual calm, collected, and strangely ordinary demeanor. A wise decision. Silvers devote so much energy to their appearance, to the false pride of visible strength and power. And none so much as the Samos king and his family in the tower above us. Next to Volo, Evangeline, Ptolemus, and the hissing Viper queen, Davidson barely registers. He could blend into the walls if he wanted to. *They won't see him coming. They won't see us coming.*

I take a shaky breath and swallow, forcing the next thought. *And Cal won't either.*

Tiberias, I snap at myself. One fist clenches, digging nails into flesh with a satisfying sting. *Call him Tiberias.*

The black walls of Corvium feel strangely silent and bare without the siege. I turn away from Davidson's retreating form to eye the parapets ringing the inner ward of the fortress city. The shiver attacking snowstorm is long gone, the darkness lifted, and everything here seems smaller now. Less imposing. Red soldiers used to be herded through this city, most on the march to inevitable death in a trench. Now Reds patrol the walls, the streets, the gates. Reds sit alongside Silver kings and speak of war. A few soldiers with crimson scarves walk back and forth, their eyes darting, well-used guns ready in hand. The Scarlet Guard will not be caught unawares, though they have little reason to be so on edge. For now, anyway. Maven's armies have retreated. And not even Volo Samos is bold enough to attempt an attack from the inside of Corvium. Not when he needs the Guard, needs Montfort, needs us. And especially not with Cal—*Tiberias, you fool*—and all his empty talk of equality. Like us, Volo needs him. Needs his name, needs his crown, and needs his damn hand in that damn marriage to his damn daughter.

My face burns hot. I feel embarrassed by the plume of jealousy rising up inside me. Losing him should be the least of my worries. Losing him shouldn't hurt as much as the possibility of dying, of losing our war, of letting everything we've worked for be in vain. But it does. All I can do is try to bear it.

Why didn't I say yes?

I walked away from his offer. From him. I was torn apart by another betrayal—Cal's betrayal, but also mine. *I love you* is a promise we both made, and we both broke. It should mean *I choose you above all else. I want you more. I need you always. I cannot live without you. I will do anything to keep our lives from parting.*

But he wouldn't. And I won't.

I am less than his crown, and he is less than my cause.

And less, far less, than my fear of another cage. *Consort,* he said, offering me an impossible crown. He would make me a queen, if Evangeline could be pushed aside *again*. I already know what the world looks like from a king's right hand. I don't care to live that life again. Even though Cal is not Maven, the throne is still the same. It changes people, corrupts them.

What a strange fate that would have been. Cal with his crown and his Samos queen and me. In spite of myself, a small part of me wishes I'd said yes. It would have been easy. A chance to let go, step back, *win*—and enjoy a world I never could have dreamed of. Give my family the best life possible. Keep us all safe. And stay with him. Stand at Cal's side, a Red girl with a Silver king on her arm. With the power to change the world. To kill Maven. To sleep without nightmares, and live without fear.

I bite my lip sharply to drive away the want. It seduces, and I almost understand his choice. Even ripped apart, we suit each other.

Farley shifts loudly, drawing my attention. She sighs as she puts her back to the alley wall, arms folded across her chest. Unlike Davidson, she hasn't bothered to change out of her bloody uniform. Hers isn't as disgusting as mine, free of mud and muck. There's silver blood on her, of course, now dried black. It's only been a few months since Clara was born, and she wears the lingering weight around her hips proudly. Whatever sympathy she had disappears, replaced by a rage sparking in her blue eyes. Not directed at me, though. She looks skyward, at the tower above us. Where the strange council of Silvers and Reds now tries to decide our fates.

"That was him in there." She doesn't wait for me to ask who. "Silver hair, thick neck, ridiculous armor. And somehow still breathing, even though he put a blade through Shade's heart."

My nails dig deeper at the thought of Ptolemus Samos. Prince of the Rift. My brother's killer. Like Farley, I feel a sudden rage too. And an equal burst of shame.

"Yes."

"Because you made a bargain with his sister. Your freedom for his life."

"For my vengeance," I mumble in admission. "And yes, I gave Evangeline my word."

Farley bares her teeth, her disgust evident. "You gave a Silver your word. That promise is less than ash."

"But a promise still."

She makes a guttural sound deep in her throat, like a growl. Her broad shoulders square and she turns her body to face the tower fully. I wonder how much restraint it's taking to stop her from marching back up there to rip Ptolemus's eyes out of his skull. I wouldn't stop her if she could. In fact, I'd pull up a chair and watch.

I let my fist open a bit, putting away the slice of pain. Quietly, I take a step forward, closing the space between us. After a split second of hesitation, I put a hand on her arm. "A promise *I* made. Not you. Not anyone else."

Farley stills a bit, and her snarl becomes a smirk. She turns to look at me head-on, her eyes brightly blue as they catch a shaft of sunlight. "I think you might be better suited to politics than war, Mare Barrow."

I offer a pained smile. "They're the same thing." A hard lesson I think I've finally learned. "Do you think you can do it? Kill him?"

Once, I would have expected her to scoff and boldly sneer at the implication she couldn't. Farley is a hard woman with a harder shell. She's what she needs to be. But something—Shade probably, Clara definitely, the bond we now share—affords me a glimpse past the general's stony and sure exterior. She falters, her smirk fading a little.

"I don't know," she murmurs. "But I'll never be able to look at myself, look at Clara, if I don't try."

"And neither will I, if I let you die in the attempt." My grip tightens on her arm. "Please, don't be stupid about this."

Like the flip of a switch, her smirk returns in full force. She even winks. "Since when am I stupid, Mare Barrow?"

Looking up at her sends a twinge through the scars at the back of my neck, scars I almost forgot about. The pain of them seems small compared to everything else. "I just wonder where it will end," I murmur, hoping to make her understand.

She shakes her head. "I can't respond to a question with too many answers."

"I mean . . . with Shade. Ptolemus. You kill him, and then what? Evangeline kills you? Kills Clara? I kill Evangeline? On and on, with no end?" I'm no stranger to death, but this feels oddly different. Calculated endings. It feels like something Maven would do, not us. Even though Farley marked Ptolemus for death long before, when I masqueraded as Mareena Titanos, that was for the Guard. For a cause, for something other than blind and bloody revenge.

Her eyes widen, vibrant and impossible. "You want me to let him live?"

"Of course not," I almost snap. "I don't know what I want. I don't know what I'm talking about." The words tumble over one another. "But I can still wonder, Farley. I know what vengeance and rage can do to a person, to the people around you. And of course I don't want Clara to grow up without her mother."

She turns away sharply, hiding her face. But not quickly enough to hide a sudden surge of tears. They never fall. With a jerk of her shoulder, she shrugs me away.

I push on. I have to. She needs to hear this. "She already lost Shade, and if given the choice between revenge for her father and a living mother—I know what she would choose."

"Speaking of choices," she grinds out, still not looking at me. "I'm proud of the one you made."

"Farley, don't change the subject—"

"Did you hear me, lightning girl?" She sniffs and forces a smile, turning back around to reveal a now very red and splotchy face. "I said I'm proud of you. Write that down. Commit it to memory. You probably won't hear it again."

In spite of myself, I chuckle darkly. "Fine. Proud of what exactly?"

"Well, besides your fashion sense"—she dusts off my shoulder, brushing away a bit of bloody dirt—"and of course your kind and calm disposition . . ."

Another chuckle.

". . . I'm proud of you because I know what it's like to lose the person you love." This time she takes me by the arm, probably so I can't run away from a conversation I don't think I'm equipped to have.

Mare, choose me. The words are only an hour old. They haunt me so easily.

"It felt like a betrayal," I whisper.

I focus on Farley's chin so I don't have to look into her eyes. The scar at the left corner of her mouth is deep, pulling her lips to the side a little. A clean drag. Knife work. She didn't have it when I first met her, by the light of a blue candle in Will Whistle's old wagon.

"From him? Of course—"

"No. Not from him." A cloud crosses the sky overhead, sending shifting shadows across us both. The summer breeze blows oddly cold. I shiver against it. As if on instinct, I wish for Cal and his warm presence. He never let me get cold. My stomach lurches at the thought, sick to think of what we both walked away from. "He made promises to me," I continue, "but I made promises to him too. I broke them. And he has other promises to keep. To himself, to his dead father. He loved the crown before he loved me, whether he knows it or not. And in the end, he thinks he's doing the right thing for us, for *everyone*. How can I really fault him for that?"

With a will, I meet Farley's eyes and search. She doesn't have an answer for me, at least not one I would like. Her teeth worry at her lip, biting back whatever she wants to say. It doesn't work.

She scoffs, trying to be her version of gentle. As prickly as ever. "Don't apologize for him and what he is."

"I'm not."

"It certainly sounds like it," she sighs, exasperated. "A different king is *still* a king. He might be a brick, but he knows that much."

"Maybe it could have been the right thing for me too. For Reds.

Who knows what a Red queen could have done?"

"Very little, Mare. If anything at all," she says with cold surety. "Any change that might come from putting a crown on your head would be too slow, too small." Her voice softens. "And too easily undone. It wouldn't last. Whatever we accomplished would die with you. Don't take this the wrong way, but the world we want to build has to outlive us."

For the ones who come after.

Farley's eyes bore into me, intense with her almost inhuman focus. Clara has Shade's eyes, not Farley's. Honey, not ocean. I wonder which pieces of her will one day belong to Farley or to Shade.

The breeze rustles Farley's freshly shorn hair, dark gold in the shadow of the clouds. Beneath the scars, she's still young, just another child of war and ruin. She's seen worse than me, done more than I ever have. Sacrificed and suffered more too. Her mother, her sister, my brother and his love. Whoever she dreamed of being when she was a little girl. All gone. If she can keep pushing forward, still believing in what we're doing, so can I. For as much as we butt heads, I trust Farley. And her words are an unfamiliar but needed comfort. I've already spent so much time in my own head, arguing with myself, that I'm beginning to get sick of it.

"You're right." Something inside me lets go, allowing the strange dream of Cal's offer to spiral into darkness. Never to return.

I will not be a Red queen.

Farley gives my shoulder an almost painful squeeze. Despite the healers, I'm still sore, and she still has a wickedly strong grip. "Besides," she adds, "it wouldn't be you on the throne. The Lerolan queen and the king of the Rift were very clear. It would be her, the Samos girl."

I snort at the notion. Evangeline Samos made her intentions obvious enough back in the council chamber. I'm surprised Farley didn't notice. "Not if she can help it."

"Hmm?" Her gaze sharpens and I shrug.

"You saw what she did in there, how she provoked you." The fresh memory flashes. Evangeline calling upon a Red servant in front of everyone, smashing a goblet, forcing the poor maid to clean it up, simply for the sport of it. To anger every red-blooded person in the room. It's not hard to understand why she did it, or what she hoped to accomplish. "She wants no part of this alliance, not when it means she has to marry . . . Tiberias."

For once, Farley seems caught off guard. She blinks, perplexed. Albeit intrigued. "But she's back where she started. I thought—I mean, I don't pretend to understand Silver behavior at all, but still—"

"Evangeline is a princess in her own right now, with everything she ever wanted. I don't think she wants to go back to being someone else's. That's all their betrothal ever was to her. And him," I add, with a pang of heartache. "An arrangement for power. Power she already has now, or"—my words falter a little—"power she doesn't want anymore." I think back on Evangeline, on my time spent with her in Whitefire. She was relieved when Maven married Iris Cygnet instead of her. And not just because he was a monster. I think because . . . there was someone else she cared about more. More than herself or Maven's crown.

Elane Haven. After her house rebelled against him, I remember Maven called her Evangeline's whore. I didn't notice Elane at the council, but much of House Haven stands behind House Samos, allied to them. Shadows all, able to disappear at will. I suppose Elane could have been there the whole time and I wouldn't even know it.

"You think she would try to *undo* her father's work? If she could?"

Farley looks very much like a cat that just caught a particularly fat mouse for supper. "If someone . . . *helped* her?"

Cal didn't deny the crown for love. But would Evangeline?

Something tells me she might. All her maneuvering, the quiet resistance, walking a razor's edge.

"It's possible." The words take on new meaning to both of us. New weight. "She has motivations of her own. And I think that gives us a bit of an advantage."

Farley's lips curve, taking on the shadow of a true smile. In spite of all I've learned, I feel a sudden burst of hope. She thumps me on the arm, her grin spreading.

"Well, Barrow, write it down again. I'm damn proud of you."

"I do prove useful from time to time."

She barks a laugh and steps away, gesturing for me to follow. The avenue outside the alley beckons, its flagstones gleaming as the last of the snow melts beneath the summer sun. I hesitate, reluctant to leave this corner of dark safety. The world beyond this narrow space still seems too big. The inner ward of Corvium looms, and the core tower stands at the center of it all. With a shaky breath, I force myself to move. The first step aches. So does the second.

"You don't have to go back up," Farley mutters, falling in at my side. She glares at the tower. "I'll let you know how it shakes out. Davidson and I can handle it."

The thought of going back to the council chamber, sitting there in silence as Tiberias throws everything we've ever done in my face—I don't know if I can bear it. But I have to. I notice things the others can't. Know things others don't. I have to go back. For the cause.

And for *him*.

I can't deny how much I want to go back for him.

"I want to know everything you know," I whisper to Farley. "Everything Davidson has planned. I'm not going into anything else blind."

She agrees quickly. Almost too quickly. "Of course."

"I'm yours to use. In any way. On one condition."

"Name it."

My steps slow, and she matches my pace. "He lives. At the end of all this."

Like a confused dog, she tips her head.

"Break his crown, break his throne, rip his monarchy apart." I stare up at her with as much strength as I can muster. The lightning in my blood responds with fervor, begging to crack loose. "But Tiberias lives."

Farley sucks in a searing breath, drawing herself up to her full, formidable height. It feels like she can see right through me. To my imperfect heart. I hold my ground. I've earned the right.

Her voice wavers. "I can't make that promise. But I'll try. I'll certainly try, Mare."

At least she doesn't lie to me.

I feel cut in two, torn in different directions. An obvious question hangs in my mind. Another choice that I might need to make. *His life or our victory?* I don't know which side I might choose, if I ever have to. Which side I might betray. The knife of that knowledge cuts deep, and I bleed where no one else can see.

I suppose this is what the seer was talking about. Jon spoke very little, but everything he said had calculated meaning. As much as I don't want to, I suppose I have to accept the fate he foretold.

To rise.

And rise alone.

The flagstones roll beneath me, passing with each step. The breeze kicks up again, blowing in from the west this time. It carries with it the unmistakable tang of blood. I fight the urge to retch as it all comes rushing back. The siege. The bodies. The blood in both colors. My wrist snapping clean in a stoneskin's grasp. Necks broken, chests obliterated in bursts of flesh, glistening organs, and spiked bone. In the battle, it was easy to detach from such horror. Necessary, even. The fear would only get me killed. Not anymore. My heartbeat triples in speed and cold sweat breaks across my body. Even though we survived and *won*, the terror of loss ripped open canyons inside me.

I can still feel them. The nerves, the electric paths my lightning traced in every person I killed. Like thin, glowing branches, each one different but also the same. Too many to count. In red and blue uniforms, Nortan and Lakelander. All Silvers.

I hope.

The possibility hits me like a punch in the gut. Maven has used Reds for cannon fodder before, or as human shields. I didn't even think about it. None of us did—or maybe the others didn't care. Davidson, Cal, maybe even Farley, if she thought the outcome was worth the cost.

"Hey," she murmurs, taking my wrist. Her skin on mine makes me jump, her fingers circling like a manacle. I break her grip forcefully, twisting away with what sounds like a snarl. I flush, embarrassed that I still react this way.

She pulls back, palms up, eyes wide. But no fear, no judgment. Not even pity. Is that *understanding* I see in her? "I'm sorry," she says quickly. "I forgot about the wrists."

I barely bob my head, shoving my hands into my pockets to hide the purple sparks at my fingertips. "It's fine. That's not even—"

"I know, Mare. It happens when we slow down. The body starts to process more again. Sometimes it's too much, and there's no shame in it." Farley tips her head, gesturing away from the tower. "There's no shame in getting some rack time either. The barracks are—"

"Were there Reds out there?" I gesture blankly, toward the battlefield and the now-broken walls of Corvium. "Did Maven and the Lakelanders send Red soldiers with the rest?"

Farley blinks, truly taken aback. "Not to my knowledge," she finally replies, and I hear the unease in her. She doesn't know either. She doesn't *want* to know, and neither do I. I can't bear it.

I spin on my heel, forcing her to keep up with my pace for once. Silence falls again, this one brimming with anger and shame in equal measure. I lean into it, torturing myself. To remember this disgust and pain. More battles will come. More people will die, no matter the color of blood. That's war. That's revolution. And others will be caught in the crossfire. To forget is to doom them again, and doom others to come.

As we ascend the steps of the tower, I keep my hands firmly fisted in my pockets. The prick of an earring stings my flesh, the red stone warm against my hand. I should throw it out a window. If there's one thing I should forget, it's him.

But the earring remains.

Side by side, we enter the council chamber again. The edges of my vision blur, and I try to fall into a familiar place. Observe. Memorize. Look for cracks in the words spoken, find secrets and lies in what they leave unsaid. It's a goal as much as a distraction. And I realize why I was so keen on coming back here, even when I had every right to run away.

Not because this is important. Not because I can be of use.

But because I am selfish, weak, and afraid. I can't be alone with myself, not now, not yet.

So I sit, and I listen, and I watch.

And through it all, I feel his eyes.

TWO
Evangeline

It would be easy to kill her.

Spindles of rose gold weave between the red, black, and orange jewels at Anabel Lerolan's neck. One twitch and I could slice the oblivion's jugular. Bleed out her body and her scheme. End her life and her betrothal in front of everyone in the room. My mother, my father, Cal—not to mention the Red criminals and foreign freaks we find ourselves tied to. Not Barrow, though. She hasn't returned yet. Probably still wailing over her lost prince.

It would mean another war, of course, shattering an alliance already spiderwebbed with cracks. Could I do such a thing—trade my loyalties for happiness? It feels shameful just to ask the question, even in the safety of my own head.

The old woman must feel my gaze. Her eyes flick to me for a second, the smirk on her lips unmistakable as she settles back into her chair, resplendent in red, black, and orange.

Those are Calore colors, not just Lerolan. Her allegiances are abrasively clear.

Shivering, I drop my gaze and focus on my hands instead. One of my nails is horribly cracked. Broken in battle. With a breath, I mold one of my titanium rings into a claw, drawing it over my finger into a talon. I click it against the arm of my throne, if only to annoy Mother. She glances at me out of the corner of her eye, the only evidence of her disdain.

I fantasize about killing Anabel a little too long, losing track of the council as they scheme in their wretched circles. Our numbers have dwindled, leaving only the collected leaders of our hastily united factions. Generals, lords, captains, and royalty. The Montfort leader speaks, then Father, then Anabel, and over again. All in restrained tones, forcing false smiles and empty promises.

I wish Elane were here. I should have brought her. She asked to come. In truth, she begged. Elane has always wanted to keep close, even in the face of lethal danger. I try not to think of our last moments together, her body in my arms. She's thinner than I am, but softer. Ptolemus waited outside my door, making sure we weren't disturbed.

"Let me go with you," she whispered in my ear, a dozen times, a hundred times. But her father and mine forbade it.

Enough, Evangeline.

I curse at myself now. They would have never known in the middle of the chaos. Elane's a shadow, after all, and an invisible girl is easy to smuggle. Tolly would have helped. He wouldn't stop his wife from coming along, not if I asked for his aid. But I couldn't. There was a battle to be won first, a battle I didn't know if we could win. And I wasn't about to take that risk with her. She's talented, but Elane Haven is no warrior. And in the thick of it, she would only be a distraction and a worry for me. I could afford neither then. But now . . .

Stop it.

My fingers curl against the arms of my throne, begging to carve the iron into ragged pieces. At home, the many metal galleries of Ridge House made for easy therapy. I could destroy in peace. Channel any fresh rage into constantly changing statues, without having to worry about what anyone else might think. I wonder if I might find some privacy here in Corvium to do just that. The promise of such release keeps me sane. I scratch the clawed ring on my chair, metal on metal. Soft enough that only Mother hears. She can't scold me for it, not in front of the rest of our strange council. If I have to be on display, I might as well enjoy the few advantages.

Finally, I wrench my thoughts away from Anabel's vulnerable neck and Elane's absence. If I'm going to figure a way out of my father's plan, I have to at least pay attention.

"Their army is on the retreat. King Maven's forces cannot be allowed the time to regroup," Father says coolly. Behind him, the tall windows of the tower show the sun beginning its descent into the clouds lingering on the western horizon. The obliterated landscape still smokes. "He's licking his wounds."

"The boy is already into the Choke," Queen Anabel is quick to reply. *The boy.* She refers to Maven like he isn't her grandson. I suppose she won't acknowledge that anymore. Not after he helped kill her son, King Tiberias. Maven isn't her blood, but Elara's and Elara's alone.

Anabel leans forward on her elbows, clasping her wrinkled hands together. Her old wedding ring, battered but gleaming, winks on one finger. When she took us all by surprise at Ridge House, announcing her intention to back her grandson, she wore no metal to speak of. To hide from our magnetron senses. Now she wears it openly, daring us to use her crown or her jewelry against her. Every part of her is a calculated choice. And she is not without weapons of her own. Anabel was a warrior before she was a queen, an officer at the Lakelander front. She is an oblivion, and her touch is deadly, able to obliterate and explode something—or *someone*.

If I didn't hate what she's forcing me into, I would respect her dedication at the very least.

"And at this hour, most of his forces will be beyond Maiden Falls and over the border," she adds. "They're in the Lakelands now."

"The Lakelander army is wounded too, just as vulnerable. We should strike while we can, even just to pick off the stragglers." My father looks from Anabel to one of our Silver lords. "The Laris fleet can be ready inside the hour, can't they?"

Lord General Laris sharpens under my father's gaze. His flask is empty now, leaving him to enjoy the drunken haze of victory. He coughs, clearing his throat. I can smell the alcohol on his breath from across the chamber. "It can, Your Majesty. You need only give the command."

A low voice cuts him off. "I'll oppose it if you do."

Cal's first words since returning from his spat with Mare Barrow are certainly not wasted. Like his grandmother, he wears black trimmed with red, having long ago discarded the borrowed uniform he wore in battle. He shifts in his seat next to Anabel, taking his assigned position as her cause and king. His uncle, Julian of House Jacos, holds his left while the Lerolan queen has his right. Flanked by both of them, Silvers of noble and powerful blood, he presents a united front. A worthy king for us to champion.

I hate him for it.

Cal could have ended my misery, broken our betrothal, refused Father's offer of my hand. But for the crown, he threw Mare away. For the crown, he trapped me.

"What?" is all Father says. He is a man of few words, and even fewer questions. Just to hear him ask is unsettling, and I tense in spite of myself.

Cal draws back his shoulders, quietly spreading his broad frame. He rests his chin on his knuckles, brows knitted together in thought. He seems larger, older, smarter. On the same playing field as the king of the Rift.

"I said I would oppose an order to dispatch the Air Fleet, or any detachment of our coalition, to give chase into hostile territory," Cal replies steadily. I have to admit, even without a crown, he has a royal way about him. An air that commands attention, if not respect. Not surprising, since he was trained for this, and Cal is nothing if not a very obedient student. His grandmother purses her lips into a tight but genuine smile. She's proud of him. "The Choke is still a literal minefield, and we have very little intelligence to guide us on the other side of the falls. It could be a trap. I won't risk soldiers on it."

"Every piece of this war is risk," I hear Ptolemus say from the other side of my father. He flexes as Cal did, drawing himself up to his full height in his throne. The setting sun gives Tolly's hair a reddish tint, making his oiled silver locks glow beneath his prince's crown. The same light bathes Cal in his house colors, red in his eyes while black shadows lengthen behind him. The pair hold each other's gaze in the strange way men do. *Everything's a competition,* I scoff to myself.

"Such insight, Prince Ptolemus," Anabel says, her tone dry. "But His Majesty, the king of Norta, is well aware of what war is. And I agree with his assessment."

Already she calls him king. I'm not the only one to notice her choice of words.

Cal lowers his eyes, stunned. He recovers quickly, jaw clenched in resolution. His choice is already made. *No going back now, Calore.*

The Montfort premier, Davidson, nods from his seat at his own table. Without the Scarlet Guard commander and Mare Barrow, he's easy to ignore. I almost forgot about him entirely.

"I concur," he says. Even his voice is bland, without inflection or accent. "Our armies need time to recover as well, and this *coalition* needs time to find . . ." He stops, thinking. I still can't read his expression, and it annoys me to no end. I wonder if even a whisper could slip past his mental shields. "Balance."

Mother is not as stoic as my father, and she fixes on the newblood leader with her smoldering black stare. Her snake mimics her action, blinking at the premier. "So is there no intelligence, are there no spies across the border? Forgive me, sir, but I was under the impression that the Scarlet Guard"—she almost spits it out—"had an intricate spy network in both Norta and the Lakelands. Certainly they can be of use, unless the Reds misrepresent themselves and their *strength*." Disgust drips from her words like poison from fangs.

"Our operatives are in order, Your Majesty."

The Red general, the blond woman with the permanent sneer, pushes into the room with Mare on her heels. Both stalk from the doorway at the edge of the chamber, crossing the council room to sit with Davidson. They move quickly and silently, as if they could somehow avoid being watched by the entire room.

While she settles into her chair, Mare keeps her eyes forward, locked on me, of all people. To my surprise, I feel a strange emotion beneath her gaze. *Could this be shame? No, not possible.* Even so, heat rises in my cheeks. I hope I'm not blushing, either in anger or embarrassment. Both churn inside me, and for good reason. I look away, turning on Cal, if only to distract myself with the one person more wretched than I feel.

He certainly *tries* to look unaffected by her presence, but Cal isn't his brother. Unlike Maven, Cal has little skill in masking his emotions. A silver blush blooms beneath his skin, coloring his cheeks, neck, and even the tops of his ears. The temperature in the room rises a little, rippling with whatever emotion he's fighting. *What a fool,* I sneer in my head. *You made your choice, Calore. You doomed us both. You can at least pretend to keep it together. If anyone is going to lose their mind to heartbreak, it should be me.*

I almost expect him to start mewling like a lost kitten. Instead he blinks furiously, ripping his eyes away from the lightning girl. One fist clenches on the arm of his chair, and the flamemaker bracelet on his wrist glows red with the dying sun. He keeps himself in check. It doesn't ignite, and neither does he.

Mare is a stone compared to Cal. Rigid, unyielding, unfeeling. Not even a spark. She just keeps staring at me. It's unnerving, but not a challenge. Her eyes are strangely devoid of her usual anger. They certainly aren't kind, of course, but they aren't brimming with disgust either. I guess the lightning girl has little reason to hate me right now. My chest tightens—does she know this wasn't my choice? *She must.*

"Good of you to return, Miss Barrow," I tell her, and I mean it. She's always a guaranteed distraction for Calore princes.

She doesn't respond, only folding her arms.

Her companion, the Scarlet Guard general, is not so inclined to silence. Unfortunately. She scowls at my mother, tempting fate. "Our operatives are currently in relay, tracking King Maven's army as they retreat. We've received word that his troops are on a hard march to Detraon, moving with speed. Maven himself, and a few of his generals, boarded ships on Lake Eris. Supposedly bound for Detraon as well.

There's talk of a funeral for the Lakelander king. And they have far more healers than we do. Whoever survived the battle will be back to fighting shape quicker than we will."

Anabel scowls, cutting a glare at Father. "Yes, House Skonos still remains split between our factions, with the majority remaining loyal to the usurper." *As if that's our fault. We did what we could, convinced who we could.* "Not to mention the Lakelands have skin-healer houses of their own."

With a sweeping hand and a tight smile, Davidson inclines his head. Wrinkles form at the corner of his eyes, marking his age. I suspect he's forty or so, but it's difficult to tell for sure.

He touches his fingers to his brow in some kind of strange salute or promise. "Montfort will provide. I plan to petition for more healers, both Silver and Ardent."

"Petition?" Father sneers. The other Silvers match his confusion, and I find myself glancing down our line to meet Tolly's eye. He furrows his brow. He doesn't know what Davidson means. My stomach flops a bit, and I bite my lip against the sensation. Usually whatever one of us lacks, the other provides. But in this, we're both at sea. *And so is Father.* Angry as I am with him, this scares me more than anything else. Father can't protect us from what he doesn't understand.

Mare doesn't understand either, wrinkling her nose in confusion. *These people,* I curse to myself. I wonder if even the scowling, scarred woman knows what Davidson means.

The premier himself gives a small chuckle. *The old man is enjoying this.* He lowers his eyes, letting dark lashes brush against his cheeks. If he wanted to, he could be handsome. I suppose it doesn't serve whatever agenda he has. "I'm not a king, as you all know." He looks back up and turns his gaze on Father, then Cal, then Anabel. "I serve at the will of my people, and my people have other elected politicians to represent their interests. They must be in agreement. When I return to Montfort to request more troops—"

"*Return?*" Cal echoes, and Davidson stops short. "When did you plan to tell us this?"

After a moment, Davidson shrugs. "Now."

Mare's lips twist. Fighting a scowl or a smirk, I can't tell. But probably the latter.

I'm not the only one to notice. Cal's eyes flicker, looking between her and the premier with a growing suspicion. "And what will we do in your absence, Premier?" he demands. "Wait? Or fight with one hand tied behind our backs?"

"Your Majesty, I'm flattered you consider Montfort so vital to your cause," Davidson says, grinning. "I apologize, but the laws of my country cannot be broken, not even in war. I won't betray the principles of Montfort, and I stand by the rights of my people. After all, they're some of the people who will help you reclaim your own country." The warning in his words is just as clear as the easy smile still pasted on his face.

Father is better at this than Cal. He dons an empty smile of his own. "We would never ask a ruler to turn on his own nation, sir."

"Of course not," the scarred Red woman adds dryly. Father takes her disrespect in stride, but only for the coalition's sake. If not for our alliance, I suspect he would kill her, to teach everyone a lesson in propriety.

Cal calms a little, doing his best to keep his head. "How long will you be gone, Premier?"

"It depends on my government, but I don't expect a long debate," Davidson says.

Queen Anabel claps her hands in amusement. She laughs, deepening the lines on her face. "How interesting, sir. And what does your government consider a long debate?"

At this point, I feel like I'm watching a play led by mediocre actors. Not one of them—Father, Anabel, Davidson—trusts a breath out of the others.

"Oh, years." Davidson sighs, matching her forced humor. "Democracy is a funny thing. Not that any of you know that yet."

The final jab is meant to sting, and it does. Anabel's smile turns frosty. She taps a hand against the table, another warning. Her ability can destroy with ease. Just like the rest of us. All deadly, all with our own motives at play. I don't know how much longer I can stand it.

"I'm excited to see it for myself."

The temperature rises before the words are barely out of Mare's mouth. She's the only one who doesn't glance at Cal. He glares at her, eyes burning, while his teeth worry at his lip. She remains resolute, her expression pleasantly blank. I think she's taking a page out of Davidson's book.

Quickly, I put a hand to my mouth, stifling a surprised giggle. Mare Barrow is so wickedly talented when it comes to upsetting Calore men. At this point, I wonder if she plans it. Lies awake at night and schemes on how best to confuse Maven or distract Cal.

But does she? Could she?

On instinct, I try to smother the spark of hope that bursts in my chest. Then I let it bloom.

She did it to Maven. Kept him occupied. Kept him off balance. Kept him away from you. Why can't she do the same with Cal?

"Then you will be a good envoy for Norta instead." I try to sound bored, uninterested. Not eager. I don't want anyone to realize I'm throwing the bone far away, knowing the puppy will follow. Mare's eyes snap to me, her brows rising a centimeter. *Come on, Mare.* I'm glad no one here can read my mind.

"No, she won't, Evangeline," Cal says quickly, forcing the words through gritted teeth. "I mean no disrespect, Premier, but we don't know enough about your nation—"

I blink at my betrothed, tipping my head. Silver hair slides across the scaled armor at my collarbone. The power I have in this moment, however small, snaps through my nerves. "And what better way to know? She'll be well received, a hero. Montfort is a country of new-bloods. Her presence will help our cause. Won't it, Premier?"

Davidson fixes me with his blank eyes. I feel his stare go through me. *Look all you want, Red.* "Undoubtedly."

"You trust her to report what she finds there? Without embellishment or omission?" Anabel scoffs in disbelief. "Make no mistake, Princess Evangeline, the girl has no loyalty to anyone with Silver blood."

Both Cal and Mare lower their eyes at the same moment, as if fighting not to look at each other.

I shrug. "Then send a Silver with her. Perhaps Lord Jacos?" The older man, thin in his yellow robes, seems startled by the sound of his own name. He has a frayed appearance, like a worn piece of cloth. "If memory serves, you're a scholar, aren't you?"

"I am," he murmurs.

Mare's head snaps up. Her cheeks are red, but the rest of her seems composed. "Send whoever you want with us. I'll be going to Montfort, and no king has the right to stop me. But they can certainly try."

Excellent. Calore tightens in his chair. His grandmother looms close, smaller in comparison to him. But their resemblance is still clear. Same bronze eyes, broad shoulders, straight nose. The same soldier's heart. And, ultimately, the same ambition. She watches him as she speaks, wary of his response. "So Lord Jacos and Mare Barrow will represent the true king of Norta alongside—"

His bracelet sparks, birthing a small red flame. It walks along his knuckles slowly.

"The true king will represent himself," Cal says, his eyes on the fire.

Across the room, Mare clenches her teeth. It takes all my restraint to stay silent in my seat, but inside, I cheer and dance. *So easily done.*

"Tiberias," Anabel hisses. He doesn't bother to respond. And she can't press him. *You did this to yourself, you stupid old woman. You named him king. Now obey.*

"I admit, I have some of Uncle Julian's—and my mother's— natural curiosity," Cal says. He softens at the mention and memory of his mother. Admittedly, I don't know much about her. Coriane Jacos was not a subject Queen Elara tolerated well. "I want to visit this Free Republic, and discover if all the stories are true." Then his voice lowers. He looks at Mare with such intensity, as if he can will her to return his gaze. She doesn't. "I like to see things for myself."

Davidson nods with a flicker in his eye, his blank mask slipping a little, just for a second. "You are most welcome, Your Majesty."

"Good." Cal winks out the fire before rapping his knuckles on the table. "Then it's settled."

His grandmother purses her lips, giving her the appearance of having eaten something sour. "Settled?" she scoffs. "Nothing's settled. You need to plant your flag in Delphie, proclaim your capital; you need to win territory, win resources, win the *people*, sway more of the High Houses to your side—"

Cal is undeterred. "I do need resources, Grandmother. *Soldiers.* Montfort has them."

"You're very right," Father says, his voice a deep rumble that puts an old fear in my heart.

Is he angry with me for pushing this? Or is he pleased? As a child, I learned what it was to cross Volo Samos. You became a ghost. Ignored, unwanted. Until you earned your way back to his love with achievement and intelligence.

Out of the corner of my eye, I look at my father. The king of the Rift sits tall on his throne, pale and perfect. Beneath his meticulously manicured beard, I catch sight of a smirk. And I breathe a small, silent sight of relief.

"A plea from the rightful king of Norta himself will go far with the premier's government," Father continues. "And it will only strengthen this alliance of ours. So it's only right I send an envoy of my own, to represent the Kingdom of the Rift as well."

Not Tolly—don't! my mind screams. Mare Barrow promised not to kill him, but I hardly trust her word, especially under such opportune circumstances. I can already see it. A foolish accident that would be anything but. And Elane will have to go too, his dutiful wife at his side. *If Father sends Tolly, we'll get back a corpse.*

"Evangeline will go with you."

Nausea wipes out relief in a heartbeat.

I'm torn between calling for another cup of wine and vomiting all over my own feet. Voices scream in my head, every one saying the same thing.

You did this to yourself, you stupid little girl.

THREE
Mare

My laughter echoes down the eastern walls and over the dark fields. I double over, hands pressed against the smooth parapet, gasping for breath. I can't control it. True laughter, the deep kind from the pit of my stomach, takes over. The noise is hollow, harsh, and dusty from disuse. My scars bite, stinging along my neck and spine, but I can't hold it back. I laugh until my ribs hurt and I have to sit down, putting my back against the cold stone. It doesn't stop, and even when I bite my lips closed, little bursts still make it through.

No one can hear me but the patrols, and I doubt they care about a single girl laughing alone in the darkness. I've earned the right to laugh or cry or scream as I see fit. Little pieces of me want to do all three. But laughter wins out.

I sound deranged, and maybe I am. I certainly have an excuse, after today. People are still clearing bodies from the other side of Corvium. Cal chose his crown over everything I thought we were fighting for. Both are still bleeding wounds no healer can fix. Wounds I have to ignore right now, for my own sanity. The only thing I can do is put my face in my hands, clench my teeth, and fight my infernal, idiotic laugh.

This is complete and total lunacy.

Evangeline, Cal, and *me*, all headed to Montfort. What a terrific *joke*.

I said as much in my message to Kilorn, still safe back in Piedmont. He would want to know about everything, as much as I could say. After I convinced him to stay behind, it's only fair to keep him in the loop. And of course, I *want* him in the loop. I want someone else to laugh with me, and curse over what's to come.

I chuckle darkly again, tipping my head back against the stone-work. The stars above me are pinpricks, dimmed by the city lights of Corvium as well as the rising moon. The stars seem to watch, looking down at the fortress city. I wonder if Iris Cygnet's gods are laughing with me. If they even exist.

I wonder if Jon is laughing too.

The thought of him chills my blood, killing whatever manic giggle I have left. That wretched, prophesizing newblood is out there some-where, having escaped us. But to do what? Sit on a hill and watch? Let his red eyes tick back and forth as we all kill each other? Is he some kind of game master, content to nudge us into position and play out what-ever future he chooses? If it were remotely possible, I would try to find him. Force him to protect us from lethal fate. But that's absurd. He'll see me coming. We can only find Jon if he wants to be found.

Frustrated, I scrub my fingers over my face and scalp, letting my nails drag across my skin. The sharp sensation brings me back to real-ity, little by little. So does the cold. The stone beneath my body loses warmth as night wears on. The thin fabric of my uniform does little to keep me from shivering, while the sharp, solid edges of the wall are hardly comfortable. Still, I don't move.

Moving means sleep, but it also means going back down. To the others, to the barracks. Even if I don my best scowl and run, I'll have to face Reds and newbloods and Silvers too. Julian, certainly. I can just imagine him waiting on my cot, ready with another lecture. What he could possibly say, I don't know.

He'll side with Cal, I think. At the end of all this. When it becomes clear we won't let Cal keep his throne. Silvers are nothing if not loyal to blood. And Julian is nothing if not loyal to his dead sister. Cal is the last piece of her left. He won't turn his back on that, even for all his talk of revolution and history. He won't leave Cal alone.

Tiberias. Call. Him. Tiberias.

It even hurts to think the name. His real name. His future. Tiberias Calore the Seventh, King of Norta, Flame of the North. I picture him on his brother's throne, safe in a cage of Silent Stone. Or would he drag out the diamondglass inferno his father sat? Destroy every shred of Maven, erase him from history? He'll rebuild his father's palace. The Kingdom of Norta will return to the way it was. Except for the Samos king in the Rift, everything will go back to what it was meant to be the day I fell into the arena.

Making everything that has occurred since that day be for nothing.

I refuse to let that happen.

And, luckily, I'm not alone in this endeavor.

The moonlight glows on the black stone, making the gold accents of every tower and parapet gleam silver. Patrols wind below me, guards in red and green uniforms keeping watch. Scarlet Guard and Montfort. Their counterparts, Silvers in house colors, are less frequent, and they clump together. Yellow Laris, black Haven, red and blue Iral, red and orange Lerolan. No Samos colors. They're royal now, thanks to Volo's ambition and opportunity. No need to waste their time on something as ordinary as the nightly rounds.

I wonder what Maven thinks of that. He fixated on Tiberias so much, I can only imagine the weight of another rival king like Volo. Everything revolved around his brother, even though Maven seemingly had everything he could want. The crown, the throne, *me*. He still felt that shadow. Elara's doing. She coiled and curled him into what she needed, cutting away and building up in equal measure. His obsession helped fuel his need for power, and enabled her own. Will it extend to King Volo? Or are Maven's darkest and most dangerous desires restricted to us? Kill Tiberias, keep me?

Only time will tell. When he strikes again, and he will, I'll know.

I only hope we're ready.

Davidson's troops, the Scarlet Guard and our spreading infiltration— we're enough. We have to be.

But that doesn't mean I can't take precautions.

"When do we leave?"

It took some dreaded social interaction, but I managed to ask my way to Davidson's quarters. He commands some larger offices in the administrative sector, forming a suite currently filled with Montfort brass. And Scarlet Guard too, although Farley isn't here. The officers take my entrance in stride, giving way to the person they still call light-ning girl. Most busy themselves with packing. Papers, folders, charts, mostly. Nothing that actually belongs to anyone here. Intelligence for smarter people than me to devour. Probably left over from whatever Silver officers used this space last.

Ada, one of my newblood recruits, is at the center of the activity. Her eyes run over every scrap of paper before someone else packs it away. She's memorizing it all, using her ability of perfect memory. I catch her eye as I pass, and we share a nod. When we go to Montfort, Ada will be dispatched to Command at Farley's orders. I don't suppose I'll see her again for a long time.

Davidson looks up from his bare desk. The corners of his angled eyes crinkle, the only indicator of a smile. Despite the harsh, unforgiving light of the office, he looks handsome as ever. Distinguished. Intimidating. A king in power if not title. When he waves me over, I swallow hard, remembering what he looked like in the siege. Bloody, exhausted, afraid. And determined. Just like the rest of us. It calms me a little.

"You did well up there, Barrow," he says. With a toss of his head, he gestures in the vague direction of the core tower.

I blink, scoffing. "You mean I kept my mouth shut."

At the window, someone laughs. I glance over to see Tyton leaning against the glass, arms crossed, his usual lock of white hair drooping over one eye. He has a clean forest-green uniform too, though a little short at the wrists and legs. No lightning insignia to mark him for what he is: an electricon like me. Because it isn't his uniform. The last time I saw him, he was painted eyebrows to ankles in silver blood. He drums his fingers against his arm, brandishing them like the weapons they are.

"Is that possible?" he says without looking at me, his voice deep.

Davidson surveys me, shaking his head a bit. "Actually, I'm pleased with what you told the others, Mare. About accompanying me home."

"Like I said, I'm curious about—"

The premier puts up his hand, palm out, to stop me short. "Save it.

I think Lord Jacos is the only person here who does anything simply for the sake of curiosity." *Well, he isn't wrong.* "What do you really want from Montfort?"

At the window, Tyton's eyes flicker in the light as he finally deigns to look at me.

I raise my chin. "Only what you promised."

"Resettlement?" For once, Davidson looks truly startled. "You want to—"

"I want my family safe." My voice never wavers. I push a little of what I remember from a dead Silver and her etiquette rules into my bearing. *Straight spine, squared shoulders. Hold eye contact.*

"We are truly at war," I say. "Norta, Piedmont, the Lakelands, and your Republic too. Nowhere is safe, from either side. But you're farthest away, and you seem to be the strongest, or at least the most defended. I think it will be best if I can take my family there myself. Before I come back to finish what better people started."

"The promise was for newbloods, Miss Barrow," Davidson says quietly. The flurry of activity around us almost drowns him out.

My stomach drops, but I harden my expression. "I don't think so, Premier."

He pulls that bland smile of his, retreating behind his usual mask. "Really, you think me so heartless?" A strange joke, but Davidson is nothing if not a strange man. He flashes even teeth. "Of course your family is welcome. Montfort would be proud to accept them as citizens. Ibarem, a word?" he adds, calling over my shoulder.

A man bustles in from one of the connecting rooms, and I can't help but jump. He's the spitting image of Rash and Tahir, the newblood twins. If I didn't know Tahir was still in Piedmont and Rash embedded in Archeon, both relaying information for the cause, I would think he *was* one of the twins. *Triplets,* I quickly realize, and a bitterness fills my mouth. I don't like surprises.

Like his brothers, Ibarem has dark brown skin, black hair, and a well-manicured beard. I can just glimpse a scar beneath the hair on his chin, a single white line of raised flesh. He's marked too, cut by a Silver lord long ago to distinguish him from his identical siblings.

"Pleased to meet you," I mutter, narrowing my eyes at Davidson.

He senses my unease. "Ah, yes, this would be the brother of Rash and Tahir."

"Couldn't tell," I shoot back dryly.

Ibarem's lips twist into a small smile as he nods his head in greeting. "Glad to make your acquaintance at last, Miss Barrow." Then he turns to the premier, expectant. "What do you need, Premier?"

Davidson eyes him. "Send word to Tahir. Have him inform the Barrow family that their daughter will be collecting them tomorrow. For resettlement in Montfort."

"Yes, sir," he replies. His eyes glaze for a moment, as the message travels from his brain to his brother's. It only takes a second, despite the hundreds of miles between them. He ducks his head again. "Relayed, sir. Tahir says congratulations and welcome, Miss Barrow."

I only hope my parents accept the offer. Not that they wouldn't. Gisa wants to go, and Mom will follow her lead. Bree and Tramy will follow Mom. But Dad, I'm not sure. Not if he knows I won't be staying with them. *Please go. Please let me give you this.*

"Tell him thanks," I mumble, still disconcerted by him.

"Relayed," Ibarem says again. "Tahir says you're very welcome."

"Thank you both," Davidson cuts in, and for good reason. The brothers can go back and forth with maddening speed, although it's worse when their linked brains are side by side. Ibarem nods, taking the dismissal, before shuffling away to continue his work elsewhere.

"Are there any more of them you'd like to tell me about?" I hiss, leaning forward to grit my teeth at the premier.

He takes my annoyance in stride. "No, though I wish I had more of their like at my disposal," he sighs. "Funny, those brothers. Usually Ardents have Silver counterparts, but I've never seen their like beyond our blood."

"His brain feels different from any other," Tyton mutters.

I eye him sharply. "The way you say that is very disconcerting."

Tyton only shrugs.

I turn back to Davidson, still smarting, but unable to ignore what a gift he's just given me. "Thank you for doing this. I know you lead the country, and it may not seem like much, but this means a great deal to me."

"Of course it does," he replies. "And I hope to do the same for other families like yours, as soon as we are able. My government is currently debating how to face what is rapidly becoming a refugee crisis, as well as how to move already-displaced Reds and newbloods. But for you, for what you've done and continue to do, exceptions can be made."

"And what have I done? Really?" The words slip out before I can bite them back. Heat spreads across my cheeks.

"You've made cracks in the impenetrable." Davidson speaks like he's pointing out the obvious. "Put dents in armor. You loosened the proverbial jar, Miss Barrow. Let us break it open." His grin is true, wide and white and stretching. I'm reminded of a cat. "And it's no small thing that, because of you, a claimant to the throne of Norta will be coming to the Republic."

That sends a jolt through me. *Is that a threat?* I move quickly, leaning over his desk, my palms braced against the wood, my voice low, in warning. "I want your word he won't be harmed."

He doesn't hesitate. "You have it," he says, matching my tone. "I won't touch a hair on his head. Nor will anyone else, not while Calore is in my country. You have my solemn promise. That's not how I operate."

"Good," I reply. "Because it would be ridiculously stupid to remove the buffer between *our* alliance and Maven Calore. And you aren't a stupid person, are you, Premier?"

That cat smile widens. He nods.

"Won't it be good for the little prince to see something different?" Davidson cocks one manicured gray eyebrow. "A country without a king?"

See that it's possible. That the crown, the throne—they aren't his duty. He doesn't have to be a king or a prince. Not if he doesn't want to be.

But I think he wants to be.

"Yes" is all I can say. And all I can hope for. After all, didn't I first meet Tiberias in a dark tavern, where he pretended to be someone else so he could see what the world really looked like? See what should change?

Davidson leans back, clearly finished with me. I do the same. "Consider your request granted," he says. "And consider yourself lucky we have to return to Piedmont first anyway, or else I might not be so amenable to retrieving a metric ton of Barrows."

He almost winks.

I almost smile.

Halfway to the barracks, I realize I'm being followed through the fortress city. Footsteps trail close behind, nimble and even along the winding street. The fluorescent lights cast two shadows, mine and someone else's. I tense, uneasy, but not afraid. Corvium is crawling with coalition soldiers, and if any of them are stupid enough to wish me harm, they're welcome to try. I can protect myself. Sparks ripple beneath my skin, easy to unleash. Ready to loose.

I turn on my boot heel, hoping to catch whoever it is off guard. It doesn't work.

Evangeline stops smoothly, expectant, her arms crossed and dark, perfect eyebrows raised. She still wears her opulent armor, the kind better suited to a king's court than a battleground. No crown, though. She used to spend her free time fashioning tiaras and circlets from whatever metal she could get her hands on. But now, when she has every right to wear one, her head is bare.

"I trailed you through two sectors of the city, Barrow," she says, tossing back her head. "I thought you were supposed to be some kind of thief?"

My incessant laugh from earlier tugs again, and I can't help but smirk, huffing out a breath. Her bite is familiar, and anything familiar feels like comfort right now. "Never change, Evangeline."

Her smile flashes, quick as a knife. "Of course not. Why change perfection?"

"Well, please don't let me keep you from your perfect life, Your Highness," I tell her. Still smirking, I step aside, clearing the way for her. Calling her bluff. Evangeline Samos did not seek me out to trade insults. Her behavior in the council chamber made her motives very clear.

She blinks, and a bit of her boldness melts. "Mare," she says, softer now. Pleading. But her pride won't let her do much more than almost beg. That damn Silver spine. She doesn't know how to bend. No one ever taught her, and no one would ever allow her to try.

Despite everything between us, a sliver of pity arrows through my heart. Evangeline was raised in the Silver court, born to scheme and climb, made to fight as fiercely as she guards her mind. But her mask is far from perfect, especially compared to Maven's. After months of reading shadows in his eyes, I see Evangeline's thoughts reflected in hers clear as daylight. Pain radiates from her. Longing. She has the feel of a predator in a cage with no chance of escaping. Part of me wants to leave her trapped. Let her realize exactly what kind of life she used to want. I want to believe I'm not that cruel. And I'm not stupid. Evangeline Samos would make a powerful ally, and if I have to buy her with whatever she wants, so be it.

"If you're looking for sympathy, keep walking," I mutter, gesturing again to the empty street. A useless threat, but she bristles anyway. Her eyes, already black, darken. The gibe works, pushing her into a corner, forcing her to speak.

"I don't want an inch of it from you," Evangeline snaps. The needle edges of her armor sharpen with her anger. "And I know I don't deserve it either."

"Definitely not," I snort. "So you want help, then? An excuse not to go to Montfort with the rest of our happy crew?"

Evangeline's face twists into another biting smile. "I'm hardly idiotic enough to owe you anything. No, I'm talking about a trade."

I keep my face still, my eyes locked on hers. I channel a little bit of Davidson's serene, unfathomable blankness. "I thought you might be."

"Good to know you aren't as dense as people seem to think."

"So, what do you have?" I ask, wanting to hurry this along. We're leaving for Piedmont, and then Montfort, *tomorrow*. We don't have the luxury of our usual barbs. "What do you *want*?"

The words stick in her throat. She drags her teeth across her lips, scraping away a bit of the purple stain. In the unforgiving light of the Corvium street, her makeup seems harsh, more like war paint. I suppose it is. The purple shadows below her cheekbones, meant to sculpt her features into impossible sharpness, seem sickly in the dark. Even the shimmering white powder on her skin, smoothing her moonbeam complexion, has flaws. *Tear tracks.* She tried to cover them up, but the evidence is still there. Uneven color, a hint of black paint from her lashes still leaving their mark. Her walls of beauty and lethal magnificence have deep cracks.

"But that's easy, isn't it?" I answer my own question, taking a step closer. She almost flinches. "All this time, all your scheming. You have Tiberias. You have a *third* chance to marry a Calore king. Become queen of Norta. Achieve everything you've ever worked for."

Her throat bobs, swallowing a probably rude response. We don't have much practice being civil each other.

"And you want out," I whisper. "You don't want to be what you were born for. Why the sudden revelation? Why throw away what you used to want so much?"

Her restraint breaks. "I don't have to explain myself or my reasons to you."

"Your reason has red hair and answers to Elane Haven."

Evangeline tenses, fists clenching, and the scales of her armor tighten, responding to her sudden emotions. "Don't talk about her," she snaps, revealing her weakness, the easy leverage we can use.

She closes the distance between us. Evangeline is several inches taller than me, and she wields this slim advantage well. With her hands on her hips, eyes glaring, her shoulders square against the city lights, I'm entirely in her shadow.

I blink up at her, tilting my head. "So you want to go back to her.

And what, you think I can stop Tiberias from marrying you?"

"Don't flatter yourself," she snaps back, rolling her eyes. "You're a good distraction for Calore kings, yes. But I'm not delusional. Cal won't break our betrothal. Maven, maybe. You certainly influenced his decision to cast me aside."

"As if you were ever *really* going to marry Maven," I tell Evangeline slowly. I saw more than she realizes, back in Maven's court. Her family took the monumental slight too well. The Kingdom of the Rift was planned long before I nudged Maven in any direction.

Evangeline shrugs. "I was never going to be his queen after Elara died. Excuse me, after you killed her," she says quickly. "She could hold his leash, at least. Keep him in check. I don't think anyone alive can do that now, not even you."

I nod in agreement. There is no controlling Maven Calore.

Though I certainly tried. Bile rises in my throat at the memory, my attempts to manipulate the boy king, playing on his weakness for me. And then Maven traded House Samos for peace, for the Lakelands, for a princess just as deadly and probably twice as cunning as Evangeline. I wonder if he met his match in Iris Cygnet, the quiet, calculating nymph.

I try to picture him now, fleeing Corvium for the Lakelands. His white face above a uniform of black and red, blue eyes sparking with quiet fury. Retreating to a strange kingdom and a strange court, without the protection of his Silent Stone. With nothing to show but the corpse of the king of the Lakelands. It comforts me a bit, to know he failed so spectacularly. Perhaps the queen of the Lakelands will kill him outright, to punish him for wasting her husband's life on the siege.

I couldn't drown Maven when I had the chance. Maybe she will.

"And you can't command Cal either. Not in any way that could achieve what I want." Evangeline pushes on, her words a twisting knife. "He won't put me aside for you, not if the crown hangs in the balance. Sorry, Barrow. He's not the abdicating kind."

"I know what kind he is," I sneer back, feeling her jab as keenly as she feels mine. If my life continues this way, with almost everything I do poking at this wound, I doubt it will ever have time to heal.

"He's made his choice," she says. Both to punish me and to make a point. "When he wins back Norta, and he *will*, I'll marry him. Cement an alliance, ensure the Rift survives. Carry on the legacy of Volo Samos and his kings of steel." Evangeline looks past me, down the dark street. A patrol walks the adjoining avenue ten yards away, their voices low and even as their footsteps. Scarlet Guard, judging by the rust-colored uniforms. Most are repurposed from the Red uniforms of the Nortan army, their insignia ripped off. I doubt Evangeline notices. Her eyes glaze, and she thinks of something far away. Something she doesn't like at all, judging by her clenching jaw.

"And if you don't marry him?" I prod, bringing her back.

It's the easy, obvious thing to ask, but she blanches, perplexed by the suggestion. Her eyes widen, her mouth dropping open in shock. "Impossible," she scoffs. "There's no way around it. Short of running away to Tiraxes or Ciron or whatever backwater my father can't invade," she adds, laughing darkly at the idea. "Even that won't work. He'll find me wherever I go, drag me back, and use me as I was intended to be used. The only course I see, the only option I have, is very simple."

Of course it is, Evangeline.

Our objectives are the same, though our motivations differ. I let her talk, spooling out exactly what I want to hear. Things will be easier if she thinks this is all her own idea.

"There will be no marriage if Cal fails." Evangeline stares through me. She forces the words. They're a betrayal, of her house, of her colors, of her father, of her *blood*. It cuts her bone-deep. "If he isn't king of Norta, my father won't *waste* me on him. And if he loses his war for the crown, if *we* lose, Father will be too distracted keeping his own throne to sell me off to someone else. Or at least sell me somewhere far away."

From Elane. Her meaning is clear.

"So you want me to stop Cal from winning back his kingdom?"

She sneers, taking a step back. "You've learned many things in Silver courts, Mare Barrow. You're smarter than you seem. I won't underestimate you ever again, and you better not underestimate me." As she speaks, her armor skitters, re-forming and twisting along her limbs. The scales shrink and crawl. Like the bugs of her mother's control, each one a gleaming dot of black and silver. She re-forms her clothing into something more substantial, less grand. Real armor, meant for battle and nothing else. "When I say I want *you* to stop Cal, I mean your little circle. Although I don't know how 'little' both Montfort and the Scarlet Guard can be considered. After all, they can't really mean to prop up another Silver kingdom. Not without some serious strings attached."

"Ah." My heart drops a little. There's a card shown, one I would have liked to keep hidden.

"Yes, well. It doesn't take a political genius to know that a Red and Silver coalition will be fraught with betrayal. I'm certain all the leaders know not to trust one another." Her eyes flash as she turns, meaning to leave me behind. "Except for maybe one aspiring king," she adds over her shoulder.

A fact I know too well. Tiberias is as trusting as a new puppy, easily led by the people he loves. Me, his grandmother, and most of all his dead father. He pursues the crown for that man, to serve some bond that hasn't broken. While his confidence, his courage, and his dogged focus make him strong, they also make him blind everywhere but the battlefield. He can predict surging armies, but not scheming people. He won't see or can't see the machinations around him. He didn't before, and he won't again.

"He's certainly not Maven," I mutter, if only to myself.

I hear an echo from Evangeline all the same, bouncing off the stone walls of Corvium.

"He's certainly not," she replies.

In her voice, I hear the same things I feel.

Relief. And regret.

FOUR

Iris

The bay laps at my bare ankles, refreshing, renewing. It's cold before the sunrise, but I hardly feel the chill. I find sanctuary in the simple sensation. I know these waters as well as I know my own face. I can feel them far beyond my feet, the pulse of the softest current, the smallest ripple of the river feeding the bay, and the bay feeding the lake. The coming light of dawn bleeds across the smooth surface. The mirror image distorts in streaks of pale blue and rose pink. Such calm lets me forget who I am, but not for long. I am Iris Cygnet, a princess born, a queen made. I don't have the luxury of forgetting anything, no matter how much I may want to.

We wait together, my mother, my sister, and I, our attention fixed on the southern horizon. Fog hangs low across the narrow mouth of Clear Bay, obstructing the peninsula dotted with guard towers, as well as Lake Eris beyond. A few lights from the towers twinkle through the fog, like stars hanging low. As the fog shifts, moving in the wind off the lake, more and more towers come into view. Tall stone structures, improved and rebuilt a hundred times over hundreds of years. The towers have seen more war and ruin than even historians can say. Their lights flare, too many ablaze this close to dawn. But the beacons will remain all day, torches burning and electric lights beaming. The flags streaming in the breeze are different from the usual standard of the Lakelands. Each tower flies cobalt blue slashed with black. To honor so many dead in Corvium, to mourn.

To say good-bye to our king.

I shed my tears already, in hours spent crying last night. I shouldn't have any more tears left to give, but still they come. My sister, Tiora, keeps herself in better check. She raises her chin, a diadem crown winking across her brow. It's a braid of dark sapphire and jet, hung low across her forehead. Even though I am a queen now, my crown is more simple, barely a string of blue diamonds punctuated by red gems to symbolize Norta.

We have the same cold, bronze skin, the same face, high cheekbones and sharply arched eyebrows, but her deep mahogany eyes belong to our mother. I have father's gray. Tiora is twenty-three, four years my elder, and the heir to the throne of the Lakelands. I used to say she was born grim and silent, loath to cry, unable to laugh. Her serious nature serves her well as my mother's heir. She has far more skill in controlling her emotions, though I do my best to keep still as the lakes. Tiora locks her gaze forward, her spine straight with the pride not even a funeral can break. Despite her stoic nature, even she cries for our lost father. Her tears are less evident, quickly dropping into the bay swirling around our feet. She's a nymph like the rest of our family, and uses her ability to cast the tears away and leave nothing of them behind. I would do the same if I had the strength, but I can't summon anything right now.

Not so for our mother, Cenra, the ruling queen of the Lakelands.

Her tears hover in the air, a cloud of crystal droplets to catch the spreading light of dawn. One by one, the cloud grows and the tears turn steadily, flashing in time, sending faint rainbows arching across her brown skin. Diamonds born from her broken heart.

She stands in front of us, knee-deep in the water, her mourning gown floating out behind her. Like Tiora and me, Mother wears mostly black slashed with our regal blue. The dress is finely made in intricate layers of thin silk, but it's shapeless, hanging off her like an afterthought. While Tiora took care to make sure we were both prepared for the funeral, choosing jewels and gowns to suit, Mother did no such thing. She looks plain, her hair undone in a sleek trail of raven and storm. No bracelets, no earrings, no crown. A queen only in bearing. And that's enough. I'm tempted to cling to her skirts like I did when I was a child. I could hold on to her and never let go. Never leave home again. Never return to a court falling to pieces around an already broken king.

The thought of my husband turns me cold. And resolute.

The tears dry on my cheeks.

Maven Calore is a child playing with a loaded gun. Whether or not he knows how to shoot remains to be seen. But I certainly have targets in mind, people to point him at. The Silver who killed my father, of course. Some Iral lord. He cut his throat. Attacked him from behind like some honorless dog. But Iral served another king. Samos. *Volo*. Another without any claim to honor or dignity. He rebelled for a petty crown, for little more than the right to call himself master of some insignificant corner of the world. And he isn't alone. Other Nortan families stand with him, ready to replace Maven with the other Calore brother, the exile. Before my father died, I wouldn't have minded if Maven had suddenly found himself deposed or dead. If the Nortan and Lakelander peace held, what difference would it make to me? But not now. Orrec Cygnet is gone. My father died because of men like Volo Samos and Tiberias Calore. What I would do to line them up and drown them with my fury.

What I will do.

Boats break through the fog, moving quietly. The three crafts are familiar, their bows painted silver and blue. Only a single deck to each. Dawnboats aren't built for war, but for speed, silence, and the will of powerful nymphs. Their hulls are specially grooved to catch forced currents as they do now.

It was my idea to send the boats. I couldn't bear the thought of Father's body dragged on the long march from Mour, the land the Nortans call the Choke. He would have to pass through many towns on the way, news of his death racing ahead of that gruesome parade. No, I wanted him to come home, so we could say good-bye first.

And so I wouldn't lose my nerve.

Nymphs in Lakelander blue, our cousins of the Cygnet Line, crowd the deck of the lead dawnboat. Grief shadows their dark faces, each one mourning as we are. Father was well loved among our line, though he came from a lesser branch of the family. Mother is the royal one, descended from a long, unbroken lineage of monarchs. As such, she is not permitted to cross the borders of our country, except in the gravest of need. Tiora isn't allowed to leave at all, even in war, to preserve the line of succession.

At least they will never share Father's fate, to die in battle. Or mine, to live my days so far away from home.

My husband isn't difficult to spot against the dark blue uniforms. Four Sentinels guard him, their flaming robes exchanged for tactical gear. But they still have their masks studded with dark gemstones, both beautiful and gruesome. Maven wears his usual black, standing out sharply despite his lack of medals, crown, or insignia. No monarch is stupid enough to march into battle with that kind of target painted on his body. Not that I think he fought at all. Maven isn't a warrior—not on the battlefield, at least. He looks so small next to his soldiers and mine. Weak. I thought as much when we first met, eyeing each other across the pavilion in the middle of a minefield. He's still a teenager, barely more than a child, a year younger than I am. Still, he knows how to use his appearance to his advantage. He plays to those assumptions. It works on his country, the people spoon-fed his lies and painted-on innocence. Reds and Silvers outside his court lap up the tales of his brother, the golden prince seduced by a spy and driven to murder. A juicy story, a lovely piece of gossip for people to latch on to. Paired with Maven's bringing an end to the war between our countries, it makes Maven so much more appealing. And it puts him in an odd position. He is a king supported by his people, but not the ones closest to him. Not the nobles still clinging to his heels. They remain because they need him to preserve a now-delicate kingdom.

And, loath as I am to admit it, because Maven is a skilled court schemer. He balances the nobles well, playing houses off each other. All while maintaining an iron grip on the rest of the nation.

The royal court of Norta is a court of snakes, now more than ever.

Maven's machinations will never work on me, though. I know better than to underestimate him. Especially now, when his obsessions seem to rule. His mind is as splintered as his country. Making him all the more dangerous.

The first boat glides to shore, its draft shallow enough to beach it a few yards from Mother. The nymphs go first, jumping into the water. The lake leaps away from their feet, allowing the cousins to walk on dry lakebed. Not for their sake, but for Maven's.

He follows closely, jumping down to get on dry land as quickly as he can. Burners like him hold no love for water, and he eyes the liquid walls of his pathway with suspicion. I don't expect any sympathy as he walks past me, his Sentinels in his wake, and I receive none. Not even a glance. For someone called the Flame of the North, his heart is brutally cold.

The Cygnet cousins remain by the boat and release their grip on the bay waters. They rush and swell before rising up, like a creature raising its head. Or a parent reaching out to hold a child.

Soldiers lift a board from the deck, revealing a familiar sight.

I'm not an infant. I've seen dead bodies before. My country has been at war for more than a century, and as the younger daughter, the second child, I'm free to walk the battle lines. I'm trained to fight, not to rule. It's my duty to support my sister as Father did my mother, in whatever way she needs.

Tiora chokes back a rare sob. I take her hand.

"Still as the lakes, Ti," I whisper to her. She squeezes my hand in reply. Her features tighten into a blank mask.

The Cygnet nymphs raise their arms and the water mirrors their action, bulging upward. Slowly, the soldiers lower the board and the corpse draped in a single white sheet. It floats on the surface, easing down from the boat.

Mother takes a few steps forward, moving deeper into the bay. She stops when her wrists are submerged, and I catch the subtle movement of her swirling fingers. My father's body glides over the surface toward her, as if pulled by invisible strings. Our cousins march alongside the king, flanking him even in death. Two of them are crying.

When she reaches for the sheet, I fight the urge to shut my eyes. I want to preserve the memories I have of my father, not corrupt them all with the sight of his corpse. But I would regret it one day. Breathing slowly, I focus on maintaining some calm. The waters churn around my ankles, a gentle, swirling current to match the nausea in the pit of my stomach. I focus on it, tracing lazy circles with my mind to stop the worst of my grief from spilling over. I keep my teeth clenched, my chin high. The tears have not returned.

His face is strange, drained of color as well as life. His smooth brown skin, barely wrinkled despite his age, has a pale undertone, the sickly kind. I wish he were only sick, not dead. Mother puts her hands on either side of his face, staring down at him with a strength I can't fathom. Her tears continue to hover like a swarm of glittering insects. After a long moment, she kisses his closed eyelids, fingers trailing through his long iron-gray hair. Then she cups her hands over his face, forming a bowl. The tears collect, flowing into her fingers. Finally she lets them go.

I almost expect him to flinch. But Father doesn't move. He can't anymore.

Tiora follows, using her hands to scoop water from the bay and trace it over his face. She lingers, studying him. She was always closer to our mother, as her position demands. It doesn't lessen her pain, though. Her composure wavers and she turns away, holding up a hand to hide her face.

The world seems to shrink as I move through the water, my limbs sluggish and distant. Mother hovers, one hand on the sheet covering the rest of the body. She eyes me across him, her countenance still and empty. I know that look. I use it myself whenever I need to mask the storm of emotions beneath. I wore it on my wedding day. But then I was hiding fear, not pain.

Not like this.

I copy Tiora, pouring the water over my father. The droplets roll off his aquiline nose and down his cheekbones, pooling in the hair beneath his head. I brush away a strand of gray, suddenly wishing I could cut a lock for myself. Back in Archeon, I have a small temple—a shrine, more than anything—filled with candles and worn emblems of the nameless gods. Cramped as it may be, the tiny corner of the palace is the only spot I feel myself. I would like to keep him with me there.

An impossible wish.

When I pull back, Mother steps forward again. She puts her hands to the wooden board, palms flat. Tiora and I follow her lead. I've never done this before, and I wish I didn't have to. But it is as the gods command. *Return,* they bid. To what you are, to your ability. Bury a greenwarden. Entomb a stoneskin in marble and granite. Drown a nymph.

If I am alive when Maven dies, will I be permitted to burn his corpse?

We push, lowering the board with our hands and our ability. Using our own muscles and the weight of our current to sink the body. Even in the shallows, the water distorts his face. Dawn breaks to my left, the sun rising over the low hills. It flashes on the surface, blinding me for a moment.

I shut my eyes and remember Father as he was.

He returns to the water's embrace.

Detraon is a city of canals, nymph-cut into the bedrock on the western edge of Clear Bay. The ancient city that used to sit here is no more, washed away by floods more than a thousand years ago. There are still massive fields of debris downriver, choked with the rotted ruins of another time. Rust-eaten iron dust turns the earth red to this day, and magnetrons harvest those stretches like farmers do wheat. When the waters receded, the land here was still the perfect spot for our capital, sitting well beside Lake Eris, with easy access to Lake Neron through a short strait, and the rest of the lakes beyond. From Detraon, over both natural and nymph-made waterways, we can quickly reach almost every corner of our kingdom. All the way from the Hud in the north to the disputed borders along the Great River in the west and the Ohius in the south . No nymph lord could resist, and so here we stay, drawing our strength and safety from the waters.

The canals make for easy division, cutting the city into quarter sectors surrounding our central temples. Most Reds live in the southeast, farthest from the blissful waterfront, while the palace quarter and noble quarter sit on the bay itself, overlooking the waters we love so well. The Whirlpool Quarter, as it's commonly known, occupies the northeast, where both wealthier Reds and less important Silvers live in close proximity. It's merchants, mostly, businessmen, lower officers and soldiers, poor students from the university in the noble quarter. As well as Reds of quality and necessity. Skilled workers—independent, usually. Servants wealthy or important enough to live in Silver households, not their own. City governance is not my strong suit, and better left to Tiora, but I do what I can to acquaint myself with such things. Even if they bore me, I must know, at the very least. Ignorance is a burden I do not intend to carry.

We don't use the canals today, as the palace is close enough to the bayfront. *Good,* I think, enjoying the familiar walk. Arches span the turquoise-and-gold walls of the noble sector, so fluid and smooth they can only be the work of Silvers. Family homes I know by heart peek up over the walls, their windows thrown open to the morning, dynastic colors streaming proudly in the breeze. The bloodred flag of the Renarde Line, jade green for the peerless, ancient storm line of

Sielle—I name each in my head. Their sons and daughters fought for the new alliance. *How many died alongside Father? How many that I knew?*

It looks to be a beautiful day, with the sun rising through a sky of sparse clouds. The wind off Eris continues, pawing through my hair with light fingers. I expect the smell of decay, destruction, defeat to come out of the east. But all I smell are the lake waters, wet and green with summer. No sign of the army limping toward us, its blood spent on the walls of Corvium.

Our escort fans out, flint-eyed soldiers of the Lakelands paired with Maven's own contingent. Most of his nobles are still with the army, moving as fast as the rest will allow. But he still has his Sentinel guards. They hang close, as do two of his high-ranking generals, each with aides and guards of their own. The lord general from House Greco is gray-haired, deceptively lean for a strongarm, but there's no mistaking the garish yellow-and-blue emblem on her shoulder. Tiora made sure I memorized the great lines of Norta, their *houses*, until I knew them as well as our own. The other, Lord General Macanthos—blue and gray—is young, with sandy hair and nervous eyes. Too young for his position. I suspect his rank is new, and he replaced a relative who died recently.

Maven is smart enough to give my mother deference in her own country, and he walks a few steps behind her. I do as is expected, keeping pace at his side. We don't touch. Not even the harmless link of arms or hands. It is his rule, not mine. He won't touch me, not since the day he lost his grip on Mare Barrow. The last we felt of each other was a cold kiss beneath a gathering storm.

For that I am quietly thankful. I know what my duty is as a Silver, as a queen, as a bridge between our countries. It's his duty too, a burden we are both supposed to bear. But if he won't push the subject of heirs,

I'm certainly not going to. For one thing, I'm only nineteen. Of age, surely, but I have plenty of time. And for another—if Maven fails, if his brother wins back the crown, I won't have a reason to stay. Without children, I'll be free to come home. I don't want any kind of anchor to Norta if I don't need one.

Our gowns trail, leaving wet paths along the wide street abutting the water's edge. Sunlight gleams off the white stone. My eyes flit back and forth, taking in the sight of a summer day in my old capital. I wish I could stop as I used to. Perch on the low wall dividing the avenue from the bay. Practice my abilities with lazy attention. Maybe even tempt Tiora into a little friendly competition. But there isn't time, nor opportunity. I don't know how long we'll stay, or how long I have with what remains of my family. All I can do is stretch the moments. Memorize them. Tattoo them on my mind like the swirling waves inked on my back.

"I'm the first Nortan king to set foot here in a century."

Maven's voice is low, cold, the snapping threat of winter in spring. After so many weeks in his court, I'm beginning to learn his moods, studying him as I did his country. The king of Norta is not a kind creature, and while my survival is necessary for our alliance, my comfort probably isn't. I try to be in his good graces, and so far it seems easy enough. He doesn't mistreat me. In fact, he doesn't treat me to much of anything at all. Staying out of his way takes little effort in the sprawl of Whitefire Palace.

"Over a century, if my memory serves," I answer, hiding my surprise at being spoken to. "Tiberias the Second was the last Calore king to make a state visit. Before your ancestors and mine began the war."

He hisses at the name. *Tiberias.* Resentments between siblings are not unfamiliar to me. There are many things I envy about Tiora. But

I've never experienced anything like the deep and all-encompassing jealousy Maven feels toward his exiled brother. It runs bone-deep. Every mention of him, even in official capacity, provokes him like the jab of a knife. I suppose the ancestral name is one more thing for him to covet. One more mark of a true king that he will never possess.

Perhaps that's why he pursues Mare Barrow with such dogged focus. The stories seem true enough. I've seen proof of them myself. She's not just a powerful newblood, the strange kind of Red with abilities like our own, but the exiled prince loves her. A Red girl. Having met her, I can almost understand why. Even imprisoned, she fought. She resisted. She was a puzzle I would have enjoyed piecing together. And, it seems, she's a trophy for Calore brothers to scrap over. Nothing compared to the crown, but still something for jealous, feuding boys to tug back and forth like dogs with a bone.

"I can arrange a tour of the capital if Your Majesty would like," I continue. Though spending more time than I must with Maven is hardly ideal, it would mean more time in the city. "The temples are renowned throughout the kingdom for their splendor. Your presence would certainly honor the gods."

Feeding his ego doesn't work, as it usually does with nobles and courtiers. His lip curls. "I try to keep my focus on things that actually exist, Iris. Like the war we're both trying to win."

Suit yourself. I swallow the response with cool detachment. Nonbelievers are not my problem. I can't open their eyes, and it isn't my job to do so. Let him meet the gods in death and see how wrong he was before he enters a hell of his own making. They'll drown him for eternity. That is the punishment for burners in the afterlife. Just as flames would be my own damnation.

"Of course." I dip my head, feeling the cold jewels on my brow.

"The army will go to Citadel of the Lakes when they arrive, for healing and rearmament. We should be there to meet them."

He nods. "We should."

"And there is Piedmont to consider," I add. I wasn't in Norta when the lords loyal to Prince Bracken sought Maven's aid. Our countries were still at war then. But the intelligence reports were clear enough.

A muscle feathers in Maven's cheek. "Prince Bracken won't fight against Montfort, not while those bastards hold his children hostage." He speaks like I'm some kind of simpleton.

I keep my temper in check, dipping my head. "Of course," I reply. "But if an alliance could be won in secret? Montfort would lose their base in the south, all the resources Bracken has ceded to them, and they would gain a powerful enemy. Another Silver kingdom for them to fight."

His footsteps echo, loud and even over the walkway. I can hear him breathing, exhaling in low, humming sighs as I wait for some answer. Even though we're almost the same height and I probably weigh as much as he does, if not more, I feel small beside Maven. Small and vulnerable. A bird in alliance with a cat. I don't like the sensation.

"Retrieving Bracken's children could be a goose chase. We don't know where they are, or how well guarded they might be. They could be on the other side of the continent. They could be dead, for all we know," Maven mutters. "Our focus should be on my brother. When he is gone, they'll have no one left to stand behind."

I try not to look disappointed, but I feel my shoulders droop anyway. We need Piedmont. I know we do. Leaving them to Montfort is a mistake, one that could end in our death and ruin. So I try again.

"Prince Bracken's hands are tied. He can't attempt a rescue of his children, even if he knew where they were," I murmur, dropping my voice. "The risk of failure is too great. But could someone *else* do it for him?"

"Are you offering yourself for the job, Iris?" he clips, looking down his nose at me.

I tighten at such a foolish thought. "I am a queen and a princess, not a dog playing fetch."

"Of course you aren't a dog, my dear." Maven offers a sneer, never breaking his stride. "Dogs obey."

Instead of recoiling, I brush off the naked insult with a sigh. "I suppose you're right, my king." My last card to play is a good one. "After all, you have experience where hostages are concerned."

Heat flares next to me, close enough that an instant sweat breaks out over my body. Reminding Maven of Mare—and how he lost her—is an easy way to ignite his temper.

"If the children can be found," he growls, "then perhaps something can be arranged."

That's all I get from the Calore king. I consider it a successful conversation.

The walls change from polished gilding and turquoise paint to gleaming marble, marking the end of the noble sector and the beginning of the royal palace. Arches still dart the way, but they're gated and guarded, a Lakelander soldier in stoic blue at each. More walk the length of the wall, looking down at their queen as she passes. Mother's pace quickens slightly. She's eager to be inside, away from prying eyes. *Alone with us.* Tiora follows at her heels, not to stay close to Mother, but to keep her distance from Maven. He unsettles her, as he does most people. Something about the intensity in his electric eyes. It seems wrong in someone so young. Artificial, even. Planted.

With a mother like his, it very well could be.

If she were alive, she wouldn't be allowed in Detraon, let alone within striking distance of the royal family. In the Lakelands, her kind of Silvers, mind-controlling whispers, are not trusted. Nor do they exist anymore. The Servon Line was extinguished long ago, and for good reason. As for Norta, I have a feeling House Merandus may soon meet the same fate. I have yet to speak to a whisper since I came to Whitefire, and after Maven's cousin died at our wedding, I think he must be keeping the rest of his mother's brood away, if they are still living at all.

The Royelle, our palace, spirals across the vast grounds of its sector. It has canals and aqueducts of its own, their waters spilling out in fountains and falls. Some arch over our path, carried to the bay, while others run under the walkway. In winter, most of them freeze, decorating the path in icy sculptures no human hand could create. Priests from the temples will read the ice, on feast days and holidays, to communicate the will of the gods. They speak in riddles, usually, writing their words on the land and lakes for only the blessed to see, and few to understand.

It takes courage for a burner king of a recently hostile nation to enter the stronghold of the Lakelands, and Maven does it without flinching. Another might think he doesn't have the capacity for fear. That his mother removed something so weak. But that isn't true. I see fear in everything he does. Fear of his brother, mostly. Fear because that Barrow girl is gone and out of his grasp. And like everyone else in our world, he is deathly afraid of losing his power. It's why he's here. Why he married me. He will do anything to keep his crown.

Such dedication. It's both his greatest strength and his greatest weakness.

We approach the grand gates opening on the bay, flanked both by guards and waterfalls. The men bow to Mother as she passes, and even the water ripples a little, tugged by her immense ability. Inside the bay gates is my favorite courtyard: a wide, manicured riot of blue flowers of every kind. Roses, lilies, hydrangeas, tulips, hibiscus—petals in shades from periwinkle to deep indigo. At least, they should be blue. But like the flags, like my family, the flowers mourn.

Their petals are black.

"Your Majesty, may I ask for my daughter's presence in our shrine? As is our tradition?"

It's the first time I've heard Mother speak this morning. She uses her court tone, as well as the language of Norta so Maven has no excuse to misunderstand her request. Her accent is better than mine, almost imperceptible. Cenra Cygnet is a smart woman, with an ear for languages and an eye for diplomacy.

She stops to survey Maven, turning to face him in a display of common courtesy. It would not do to show a king her back while asking something of him. *Even if the request is for me, her daughter, a living person with a will of her own,* I think as a sour taste rises in my mouth. *But not really. He outranks you. You're his subject now, not hers. You do as he wishes.*

On the outside, at least.

I have no intention of being a queen on a leash.

Thankfully, Maven is less dismissive of religion in front of my mother. He offers a tight smile and a shallow bow. Next to Mother, with her graying hair and crow's-feet, he seems younger. New. Inexperienced. He is anything but. "We must honor tradition," he says. "Even in chaotic times like these. Neither Norta nor the Lakelands can forget who they are. It may be what saves us in the end, *Your* Majesty."

He speaks well, the words smooth as syrup.

Mother shows her teeth, but the grin doesn't meet her eyes. "It may indeed. Come, Iris," she adds, beckoning to me.

If I had no restraint, I would take her hand and run. But I have restraint in spades, and I keep an even pace. Almost too slow, as I follow my mother and sister through the black flowers, the blue-patterned halls, and onto the sacred ground that is the queen's personal temple in the Royelle.

Adjoining the royal apartments of the monarch, the secluded temple is simple, tucked away among salons and bedrooms. Tradition stands in the usual trappings. A gurgling fountain, waist height, bubbles away in the center of the small chamber. Worn faces, bland in their features, both strange and familiar, look down from the ceiling and walls. Our gods have no names, no hierarchy. Their blessings are random, their words sparse, their punishments impossible to predict. But they exist in all things. They are felt at all times. I search out my favorite, a vaguely feminine face, her eyes empty and gray, distinguished only by a quirk of the lips that could be a flaw in the stone. She seems to smile knowingly. She comforts me, even now, in the shadow of my father's funeral. *All will be right,* I think she says.

The room isn't as large as the other palace temple, the one we use for court services, or as grand as the massive temples in the center of Detraon. No golden altars or jeweled books of celestial law. Our gods require little more than faith to make their presence known.

I lay a hand against a familiar window, waiting. The rising sun filters weakly through thick diamondglass, the panes arranged like spiraling waves. Only when the doors of the sanctum close behind us, locking us in with no one but the gods and one another, do I breathe a low sigh of relief. Before my eyes adjust to the dim light, Mother takes my face in her warm hands, and I can't help but flinch.

"You don't need to go back," Mother whispers.

I've never heard her beg. It is a foreign sound.

My voice sticks. "What?"

"Please, my dearest one." She switches deftly back to Lakelander, favoring our native tongue. Her eyes sharpen, darker in the shadows of the narrow room. They are deep wells I could fall into and never climb out of. "The alliance can survive without you holding it together."

She doesn't let go of my face, her thumbs running over my cheekbones. For a long moment, I linger. I see the hope bloom in her eyes, and I squeeze my lids shut. Slowly, I put my hands over her own and pull them away.

"We know that isn't true at all," I tell my mother, forcing myself to look back at her face.

She clenches her jaw, hardening. A queen is never accustomed to denial. "Don't tell me what I do or do not know."

But I am a queen too.

"Have the gods told you otherwise?" I ask. "Do you speak for them?" A blasphemy. You can hear the gods in your heart, but only priests can spread their words.

Even the queen of the Lakelands is subject to such bonds. She glances away, ashamed, before turning to Tiora. My sister says nothing, and looks grimmer than ever. Quite a feat.

"Do you speak for the crown?" I press on, putting distance between us. *Mother must understand.* "Is this what will help our country?"

Again, silence. Mother won't answer. Instead she steels herself, shifting into her royal persona before my eyes. She seems to harden and grow taller. I almost expect her to turn to stone. *She won't lie to you.*

"Or do you speak for yourself, Mother? As a grieving woman? You just lost Father, and you don't want to lose me—"

"I cannot deny that I want you here," she says firmly, and I recognize the voice of a sovereign. The one she uses in court rulings. "Safe.

Protected from monsters like *him*."

"I can handle Maven. I have been, for months now. You know that." Like her, I look to Tiora for some kind of support. Her face doesn't change, maintaining neutrality. Observant, quiet, and calculating, as a queen in waiting should be.

"Oh, I read your letters, yes." Mother waves a hand, dismissive. Have her fingers always been so thin, so wrinkled, so *old*? I'm struck by the sight. *So much gray,* I muse, watching her as she paces. Her hair gleams in the dim light. *So much more gray than I remember.*

"I receive both your official correspondence and the secret reports you send, Iris," Mother says. "Neither fills me with confidence. And seeing him now . . ." She heaves a ragged sigh, thinking. The queen crosses to the opposite window, tracing the swirls of diamondglass. "That boy is all sharp edges and emptiness. There is no soul to him. He killed his own father, tried to do the same to the exiled brother. Whatever his demon mother did has cursed the king of Norta to a life of torment. I won't curse you to the same. I won't let you waste your life at his side. It's only a matter of time before his court devours him, or he devours it."

I share that fear with her, but it's no use lamenting choices already made. Doors already opened. Paths already taken. "If only you'd told me this sooner," I scoff. "I could have let him die when those Reds attacked our wedding. Then Father would still be alive."

"Yes," Mother murmurs. She studies the window like a fine painting, so she doesn't have to look at her daughters.

"And then, if he were dead . . ." I lower my voice, trying to sound as strong as she does. Like Mother, like Tiora. A queen born. Slowly, I move to my mother's side, put my hands on her narrow shoulders. She's always been thinner than me. "We would be fighting a war on two fronts. Against a new king in Norta and the Red rebellion that seems to boil all over the world." *In my own country,* I curse in my head. The Red rebellion began within *our* borders, under *our* noses. We let their rot spread.

Mother's eyelashes flutter, dark against brown cheeks. Her hand covers mine. "But I'd have you both. We'd still be together."

"For how long?" my sister asks.

Tiora is taller than us, and surveys us down the length of her arched nose. She folds her arms, rustling the blue-and-black silk. In the cloistered, small temple, she seems statuesque, towering next to the gods themselves.

"Who's to say *that* path doesn't end in more death?" she says. "In all our bodies at the bottom of the bay? You think the Scarlet Guard would let us live if they overthrew our kingdom? I don't."

"Neither do I," I mumble, laying my forehead against our mother's shoulder. "Mother?"

Her body stiffens beneath my touch, muscles coiling tight. "It can be done," she says flatly. "This knot can be untangled. You can still stay with us. But it must be your choice, *monamora.*"

My love.

If I could ask one thing of Mother, it would be to choose for me. To do as she has done for me so many thousand times. *Wear this, eat that, say what I tell you.* I begrudged her wisdom then, how she or my father would take the responsibility from me. Now I wish I could cast it away. Put my fate in the hands of the people I trust. If only I were still a child, and this were all a bad dream.

I look over my shoulder, searching for my sister. She frowns at me, heartsick, and offers no escape.

"I would stay if I could." I try to sound like a queen, but the words tremble. "You know that. And you know, deep down, that what you ask is impossible. A betrayal of your crown. What is it you used to tell us?"

Tiora answers as Mother winces. "Duty first. Honor always."

The memory warms my insides. What lies ahead isn't easy, but it's what I must do. I have purpose in that, at the very least.

"My duty is to protect the Lakelands as well as you do," I tell them. "My marriage to Maven may not win the war, but it gives us a chance. It puts a wall between us and the wolves at the door. As for my honor—I have none until Father is avenged."

"Agreed," Tiora snarls.

"Agreed," Mother whispers, her voice a shadow.

I stare over her shoulder, at the face of the smiling god. I draw strength from her smirk, her confidence. She assures me. "Maven, his kingdom, they're a shield, but a sword too. We have to use him, even though he's a danger to us all."

Mother scoffs. "Especially you."

"Yes, especially me."

"I never should have agreed," she hisses. "It was your father's idea."

"I know, and it was a good one. I don't blame him." *I don't blame him.* How many nights did I spend alone in Whitefire Palace, awake and telling myself I felt no remorse? No anger at having been sold like a pet or an acre of land? It was a lie then, and a lie now. But my anger at such things died with my father.

"When all this is over—" Mother says.

Tiora cuts her off. "*If* we win—"

"*When* we win," Mother says, spinning on her heel. Her eyes flash, catching a spangle of light. In the center of the temple chamber, the curling fountain slows its motions, the steady fall of water easing in its journey. "When your father is bathed by the blood of his killers, when the Scarlet Guard is exterminated like so many overgrown *rats*"—the water stops, suspended by her fervor—"there will be little reason to leave you in Norta. And even less to leave an unstable, unfit king on the throne in Archeon. Especially one who is so foolish with the blood of his own people, and ours."

"Agreed," my sister and I whisper in unison.

With even motion, Mother turns her head to the frozen fountain, shaping the liquid to her liking. It arcs in the air, like a glass complexity. Light plays off the water, splitting into prisms of every color. Mother doesn't flinch, unblinking against the flash of sun. "The Lakelands will wash clean those godless nations. Conquer Norta. And the Rift too. They gnaw at each other already, sacrificing their own for such petty rivalries. It won't be long until their strength is spent. There will be no escape from the fury of the line of Cygnet."

I have always been proud of my mother, even when I was a child. She is a great woman, duty and honor personified. Clear-eyed, unyielding. A mother to her entire kingdom as well as her children. I realize now I didn't know the half of it. The resolve beneath her still surface, as strong as any storm. And what a storm it will be.

"Let them face the flood," I say, an old promise of judgment. The one we use to punish traitors. And enemies of every kind.

"What of the Reds? The ones with abilities, in the mountain country? They have spies running through our own kingdom." Tiora furrows her brow, cutting a canyon in her skin. I want to smooth away her infinite cares, but she's right.

People like Mare Barrow must be accounted for. They're part of this too. We're fighting them too.

"We use Maven against them," I tell Tiora. "He has an obsession with newbloods, the lightning girl especially. He'll pursue them to the ends of the earth if need be, and spend all his strength doing it."

Mother nods in grim approval. "And Piedmont?"

"I did as you said." Slowly, I straighten, proud of myself. "That seed is planted. Maven needs Bracken as much as we do. He'll try to rescue the children. If we can win Bracken to our side, use his armies instead of our own . . ."

My sister finishes for me. "The Lakelands can be preserved. Our strength gathered and waiting. Bracken could even be made to turn against Maven."

"Yes," I say. "If we're lucky, they'll all kill each other long before we show our true selves."

Tiora clucks her tongue. "I put little stock in luck when your life hangs in the balance, *petasorre*." *Little sister.*

Though she says the word with love, meaning no disrespect, it still makes me uncomfortable. Not because she is the heir, the eldest, the daughter meant to rule. But because it shows how much she cares and how much she will sacrifice for me. Something I don't want from her, or my mother. My family has given enough.

"It must be you who rescues Bracken's children," my mother says, her voice sullen and cold. Her eyes match her tone. "A daughter of Cygnet. Maven will send his Silvers, but he won't go himself. He doesn't have the skill or stomach for such things. But if you go with his soldiers, if you return to Prince Bracken with his children in your arms . . ."

I swallow hard. *I'm not a dog playing fetch.* I told Maven that only minutes ago, and I almost say the same to my royal mother.

"It's too dangerous," Tiora says quickly, almost stepping between us.

Mother holds her ground, unflinching as always. "*You* cannot leave our borders, Ti. And if Bracken is to be swayed, to us and us alone, we must be the ones to help him. Such is the Piedmont way." She clenches her teeth. "Or would you rather Maven do it and win himself a staunch ally? That boy is dangerous enough alone. Don't give him another sword to wield."

Even though it wounds me, both my pride and my resolve, I see reason in her words. If Maven is the one to lead, or to order a rescue of the children, then Maven will certainly win Bracken's allegiance. That cannot be allowed.

"Of course not," I answer slowly. "It must be me, then. Somehow."

Tiora concedes too. She seems to shrink. "I'll have my diplomats make contact. Discreetly as they can. What else do you need?"

I nod, feeling a numbness in my fingers. *Rescue Bracken's children.* I don't even know where to start.

The seconds drag as they pass, more difficult to ignore.

If we stay in here much longer, the Nortans will get suspicious, I think, biting my lip. *Maven, especially, if he isn't already.* My legs turn to lead as I back away from Mother, my hands suddenly cold without her warmth.

As I pass the fountain, I run my fingers in the arcing water, wetting the tips. I draw the liquid over my eyelids, smudging the dark makeup on my lashes. False tears roll down my cheeks, black as the mourning flowers.

"Pray, Ti," I tell my sister. "Trust the gods if you will not trust luck."

"My trust in them is absolute," she replies, mechanical, automatic. "I'll pray for us all."

I linger at the door, one hand on the simple knob. "As will I." Then I pull, popping the bubble around us, ending what could be our last moments of security for years to come. Under my breath, I mumble to myself, "Will this work?"

Somehow Mother hears me. She looks up, her eyes inescapable as I back away.

"Only the gods know."

FIVE
Mare

The dropjet feels sluggish on the air, heavier than usual. I sway against my safety restraints, eyes lidded. The motion of the craft paired with the comforting buzz of electricity has me half asleep. The engines chug calmly, despite the extra weight. *More cargo,* I know. The hold is filled to the brim with the spoils of Corvium. Munitions, guns, explosives, weapons of every kind. Military uniforms, rations, fuel, batteries. Even bootlaces. Half is going to Piedmont now, and the rest is on another jet, returning to Davidson's mountains.

Montfort and the Scarlet Guard are not wasteful in their endeavors. They did the same thing after the Whitefire attack, stripping what they could from the palace in such limited time. Money, mostly, hauled out of the Treasury once it was clear Maven was beyond our reach. It happened in Piedmont too. It's why the southern base seems empty, in the lodgings, in the administrative buildings once meant for grand war councils. No paintings, no statues, no fine plates or cutlery. None of the trappings great Silvers require. Nothing but what is necessary. The rest was pulled apart, sold, repurposed. Wars are not cheap. We can only maintain what is useful.

That's why Corvium crumbles behind us. Because Corvium is no longer useful.

Davidson argued that leaving a garrison of soldiers was foolish, a waste. The fortress city was built to funnel soldiers into the Choke to fight Lakelanders. With that war ended, it has little purpose. No river to guard, no strategic resources. Just one of many roads to the Lakelands. Corvium had become little more than a distraction. And while we held the city, it was deep in Maven's territory, and too close to the border. The Lakelands could sweep through without warning, or Maven could return in force. We might win again, but more would die. For nothing more than some walls in the middle of nowhere.

The Silvers opposed. Naturally. I think they must be honor-bound to disagree with anything someone with red blood says. Anabel argued the *optics*.

"How many dead, how much blood spent on these walls, and you want to give up the city? We'll look like fools!" she scoffed, glaring across the council chamber. The old woman looked at Davidson like he had two heads. "Cal's first victory, his flag raised—"

"I don't see his flag anywhere," Farley interrupted, dry as bone.

But Anabel ignored her. She pressed on, seeming like she might obliterate the table beneath her fingers. Cal sat silent at her side, his eyes ablaze as he stared at his hands. "It will look like weakness to abandon the city," the old queen said.

"I care very little for how things appear, only for how they *are*, Your Majesty," Davidson replied. "You are very welcome to leave a garrison of your own to hold Corvium, but no soldier of Montfort or the Scarlet Guard will remain here."

Her lip curled at that, but any retort died in her throat. Anabel had no intention of wasting her own army in such a way. She slid back in her seat and turned away from Davidson, her eyes flitting toward Volo Samos. But he wouldn't volunteer his own soldiers either. He kept silent.

"If we leave the city, we leave it in ruins." Tiberias clenched his fist on the table. I remember that clearly, his knuckles bone-white beneath his skin. There was still dirt under his fingernails, and probably blood too. I focused on his hands so I wouldn't have to look at his face. His emotions are too easily read, and I still want no part of them. "Special contingents from each army," he said. "Lerolan oblivions, the new-blood gravitrons and bombers. Anyone who can destroy. Strip the city of resources, then turn it to ash and wash away whatever's left. Leave nothing Maven or the Lakelands can use."

He didn't look up as he spoke, unable to hold any gaze. It must have been difficult to order the destruction of one of his own cities. A place he knew, a place his father had protected, and his grandfather before him. Tiberias values duty as much as tradition, both ideals planted bone-deep. But I had little pity for him then, and have even less now as we hurtle toward Piedmont.

Corvium was nothing more than the gate to a Red graveyard. I'm glad it's gone.

Even so, I feel unease deep in the pit of my stomach. Corvium still burns behind my eyelids, its walls crumbling, torn apart by explosive bursts, the buildings ripped away by manipulated gravity, the metal gates twisting into snaking knots. Smoke races the streets. Ella, an electricon like me, used her own storm to strike the central tower, furious blue lightning cracking stone. Montfort nymphs, newbloods of great power, used the nearby streams and even a river to sweep rubble away to the distant lake. No part of Corvium escaped. Some of it even sank, collapsing into the tunnels beneath the city. The rest was left in warning, like ancient stone monoliths weathered by a thousand years instead of a few hours.

How many other cities will share the same fate?

First I think of the Stilts.

I haven't seen the place where I grew up in almost a year. Not since my name was Mareena, and I stood on the deck of a royal ship, eyeing the banks of the Capital River with a ghost at my side. Elara was alive then, and the king too. They forced me to watch as we passed my village, its people gathered at the water's edge under the open threat of a whipcrack or a cell. My family stood among them. I focused on their faces, not on the place. The Stilts was never my home. They are.

Would I care now if the village disappeared? If no one was harmed, but the stilt houses, the market, the school, the *arena*—if it was destroyed? Burned, flooded, or simply gone?

I really can't say.

But there are certainly places that should join Corvium in ruins. I name the ones I want to destroy, cursing them.

Gray Town, Merry Town, New Town. And all the rest of their like.

The techie slums remind me of Cameron. She sleeps across from me, jostled in her restraining belts. Her head lolls, her snore almost indistinguishable over the sound of the jet engines. From underneath her collar, her tattoo peeks out. Black ink against dark brown skin. She was marked with her profession, or rather her prison, a long time ago. I only saw a tech town from a distance, and the memory still makes me gag. I can't imagine growing up in one, bound to a life in smoke.

The Red slums must be ended.

Their walls must burn too.

★ ★ ★

We land at the Piedmont base in a late-morning downpour. I'm drenched after three steps across the runway, heading for the line of waiting transports. Farley outpaces me easily, eager to get back to Clara. She has a mind for little else, bypassing the Colonel and the rest of their soldiers as they move to greet us. I work to keep at her heels, forced to move at an uneasy trot. I try not to look back at the other jet, the Silver one. I hear them over the rain, trooping out onto the paved field in all their style. The rain darkens their colors, muddying Lerolan orange, Jacos yellow, Calore red, and Samos silver. Evangeline smartly abandoned her armor. Metal clothes aren't exactly safe in a thunderstorm.

At least King Volo and the rest of his Silver lords haven't followed us here. They're on the way back to the Kingdom of the Rift, if they haven't arrived already. Only the Silvers going on to Montfort tomorrow made the journey to Piedmont. Anabel, Julian, their various guards and advisers—as well as Evangeline and, of course, Tiberias.

When I get into my transport, sliding into the dry interior, I catch a glimpse of him, brooding like a storm cloud. Tiberias stands apart, the only one of them familiar with the Piedmont base. Anabel must have brought more courtly clothes for him. It's the only explanation for his long cloak and polished boots, and the finery underneath. At this distance, I can't tell if he has a crown. Despite the royal clothing, no one would mistake him for Maven. Tiberias's colors are reversed. The cloak is bloodred, as are his clothes, all trimmed with black and royal silver. He glows through the rain, bright as any flame. And he stares, dark brows furrowed, unmoving as the storm opens above us.

I feel the first crack of lightning before it splits across the sky. Ella was holding it back to let the jets land. She must have let it go.

I turn from the transport window and lean against the glass. As we speed off, I try to let go of something too.

The row house ceded to my family looks the same as it did when I left a few days ago, albeit very wet. Rain lashes the windows, drowning flowers in their window boxes. Tramy won't like that. He dotes on those flowers.

He can grow as many as he likes in Montfort. He can plant an entire garden, and spend his life watching it bloom.

Farley gets out of the transport before it fully stops, her boots splashing through a puddle. I hesitate, for many reasons.

Of course I have to talk to my family about Montfort. And hope they agree to stay there, even when I leave again. We should be used to it by now, but walking away never gets easier. They can't stop me from doing it, but I can't stop them either. If they refuse to go. I shudder at the thought. Knowing they're safe is the only sanctuary I have left.

But that inevitable argument is a dream compared to what else I have to admit.

Cal chose the crown. Not me. Not us.

Saying it makes it real.

The puddle outside the transport is deeper than I thought, splashing up the sides of my short boots, sending a cold chill over my legs. I welcome the distraction, and follow Farley up the steps to an opening door.

A blur of Barrows pulls me inside. Mom, Gisa, Tramy, and Bree whirl around me. My old friend Kilorn joins the mix as well, stepping in to give me a short but firm squeeze. I feel a burst of relief at the sight of him. He wasn't ready to fight in Corvium, and I'm still glad he agreed to stay behind.

Dad hangs back again, waiting to hug me properly without anyone else worming in. He might have to wait a long time, since Mom doesn't seem too concerned with letting me go. She drapes an arm across my shoulders, pulling me close. Her clothes smell fresh, clean, like a dewy morning and soap. Nothing like home in the Stilts. My status in the army, whatever it is, affords my family a level of luxury we were never accustomed to before. The row house itself, a former officer's quarters, is opulent compared to our old stilt home. Though it is sparsely decorated, the essentials are all finely made and well cared for.

Farley only has eyes for Clara. While I'm barely through the front door, Farley already holds Clara against her chest, letting the baby girl rest her head on her shoulder. Yawning, Clara nuzzles, trying to return to her interrupted nap. When she thinks no one is looking, Farley dips her neck, pressing her nose against Clara's tiny head of brown hair. She shuts her eyes and inhales.

Meanwhile, Mom plants another of a dozen kisses on my temple, grinning. "Home again," she murmurs.

"So they really did it," Dad says. "Corvium is gone." I untangle myself from Mom long enough to give him a proper hug. We're still unaccustomed to touching this way, without my father huddled in his wheelchair. Despite his long months of recuperation with the aid of Sara Skonos, as well as the healers and nurses of the Montfort army, nothing can erase the years we all remember. The pain is still there, sitting in his brain. And I suppose it should. Forgetting doesn't feel right.

He leans on me, not as heavily as he used to, and I lead him into the sitting room. We share a bitter smile, a private one that passes only between us. My father was a soldier once too, longer than any of us. He understands what it is to see death and return from it. I try to imagine who he was, beneath the wrinkles and the scraggly whiskers fading into gray, behind his eyes. We had few photographs at home. I don't know how many made it to the refuge on Tuck Island, then to the other base in the Lakelands, and then here. One of them sticks out in my memory. An old scrap of a picture, worn at the edges, fuzzy and faded in the image. My mother and father posed for it a long time ago, before even Bree was born. They were teenagers, kids of the Stilts like I was. Dad must not have been eighteen. He wasn't conscripted yet, and Mom was just an apprentice. Dad used to look so much like Bree, my oldest brother. Same grin, his mouth almost too wide, framed by dimples. Thick, straight eyebrows across a high forehead. Ears that could be a little too big. I try not to think of my brothers aging like my father has, subjected to the same pains and worries. I can make sure they don't share our father's fate—or Shade's.

Bree flops into an armchair near us, crossing his bare feet on the simple rug. I wrinkle my nose. Men do not have lovely feet.

"Good riddance to that heap," Bree says, cursing Corvium.

Tramy bobs his head in agreement. His dark brown beard continues to fill in. "Won't miss it," he agrees. Both of them were conscripted like Dad. Both of them know the fortress well enough to hate its memory. They trade smiles, as if they've won some kind of game.

Dad is less celebratory. He eases himself down into another chair, stretching out his regrown leg. "Silvers will just build another. It's their way. They don't change." His eyes flash, finding mine. My stomach drops when I realize what he's trying to say. My cheeks burn at the implication. "Do they?"

Shamed, I look back at Gisa, searching her quickly. Her shoulders droop and she sighs, barely nodding. She picks at the sleeve of her shirt, avoiding my eyes.

"So you've heard," I say, my voice flat and empty.

"Not everything," she replies. Her eyes dart to Kilorn, and I'm willing to bet he tipped everyone off, relaying the less painful parts of my message last night. Nervous, Gisa twists a lock of hair around her finger. The dark red strands gleam. "But enough to figure it out. Something about another queen, a new king, and Montfort, of course. Always Montfort."

Kilorn's lips twist, pursing together. He runs a hand through his choppy blond hair, mirroring Gisa's discomfort. There's anger too. It simmers in him, lighting up his green eyes. "I can't believe he said yes."

I can only nod.

"Coward," Kilorn snaps. He clenches a fist. "Idiot coward. Wasteful, spoiled-brat bastard. I should break his jaw."

"I'll help," Gisa mutters.

No one scolds them. Not even me, though Kilorn certainly expects it. He glances my way, surprised by my silence. I hold his gaze, trying to speak without saying the name. *Shade gave his life for our cause, and Tiberias can't even give up the crown.*

I wonder if Kilorn knows my heart is broken in two. He must.

Is this what it felt like, when I pushed Kilorn away? When I told him I didn't feel the same? That I couldn't give him what he wanted?

His gaze softens with pity. I hope he doesn't know what this feels like. I hope I didn't put him in this much pain. *It's just not in you to love me,* he said once. Now I wish that weren't true. I wish I could save us both from this agony.

Thankfully, Mom puts a hand on my arm. A light touch, but enough to guide me to the long sofa. She doesn't say anything about the Calore prince, and the glare she shoots around the room communicates her point. *Enough.*

"We got your message," she says, her voice a little too loud and bright as she forces the change in subject. "From that other newblood, with the beard—"

"Tahir," Gisa offers as she sits down next to me. Kilorn hovers behind us both. "You've decided on resettlement for us." Even though it's what she wanted, I don't miss the sharp edges to her tone. My sister blinks at me, one eyebrow raised.

I sigh aloud. "Well, I'm not making decisions for you. But if you want to go, there's a place for you all. The premier said you'll be welcomed with open arms."

"What about everyone else?" Tramy asks. He narrows his eyes as he perches on the arm of Bree's chair. "We're not the only ones evacuated here."

He catches an elbow in the side and doubles over as Bree snickers. "Thinking about that clerk? What's-her-name, with the curly hair."

"No," Tramy grumbles back, his golden cheeks flaming beneath his beard. Bree tries to poke at his flushed face but gets swatted away. My brothers have a terrific talent for acting like children. It used to annoy me, but not anymore. The normalcy of them is soothing.

"It will take time." I can only shrug. "But for us . . ."

Gisa scoffs aloud. She tosses back her head, exasperated. "For *you*, Mare. We're not silly enough to think the leader of the Republic wants to do *us* a favor. What does he get in return?" With nimble fingers, she grabs my hand, tightening her grip. "What does he get from you?"

"Davidson isn't Silver," I say. "What he wants, I'm willing to give."

"And when do you get to stop *giving* things?" she snaps back. "When you die? When you end up like Shade?"

The name drops a hush over the room. At the door, Farley turns her face, hiding in shadow.

I stare at Gisa, searching my sister's pretty face. She's fifteen now, settling into herself. Her face used to be rounder, her freckles less numerous. And she didn't have the cares she has now. Just the usual worries. It used to be little Gisa we relied on. Her skill, her talent. Her ability to save our family. Not anymore. She doesn't begrudge the loss of that weight. But her concern is clear. She doesn't want it on my shoulders either.

Too late.

"Gisa," Mom says, her voice a low warning.

I recover as best I can, pulling my hand away. My spine turns to steel. "We need to request more troops, and Premier Davidson's government has to approve before they can be sent. I'll help present our coalition, show them who we all are. Make a convincing argument for the war against Norta and the Lakelands."

My sister is unconvinced. "I know you're good at arguing, but you aren't *that* good."

"No, but I'm the crossroads," I say, dancing around the truth of it. "Between the Scarlet Guard, the Silver courts, the newbloods, and Reds too." I'm not lying, at least. "And I've had enough practice putting on a good show."

Farley balances her baby in one arm, putting her other hand on her hip. She drums a finger against the holster of the pistol glued to her side. "Mare's trying to say she's a good distraction. Where she goes, Cal follows. Even now, when he's trying to win back his throne. He's coming with us to Montfort, and so is his new betrothed."

Behind me, I hear Kilorn suck in a hissing breath.

Gisa is just as disgusted. "Only *they* would stop to arrange marriages in the middle of a war."

"For another alliance, right?" Kilorn sneers. "Maven did it already. Locked up the Lakelands. Cal needs to do the same. So who is it? Some girl from Piedmont? Really cement what we're doing down here?"

"It doesn't matter who she is." My fist clenches in my lap as I realize that I'm *lucky* it's Evangeline. A girl who wants nothing to do with him. Another chink in his flaming armor.

"And you're just going to let this happen?" Kilorn paces out from behind the sofa, his long limbs making even strides. He glares between Farley and me. "No, excuse me, you're going to *help*? Help Cal fight for a crown *no one* should have? After everything we've done?" He's so upset, I almost expect him to spit on the floor. I keep my face still, impassive, letting him fume. I can't remember him ever being so disappointed in me. Angry, yes, but not like this. His chest rises and falls rapidly as he waits for my explanation.

Farley does it for me. "Montfort and the Scarlet Guard won't fight two wars," she says evenly, emphasizing the words. Conveying a message. "We have to take on our enemies one at a time. Do you understand?"

My family seems to tighten in unison, their eyes going dark. Dad especially. He runs a thumb along his jaw, thoughtful, as his lips press into a thin line. Kilorn is less subdued. Green fire sparks behind his eyes. "Oh," he murmurs, almost smiling. "I see."

Bree blinks. "Uh, I don't?"

"No one is surprised," Tramy mutters under his breath.

I lean forward, eager to make them all understand. "We aren't going to give the throne to another Silver king. At least not for long. The Calore brothers are at war, spending their forces fighting each other. When the dust settles . . ."

Dad drops his hand on his knee. I don't miss the tremble in his fingers. I feel it in mine too. "It will be easier to deal with the victor."

"No more kings," Farley breathes. "No more kingdoms."

I have no idea what that world could look like. But I might soon, if Montfort is everything I've been promised.

If only I still believed in promises.

We don't bother trying to sneak out. Mom and Dad snore like trains, and my siblings know better than to stop me. The rain hasn't let up, but Kilorn and I don't mind. We walk down the row-house street without speaking, the only noise coming from our feet squelching through puddles as the storm rumbles in the distance. I can barely feel it anymore, as the lightning and thunder spiral away toward the coast. It isn't that cold, and the well-illuminated base keeps out the darkness. We don't have any real destination. No direction but forward.

"He's a coward," Kilorn mumbles. He kicks at a loose pebble. It skitters away, spreading ripples across the wet street.

"You said that already," I reply. "Along with a few other things."

"Well, I meant it."

"He deserves every word."

Silence drags over us like a heavy curtain. We both know this is strange territory. My romantic entanglements aren't exactly his favorite subject, and I don't want to inflict any more pain than I already have on my closest friend.

"We don't have to talk—"

He cuts me off, putting a hand on my arm. His touch is firm but friendly. The lines between us are clearly drawn, and Kilorn values me enough to never cross them. He might not even feel the same as he did before. I've changed so much in the last few months. It's possible the girl he thought he loved is gone. I know what that's like too, to love someone who doesn't really exist.

"I'm sorry," he says. "I know what he means to you."

"Meant," I growl, trying to push past him.

But his grip tightens. "No, I didn't make a mistake. He still means something to you, even if you won't admit that."

It isn't worth the argument. "Fine. I admit it," I force through clenched teeth. It's dark enough that he might not notice my face turning scarlet. "I asked the premier," I mumble. *Kilorn will understand. He has to understand.* "I asked to keep him alive. When the time comes, when we turn. Is that weakness?"

Kilorn's face falls. The harsh streetlights illuminate him from behind, giving him a halo. He's a handsome boy, if he isn't already considered a man. If only my heart fell to him instead of someone else.

"I don't think so," he says. "Love can be exploited, I guess, used to manipulate. It's leverage. But I would never call loving someone else a weakness. I think living without love at all, any kind of love, is weakness. And the worst kind of darkness."

I swallow thickly. The tears don't feel so immediate anymore. "When did you become so wise?"

He grins, shoving his hands in his pockets. "I read books now."

"Do they have pictures?"

Barking a laugh, he starts walking again. "You're such a kind person."

I match his pace. "That's what I hear," I reply, glancing up at his lanky form. His hair is soaked through now, darker in the wet. Almost brown. Kilorn could be Shade if I squinted. Suddenly I miss my brother so much I can barely breathe.

I won't lose anyone else the way I lost Shade. It's an empty promise, with no guarantees. But I need some kind of hope. I need some kind of hope, however small it may be.

"Will you come to Montfort?" The words blurt out of me, and I can't bite them back. It's a selfish request. Kilorn doesn't have to follow me around everywhere I go. And it's not my place to demand anything of him. But I don't want to leave him behind again.

His responding grin erases any trepidation I might have. "Am I allowed? Thought it was some kind of mission."

"It is. And I'm allowing it."

"Because it's safe," he replies, eyeing me sidelong.

I purse my lips, searching for an answer he might accept. *Yes, it is safe. Or the closest thing we have to safe.* It isn't wrong to want him out of danger.

Kilorn brushes my arm. "I get it," he continues. "Listen, I'm not about to storm a city or shoot jets out of the sky. I know what my limitations are, and how many I have compared to the rest of you."

"Just because you can't kill someone with a snap of your fingers doesn't make you less than anyone else," I fire back, almost electrified with sudden indignation. I wish I could list all the wonderful things about Kilorn. All the *important* things he is.

His expression sours. "Don't remind me."

I grab his arm, nails digging into wet fabric. He doesn't stop walking. "I'm serious, Kilorn," I say. "So you'll come?"

"I'll check my schedule."

I dig my elbow into his side and he jumps away, forcing an exaggerated frown.

"Stop it. You know I bruise like a peach."

I elbow him again for good measure, both of us laughing as much as we dare.

We continue on quietly, lapsing into an easy silence. This time it isn't so stifling. My usual worries melt away, or at least step back for long moments. Kilorn is my home too, as much as my family. His presence is a pocket of time, a narrow place where we can exist without consequence. Nothing before, nothing after.

At the end of the street, a figure seems to materialize from the rain, shedding drops of dark and light. I recognize the silhouette before my body has time to react.

Julian.

The gangly Silver hesitates when he sees us, only for a second, but it's enough time for me to know. *His side is chosen, and it isn't mine.*

Cold bleeds through me, from fingers to toes. *Even Julian.*

As he approaches, Kilorn nudges me.

"I can head back," he whispers.

I glance at him briefly, drawing strength from him. "Please don't."

His brows knit with concern, but he nods curtly.

My old tutor still wears his long robes, despite the rain, and he shakes water from the folds of his faded yellow clothing. No use in it. The rain keeps pelting down, smoothing out the slight curls of his gray-streaked hair.

"I was hoping to catch you at home," he calls over the hissing downpour. "Well, honestly, I was hoping to catch you indisposed so I could do this in the morning. Instead of out in this infernal wet." Julian shakes his head like a dog and pushes hair away from his eyes.

"Say what you came here to say, Julian." I cross my arms. As the night falls, so does the temperature. I might catch a chill, even here in steaming Piedmont.

Julian doesn't reply. Instead his eyes flick to Kilorn, one eyebrow raised in silent question. "He's fine," I say, answering before he can ask. "Speak up before we all drown out here."

My tone sharpens, and so does Julian. He isn't a fool. His face falls, reading the disappointment etched on me. "I know you feel abandoned," he begins, choosing his words with maddening care.

I can't help but bristle. "Stick to history. I won't let you lecture me on what I'm allowed to feel."

He only blinks, taking my response in stride. Again he pauses, long enough to let a raindrop roll down his straight nose. He does it to gauge me, to measure, to study. For the first time, his patient manner makes me want to seize him by the shoulders and shake some impulsive words out of him.

"Very well," he says, his voice low and wounded. "Then, in the interest of history, or what will very soon *be* history, I am still accompanying my nephew on your journey west. I would like to see the Free Republic for myself, and I think I can be of use to Cal there." Julian starts to take a step forward, toward me, but thinks better of it. He keeps his distance.

"Does Tiberias have some interest in obscure history that I don't know about?" I scoff, the words coming out harsher than usual.

He looks torn; that much is very clear. He can barely look me in the eye. The rain plasters his hair to his forehead, clings to his lashes, pulls at him with tiny fingers. It smooths him out somehow, as if washing away his days. Julian seems younger than when I met him, almost a year ago. Less sure of himself. Full of worry and doubt.

"No," he concedes. "While I normally encourage my nephew to pursue all knowledge he can, there are some things I'd like to steer him away from. Some stones he should not waste time trying to overturn."

I raise an eyebrow. "What do you mean?"

Julian frowns. "I assume he mentioned his hopes for Maven. *Before.*"

Before he chose the crown over me. "He did," I whisper, sounding small.

"He thinks there might be some way to fix his brother. Heal the wounds of Elara Merandus." Slowly, Julian shakes his head. "But there is no completing a puzzle with missing pieces. Or putting a shattered pane of glass back together."

My stomach twists, tensing with what I already know. What I've seen firsthand. "It's impossible."

Julian nods. "Impossible, and hopeless. A doomed pursuit, one that will only break my boy's heart."

"What makes you think I still care about his heart?" I sneer, tasting the bitter lie.

Julian takes a wary step forward. "Go easy on him," he murmurs.

I snap back without blinking. "How dare you say that to me?"

"Mare, do you remember what you found in those books?" he asks, pulling his robes tight around himself. His voice takes on a pleading edge. "Do you remember the words?"

I shiver, and it isn't because of the rain. "'Not a god's chosen, but a god's cursed.'"

"Yes," he replies, nodding along with fervent motion. It reminds me of the way he used to teach, and I brace for a lecture. "This is not a new concept, Mare. Men and women have felt that way, in some capacity, for thousands of years. Chosen or cursed, fated or doomed. Since the dawn of sentience, I suspect, and long before Silver and Red or any type of ability. Did you know kings and politicians and rulers of every kind used to think they were blessed by the gods? Ordained to their place in the world? Many thought themselves chosen, but a few, of course, saw the duty as a curse."

Next to me, Kilorn puffs out a low scoff. I'm more obvious, rolling my eyes at Julian. When I shift, so does the collar of my shirt, sending a steady drip of rainwater down my spine. I clench my fists to keep from flinching.

"Are you saying your nephew is cursed to his crown?" I sneer.

Julian hardens, and I feel a tinge of regret for being so callous. He shakes his head at me, like I'm a child to be scolded. "Forced to choose between the woman he loves and what he thinks is right? What he thinks he must do, because of everything he's been taught to be? What else would you call that?"

"I call it an easy decision," Kilorn growls.

I bite down hard on the inside of my cheek, trying to gnaw back a dozen rude responses. "Did you *really* come here to defend what he did? Because I'm certainly not in the mood for it."

"No, of course not, Mare," Julian replies. "But to explain, if I can."

My stomach churns at the thought of Julian of all people *explaining* his nephew's heart to me. With his dissections and ruminations. Will he boil it down to simple science? An equation to show that the crown and I are not equal in the prince's eyes? I simply can't stand it.

"Save your breath, Julian," I spit. "Go back to your king. Stand at his side." I look him dead in the eye. So he knows I'm not lying. "And keep him safe."

He sees the offer for what it is. The only thing I can do.

Julian Jacos bows low. He sweeps out his soaking robes in an attempt at courtly manner. For a second, we could be back in Summerton, just him and me in a classroom piled with books. Back then, I lived in terror, forced to masquerade as someone else. Julian was one of my only refuges in that place. Alongside Cal and Maven. My only sanctuaries. The Calore brothers are gone. I think Julian might be too.

"I will, Mare," he tells me. "With my life, if I must."

"I hope it doesn't come to that."

"So do I."

Our words are warnings to each other. And his voice sounds like a good-bye.

I think Bree keeps his eyes closed for the entire flight. Not to sleep. He just really despises flying, so much so he can hardly look at his own feet, let alone peek out the window. He doesn't even respond to Tramy's and Gisa's gentle teasing. They sit on either side of him, content to poke and prod. Gisa stage-whispers to Tramy, leaning across Bree to say something about jet crashes or engine malfunctions. I don't join in. I know what a jet crash feels like, or at least close to it. But I won't spoil their fun either. We get so little of it these days. Bree keeps still in his seat, arms tightly crossed, his lids glued shut. Eventually his head lolls forward, chin resting on his chest, and he sleeps the rest of the way.

It's no small accomplishment on his part, considering the route from the Piedmont base to the Free Republic of Montfort is one of the longest flights I've ever taken. Six hours of flying at least. Too long a journey for a dropjet, so we're on a larger carrier, a transport more like the Blackrun. But this isn't the same craft, thankfully. The Blackrun was torn apart last year, by a contingent of Samos warriors and Maven's own fury.

I glance down the fuselage to the silhouettes of two pilots working the jet. Men of Montfort. I don't know either of them. Kilorn hangs at their backs, watching them fly.

Like Bree, Mom isn't keen on the flight, but Dad twists with his forehead glued to the glass, eyes on the land as it sprawls out below. The rest of the Montfort escort—Davidson and his advisers—spend the time sleeping. They must intend to hit the ground running when they get home. Farley sleeps too, her face pressed up against her seat. She took a spot without a window. Flying still makes her ill.

She is the only representative from the Scarlet Guard. Even in sleep, she curls her arms around Clara, rocking with the motion of the jet to keep her settled. The Colonel is back at the base, and probably ecstatic about it. With Farley gone, he's the highest-ranking member of the Scarlet Guard left behind. He can play Command all he likes, while his daughter relays information back to the organization.

On the ground, the verdant green of Piedmont, braided with muddy rivers and rolling hills, steadily gives over to the floodplain of the Great River. The disputed lands line both banks, their borders strange and always changing. I know little about them, except the obvious. The Lakelands, Piedmont, Prairie, and even Tiraxes farther south fight over this stretch of mud, swamp, hill, and tree. For control of the river, mostly. *I hope.* Silvers fight for nothing most of the time, spilling red blood for less than dirt. They control this land too, but not as tightly as they do Norta and the Lakelands.

We fly on, heading west over the flat grasslands and gentle hills of Prairie. Some is farmland. Wheat sprouts in golden waves, patchworked with corn in endless rows. The rest looks like open landscape, pocked by the occasional forest or lake. Prairie has no kings that I know of, no queens, no princes. Their lords rule by right of power, not blood. When a father falls, his son does not always take his place. It's another country I never thought I'd see, but here I am, looking down at it.

It never goes away, this strange feeling bubbling up from the odd divide between who I was before and who I am now. A girl of the Stilts, of familiar mud, trapped in a small place until the doom of conscription. My future was so empty then, but was it easier than this? I feel detached from that life, a million miles and a thousand years ago.

Julian isn't on our carrier, or else I might be tempted to ask about the countries beneath us. He's on the other airjet, the Laris jet striped yellow, with the rest of the Calore and Samos representatives, as well as their guards. Not to mention their baggage. Apparently a would-be king and a princess require a good deal of clothes. They trail behind us, visible from the left-side windows, metal wings flashing as we chase the sun.

Ella told me she came from the Prairie lands before Montfort. The Sandhills. Raider country. More terms I don't really understand. She isn't here to explain, left behind at the Piedmont base with Rafe. Tyton is the only electricon coming with us. Besides me, of course. He's Montfort-born. I suspect he has a family to visit, and friends too. He sits near the rear of the jet, sprawled across two empty seats, his nose buried in a tattered book. As I look at him, he feels my gaze, and he meets my eyes for a brief second. He blinks, gray orbs calculating. I wonder if he can feel the tiny pulses of electricity in my brain. *Does he know what each one means? Can he distinguish between bursts of fear or excitement?*

Could I, one day?

I hardly know the depth of my own abilities. It's the same for all newbloods I've met and helped train. But maybe not in Montfort. Maybe they understand what we are, and how much we can do.

The next thing I know, someone nudges my arm, jolting me out of an uneasy sleep. Dad points at the rounded window between us, set into the curved wall behind our seats.

"Never thought I'd see anything like that," he says, rapping the thick glass.

"What?" I ask, adjusting myself. He snaps the buckle on my belts, giving me full range of motion to turn and look out.

I have seen mountains before. In the Greatwoods, from the Notch. Green ranges fading into autumn's fire and then winter's barren, bone-branched chill. In the Rift, where hunched ridges ripple into the horizon, rising and falling like leafy waves. In Piedmont, deep in the backcountry, their slopes shifting into blue and distant purple, glimpsed only from the windows of a jet. All of them were part of the Allacias, the long line of ancient mountains marching from Norta to the Piedmont interior. But I have never seen mountains like the ones before us. I don't think they can even be called mountains at all.

My jaw hangs open, eyes glued to the horizon as the jet arcs toward the north. The flat Prairie lands end abruptly, their western edge punctured by the wall of a vast and sheer mountain range, bigger than anything I've ever seen before. The slopes rise like knife edges, too sharp, too high, rows upon rows of jagged, gigantic teeth. Some of the peaks are bare, without trees. As if trees can't grow up there. A few mountains in the distance are capped in white. *Snow.* Even though it's summer.

I draw in a shaky breath. *What kind of country have we come to? Do Silvers and Ardents rule so completely, with enough strength to build an impossible land like this?* The mountains put a fear in me, but a little excitement too. Even from the air, this country feels different. The Free Republic of Montfort stirs something in my blood and bone.

Next to me, Dad puts a hand to the glass. His fingers brush over the silhouette of the range, tracing the peaks. "Beautiful," he murmurs, so low only I can hear. "I hope this place is good to us."

It's cruel to give hope where none should be.

My father said that once, in the shadow of a stilt house. He sat in a chair, missing a leg. I used to think he was broken. I know better now. Dad is as whole as the rest of us, and always has been. He just wanted to protect us from the pain of wanting what we could not have. Futures we would never be allowed. Our fates have been quite different. And it seems my father has changed with them. He can hope.

With a deep breath, I realize the same. Even after Maven, my long months of imprisonment, all the death and destruction I've seen or caused. My broken heart, still bleeding inside me. The unending fear for the people I love, and the people I want to save. It all remains, a constant weight. But I won't let it drown me.

I can still hope too.

SIX
Evangeline

The air is strange. Thin. Oddly clean, as if removed from the rest of the world.

I smell it around the edges of my iron, my silver, my chrome. And of course the metallic tang of the jets, their engines still hot from the journey. The feel of them is overpowering, even after long hours cramped in the belly of a Laris carrier. So many plates and pipes and screws. On the flight, I spent longer than I care to admit counting rivets and tracing metal seams. If I tore there, or there, or there, I could send Cal or Anabel or anyone I wished plummeting to their death. Even myself. I had to sit near a Haven lord for much of the trip, and his snore rivaled thunder. Jumping out of a jet almost seemed like a better choice.

Despite the time of year, the air is colder than I expected, and goose bumps rise beneath the sheer silk draped around my shoulders. I took care to dress as a princess should, even though now I suffer the chill for it. This is my first state visit, both as a representative of the Rift and as the future queen of Norta. If that cursed future comes to pass, I must look the part, impressive and formidable down to my painted toes. I have to be prepared. I am well beyond the bounds of the world I understand. I inhale again, sucking down an oddly shallow breath. Even breathing here is unfamiliar.

It isn't late enough for sunset, but the mountains are so tall, and already the light wanes. Long shadows race across the landing field cut deep into the valley. I feel as if I could touch the sky. Run my jeweled claws across the clouds and make the sky bleed red starlight. Instead I keep my hands at my sides, my many rings and bracelets hidden beneath the folds of my skirt and sleeves. Decoration only. Pretty, useless, silent things. Just like my parents want me to be.

At the far end of the jet runway, the land drops away in a cliff. The carved edges of the mountainsides frame the horizon like a window. Cal stands silhouetted, looking eastward, where evening falls in shades of hazy purple. The mountain range casts shadows of its own, and all the world seems to fade in a darkness of Montfort's making.

Cal isn't alone. His uncle, the infinitely odd Jacos lord, stands at his side. He jots something in a notebook, moving with the excited, nervous energy of a tiny bird. Two guards, one in Lerolan colors, orange and red, with the other in Laris yellow, flank them from a respectful distance. The exiled prince stares out, still but for the wind in his scarlet cape. Reversing his house colors was a smart decision, to distance himself from everything King Maven is.

I shudder at the memory of that white face, those blue eyes, how every part of him seemed to burn with an all-consuming flame. There is nothing in Maven but hunger.

Cal doesn't turn around until Mare is off her jet with her family, hustled to a waiting escort of Montfort attendants. The Barrows' voices echo off the stone walls of the high mountain valley. That family is quite . . . vocal. And for someone so short and compact, Mare has surprisingly tall brothers. The sight of her younger sister turns my stomach. The girl has red hair. Darker than Elane's, without any of her bright gleam. Her skin doesn't glow, not with ability or some inner charm I can't explain. She isn't pale or alluring either. Her face is plainly pretty, more golden, an average sort of beauty. *Common. Red.* Elane is singular, in appearance and mind. She has no equal in my eyes. But still, the Barrow girl reminds me of the person I want most, the person I can never truly have.

Elane isn't here, and neither is my brother. That is the price. For his safety, for his life. General Farley will certainly kill him if given the opportunity, and I don't intend to let her have it. Not even for my own heart.

Cal turns around to watch Mare disappear, his eyes on her back as the escorts lead her and her family away. My lip curls at his idiocy. She's right in front of him, and he still pushes the girl away with both hands. For something so fragile and fickle as a crown. Even so, I envy him. He could still choose her if wanted. I wish I had the opportunity to do the same.

"You think my grandson is a fool, don't you?"

I turn to see Anabel Lerolan watching me, her lethal fingers knitted in front of her, a rose-gold tiara winking on her head. Like the rest of us, she made an effort to look her best.

Gritting my teeth, I dip into a shallow but perfect curtsy.

"I have no idea what you mean, Your Majesty." I don't bother trying to sound convincing. I see little consequence to it, for good or ill. It makes no difference what she thinks of me. She controls my life either way.

"You're attached to the Haven girl, yes? Jerald's daughter." Anabel takes a daring step closer to me. I want to cut Elane's face right out of her head. "If I'm not mistaken, she's married to your brother, a future queen as much as you are."

The threat laces through her words like one of my mother's snakes.

I force a laugh. "My passing fancies are not your business."

One of her fingers ticks, tapping against a wizened knuckle. She purses her lips and the wrinkles around her mouth deepen. "They are very much my business. Especially when you lie so quickly to keep Elane Haven from any kind of scrutiny. A passing fancy? Hardly, Evangeline. You are clearly smitten." She narrows her eyes. "I think you'll find you and I have more in common than you believe."

I smirk in her face, flashing my teeth in a veiled snarl. "I know old court gossip as much as anyone else. You speak of consorts. Your husband had one, a man named Robert, and you think that gives us what—an understanding?"

"I married a Calore king and sat by his side while he loved another. I think I know how this"—she dances two fingers in front of me—"might work. And let me tell you, it works best when all parties involved are in agreement, and *in the know*. Whether you like it or not, you and my grandson need to be allies in all things. It's the best way to survive."

"Survive in his shadow, you mean," I snap, unable to help myself.

Anabel blinks at me, her face pulled in rare confusion. Then she smiles and dips her head. "Queens cast shadows too."

Her demeanor changes in an instant. "Ah, Premier." She turns to my left, toward the man standing behind me.

I do the same, watching as Davidson steps forward. He nods at both of us, though he never breaks his gaze. His angled eyes, oddly gold, dart from Anabel to me. They are the only part of him that seems alive. The rest, from his empty, bland expressions to his still fingers, seems schooled by restraint.

"Your Majesty, Your Highness," Davidson says, bobbing his head again. Over his shoulder, I glance at his Montfort guards in green, as well as his officers and soldiers with their insignia. There are dozens of them. Some accompanied him from Piedmont, but most were already here waiting for his arrival.

Did he always have so many guards at his back? So many guns? I feel the bullets in their chambers. I count them off, a force of habit, and thicken the pools of iron in my dress, covering my most sensitive organs.

The premier gestures with one hand, sweeping his arm. "I hoped to escort you both into our capital, and be the first to bid you welcome to the Free Republic of Montfort." Though he still does his best to remain emotionless, I sense a pride in him. Pride in his home, his country. I understand that, at least.

Anabel surveys him with a look that would level noble Silvers, men and women of terrible power and even worse arrogance. The premier doesn't even flinch. "This," she sniffs, eyeing the naked cliffs on either side of us, "is your Republic?"

"This," Davidson replies, "is a private runway."

I spin a ring on my finger, distracting myself with the braid of jewels to keep from laughing.

Buttons gleam at the edge of my awareness. Heavy iron, well formed, forged into the likeness of flame. They approach, fastened to my betrothed's clothing. He stops at my side, radiating a low but constant heat.

Cal says nothing to me, and I'm glad for it. We haven't truly spoken in months. Not since he escaped death in the Bowl of Bones. Before, when he was my betrothed for the first time, our conversations were few and dull. Cal has a mind for battle and Mare Barrow. Neither interests me much.

I sneak a look at him and can tell his grandmother has seen to his appearance well. Gone is the rough-cut hair and the uneven stubble across his jaw. His cheeks are smooth, his black hair neat and glossy, brushed back from his forehead. Cal looks like he just stepped out of Whitefire, ready for his own coronation, instead of a six-hour flight on a jet carrier with a siege behind him. But his eyes are dull, hard bronze, and he doesn't wear a crown. Either Anabel could not procure one for him, or he refused to put it on. I assume the latter.

"A private runway?" Cal asks, looking down at Davidson.

The premier doesn't seem bothered by the height discrepancy. Maybe he is without the infinitely male preoccupation with size.

"Yes," Davidson says. "This airfield is at higher altitude, and has easier access to the city of Ascendant than the fields on the plains or the valleys deeper in the mountains. I thought it best to take us here, although the eastern ascent up the Hawkway is considered a splendid sight."

"When the war is over, I'd like to see it," Cal replies, trying to be polite. It does little to hide his naked disinterest.

Davidson doesn't seem to mind. "When the war is over," he echoes, his eyes glittering.

"Well, we wouldn't want to make you late for your address to your government." Anabel puts her arm through Cal's, ever the doting grandmother. She leans on him more than she needs to. A fitting and calculated picture.

"I wouldn't worry about that," Davidson says with one of his easy, languid smiles. "I'm scheduled to speak before the Montfort assembly in the morning. I'll make our case then."

Cal jolts. "Tomorrow morning? Sir, you know as well as I do that time—"

"The assembly convenes in the morning. Tonight I hope you'll join me for dinner," Davidson says placidly.

"Premier—" Cal begins, gritting his teeth.

But the newblood is forceful and stern, albeit as apologetic as he can be. "My colleagues already agreed to hold a special session, out of season. I assure you, I'm doing what I can within the bounds of my country's laws."

Laws. Can they even exist in a country like this? With no throne, no crown, no one to make the ultimate decision while all the rest squabble over details? How can Montfort hope to survive? How can they hope to move forward with so many pulling in different directions?

But if Montfort cannot move, if Davidson cannot win Cal more troops, then this war may end the way I want. It may end sooner than I thought.

"To Ascendant, then?" I ask, hoping to get out of the settling cold. And get Cal closer to all the distraction this place can give. As Anabel has already claimed Cal, I offer my arm to Davidson instead. He takes it with a slight bow, his hand featherlight on my wrist.

"This way, Your Highness," he replies.

I'm surprised to find that the touch of a newblood is not as revolting as the touch of my betrothed. He sets a good pace, leading us away from the jets and onto the paths leading into Ascendant.

The city is set high on the eastern edge of the massive mountain range, looking over the lower peaks and out over the borders. Prairie fades on the horizon, its edges known as raider country, where roving bands of Silvers aligned to no nation prey upon all who cross. The rest is empty plain, marred only by the cratered remains of what was once a city, long ago. I do not know its name.

Ascendant seems born of the mountains themselves, built upon slopes and into valleys, arching over gushing streams and the larger river picking its way back east through winding canyons. The few roads tunnel, and transports weave in and out of sight. There must be more beneath the surface, carved into the rock hearts of these mountains.

Most of the Ascendant city buildings are quarried stone—granite, marble, and rock quartz—cut and sculpted into impossibly smooth slabs of white and gray. Pine trees, some taller than spires, sprout up between buildings, their needles the same dark green as Montfort's flag. The sunset and the mountains wash the city in alternating stripes of deep pink and darkening purple, light and shadow. Above us, marching into the western distance, snowy peaks stand triumphant beneath a sky that seems too big and too close. A few early stars pinprick the dusk. They are familiar, forming patterns I know.

I have never seen a city like this, and it worries me. I do not like surprises, nor do I like to be impressed. It means something is better than me, or my blood, or my homeland.

But Ascendant, Montfort, Davidson, they've done it.

I can't help but be awed by this strange, beautiful place.

It's less than a mile to the city, but the many steps make it seem longer. I think the premier wants to show off, so rather than stuff us all into transports, he forces us to walk and see the city fully.

If I were back in the court of a Calore king with some other noble on my arm, I wouldn't bother making conversation. The presence of House Samos is well reputed. But here? I have to prove myself. I sigh, grit my teeth, and look to Davidson at my side.

"I understand you were *elected* to your position." The word is foreign to me, rolling around my mouth like a smooth stone.

Davidson can't help but chuckle, a small crack in his inscrutable mask. "Yes, indeed. Two years ago. The nation voted. And on the third year, next spring, we do so again."

"Who voted, precisely?"

His mouth tightens. "All kinds, if that's what you mean. Red, Silver, Ardent. A ballot is color-blind."

"So you do have Silvers here." They said as much before, but I doubted any Silver would condescend to a life alongside any Red, let alone to be ruled by one. Even a newblood. Still, it puzzles me. *Why live here as an equal when they could live elsewhere as a god?*

Davidson dips his chin. "We have many."

"And they just *allow* this?" I scoff, not bothering to hold my tongue. I only do that around my parents, and they aren't here, having thrown me to these red-blooded wolves.

"Allow our equal existence, you mean." The premier's voice takes on a sharper edge, hissing through the mountain air.

His eyes bore into mine, gold into charcoal gray. We continue walking, both of us sure over the many steps. He wants me to apologize. I do not.

Finally we reach a landing, a marble terrace overlooking a wide garden in full bloom. Unfamiliar flowers, purple and orange and pale blue, spiral out before us, wild and fragrant. Some yards ahead, Mare Barrow and her family pick their way through the garden, led by their own Montfort escorts. One of her brothers stoops to inspect the flowers more closely.

While the rest of our group takes in the expanse of the garden, Davidson draws closer to me, his lips almost brushing my ear. I resist the urge to slice him in two.

"Forgive me for my bluntness, Princess Evangeline," he whispers, "but you have a female lover, don't you? And you are forbidden to marry her."

I swear, I'm going to cut the tongues from the mouths of everyone here. Is no secret sacred?

"I don't know what you mean," I growl through a clenched jaw.

"Of course you do. She's married to your brother. Part of an arrangement, yes?"

My hands tighten around a stone railing. The cool smoothness does nothing to sooth me. I dig in my fingers, and the sharp, jeweled points of my decorative claws scratch deep. Davidson keeps on, his words a tumult, low and fast and impossible to ignore.

"If all were as you wished, if you were not a bargaining chip in a crown, and she were not wed, could you marry her? Under the best of circumstances, would the Silvers of Norta allow what you desire?"

I turn to him, teeth bared. The premier is far too close. He doesn't flinch, or step back. I can see the tiny imperfections in his skin. Wrinkles, scars, even pores. I could claw his eyes right out of his head if I wanted to.

"Marriage has nothing to do with desire," I snap. "Marriage is for heirs and nothing else."

For reasons I can't fathom, his golden eyes soften. I see pity. I see regret. I hate it. "So you are denied what you want because of what you are. A choice you never made, a piece of yourself you cannot change— and do not want to change."

"I—"

"Look down on my country all you want," he murmurs, and I see a shadow of the temper he works to keep hidden. "Question the way things are. Perhaps the answers will be to your liking." Then he steps back a little, returning to the picture of a politician. An ordinary man of ordinary charm. "Of course, I hope you enjoy our dinner this evening. My husband, Carmadon, has been busy enough preparing for you all."

What? I can only blink. *Of course not. I misheard.* My cheeks flush with heat, turning gray with shame. I can't deny that my heart leapt in my chest, a burst of adrenaline coursing through me only to die in a heartbeat. *It's no use wishing for impossible things.*

But the premier moves his head, the slightest nod.

I didn't mishear and he didn't misspeak.

"Another small thing we *allow* here in Montfort, Princess Evangeline."

He drops my arm without ceremony, quickening his pace to put some distance between us. I feel my heart hammer in my chest. *Is he lying? Is what he said even possible?* To my bewilderment, sharp tears prick at my eyes and my chest tightens.

"Diplomacy was never your strong suit."

Cal glowers at my shoulder, his grandmother hanging back to whisper with one of the Iral lords.

I turn my head, hiding for a moment in a curtain of silver hair. Just long enough to regain some semblance of control. Luckily he's decidedly occupied with staring after Mare, tracking her movements with pitiful longing.

"Then why did you pick me?" I finally sneer back at him, hoping he feels every ounce of my rage and pain. "Why make someone like me a queen when all I'll be is a thorn in your side?"

"Playing dumb isn't your strong suit either, Evangeline. You know how this works."

"I know you had a choice, Calore. Two paths. And you chose the one that leads right through me."

"*Choice,*" he barks. "You girls love that word."

My eyes roll in my skull. "Well, you seem to be a stranger to it. Blaming everyone and everything else for a decision *you* made."

"A decision I had to make." He turns to me, eyes flashing. "Or what? You think Anabel and your father and the rest would have allied with the Reds anyway? Without getting something in the bargain? You think they wouldn't find someone else to back, someone *worse*? At least, if it's me, I can—"

I step neatly in front of him, putting us chest to chest. My shoulders square, ready for battle. A lifetime of Training hardens beneath my skin. "What? Make things better? When all the fighting is done, you think you can sit on your new throne and wave your stupid flames and change the way the world is?" With a sneer, I size him up, my eyes ripping a path from his boots to his forehead. "Don't make me laugh, Tiberias Calore. You're a puppet as much as I am, but at least you had a chance to cut your strings."

"And you don't?"

"I would if I could," I whisper, and I think I mean it. *If Elane were here, if there were some way we could stay . . .*

"When—when the time comes, when we have to marry . . ." He stumbles over the words. It isn't like a Calore to stammer. "I'll try to make things as easy as I can. State visits, meetings. You and Elane can do as you like."

A chill runs through me. "As long as I hold up my end of the bargain."

The prospect disgusts us both, and we look away from each other. "I'm not doing anything without your consent," he mutters.

Even though I'm not surprised, a tiny burst of relief blooms in my heart. "I'd cut something off if you tried."

Cal offers a weak laugh, little more than an expulsion of air.

"What a mess," he mumbles, so low he might not expect me to hear.

I suck in a shaky breath. "You can still choose her."

The words hang in the air, torturing us both.

He doesn't reply, now glaring at his booted feet. In the garden, Mare keeps her back to him, following close at her sister's heels. Despite their differing hair colors, I see the resemblance. They move in the same way. Careful, quiet, deliberate, like mice. The sister picks a flower as they go, a pale green bloom with vibrant petals, then tucks it into her hair. As I watch, the tall Red boy, the one Mare insists on dragging everywhere, does the same. The flower looks silly behind his ear, and both Barrow sisters double over. Their laughter echoes over us, a taunt more than anything.

They are Red. They are lesser. And they are happy. How can this be?

"Stop moping, Calore," I grind out through gritted teeth. The advice is for both of us. "You forged this crown yourself—now wear it. Or *don't*."

SEVEN
Iris

The banks of the Ohius are high. It was a wet spring, with the southern farms of the Lakelands almost flooding many times. Tiora was here in the unstable borderlands just a few weeks ago, to help save the new crops as much as she was to smile and wave. Her small, rare grin won us some favor here, but not enough. Reports to the crown say that Reds are still fleeing, crossing the hills into the Rift to the east. They are fools if they believe the Silver king there will offer them a better life. The smarter ones cross the Ohius into the disputed territories, where no king or queen rules. But they have to risk the chaos of such a journey, facing Red and Silver alike between the Lakelands and northern Piedmont.

The rise above the river offers a commanding view of the valley. A good place to wait. I look south, into the woods gleaming golden beneath the waning light of afternoon. Today was easy, filled with travel across the corn and wheat. And Maven was kind enough to take his own transport, allowing me long hours of peace as we rolled south. The journey was almost a reprieve, even if it meant leaving my mother and sister behind. They're back in the capital. I can't say when I'll see them again. *If I ever do.*

In spite of the pleasant breeze and the warm air, Maven elects to wait in his vehicle. For now. Certainly he'll try to make some kind of entrance when the Piedmontese arrive.

"He is late," the old woman mutters at my side.

In spite of the circumstances, I feel a corner of my mouth lift. "Patience, Jidansa."

"My, how the current has changed, Your Majesty," she chuckles, the wrinkles on her brown face deepening as she grins. "I can remember giving you the same counsel more than once. Usually in regard to food."

I break my vigil, looking away from the horizon to glance at her. "In that, the current remains true."

Her dusty laugh deepens, echoing out across the river.

Jidansa of the Merin Line has been a friend of the family for as long as I can remember, close as an aunt and doting as a nanny. She used her telky ability to amuse Ti and me as children, juggling our shoes or toys with her mind. Despite her lined face, white hair, and matronly disposition, Jidansa is a fearsome opponent, a telky talented beyond measure, one of the best in our nation.

I would ask her to return with me to Norta, if I were not so heartless. She would agree, but I know better than to make such a request. Most of her family died in the war. Living among Nortans would be a punishment she doesn't deserve.

Her presence is calming. Even if we are in the Lakelands, I still feel unease around Maven.

The rest of my escort fans out behind me, allowing a respectful distance. The Sentinels should make me feel safe, but I can never feel at ease beneath their jeweled gaze. They would kill me if my husband commanded it. Or try, at the very least.

I fold my arms in front of me, feeling the edges of my blue traveling jacket. Even though I'm about to meet a prince of Piedmont, the *ruling* prince, I look woefully underdressed. Hopefully he isn't as dedicated to appearance as most Silvers I know.

I don't have to wait much longer to find out.

From our vantage point, we can see his convoy picking its way across the disputed territories. The land is otherwise indistinguishable from the woods of the southern Lakelands. There are no walls, no gates, no roads to mark this part of the border. Our own patrols are well hidden for now, and instructed to let the Piedmont prince pass unimpeded.

His convoy is small, even compared to our meager group of six transports and fifty or so guards. I spot only two transports, fast and agile machines, tearing low across the sparser edges of the forest. They're painted in camouflage, a sickly green to match the landscape. As they get closer, I can see the yellow, white, and purple stars dotting their sides.

Bracken.

Behind me, metal groans and Maven steps down from his transport. He crosses the flattened grass in a few quick strides, stopping next to me with even grace. Slowly, he folds his hands. His white skin looks more golden in this light. He could almost seem human.

"I did not take Prince Bracken to be such a trusting man. He is a fool," he says, gesturing to the prince's small party.

"Desperation makes fools of most," I answer coolly.

Maven barks out a single laugh. His eyes drag over me in an almost lazy fashion. "Not you."

No, not me.

This needle must be gently threaded. Like Maven, I fold my hands together, projecting an image of strength. Determination. Steel.

Bracken's children have been missing for months, imprisoned and used as leverage. Every moment they are gone is another bit of Piedmont bled away. Montfort has already cost them millions of crowns, using whatever they get their hands on. Guns, jets, food stores. The military base in the Lowcountry was stripped, with much of its contents shipped back to the mountains. The Montfortans are locusts, feeding upon all they can. Whatever resources Bracken has left are almost spent.

The transports coast to a halt some yards away, keeping a safe distance from our own convoy. When they open, a dozen guards troop out, resplendent in dark purple edged in gold. They carry swords and guns, though a few seem to favor war hammers or axes instead of blades.

Bracken carries no weapons at all.

He is tall, black-skinned, with a smooth complexion, full lips, and eyes like two polished stones of jet. Where Maven is draped in his cape, his medals, and his crown, Bracken seems less reliant on style. His clothes are finely made, dark purple edged in gold to match his guards, but I see no crown, no furs, no jewels. This man is here on a dire mission and has no cause for pageantry.

The prince towers over us both, with the muscular physique of a strongarm, though I know for a fact that Bracken is a mimic. If he were to touch me, he would be able to use my nymph abilities, albeit only for a time, and to a lesser extent. The same goes for any Silver. Perhaps even newbloods too.

"I wish our first meeting were under better circumstances," he says in a deep, rumbling voice. As is custom, he ducks into a shallow bow, observing both our ranks. He might rule Piedmont, but his country is no match for ours.

"As do we, Your Highness," I reply, offering a nod of my own.

Maven copies my motions, but too quickly. As if he wants this to be over with as soon as possible. "What do you have for us?"

I wince at the lack of tact. On instinct, I open my mouth, ready to smooth over the rough edges of such a precarious conversation. But to my surprise, Bracken grins.

"I don't like to waste time either," he replies, his smile taking on a hard edge. Over his shoulder, one of his guards approaches, carrying a leather-bound folio in hand. "Not when my children hang in the balance."

"This is your intelligence on Montfort?" I ask, eyeing the papers as the guard passes them to her prince. "You pulled this together so quickly."

"The prince has been searching for his children, and for people to help in his endeavor, for months," Maven drawls. "I remember your envoys, the princes Alexandret and Daraeus. I'm sorry I couldn't be of any . . . help to them."

I almost snort aloud. One of the princes died in the Archeon palace, killed in a failed coup to overthrow Maven himself. And the other is dead too, as far as I know.

Bracken dismisses the apology with a wave of one large hand. "They knew the risks, as do all in my service. I've lost dozens to the search for my son and daughter." There is true sorrow in his words, laced beneath the anger.

"Let us hope we don't lose any more," I mutter, thinking of myself. And what my mother said. *It must be you.*

Maven raises his chin, his eyes flashing between Bracken and the folio. It has to be filled with information on Montfort, their mysterious cities, their mountains, their armies. Information we need.

"We're prepared to do what you cannot, Bracken," he says. Maven is a skilled performer, and he layers his words with just the right amount of sympathy. If given the chance, the young king might lure Bracken to his side before I even get a chance to play my hand. "I understand that, while the Montfortans hold your children, you can't move against them. The smallest rescue mission could jeopardize their lives."

"Yes, exactly true." Bracken nods rapidly. He's eating up everything Maven gives him. "Even gathering intelligence was almost too dangerous."

The Nortan king raises an eyebrow. "And?"

"We were able to track the children to their capital, Ascendant," the prince offers. He extends his hand, holding out the folio to us. "It's deep in the mountains, protected by a valley. Our maps of the city are old, but usable."

I take the information before one of the Sentinels can, weighing the folio. It's heavy, worth its weigh in gold.

"Were you able to find where they're being held?" I ask, eager to crack open the pages and get to work.

Bracken dips his head. "I believe so. At great cost."

I cross my arms, cradling the substantial book to my chest. "I won't waste it."

The Piedmont prince looks me up and down, his face pulled in respectful confusion. Maven is less obvious. He doesn't move and his expression doesn't change. The temperature doesn't rise a single degree. But I can smell the suspicion rolling off him. And the warning. He's smart enough to keep his mouth shut in front of the prince, unable to stop me from spinning my web.

"I'm leading the team myself," I offer, fixing Bracken with my most determined stare. He doesn't blink, resolute as a statue. Examining me, weighing me. The simple clothing was a good choice on my part. I look more like a warrior than a queen. "I'll use Nortan soldiers and soldiers of the Lakelands, a small-enough force to pass through unnoticed. Rest assured, we've been hard at work since yesterday."

Even though it makes my skin crawl, I put a hand on Maven's arm. His flesh is cold beneath his sleeve. I can't see it, but I feel the tiniest tremble in him. My smile widens.

"Maven came up with a brilliant plan."

He slides his hand over mine, fingers like ice. A threat plain as day.

"Indeed I did," Maven says, his lips pulling into a feral smile to match my own.

Bracken sees only the offer, and the possibility, of his children's rescue. I don't blame him. I can only imagine what my mother would do, if Tiora and I were in the same position.

The prince breaths a long sigh of relief. "Magnificent," he offers, bowing his head one more time. "And in return, I can pledge to uphold the alliance we've had for decades. Until the blood freaks decided to intervene." Bracken hardens. "But no more. The tide turns today."

I feel his words as keenly as I feel the river below, flowing in its course. Unbreakable. Unstoppable.

"The tide turns today," I echo, the folio tight in hand.

This time, Maven climbs into my transport after me, and I'm tempted to kick him back out in the grass. Instead I retreat to the farthest corner of my seat, Bracken's intelligence laid across my knees. Maven keeps his eyes on me as he sits down . His calm manner almost makes me sweat.

I wait for him to speak, matching his icy gaze with my own.

Inwardly, I curse his presence. I want to crack into the papers and start filling in the gaps in my rescue plan, but I can hardly start with Maven sneering at me. And he knows it. He's enjoying this, as he always enjoys bothering people. I think it makes him feel better about his own demons, to make demons for everyone else.

Only after the transport is moving, hurtling away from the border-lands at high speed, does he speak.

"What exactly are you doing?" he asks, his voice smooth and devoid of all emotion. It's his favorite tactic, giving no indication as to his mood. It's useless to search his eyes or his face for any feeling, to try to read him as I would any other person. He's too skilled for that.

I answer simply, head held high. "Winning Piedmont for us."

Us.

Maven *hmms* deep in his throat, before settling back for the long journey. "Very well," he says, and speaks no more.

EIGHT
Mare

The Montfort escort leads us toward a palatial compound set high on a ridge overlooking the central valley, where the rest of Ascendant clings to the slopes. Everywhere, dark green banners drift in the sweet evening breeze, bearing the mark of the white triangle. *A mountain,* I realize, feeling silly for not having figured out their symbol sooner. Their uniforms have the same marking.

My own clothes are plain, not even a uniform, just items cobbled together from stores in both Corvium and Piedmont. Probably owned by a Silver, judging by the fine make of the jacket, pants, boots, and shirt. Farley tromps along in her version of a uniform, with Clara swaddled on her hip. She wears red all over, with three metal squares at her collar. The mark of a Command general.

The Silvers behind us are more *flashy,* and I expect nothing less from their kind. They cut a rainbow of vibrant, sharp colors against the white walkways of Ascendant that wind through the city. Cal is difficult to ignore in his burning red cloak, but I certainly try. He walks with Evangeline, and I half expect her to shove him off one of the more treacherous terraces or stairways.

I keep close to my father's side, listening to him breathe. The steps of Ascendant are many, and he is an old man with a regrown leg, not to mention his repaired lung. The thin air can't be helping either.

He works hard not to stumble, his red face the only hint of how much effort this takes. Mom flanks him on the left, sharing my thoughts. Her hands trail behind him, fingers splayed to help him if he falters.

I would call for some kind of aid, a strongarm maybe, or even just Bree and Tramy, if Dad asked. But I know he won't. He forges ahead, touching my arm once or twice. Grateful for my presence, and equally grateful for my restraint.

The steps level eventually, carrying us through an archway carved to look like tree trunks and leaves. We pass through into a central plaza, its stonework a checkered spiral of hewn green granite and milky limestone. Pines of every kind line the arches bounding the place, some of them tall as towers and just as thick. I'm struck by the overpowering swell of birdsong, chittering against the purpled sky.

Behind me, Kilorn lets loose a low whistle. He stares through the trees to a long, pillared building set into and up the cresting slope. It's a strange mix of tumbled stone, like the bottom of a riverbed, with lacquered timber and marble detail. Balconies dot its many wings, some bursting with wildflowers. All of them face into the valley, to watch over Ascendant.

This is the premier's house, I'm certain of it. A palace in all but name. It makes me uneasy, while the rest of my family is rightfully dazzled. I've had enough of palaces to know I shouldn't trust what lingers behind sculpted beauty and gleaming windows.

There are no walls around the palace, and no gates. There don't seem to be any surrounding Ascendant either. Or at least not the kind I can see. I get the feeling the geography of this city, this country, is its own kind of boundary. Montfort is strong enough not to need walls. Or stupid enough not to build them. Judging by Davidson, I doubt the latter very much.

Farley must be thinking the same thing. Her eyes pass over the arches, the pines, the palace, noting each one with focused precision. Then she looks back at the Silvers as they troop in after us, all of them trying not to seem impressed by Davidson's home.

The premier only waves us forward, deeper and deeper into the heart of his country.

As in Piedmont, the Barrow family is given much nicer living quarters than we're used to. The apartments within Davidson's home are vast, large enough to give each of us our own bedroom. Kilorn and Gisa busy themselves with exploring, poking around the various rooms. Bree is less inclined to move, taking over one of the velvet couches in the long salon. I can hear him snoring now, from where I stand on our terrace. This is temporary, until more permanent lodging can be procured in the city.

Everyone leaves me alone, either unknowingly or on purpose. I don't mind either way.

Ascendant glitters below, a constellation on the mountainside. I can feel the electricity in it, distant and constant, winking in the many lights. It all looks like a reflection of the sky above. The stars seem impossibly clear here, close enough to touch. I breathe deep, sucking in the wild freshness of the mountains. *This is a good place to leave them. The best place I could ask for.*

Along the balcony edge, flowers bloom from pots and boxes, in all colors. The ones before me are purple and strangely shaped, with odd petals like a tail.

"They call them elephant flowers."

Tramy sidles next to me, planting an elbow on the railing. He leans out to stare at the city below. Despite the season, a deep chill settles with the night. I must be shivering, because he offers a shawl with one hand.

As I take it, wrapping the knitted fabric around my shoulders, he furrows his brow. "I don't know what *elephant* means."

The word rings a distant bell, but I shake my head and shrug. "Neither do I. It could be an animal, I think. Julian would know." I speak his name without thinking, and I almost wince. A twinge of pain snaps in my chest.

"You can ask him tonight at dinner," my brother says, thoughtful as he runs a hand through his scratchy beard.

I shrug again, trying to brush off all mention of Julian Jacos. "You need to shave, Tramy," I snicker. Inhaling the sweet air again, I turn back to the city lights. "And ask Julian yourself at dinner tonight."

"No."

Something in his voice gives me pause, a low tremor of resolve. Boldness. Tramy isn't the kind to refuse any of us. He's too used to following Bree around, or smoothing over family troubles. He is a peacemaker, far from the kind to plant his feet and dig in.

I glance up at him, expecting an explanation.

He clenches his jaw, dark brown eyes boring into mine. He has Mom's eyes, like I do. "It's no place for us."

Us.

His meaning is clear. *This is as far as we go.* The Barrows aren't politicians or warriors. They have no reason to share the spotlight, or the danger I live with. But the prospect of standing alone, without them—the fear is endless and selfish and sudden.

"It can be," I say too quickly, taking his wrist. Tramy quickly covers my hand with his own. "It should be your place. All of you. You're my family—"

A door creaks open onto the terrace, then shuts behind Gisa and Kilorn. My sister surveys us, eyes shining. "How many people have power they shouldn't simply because their family gives it to them?" she asks.

She means the Silvers. The royals and the nobles who hand power to their children, no matter how unsuited they might be. The obsession with blood, with dynasty, is the reason Maven is on the throne in the first place. A twisted boy king ruling a country when he can't even rule his own mind.

"That's different," I mutter back, though my retort is halfhearted. "You're not like them."

Gisa reaches out to me, adjusting my shawl. She dotes on me the way a big sister should, even though I'm years older. The flower is still tucked behind her ear, pale as dawn. Slowly, I touch the petals, then run a lock of her hair through my fingers. The flower suits her. *Will Montfort?*

"Like Tramy said," she replies, "your meetings, your councils, the war you're fighting, that's no place for us. And we don't want it to be." Gisa stares back at me, eye to eye. We're the same height for now, but I hope she keeps growing. She doesn't deserve to see the world the way I do.

"Okay," I breathe, pulling her close. "Okay."

"They agree," she mumbles against me.

Mom. And even Dad.

Something in me releases, letting go of a great weight. But is it an anchor pulling me down, or an anchor keeping me steady? It could be both in equal measure. Without my parents or siblings hanging in the balance, who will I become?

Who I must.

With my head tucked on Gisa's shoulder, it's hard not to look at Kilorn standing behind her. His face is dark, a storm cloud as he watches us both. We lock eyes when he feels my gaze, and I see determination in him. He joined the Scarlet Guard long ago, and he won't take the opportunity to break that pledge. Not even to stay here, in safety, with the only family he knows.

"Now," Gisa says, pulling back. "Let's get you ready for this mess of a dinner party."

Months of life on rebel bases has only sharpened my sister's keen eye for color, fabric, and fashion. Somehow she scares up a few different outfits from the palace to choose from, all of them relaxed but formal, in a range of styles. None of the gemmed monstrosities the Nortan Silvers wear, of course, but still suitable for a table of kings and leaders. I have to admit, I like dressing up in this way. Running my fingers over cotton or silk. Deciding how to wear my hair. It's a good distraction. And necessary.

Tiberias will certainly be sitting at the table with me, glowering in his crimson clothes. Pouting because I held to my principles, while he spit on them. Let him see exactly what he turned his back on, and who.

I get a sick, but satisfying, pleasure from the thought.

Though Gisa favors the more complex outfits for me, we eventually settle on a dress both of us like. Simple, a deep plum red, long-sleeved with a trailing skirt. No jewelry but my earrings. Pink for Bree, red for Tramy, purple for Shade, green for Kilorn. The final red stone, scarlet as fresh blood, is tucked away in my things. I won't wear the earring Tiberias gave me, but I can't throw it away either. It sits, undisturbed but not forgotten.

Gisa quickly sews some gold braid, an intricate piece of already-made embroidery, to the cuff of each sleeve. I don't know where she swiped a sewing kit from, or if Davidson's staff knew to leave her one. Her nimble fingers are equally skilled at fixing my hair, twisting my mud-brown locks into something like a crown. It hides my gray ends nicely, even though they've spread so much. The strain of the days has certainly taken its toll on me, something I don't miss in the mirror. I look washed out, sunken, my eyes circled by bruise-like shadows. I have scars of every kind, from Maven's brand, from wounds not properly healed, from my own lightning. But I am not a ruin. Not yet.

The premier's palace is vast, but the layout is simple enough, and it takes little time for me to descend to the ground floor, where the public rooms are. Eventually I can just follow the smell of food, letting it lead me through room after room of grand salons and galleries. I pass a dining area the size of a ballroom, dominated by a table big enough for forty, as well as a massive stone fireplace. But the table is bare and no flame crackles in the grate.

"Miss Barrow, isn't it?"

I turn to the kindly voice, finding an even kinder face. A man beckons from one of the many arched doorways leading out onto another terrace. He is perfectly bald, with midnight skin, almost purple in hue, and his smile flashes like a white crescent above an even whiter silk suit.

"Yes," I reply evenly.

He grins wider. "Very good. We'll be eating out here, under the stars. I thought it best to do so, on your first visit."

The man gestures and I follow, crossing the grand dining room to meet him. With smooth motions, he takes my arm, locking his elbow with mine as he leads me out into the cool night air. The smell of food intensifies, making my mouth water.

"So tense," he chuckles, moving his arm a little to contrast my own tight muscles. His air is easy, so much so that I want to mistrust him. "I'm Carmadon, and I cooked the dinner. So if you have any complaints, keep them to yourself."

I bite my lip, trying to hide a smirk. "I'll do my best."

He only taps his nose in reply.

The spider veins in his eyes are gray, branching across white. *His blood is silver.* I swallow around a sudden lump in my throat.

"May I ask what ability you possess, Carmadon?"

His response is a thin smile. "Is it not obvious?" He gestures to the many plants and flowers, both on the terrace and dangling from the many balconies and windows. "I am but a humble greenwarden, Miss Barrow."

For the sake of appearance, I force a smile of my own. *Humble.* I've seen corpses with roots curling from their eyes and mouths. There is no such thing as a humble Silver, or a harmless one. They all have the ability to kill. But then, I suppose, so do we. So does every human on earth.

We walk across the terrace, toward the smell and soft lights and the low murmur of stilted conversation. This part of the palace juts out over the ridge, allowing an unobstructed view over the pines, the valley, and the snowy peaks in the distance. They seem to glow under the light of a rising moon.

I try not to look eager or interested or even angry. Nothing to hint at my emotions. Still, I feel my heart jump, adrenaline pumping, at the sight of Tiberias's familiar silhouette. Again he stares out at the landscape, unable to face anyone else around him. I feel my lip curl in distaste. *Since when are you a coward, Tiberias Calore?*

Farley paces back and forth some yards away, still wearing her Command uniform. Her hair has been freshly washed, and it gleams beneath the lamps strung over the terrace table. She gives me a nod before moving to sit.

Evangeline and Anabel are already in their chairs, on either side of one end of the table. They must intend to flank Cal and trumpet their importance at his right and left. While Anabel seems comfortable in her gown from earlier, the heavy red and orange silk, Evangeline nuzzles into a collar of smooth black fox fur. She watches me as I approach the table, eyes glittering like two devious stars. When I sit, taking my place diagonal from her, as far as possible from the exiled prince, her lips twist into what could be a smile.

Carmadon doesn't seem to notice or care that his dinner guests are hell-bent on hating one another. He sits gracefully in the chair across from mine, at the right hand of where I assume Davidson will be. A servant springs from the shadows to fill his intricately etched wineglass.

I watch with narrowed eyes. The servant has red blood, judging by the flush in her cheeks. She is neither old nor young, but she smiles as she works. I've never seen a Red servant smile like that, unless commanded.

"They're paid, and paid fairly," Farley says, sitting down beside our host. "I've already checked."

Carmadon swirls the wine in his glass. "Poke and prod at whatever you like, General Farley. Check behind the curtains, for all I care. There are no slaves in my house," he says, his voice taking on a stern edge.

"We haven't been properly introduced," I say, feeling more rude than usual. "Your name is Carmadon, but—"

"Of course, excuse my manners, Miss Barrow. Premier Davidson is my husband, and he is currently very late. I would apologize if the dinner goes cold waiting for him"—he waves a hand at the table of food nearby, holding our first course—"but his punctuality is neither my fault nor my problem."

His words are harsh, but his manner friendly and open. If Davidson is difficult to read, his husband is an open book. And so is Evangeline right now.

She stares at the man with such naked envy I think she might turn green. And no wonder. Their lives, a marriage such as this, are impossible in our country. Forbidden. Considered a waste of silver blood. *But not here.*

I fold my hands in my lap, trying not to fidget despite the nervous energy settling over the table. Anabel has not spoken, either because she disapproves of Carmadon or because she disapproves of eating alongside Reds. It could be both.

Farley barely nods her head in thanks when Carmadon fills her glass with rich, almost black wine. She drinks deep.

I stick to ice water, speckled with slices of bright lemon. The last thing I need is a spinning head and blurred thoughts with Tiberias Calore anywhere nearby. I glance at him as he enters, running my eyes over his familiar shoulders thrown wide beneath the edges of a red cape. It seems more like flame in the warm lights of the terrace.

When he turns around, I drop my gaze. I can only listen as he approaches, his presence heavy on the air. A wrought-iron chair scrapes against the stone terrace, its movement agonizingly slow and deliberate. I almost jolt when I realize exactly where he has decided to sit.

His arm brushes mine, just for a second, and his warmth settles around me. I curse the familiar comfort of it, especially against the mountain chill.

Finally I dare to look up, only to find Carmadon with his head tilted, chin resting on one fist. He seems infinitely amused. At his side, Farley looks more inclined to vomit. And I don't have to see Anabel's face to know she's scowling.

I lock my hands together beneath the tabletop, knitting my fingers so tightly my knuckles turn white. Not with fear, but with anger. Next to me, Tiberias leans, one elbow on the arm of the chair closest to me. He could whisper in my ear if he wanted. I grit my teeth, resisting the instinct to spit.

Across the table, Evangeline almost purrs to herself. She runs a hand through her furs, her decorative claws gleaming. "How many courses does this meal have, my lord Carmadon?"

Davidson's husband doesn't look away from me, and his lips twitch in what could be a smirk. "Six."

With a scowl, Farley knocks back the rest of her wine.

Grinning, Carmadon gestures to the servants in the shadows. "Dane and your lord Julian can catch up," he says, calling for the first course with a flick of his fingers. "I hope you enjoy. We've taken great care to prepare some Montfort delicacies."

The service is smooth and quick, just as efficient but less formal than I've seen in the palaces of Silver kings. Carmadon presides as small plates of elegant bone china are laid out in front of us. I look down at a pink slice of fish the size of my thumb, topped with some kind of creamy cheese and asparagus.

"Fresh-caught salmon, from the Calum River in the west," Carmadon explains, before popping the entire thing in his mouth. Farley quickly follows suit. "The Calum drains to the western coast, into the ocean."

In my head I try to picture what he's talking about, but my knowledge of his lands is poor at best. There's another ocean, yes, bordering the western edge of the continent, but that's all I can grasp right now.

"My uncle Julian will be eager to learn more of your country," Tiberias replies. He speaks slowly, with conviction. It ages him a decade. "I suspect his questions are what delay both him and the premier now."

"Perhaps. My Dane does delight in his library."

And so would Julian. I wonder if the premier is trying to form ties of his own, perhaps make an ally of a friendly Nortan Silver. Or maybe Davidson is just enjoying time with another scholar, eager to share word of his country.

After the salmon comes a hot vegetable soup, steaming in the chilly air, and then a salad of fresh greens and wild huckleberry grown on this very mountain. Carmadon doesn't seem to mind that no one else is speaking. He fills the silence with his own chatter, pleasantly comfortable as he details every bit of the meal he prepared. The particulars of a salad dressing, the best time to pick berries, how long the vegetables must cook, the size of his personal garden, and so on. I doubt

Evangeline, Tiberias, or Anabel has ever cooked a day in their life, and I wonder if Farley's ever eaten anything that wasn't stolen or rationed.

I do my best to seem polite, although I have little to say. Especially with Tiberias so close, inhaling everything on his plate. I glance at him here and there, hoarding brief flashes of his face. His jaw clenched, his throat working. He never shaved so closely before. If I didn't have my pride or conviction, I might run my knuckles over his cheek, close against smooth skin.

This time, he catches my eye before I can look away.

My instinct is to blink, break the stare. Turn back to my plate or maybe even excuse myself from the table. But I hold my ground. If the would-be king wants to put me on edge, knock me back on my heels, then fine. I can do that too. I set my shoulders, straighten my spine, and, most important of all, remember to breathe. Tiberias is just one more Silver who will leave my people enslaved, no matter what he preaches. He is an obstacle and a shield. A delicate balance must be kept.

He blinks first, returning to his food.

I do the same.

It burns to be near him, so close to a person I used to trust. A body I know so well. One choice, one word, and things would be so different. This dinner would be spent trading glances, communicating in our way about Evangeline or Anabel or Davidson's absence. Or they wouldn't be here at all. It would be us on this terrace, under the stars, surrounded by a new kind of country. An imperfect one, maybe, but a goal just the same. Carmadon is Silver, his husband a Red newblood. The servants are not slaves. I've seen little of Montfort, but enough to know this place might be different. And we could be different in it. If only he would let us.

Tiberias still wears no crown, but I see it on him just the same. In his shoulders, in his eyes, in his slow, firm manner. He is a king as much as anyone can be. To the blood. To the bone.

When the servants clear the salad plates, Carmadon glances at the door, as if expecting Davidson to join us. He frowns a little when no one appears but gestures for the next course anyway. "This is a particular Montfortan treat," he says with a pasted smile.

A plate slides onto the table in front of me. It looks like a particularly thick and juicy cut of steak, flanked by golden fried potatoes and mushrooms, onions, and leafy greens cooked in sauce. In a word, delicious.

"Steak?" Anabel asks, leaning forward with an unkind smile. "I promise, my lord Carmadon, we do have steak in our country."

But our host ticks one dark finger. It incenses the old queen as much as his disregard for titles does. "On the contrary. You have cattle. This is bison."

"What is bison?" I ask, eager to try it for myself.

His knife scrapes the plate as he slices a cut. "A different species, albeit close in relation to the cattle you know. Bigger by far, better in taste. Much stronger and hardier, with horns and shaggy coats and enough muscle to knock over a transport if they so choose. Most here are wild, though some farms exist. They roam the Paradise Valley, the hills, and the plains as well. They thrive even in winters that could kill man or beast. You'd never look a live bison in the face and call her cattle, that I can assure you." I watch, fascinated, as his blade cuts through such strange meat. Red juice bleeds across his meal, staining the white china. "An interesting thing, the bison and the cow. So similar. Two branches of the same tree, though entirely different from one another. And separate as they are, divided as the two species can be, they can live alongside each other just fine. Mingle their herds. They can even breed."

Next to me, Tiberias coughs, almost choking on a piece of food.

My cheeks flame hot.

Evangeline laughs into her hand.

Farley finishes the bottle of wine.

"Have I said something impertinent?" Carmadon glances between us, his black eyes dancing. He knows exactly what he said and what it means.

Anabel cuts in before anyone else can, under the guise of easing her grandson's embarrassment. She surveys the palace over the lip of her glass. "Your husband's lateness is quite rude, my lord."

The smiling Carmadon doesn't miss a beat. "I agree with you. I'll make sure his punishment is swift."

The bison is lean, and Carmadon is right. Better than beef. I don't bother with manners, as Carmadon seems quite at ease eating potatoes with his hands. It only takes a minute for me to devour half the bison steak, and all the browned onions. I'm so focused on cleaning my plate with my fork, scraping together the perfect bite, that I barely notice the door open again behind us.

"Apologies, of course," Davidson says, his pace even but quick, as he walks toward the table. Julian trails him closely. Side by side, I'm struck by how similar Julian and Davidson look. In air, not appearance. They both have a hunger about them, the intellectual kind. Otherwise they could not be more different. Julian is too slim, his graying hair thinning and wispy, his eyes watery and brown. Davidson is a picture of health, his gray hair neatly cut and gleaming, and despite his age, he is all lean muscle. "What have we missed?" he asks, taking the seat beside his husband.

With some awkward glances, Julian surveys the table and claims the only open seat. The one meant for Tiberias, if Tiberias weren't so hell-bent on annoying me.

Carmadon sniffs. "Discussion of the menu, the breeding habits of bison, and your lack of punctuality."

The premier's laugh is open, honest. He either feels no need to perform or he performs perfectly in his own home. "Normal dinner conversation, then."

At the far end of the table, Julian leans forward, looking sheepish. "The fault is mine, I'm afraid."

"The library?" his nephew offers with a knowing grin. "We heard."

My heart twists at the warmth in Tiberias's voice. He loves his uncle, and any reminder of the person Tiberias is beneath his bad choices makes me ache.

A corner of Julian's mouth lifts. "I'm the predictable kind, aren't I?"

"I prefer predictable," I mutter. But loud enough for the table to hear.

Farley smirks at her plate. And Tiberias scowls, turning to me with a quick, even snap of his neck. His mouth opens, as if he's about to say something rash and stupid.

His grandmother speaks before he can, eager to protect him from himself. "And what makes this library so . . . interesting?" she asks, her disdain evident.

I can't help myself. "Probably the books."

Farley barks out a laugh with little regard while Julian tries to hide a smirk in his napkin. The rest are more demure. But Tiberias's low chuckle stops me cold. I glance at him to see him smiling, eyes crinkled at the corners as he looks down at me. I realize that, for a moment, he has forgotten where we are—and *who* we are. His laughter dies in an instant, his face falling back into a more neutral expression.

"Ah yes," Julian pushes on, if only to distract us all. "The volumes are quite extensive. Not just regarding science, but history as well. I'm afraid we lost track of ourselves." He bobs his head and samples the wine. Then he tips his glass toward Davidson. "Or the premier obliged me, at least."

Davidson raises his glass in reply. A watch ticks on his wrist. "Always happy to share books. Knowledge is a rising tide. Lifts all boats, as it were."

"You should visit the Vaults of Vale," Carmadon puts in. "Or even Horn Mountain."

"We do not intend to be here long enough for *sightseeing*," Anabel says with a sniff. Slowly she lays her silverware on her plate of half-eaten food. Indicating how supremely finished she is with all this.

In her furs, Evangeline lifts her head. Like a cat, she surveys the old queen. Weighing something. "I agree," she says. "The sooner we're able to return, the better."

Return to someone, she means.

"Well, that isn't up to us, is it? Excuse me," Farley adds as she leans across the table. Anabel's eyes almost bug out of her head as she watches a Red rebel grab her abandoned plate and scrape the leftovers onto her own. With sure hands, Farley slices up the extra cut of bison, the knife dancing through meat. I've seen her do worse to human flesh. "It's up to the Montfort government," she says, "and whether or not they decide to give us more soldiers. Eh, Premier?"

"Indeed," Davidson says. "Wars cannot be won on familiar faces alone. No matter how bright the flag, how high the standard." His gaze flickers from Tiberias to me. What he means is clear. "We need armies."

Tiberias nods. "And we'll get them. If not from Montfort, then from anywhere we can. The High Houses of Norta can be swayed."

"House Samos tried." Evangeline gestures for more wine with a lazy, familiar twist of her fingers. "We aligned who we could, but the rest? I wouldn't rely on them."

Tiberias blanches. "You think they'll stay loyal to Maven when—"

"When they have you to choose?" the Samos princess scoffs, cutting him off with an imperious glare. "My dear Tiberias, they could have chosen you months ago. But in the eyes of many, you're still a traitor."

Across from me, Farley scowls. "Are your nobles so stupid as to still think Tiberias killed his own father?"

I shake my head, knife in hand. "She means because he's with us. Allied to Reds." The blade slices through the rest of the meat on my plate. I cut with vicious force, tasting bitterness in my mouth. "Trying so desperately to find balance between our peoples."

"That is what I hope to do," Tiberias says, his voice oddly soft.

I pull my gaze away from the cooked flesh to stare at him again. His eyes meet mine, wide and disgustingly gentle. I harden myself to his charms.

"You have an interesting way of showing it," I sneer.

Anabel is quick, barking a retort. "Enough, both of you."

My jaw tightens, and I look past Tiberias to his grandmother, now glaring at me. I meet her gaze with equal fire. "This is Maven's strength, one of his *many* strengths," I say. "He divides so easily, without even trying. He does it to his enemies, and to his allies."

At the head of the table, Davidson steeples his fingers. He surveys me over his knuckles, unblinking in his focus. "Go on."

"Like Evangeline said, there are noble families who will never abandon him, because he won't change the way things are. And he's *good* at ruling, winning over his subjects while keeping the nobles satiated. Ending the Lakelander War earned him a great deal of respect among the people," I point out, remembering how even Reds cheered him when he toured the countryside. It still turns my stomach. "He plays on that love, just as he plays on fear. When I was his prisoner, he was careful to keep many children in court, heirs to different houses, hostages in all but name. It's an easy way to control a person, seizing what they hold most dear."

I know that firsthand.

"And on top of everything else," I add, swallowing around the lump in my throat, "there is no predicting Maven Calore. His mother still whispers in his head, pulling his strings, even though she lies dead and cold."

A low current of heat ripples at my side. Tiberias stares at the table-top, looking as if he might burn a hole through his plate. His cheeks are drained of color now, pale as bone.

With her eyes still on me, watching me devour the last bites of steak, Anabel curls her lip. "Prince Bracken in Piedmont is under our control," she says. "He will give us whatever we need."

Bracken. Another one of Montfort's schemes. The ruling prince of Piedmont is under our thumb as long as Montfort still holds his son and daughter captive. I wonder where they are, who they are. *Are they young? Are they just children? Are they innocent in all this?*

The temperature begins to rise, a small but steady increase. Next to me, Tiberias tightens. He fixes his grandmother with a firm stare. "I don't want soldiers who haven't agreed to fight for me. Especially Bracken's Silvers. They can't be trusted. Neither can he."

"We have his children," Farley says. "That should be enough."

"*Montfort* has his children," Tiberias replies, his voice deepening.

Before, on the base, it was easy to ignore the price someone paid. The evils done for good reasons. I look to Davidson, who glances at his watch. *This is war,* he said once, trying to justify what must be done.

"If they were returned, could we convince Piedmont to stand aside?" I ask. "Remain neutral?"

The premier turns his empty wineglass around in his hands, letting the many facets catch the soft light of lanterns. I think I see regret in him. "I doubt that very much."

"Are they here?" Anabel asks the question with a calm so forced I almost expect her to pop a vein in her neck. "Bracken's children?"

Davidson doesn't reply, moving only to refill his glass.

The old queen tips a finger, her eyes shining. "Ah. They are." Her grin spreads. "Good leverage. We can bargain for more of Bracken's soldiers. An entire army if we wish."

I look at the napkin in my lap, stained with fingerprints of grease and bits of lipstick wiped away. *They could be in this palace. Looking down at us right now. Children at the window, trapped behind a locked door.* Are they strong enough to require silent guards, or even the torture of chains like the ones I used to wear? I know what that kind of prison is like. Under the table, I touch both my wrists, feeling the empty skin there. Flesh instead of manacles. Electricity instead of silence.

Tiberias suddenly slams a closed fist on the table, making the plates and glassware jump. I jolt too, surprised. "We will do no such thing," he snarls. "The resources are enough."

His grandmother scowls at him, deepening the lines of her face. "You need bodies to win wars, Tiberias."

"The discussion of Bracken is over" is all he says in reply. With finality, he cuts the last piece of steak in two, sawing with his knife. Anabel sneers, showing teeth, but says nothing. He is her grandson, but also a king by her own declaration. She has long passed the line of what is proper debate with a sovereign.

"So we must beg tomorrow," I mumble. "It's the only choice left."

Frustrated, I signal for a glass of wine of my own, and don't waste time gulping it down. The sweet red soothes enough that I can almost ignore the feel of eyes on my face. Bronze eyes.

"I suppose you could call it that," Davidson says, his gaze faraway. He looks down, first at his watch again, then sidelong to Carmadon. Their glance speaks volumes I cannot fathom. It makes me envious, and again I find myself wishing things were different.

"What chance do we have?" Tiberias is blunt, forceful, and direct. All the things he's been taught a king should be.

"For a full deployment of every soldier in our armies?" Davidson shakes his head. "No chance at all. We have borders of our own to guard. But half? A bit more? I could see the scales tipping in our favor. If."

If. I hate that word.

I brace myself in my seat, suddenly more on edge than usual. I feel like the terrace might crumble beneath me and send us all plunging into the valley.

Farley's face mirrors my fear. She keeps her knife in hand, wary of our ally. "If what?"

The bells sound before Davidson can answer. And while the rest of us jump, startled by the noise, he doesn't move. He's used to it.

Or he expected it.

This isn't a chime to mark the hours on a clock. These bells ring deep and low, their voices trembling down the mountainside, echoing across Ascendant, calling to other bells throughout the city. The din spreads like a wave, running down this slope and back up the other. Lights spread with the noise. Bright, harsh lights. Floodlights. Security lights. The alarm that follows is mechanical, whining. It shatters the calm mountain valley with its wail.

Tiberias jumps to his feet, cloak swirling around his shoulders. He frees one hand, fingers wide, the flamemaker bracelet glinting beneath his sleeve. If he calls to fire, it will come. Evangeline and Anabel do the same, both of them lethal. Neither looks afraid, only determined to protect themselves.

I feel the lightning in me rise the same way, and my thoughts fly to my family in the palace behind us. *Not safe. Not even here.* But we have no time for one more of my heartbreaks.

Farley stands too, leaning hard on her hands. She glares at Davidson. *"If what?"* she snaps again, yelling over the alarm.

He looks up at her, oddly serene among the chaos. Soldiers replace servants in the shadows, flanking our table. I tense, fists clenching at my sides.

"If Montfort will fight for you," the premier says, turning his eyes on Tiberias, "you must also fight for us."

Carmadon doesn't seem startled by the bells. He only glances toward the palace before sighing in what could be annoyance. "Raiders," he scowls. "Every single time I try to throw a dinner party."

"That's hardly true." Davidson cracks a grin, though he never breaks his gaze. His eyes remain on Tiberias, a challenge as much as anything.

"Well, it feels true," says Carmadon, pouting.

As security lights blaze all around us, Davidson's gaze flames gold. Tiberias's burns red.

"They call you the Flame of the North, Your Majesty. Show us fire."

Then the premier looks at me.

"And show us storm."

NINE
Mare

"I said no more surprises," I hiss to Davidson, following close on his heels as he leads us through his palace. Farley marches next to him, her hand resting on the pistol at her hip, as if she expects raiders to start popping out of the closets.

The Silver members of our party are just as on edge. Anabel keeps their ranks tight. She repeatedly slows Tiberias, nudging him back behind a protective wall of loyal guards from House Lerolan. Evangeline is better at hiding her fear, her face the usual twist between sneer and smirk. She has two escorts of her own—Samos cousins, I think. Her dress changes quickly, re-forming into scaly armor as we weave through the halls of the Montfort palace.

The premier looks over his shoulder when I speak and surveys me with a withering glance. The bells and alarm echo strangely in the hall, dancing around his words. "Mare, I can hardly control the whims of raiders, and I do not schedule their attacks, frequent as they may be."

I hold his gaze and quicken my pace, hot anger pulsing through my veins. "You don't?" It wouldn't surprise me. I've seen kings do worse to their own people in exchange for power.

Davidson turns steely and presses his lips into a grim line. A sudden flush spreads across his broad cheekbones. His voice drops to a whisper. "We had warning, yes. We knew they were coming. And we had enough lead time to make sure the outskirts were protected. But I resent the implication that I would spill the blood of my own people, risk their lives, for what? Dramatic effect?" he hisses, his voice deadly as a knife edge. "Yes, this presents an opportunity for the Scarlet Guard and for Calore to uphold their ends of the bargain, and to prove something before we go to my government and beg. But it is not a trade I'm happy to make," he snaps. "I'd much rather be sitting out on the terrace getting pleasantly drunk with my husband, watching overpowered children sneer at each other, than do this."

I feel scolded but also relieved. Davidson glares at me, fire burning in his golden eyes. He's usually so serene, unflappable, impossible to discern. His strength lies not just in ability or charisma, but in a well-practiced calm that few can see beyond. Not now. Merely the suggestion of any betrayal, however small, to his country has him incensed. I understand that kind of loyalty. I respect it. I can even almost trust it.

"So what are we going to do?" I ask, satisfied for the moment.

The premier slows, then halts, turning his back to the wall. So he can see all of us. It stops everyone short, crowding the wide passageway with waiting Reds and Silvers. Even Queen Anabel looks on Davidson with grave attention.

"Our patrols reported raiders crossing the border an hour ago," he says. "They usually head for the towns down on the plain, or to the city itself."

I think about my parents, my siblings, and Kilorn. Either sleeping through the noise or questioning it. I don't want to fight, not if it means leaving them behind and in danger. Farley catches my eye, and I see the same fear in her. Clara is upstairs too, tucked into a crib.

Davidson does his best to assuage us. "The alarms are cautionary, and our citizens know it," he says. "Ascendant is well defended from attack. The mountains alone provide enough protection to keep most assaults to the plains or low on the eastern slopes. They would have to climb into our own teeth to get within striking distance of the city."

"Are the raiders particularly stupid, then?" Farley asks, trying to bluster away her concern. She doesn't take her hand off her gun.

A corner of Davidson's mouth lifts, and I think I hear Carmadon cough *yes* into his hand.

"No," the premier replies. "But they are very keen on optics. Attacking the Montfort capital is somewhat of a habit for them. It wins favor among their own, as well as the Prairie lords."

Tiberias lifts his chin. He shifts slowly, edging in front of one of his guards. I can tell by the tightness in his shoulders that he hates being hemmed in like that. Hates being anywhere but the front line. It isn't in Tiberias Calore to ask another to do what he won't, to face danger if he doesn't. "And who are *they* exactly?" he asks.

"You've all asked about Silvers in Montfort," Davidson says, his voice loud enough to carry over the warning alarms. "You wonder how they live this way. How we changed things decades ago. Some Silvers agreed to freedom, to democracy. Many, I should say. *Most.*" He clenches his jaw. "They saw what the world should be like. Or they saw the world beyond, and decided it was better to stay, easier to adjust."

His eyes land on Evangeline, and for some reason she flushes under his scrutiny, almost hiding her face.

"Some did not. Old Silvers, royals, nobles who could not stand our new country. They fled or fought their way to the borders. North, south, west. To the east, in the empty hills between our mountains and Prairie, they formed bands. Attempts at their own lands and lordships. Always fighting, gnawing at each other and us. They live as leeches, feeding on what they find. They do not grow anything; they do not build. They have little holding them together but anger and dying pride. They attack transports, farms, cities, in both Prairie and Montfort. They focus on Red towns and villages mostly, on those who cannot defend against Silver onslaught. They move; they strike; they move again. And so we call them the raiders."

Carmadon tsks loudly. He runs a hand over his gleaming purple-black skull. "So far to fall for my Silver kin. For nothing more than pride."

"And for what they think is power," Davidson adds. His eyes land on Tiberias. The exiled prince straightens, setting his jaw. "For what they think they deserve. They would rather lose everything than live beneath people they think are lesser."

"Idiots," I curse.

"History is marred with people like that," Julian offers. "Resistant to change."

"But they make those *willing* to change all the more heroic, don't they?" I reply, letting the words land as they should.

Tiberias doesn't take the bait. "Where will they strike?" he says, never moving his eyes from Davidson's face.

The premier grins darkly.

"We've received word from one of the towns down on the plain. Raiders are close," he says. "Your Majesty, I believe I may get to show you the Hawkway after all."

No palace is complete without an armory.

Davidson's guards are already there, suiting up throughout the long room stocked with weaponry and gear. They don't pull on the green coveralls, the uniforms I've become accustomed to, but tight black suits and high boots. Good for defending against a night raid. They remind me of what I used to wear in Training, my purple-and-silver-striped outfit to mark me as a child of House Titanos. A Silver through and through. A lie.

At the door, Anabel puts a hand on Cal's arm. She pleads with her eyes, but he moves past her, firmly but gently pushing her away. Her fingers trail along the edge of his red cape, letting the black brocade run through her fingers as he escapes her grasp.

"I need to do this," I hear him murmur. "He's right. I need to fight for them if they'll fight for me."

No one else speaks, and the silence falls thick as a low cloud. All I hear is the shuffle of clothing. My dress puddles around my ankles as I quickly pull the suit up over my underclothes. As I move, I shift, and my eyes lock on familiar muscles.

Tiberias faces away from me too, his shirt discarded, the suit tight around his waist. I trace the length of his spine, noting the few scars along otherwise smooth and sculpted skin. They're old, older than mine. Won in Training in a palace and on a war front that no longer exists. Even though the touch of a healer could erase them quickly, he keeps them, collecting scars as another would medals or badges.

Will he earn more scars today? Will Davidson keep his promise?

Part of me wonders if this is a trap for the true Calore king. An easy assassination disguised as a real threat. But even if Davidson lied about not harming Tiberias, he's not an idiot. Removing the older Calore would only weaken us, destroying a vital shield between Montfort and the Scarlet Guard, and Maven.

I keep staring, unable to stop myself. The scars might be old, but not the almost-purple, bruise-like mark where his neck meets his shoulder. That's new. Only a few days old. *That's mine,* I think, gulping around a memory both close and infinitely far away.

Someone bumps my shoulder, jolting me out of the quicksand that is Tiberias Calore.

"Here," Farley says gruffly, a warning. She hasn't discarded her dark red uniform of Command, and she stares down at me, blue eyes wide. "Let me."

Her fingers zip up the back of my suit with speed, tightening the ensemble around my frame. I shuffle a little, adjusting the thick-woven fabric of my too-long sleeves. Anything to keep my attention away from the exiled prince currently shoving his arms into his own suit.

"Nothing in your size, Barrow?"

Tyton's deep drawl offers a well-needed distraction. He leans up alongside us, back braced against the wall with one long leg stretched out. His suit is the same as mine, albeit better fitted to his trim form. No lightning insignia. No markings. No indication of how deadly a man this newblood is. With him around, I realize Davidson has no need to arrange useful *accidents* to remove opponents. He only needs Tyton. The chilling thought is somehow a balm. This isn't a trap, at the very least. It doesn't need to be.

I slide on my boots, smirking. "I'll have words with the tailor when we get back."

Across the room, Tiberias rolls his sleeves, exposing his flamemaker bracelet. Evangeline looks almost bored at his side, her furs tossed to the floor to reveal the full armor covering her from fingertips to toes.

She catches my glance and holds my gaze.

I don't expect her to stick her neck out for anyone but Elane Haven, and yet I feel safer with her around. She's saved me twice before. And I'm still of value to her. Our agreement still stands.

Tiberias must not win the throne.

The room clears as we prepare, moving from the changing area to the rows and rows of arms at the back of the room. Farley weighs herself down with ammunition, putting a pistol on her other hip and a snub machine gun across her back. I assume she already has her knives tucked away. I don't take any weapons, but Tyton grabs a belt, pistol, and holster off the rack, shoving them toward me.

"No thanks," I grumble, begrudging. I don't like guns or bullets. I don't trust them. And I don't need them. I can't control either one the way I can control my lightning.

"Some raiders are silents," he replies, his voice a low whipcrack. Just the thought turns my insides. I know the feel of Silent Stone all too well. It isn't a sensation I would like to bear again, not for any reason.

Without warning, Tyton fastens the gun belt around my waist, his eyes and fingers quick on the buckles. The gun slides into its holster, feeling heavy and unfamiliar at my side. "If you lose your ability," he adds, "it's best to have a backup."

Behind us, the temperature rises, a rippling heat that can only mean one thing. I look up just in time to watch Tiberias shoulder by, keeping his distance, furiously intent on staring at the floor as he goes. Trying to ignore me.

He might as well wear a sign around his neck.

"Careful with those hands, Tyton," he growls over his shoulder. "She bites."

Tyton just chuckles darkly. He doesn't need to respond, and doesn't attempt to. It only incenses Tiberias further.

For once, I don't care about the scarlet flush heating my cheeks. I step away from Tyton, who is still laughing.

Tiberias watches me as I catch up to him, his bronze eyes alight with something more than his usual fire. Electric energy pulses through my limbs. I keep it in check, using it to fuel my resolve.

"Don't be such a possessive ass," I snap, driving my elbow into his ribs as I stalk by. It's like hitting a wall. "If you insist on calling yourself a king, you can at least act like one."

Behind me, he lets loose something between a snarl and a frustrated sigh.

I don't respond, don't look back, and don't stop until I've followed the steady current of soldiers outside onto the central plaza where we first arrived hours ago. Black and forest-green transports crowd the stone, the vehicles fanned out evenly. Davidson waits by the lead, Carmadon at his side. They embrace quickly, touching foreheads and kissing, before Carmadon backs away. Neither of them seems bothered by the impending skirmish. This must be a common occurrence—or they're very good at masking their fear. It could be both.

The palace overlooks the growing number of soldiers, and shadows move on the balconies. Servants and guests alike. I squint, trying to find my family among the silhouettes. Gisa's hair should stand out, but I spot Dad first. He hunches over a railing, leaning out to watch. When he sees me, he tips his head, but only a little. I want to wave, but it feels silly. And when the transports rev to life, their engines a growl across the pines, I know that calling to them is no use either.

I find Farley at the lead transport, waiting alongside Davidson. She clambers inside, hoisting herself up and into the raised vehicle. These transports are different from the ones I'm used to. The wheels are much bigger, almost my height, with deep treads for the rocky, jagged mountain terrain. The rest of the body is reinforced, piped with steel, and decorated with many handholds, toeholds, and dangling straps, for obvious purpose.

Tyton jumps up, scrambling onto the back of the lead. He links himself to the frame alongside another Montfort soldier. The straps connect to their waists, giving them enough slack to lean but not enough to bounce. Other soldiers, with all kinds of blood, do the same across the transports. Without their insignia, I can't tell for certain, but I assume they are the best shots, with both bullets and ability.

Premier Davidson holds the door, waiting for me to join him inside the transport. Something hungry and wild drives me to do the opposite.

I climb up next to Tyton, tying myself in on his right. One corner of his mouth lifts, the only acknowledgment of my choice.

The transport behind us is for Tiberias and Evangeline, their guards flanking the vehicle in unmistakable colors. I watch as Evangeline halts, one foot on the step up. She looks, not at me, but back at the palace. At Carmadon waiting by the grand entrance, arms crossed, his white suit glowing in the floodlights. Anabel stands nearby, a few feet distant. On the edge of impolite. She raises her chin when Tiberias appears, striding across the plaza with long steps.

Without his colors, he seems like all the rest. A soldier with orders to answer to. Fitting. That's who he thinks he is. Just another person under his father's command, obeying the will of someone dead. Again we lock eyes, and something in both of us burns.

Despite everything, his presence feels like safety. No matter what, he chases away any fear I have for myself.

Of course, that only leaves fear for the people I love.

For Farley, for my family.

And still, always, for him.

A settlement down on the plain is at risk, calling for aid on the other side of the mountain. There isn't time to go down the slope and wind around through the valley. So we go over it.

There are roads above the palace, weaving high into the pines. We scream over the steep landscape, beneath branches so tight they obscure the stars. I lean flat to the transport, afraid of being dashed into an overhanging bough. Soon the trees are gone entirely, and the earth beneath our transports turns rocky. My head tightens, my ears popping like they do during jet takeoffs. Snow pocks the sloping ground, gathered in hollows at first, until it blankets the final peak. My exposed face goes red with cold, but the suits are special-made, keeping me warm. Still, my teeth chatter, and I wonder exactly what possessed me to ride on the back of the transport rather than inside it.

The tip of the mountain looms above, a white knife against a sky pinpricked with blazing stars. I lean back as far as I dare. The sight makes me feel small.

My balance shifts, marking the descent. Snow sprays in our wake, then rocks and dirt, kicking up a cloud of debris to follow the transports down the eastern slope. My stomach plummets as we approach the tree line again. The plain stretches out beyond the pines, endless and dark as an ocean. I feel as if I could see across a thousand miles. Back to the Lakelands, to Norta. To Maven and whatever he has in store for us. Another hammer will fall, and soon. But where? On who? None of us can say yet.

We plunge into the trees, the transport bouncing over roots and boulders. There are no roads on this side, only barely cleared paths through the arched branches. My teeth rattle with every bump, and the restraints are certainly bruising my hips.

"Call to it," Tyton growls, nudging up against me so I can hear him over the roar of engines and howl of wind. "Be ready."

I nod, steeling myself. The thrum of electricity is easy to pull. I make sure not to draw from the engines around me, but on the lightning only I can summon. Purple and dangerous, it thunders under my skin.

The massive pines thin, and I glimpse starlight between their needles. Not above, but beyond. Out. Forward.

I shriek, pressing myself against the transport as it skids, turning a hard left onto a sudden, smooth road along the cliff side. For a terrifying moment, I think we might spin right off the mountain and plummet into the darkness below. But the vehicle holds firm, tires catching the road, as one by one the other transports follow, hard drifting over the paved way.

"Easy," Tyton says, eyes flickering over my body.

Purple sparks are running up and down my skin, responding to my fear. They burn off harmlessly, flickering in the dark.

"There wasn't a better way to do that?" I mutter.

He barely shrugs.

Hewn stone arches over the road at intervals, the structures smooth-cut, in alternating curves of marble and limestone. Each one is crowned with a pair of carved wings, the feathers etched deep into the rock to surround blazing lights illuminating the path.

"The Hawkway," I breathe aloud. A worthy name for the road as high as hawks and eagles fly. In the daylight, it must be astounding.

The road zigzags back and forth down the almost cliff-like mountainside, precarious with sharp switchbacks. This must be the quickest way down to the plain, and also the most insane. But the transport drivers are infinitely skilled, hitting each razor-edged corner with precision. Perhaps they are all silks or a newblood equivalent, their agility translating to the machines they drive. I try to stay vigilant as we tear down the Hawkway, on the lookout for hostile Silvers hiding in the rocks and gnarled trees. Lights on the plains come into focus. The few towns Davidson mentioned dot the landscape. They seem peaceful, untouched. And vulnerable.

We're rounding another switchback turn when something like a scream pierces the night. The sound of tearing metal, shredding at the seams, shrieks around us. I look up to see a transport falling, tipping over and over, knocked out of its place halfway back the line. All seems to slow down as it comes into blinding focus, my senses narrowing to the transport spiraling in midair. The Montfort soldiers on board fight with their restraints, hoping to beat gravity. Another, a strong-arm, grabs for the road edge. It slips through his fingers, the pavement cracking beneath his touch. The transport continues to fall, spinning on its axis. It can't be an accident. The trajectory is too perfect.

It's going to flatten us.

I barely have time to duck while my own transport lurches beneath me, our brakes squealing, trying to stop in time. Smoke burns from the tires as the brakes lock up.

The road jumps when the transport smashes down, and we smash into it. Tyton grabs the back of my suit, yanking me upward, while I snap my arms over my restraints, using my electricity to cut through the thick weave. We scramble forward as Tiberias and Evangeline's transport smashes into our rear, pinning us between the fallen vehicle and theirs.

More screaming brakes and resounding crashes echo behind us, one after the other, a chain reaction of twisted engines and burned rubber. Only the last transports in the line, six or so, are saved from the onslaught. They're able to brake in time to save their machinery.

I look back and forth, ahead and behind, not sure where to go. The fallen transport lies on its back, an overturned turtle. Davidson is already out of the lead, stumbling toward the soldiers crushed beneath the vehicle. Farley moves with him, gun ready in her hand. She drops to a knee, training her sights on the cliffs above us.

"Magnetrons!" Davidson roars, one hand raised for aid. He pushes out a palm, forming a clear blue shield along the deadly edge of the road.

Somehow Evangeline is already at his side, her hands dancing. She hisses as she raises the heavy transport off the road, revealing twisted limbs and a few flattened skulls seeping brain like popped grapes leaking juice. Davidson doesn't waste time, lurching forward to pull survivors from beneath the floating transport.

Moving slowly, Evangeline lowers the transport again. With a twitch of her fingers, she rips off one of the doors, allowing those inside to tumble out. The soldiers are bloody and disoriented, but living.

"Get out of the way!" she snaps, waving them back from the transport. When they do, limping out of her path, she slaps her palms together in a resounding clap.

The transport does as she wills, crushing itself into a dense, jagged ball the size of one of its doors. She lets it drop with a crack. Only the glass and the tires fly in every direction, beyond Evangeline's metallic control. One tire rolls down the road, an odd sight.

I realize I'm standing up on my pinned transport. Evangeline turns around, her armor reflecting the starlight. Despite Tyton next to me, I feel exposed. An easy target.

"Get the healers up here!" I shout, looking back along the line of crushed vehicles piled up beneath the arches. "And get some more light on the road!"

Above us, something flares, a rising beam like the sun. The work of shadows, no doubt, manipulators of light. It sends harsh light and harsher darkness dancing across us all. I squint and clench a fist, sparking some electricity of my own around my knuckles. Like Farley, I keep my eyes on the rocky ledges rising all around. If the raiders somehow have the high ground, if they're above us, then we lose a great advantage.

Tiberias already knows that. "Eyes up, sights on the cliffs!" he shouts, his back to his transport. He too has a pistol in one hand, while flames twist around the fingers of the other. Not that the soldiers need such instruction. Anyone with a gun has it raised, fingers ready on triggers. We just need a target.

But the Hawkway is oddly silent, quiet except for the occasional shout and echo as orders pass along the line.

A dozen or so Montfort soldiers work their way down the zagging road, silhouettes in their black suits. They stop at each transport, using their abilities to try to pull apart the mashed vehicles. Magnetrons and strongarms, or the newblood versions of each.

Evangeline and her cousins stomp by below, focusing on extricating my transport from theirs.

"Can you fix it?" I call down.

She just sneers as she forces the twisted metal to slither apart. "I'm a magnetron, not a mechanic," she grunts, shouldering between the wrecks.

Suddenly I wish for Cameron and her tool belt. But she is far away, out of danger with her brother back in Piedmont. I bite my lip, brain buzzing. This is a blatant trap, an easy one, leaving us vulnerable on the mountainside. Or just stuck here, while the raiders wreak havoc on the towns below, if not the city behind us.

Tiberias is thinking the same thing. He hastens to the edge of the road, looking down into the darkness. "Can you radio your settlements? They need to be warned."

"Ahead of you," Davidson barks back. He crouches over one of the wounded soldiers, holding his arm while a healer works at the man's broken leg. At the premier's side, an officer speaks rapidly into her communications gear.

Tiberias frowns, turning from the cliff back to the carnage. "And send word back to the city. Call out a second detachment. Dropjets if they can get here in time."

Davidson barely nods. I get the feeling he's already done that too, but he holds his tongue, keeping his focus on the soldier beneath him. Healers, half a dozen or so, work diligently down the line, tending to anyone injured in the massive wreck.

"What about us? We can't stay up here for long." I slide off my vehicle, landing gently. It feels better to be on solid ground. "Something tipped that transport."

Still on the roof, Tyton braces his hands on his hips. He looks at the zagging road above, investigating the otherwise empty spot the first transport fell from. "Could be a small-charge mine. Detonated at the right moment, it could flip a vehicle."

"Too clean," Tiberias growls. He paces along the road, his entire body on edge. His Lerolan guards follow him a little too closely, almost catching his heels. "Coordinated. Someone's up here with us. We need to get down before they strike again. We're sitting ducks."

"Sitting ducks on the edge of a *cliff*," Evangeline adds. She kicks at her own transport in frustration, putting a solid dent in the already crumpled front. "We can get the working transports up front. Load them as much as we can."

Tiberias shakes his head. "It's not enough."

"It's *something*," I snap at him.

"We're only a few thousand feet up now. Some of the regiment can start running, get to the ground," Davidson says, helping one of the soldiers limp away from the head of the line. His communication officer follows, still jabbering into her radio. "The outpost at Goldengrove has transports. It isn't far from the foot of the mountain."

On the ground, Farley whirls, lowering her gun in her haste. "You want us to split up?"

"Not for long," Davidson replies.

She pales, rising to her feet. "But long enough if—"

"If?" he asks.

"If this is a trap. A feint. You got word from the towns that raiders were close. But where is the attack?" She gestures to the black horizon. "There isn't one. Not out there."

Davidson frowns, eyes shifting. "Not yet."

"Or they didn't plan to attack at all. They wanted to draw us out of the city," Farley says. "Catch us on the cliffs. You said yourself, they fight for their pride. And the city is too well defended. This is a hell of a way to get valuable targets out in the open."

The premier steps to her, his face grim and stern. Then he puts a hand on her shoulder, squeezing a little. A friendly if apologetic gesture. "I won't leave my people out there alone because we *might* be in danger. I can't do that, General Farley. I know you understand my position," he sighs.

I expect more of a fight from Farley, but she drops her chin, almost nodding. She chews her lip and says nothing more.

Satisfied, Davidson looks over his shoulder. "Captain Highcloud, Captain Viya," he calls. Two officers in their black suits step forward, ready for their orders. "Take your units down. Hard march, all speed. Rendezvous at Goldengrove."

They salute in response, turning to gather their soldiers. As the two units group near the head of the line, Tiberias winces. He hastens to the premier, clasping his arm. Not to threaten him, but to beg.

I know what fear looks like on Tiberias Calore, and I see it in him now.

"Leave the gravitrons, at least," he pleads. "In case they decide to blow us all off the mountain . . ."

After a brief moment of reflection, Davidson clicks his teeth. "Fine," he says. "And Your Highness, if you wouldn't mind," he adds, turning to face Evangeline, "those transports aren't going to climb over this mess without help. Use the gravitrons too. They'll make quick work for you."

She eyes him with steel annoyance, unaccustomed to taking orders from anyone but her father. Still, she sighs and trots off to do as he wills.

"What about me?" I ask, planting myself between Tiberias and Davidson. Both of them jolt, forgetting I was even here to begin with.

"Stay vigilant" is all Davidson offers, shrugging. "Unless you can lift a transport off the ground, there's not much any of us can do right now."

Helpful, I growl in my head. But the frustration is with myself. My ability is meant to destroy. It has no purpose right now. I'm useless, for the moment.

So is Tiberias.

He watches Davidson stalk off, his communications officer in tow, leaving us standing alone, our backs to the wrecked hulk of my transport. Adrenaline and electricity still course through me. I have to lean against the metal, my fingers knotted together to keep from twitching.

"I don't like this," Tiberias mutters.

I scoff, scuffing my new boots on the road. "Stuck on a cliff, half of the soldiers gone, transports ruined, raider attack imminent, and I didn't get to finish my dinner. What's not to like?"

In spite of our circumstances, he grins, his smile crooked and familiar. I cross my arms, hoping he can't see me flush in the dim light. He stares at me, his eyes an intent, burning bronze as they trace my face. Slowly, his lips fall and the smile fades as he remembers our decisions. Our choices. But his stare remains, and I feel fire rise inside me. Rage and want and regret in equal measure.

"Don't look at me like that, Tiberias."

"Don't call me Tiberias," he shoots back, dropping his gaze.

I laugh bitterly. "It's the name you chose."

To that he has no response, and we lapse into uneasy silence. The occasional shout or metallic groan echoes across the mountainside, the only sound in the empty darkness.

On the zagging road above us, Evangeline, her cousins, and the gravitrons slowly leapfrog the all-terrain vehicles, moving the wrecks behind the transports that can still function. Davidson must have told her to preserve all the wrecks she could, or else she could just crush them all to dust and let the rest roll through.

"I'm sorry about before, in the armory," he says after a long moment. He keeps his eyes on the ground, head bowed in shadow. But not enough to hide the cold flush across his cheeks. "I shouldn't have said that."

"I don't care what you said. I care about the intention behind it," I tell him, shaking my head. "I don't belong to you."

"I think anyone with eyes can see that."

"Can *you*?" I ask sharply.

He exhales slowly, as if gathering himself for a fight. Instead he turns his head to look down at me. The glowing lights of the Hawkway cast jagged shadows across his face, emphasizing his cheekbones. It makes him look old and tired, a king for years instead of days. "Yes, Mare," he finally says, his voice a low rumble. "But remember it wasn't just me."

I blink. "What?"

"You chose something over me too," he sighs. "Many things."

The Scarlet Guard. The Red dawn. The hope of a better future for the people I love. I bite my lip, chewing my own flesh. I have nothing to deny. Tiberias isn't wrong.

"If you two are done," Tyton says loudly, leaning down from his vantage point on the transport, "I think you'd both be interested to know there are people in the trees."

I suck in a breath, tensing up. Tiberias puts out a hand quickly, touching my arm in light warning. "Don't startle," he says. "I'm guessing they have us targeted."

Metal groans, and I jump beneath Tiberias's fingers. His grip tightens. But it's just the transports being moved.

"How many?" I ask through gritted teeth, trying my best to mask my fear.

Tyton looks down at me, eyes bright. His white hair gleams in the artificial light illuminating the Hawkway. "Four, two on each side. At a good distance, but I can just feel their brains." Next to me, Tiberias frowns, the corners of his lips curving downward in distaste. "Fifty yards, maybe."

I look past Tiberias, and he looks past me, both of us searching the shadowed pines as furtively as we can. I can't see anything beyond our circle of light. Not the gleam of eyes or the flash of steel down a gun barrel. Nothing.

I can't feel them either. My ability is nowhere near as strong or as focused as Tyton's.

Farley catches my eye and approaches with a hand on her hip, the other still clutching her pistol. "You three look like you've seen a ghost," she says, sweeping her gaze back and forth. "Snipers in the trees?" she offers, as if she's asking about the weather.

"Did you see them?" Tyton breathes.

"No." She shakes her head. "But it's what I'd do."

"You can drop them, right?" I ask, nudging Tyton's boot. I remember the electricons taught me about his ability. Brain lightning. Tyton can affect the electricity in a person's body, the tiny sparks inside our brains. He can kill without anyone knowing. Without any trace.

He frowns and furrows his dark brows, a sharp contrast to his dyed hair. "I might be able to, from this distance. But only one at a time," he says. "And only *if* they are raiders."

Tiberias scowls. "Who else would they be up here?"

"I don't enjoy killing people without cause, Calore," Tyton replies. "And I've lived on these mountains my entire life."

"So you'll wait for them to shoot us?" The prince shifts slightly, squaring his shoulders so that I'm sheltered on one side.

Tyton doesn't budge. As he speaks, a breeze plays up, carrying with it the strong, sharply sweet scent of pine. "I'll wait for your magnetron princess to tell me if they're holding sniper rifles or not."

On the one hand, I agree with Tiberias. We're exposed up here, and who else would be waiting in the trees, watching us scramble? But I understand Tyton too. I know what it is to pour lightning into a person, to sense their nerves sparking off and dying. It feels like a small death of your own, an ending you can never forget.

"Get Evangeline," I mutter. "And tell Davidson. We need to be sure."

Next to me, Tiberias huffs. But he doesn't argue. He pushes off the transport, intending to stalk after Evangeline.

The breeze strengthens, playing across my face. Pine needles brush my skin, soft as trailing fingers. I try to catch one, but it dances off on the growing wind.

And it sprouts before my eyes, a sapling growing in midair. It spears a soldier before any of us can react.

The attack is not the storm of bullets we expected, but the spray of pine needles blasting in a strong, sudden gale. It catches Tyton head-on, tossing him off the wrecked transport. He rolls onto the road, head smacking against the pavement. He stumbles to a knee, then falls, oddly off balance. I throw up an arm to protect my eyes and drop to a knee as needles scratch across my exposed skin. Where they land, roots and trunks burst forth in curling, living explosions. The Hawkway cracks and transports heave, tossed by the forest growing before our eyes. My balance shifts with the road, and I fight to keep upright, bracing against the wrecked transport at my back.

Tiberias reacts without thinking. He tosses a fireball, charring the pines sprouting up around us as fast as they can grow. The ash swirls in the growing wind, obscuring the road lights, making my eyes water.

The air shudders with the sound of crushing metal and shattering glass. Evangeline and her crew are done wasting time. They flatten the wrecks that remain in the way, reducing them to solid puddles of iron and steel. The transports that still work roar, revving their engines as they lurch forward, fighting over pulsing roots and ripping branches. Evangeline leaps through the smoky air, climbing up onto a transport frame. Gunshots ring out, but the bullets fall to the wayside, tossed off by her ability.

Blue shields spring to life on either end of the Hawkway, tall and ethereal against the smoke and ash. Davidson controls each one with an outthrust fist. More shots sound, rippling over the shield. They can't penetrate. The guns can't reach us.

"Tyton!" I scream, looking for the electricon. "Tyton, kill them!"

He hoists himself to his feet, teetering as he wags his head back and forth. Trying to shake away the daze. Using the nearest transport, he props himself up, leaning heavily.

"Give me a second!" he yells back, shaking his head again.

We still can't see the raiders, safe from their nests in the trees. There have to be greenwardens, at least. Tiberias's flames spread across the surge of pines on the road, twisting like a snake, attempting to devour each new tree as it sprouts. His Lerolan guards run between the trunks, laying hands on each. They explode at their touch, splintering in clouds of bark and blooming fire.

"Get on the transports!" Davidson roars over the chaos. He still holds the shields, defending us from a hail of bullets. "We have to get off the mountain!"

I suck in a deep breath, steeling myself. *Focus.* In the dark, I can't see the clouds gathering overhead, but I can feel them. Storm clouds, thunderheads. Growing at my command, ready to strike.

Someone pulls Tyton onto the approaching transport, buckling him in. On the road, Tiberias directs his inferno through the lethal forest trying to trap us on the cliff or push us off it. The rest of our detachment does their best to dodge the trees or destroy them, clearing the way for the transports and our escape.

My heart thunders against my rib cage, adrenaline charging in my blood. It rises until I feel like I might burst. I take one more breath, deeper than before, and raise my hands, palms flat. My storm breaks overhead, twin bolts of lightning shattering down into the trees on either side of the Hawkway. The pines crack. Embers flare. Trunks slide and lean before crashing into the underbrush. Fire springs up among the boughs, small at first. Then gigantic. Fueled by the strength of a Calore prince.

The bullets on our left stop long enough for Davidson to drop one shield and clamber onto the transport behind Evangeline's. The six vehicles bristle with soldiers, familiar and unfamiliar. In their black suits they look like bugs, crowding for space on a stone in the middle of a churning river.

Tyton hangs off the side of Evangeline's transport, one arm looped through a set of straps. As they drive past Tiberias, still fighting, Tyton extends a hand. The prince takes it without question, swinging up onto the transport with ease. I'm next.

I land hard, tucked between Tiberias and Tyton, with Evangeline upright above us. She fuses her metal boots to the body of the transport, which allows her to stand with confidence despite our growing speed. She clenches a fist, clearing the last wreck out of our way, slamming it against the cliff side. Glass sprays the air like jagged rain.

Davidson's final shield drops, shifting from the trees ahead to the lead transport. But in that brief second, another storm of bullets peppers our convoy. A few hit dangerously close, pinging off the metal by my head. Adrenaline eats my fear. I focus on keeping my grip on the transport, fingers tight on makeshift handholds, my body pressed against the cold steel. Flame chases alongside us, flanking the cliff edge of the transport. Tiberias keeps hold of it, dragging the swirl of fire with us, charring anything in our path. We scream over the road, taking the switchbacks with blinding speed.

"More in the trees," Tyton growls, his teeth gritted against the wind. He squints into the darkness, his eyes narrowing to slits. I know what he's doing, even if I can't do it myself. Tyton reaches out to the brains, feeling them as I feel the storm. He blinks once, twice. Killing anyone within his reach, leveling them with a fury of electricity in their skulls. I imagine raiders dropping to the forest floor, their bodies twitching through a deadly seizure before finally lying still.

I rain lightning into the pines, more bolts striking through trunks and branches. The blinding flashes illuminate the forest for a moment, enough to see the silhouettes of falling trees and fleeing figures. A dozen at least.

The Hawkway levels for the last mile as we leave the sharp corners and cliffs behind. The transports roar beneath us, eating up the straightaway in a mad race to the foot of the mountain. Fire and storm run with us, two guardians on deadly wings.

More engines flare on the edge of my awareness. Not as strong as the transports, but just as fast, and moving toward us with furious speed.

The first cycle snarls out of the tree line, its single headlight blinding. The raider on it is small, with spindly limbs, armor, and goggles. He is also boldly stupid, driving the cycle up and off a boulder, sending himself arcing over the road.

Above me, Evangeline slices her hands through the air. The cycle shreds at her command, spokes and pipes peeling apart.

But she isn't the only magnetron here.

The raider keeps his seat, and the cycle knits back together beneath his body, continuing its leap over the hood of the transport. As he goes, he tosses something. The steel glints in the dim light, fast as any bullet.

Knives sail through the air, their razor edges cutting the wind. We duck together, Tiberias, Tyton, and I. One grazes my shoulder. The suit saves me from the worst of it, but I still feel the sting. I bite my lip hard, forcing back a yelp of pain.

The cycling raider hits the other side of the road hard, wheels skidding through dirt as he circles to make another pass. Instead he crunches into a thin blue wall, the cycle crumpling beneath him as he falls backward, gushing blood.

Davidson moves the shields with us, trying to block the other cycles spitting out of the trees. Some of the riders drop, their bodies spasming, as Tyton takes hold of them. The rest of our focus is on getting onto the plain, out into the open. To the outpost, our reinforcements, and safety. The Montfort newbloods defend the convoy, pushing back the raider attacks with everything they have. Tiberias's fire spreads through the trees, the ash falling around us like snow, coating us in white and gray. I let my lightning crack across the sky, the sound and force of it enough to send the raiders scurrying back into the trees.

In the darkness, it's hard to discern their shadows. They don't look like the Silvers I'm used to, in fine robes, polished armor, and gleaming jewels. They don't even have the neat severity of Training suits and uniforms. These Silvers are different, their clothes a patchwork, their weapons and gear mismatched. I'm reminded, more than anything, of the Scarlet Guard in their scraps of red, united only by a color and a cause.

The cycles disappear into the smoky underbrush, their headlights bobbing and weaving out of sight. I reach for the engines, trying to grab hold before they pass beyond my grasp. But another rumble makes me pause, a pounding thrum lurching close.

I can feel it in my teeth.

Monsters burst from the ash, their shaggy heads massive, horns lowered, hooves stamping. Dozens of them, snorting and braying in hulking ranks. The stampede pummels into the convoy, knocking over each transport even as they meet bullets and fire and lightning and knives. The monsters are too strong, too strange. Their hides thick, muscles thicker, with bone like living armor. I watch one catch a bullet in the forehead and keep on ramming, horns tearing through metal like paper. I barely have the wherewithal to scream.

Our transport tips beneath us, knocked off the road by the monstrous charge. We topple with it. I hit the dirt hard and taste blood. Someone holds me down, their hand on my neck. Through my hair, I glimpse the transport as it sails over us. Evangeline is silhouetted against the sight, arms outstretched, fists clenched. She swings, using the transport like a battering ram, and tosses it into the stampeding herd of fearsome creatures. They circle and charge again, their eyes wide and furious, clearly under the control of a Silver animos.

I scramble up, using Tiberias's arm to leverage my weight and get back on my feet. Some yards away, Farley fires her gun from a knee. Her bullets have no effect on the beasts as they run, closing the distance quickly.

Gritting my teeth, I toss and spread, weaving purple-white lighting across their path. The beasts rear in terror, still animals despite whoever is controlling them. A few attempt to run through. They scream in pain, collapsing in heaps of twitching hide and tossing horns.

I try to ignore the terrible sound and narrow my eyes, squinting through the semidarkness as fear gives way to instinct. My movements come without thought, every step and sweep of my arms immediate. In my focus, I almost don't notice the creeping sensation, the heavy weight falling around my shoulders. The press is gentle at first, easy to mistake for exhaustion.

But my lightning wanes, not as bright as before. Not as easy to control. It flickers, sparking weakly as I brush aside another raider. He falls but gets back up quickly, a fist clenched in my direction.

The force of his ability sends me to my knees, and I lose all sensation of electricity. Like a candle snuffed out, unable to spark and burn.

I can't breathe. I can't think.

I can't fight.

Silence, a voice in me screams. A familiar pain and familiar fear level me again, bending me over.

My useless hands hit the dirt, brushing against cold earth. I gasp weakly, barely able to move, let alone defend myself. Fear sends me spiraling, my vision going black for a second. I feel manacles again, Silent Stone around my wrists and ankles, keeping me prisoner behind a locked door. Chaining me to a false king, dooming me to a life of slow, wasting death.

The Silver stalks toward me, his footsteps thunderous in my ears. I hear the sing of rasping metal as he draws a knife, intending to make quick work of my throat. It flashes in the night, reflecting the flames with a red sheen. He grins at me, his face bloodless and white as he grabs my hair, forcing my head back. I want to fight him. I should reach for the gun at my hip, still holstered. But my limbs won't move. Even my heartbeat feels sluggish. I can't even scream.

The combination of crushing silence and fear keeps me still. All I can do is watch. The blade edges my skin, almost burning me with its cold.

He leers down at me, his hair greasy beneath the scarf wrapped around his forehead. I can't tell what color the fabric is, if it means anything. A useless thing to wonder right now.

Then his face explodes; shards of bone and torn flesh arc forward. His body follows the momentum, slumping over me, and the thunderous touch of electricity returns as quickly as he falls. I scramble, unthinking, sliding out from under the Silence's corpse even as his warm blood and splintered teeth catch in my hair.

Someone grabs me beneath the arm, dragging me through the dirt. I let them, still in shock, still paralyzed by fear, unable to do much more than kick weakly at the ground. In the distance, Farley watches me with a murderous expression, her pistol still raised and aimed at a man already dead.

"It's me," a deep voice says, laying me down some yards away. Or, rather, letting me drop. Tiberias stands back, eyes wide and almost glowing in the dim light. His breath comes in quick puffs as he looks me over.

Stand up, I tell myself. *Get back on your feet.*

If only I could. If only the memory of Silent Stone were so easy to brush off. Slowly, I brush my hands together, calling sparks to my skin. I have to see them. I have to know they aren't gone again.

Then I touch my throat, my fingers coming away slick with my own blood.

Tiberias watches in silence, unblinking.

I stare back until he turns away, putting reluctant distance between us. When I get my bearings, I realize I'm somewhat defended. He dumped me next to the transports, using the wrecks for cover. All around me, soldiers of Montfort re-form along the line. Davidson stalks among them, a streak of blood across his face. He looks disgusted with himself, and with the raiders.

Shaky, I climb to my feet, using the hulking vehicle above me for support. The battle still rages before us, and the monstrous beasts snort and stamp, at odds with their own nature and their Silver masters.

A net of white lightning forms ahead of them, like a fence to hold them back. They toss their heads at the display, frightened beyond sense. I know the feeling.

"Poor things," I hear Tyton mutter as he stops next to me. He stares at the beasts, strangely forlorn. When one tries to charge, he blinks, and it drops, its massive body crumpling.

The raiders return for another pass, their cycles snarling and leaping through the thinning trees. Evangeline and her cousins do battle with the other magnetrons, wrestling for dominance over the cycles.

One hand on my chest, nails clutching at my suit, I try to grab hold of a cycle as it leaps over the road. Glaring, I trace the lines of electricity into its engine. With a great push of resolve, I feel them die in quick succession, a sudden burst and then nothing.

The rider twists, startled, as his machine fails. Breathing hard, I do the same to the next. They fall one by one, either coasting to a stop or toppling in midair.

Our own soldiers descend on the raiders. They must have orders to capture, not kill. Davidson himself imprisons one in a cage of shields, letting the raider pound uselessly at his blue prison.

Evangeline pursues one of the small raider magnetrons, running him down over the dirt. He tries to duel her, swirling twin blades that bleed between sword and whip. She is faster and more deadly. His swords are no match for her knives as they pepper his skin, her ability too strong for him to overcome. Evangeline Samos owes no allegiance to Davidson, and she doesn't have his mercy. She cuts the raider apart, letting him bleed silver beneath the starlight.

Between the blood and the ash, the low foothills smell and taste like death. I gulp down the wretched air anyway, trying to catch my breath.

The remaining raiders know the battle is lost, and their engines begin to ebb away, attempting to escape into the wilderness. As they disappear, so does their influence, and the herd of beasts calms. They turn, charging away into the forest, leaving only corpses and trampled underbrush behind.

"Was that what you call a bison?" I pant, glancing at Davidson.

He nods grimly and I swallow around the irony. I can still feel the bison steak in my stomach, heavy as a stone.

In the distance, some ways down the road, headlights flare out of the plain. I clench a fist, tensing for a second wave.

But Tyton puts a hand on my arm. He looks down at me with flashing eyes. "It's the Goldengrove transports. Reinforcements."

Relief floods me and I drop my shoulders, exhaling. The movement sends a twinge through the cut on my back. I hiss, wincing, and put up a hand to feel the damage. The gash is long, but not so deep.

A few yards away, Tiberias watches me take stock of my wounds. He jumps when I meet his gaze and spins on his heel. "I'll get you a healer," he mutters, stalking off.

"If you're done crying over paper cuts, I could use some help." Still on the ground, Farley gestures with one hand, her teeth clenched together tightly. Her gun lies in the dirt, surrounded by spent bullet casings. One of them saved my life.

She leans to one side, careful not to move her right leg.

Because her knee is . . . wrong.

My vision swims for a second. I've seen many forms of injury, but the way her knee twists, the lower half of her leg out of position, something about it turns my stomach. I immediately forget the ache in my own muscles, the blood on my shoulder, even the touch of Silence, and rush to her side.

"Don't move," I hear myself say.

"No shit," she growls back, her hands tight on mine.

TEN
Iris

The mountains are steep and perilous, guarding the valley cities from siege or an army's onslaught. The thick pines make for dangerous obstacles to any transport that dares to turn off their defended roadways. And the elevation alone is a deterrent, weakening any who might hope to climb their way up into the city's jaws. They think themselves safe in their fortress of cliff and sky. They see no danger, for no army could hope to march to their door. But we are often made weak by what also makes us strong.

Montfort is no exception.

We land to the east outside their borders, well within the bounds of Prairie. Our dropjet is unmarked, freshly painted in Prairie gold for appearance sake. It blends well with the tall grass as it sways like waves beneath the morning light. No one notices our arrival, out on the distant plains. We flew carefully, first through the wilds of the Lakelands before crossing the open and empty landscape. The Prairie lords are far-flung, their lands too vast and sprawling to patrol properly. And they are preoccupied with their own doings. They don't know we crossed their lands. No one knows we're here.

Except the raiders, of course.

Their involvement is necessary, to lure as many as we can out of Ascendant. With any luck, Tiberias Calore will be one of them. According to Maven, his brother would never pass up an opportunity to fight. *To show off,* he added, scowling at the idea when we discussed this. I don't know the exiled prince. I've never met Tiberias Calore. But the Lakelands is not a blind country. We collected intelligence on him and all the royal family. They were our enemies for more than a century, after all. The reports revealed an altogether predictable prince. Raised to be a military leader like his father. Hammered by duty and expectation. Formed into a person who values the crown above all else. The brothers have that in common, I think, along with a very peculiar Red girl.

I have to agree with Maven's assessment. If Tiberias really is here to bargain with Montfort, to strengthen their alliance, he will certainly try to prove himself and win their loyalty. What better way than to fight for them?

The raiders meet us at the agreed-upon location, a rise allowing full view of the surrounding landscape. They are masked and veiled, sitting astride smoke-spitting, old-fashioned cycles with even their eyes obscured by riding goggles. Silvers, all of them. Exiled from their own lands when the mountain kingdoms fell. Stripped of their own birthrights as lords and rulers. They outnumber us, but I feel little fear. I am a warrior by birth, bred by the strongest nymphs in my kingdom. And my five escorts are just the same—strong, noble, and useful.

Jidansa is still with me, eager to serve as well as protect. She's careful to position herself between me and any raider who might come too close.

I keep my head down, my own face shadowed. The raiders are an isolated kind, and they probably wouldn't know a princess of the Lakelands or the queen of Norta on sight, but it's best this way. The others speak for me, going over the arrangement.

Our team of six is easy to transport, each of us clinging to one of the raiders as they ferry us across the plain. They know this land better than any of us, and we don't even need to use our shadow of House Haven to hide our journey. Not yet.

The mountains in the distance loom closer with every passing second. They look more like a wall than any mountains I've ever seen. Fear tries to eat at my resolve, but I don't let it. Instead I narrow my eyes and sharpen my focus on the task at hand, leaving little room for anything else.

As the hours bleed together, I run over the plan in my head. Each obstacle to be surmounted.

Cross the border.

That is done easily. The raiders know their paths and they know Montfort's blind spots. They follow a stream through tight, dense pine forest, and only when we start climbing into the foothills do I realize we're on the other side of the invisible dividing line between Prairie and Montfort.

Pay for your passage.

The string of jewels is mine. Sapphire, silver, and diamond. I hand them over at gunpoint. Our Haven shadow, a young, stocky Sentinel on loan from my royal husband, gives up the more valuable piece of the bargain. His own house is split, torn in two by the civil war erupting across Norta. The head of his house fights for Tiberias, but the majority of his kin remain at Maven's side. An admirable thing, to be loyal to country and king over family. Even if that king is Maven Calore.

He doesn't wear his Sentinel mask, leaving the black-jeweled tradition behind. Without it, he seems human. Blue eyes, red hair gleaming in the sunlight. Sentinel Haven gives the raiders the location of our resource drop some miles north. Crates of food, coin, batteries, as well as arms and ammunition to feed their endeavors. The raiders waste no time leaving us on the eastern mountainside, as high as they could ride. I never see their faces. But at least one has blond hair, a few strands of it visible beneath his wrapped head coverings.

Climb.

The waterfalls are simple enough. They act as moving ladders, and I use the water to pull us up and over a great many cliffs. I eventually lose count of them. We follow the stream backward, against the current, with little difficulty. Between my ability and that of another nymph, Laeron of the Nortan House Osanos, all six of us manage to get into the high valley as the stars prick to life overhead. Still, the way is rough. The air thins and my breathing turns shallow, making my steps harder with every inch of the ascent. But I am no stranger to physical exertion. I trained at Citadel of the Lakes from childhood.

The Haven man keeps his hands free, fingers twitching now and then. He blankets us in invisibility, allowing us to move through the pines unseen. It's an odd thing, to look down at your own feet and see nothing but the underbrush. At least I don't have to look at Rydal, the Rhambos strongarm. On the way up, his bulk was distorted by the two bodies strapped across his shoulders like a pack. Another part of my own plan. A bloody part.

Again, I push away a shiver of fear.

We began our climb farther north of the city, forcing us to cut back south to reach the river. It is dammed downstream, in the valley where Ascendant lies, creating a crooked lake. I feel some weight lift when we reach the water, its banks quiet and empty. Together, the six of us descend beneath its surface, leaving no trace of ourselves behind.

I turn my attentions on the current, creating a channel of flowing water along the riverbed. Laeron does as we planned. Bubbles form around our heads, giving each of us a shield of breathable air. It's an old nymph trick, something a child could do. And so we pass in secret along the waterway, riding the current through the turns of the valley. It's almost pitch-black, but I trust the water. The last miles pass in forced silence, filled only with the sound of my own breathing and my own pounding heartbeat.

The Ascendant city lake is deep and full of fish. Once or twice, I jump at the brush of scales in darkness as we navigate to the edge of the water. I shrug off the sensation, focusing on the next step in my plan. Several fine estates have docks on the lake, and we use them as cover. I surface first, raising my eyes just above the waterline. After hours in the wilderness and underwater, even the soft lights of the city are glaring. I don't blink or flinch. I force my eyesight to adjust as quickly as I can. We have a schedule to keep.

No alarms yet. No warning signals. *Good.*

Sentinel Haven shrouds us again as we leave the water, but even he can't hide the wet footprints that trail us through the alleyways. That is left to Laeron and me. We wring ourselves dry with a few twists, using our abilities to squeeze every drop out. I condense the resulting puddles, casting away floating orbs of water into the nearest plant or gutter. Leaving no trace.

I spent the flight to Prairie memorizing the layout of Ascendant, using the map from Bracken. It unsettles me to know so much of my plan is built on someone else's work. I have to trust the information I was given, even if one wrong piece could mean failure. Though the Montfort capital is confusing, a jagged network of streets and steps along both sides of the valley floor, I was able to trace the quickest route from the dammed lake up to where Bracken's children are being held.

Not in the palace, according to the Piedmont spies, but in an observatory.

From the safety of a dark and silent alleyway, I glance up the stepped slopes to the domed building high on the mountainside.

My legs shudder at the thought of climbing another few thousand feet. But I push forward without a sound, schooling my breath to a low, even pace. In through the nose, out through the mouth, in tandem with my steps.

The strongarm has little trouble with the stairs, despite the extra weight of his *cargo*. And the Haven Sentinel is better trained than any of us; raised to defend the king and his family, he is in prime physical form. The same can be said of Laeron. I'm loath to trust a Nortan, let alone three at my side, but it couldn't be helped. An even representation was required for politics' sake.

Jidansa is the only companion I trust completely. The other Lakelander with us sets my teeth on edge. I loathe Niro of the Eskariol Line, but we need him and his talents. He's a skin healer, a strange one. A person gifted with the ability to save life should not enjoy taking it as much as he does.

I can hear him breathing, inhaling and exhaling rapidly as we ascend. Though I'm glad to have a healer as talented as he is at our backs, I wish he weren't necessary. Niro takes too much delight in what he must do before the night is done.

"With luck, they won't be noticed until midday," he whispers. "My work will be perfect." His voice is smooth, silken. Niro comes from a long line of diplomats just as adept at healing political alliances as they are at fixing broken bones.

"Keep silent," I murmur back at him. The ghost of his presence is somehow colder than the mountain air.

Ascendant is not undefended. Guard posts and patrols dot the way, though far less than I've seen in the Lakelands or the Nortan capital. These foolish Montfortans think their mountains and their secrets are enough to keep them safe.

I glance over my shoulder, at the other side of the valley. I feel the swish of my black braid but can't see it. What must be the premier's palace sprawls across the height opposite us, with other estates and government buildings lining its edges. It gleams white in the starlight, with many lights glowing from balconies, windows, and terraces.

Mare Barrow is in there. The lightning girl with a knack for survival.

I thought her a delightful curiosity in Archeon. The Red girl leashed to a Silver king who seemed just as trapped by her as she was by him. I won't pretend to understand why she bewitches Maven in such a way, but it must be his mother's doing. No person of sound mind carries such obsession. And it cannot be love. No person capable of love acts the way he does.

I never thought I would marry for love. I'm not naive enough for such daydreams. My parents grew to love and respect each other through their arrangement, and I hoped for that at least. Of course,

Maven makes that hope impossible. I've had only small glimpses into his heart, and they are enough to know that his heart is dead.

If the Bracken children were not our objective, if I actually hoped to maintain my Nortan crown, I might entertain the idea of killing Mare Barrow. Not for spite, but to hopefully give Maven some clarity. She is a motivation now, a carrot for him to follow, but she is a weakness too. And I need him weak. I need him distracted.

As Mother said, Maven Calore will face the flood.

They all will.

The military contingent left ten minutes ago, their transports screaming up the mountain. I can still hear the echoes coming down the slope, reverberating through the streets and allies of the Montfort capital. The rest of the city clangs with alarm bells and warning signals. Just as planned. I blink, still shrouded in Sentinel Haven's impenetrable shadow.

The observatory guards abandoned their posts to assist the city, leaving behind a skeleton shift of two Montfort soldiers. At night, their green uniforms seem black. They stand out against the polished moonstone columns holding up the spangled dome of stained glass.

Without a singer or a whisper to wipe the memories of both guards, we have no choice but to slip by them instead. It isn't difficult, but I hold my breath as we do, weaving through the observatory columns.

They flank the entrance, still and steady, accustomed to the clanging alarms. Raider attacks are common, I'm told, and of little threat to the capital.

"On the plain?" one says to the other, turning his face.

His compatriot shakes her head. "On the slopes. They hit the plains twice last month."

The male guard grins, shoving his hand in his pocket. "Plain. Bet you ten coppers."

"Don't you get tired of losing your money to me?" she replies.

As they laugh, grins wide, I press my hand to the lock of the door. With my other hand, I flick open the canteen holstered at my side. Under Sentinel Haven's power, I can't see what I'm doing, and so must rely on touch. It complicates things, but only enough to slow me down.

The water swirls around my wrist, kissing my skin, before worming between my fingers and into the keyhole. It fits to the mechanism, filling the space as I exhale. Through the water, I press along the tumblers of the lock, touching each one, forming a key of my own making.

I nudge sideways with my foot, reaching for Jidansa. She nudges back.

Some yards away, a tree branch cracks under her ability, crashing to the paved stone. Perfectly masking the sound of a turning lock.

"Raiders in the city?" the female guard says, her laughter replaced by panic.

"No bet," the man responds.

They rush to investigate, leaving us to slip into the observatory undetected, unseen, unlooked for.

Wary of any kind of security cameras, Sentinel Haven keeps us shrouded as we enter.

"Laeron, through," whispers the Nortan nymph. We sound off in turn, unable to see one another.

"Jidansa."

"Rydal."

"Niro."

"Iris."

"Delos," says the Haven Sentinel.

Grinning, I ease the door shut behind us.

Infiltrate the observatory prison. Done.

I don't allow myself a sigh of relief. That won't come until I'm on the ground at home, with Bracken's children safely returned. And even that is premature. As Mother would say, no use sleeping while there are wars to be won. And we certainly have a war exploding around us.

Jidansa's footsteps echo slightly as she rounds the room. Her search takes several long minutes, enough to put us on edge. The tension ratchets with the passing seconds, until she returns. I can hear the smile in her voice.

"They're truly foolish," she says. "No cameras. Not one."

"How can that be?" I hear Laeron mutter.

My teeth grit together. "Perhaps they don't want a record of the children being here," I reply, giving the only explanation I can think of. It shouldn't affect me. Horrible things are done in war, even to Silvers. I know that firsthand. "Or what they've done to them."

The realization settles over us, another curtain of dread upon the pile.

I raise my chin, smoothing my unseen hair, tucking pieces behind my ears. "Sentinel Haven, you may cease."

"Yes, Your Majesty." I can hear him bow, and then I see it.

We bleed into vision, all of us at once, as if a window has suddenly been wiped clean. Most look at their own limbs, examining themselves, but Niro is staring at me. He looks paler in the dim light filtering through the glass dome, which dapples his face in sickly green. His gaze feels like a challenge or perhaps an amusement. I dislike either option.

"This way," I tell them, focusing on the task at hand. They fall into line, even Niro, and I'm glad to have Jidansa on my heels. The Sentinel too. I'm the queen of Norta, and he is sworn to protect me as well as Maven.

We round a massive telescope, pointed at the domed roof, made of tubes of brass and glass fixtures. *A waste,* I think. The stars are well beyond the reach of anyone, even Silvers. They are the realm of gods and gods alone. They are not for us to fathom. To try is to squander time, resources, and energy.

Several chambers lead off the round central room, but we ignore them. Instead I cross the floor, searching the marble beneath my feet for visible cracks. I don't expect any, and loose the canteen again. With a nod at Laeron, I have him do the same.

Our water spreads around our feet and across the marble, expanding to the thinnest of covers. It prods and puddles over the stone, working into grooves and seams between the slabs.

"Here," Laeron says, taking a few steps toward the wall. His own water bunches up like a giant droplet. As I approach, squinting, I can see tiny air bubbles trailing up through the water.

There is open space below.

Jidansa makes quick work of the slab, drawing it up and out of place with a wave of her fingers. Beneath, darkness looms, but not blackness. There are lights in the chamber below the observatory, somewhere farther down the passage. Enough to see by, but not to bleed through the tiny seams of the trapdoor slab.

Stairs lead downward, as if beckoning.

Rydal goes first, according to our plan, with Niro behind, one hand on his holstered gun should Rydal meet opposition. Sentinel Haven follows. I notice that his hands seem to darken, pooling with shadow like curling smoke. I keep close on his heels, with Jidansa at my side and Laeron bringing up the rear.

This is the easy part, I tell myself. And I'm right.

The passage curves, tracking below the observatory and beyond its bounds. There are no guards, no cameras. Nothing but the dim lights and the echo of our own feet.

I wonder if this place was made specifically for Prince Bracken's children. Somehow I doubt it. The stone is old, though the walls are freshly painted the warm color of butter. It has an odd, calming effect I wouldn't expect for enemy prisoners.

The Montfortans are strange indeed.

About a hundred yards on, the passage widens into some kind of receiving chamber walled by a bank of windows. I balk at them, looking out onto the glimmer of the city. The windows must be thick, because I can't hear any alarms, though I still see the lights of them flashing up and down Ascendant.

I exchange a confused glance with Jidansa, who looks just as puzzled as I feel. She shrugs and jerks her chin to our right, where the chamber dead-ends at a single door.

It is unremarkable, not even reinforced that I can see.

When I lay my palm against the lock, intending to key it open again, I realize why.

"Silent Stone," I hiss, drawing back as if burned. Just the distant ache of the ability-smothering weapon makes my skin crawl. "Torturous bastards."

Jidansa makes a disgusted sound deep in her throat. "Those poor children. It's been months."

The others echo her sentiment.

All but one.

"Bad for them, good for us," Niro says without any kind of sympathy. I round on him, sneering.

"What's that supposed to mean?" I growl.

"Silent Stone will have made them lethargic, sleepy. No one will notice when these two don't move in the morning," he says, poking at the covered bulk on Rydal's back. His fingers tap against human flesh with little regard.

Right as he may be, I still scowl. "Let's get them out," I say, snapping my fingers. "Sentinel Haven, your assistance, please. And Niro, be ready to heal them. They'll need it."

I know what a prison of Silent Stone does to a person. I saw it firsthand in Barrow. Her sunken cheeks and dull eyes. The way her bones jutted, her cold skin veined with sickness. And she was a stubborn hellion, feeding on fury to keep herself sane, with a cause to hold on to, albeit a foolish, doomed one. Prince Bracken's children are young, only ten and eight years old. Silvers born, reliant on their ability, with no memory of life without. I don't want to know what the Silent Stone has done to them, but I have no choice.

I must look into the face of war's horrors and never blink. My father did not. My mother and sister do not. I have to keep my eyes open if I can ever hope to win.

Win and go home.

Laeron opens this door, using his own canteen to form a watery key. It takes him a bit longer, battling the edges of Silent Stone.

Finally, he swings open the door and steps back, allowing me to enter first. I shudder as I step inside, steeling myself against the unnatural sensation. It's more uniform than fighting with a Silence. Their abilities pulse with their hearts and concentration. This is constant. Unyielding. I swallow hard against the ugly, unnatural sensation.

In spite of my team at my back, waiting in the blissful safety of the passage, I feel more vulnerable than ever, a newborn baby exposed on a cliff.

The children sleep soundly, each one tucked into a nicely made bed. I glance around, expecting some kind of guard in the shadows. There's nothing but the dim silhouettes of a well-furnished room and curtained windows. As in the passage, they look out through the pines and down into the city valley. Another torture. To see the world beyond your reach.

"Help me carry them out," I mutter, eager to be rid of this place.

I reach for the dark-haired child in the bed closest to me, putting a hand to her face. Ready to clamp my fingers over her mouth, should she scream. Bracken's daughter shifts at my touch but doesn't wake. In the dim light, her skin is the color of polished jet.

"Wake up, Charlotta," I murmur. My heartbeat doubles. *We need to go.*

Sentinel Haven is not so steady with Prince Michael. He slides one arm behind his shoulders and another under his knees before scooping him up. Like his sister, the boy is slow to wake. Groggy, sluggish. The Silent Stone has wreaked its havoc upon them both.

"Who . . . ?" the boy mumbles, his eyes fluttering open and shut.

Beneath me, his sister stirs, roused as I shake her shoulders gently. She blinks up at me, brows knitting in confusion. "Is it time for our walk?" she asks, her voice high and breathy. "We won't fuss, promise."

"Yes," I tell her quickly, seizing the opportunity. "We're going to go for a walk away from the Stone. But you both have to be very quiet, and do exactly as we say."

It isn't a lie, and it energizes both of them as much as possible. Charlotta even wraps her arms around my neck, allowing me to lift her.

She's lighter than I expected, more like a bird than a girl. She smells fresh, clean. I would think the children well treated if not for the Silent Stone.

Michael curls in Sentinel Haven's arms. "You're new," he says up to the Sentinel.

I can't get out of the room fast enough, and I suck in a healing breath as we step back into the passage. The children both exhale, and Charlotta relaxes in my arms.

"Remember, do as we say," I mumble, averting my eyes from what Rydal and Niro have prepared.

The boy nods, wordless, but the girl looks up at me with a keen glance I wouldn't expect from a child. "Are you rescuing us?" she whispers.

I see no reason to lie. The words stick anyway. Because I might fail. I might get them killed. I might die in this attempt. "Yes," I force out.

"Let me see them."

Niro wastes no time, flashing a light in both their faces that startles even me. "Quiet," I murmur when Michael yelps. I glare at Niro over the girl's head but he ignores me, turning his focus on them. His eyes dart back and forth like some kind of ticking machine as he memorizes their features.

When he turns back to the bundle on the ground, I can't look away fast enough. Still, I catch the sight of them. The two little Red bodies.

They are still breathing. Heavily drugged, already too far gone to wake up without aid. But still breathing.

Niro needs living flesh to do his work.

Sentinel Haven catches my eye, and he turns as I do, putting his back to the skin healer and the Reds. We can't let the children see what is being done for them. And we don't want to watch it happen.

Weakness, something whispers in me when I flinch at the sound of a blade singing out of its sheath. *Keep your eyes open, Iris Cygnet.*

"Such artistry," I hear Niro tell himself, his voice wolfish and full of glee.

His work is mostly silent.

Mostly.

ELEVEN
Mare

I barely slept, despite my exhaustion. It took us almost until dawn to get back to Ascendant, the healers working on us along the way. When we arrived, we only had a few hours until Davidson's planned address to his assembled government. I tried to sleep, but by the time the adrenaline from the raider battle wore off, I was racked with nerves for the coming meeting. I spent what was left of the night staring at the edges of my curtains, watching the blue light of predawn grow. Now I can barely sit still as I wait on the lower terrace, fussing with the edges of my dress. It is a harsh gown, a deep, spangled purple belted in gold at my waist, with ballooning sleeves gathered at the wrists. The collar plunges, showing the edge of Maven's brand, and I've braided my hair back away from my face. I proudly display the scars branching down my neck. My idea, not Gisa's. I want to show the Montfort politicians how much I've already sacrificed. And I want to look like as much of the lightning girl as I can, even if that person isn't real. I can draw strength from her, as I draw strength from Mareena too. They may be false versions of myself, but they are also pieces of someone real, however small.

The sunrise is strange in the mountains. It spreads behind me, sending jagged rays of light up and over the peaks. Slowly but steadily, darkness bleeds from the valley, fleeing with the morning mist along the slopes of the city. Ascendant seems to wake up with the light, and the low hum of activity buzzes up to the palace.

Queen Anabel is not one to be late, especially for something as important as this. She descends from the palace entrance, her grandson and their guards close at hand. Julian hangs back a bit, arms folded into his long, golden robes. He meets my eye and nods in greeting. I return the gesture. I might not agree with his choosing to back his nephew, but I understand the choice. I understand supporting family over everything else.

In her Lerolan colors, red and flaming orange, Anabel seems more like a Sentinel guarding her king than his grandmother. She is just as deadly. She doesn't wear a gown, but a brocaded coat with a matching tunic and black leggings beneath, their hems set with glinting bronze like pieces of armor. Anabel Lerolan is ready for the kind of battle not fought on the field. Her smile at me, across the terrace, does not meet her eyes.

"Your Majesty," I say, greeting her with a dip of my head. "Tiberias," I add, my eyes flicking to him.

He smirks to himself, darkly amused by my refusal to call him anything else. Not his nickname. Not even his title.

"Good morning," he replies. He looks handsome as ever. Perhaps more so. The raider battle hangs on him, and I can almost smell the ash he spent the night scrubbing away. *Maybe don't think about him bathing,* I snap to myself.

The dawn suits the fire prince, in his scarlet cloak and raven silk underclothes. He has his crown on his neat, black hair. Magnetron-made, I bet. Another of Evangeline's creations. It suits him too. No jewels, no intricacies. Just a simple band of raw iron sculpted like a braid of flame. I trace it with my eyes, focusing on such a small thing that he loves so much.

While there is still a hissing tension between us, I don't feel the same anger or rage I did yesterday. Our words on the mountain, few as they were, had some calming effect. I wish we had more time to come to some sort of understanding.

But what understanding can there be?

Try as I might, I can't stamp out the hope still burning in my heart. I still want him to choose me. And I would still forgive him if he admitted his mistake. That hope refuses to die, stupid as it might be.

Farley's appearance shocks me most of all. Not because her leg is healed, good as new. That I expected. She follows the immaculate Premier Davidson out, and at first I don't recognize her. Gone is the battered uniform, her dark red coveralls stained by use and worn by battle. This is a dress uniform instead, more akin to something I've seen Tiberias or Maven wear. Never Farley.

I blink at her, watching her adjust the sleeves of the snug crimson coat, intimately tailored to her form. Her general's badges are fastened at the collar, three iron squares set in the fabric. There are others on her breast, medals and honors, both metal and ribbon. I doubt they're real, but they make her look impressive. Clearly Davidson and Carmadon helped her dress for the meeting, working to legitimize the Scarlet Guard through her. Add to that the scar at the corner of her mouth and the hard steel of her blue eyes, and I wonder how any politicians might deny what she asks for.

"General Farley," I say, offering her a crooked smirk. "Nice outfit."

"Careful, Barrow, before I force you into one of these too," she grumbles, fighting her sleeves again. "I can barely move in this thing." The jacket runs tight across her shoulders, perfectly fitted. But not enough to allow the kind of movement she's used to. The kind of movement required in a fight.

I glance at her hips, snug in equally tailored pants tucked into boots. "No gun?"

Farley scowls. "Don't remind me."

To the surprise of no one, Evangeline Samos arrives last. She glides through the grand oak doors, her Samos cousins flanking her in matching gray coats and black trim. Evangeline's gown is blinding white fading to deep, inky black at the sleeves and long train. As she grows closer, I realize that the silk of her dress isn't dyed, but patterned with chips of resplendent, shimmering metal in a perfect shift from pearly white to gray steel to black iron. She approaches with purpose, letting the gown spread behind her, hissing over the green and white stones.

"If only we could replicate such an entrance in the People's Gallery," Davidson mutters to Farley and me. He watches Evangeline approach. She squares her shoulders, letting the ramrod of determination mark her steps.

The premier himself keeps to his plain but splendid persona, clad in a dark green suit with white enamel buttons. His gray hair gleams, slicked back against his head.

"Shall we?" he says, gesturing to the arches leading away from the palace.

In our varying colors and varying degrees of readiness, we follow him down the winding steps into the city.

I wish the walk were longer, but the People's Gallery, the building where the entire Montfort government gathers for matters such as this, isn't far. Just a few hundred yards down the slope, set onto more terraces cut below the premier's palace. Again, there are no walls to defend such an important place. Only white stone archways and sweeping verandas surround the domed building overlooking Ascendant and the valley. The sun continues to rise, gleaming off the green-glass dome hundreds of feet across. The glass is too flawed to be Silver-made, but it is more beautiful for the whorls and curves of imperfection, which catch the light in more interesting ways than flat, meticulous panes of pure glass. Silver-barked aspen trees with golden leaves spring up at even intervals, lining the structure like living columns. Those *are* the work of Silvers. Greenwardens, no doubt.

Soldiers flank each tree, still in their dark greens. Proud, unyielding. We cross the long, marble walkway to the wide-open doors of the Gallery.

I take a breath, steeling myself. This shouldn't be difficult. Montfort is not our enemy. And our objective is clear. Acquire an army, as much as we can. Overthrow a mad king and his allies, all of them hellbent on maintaining their power at the cost of Red and newblood life. Agreeing to help should be easy for the Free Republic of Montfort. Isn't equality what they stand for?

Or so I've been told.

Gritting my teeth, I reach out and grab Farley's hand. I squeeze her callused fingers, just for a second. Without hesitation, she squeezes back.

The first hall is columned, hung with green and white silks gathered with silver and red ties. The colors of Montfort and the colors of both kinds of blood. Sunlight beams down from skylights, filling the space with an ethereal glow. Many chambers branch off, visible through arches between the columns or locked behind polished oak doors. And of course there are people in the hall, clustered together, their eyes on all of us as we pass. Men and women, Red and Silver, their skin a vast array of hues ranging from porcelain to midnight. I try to feel armored in my skin, protected from their gaze.

Ahead of me, Tiberias holds his head high, his grandmother on his right arm while Evangeline takes his left. She is careful to keep in step with his long stride. No daughter of House Samos walks behind. Her gown's train forces Farley and me to keep our distance. Not that I mind.

Julian walks behind us both. I can hear him muttering to himself as he looks back and forth. I'm surprised he doesn't take notes.

The People's Gallery is aptly named. As we approach the entrance to the chamber, I hear the low hum of hundreds of voices. It rises quickly until it drowns out everything but the thunder of my own pulse in my ears.

Massive doors of white and green enamel glide open on oiled hinges, as if bowing before the will of Premier Davidson. He enters to the cascading noise of applause. It spreads as we follow into the amphitheater that is the Gallery.

Hundreds crowd the many seats ringing the room, most of them in suits like Davidson's, in varying shades of green and white. Some are military, clearly marked by dress uniforms and insignia. All rise when we enter, their hands clapping together to celebrate . . . us? Or the premier?

I don't know.

Some don't clap, but they still stand. Out of either respect or tradition.

The steps down the bowl of the amphitheater are shallow. I could run them with my eyes closed. Even so, I keep my focus on my feet and the folds of my shimmering dress.

Davidson reaches the floor of the chamber, making for his own seat at the center, flanked by still-standing politicians. There are empty chairs for us as well, each one marked by a drape of colored cloth. Orange for Anabel, silver for Evangeline, purple for me, scarlet for Farley, and so forth. While Davidson greets the men and women on the floor, shaking hands with an open, charismatic grin, we take to our chairs.

No matter how many times people put me on parade, I never get used to it.

Not so for Evangeline. She sits next to me, arranging the falling folds of her dress with a flick of her hands. She raises an eyebrow, imperious, a living painting. She was born for moments like this, and if she is afraid of them, she will never show it.

"Kill that fear, lightning girl," she mutters to me, fixing me with an electric stare. "It's not like you haven't done this before."

"True," I whisper back, remembering Maven, his throne, and all the vile things I said at his side. This will be easy in comparison. This won't rip me apart.

Davidson doesn't sit down, watching as the others in the room take their seats in thunderous unison.

He clasps his hands before him, bowing his head. A lock of gray hair falls over his eyes. "Before we begin, I would like to observe a moment of silence for those who fell last night, defending our people from raider attack. They will be remembered."

All over the room, his politicians and officers nod approvingly before lowering their own heads. Some close their eyes. I'm not sure which is appropriate, so I mimic the premier, knitting my fingers together and dipping my chin.

After what feels like an eternity, Davidson raises his head again.

"My fellow countrymen," he says, his voice carrying across the amphitheater with ease. Something about the room, I suspect, built to maximize acoustics. "I would like to thank you. Both for agreeing to this special session of the People's Gallery—and for showing up."

He pauses, grinning at the responding wave of polite laughter. The bland joke is an easy tool. I can pick out exactly who his supporters are, simply by how much they laugh or grin. A few politicians remain stoic. To my surprise, they are both Red and Silver, judging by the undertones of their skin.

Davidson pushes on, pacing as he speaks. "As we're all aware, our nation is a young one, built by our own hands over the last two decades. I am only the third premier, and many of you are in your first terms of office. Together we represent the will of our diverse people, and their interests, and of course we work to provide for their safety. In the past months, I have done what I've thought is necessary to uphold what our country is, and to safeguard what our country strives to be." His face turns stern, the lines on his forehead deepening. "A beacon of freedom. A hope. A light in the darkness surrounding us. Montfort is a country, the only one on this continent, where the color of blood does not rule. Where Red and Silver, and Ardent, work in tandem, hand in hand, to build a better future for *all* of our children."

My knuckles turn white in my lap as I squeeze my hands together. The country Davidson speaks of, what it represents—could it really be possible? A year ago, Mare Barrow, knee-deep in the mud of the Stilts, would not have believed it. Could not have. I was constrained both by what I was taught and by the only world I was allowed to see. My life was limited to the bounds of work or conscription. Each a different kind of doom. Both lives already lived by thousands, millions. There was no use dreaming that life could be different. It would only break an already broken heart.

It's cruel to give hope where none should be. My father told me that. And even he would never say it again. Not now, when we've seen that hope is real.

And this place, this step toward a better world, is somehow real too.

I see it before my eyes. Red representatives with their blooming flushes alongside Silver. A newblood leader walking the floor before us. Farley, her blood red as the dawn, sitting so close to a Silver king. And even me. I'm here too. My voice matters. My hope matters.

I glance across Evangeline to the true king of Norta. He followed me here because he still loves me, a Red girl. And because he truly does try to see things for himself.

I hope he sees what I see here. And if he does take the throne, if we are unable to stop him, I hope he hears what the premier is saying.

He looks at his hands, his fingers clawed on the arms of his seat. His knuckles are just as white as mine.

"And yet we cannot claim to be free, we cannot claim to be any kind of beacon, if we allow atrocity on our borders," Davidson continues. He stalks toward the lower seats, gazing at each politician in turn. "If we can look at the horizon and know there are Reds living as slaves, Ardents slaughtered, lives crushed beneath the feet of Silver overlords."

The royal Silvers with us do not flinch. But they don't do anything to deny what the premier is saying either. Anabel, Tiberias, and Evangeline keep their eyes forward, their expressions locked in place.

Davidson paces back, completing a circle of the floor. "One year ago, I petitioned for the ability to interfere. To use a fraction of our armies to aid the Scarlet Guard in their infiltration of Norta, the Lakelands, and Piedmont, all kingdoms built on tyranny. It was a risk. It exposed our nation, which had been growing in secret. But you graciously agreed." He steeples his fingers, half bowing to the Gallery. "And so I ask again. For more soldiers, more money. For the ability to overthrow murderous regimes, and for the right to look ourselves in the face. So we can tell our children we did not stand by and watch as children just like them were murdered or condemned. It is our duty to witness, and to fight now that we can."

In the seats of the Gallery, one of the politicians stands. A Silver man, with wispy blond hair, bone-white skin, and robes of deep emerald green. His nails are oddly long and polished to a high shine. "You speak of overthrowing a regime, Premier," he says. "But I see beside you a young man with Silver blood and a crown upon his head. I see no other crowns in this room. And you know, as well as I do, the crowns we had to destroy to forge our country. How much we had to burn to rise from the ashes."

The politician touches his own brow. His meaning is clear. One of the crowns given up was his own. I clench my teeth, fighting the urge to look at Tiberias. I want to yell at him, *See? It can be done.*

Davidson offers a deep bow of his head. "Very true, Representative Radis. The Free Republic is a nation made from war, from sacrifice, and above all things from opportunity. Before we rose up, the mountains were a patchwork of petty kingdoms and worse, fighting for dominance. There was no unity. It was easy to worm ourselves into the cracks and break apart what was already breaking." He pauses, eyes alight. "I see a similar opportunity now, in the Silver kingdoms of the east. Room to change things in Norta. To remake things for the better."

Another politician stands from the Gallery ranks, a Red woman with smooth copper skin, close-cropped black hair, and a white gown crossed with an olive sash. "Does Your Majesty agree?" she asks, fixing her eyes on Tiberias.

He hesitates, surprised at her directness. Tiberias isn't as quick with his words as his cursed brother. "Norta is in a state of civil war," he replies, his voice wavering. "More than a third of the nation has seceded, some pledging fealty to the Kingdom of the Rift. Where my betrothed's father is king." Clenching his jaw, he gestures to Evangeline next to him. She doesn't react. "The rest are pledged to me. To putting me back on my own father's throne, and casting out my brother." A muscle jumps in his cheek. "Who murdered his way to it."

Tiberias lowers his eyes slowly. I can see his chest rising and falling rapidly beneath the folds of his red cape. The thought of Maven still wounds us both, Tiberias even more than me. I was there when Maven and Elara forced him to murder his own father, the old king. I see that terrible moment written on his grim face, clear as letters in a book.

The representative is not satisfied. She tips her head, bringing long fingers together. "Reports say that King Maven is beloved among the people. The ones still loyal to him, I mean," she adds. "Curious, that the Red populace of Norta is counted in that regard."

A low current of heat ripples across my exposed skin. Not a lot, but enough to communicate Tiberias's discomfort. I curl my fingers into a fist, speaking before he is forced to.

"King Maven is greatly skilled in manipulation," I tell the woman. "He easily uses his own image, the boy king forced to the throne, and tricks anyone who doesn't truly know him."

And even sometimes those who do. Tiberias, most of all. He told me once he was looking for newblood whispers, stronger than Queen Elara, perhaps able to fix what she broke in his brother. An impossible wish, a terrible dream. I've seen Maven without her machinations. She is dead, and he is still the monster she forced him to be.

The politician turns her eyes on me, and I continue. "He brokered the Lakeland alliance, ending a war my people were sent to fight. He lifted the restrictions his father made on their lives. It isn't hard to understand why he has support. It's easy to win the favor of the people you feed." As I speak, I think about myself, my family. The Stilts. Cameron and the slum towns full of Reds trapped to their lives. Where would we be, if someone had not broken through the wall around us? Shown us how the world really should be? "Especially when you control what they are given, both on the table and on the video screen."

She grins at me, showing gapped teeth. "You've been a thorn in his side, Mare Barrow. And a boon to him as well. We've seen videos from your capture. Your words swayed people to him too."

The heat I feel next isn't from Tiberias, but from my own embarrassment. It claws over my face, warming my cheeks. "Yes. And I am ashamed of it," I tell her bluntly.

On my left, Farley clenches a fist on the seat of her chair. She leans forward. "You can't blame her for things said to the business end of a gun."

The Red woman tightens. "I do not, of course. But your face and your voice have been used so many times, Miss Barrow. You will be little use in trying to sway your own people back in Norta. And, I apologize, but it makes it difficult to trust what you say now, and who you speak for."

"Then speak to me," Farley snaps, her voice echoing throughout the Gallery. My flush recedes, chased away by cool relief. I glance sidelong, more grateful for Farley than ever before. She keeps her temper in check, using it as fuel. "I am a general of the Scarlet Guard, a high officer of Command. My organization has been working in the shadows for years, from the frozen shores of the Hud to the Piedmont lowlands, and everywhere in between. We've done very much with very little. Imagine what we can do with more."

On the opposite side of the chamber, another one of the Montfort representatives puts up a hand winking with golden rings. He's Red, his smile sharp and slick. "Much, you say? Forgive me, General. But before you began working with us, your Scarlet Guard was little more than a network of allied criminals. Smugglers. Thieves. Murderers, even."

Farley just sniffs. "We did what we had to. The premier speaks of working through cracks—we made them. And we transported thousands out of danger. Reds who needed our help. Newbloods too. Your own premier is Nortan-born, isn't he?" She points her chin at Davidson, who holds her gaze. "Nearly executed for the crime of what he was born as. We saved people like him every day."

The sly man shrugs his shoulders. "Our point is that you cannot do this alone, General," he says. "And while your cause is just, accordances must be made. You are a group with no nation, no citizens to answer to. Your methods are beyond the usual bounds of war. We have our own to think of."

"We answer to everyone, sir," Farley replies coolly. She turns her head just so, letting the scarred side of her mouth catch the light from the dome overhead. "Especially those who think no one is listening. *We* are listening, and we are doing, and we will keep fighting. To the last rattle of our last breath, the Scarlet Guard will do what it can to fix what is broken. With or without your aid."

Still pacing, Davidson passes by her. He shoots her a glance I cannot decipher, lips pressed into a neutral line, eyes locked on her face. I can't tell if he's pleased or infuriated.

The Silver representative named Radis stands again. He doesn't look a day over thirty-five, and he's old enough to remember what this country was before Montfort. He eyes us all. "So you propose we support another Silver monarch and help him to a throne."

On my right, Evangeline grins, and I can see she capped her eyeteeth with pointed silver. *Gruesome,* I think to myself. And a message like the rest of her image. She will bite out the heart of anyone in her way. Including all of us.

"Two, actually," she says, projecting her voice across the amphitheater. "My father, the king of the Rift, must also be recognized as a legitimate ruler."

A corner of Tiberias's mouth twitches, and Anabel purses her lips. As before in Corvium, Evangeline does her best to sidetrack any progress her betrothed might make.

Radis sneers back at her, gray eyes flashing. "But as you told us, Premier," he says, "the Free Republic was built from such kingdoms. We know what they are, what they become." His gaze ticks from Evangeline to Tiberias. "No matter how noble, how true, how honorable the king or queen."

Premier Davidson's blank mask threatens to slip, betraying a frown. He bows his head slightly, acknowledging Radis's point. Others murmur around the room, ruminating on the same flaw in this alliance. Of course, Davidson and the Guard have a longer game, with no intention of propping up more kings and queens, but we can't exactly argue that in front of the Silvers.

The lie comes easily for me, because it isn't entirely false.

"You said something else before, Premier," I say quickly, pushing out of my chair. "Before the second battle of Corvium, when we were still in Piedmont."

Davidson whirls to me, an eyebrow raised.

"Inches for miles," I explain, sharpening each letter on my tongue.

The full strength of the Gallery's attention makes me shiver with desperation. They must agree. We need their support if we're going to end Maven's reign and stop Tiberias from picking up the crown he leaves behind. "Change can be quick, or it can be slow. But the movement should always be forward. I know some of you look at King Tiberias, at Queen Anabel and Princess Evangeline, and wonder, how are they different? How is spilling your own blood to give them a throne better than staying alive and letting Maven keep his?"

Radis looks down his long nose at me. "Because you claim Maven Calore is a monster. A wayward boy with no leash."

I toss my head, flicking my braid over my shoulder. Like Farley, I let my scars tell their own story. The *M* on my collarbone cooks beneath a hundred pairs of eyes. "Because Maven Calore is, without question, without argument, the worse option," I say, directing my words to all of them. "Not only will he never move his country forward, but he will also drag Norta backward. He has no regard for Red life, or even Silver. No thoughts of equality. Not even an inkling of anything beyond his broken circle of vengeance and the desire to be loved. And unlike Tiberias, unlike King Volo in the Rift, unlike perhaps any Silver monarch breathing today, he is willing to do anything to keep his crown."

Slowly, Radis sits. He gestures with a white hand, asking me to continue. Not that I need his permission. Still, pride surges in me.

"Yes," I tell them. "Under most circumstances, you would be better off staying here, protected by your mountains, insulated against the world. *If* you can find it in your stomachs to ignore the atrocities of Norta and her allies." Some of them squirm in their chairs. "But not now. Not with the Lakelands on his side. You can take your time deciding whether to give us more aid, but that bell has already rung. You voted to help us before. Your soldiers were there when I was rescued from Whitefire Palace. Your army helped us hold the walls of Corvium. And Maven Calore will never forget what you did. He will never forget how you stole me from him."

You're like Thomas was, Maven told me once. I hear him still muttering in my head. *You are the only person I care about, the only person who reminds me I am alive. Not empty. And not alone.*

He was a monster then, keeping me trapped in his palace, trapped inside my own skin. I wonder what kind of beast he is now, with nothing and no one but the splintered pieces in his head.

I grit my teeth, trying to picture his next moves. Not in the coming days, but months from now. Years. "One day, his armies will be at your door. The Nortans, the Lakelanders." They swim before my eyes, the High Houses in their colors, the Lakelanders in their royal blue. "All of them with all their fury, marching behind a shield of Red soldiers you'll be forced to kill. You might win, but many of your own will die with them. How many, I can't say. I can only assure you, it will be more."

The Red woman with black hair tips her hand, calling for attention. She looks past me, to Farley still in her seat. "Do you agree, General?" she asks, and then points to Tiberias. "Will *this* Silver king be better than the one already on the throne?"

Farley scoffs, all but rolling her eyes. "Ma'am, I care very little for Tiberias Calore," she replies. I can't help but wince, hissing out a breath. *Farley.*

But she isn't finished. "So you can believe me when I say he will be."

The representative bobs her head, satisfied with such an answer. She isn't the only one. Many of the politicians around the room, both Red and Silver, exchange whispers. "Well, Your Majesty?" the woman adds, turning her attention on Tiberias.

He shifts in his chair. On his right, Anabel touches his arm with fleeting fingers. I have enough experience with Silver mothers to know that Queen Anabel would be considered overly maternal, too gentle, too loving with her kin.

I sit as he gets up, stepping onto the floor. Davidson acquiesces, finally taking his own chair to let Tiberias stand alone. He cuts a magnificent sight against the white marble and granite, and the swirling green dome over our heads. The red of his cape seems a livid flame, a swath of fresh blood.

Tiberias raises his chin. "I've spent almost a year in exile, betrayed by my brother. But I was betrayed by my . . ." He pauses, chewing the words. "My father as well. He raised me to be a king like every king before. Unyielding, unchanging. Bound to the past. Locked into endless war, married to tradition." For the first time, Evangeline flinches, her clawed nails curling on the arms of her seat.

The true king pushes on. "The truth is Norta was split in two long before my father was murdered. Silver overlords, with Reds below. I knew it to be wrong, as we all know, in the deepest places of ourselves. But there are limits to the power of kings. I thought changing the bedrock of a country, rearranging the ills of our society, was one of them. I thought the current balance, however unfair, was better than the risk of tipping the kingdom into chaos." His voice hums with determination. "And I was wrong. So many people taught me that.

"You were one of them, Premier," he says, glancing back at Davidson. "And so are all of you. Your country, strange as it seems to us, is proof that new lines can be drawn. A different kind of balance can be maintained. As king of Norta, I intend to see what I couldn't before. And to do everything I can to bridge the canyons between Red and Silver. Heal the wounds. Change what must be changed."

I've heard him speak eloquently before. He did it in Corvium, saying much the same thing. He swore to change the world with us. To erase the divide between Red and Silver. It stirred pride in me then, but not now. I know what his words mean and exactly how far his promises extend. Especially with the crown in the balance.

Even so, I gasp to myself when he sinks, dropping to a knee at the center of the floor. His cape pools around him, vibrant and bloody against the marble.

Murmurs rise as he bows his head.

"I don't ask for anyone to fight for me, but alongside me," he says slowly.

The black-haired woman is first to speak, her head tipped to one side. "We already know you're not the kind to send another in your stead, Your Majesty," she replies. "That was made clear last night. My daughter, Captain Viya, fought with you on the Hawkway."

Still kneeling, Tiberias says nothing. He only nods, a muscle jumping his cheek.

On the opposite side of the chamber, Radis gestures to Davidson, flicking out one hand. As he does so, a sudden breeze rustles through the Gallery. He is a windweaver, I realize. "Put it to a vote, Premier," the Silver says.

In his seat, Davidson dips his chin. He stares out, searching the many assembled politicians. I wonder what he reads in their faces. After a long moment, he exhales. "Very well, Representative Radis."

"I vote yes," Radis says quickly, firmly, and sits.

On the floor, Tiberias blinks quickly, trying to mask his surprise. I feel the same.

It only grows with every resounding yes, spoken from dozens of lips. I count under my breath. *Thirty. Thirty-five. Forty.*

There are nos scattered among the politicians, enough at first to temper any hope I might feel. But they are quickly eclipsed, drowned out in favor of the answer we so desperately need.

Finally, Davidson grins and stands back up out of his chair. He crosses the floor and touches Tiberias lightly on the shoulder, gesturing for him to rise.

"You have your army."

TWELVE
Evangeline

Even though Montfort is beautiful, I'm keenly glad to be leaving so soon after our arrival. What's more, I'm going home. To Ridge House, to Ptolemus, to Elane. I'm so happy I barely notice that I have to pack up my things myself.

It's the smart move. Even the Reds know it. The Rift is closer to Montfort than the Piedmont base, not to mention it isn't surrounded by Bracken's territory. And the kingdom is a place of strength, well defended. Maven won't order an assault on our lands, and we'll have time to gather our resources and our armies.

Still, my skin prickles with discomfort all afternoon. I can hardly stomach Cal's grin as we step out into the courtyard of Davidson's palace. Sometimes I wish he had just an ounce of Maven's cunning, or even sense. Then he might understand what happened this morning in the People's Gallery. But no, he's too trusting, too *good*, and much too pleased with his little speech to realize how well Davidson maneuvers.

The vote was already decided. It must have been. The politicians of Montfort already knew what Davidson would request, and they already knew how they would answer. The army was decided before we even arrived. Everything else, the entire visit to the city, was a performance, and a seduction.

It's what I would do.

Just as Davidson's own words to me were a seduction of their own. *Another small thing we allow here,* he said to me when I first arrived. He knows about Elane, and he knows exactly what to say to make me falter. Make me wonder. Make me think, even for an instant, about throwing my life away for a place here.

The premier is a good salesman, to say the least.

Cal crosses the courtyard to bid good-bye to Davidson and his husband, Carmadon. Looking at the couple, I feel the familiar surge of jealousy and then nausea. I turn away, if only to look somewhere else.

My eyes land on another despicable public display of emotion. Another nauseating round of farewells before this troop of dancing monkeys heads to the Rift.

I don't understand why Mare couldn't have said her good-byes inside, where the rest of us didn't have to see such a *performance*. As if she is original in her grief. As if Mare Barrow is the only one here who has ever had to leave someone behind.

She hugs her family one by one, each embrace longer than the last. Her mother cries; her father cries; her brothers and her sister cry. She does her best not to, and fails. Their half-hidden sniffles echo across the mountain jetway, and the rest of us are forced to act as if we aren't waiting for the weeping family.

It's all very *Red*, I suppose. They don't have to worry about what showing weakness might do, because, for the most part, they're already weak. Someone should talk to Barrow about that. She should know by now how important maintaining an image is.

The tall Red boy, Barrow's tan, blond pet, follows alongside, hugging her family as if they were his own. I suppose he's still tagging along.

Cal finishes with Davidson, pulling back from their whispered conversation. The premier isn't coming back with us, not yet. Now that his government has agreed to fully aid us, he has much to organize, and he pledges to follow us back to the Rift in a week or so. But I don't think that's what they're talking about. Cal is too fervent, too on edge, his grip on Davidson tight and unyielding. His eyes are soft, though. He's asking for something, something small and unimportant to anyone but him.

When the prince walks away, he passes by Mare with long, quick strides. Her brothers watch him go, eyes trailing in the prince's wake. If they were Calore burners, I think they might set him on fire. The sister is less hostile, but more disappointed. She frowns at his retreating form, lip between her teeth. She looks more like Mare when she does that, especially when her frown deepens into a sneer.

Cal stops at my right, settling into a wide-legged stance, crossing his arms over a plain black uniform.

"You need a better mask, Calore," I mutter to him. He only scowls. "And she needs to keep to our schedule."

"She's leaving her family behind, Evangeline," he growls in reply. "We can spare the minutes."

I heave a sigh and examine my nails. No claws today. No need for them on the journey back home. "So many allowances where Barrow is concerned. I wonder where that line is, and what happens when she inevitably crosses it."

Instead of snarling back, as I expect, he chuckles low in his throat.

"Try to spread your misery all you want, *Princess*. It's the only thing you have left."

Gritting my teeth, I clench a fist. And I wish I'd donned my claws.

"Don't pretend I'm the only one miserable here," I snap.

That cows him into silence, the tips of his ears flushing a stubborn gray.

With a last embrace, Mare *finally* finishes all her hysterical nonsense. She turns tightly, shoulders squared away from her brood. Their faces vary, but they all have a likeness. Similar coloring, dark eyes and golden-toned skin. Dark brown hair but for the sister and the graying parents. There's a common roughness to them, born in their blood. As if they were shaped from earth and we were shaped from stone.

The Red boy keeps pace as Mare walks toward us, tugged along on an invisible leash. He looks over his shoulder to wave back at the family, but Mare doesn't. I respect that instinct, at least. Her dogged and sometimes ill-advised habit of pressing forward at all costs.

Cal looks up as she passes, stomping her way into the jet. His hand flexes, fingers grazing her arm as she goes. His skin is pale against the sleeve of her rust-colored jacket. But she doesn't stop and he doesn't stop her. He only stares at her disappearing form, throat bobbing with the words he can't find it in himself to say.

Part of me wants to prod him after her with a sharp knife. The rest wants to cut out that heart of his, since he insists on ignoring it and subjecting me to a similar pain.

"Shall we, my future husband?" I growl, offering him my arm. The spikes of my metallic coat lie flat, glistening against one another in invitation.

Cal eyes me darkly, his teeth clenched into a forced grin. Dutiful to the last, he slips his arm around mine, resting his hand below my wrist. His skin blazes with heat, almost too hot to touch. I feel sweat prickle on my neck and fight the urge to shiver in disgust. "Of course, my future wife."

How I used to want this, I don't know.

Any revulsion I feel is quickly swallowed by excitement as we board the jet, our steps matched as we climb into the iron hulk. All that stands between me and a reunion with the ones I love most is a few short hours of flight. Squeezed alongside Cal and Mare and whatever dramatic sighs and meaningful stares they might toss at each other, yes, but I can handle it. Ptolemus is waiting.

Elane is waiting.

Even thousands of miles away, I feel the cool balm of her presence, a cold towel on fevered skin. White skin, red hair, all the stars in her eyes, the moon in her teeth.

When I was thirteen, I cut Elane to ribbons in the Training ring. For Father, for even the chance of his approval. I cried for a week afterward, and spent another month apologizing. She understood, of course. We know what our families are, what they demand, what we must *be* for them. And as the years wore on, such things became expected. Ordinary. We fought daily, hurting each other, hurting ourselves. In Training, with healers at the ready. We desensitized ourselves to the necessary violence of our days. But I wouldn't do it to her now. Wouldn't hurt her for anyone on this earth, even with the best healers in the world waiting to attend her. Not for my father, or for my crown. *If only Calore felt as strongly for Mare. If only he loved her as I love Elane.*

As soon as we're safely in the belly of the jet, the curved walls lined with cushioned seats and restraints, bolted-down tables and thick-glassed windows, Cal peels away from me. He eases himself down next to his grandmother, holding solitary court at one of the few tabled areas.

"Nanabel," I hear him mumble in greeting, using the utterly ridiculous and unbecoming pet name.

She looks weary for the first time I can remember. She offers her grandson a kind, private smile as he sits.

I find a seat of my own, favoring a window and a table at the corner, where I can sleep without much disturbance. Our jet is more comfortable than the military transports, though also commandeered from the Piedmont Air Fleet. The inside is white and cheery, accented with yellow and tiny bursts of purple stars along the interior. Prince Bracken's colors and symbols.

I've never met the prince, only his various diplomats through the years, and of course his envoys, Prince Alexandret and Prince Daraeus. They're both dead now. I watched Alexandret die in Archeon, shot through the skull during the first attempt on Maven's life. The memory turns my stomach.

An Iral lord stood up, pointed a gun, and fired a bullet at the king sitting two feet to my left. Fired and *missed*, of course, forcing us to act like the allies we pretended to be.

He should have died that day. I wish he'd died that day.

I can still taste the iron tang of his blood, mercurial upon the stones, gushing in an open river at my feet.

The assassination attempt failed. The rebelling houses fled, retreating to their lands and strongholds. Elane is no warrior and she was already gone, fleeing before the attack. But House Samos had to keep our cover. I still had to stand at Maven's council—stand because the weasel denied me the courtesy of a single *chair*—and watch him interrogate her sister. Watch his Merandus cousin spill out her memories before they executed her for treason.

Elane never speaks of it, and I won't push. I can't imagine what I would do if Ptolemus met the same fate. No, that's not true. I can imagine a thousand things. A million different forms of violence and pain. And not one would fill the void. The bonds of Silver blood, when strong, are unbreakable. Our loyalty to the few we love runs bone-deep.

What will Bracken do for his children, then?

I didn't ask after them, or their treatment in Montfort. It's easier not to. One less worry in a world full of worries.

My pursuit of silent privacy is interrupted by a hurricane of muscular limbs and cropped blond hair. The Scarlet Guard general sits with a collapsing thump, shuddering the floor beneath my feet.

"You move with the grace of one of those bison," I sneer, hoping to chase her out of the seat opposite mine.

She doesn't flinch or reply. The woman just glares at me with a flash of anger, her eyes galaxy blue. Then she turns to the window, leaning her forehead against the glass with a low huff of breath. She isn't crying. Not like Barrow, who enters the jet with hiccups and red-rimmed eyes.

There is no such display of sorrow on General Farley. Still, I can see the agony rolling off her like a tide. Her face goes blank, empty without the usual stony expression and obligatory disgust she tosses at Silvers, especially me.

I know she has a daughter, an infant, stowed away somewhere.

Not here. Not on this craft.

Barrow follows the Red woman, taking the seat beside her, and I snarl to myself. We traveled here with two jets, enough to keep the

Reds and Silvers apart, as well as carry the bounty of Corvium. I find myself wishing that were still the case, and we weren't all crammed together for the journey to the Rift.

"There are approximately sixty other seats on this plane," I mutter.

Mare cuts her own glare at me, torn between anger and heartache. "You're welcome to move if you want," she replies. "But I doubt you have somewhere better to sit." She gestures with her chin, indicating the rest of the plane as it fills with various representatives of those loyal to Cal and the Scarlet Guard.

I sink back into the plush seat, almost huffing. She isn't wrong. I hardly want to spend the hours donning a court mask, wielding a smile like a shield to trade information and veiled threats with the other Silvers. Nor do I have any desire to shut my eyes among Reds who would rather slit my throat. No, strangely, Mare Barrow is my safest haven here. Our bargain protects us both.

Mare shifts her attention, moving so her body is squared to the general. They don't speak, and Diana Farley doesn't look at Barrow. Her focus on the window is perfect, enough to shatter the glass. She doesn't seem to notice when Mare takes her hand.

As the jet purrs to life, its engines humming to a roar, she doesn't move. Her teeth clench, the muscles in her jaw jumping as she grinds them together.

Only when we take off, climbing into the clouds, leaving the mountains behind, does she shut her eyes.

I think I hear her whisper good-bye.

I'm the first down the steps of the jet, gulping the fresh scent of the Rift in summer. I smell dirt and river and leaves and damp heat, undercut with the distant hint of iron beneath the hills. The sun is strong, bright in a hazy, humid sky. It makes everything gleam in odd contrast. The ridges march off into the distance, lush and green against the flat, hot black of the paved runway. If I were to lay a palm to the ground, it would burn my skin. Waves of heat distortion rise from the pavement, wobbling the world around me. Or that could just be me, trembling with want. I try not to run. Try to hold on to some sense of propriety.

My relationship with Elane Haven is an open secret now, and a small one in comparison to the myriad of alliances and betrayals that seem to tangle our lives in so many webs.

A small secret, but a shameful one. An obstacle. A difficulty.

In Norta. In the Rift, a voice says in my head. *Not so elsewhere.*

She won't be waiting out here for all to see. It's not her way. Still, my heartbeat hammers, pounding at my pulse points.

Ptolemus is not so restricted. He stands on the runway, sweating stubbornly in a summer uniform of gray linen and reserved regalia. The only metal on him winks at his wrists. Thick-braided iron rope, more weapon than jewelry. A caution, especially alongside the dozen or so guards in Samos colors. A few are cousins, marked by their silver hair and black eyes. The rest are pledged to our house, to my father's crown, in the same way Maven's guards were. I don't bother noting their colors. They don't matter.

"Eve," he says, opening his arms to me. I return the gesture, holding him around the middle, letting all the muscles in my body release for one long moment of relief. Ptolemus is safe and whole beneath my fingertips. Solid. Real. Alive.

Now, more than ever, I won't take that for granted.

"Tolly," I breathe in reply, pulling back to look up at him. The same relief I feel flashes in his stormy eyes. We despise being parted. It's like separating a sword from a shield. "I'm sorry I left."

No, you didn't leave him. That denotes choice. You had no choice in this. My fingers tighten on my brother's upper arm. Father sent me to Montfort. To send a message. Not just to our coalition, but to me. He is my king and lord of my house. It is my duty to obey him. To go where he wishes, do as he says, and marry who he commands. Live as he wills.

But I see no other way, no other path than the one he sets.

"Sad to miss the chaos?" Ptolemus says, pushing me back softly. "Father's gone a bit wild making up a proper court. Silver all over the place. And he can't decide on a throne."

"What about Mother?" I ask, tentative.

Despite the heat, Ptolemus tucks my arm under his, leading me toward our transport. Behind us, others fall in line, but I have little regard for them.

"More of the same," he says. "Prodding after grandchildren. She escorts Elane to my rooms every night. I think she might even stand guard outside the door."

Bile rises in my throat, but I force it down.

"And?" I try to keep my voice from wavering. His grip tightens.

"We do as we all agreed." His breath catches. "What has to be done, for this to work."

Hot, green envy roars in my chest.

I thought I wouldn't be jealous. Months ago, when all three of us came to this decision. When we decided to go through with Elane's betrothal to my brother. At first, the betrothal was simply meant to protect her. Take her out of consideration for any other houses until we could figure something out. It would not do to have her married off to some simpering Welle greenwarden or boorish Rhambos strongarm. Both out of my reach and out of my control. She is a beautiful girl, a talented shadow. Her house is of great value. And Ptolemus is the heir to House Samos. It was an equal match, understandable, predictable. Useful for a time. When the three of us thought there were no other options. I was still betrothed to Maven, doomed to be his queen. But Ptolemus was near as his right hand, close to court. A marriage would keep Elane close too.

We didn't know what machinations our father had in store. Not really. Not the details.

If I knew then what I know now . . . what decisions would have been different?

Ptolemus would be unwed, an eligible prince. And Elane free to follow you, her princess, wherever you may go. To marry whatever courtier you chose. Not chained to your brother, in another kingdom, another country, another bedroom, for the rest of all your lives.

Father could have stopped us, but he didn't. He let us make this mistake. I bet he enjoyed it, knowing I was separating myself from the one person I wanted more than any crown.

"Eve?" Ptolemus whispers, bending down. He's at least six inches taller than me. Broader, too. The firstborn, four years my elder. The son of Volos Samos, the heir to the Kingdom of the Rift. I love my brother, but his life will always be easier than mine. And I'm allowed to resent him for it, in my small way.

"It's fine," I force out between clenched teeth. It's a good thing I'm not wearing my usual metals, or they all might crush to dust. Out of the corner of my eye, I note Tolly adjusting his bracelets as they tighten on his skin. "We chose this. We have to live with it."

The odd, faraway voice rises again.

Do you?

In my mind, I see a flash of a white suit and a green one, two men, their hands different colors, fingers interlaced. They cloud across my vision, and I rely on Ptolemus to lead me the last few steps. He almost has to lift me into the transport.

The vision of Davidson and Carmadon is replaced with another. My brother and Elane in a familiar bedroom. My own wretched mother's shadow at the door. There's only one way to erase the vision threatening to burn itself onto my eyes.

While the rest make for the newly fashioned throne room, to greet my father as a king deserves, I do the opposite. I know Ridge House as well as my own face, and it isn't difficult to slip away in the receiving courtyard, disappear into the regimented trees and flowers. The servants' garden connects to the kitchens, and I barely notice the Reds as I pass. They shrink from my presence, well accustomed to my moods. Currently, I feel like a storm cloud, dark and brooding, threatening to burst.

Elane waits in my room. Our room, the windows clear, curtains open. She knows I like the sun, especially on her. She perches in one of the window seats, leaning back against a pillow, one leg dangling free, bare to her upper thigh beneath a sheer black gown. She doesn't turn to look at me when I walk in, allowing me the time I want to adjust to her presence.

My eyes trace her leg before jumping to her hair, red and gleaming, loose around her pale shoulders. It looks like liquid fire. Her skin seems to glow, because it does. This is her ability, her art. She manipulates the light just so, accentuating herself without any need for makeup or finery. Rarely do I feel ugly. I'm a beautiful girl, by design and nature. But after the long flight, without my usual armor of an intricate dress and painted face, I feel diminished next to her. Unworthy. I fight the urge to duck into my bathroom and sweep a little makeup on.

Finally she turns, giving me full view of her face. Again I feel a little bit of shame in coming to her so disheveled. But want quickly chases away any other sensation. She laughs as I kick the door shut and cross the room to take her face in my hands. Her skin is smooth and cool beneath my fingers, a perfect alabaster. Still, she doesn't speak, letting me look over her features.

"No crown," she says, raising her hand to my temple.

"No need for it. They all know who I am."

Her touch brushes lightly, sweeping down my cheekbone as she tries to smooth away my cares. "Did you sleep on your journey back?"

I huff, running my thumbs along the underside of her jaw. "Is that your way of saying I look tired?"

Her fingers continue over my face, down to my neck. "I'm saying you can sleep if you want."

"I've slept enough."

She smirks, lips twisting in the split second before I kiss her.

It breaks my heart to know she isn't really mine.

A fist collides with my door, pounding directly on the entrance to my bedroom. Not even the salon outside, where visitors are meant to wait. My bedroom, *our bedroom*, directly. I shoot up from my pillows, untangling myself from the sheets with fury. With a flick of my wrist, I draw a knife from the chest across the room and make quick work of the silk twisting around my legs.

Elane doesn't blink when the blade passes within an inch of her bare skin. She just yawns, my lazy cat, and rolls over to cradle a pillow. "So rude," she murmurs, meaning both me and whatever idiot decided to interrupt us.

"Practicing for that foul creature," I reply, cutting the last sheet. "What an unlucky messenger."

I stand, naked, before tying a soft robe around myself with the blade still in hand.

The knocking continues, followed by a muffled voice. I recognize it, and some of my delicious, righteous anger evaporates. No scaring the colors out of anyone right now. Annoyed, I throw the knife at the wall. It sticks, blade sinking into the woodwork.

"What, Ptolemus?" I sigh, wrenching open the bedroom door. He looks similarly disheveled, his hair messy and his eyes burning. I suspect he was interrupted as I was. He and Wren Skonos like their afternoon trysts.

"We're needed in the throne room," he says firmly. "Right now."

"Is Father that upset I haven't kissed his feet yet? It's only been a few minutes."

"It's been two hours," Elane calls, not bothering to raise her head. "Hello, Husband," she adds, tipping a dainty hand. "Be a dear and call for some lunch?"

I tighten the robe, annoyed. "So, what am I walking into? A public lashing? Will he finally make good on the promise to spike our heads to the gate?" I sneer, chuckling darkly.

"Strangely, this isn't about you," my brother replies, his voice sharp and dry. "There's been an attack."

Quickly, I look over my shoulder. Elane lies sprawled, partially covered by the sheets. She isn't glowing now, without any reason to concentrate as she drifts back to sleep. She is defenseless, vulnerable. Even to words. "Out here," I mutter, pushing my brother into the adjoining salon. I can protect her from this, at least, if nothing else.

I lead him to one of the couches, a cool green to match the hilly vista in the window. Rough river stone paves the floor, strewn with soft blue carpets. "What happened? Attack where?" For some reason, I picture Montfort, and my heart plunges in my chest.

Ptolemus doesn't sit. He paces instead, hands on his hips. The tendons in his forearms flex. "Piedmont."

I can't help but scoff. "Maven's a *fool*," I snarl. "He's only hurting Bracken's resources, not ours. I didn't think he was this *stupid*—"

"Maven didn't hit Bracken," my brother snaps. "Bracken hit us. The Piedmont base. Two hours ago, but we just got the call for help."

"What?" I blink, admittedly confused. I raise a hand, clutching the collar of my robe, pulling it shut. As if silk can save me from anything.

"He cut off the base, stormed it with his own army and an alliance of the other Piedmont princes. He's taking it back. Killing anyone they could get their hands on. Nortan Red, Montfort Silver. Newbloods." Ptolemus prowls to the window, putting a hand to the glass. He stares east, at the haze of a hot afternoon. "We suspect Maven and the Lakelands are helping behind the scenes."

I look at the floor, my bare feet on the carpet. "But his children. Montfort will have to kill them." *What a trade. Your children for your crown.* I wonder if my own father would make the same choice.

Slowly, Ptolemus shakes his head. "We received word from Montfort too. The children—they're gone. Replaced with Red corpses healed to *look* like Princess Charlotta and Prince Michael. Someone got to them, and got them out." He growls low in his throat. "Montfort idiots don't know how it happened. How anyone got into their precious mountains and out again."

I wave a hand, dismissing the point. It doesn't matter right now. "So Piedmont is finished?"

His jaw tightens. "Piedmont is with Maven now."

"And what can we do?" I suck in a dragging breath. My mind whirls. There was a garrison left back in Piedmont, soldiers from the Scarlet Guard and Montfort. Red, newblood, and Silver, people we need for our armies. I grit my teeth, wondering how many might have survived.

At least my father's own army is here in the Rift, having returned after we destroyed Corvium. The same can be said of Anabel's alliance. Our Silver strength is preserved, but the loss of the base—and Piedmont—will have devastating consequences.

I swallow hard, my voice shaking as I speak again. "What can we do against the Lakelands, Maven's Norta, and Piedmont?"

My brother's look is grim, and I shiver to my core.

"We're about to find out."

THIRTEEN
Iris

I've never been this far south.

The Piedmont base is so thick with humidity I feel as if I could weaponize the air itself. My bare arms prickle with the sensation of moisture, minuscule droplets too small to see dancing over my skin. I stretch a little, moving my fingers in tiny circles, stirring up the cloying warmth hanging over the balcony of the base headquarters.

Thunderheads chase across the horizon, trailing gray shadows of lashing rain out over the swamps. Lightning forks once or twice, and the distant rumble takes four or five seconds to reach us. The light breeze smells of fires doused by the passing rain, and smoke trails over near the main gate of the base. Bracken's own soldiers marched in through open gates before turning on all inside in a blitz of swift and strongarm, revealing exactly where their bought allegiances lie. With Maven. And with me.

The king of Norta lays his bone-white hands flat on the balcony railing, leaning forward an inch or two over the edge.

It isn't far to the ground. Just two stories. If I pushed him over the rail, he would live, albeit with a few broken bones. He squints, dark brow furrowed beneath a simple crown of iron and ruby. No cloak today. Too hot. Instead he has his usual black uniform, unbuttoned at the throat, the fabric flapping in the slight, damp breeze. A sheen of sweat gleams on his neck. Not from the heat. A fire king would be far more comfortable than anyone else at these temperatures. The sweat isn't from exertion either. He took no part in the storming of the base. Neither did I, though both our nations provided Silver soldiers for Bracken's endeavor. We waited until it was clear, until victory was sure, before setting foot here.

I think Maven is nervous. Afraid. And enraged.

She wasn't here.

I watch him quietly, waiting for him to speak. His throat works, bobbing between the open folds of his collar. He looks oddly vulnerable in spite of our triumph.

"How many escaped?" he asks without meeting my gaze. His eyes stay fixed on the storm.

I bite back a rush of annoyance. I'm not some lieutenant, some officer's aide meant to stand and give figures. But I tell him what he wants, and I do it with a tight smile.

"One hundred into the swamps," I reply, running a hand through the flowers blooming from boxes along the balcony. The dirt around them is still wet from the passing rains and a particularly exuberant gardener. Behind us, more flowering vines run up the brick walls and columns of the administrative building. The Piedmontese love their flowers. They explode in various shades, thriving in this climate. White, yellow, purple, pink, and a bit of comforting blue. The sun strengthens overhead, and I wish I'd worn white instead of my royal blue dress. The linen is light, at least, thin enough that I can feel the wind on my skin.

Maven plucks a single indigo bloom from the flowers at his side. "And another two hundred dead." Not a question. He knows the death toll well enough.

"They're being identified now to the best of our ability."

He shrugs. "Use the prisoners. Perhaps a few will do the work for us."

"I doubt that," I reply. "The Scarlet Guard and the Montfortans are loyal creatures. They won't do a thing to help us."

With a long, low sigh he straightens up, pushing back from the balcony. He squints as another crack of lightning flashes, closer this time. What little color he has left drains from his face when the sound of thunder rolls over us. *Is he thinking of the lightning girl?*

"I have some Merandus cousins who could be the judge of that."

I grit my teeth. "You know how I feel about whispers," I say, too quick and too harsh. *His mother was one,* I remind myself, bracing for some kind of reprimand.

But Maven remains silent. He lays the flower on the railing, petals up, and fusses with his fingernails. They're short, worn by teeth and anxiety. I would expect a king to keep his nails finely manicured, suited to the arms of a throne. Or maybe roughed by Training or combat, as I'm sure his brother's are. Not ruined by nervous habits better suited to a child.

"And I think I know how you feel as well, Maven," I hear myself say. Daring to turn over one of my many cards on the table.

Again he doesn't respond, and I know I'm right. Whatever his mother did, however her whispers crawled across his brain, left scars and marks. He doesn't want to risk more.

I sense a chink in his armor, a hole in the wall he keeps up. *What if I could slip through? If I could grab hold of a piece of him the way Mare Barrow has—could I hold the reins of a king?*

"We can remove them from court, if you want," I murmur slowly. I school my features into something softer, more caring, as I shift closer to him. I angle my body so my collarbone juts out, and my dress slips just so, showing exactly as much skin as I need. "Blame it on me. My Lakeland superstitions. Call it a short-lived measure to please your new wife."

It's like circling a whirlpool, trying to keep to its edges. To stay within its bounds without drowning.

The corner of his mouth lifts, tugging his lips. He cuts a sharp profile, all edges of straight nose, proud brow, and sculpted cheekbones. "You're nineteen, aren't you, Iris?"

I blink at him, confused. "And?"

Grinning, he moves faster than I expect, putting one hand to my face. I flinch as his fingers slide behind my ear, his thumb beneath my chin. The latter digs a little, pressing into the flesh of my throat. His skin flares, hot but not burning. We're almost the same height, but he has an inch or so over me, and I'm forced to look up into eyes like a tundra sky. Frozen, unforgiving, endless. To anyone watching, we might look like enamored newlyweds.

"You're very good at this already," he says, his oddly cool breath washing over my face. "But so am I."

I step back, meaning to pull from his grip, but he releases me before I force any kind of struggle. He seems amused, which makes my stomach churn. I give no indication of my disgust. Only cold indifference. I raise an eyebrow and smooth my hair over one shoulder, gleaming black and oil-smooth. I try to channel my mother's regal, fearless nature.

"Touch me without my consent again, and we'll see how long you can hold your breath."

Slowly, he lifts the flower again, and his fist tightens around it. One by one, the petals fall, and he flicks his wrist, sparking his bracelet. The petals burn before they hit the ground, disappearing in a burst of red flame and ash and open threat.

"Forgive me, my queen," he says, smiling. Lying. "The stress of this war can be such a ruin on my nerves. I only hope my brother can be made to see reason, and the traitors with him are brought to justice so we might finally have some peace in our lands."

"Of course." My words are just as false as his. I dip my head, ignoring any shame I feel in the action. "Peace is the goal we all share."

After my mother feasts on your country and tosses your throne into the ocean. After we bleed the Samos king dry and kill every person responsible for my father's death.

After we take your crown, Maven Calore, and drown you and your brother both.

"Your Majesty?"

We both turn to find one of Maven's Sentinels, his mask black and glittering, standing in the doorway to the balcony. He bows low, his robes a swirl of woven fire. I can't imagine how sweltering their armor and robes must be right now.

Maven gestures, hands open. His voice is a bucket of ice water. "What is it?"

"We've located what you asked for." I can only see the Sentinel's eyes beneath his mask, and they flash with fear.

"Are you sure?" The king picks at his nails again, feigning disinterest. This only piques mine.

The Sentinel bobs his head. "Yes, sir."

With a cutting smile, Maven looks up from his hands and turns, putting his back to the railing. "Well, then, my thanks. I'd like to see it."

"Yes, sir," the Sentinel says again, nodding once more.

"Iris, care to join me?" Maven asks, one hand outstretched. His fingers hover half an inch from my arm, taunting me.

Every warrior instinct I have tells me to refuse. But then I openly admit I am afraid of Maven Calore, and give him power over me. This I cannot allow. And whatever he's looking for on the Piedmont base could be important to the Lakelands. A weapon, perhaps. Intelligence, maybe. "Why not?" I say with an exaggerated shrug.

I ignore his hand, following the Sentinel off the balcony. My dress snaps behind me, cut low to show the whorls of water tattooed across my back.

The base is a good size, though half as big as the major citadels where we house our fleets and armies back in the Lakelands. Wherever we're going must be close enough to walk, as Maven's contingent of Sentinels doesn't bring a transport. I wish they would. Despite the many trees dotting the streets of the base, the shady areas aren't much cooler than the sunlit streets. As we walk, flanked by a dozen Sentinel guards, I run a hand along my neck. Droplets of water form in the wake of my fingertips, each one running a soothing race down my inked spine.

Maven follows close at the heels of his lead Sentinel, hands fisted in his pockets. He's eager. He wants whatever we're about to find.

They turn us onto a street of row houses. At first it seems oddly cheerful. Red brick and black shutters, paved sidewalks, flowers blooming, and columns of pruned trees. But the emptiness is unsettling, like a city block removed of its inhabitants. A dollhouse without dolls. The people who lived here were either killed or captured, or they fled into the stinking, sinking swamps. Perhaps they left something of value behind.

"These were officer homes," one of the Sentinels explains. "Before the occupation."

I raise an eyebrow at him. "And after?"

"Used by the enemy. Red rats, blood traitors, newblood freaks," one of the Sentinels hisses behind his mask.

Maven stops so quickly his leather boots leave black scuff marks on the sidewalk. He turns to the hissing guard, hands still concealed. Despite the Sentinel's towering height, Maven doesn't seem at all perturbed. In fact, he wears no expression at all as he stares.

"What was that, Sentinel Rhambos?"

Strongarm. The Sentinel could tear Maven's arms off if he wanted. Instead his eyes widen behind his mask, a watery brown full of terror.

"Nothing of importance, Your Majesty."

"I decide what is important," Maven clips. "What did you say?"

"I answered Her Majesty, the queen." His eyes shift to me. Begging for some kind of protection, but I have none to give. The Sentinels are Maven's to command. "I told her Reds lived here during the Montfort occupation. And Silvers. And newbloods."

"Rats. Traitors. *Freaks*," Maven offers, still without any inflection or emotion. I almost wish he would explode with rage. This is far more frightening. A king who cannot be read, a king without anything in him. "Those were your exact words, weren't they?"

"They were, Your Majesty."

With a crack of his neck, Maven looks at another guard. "Sentinel Osanos, can you explain why this was a mistake?"

The blue-eyed nymph sputters at my side, stunned to be called upon. She tries to gather herself as quickly as possible. And answer correctly. "Because . . ." She trails off, her fingers twitching in her robes. "I can't say, sir."

"Hmm." His hum is low, guttural, vibrating in the damp air. "No one?"

I truly despise him.

I click my tongue. "Because Sentinel Rhambos insulted Mare Barrow in your presence."

I suddenly regret wishing Maven would show anger instead of emptiness. His eyes go black, the pupils blowing out in fury. His mouth opens a little, showing teeth, though I expect fangs. The Sentinels around us tense, and I wonder if they would try to stop him if he moved to strike me. I don't think they would. I'm their charge as well, but he comes first. *He will always come first in this marriage.*

"My wife has such an imagination," he sneers, though I've struck upon the truth. An ugly one. I knew he was obsessed with her, in love with her in some corrupt and vile way, but his reaction hints at something deeper. An internal flaw of someone else's making. His mother did this to him, for a reason I can't fathom. Speared the pain and agony and torture of loving Mare through his heart and brain.

In spite of my better instincts, I feel the smallest pang of pity for Maven Calore. He is not of his own making. Not entirely. Someone else perfectly cut him apart and poorly put him back together.

His anger passes like the storm clouds, leaving the threat of trembling thunder in its wake. The Sentinels relax when it does. Maven rolls his shoulders and smooths a hand through his hair.

"Your mistake, Sentinel Rhambos, lies in your disdain," he says, his voice returning to the dismissive, boyish tone he uses to ensnare people. Stepping lightly, he gets us moving again, though I think the

Sentinels are keeping a distance. "We are at war, yes, and these people are our enemies. But they're still people. Many of them my rightful subjects and your own countrymen. When we claim our victory, we will welcome them back into the Kingdom of Norta. With some exceptions, of course," he adds with a conspiratorial smirk.

The lie comes so easily and so well I shiver in the heat.

"Here, sir," one of the guards finally says, indicating a row house that looks identical to the others at first glance. But upon closer inspection, I realize the flowers are better tended to. Vibrant, lush petals and verdant green leaves burst from the window boxes.

Maven glares up at the windows, as if inspecting a corpse. He mounts the steps to the door, moving slowly. "And what *freak* lived here?" he finally says.

At first the Sentinels do not answer. Fearing the trap for what it is.

Only Osanos is brave enough to speak. She clears her throat, then responds.

"Mare Barrow."

Maven nods, still for a second. Then he raises a foot, slamming his boot next to the doorknob, kicking the lock and the door open with a shatter of wood. His form recedes like a fading shadow as he enters the house.

I remain on the pavement for a moment. *Stay here.* The Sentinels hesitate with me, reluctant to follow their king. Though I would personally love nothing more than an assassin to jump out of a closet and cut Maven's throat, I know how that would destroy any chance of winning this war and keeping the Lakelands safe from the other brother and his pets in the Rift.

"Keep up," I growl, ascending the steps after my foul husband. The

Sentinels clatter after me, their armor clinking beneath their robes of flame.

I focus on the sound of them as we enter the dim house, empty and silent without its occupants. The walls are oddly bare; Bracken did say his base, and many of his own treasures, were stripped of valuables. Sold off for resources. I wince at the thought of my own home facing such vultures. Our shrines and temples desecrated to fund a war. *Not while I live and breathe. Not while Mother holds her throne.*

I don't bother entering the small salon or searching out the kitchen. Maven's footsteps echo on the stairs, and I follow, pulling the Sentinels along with me. If the king wants to be alone, he doesn't say so.

He bangs open each door on the second floor in turn, poking his head into various bedrooms, closets, and a bathroom. Once or twice, he snarls under his breath, like a predator denied prey.

At the final door, in the corner, he pauses, hesitating.

This door he opens with one hand, gently, as if entering a holy place.

I hang back a moment, letting him go first.

Inside is a bedroom, with two small beds flanking a single window. I notice the oddity first. The patterned curtains are cut up, with precise chunks removed.

"The sister," Maven murmurs, running his hand along a sliced edge. "The seamstress."

As he runs the fabric through his fingers, sparks spit from his wrist. They catch and spread, eating through the curtains with speed and skill. Burning holes spread like disease. Acrid smoke stings my nostrils.

He does the same to the wallpaper, letting it burn and peel beneath his touch. Then the window, laying a flaming hand to the glass. It cracks under the tremendous heat he throws off, shattering outward into the sunlight. The room seems to pulse and boil, like the inside of a bubbling pot. I want to step away, but I want to see him. Maven. I must know who he is if I am to defeat him.

The first bed he ignores, somehow knowing it wasn't hers.

The second he sinks into, as if testing the firmness. He smooths the coverlet beneath his hands, then the pillow. Feeling where her head used to rest. I almost expect him to lie down and breathe in whatever scent might linger.

Instead his fire consumes. Feather and fabric. Wood frame. It leaps across to the other bed, gobbling it up.

"Give me a minute, please," he whispers, almost inaudible over the roar of controlled flame.

We do as we are told, fleeing before the shining heat.

A minute is all he needs. We're barely back on the street before he emerges from the door, an inferno jumping to life behind him.

I realize I'm sweating with fear as we walk away and the row house crumbles.

What will Maven burn next?

The snarl of transports echoes outside the holding bunker. The soldiers must have returned, and I wonder if they managed to track down any-one in the swamps. The noise filters through the high windows cut into the concrete slab walls. This room is cool, partially underground, bisected by a long aisle dividing two rows of barred cells. By the offi-cial count, we have forty-seven captured held here, two or three to a cell. All red-blooded, but still under heavy Silver guard. Some could be newbloods, quietly waiting for a chance to use their abilities and escape. The Silvers of Montfort—the blood traitors, as the Sentinel called them—are being held elsewhere, restrained by silents and the most powerful of guards.

Maven idly knocks his knuckles against each bar as we pass. The prisoners shrink back or stand firm, afraid or defiant in the face of the king of Norta. Strange, he seems relaxed here, surrounded by cells. He barely seems to notice the prisoners at all.

I do the opposite. I count as we go, to see if they match the official tally. To look for any flash of rebellion or determination that might spark into something inconvenient. I wish I could separate Red from newblood. Every cell I pass makes me uneasy, knowing a snake could be waiting in each one.

At the far end of the bunker, another contingent of royal Silvers approaches, their colors yellow, white, and purple, all done up in gold armor and weapons better suited to decorating a banquet hall. Prince Bracken smiles broadly, but the children clutching his hands cower. Michael and Charlotta alternate between burying their faces in their father's purple-spangled robes and looking at their golden-shod feet.

While I feel a surge of sorrow for the children and what they endured at the hands of the Montfort monsters, I am also grateful to see that they are well enough to accompany their father. When we slipped out of the mountain kingdom with them, they could barely speak, despite the wretched healer's fine work. For no skin healer can mend a mind.

If only they could, I think to myself, glancing sidelong at my husband.

"Prince Bracken," Maven says, dipping his head with all the charm he can muster. Then he sinks further, to eye level with the approaching children. "And Michael, Charlotta. The bravest pair of siblings I ever saw."

Michael hides his face again, but Charlotta offers the smallest of smiles. The polite kind, hammered into her by some etiquette instructor, no doubt.

"Very brave indeed," I add, winking at the pair of them.

Bracken stops before us, still smiling, and his guards and retainers glide to a halt with him. I spot another Piedmont prince in their midst, marked by a crown of emeralds, but I can't say which one.

"Your Majesties," Bracken offers, sweeping out his hands to bow as low as he can. His children, still holding his fingers, do the same with practiced grace. Even shy, shivering little Michael. "There are neither enough words nor enough gold in the world to express my gratitude, but rest assured, you have it." The prince's eyes stray to me and I meet his gaze, raising my chin. I saved his children with my own two hands. That will not be forgotten. "Just as you have use of my military installation, and any resources Piedmont can offer in this war against the very nature of our world."

With a flick of his fingers, Maven gestures for Bracken to stand.

"You have my gratitude as well for such a mighty pledge," Maven replies, all performance and posture. "Together we can end what my brother began."

Something flashes in Bracken's eye. Amusement, maybe. Does he see the lie for what it is? *Tiberias Calore did not start this war, not by any stretch of the imagination. That sin lies with the Red rebels.* I swallow, my throat suddenly dry. The Scarlet Guard began in the Lakelands, spurred on by necessary actions my own father took. Still, if they are sinners, we enabled their existence, allowing it to spread. We share in the sin and shame.

"Together with the Lakelands," Bracken adds.

Another flash of amusement in the prince, and I feel heat rise in my cheeks. "Of course. We back Maven Calore to the last." *With as little as we can afford to send. Fewer troops, less weaponry, less money. The rest of it jealously guarded and hoarded for when we need it most.*

My cheek burns, flaming hot, as Maven's lips brush my face in a chaste but symbolic kiss. "We're a good match, aren't we?" he says, turning back to Bracken.

I fight the urge to make good on my promise and pin Maven to the floor where I can drown him to my heart's content.

"Quite," Bracken murmurs, his black eyes darting between us. "Unfortunately, we don't seem to be making much headway. I've sent for whispers and singers from Prince Denniarde's lands." He gestures to the prince behind him, resplendent in his emeralds and sheer, green silk. "But they've yet to arrive, and I'm afraid I don't want to risk further damaging any of the prisoners before they can be properly interrogated."

I turn to the nearest cell, hoping to hide my disgust at the thought of whispers and singers coming here. Neither should be trusted, but I hold my tongue.

The man in the cell stares back at me, his eyes like bright coals in the dim light of his prison. His skin is as brown as mine, although with a reddish undertone, and his black hair is curly, as is his oiled and groomed beard. The uniform he wears is dark green, the color of Montfort. It has rips in it, missing patches on the breast and upper arms. They dangle broken thread. From insignia removed, badges and honors torn away. I narrow my eyes, and he does the same.

"What's your rank, soldier?" I sneer, crossing to the bars.

Behind me, Bracken and Maven quiet.

The bearded man says nothing. As I come closer, I realize he has a scar below his eye. Too uniform to be an accident. A well-healed and perfectly straight line.

I jerk my chin at it. "Someone gave you that mark, didn't they?"

"You speak as if a Silver holding me down and scarring my face were a gift," he replies slowly. His words are oddly stilted, broken apart. As if he has to think through each as it weighs on his tongue.

I trace the scar again, looking it over. I wonder what he did, or didn't do, to warrant such a punishment.

"When your whispers come," I say, looking over my shoulder to Bracken. "Start with him. He's of higher rank. He'll know more than most."

Maven's lips twitch and he almost smiles.

"Of course," Bracken replies. "We'll start with that foolish Red, won't we?" he adds, crooning to his children as he leads them away. They nod in tandem, seeming far younger than ten and eight. "Then you'll see they are nothing to be frightened of. Not anymore. They're nothing to you. *Nothing*."

Again Michael hides his face, shoving his head under his father's arm.

Charlotta does the opposite, putting her tiny chin in the air. She has freckles, a dusting over her brown skin. In Montfort, her hair was simple, smoothed back into a single, tight knot. Here she dresses like the princess she is, in patterned white silk, with amethysts studding her many braids. I watch her as she follows her father, small gown trailing over concrete. Her outfit reminds me of a bride's dress, and I wonder who she will be traded to, as I was traded, when the time comes.

We continue on our way, surveying the cells, and I return to my counting. Maven swings his arms back and forth, almost joyful. So the victory has had an effect after all.

"I didn't know you were capable of happiness," I mutter, and he laughs outright. It cuts like glass.

He grins at me unkindly, a wild, manic gleam in his eye. "Your impression of Mare Barrow is very good."

I sneer back, dancing on the knife edge. "Well, you want her to be your queen, so I might as well play the part."

Another peal of laughter. He blinks at me, as if inspecting a painting. "Is this jealousy, Iris?" I tighten under his scrutiny, my muscles tense as coiled wire. "No, no, it's not," he sighs, still smiling. "As I said before, we're a good match."

Hardly.

"Did someone say my name?"

Maven stops short next to me, his brows furrowing in open confusion. He tips his head to one side and looks over his shoulder, blinking back at the cell behind us.

The voice belongs to the bearded man. He leans against his bars, dangling his hands into the central aisle. He peers at us, an eyebrow raised like some kind of challenge.

"You heard me, Maven," he says, and his voice is different from before. Still his own, but stronger, faster, more forceful. A sharp edge on stone.

We look back at him, perplexed. At least, I am.

Maven looks torn between murderous fury and . . . hope?

The man grins.

"Have you missed me?" he says. "I think you have."

I hear bone on bone. Grinding teeth. Maven clenches his jaw and forces out a single word.

"Mare."

FOURTEEN
Mare

"He knows it's you."

We all seem to inhale at the same time, and my breath feels ragged. Suddenly, the small room tucked away in the Samos palace is much too tight. On instinct, my eyes snap to Farley. She stares back at me. Her throat works, swallowing hard, and I trace the action. She steels before my eyes, hardening with determination.

I bite my lip and wish I could do this alone. But she isn't going anywhere, standing over Ibarem. Close enough to stop this if things get beyond my control. Ibarem's eyes burn into mine, alight and intense as his mind bridges the divide between Ridge House and Piedmont. He already vomited out as much information as he could about the prison on the Piedmont base, the bunker half buried with east-facing windows. Which prisoners his brother can see, exactly who he's captured with, who he saw die, who he saw escape. To my relief, Ella and Rafe were among the survivors who made it into the swamps. That intelligence alone was vital, but this—*Maven*, right in front of us. So close I feel like I could almost reach out and touch him.

I want to see what Ibarem sees. I want to tip forward, plunge through the russet depths of his eyes, and emerge in the matching pair staring out of a cell hundreds of miles away. Look Maven in the face again. Read him as I know I can. Every tick and pull of muscle under skin. The smallest flashes across ice-blue eyes, speaking of secrets and weaknesses he tries to bury.

Ibarem's connection to his brother will have to do. Their bond is strong despite the distance, almost immediate. Ibarem describes everything he senses through Rash as it comes.

"Maven is approaching the bars—he's leaning in, inches away. There's sweat on his neck. It's hot in Piedmont. It just rained." Ibarem tightens before me, laying his palms flat on his thighs. He draws back, and I imagine Maven right here in the room with us, crowding into his face. Ibarem's lip curls in distaste. "He's searching us. Our eyes."

I flinch and feel the cold phantom of familiar breath on my skin.

In spite of the sunlight streaming in through the single window, I feel darkness pool in this small, forgotten room hidden in Ridge House. I wish I'd never thought of this, had never summoned Ibarem to do this. He was supposed to be our link to Tahir and Davidson, an easy connection to Montfort. Not to his other brother, captured in Piedmont. Not to Maven.

I force myself to keep still, locking my muscles and my expression. But my heart gallops in my chest, rising to a dull, constant thud.

Farley tries not to pace, and her odd lack of activity makes me even more nervous than I already am. This place disagrees with both of us. Ridge House seems like little more than a trap waiting to be sprung. Every room has metal in some form, beamed or columned or even woven into the floor itself. The house is a weapon only a few can wield. And they surround us at all times.

Even the chair beneath me is cold steel. I shiver where it touches my bare skin.

The knock on the door makes us both jump, startled out of our skin. I whirl, teeth clenched, to see the knob turn, catching fast against a lock. Farley crosses to the door in two long strides, ready to turn away whatever servant or snooping noble waits on the other side.

To my dismay, she throws the door wide and steps back, allowing a broad, familiar silhouette to step into the room.

I all but snarl at her, my fists clenching on my knees.

"What are you doing?" I hiss, my voice low and firm.

Tiberias glances between Farley and me, as if weighing the two of us. Which female frightens him more. "I was invited," he says thickly. "And we are going to be extremely late for a council meeting."

"Then go!" I dismiss him with a wave, turning on Farley. "What are you doing?" I force through gritted teeth.

She cuts me off with the sharp slam of the door. "You know Maven, but so does he," she says with cold efficiency. "Let him listen."

In front of me, Ibarem blinks. "Miss Barrow," he says, prodding for us to continue.

As if this weren't stressful enough.

"Fine," I mutter through gritted teeth, turning back to face the Montfort newblood. I do my best to ignore the other Calore, now leaning against the wall to put as much space between us as he can. His foot taps in the corner of my eye in a burst of nervous energy.

"Maven is saying something," Ibarem murmurs, his natural voice soft and halting. It shifts quickly into the best impression he can make of Maven. "How are we speaking right now?" he says, the words suddenly cruel and sharp. He even forces a cold laugh. It's a good likeness.

"Or are you just trying to toy with a king, Red? Not a good decision, I'm afraid."

Ibarem shifts again, his eyes darting, seeing across the miles. "He has guards. Sentinels. Six of them. Prince Bracken and his children just passed through as well, with four guards of their own."

Tiberias says something behind his hand and Farley nods. Adding to the count of hostiles, probably. "Firm alliance with Bracken," I hear Tiberias mutter. "They'll strike again, and soon."

"The queen is with him," Ibarem continues. "The Lakelander princess. She isn't speaking, just standing. Watching." Ibarem narrows his eyes. "Her face is blank. She almost seems frozen."

"Tell Iris . . ." I stumble, tapping my fingers together. They must be convinced. Irrevocably sure it's me speaking through the brotherly bond. "Tell her all dogs bite."

"All dogs bite, Iris," Ibarem repeats. He tips his head as I tip mine. Imitating me now. A common girl with an uncommon life. The truth unsettles Maven as much as anything, and I must unsettle him if I'm to get anything out of this exchange.

"The queen is smirking. She nods her head," Ibarem says. He shifts into an impression of Iris, his voice climbing an octave. "All dogs bite, but some dogs wait, Mare Barrow."

"And what is that supposed to mean?" Farley grumbles into her hand.

But I know.

I'm just a well-dressed and tightly leashed lapdog, I told Iris once, during my imprisonment. She smirked then too. *Even lapdogs bite,* she replied. *Will you?*

I'm finally free to answer. And so is she.

Iris Cygnet is waiting for her own opportunity to strike. I wonder if she has the Lakelands behind her, or just her own rage.

I glance over my shoulder, looking to Farley. "It's something she said to me in Archeon. Before I came back."

"It's definitely her, but how, I can't say," Ibarem continues, relaying Iris's voice the best he can. "This must be some newblood ability we don't know yet."

"What you don't know could fill an ocean," I reply. "About Montfort, about the Scarlet Guard." It feels shameful, dirty even, to jab like this, but I do it easily. "About your brother. He's standing right next to me, you know."

Ibarem sneers, mimicking Maven. "Is that supposed to mean something?" I think there may be a tremor of fear in the echoed words. "I have little regard for who you decide to stand next to. Though," he adds, and his sneer curves into a wicked smile, "I understand you aren't standing next to him much anymore."

I force a smile, using it to mask my wince. "Good to know you have spies in our coalition," I say boldly. "Although nowhere near as many as we have in yours."

A laugh like nails on glass bursts from Ibarem. "You think I waste my spies on tracking your emotions, Mare? No, my darling, I just know you better than anyone else." He laughs again, showing white eye-teeth. I focus on the scar on Ibarem's chin to keep a picture of Maven's beautiful, haunted, hissing face out of my head. "I knew you wouldn't stomach it when Cal showed who he truly was."

At the edge of my vision, Tiberias doesn't move. Doesn't even breathe. He keeps his eyes lowered, intent on glaring a hole in the floor.

"He is created as much as I am. Made by our father, molded and broken into that walking, talking brick wall you thought you loved so well." Maven pushes on, speaking through Ibarem. "He hides behind that shield he calls duty, but the truth is less noble. Cal is made of want, same as the rest of us. But he wants the crown. He wants the throne. And no price is too high to pay. No blood too valuable to spill."

A snap rips through the air as Cal cracks a single knuckle with his thumb.

"We always come back to the same conversation, Maven," I grumble, leaning back with exaggerated nonchalance. Ibarem mirrors my motions. "I wonder, Iris, does he whine about Tiberias as much to you, or am I the only one who has to deal with this nonsense?"

Ibarem turns his head, as if looking to Iris. "Her lips twitched. Perhaps a smile," he reports. "Maven is shifting, putting an arm to the bars. The temperature is rising."

"Did I strike a nerve?" I ask. "Oh, I forgot, you don't know which nerves are even yours. And which are hers."

With a grimace, Ibarem smacks his open palms on his thighs. "Maven hit the bars. The temperature is still rising. The other prisoners are doing their best to watch." The newblood blinks, flaring his nostrils, forcing heavy breaths. "He's trying to calm himself."

"It isn't wise to antagonize someone with so many hostages at his disposal. I could let them all burn if I wanted," Maven hisses through gritted teeth. I can smell his shaking anger from hundreds of miles away. "It would be easy to report that there were no survivors of Bracken's glorious reclamation of his lands."

It's true. There is nothing to stop Maven from murdering every prisoner in sight. They live on his whims alone.

Leaving an intricate needle for me to thread.

"Or you could free them."

Maven barks a surprised laugh. "I think you need to get more sleep, Mare."

"In a trade, of course." I glance up at Farley, weighing her expression. Her brows twitch, knitting together in thought.

I see Tiberias pale too. The last time we brokered a trade with Maven, I ended up imprisoned for months on end.

"Because that ended so well for us last time," Maven chuckles through Ibarem's bond. "But if you'd like to return, and pretend you're doing it to save some nameless soldiers, then I'm happy to welcome you back."

"I thought Elara killed your ability to dream," I snap back. "No, Maven, I'm talking about what the Scarlet Guard left behind on Bracken's base."

Ibarem's face falls, matching the boy king's. "What?"

Farley grins, crouching next to me. Addressing Ibarem, and therefore Maven. "The Scarlet Guard has a difficult time trusting Silvers. Especially ones kept in check the way Bracken was. It was only a matter of time before something happened and he decided to stop taking orders from the people holding his children."

"Who am I speaking to now?" Maven demands through Ibarem.

"Oh, I'm hurt you don't remember me. But it's *General* Farley now, so maybe I sound different."

"Ah yes." Ibarem clucks his tongue. "How foolish of me to forget the woman who let a wolf like me into her pack of particularly stupid sheep."

Farley smiles like she's just been served a particularly delicious meal. "These stupid sheep wired your base with explosives."

For a second, the room goes deathly silent. Tiberias looks up, his face twisted in alarm. "Do you have any idea how dangerous that was?"

"Plenty," she snaps, not looking away from Ibarem. "Don't repeat that."

He barely nods.

"Well, Maven?" I ask, pasting on a sweet smile. "You can recall whoever you sent into the swamps after our people, and try to search the base before we obliterate it. Or you can release the prisoners, and we'll tell you exactly how close you're standing to a bomb."

"Explosives don't frighten me."

"They would if you cared about the soldiers sworn to your crown," Tiberias growls, prowling close to my shoulder. His forearm brushes against me, sending a flare of heat down my spine.

A shadow seems to pass over Ibarem as he relays the prince's words and presence. "Good of you to step forward, brother," Maven whispers. "I thought you'd never find the spine to speak to me."

"Name the place and we'll see exactly who has the stronger spine," Tiberias fires back, his growl feral and unchecked.

In reply, Ibarem just wags a finger back and forth. "Let's leave the posturing for your inevitable surrender, Cal. When you have to kneel before Norta, the Lakelands, and Piedmont." He rattles off each country with a spreading grin. I feel the weight stacking against us, the wall getting higher and higher.

Farley puts a hand on my shoulder, holding me back to my chair. Bidding me to wait.

Finally, Ibarem moves, crossing his arms and shifting his weight. His body language is all Maven. Dedicated to a performance. Now he isn't wearing the false mantle of the young man called to duty. He dons the mask of the heartless, impenetrable son of Elara Merandus. Someone who cares only for power and nothing else.

It is an act as much as Mareena was to me.

"How many bombs did you say, General?"

He uses her rank to throw her off, but Farley is more difficult to rattle. "I didn't."

"Hmm," Maven murmurs. "Well, Bracken won't take kindly to any further damage done to his installation. Though we bought enough goodwill returning his children, so he might not mind."

I don't know exactly where the explosives might be, only that the Guard planted them some time ago. Buried them below the roads, the runways, and most of the administrative buildings. Where they could do the most damage, not just to enemy soldiers, but to the base itself. They're tuned to a specific frequency, triggered and ready to blow. A perfect and deadly piece of foresight.

"The decision is yours, Maven," I answer. "The prisoners for your base."

Ibarem mimics Maven's grin. "And this newblood, of course," he says. "Though I'd like to keep him, if you don't mind. This is much easier than sending you letters."

"Not part of the deal."

Pouting, Ibarem huffs. "You make things so difficult sometimes."

"It's my specialty."

At my side, Tiberias scoffs quietly. I'm sure he agrees.

We wait in blistering silence, hanging on every breath from Ibarem's body. He turns in his seat, looking back and forth. Pantomiming Maven as he paces.

Farley looms above me, a storm cloud as much as I am.

"Where would you like them released?" he says finally.

Silently, Farley punches the air with a pair of brutal, triumphant jabs. I'm reminded of her young age. Only twenty-two, just a few years older than me.

"East gate," Farley replies, and I try to keep my triumph in check. "The swamps. Dusk."

I hear Maven's confusion. "That's it?"

Tiberias is just as puzzled. He glances sidelong at Farley. "That's no rescue," he murmurs, gesturing for Ibarem not to relay his words. "*General*, we need to get dropjets in place. A clear path. A cease-fire while we evacuate the prisoners and those who managed to escape."

She slices a hand through the air. "No need, Calore. You keep forgetting the Scarlet Guard isn't the kind of army you're used to." Proud, she plants her hands on her hips. "There's already infrastructure in place, and we have boots on the ground in the swamps already. Moving Reds across enemy territory is sort of what we're best at."

"Good to hear," Tiberias grinds out. "But I don't like being left out of the loop. We work better with everyone on even ground."

"You call this even ground?" Farley says, gesturing between him and us. His blood, our blood. His rank, our rank. The canyon between a Silver born to be a king and Reds born to nothing at all.

His eyes flicker, dancing from her to down to me. He towers over me in my seat, his height exaggerated by the distance. So much space between us and yet none at all. Though it pains him, Tiberias bites his tongue, and a muscle feathers in his cheek as he wrenches his gaze from mine. I see the struggle in him and I expect him to push. Keep arguing. To my surprise, he settles back, gesturing for us to continue.

In front of me, Ibarem heaves a breath. He touches the scar on his chin, brown skin knobbled white between the curls of his black beard. Then he brushes the flesh below each of his eyes. Where the scars of his brothers lie. "The king lingers, thinking. Miss Barrow, tell him he won't be able to use us this way again," he says, now pleading. "Or this wretched young man will keep my brother as his prisoner. As a channel to you and His Majesty."

"Of course," I reply, bobbing my head. Eager to save Rash from becoming another newblood pet. "We'll know if you keep the newblood, Maven. And if you do, the deal is broken."

The responding voice is bitter, but unsurprised. "But I've missed our conversations. You keep me sane, Mare," he tells me, trying for dark humor. It lands poorly.

"We both know that isn't true. And you will never communicate with me through him again."

He scowls. "Then we'll have to find new ways to talk."

Above me, Tiberias lifts a finger, signaling for Ibarem's attention. "If you want to talk, no one will stop you, Maven," he says, and the newblood relays. "Wars are fought with diplomacy as much as weaponry. Meet us on neutral ground, face-to-face."

"So eager to negotiate surrender, Cal?" Maven taunts, waving away the offer. "Now, General, the explosives?"

Farley nods. "You'll be given their locations after we can verify that our people are in the swamps and out of harm's way."

"I won't be held responsible for anything an alligator does."

At this, she truly laughs. "It's a pity you have no soul, Maven Calore. You could've been someone worth saving."

Tiberias shifts, unsettled. *If someone can fix him, isn't it worth it to try?* He asked me that a few weeks ago, skin to skin. It feels like another life. It isn't a subject I care for. There is no fixing Maven. No redemption for the boy king, for the false person we both loved. We can't save him from himself.

And I don't think I'll ever have the heart to tell Tiberias that.

As broken as Maven's ability to love is, Tiberias's is that much stronger. To a fault, perhaps. It makes him cling too tight.

"First you burn Corvium; now you threaten the Piedmont base?" Maven sneers through the bond. "The Scarlet Guard is so talented at destruction. But then it's always easier to tear down what is already built."

"Especially when what you build is rotten to the core," Farley sneers back.

"East gate. The swamps. Dusk," I repeat. "Or the base burns beneath you."

My foot twitches beneath me. *How many are on the base now? Soldiers oathed to Maven and Bracken and Iris. Silvers, probably. And Reds too. Their shield wall of innocents following orders.*

At first I tell myself not to think about it. War is difficult enough without weighing how many lives hang in the balance. But closing my eyes isn't the answer either. No matter how hard it is to see, I have to look. Even if I have to make the hard decision, I must do it with my eyes open. No more pushing down the pain or the guilt. I have to feel it if I want to get through it.

"Very well," Maven growls. Again I picture him standing outside a cell. White-faced in the dim light, his eyes rimmed with the usual shadows of exhaustion and doubt. "I am a man of my word."

The familiar refrain smarts like his brand, drawing out a dozen harsh memories of his letters and his promise.

Slowly, I nod.

"You're a man of your word."

We leave Ibarem with instructions to find us if his brother isn't freed with the rest, before hurrying along the corridors of Ridge House, trying to navigate our way to the Samos throne room. Tiberias is less helpful than he should be, his mind clearly elsewhere. With his brother in Piedmont, I suspect.

I do my best to keep up with his long strides and Farley's, but I keep bumping into his back as he slows, lost in thought.

"We're already late," I grumble, putting a hand to the small of his back on instinct. Shoving him forward.

He jumps at the contact, as if burned by my touch. His larger hand covers mine when he recovers, pulling my fingers away. Then he drops them quickly as he halts, turning to face me.

Farley keeps on, outpacing us with an exasperated groan. "Fight when we have the time," she calls, urging us to keep up.

He ignores her, glaring down at me. "You were going to speak to him without me."

"Do I need your *permission* to talk to Maven?"

"He's my brother, Mare. You know what he still means to me," he whispers, almost begging. I try not to soften in the face of his pain. It almost works.

"You have to forget who you thought he was."

It kindles something in him, a deeper anger. A desperation. "Don't tell me how to feel. Don't tell me to turn my back on him." Then he straightens, pulling back so I have to crane my neck to meet his gaze. "Besides, confronting him alone, just the two of you?" He looks over his shoulder at Farley. "It isn't wise."

"Which is why I sent for you," Farley snaps harshly. "We need to go. That took long enough, and the council started twenty minutes ago. If Samos and your grandmother are scheming, I want to be there."

"And what about Iris?" Tiberias says, recovering. He braces his hands on his hips, broadening his frame. To cut off any escape if I try to slip around him. He knows my tricks too well. "What was all that about dogs biting?"

I hesitate, weighing my options. I could always lie. It might be better to lie.

"Something Iris said before, when I was still at Whitefire," I admit. "She knew I was a pet to Maven. A lapdog. And she told me all dogs bite. It was her way of communicating that she knew I would turn on him if I could." The words catch, but I force them out. Why, I can't say. "So will she."

Instead of thanking me, Tiberias seems to darken. "And you think Maven wouldn't catch that?"

I can only shrug. "I think right now he doesn't care. He needs her, needs her alliance. There's only today and tomorrow, in his eyes."

"I can understand that," he mutters under his breath, so only I can hear.

"I'm sure you do."

He heaves another sigh, running a hand through his short hair. I wish he would let it grow into dark waves again. He'd look more handsome, less rigid. Less like a king.

"Do we tell them what just happened?" he asks, pointing a thumb back toward the room.

I frown. I would rather not retell our conversation to a larger audience, especially one that includes the Samos brood. "If we do, we risk Rash and Ibarem. Volo would enjoy using that particular advantage if he could."

"I agree. But it is an advantage. To be able to speak to him, watch him." He lowers his voice. Gauging my reaction. Letting me make the decision.

"Leave him in peace. We can relay with the Scarlet Guard on the ground. Get our people back."

He nods along. "Of course."

"No word about Cameron," I add, wincing as I say her name. She went back to Piedmont to be with her brother when we went on to Montfort. Chasing peace instead of war. And war found her again.

Tiberias turns thoughtful—sympathetic, even. Not for show, but truly. I try not to look at his handsome features as he looms above me. "She'll be okay," he says, just for me. "Can't imagine anyone taking her down."

Ibarem didn't mention seeing her among the prisoners, but he didn't think she was among the dead either. I can only hope she's among the ones who escaped, hiding in the swamps, slowly making her way back to us. Besides, Cameron can kill a man as easily as I can. More easily. Any Silver hunter would find her to be dangerous prey, with her ability to smother the strongest of their powers. She must have escaped. I will entertain no other possibility. I simply can't.

Especially because I need her for what I have planned.

"Farley might pop a blood vessel if we keep her waiting any longer."

"I would prefer not to see that," Tiberias grumbles after me.

FIFTEEN
Evangeline

Anabel stalls with such talent, as we wait for her chronologically impaired grandson. I'm torn between asking for a lesson and skewering her to the wall with the steel of my throne.

There are maybe a dozen people in the throne room, only those necessary for a war council. Red and Silver, Scarlet Guard and agents of Montfort alongside noble houses of the Rift and rebel Norta. No matter how many times I see it, I can hardly get used to the sight.

Neither can my parents. Today, Mother coils on her throne of emeralds like one of her snakes. She sinks back into black silk and rough gems, looking incomplete without some threatening predator pet at her knee. The panther must be indisposed today. She sneers while Anabel spins her wheels.

Father, on the other hand, sits in rapt attention, his acute focus locked entirely on Anabel even as she steps back. Trying to make her squirm. The head of House Lerolan does not, to her credit. I'm a magnetron. I know steel when I see it. And she has steel in her bones.

"Tiberias the Seventh needs a capital. A place to plant his flag."

She pauses, pacing for effect as she surveys the throne room. I want to scream, *Get on with it, old woman!*

What she should really do is go find Cal, wherever he might be, and drag him back here by the ears. The Piedmont base is lost, and this is a meeting of *his* own war council, not to mention my father's court. Making us wait isn't just rude; it's politically stupid. And a waste of my own precious time.

He's probably off arguing with Mare again, pretending not to look at her lips while he does it. The prince is terribly predictable, and I hope the pair of them will boil over into some not-so-secret secret relationship once more. *Will I be expected to guard the door?* I sneer to myself.

In a flash, I envision the life he wants for us all. The life he would subject all of us to. The crown on my head, his heart in her hand. My children threatened every second by any child she might have. My days spent bending to his will, no matter how gentle it might be. No matter how many days he might let me spend with my Elane, as long as he can spend his with Mare.

If only he wanted her more. If only I could make him want her more. But, as I told Mare back in Corvium, Cal isn't the abdicating kind. *You weren't either,* I remind myself. *Until you had a taste of the other side.*

At the thought, my insides flip. With excitement, with hope—and with exhaustion. I'm already annoyed by the prospect of tangling myself up with Cal and Mare more than I already am. Even if it's for my own happiness.

Stop complaining, Samos.

When General Farley and Mare finally enter the room, with Cal on their heels, I sigh to myself. Mare Barrow is not unfortunate-looking, but she's no lady. Cal must like that sort of thing. A rougher edge.

Warmth, dirt under fingernails, a rotten temper. I don't see the appeal. But he must.

"Ah," Anabel says, turning gracefully on her heel. "Your Majesty." Her face relaxes in relief as she beckons Cal to join her before the Samos thrones. The rest of the chamber looks on.

"So kind of you to join us, King Tiberias," my father says. He runs a hand through his silver beard, pulling at the strands. "I'm sure you've been made aware of our dire situation."

Cal sweeps into a low bow, surprising us. Kings and queens of the blood do not bow, not even to each other. Still he does it. "My apologies. I was detained," he says, offering nothing else. And giving us no opportunity to ask further as he waves Farley forward. "I believe General Farley has some good news, at least."

"Weighed against the loss of our foothold in Piedmont?" Father scoffs. "As well as any leverage we had over Prince Bracken? It must be very good news."

"I consider over a hundred of our people saved from Piedmont to be good news, sir," she says, also stooping into a quick, pitiful bow. "The Scarlet Guard and our Montfortan allies left only a skeleton garrison behind in Piedmont. There were a few hundred soldiers left behind at the base when Bracken struck. Right now, according to our intelligence, at least a third have made it into the swamps. The Scarlet Guard has contingents all over the region; we are more than able to retrieve and transport those who escaped to safety."

"How many dead, do you estimate?" Anabel says, now standing to the side with her hands clasped.

"A hundred, we think," she forces out, as if she can run right past the thought. But it seems to catch up to her as she repeats, more slowly, "A hundred dead."

"We lost more in Corvium," I say, tapping my fingers in time. "A hard trade, to be sure," I add, feigning sympathy before I send the Red woman into a rage spiral.

"It will be difficult, going forward, without the base," Ptolemus offers, making the painfully obvious point. Sometimes I think he just wants to hear himself talk, even in situations like this.

"Yes, that's true," Cal offers. "We still have the Rift, and all that entails, but we've lost two of our conquests in so many weeks. First Corvium—"

"We chose to destroy Corvium; we didn't lose it," Mare puts in, eyeing him with venom. I'd wager she's glad to be rid of that city.

Cal nods in begrudging agreement. "And now Piedmont," he continues. "It doesn't exactly present the image of strength, especially to any houses aligned to Maven who might still be swayed."

Mother angles on her throne, her knuckles glinting with a ransom of green gems. "What of Montfort?" She raises an eyebrow, searching the room. "I'm told you were successful in procuring their army?"

"I don't count my soldiers before they form up," Cal shoots back, harsher than he should be. "I trust Premier Davidson will deliver what his government promises, but I won't make decisions based on resources we can't see yet."

"What you need is a capital," Anabel says, circling the conversation back to her original song and dance. She paces, her red-and-orange regalia matching the light outside as it shifts toward sunset. "The city of Delphie will provide. The seat of House Lerolan will support the rightful king."

Cal avoids her gaze. "That's true. But—"

"But?" She snaps to him, stopping in her tracks.

He throws his shoulders wide, self-assured. "It's too easy."

Like a true grandmother, Anabel pats him on the arm with the manner of someone teaching a toddler a syrupy life lesson. "Nothing in life is truly easy, but you take the breaks you manage to find, Tiberias."

"I mean it *says* nothing," he answers, extricating himself from her grasp. "Not to the people of Norta, not to our allies, and certainly not to our enemies. It's an empty move. An expected move. Delphie is already mine in all but name, correct? I simply have to raise my flag and proclaim it."

"Yes," she says with a blink. "Why throw away such a gift?"

He sighs, a little exasperated, and I share the feeling. "I'm not. The gift is already given. You're right: We do need another stronghold, preferably in Norta. Another victory to prove our strength. Put fear in the Lakelands and Piedmont, as there is already fear in Maven."

"Where do you suggest?" I ask, leaning forward. If only to move along his proposal and end this miserable show.

He nods at me. "Harbor Bay."

"That was your mother's favorite palace," Anabel mutters at his side, forgetting herself. Cal doesn't respond, as if he doesn't hear her. "And governed by families loyal to Maven."

"It's strategic," he offers.

General Farley narrows her eyes. "It's another siege and another battle that could get hundreds of us killed."

"It has Fort Patriot," Cal fires back. "It services the army, the Air Fleet, and the navy armada." He ticks each one off on his fingers. His fervor is palpable, almost contagious. I can understand why he was made a general at such a young age. Maybe if I were a simple soldier, if I didn't know any better, I would willingly follow such a man into the jaws of death. "We can choke off a large piece of Maven's military, and perhaps win some of it in the process. At the very least, we'll be able to replace what we lost in Piedmont. Weapons, transports, jets. It's all there for the taking. And the city itself is a Scarlet Guard hot spot."

Father arches one sharp eyebrow. He is almost grinning, a ferocious sight. "A wise decision," he says. King Volo's agreement seems to take Cal by surprise, but it shouldn't. I know my father and see the hunger in him, the lust for power that he always keeps close. I bet he already dreams of Harbor Bay laid bare, a Samos flag raised over the conquered city. "Maven has taken a fort from us. We'll take a city from him."

Cal dips his head. "Yes, exactly."

"*If* you can take it," Mare replies, looking over her shoulder at him. Her brown-and-gray hair spins with her momentum, gleaming with a reddish hue in the sunset.

He tilts his head, eyes narrowed. "What are you saying?"

"Attack Harbor Bay. Attempt to overthrow the city. It's a good risk and we should try," she says. "But even if we fail, we can still strike a real blow to Maven's forces."

In spite of myself, I find this intriguing. I smooth my skirts, rippled sheets of speckled silver and white silk, as I lean toward her. "How, Barrow?"

She seems almost grateful, and shows me her teeth in what could be a reluctant smile. "Split open New Town, the techie slum outside Harbor Bay. Loose the Reds. It's a manufacturing hub, and it fuels Norta as much as any Silver fort. If we hit New Town, Gray Town, Merry Town—"

Again, Father is taken off guard. "You want to get rid of the tech centers?" he sputters, blinking at her like she told him to cut out his own beating heart.

Mare Barrow stands firm beneath his confounded gaze. "Yes."

Anabel eyes Mare in disbelief, almost laughing. "And what about after this war is done, Miss Barrow? Will you pay to rebuild them?"

Mare almost bites off a chunk of her own tongue to keep back a sudden, unchecked retort. She takes a breath, willing herself to something within the realm of calm.

"If destroying them means victory?" she says slowly, ignoring Anabel's questions. "Winning the country?"

Cal's eyes shift and he steadily nods his head. Agreeing because she's right—or because he's still a lovesick puppy. "Breaking up even one tech center will greatly disrupt Maven's ability to fight back, and it will spread unrest through his supporters. If the Reds see us as liberators, that can only help us," he says. "Add that to taking over Fort Patriot—he could lose control of everything north of the Bay, all the way to the Lakelander border." Thoughtful, he looks to his grandmother, opening his stance to her. "Cut off the entire region. And sandwich Maven between our already loyal Delphie, the Rift, and our new conquest."

I imagine Norta in my head, or Norta as she was a year ago. Lines carve across her lands, like a cook slicing up pieces of pie. One chunk to us, two more to Cal. *And the rest?* My eyes linger on the Red general and Mare Barrow. And I think of that insufferable premier a thousand miles away. *Which piece will they take?*

I know what they want, at least.

The whole damn pie.

Ptolemus makes a show of mulling over my proposition. He runs a finger around the rim of his water glass, listening to the crystal sing. The sound is haunting, an ethereal echo weaving through our dinner. The sky behind him is blood red against his silhouette. My brother is strong-jawed, broad, with my father's long nose and mother's tiny rosebud mouth. He looks more like her in this light, with the growing shadows gathering beneath his eyes, in the hollows of his cheeks and throat. His clothes are fresh and casual for him: clean, white linen, light enough for the summer season.

Elane watches him play the glass with distaste, one side of her mouth curled into the beginnings of a sneer. The waning light gleams in her hair, giving her a ruby halo finer than any crown. She drains her own wine, staining her lips with berry, grape, and plum.

I refrain for the moment, leaving my wineglass full and undisturbed. Usually a quiet dinner away from my parents and the prying eyes of an assembled court is an excuse to drink as much as I like, but we have business to attend to.

"It's a foolish plan, Evangeline. We don't have time to play matchmaker," Ptolemus mutters, his fingers gliding to a halt on the crystal rim. "Harbor Bay could be the end of us all."

I cluck my tongue. "Don't be a coward—you know Father wouldn't risk you or me in an ill-fated siege." *We are well-cared-for investments, Tolly. His legacy depends on our survival.* "Whether Cal wins Harbor Bay or not is of no interest me."

"We *do* have time, at least," Elane offers. She regards me with dark eyes that glimmer like star fall across a cornflower sky. "There can be no movement without the Montfort armies. And we still have to outfit our own soldiers, to build up for the siege."

I slip my hand under the table, feeling the smooth softness of silk on her knee. "This is true. And I'm not suggesting we ignore the war, Tolly. Just divide our attention. Look elsewhere when we can. Nudge pieces on the chessboard."

"Nudge pieces into bed, you mean," Ptolemus says with a dry grin. He moves his hand from his water to the stout glass of biting clear liquor and ice he's drinking. "You think I can influence Mare Barrow without getting my throat slit?" he asks, tossing back a fiery gulp. He winces, hissing air through his teeth. "I think it's best I stay away from her."

"I agree with that," I answer. Barrow promised to let my brother live. It's a promise I trust less and less every day. "But you can keep an eye on Cal. I thought he was immovable, completely dedicated to winning Norta, but . . . we may have an opportunity to stop that."

My brother throws back another blistering swig. "We aren't exactly friends."

I shrug. "But close enough to it. At least you were a year ago."

"And what a year it has been," he mutters, inspecting his reflection in the flat of his dinner knife. His face has not changed, his beauty is undiminished by war, but so many other things are different now. A new king, a new country, new crowns for us both. And a mountain of problems to go with each.

The tumultuous year has been worth the cost, at least to me. A year ago, I was Training harder than I ever had, preparing for the inevitable Queenstrial. I could barely sleep for fear of losing, even when victory was all but guaranteed. My life then was decided, and I reveled in knowing what was to come. In hindsight, I feel stupid and manipulated, seeing myself as the doll I was. Pushed toward a boy I could never love. And here I am again, trapped in the same place I've always been. But now I know better. I can fight it. *And maybe I can make Cal see reason the way I did. See what our worlds are, the strings we all dance upon.*

Ptolemus picks around his specially made meal of lean, barely seasoned chicken, wilted vegetables, and pale fish meat. It lies mostly untouched. Usually he wolfs down his bland, healthy foods, as if eating them quickly can disguise the lack of taste.

Elane is quite the opposite. Her plate is clean, showing no evidence of the rack of wine-soaked lamb we shared. "Indeed," she says. Her voice is quiet and measured. I try to read her thoughts on her face, her carefully worn expression of thoughtfulness. Is she remembering our lives a year ago? When we thought we would be happy beneath the Nortan throne together, living in a future built on our secrets? *As if we were ever truly a secret to anyone with eyes.*

"What about me?" Elane prods, putting her hand over my own. Her skin is the perfect balance of warmth against mine. "What part will I play in this?"

"You don't have to do much of anything," I answer, almost too quickly.

She puts her hand over mine. "Don't be stupid, Eve."

"Very well," I grit out. "Do as you have before, I suppose." Shadows are perfect spies, well suited to the intrigues of a royal court. To listen, to watch, safe behind a shield of invisibility. I don't like the prospect of using her in any capacity that might be dangerous, but like she said, we have time. We're at Ridge House. She wouldn't be any safer if I locked her up in my rooms.

Not exactly a bad idea . . .

Elane smirks a little and pushes away her plate, half in jest. Her nose wrinkles. "Should I go now?"

I tighten my grip on her hand, smirking. "You can finish off the wine, at least. I'm not completely heartless."

With a smile that stops my breath and leaves my pulse racing, she leans into me, her eyes drifting lazily to my lips. "I know exactly how much heart you have."

Across the table, Ptolemus finishes his drink, rattling the ice. "I'm right here," he grumbles, averting his eyes.

★ ★ ★

We have a week at least, if not two, before Davidson and his army return. Enough time to do what I can, with the added advantage of my own territory. Cal and Mare want each other, no matter how many obstacles might stand in the way. He requires only a very little push. If anything, a single word from Mare would send him scurrying to her bedroom. Mare, on the other hand, will be infinitely more difficult, married as she is to her pride, her cause, and that constant, unflagging rage she keeps burning in her chest. Of course, shoving the pair of them back together is only the first half of the endeavor. It's getting Cal to realize, as I have, the weight of a heart. And how much heavier it is than a crown.

A small part of me wonders if this is impossible. Cal might never wake up the way I did. His choices could be set in stone. But that can't be true. I see the way he looks at her, and I won't give up so easily. I only wish I could solve all this with my own two fists and a knife. That might even be enjoyable.

Quite honestly, anything would be more enjoyable than what I'm doing now, prowling through Ridge House at dusk, searching for Mare Barrow. This is a chore and a bore.

Elane is gone, somewhere on the other side of the estate. Keeping an eye on General Farley while Ptolemus works through his evening routine in the training arena. A routine that nicely aligns with Cal's own schedule. The would-be king is oh-so-married to his workouts, especially now that he can't burn off his energy with a certain lightning girl.

I pass through the gallery halls, dragging my fingers across statues of reflective steel and polished chrome as I go. Each one responds to my touch, rippling like water disturbed on a still pond. Outside, the sky purples, and stars prick to life across the western horizon. The city of Pitarus glows in the distance, several miles away. A reminder of the world still marching on. Reds and common Silvers now living under the spreading shadow of war. I wonder what that must be like, to read about battles and hear of cities torn apart, and know you have no part in the conflict. No influence. No power should war come to knock on your own door.

And it certainly will.

This war has many sides, and there's no way to stop what has already begun. Norta will be a rotting carcass one day, with the Rift, the Lakelands, Montfort, Piedmont, and whoever else is left all howling over her corpse.

I step onto the upper terraces, facing into the eastern darkness. A chill hovers on the air, and I think we might face a summer cold front before the week is out.

Barrow isn't alone when I find her, to my chagrin. She looks up at the stars while her Red boy stretches out at her side, long limbs splayed without thought for appearance. He seems a tangle of blond hair and bronzed, sun-damaged skin.

Kilorn glances at me first, pointing his rounded chin in my direction. "We have an audience."

"Hello, Evangeline," Mare replies. Her knees are drawn up to her chest. She doesn't move, her face tipped to the sky and the growing starlight. "To what do we owe this honor, Your Highness?" she drawls.

I chuckle and pause to lean against the railing edging the terrace tile. Biting to the last. "I find myself in need of distraction."

Mare shakes her head, amused. "I thought that's what Elane is for."

"She has a life of her own," I muse airily, forcing a shrug. "I can't expect her to live at my beck and call."

"You spent all your time pretending not to pine for her, and now here you are, in the same place again. But you're bothering me instead.'

Shrewd, she turns her gaze on me for a second, her brown eyes black against the deepening night sky. Then she looks back at the stars. "What do you want to know?"

"Nothing at all. I don't care where you and Cal scampered off to today, or why you both were so incredibly late to a meeting about the survival of your own people."

At her side, the Red boy tenses, his brows knitting together.

Mare tries not to rise to the bait or the implication. She waves a hand, dismissive. "It wasn't important."

"Well, if you ever need assistance with your unimportant doings, there are a few passages I can show you. Ways to get around the Ridge unseen." I tip my head, surveying her as she pretends not to listen to me. "Cal sleeps in the east wing, near my rooms, in case you're interested."

Her head snaps up. "I am not."

"Of course," I reply.

The Red boy glowers, his eyes a dark green, the color of my mother's stormiest emeralds. "Is this what you call distraction? Taunting Mare?"

"Not at all. I was wondering if Mare felt like sparring a bit."

She balks. "I beg your pardon?"

"For old time's sake."

She huffs, as if annoyed. But I see the familiar twitch in her. The need. A coil in the pit of her stomach, begging to be unwound. Barrow looks at her feet, blinking slowly. She runs one hand over the other, smoothing her fingers against her palm. Imagining the lightning, no doubt.

There is a particular pleasure in using our abilities for sport rather than survival.

"I've almost beaten you twice, Evangeline," Mare says.

I grin. "Third time's the charm."

She glares up at me, annoyed at the hunger inside herself. "Fine," she forces through gritted teeth. "One match."

Cal is also in the training arena, not that Mare or Kilorn knows it, though. The Red boy follows us wordlessly, fuming, but he does nothing to stop Barrow when I lead her into the specially made chamber.

The walls are glass, much like the rest of the Ridge. In the morning, it enjoys a full view of the sunrise. Perfect for early sessions. Now it looks out on the darkness, a vague, bruising blue, fading to black. Ptolemus and Cal occupy different ends of the training floor, ignoring each other as men do. My brother steadily works through a rotation of push-ups, his back straight and lean. Wren perches nearby, seated in the raised viewing area. She must be the healer on duty, to attend to anyone on the floor. But her attention is firmly fixed on Ptolemus and his flexing muscles. I could probably spear Cal through the middle and she wouldn't blink an eye.

The would-be king faces away from us at first, running a towel over his hair and his sweaty, flushed face. I watch Mare go stock-still next to me, as if frozen solid. Her eyes widen, running over his figure. I can only grimace, noting the damp material clinging to Cal's back and shoulders. Maybe if I felt some attraction to him—or to any man, for that matter—I might understand exactly why Mare looks like she's going to pass out.

At least this part of the plan is working. Barrow clearly has no objections to Cal's body.

"This way," I say to her, taking her by the arm.

Cal spins at my voice, towel still in hand. He startles at the sight of us. Well, the sight of *her*. "We're almost finished," he manages to sputter.

"Take your time. It doesn't make a difference to me," Mare replies, her voice and expression decidedly neutral. She lets me lead her away without protest, but her hand shifts, her arm moving quickly. Her fingers dig into my flesh, nails biting in warning.

"Kilorn," I hear Cal say behind us, greeting the Red boy with what sounds like a handshake.

Ptolemus looks up from his spot on the floor, not breaking his pace. I give him the slightest nod, pleased by our machinations. His eyes slide past me, though, to rest on Mare instead.

She looks back at him, murderous. It chills my blood.

I try not to shudder. Try not to think of my brother bleeding like hers did, dying as he falls, dying for nothing at all.

Pull yourself together, Samos.

SIXTEEN
Mare

"I'm not an idiot, Evangeline," I growl as the changing-room door slams behind us.

She just sighs, shoving a training suit into my chest. With practiced, even motions, she strips out of her simple gown and tosses it to the side, discarding the puddle of silk like a pile of trash. Naked but for her underclothes, she pours herself into a training suit of her own. Clearly custom-made for her, printed with a scaled design of black and silver.

Mine is less ornate. A simple navy blue. Furious with her scheming, I pull off my own clothes before forcing the suit on.

"You might as well just shove us into a closet and lock the door," I snarl, watching her braid her silver hair away from her face. She does it quickly, without thought, forming a crown around her head.

Evangeline only twists her lips. "Trust me, I would if I thought that might work on you. Him, yes. A closet would be enough. But *you?*" She throws her hands wide, shrugging. "You can never make anything easy."

"So, what, you're going to try to beat the shit out of me and hope he feels some pang of sympathy? Maybe have him nurse me back to health?" I shake my head, disgusted.

"It seemed to be working in Montfort." Her eyes paw over me. "Those Silences did a real number on you."

My eyes narrow. "Well, I have my reasons," I snap back, defensive. The memory is like a slap to the face, followed by a deep kick to the gut. I dig my nails into my palm, trying not to slide back into the sensation of being suffocated. In the mountain foothills, in a palace bedroom. From Silvers or from manacles. Without thinking, I circle my fingers around my wrist and squeeze. It almost makes me vomit onto the polished tile floor.

"I know," she replies, softer than before. If she were anyone else, I might think that was concern shadowing her voice. But not Evangeline Samos. She doesn't have the ability to feel sympathy toward Reds.

I cough, regaining some of my composure. "Even if you somehow did drive us back together, it wouldn't accomplish anything. You said yourself, he's not the abdicating kind. It's a stupid plan, Evangeline," I add, for both our sakes.

She looks at me sidelong, buckling a brace of daggers into place around her thigh. One side of her mouth lifts. I can't decide if it's a smirk or a smile. "We'll see."

All grace and agility, she crosses back to the door, gesturing for me to follow her out onto the waxed wood.

I do so reluctantly, pulling my hair back into a neat tail. Half of me hopes Tiberias is already gone. I focus my eyes on a spot between her shoulder blades.

"It's a stupid plan, not just because Tiberias already made his choice," I continue, sliding by her onto the training floor. Instinctively I shift my weight to the balls of my feet, almost bouncing as we walk. I grin back at her. "But also because you're never going to lay a finger on me."

She clutches a hand to her chest in false pain. The changing-room door slams shut behind her. "Mare, *I'm* supposed to be the overly confident one."

I keep grinning, walking backward to keep my eyes on her. I don't trust anyone to fight fair, especially her. "Maybe Elane can lick your wounds?"

Evangeline only raises her chin, looking down her nose at me. "She does, and frequently. Jealous?"

My face flares red. I feel the heat of it all down my neck. "No."

Now it's her turn to grin. She shoulders past me, knocking her arm into mine with marked force. I twist, but she keeps her body squared to me, never letting me pass out of her eye line. We start to resemble dance partners turning in a ballroom. Or wolves circling in the dark, predators testing each other. Searching for openings and weaknesses. Opportunities.

I have to admit, the prospect of blowing off some steam, and maybe getting a few good rounds in, has me excited. Adrenaline already surges through my veins in anticipation. A good fight, the kind without consequences or any real danger, sounds especially delicious. Even if it means admitting Evangeline was right about sparring.

Across the floor, I spy Kilorn looking on, with Tiberias standing beside him. Ptolemus keeps his distance. I don't waste my attention on them, even though Evangeline wants me to. She'll probably slice my face the second I drop my guard.

"You should train more," she says, her voice a bit louder. It echoes through the open space. I wonder if Evangeline was simply born without shame. "Work that stress out of your system in other ways. Or with other people."

I blink a rapid tempo, truly surprised. My entire body floods with warmth, and for once, it isn't Cal's fault. She grins at my discomfort, even tipping her head toward Cal and Kilorn a few yards away. Both of them are clearly listening to our conversation, while simultaneously trying to look like they aren't. Evangeline raises an eyebrow toward Kilorn, surveying him with a keen eye.

The implication dawns on me. "Oh, he's not—"

"Don't make me laugh," she sneers, taking another step backward. "I'm talking about that other newblood. The Montfort one. White hair, deep voice. Thin and tall."

Suddenly the heat coursing through my body turns icy, and I feel the hair on my neck rise. Cal pushes off the far wall. His eyes slide past me as he turns, dropping into his final routine. Push-ups. He works at a steady but fast pace, rising and falling. In the silence, I can just hear his rhythmic puffs of breath over the embarrassing thud of my own heart.

Why are my palms so sweaty?

Evangeline leers, more than satisfied. She dips her chin a little, nodding. Goading me on. *Do it,* she mouths to me.

"His name is Tyton, and he isn't here," I growl, hating myself as the words come out. Across the room, Cal quickens his pace. "This an even stupider plan," I add, leaning in to whisper as low as I can.

Evangeline tosses her head. "Is it?"

She breaks my nose with her skull before I can answer.

My vision spots: I see black, red, all colors in a dizzy spiral as I slump sideways, falling to my knees. Crimson blood spurts down my face, running into my mouth and over my chin. The familiar tang wakes something up. Instead of collapsing, I gather my legs under me and spring.

My head collides with her chest bone, and I hear a whoosh as the air goes out of her lungs. She stumbles, arms pinwheeling as she lands flat on her back. I swipe a hand across my face. It comes back sticky with blood, and I wince, trying to think through the yowling pain.

Across the floor, Cal is on his knee, eyes wide, jaw tight, about to get up. I shake my head at him and spit blood on the ground. *Stay where you are, Calore.*

He does.

The first dagger sings past my ear, a warning. I drop beneath the second, rolling across the smooth, almost slippery wood floor. Evangeline's laughter rings in my ears. I silence it quickly, lunging forward to grab her by the neck. She twists before I can get a good grip and shock her into submission. Only a few sparks touch her as she slides away, using the polished floor beneath us to her advantage. Still, my sparks are not gentle. She twitches as she moves, as if trying to brush off a particularly tenacious insect.

"You're better than I remember," she pants, coming to a stop a few yards away.

I clench one fist, the other pressed to my nose in an attempt to stem the river of blood. Not a pretty picture by any standard. Red spatters the floor already. "I could drop you where you stand if I wanted," I tell her, remembering what I learned with the electricons. Web lightning, storm lightning. But not Tyton's impossible brain lightning, which I still have no control over.

Evangeline shakes her head, smiling. She's enjoying this. "You're welcome to try."

I match her grin. *Fine.*

My lightning erupts, purple and white, blinding, burning, hissing through air already damp with sweat. She reacts with near-inhuman speed, her knives suddenly melded into a single, long band of steel. It pierces the floor as the lightning hits, making it ripple into the metal. It misses its mark with a flash that blinds even me.

Then her elbow cracks into my chin, throwing me backward. I see stars again.

"Nice trick," I mumble, rolling the blood around my mouth. When I spit this time, I think I hear a tooth ping off the floor. I confirm my suspicious with my tongue, feeling the sudden, unfamiliar gap in my bottom teeth.

Evangeline rolls her shoulders, her breath coming in uneven gasps. "Had to even the playing field somehow." With a small grunt, she yanks the spear out of the floor and twists it around her wrist. "Finished warming up?"

Slowly, I laugh.

"Oh yes."

I wait my turn, watching as Wren works on Evangeline's face. One of her eyes is swollen shut, colored a black and sickly gray-purple that deepens with the passing minutes. The other eyelid twitches every few seconds. Some busted nerve. She huffs at me, shoulders rising and falling, then winces, pressing a bloody hand to her side.

"Stay still," Wren mutters for the third time. She traces the side of Evangeline's face, and the swelling recedes in her wake. "You broke a rib."

Evangeline glares as best she can with one barely working eye. "Good fight, Barrow."

"Good fight, Samos," I answer with some difficulty. Between a split lip, the nose, and the bruised jaw, even talking stings. I have to lean, keeping my weight off my left ankle, which is steadily dripping blood from a neat gash above the knobbly exposed bone.

The three men stand back, giving us all the space we need to breathe.

Kilorn looks between Evangeline and me, his mouth hanging open in disbelief. And maybe fear. "Girls are weird," he mutters to himself.

Tiberias and Ptolemus bob their heads, agreeing.

I think Evangeline is trying to wink. Or the twitch is worse than I thought. Maybe I'm exhausted from the fight, but I almost laugh. With her, not at her. The realization sobers me up, and the pulsing, electric feel of adrenaline starts to fade. I can't forget who she is, and what her family has done to mine. Her brother, sitting just a few feet away, killed Shade. Robbed Clara of a father, Farley of a partner. Took a son from my mother and father. Stole a brother from me.

And I've tried to do the same.

Evangeline senses the shift in me, and her gaze drops, her face returning to carefully sculpted stone.

Wren Skonos is skilled: her skin-healer abilities restore Evangeline to fighting shape in a few minutes. The two young women contrast each other, Evangeline with her braided silver hair and pale skin, Wren with a long braid of gleaming jet hair cast over one bare blue-black shoulder. I don't miss the way Ptolemus watches the skin healer as she finishes up with his sister. His eyes linger on her neck, her face, her collarbone. Not her fingers or her handiwork. It's easy to forget he's married to Elane. At least in name. Though I suppose his sister spends more time with his bride, while he spends his own with Wren. *What a confusing family.*

"Now you," Wren says, gesturing for me to take Evangeline's spot. The Samos princess stands, stretching out her newly healed abdomen with the grace of a cat.

I sit gingerly, wincing as I do.

"Big baby," Kilorn chuckles.

In response, I grin aggressively, careful to show the new gap in my bloodstained teeth. He pretends to shudder.

Ptolemus laughs at the display, earning a glare from both of us.

"Something funny?" Kilorn sneers, stepping closer to the silver-haired man. My friend is too brave for his own good, with no regard for the magnetron prince who could cut him in two.

"Kilorn, I'll be along in a second," I cut in loudly, hoping to kill any conflict before it starts. I don't fancy wiping Kilorn's blood off the training floor. He glances at me, annoyed by my nannying, but I stay resolute. "It's okay, go on."

"Fine," he grinds out, careful to glare back at Ptolemus as he walks away.

When the echo of his footsteps dies, Evangeline smoothly stands, her intentions clear. She barely smirks as she leaves us too, her brother in tow, and they head in a different direction. She glances over her shoulder. I catch her gaze as it flicks between me and Tiberias, who is still silent, hanging close. Hope flares in her eyes. It only makes my heart sink.

It's a stupid plan, I want to say again.

Relief pulses from Wren's fingers, soothing each aching muscle and blooming bruise. I shut my eyes, letting her prod and pull me in different directions. Wren is Sara Skonos's cousin, a daughter of a noble house torn between two Calore kings. She served Maven before, working as my healer in Archeon. She watched me through those days. Kept me alive when the weight of Silent Stone would otherwise kill me. Kept my face and my body presentable for Maven's broadcasts. Neither of us could predict where we would be today.

Suddenly, I don't want the pain to go. It's an easy distraction from the want in my heart. As Wren's fingers dance along my jaw, stimulating bone growth to replace my lost tooth, I try not to picture Tiberias. But it's impossible. He's close enough to feel, the familiar warmth of him steady and constant.

Before, Evangeline said I was the difficult one. I think she's wrong. If she trapped Tiberias and me in a room together, I'd probably snap.

And would that be so terrible?

"You blush a great deal."

My eyes wrench open to see Wren hovering in front of my face, her full lips pursed. She blinks at me, her eyes the same stormy gray as Sara's.

"It's hot in here," I reply.

Tiberias blushes too.

We walk in silence. The glass walls of Ridge House look out on flat darkness, the long, clean lights of the passages bouncing back at us. Our reflections keep pace, and I'm struck by the sight of us side by side. I never forget how tall he is, but this is a firm reminder of how ill suited we are. Despite the training session, the sweat still clinging to his skin, Tiberias is a prince born, descended from three centuries of kings. He was bred to be better than anyone else, and it shows.

I feel smaller than usual beside him. A dirty little speck of scars and heartache.

He feels my gaze and glances down. "So, New Town."

Sighing, I brace myself for the discussion. "We need to do it," I reply. "Not just for the war, but for us. Reds. The tech towns are little more than enslavement." I've never set foot inside one, but I've seen Gray Town, a city of ash and smoke crowded onto the poisoned riverbank. I've seen Cameron's neck and her brother's, both harshly tattooed with their assigned place. Their "profession." Their prison.

I intend to leave New Town and the other slums as little more than corpses. Empty, dead. Doomed to rot and disappear and be forgotten.

"I know," Tiberias says softly, his voice tinged by blue regret. As I watch, his eyes darken. He knows what I'm really saying. If there were no crown between us, I would take his hand, kiss his shoulder. Thank him for even such a small display of support.

I bite my lip, blinking quickly to chase off the urge to touch. "I'll need Cameron."

Her name wakes him up. "Is she . . ."

"Alive?" I offer, letting the word echo off the tumbled stone of the passageway. It lingers, a question as much as a hope. "She has to be."

He slows his pace. "Farley still hasn't heard anything?"

"She will soon."

The Scarlet Guard contingents in Piedmont, now converging on the Lowcountry to evacuate anyone who escaped the base, should have reports back in a matter of hours. And Ibarem should have more intelligence to relay when Rash gets to the other survivors. There is no realm of possibility where Cameron isn't on the list. She's too strong, too smart, and too damn stubborn to get herself killed.

I can't even entertain the idea.

Not because we'll need her to help destroy her wretched home, New Town, but because she'll be one more body on my conscience. Another friend I pushed toward death.

I squeeze my eyes shut, trying not to think about the others who were still in Piedmont when Bracken took the base. Cameron's brother, Morrey. The teenagers of the Dagger Legion, rescued from one siege only to be caught in another.

Nothing compares to the agony of losing Shade, but losing the others could destroy me just as easily. How long will this last? How many people will we risk losing?

This is war, Mare Barrow. You risk everyone, every single day.

Especially the person next to me.

I bite my lip, almost drawing blood, to stave off the thought of Tiberias, *Cal*, dead and gone.

"It doesn't get easier," he says, the words ragged.

I open my eyes to find him staring ahead with the dogged focus he usually saves for a battlefield or a war council.

"What?"

"Losing people," he growls. "There's never a moment where it goes away, no matter how many times it happens. You never get used it."

An eternity ago, when I was Mareena Titanos, I stood inside a prince's bedchamber. He had books all over the place: manuals, treatises on war, strategy, diplomacy. Maneuvers and manipulations for gigantic armies and single soldiers. Calculations weighing the risk and reward. How many people could die and yet he'd still be able to claim victory. Back then it was a stark reminder of who he was, and whose side he was on.

It disgusted me to think of him as a person who would trade life so carelessly. Spill blood for another inch of progress. Now I've done the same thing. So has Farley. So has Davidson. None of us are innocent.

None of us will ever be able to forget what we do in these days.

"If it never goes away," I murmur, feeling as if I might be drowned, "it will eventually be too much."

"Yeah," he says hoarsely.

I wonder how close he is to his line, and how close I am to mine. Will we cross it on the same day? Is that the only answer?

Do we walk away, broken and beyond repair, together? Or apart?

His eyes smolder over me. I think he's asking himself the same thing.

Shuddering, I quicken my steps. A firm signal to both of us. "What's the plan for Harbor Bay?" I ask, looking down the long hall. It bridges this wing of Ridge House to the next, arcing over a weaving garden of trees and fountains barely visible in the darkness.

Tiberias matches my pace easily. "Nothing is set until Davidson comes back. But Farley has ideas, and her contacts in the city will certainly be of help."

I nod in agreement. Harbor Bay is the oldest city in Norta, a warren of Red criminals and their gangs. A few months ago, one of those gangs, the Mariners, tried to sell us to Maven as we searched for newbloods. But the tide is changing. The Reds of Norta are falling into line as the Scarlet Guard grows in power and notoriety. Our victories are having an effect on some, at least.

"There will be civilian casualties," Tiberias adds, matter-of-fact. "It isn't Corvium or Piedmont. Harbor Bay is a city, not a fort. Innocent people, Silver and Red, will be stuck in the middle of this." He flexes a hand, stretching out long, keen fingers before cracking his knuckles one by one. "We'll start with Fort Patriot. If we can take control there, the rest of the city will fall."

I've only see Patriot from afar, and the memory is vague. It's smaller than the Piedmont base, but better equipped and far more important to Maven's armies.

"Governor Rhambos and his house are sworn to Maven," I reply. "They're still firm allies." Due in no small part to me, since I killed his son in the arena during a failed execution. Of course, he was also trying to kill me. "They won't surrender easily."

Tiberias scoffs. "No one ever does."

"And if you win the city?" I prod. *If you survive?*

"Then I think we can get Maven to the table."

The name sends a jolt through me. At my collarbone, Maven's brand smarts and warms, itching for attention.

"He won't negotiate. He won't surrender at all." I feel sick at the thought of Maven's empty eyes, his wicked smile. The cloying, unbreakable obsession plaguing us both. "There's no point in it, Tiberias."

He winces at my use of his full name, eyes sliding shut for a second. "That's not why I want to see him."

The implication is clear. "Oh."

"I have to be sure," he grinds out. "I asked the premier about whispers in his country. If there are any newbloods like Elara. Anyone who might be able to help him."

"And?"

When I walked away from Tiberias in Corvium, he looked heartbroken, agonized. This is no different. Love has a way of cutting us apart like nothing else. "He didn't think so," he admits quietly. "But he said he would keep looking."

I lay a hand on his arm, still damp with sweat. My fingers know his skin as well as my own by now. He feels like quicksand. If I linger too long, I won't be able to escape.

I try to be gentle. "I doubt even Elara could fix him now. If he would let her."

His flesh flares hot beneath my hand and I pull away, remembering myself. He doesn't react. There's nothing he can say, and nothing he has to say to me. I know what letting go of Maven Calore looks like.

The passage ahead of us dead-ends at a T-shaped junction, trailing off to the left and right. His rooms to one side, mine to the other. We stare at the wall in silence, neither of us daring to move.

Speaking to him feels like a dream, a painful one. Even so, I don't want to wake up.

"How long?" I whisper.

He doesn't look at me. "Davidson will be here in a week's time. With another week to plan." His throat bobs. "Not long."

The last time I set foot in Harbor Bay, we were on the run. But my brother was alive. I wish I could go back to those days, hard as they were.

"I know what Evangeline's trying to do," Tiberias says suddenly, his voice thick with too many emotions to place.

I glance sidelong at him. "She's not exactly subtle about it."

He doesn't return the gesture, continuing to stare at the wall in front of us. Never leaning one way or the other. "I wish there were some middle ground."

A place where our names and our blood and our pasts don't matter. A place without weight. A place that has never been and will never exist.

"Good night, Tiberias."

Hissing, he clenches a fist. "I really need you to stop calling me that."

And I really need you.

I turn and walk toward my room, my footsteps echoing and alone.

SEVENTEEN
Iris

Archeon will never be my home.

Not because of the location, the size of the city, the lack of shrines and temples, or even my bone-deep, inborn disdain for Nortans. None of those things weigh as much as the emptiness I feel without my family at my side.

It is a hole I try to fill with training, prayer, and my other queenly duties, boring as some of them might be. But all are necessary. The most important is to stay in fighting shape. It would be easy to soften in my apartments of silk and velvet, waited on by Red servants tripping over themselves to bring me anything I want. It was the same in the Lakelands, but I never wanted to find solace in food and alcohol the way I do here. My training sessions also set a good balance, so I don't fall into the trap so many royals and nobles find themselves in. A trap Maven baits well. Many of the lords and ladies still supporting his reign seem more preoccupied with his parties and feasts than they are with the wolves at the door. *Idiots.*

Prayer is more difficult to come by in this godless country. There are no temples in Archeon that I know of, and the shrine I demanded be built for me here is small, a glorified closet tucked away in my apartments. Not that I need much space to commune with my nameless gods. But in the heat of high summer, the little room crowded with worn faces is hardly comfortable—even with my abilities circulating cool moisture through the air. I try to pray elsewhere, or at least feel my gods as the days pass, but it grows more difficult the longer I'm away from home. If I can't hear them, can they hear me?

Am I infinitely alone?

I suppose that is easier. I want no connection to Norta. Nothing to tie me to this place when Maven's brother overthrows him, unless my mother does it first.

My queenly duties are the only distraction from my isolation. Today my schedule takes me across the great bridge spanning the Capital River, to the other side of the city. As far away from Maven as I can still get within the diamondglass walls of Archeon. He appears outside the palace less and less, occupying himself with endless councils. Or long hours alone.

I hear the whispers of the servants. His clothes end up burned most days, charred beyond repair. It means he's losing control, or he doesn't care to keep himself in check. I think it could be both.

East Archeon mirrors the western side of the city, rising up from the river's edge to the cliff-like banks that roll off into gentle slopes. Everything is green this time of year. That reminds me of home, at least, though little else does. Even the water is wrong. Salt, not fresh, and tainted with the whispers of pollution from the tech slum upstream. They think the barrier trees get the most of it, but any nymph would know better with a single sniff.

The buildings here are tall and oppressive, all columns of granite and marble, their roofs crowned in sculpted birds with splayed wings and arched necks. Swans, falcons, eagles. Their feathers are copper and steel, polished to a blinding sheen.

Even in the middle of a war, the capital itself carries on in ignorant bliss. Reds walk the streets, marked by their crimson bracelets or the colors of their employing houses. Silvers in their transports roll between their destinations. Museums, the galleries, the theater are all still in operation without change or delay.

I suppose they're used to war, as the Lakelands are. Even within the borders of their own kingdom.

Today I'm attending a memorial luncheon, to honor the soldiers lost when Maven's brother and his rebels took Corvium. My Sentinels follow as always, garish in their flaming robes. Though I wear my usual colors, a nod to my native home, my blue blouse and jacket are trimmed with Maven's black and red. I feel wrong tainting myself like this, but no one would know from looking at me.

I smile and nod with the best, trading idle conversation with the many lords and ladies who wish to favor their new queen. No one says anything of any real use. It's all for show, even with the families of those who died. They clearly don't want to be here, preferring to face their grief alone. Instead they're trotted out like actors in a performance, put on display. One after the other explains how their loved ones died, all murdered by some Red terrorist or Montfort freak. A few are barely able to finish their speeches.

A clever tactic, one I'm sure my husband is behind. Anyone who might oppose this war, or even prefer Maven's brother on the throne, would have a difficult time holding to their convictions after such a show. And I play my part in it well enough.

"We are here today to mourn, but also to send a message. We will not be controlled by fear," I say as firmly as I can, staring out at a chamber crowded with sharp-eyed lords and ladies. They look on with rapt attention. Either to be polite, or to look for cracks. Hunt for weakness. Many, I know, would abandon Maven's Norta if they thought it was the right play for their houses.

It's my job to convince them otherwise. To stay. To fight. To die.

"We will not give in to the will of rebels and terrorists, and power-hungry criminals hiding behind false promises. We will not throw away everything our country is, our ideals, what Norta is built on, what our very lives are built on." My elocution lessons come to mind. Although I was never as talented at speechcraft as Tiora, I do my best. Holding a dozen gazes at once, never flinching, never stumbling. I clench a fist at my side, hidden in my skirts. "Norta is a Silver country, born from our strength, our power, our achievements, and *our* sacrifices. No Red will take what we have or change who we are. They are nothing to us, no matter who their allies are.

"Maven Calore will prevail. True Norta will prevail. Strength and power." I bite back a grin as I slip familiar words into the previously approved speech. "Let them face our flood."

Despite all my restraint, I can't help but smile as the crowd claps and cheers for Lakelander words. My mother's words. *Get used to it, Nortans. You'll bow to my colors soon enough.*

The heat wave has broken, making the walk back to my waiting convoy of transports pleasant. I want to linger on the street, enjoying the fresh air and gentle sunlight, and I move as slowly as I can. My Sentinels edge me along, their gloved hands and masked faces flanking me in practiced formation. We're ahead of schedule, by my count. I only have to return to the palace and prepare for tonight's dinner.

Still, the open transport door comes too quickly. With a huff, I step up and in, my eyes downcast as the door shuts behind me.

"Good afternoon, Your Majesty."

Two faces stare back from inside the transport, on the seats across from mine. One is familiar, and one I can guess at. Both are enemies.

I yelp, sliding back against the leather seating. On instinct I reach for the canteen of water I keep close. My other hand scrambles for the pistol under the backseat.

Fingers catch me under my chin, forcing me to look up. I expect them to belong to the singer, the uncle who can murmur away all thought in my head. Turn me inside out.

Instead I look up to find it's the grandmother who holds me, her bronze eyes alight and determined. I freeze, knowing exactly what Anabel Lerolan's touch can do. I picture her grip changing, shifting, and then my skull exploding open, spewing brain and bone all over the transport interior.

"Some advice, from one queen to another, my dear," Anabel says, still holding my chin. "Do not do anything stupid."

"Fine," I whisper, showing my empty palms. No gun, no canteen. No weapons but the air in the transport with us. I glance over her shoulder, at the silhouette of my driver and the Sentinel guard. Both on the other side of the glass.

Julian Jacos follows my gaze, then sighs. He raps his knuckles on the divider. Neither of my guards moves. "They won't be able to hear you for some time, I'm afraid," he says. "And they've been instructed to take the scenic route back to the palace." With an empty smile, he peeks out the window as we weave down unfamiliar alleys. "We're not here to hurt you, Iris."

"Good. I didn't think you were foolish enough to try," I shoot back, a little impeded by Anabel's lethal grip. "Do you mind?" I sneer at her.

With a patronizing bow of her head, she releases me, but doesn't back away. Keeping me within easy reach. Under my clothes, I try to gather moisture on my skin, pulling it from the air. And the cold, terrified sweat breaking out over my body. Maybe I can get some kind of shield ready if she tries to obliterate my fingers.

"If you want to send Maven a message, use the proper channels," I toss at her, throwing up a brazen wall of attitude.

She scoffs, looking disgusted. "This isn't a message for that wretched brat."

"Your grandson," I remind her.

She scowls but carries on. "I want you to pass along word to your mother. The way you usually do."

Sniffing, I cross my arms. "I don't know what you're talking about."

Anabel rolls her eyes and exchanges glances with Julian. He is far more difficult to read, his expression still and studious.

"I don't need to sing a confession out of you," Julian says plainly, "but you know I can if need be."

I say nothing. Do nothing. My face is still as the surface of an undisturbed pond. No confirmation either way.

The Lerolan woman barrels on anyway, looking down her nose at me. "Tell the queen of the Lakelands that the rightful king of Norta has no quarrel with her. And every intention of preserving the peace his usurper negotiated. That is, of course, if assurances can be made."

"You want us to stand down?" I sneer at her. She regards me with equal disdain. "An impossible thing."

"No, not stand down. Appearances must be maintained, of course," Anabel says, splaying those wretched fingers. I watch each one as they drum a rhythm against her leg. "But I'm sure we can find some compromise other than open war between our two sovereigns."

Once more, I glance at my guards behind glass, bewitched into ignoring us. The road through the window is unfamiliar. To me, at least. I grit my teeth. "He is no sovereign. Our alliance is not with Tiberias Calore, a traitor to his kingdom and his kind."

The uncle tips his head to one side, surveying me like a painting. He blinks slowly. "Your husband is better at that lie than you are."

Husband. The reminder of my place here and my position at Maven's side is an easy jab, but it stings nonetheless. "Lie or not, the people believe it," I hiss back at him. "Red and Silver, all over this country, they believe what they are told. And they will fight for the person they think Maven is."

To my surprise, Anabel nods. Her face falls, a picture of concern. "That's what we're afraid of. And that's why we're here. To prevent as much bloodshed as we can."

"Anabel Lerolan, you should have been an actress," I chuckle darkly.

She just waves a hand, glancing out the window. Her lips curve into the ghost of a smile. "I was a great patroness of the arts, a lifetime ago." For some reason, Julian glances at her, his eyes softening. She glances back, oddly reserved. Something passes between them. An unspoken word or a shared memory, perhaps.

Anabel recovers first, looking back to me. Her voice is stern, and I feel scolded without a reprimand. "When Tiberias wins the throne, he is prepared to offer land and money in exchange for Lakelander cooperation."

I raise one eyebrow, the only indication of any interest. After all, who knows where this might lead. Keeping options open is smart.

She knows what I'm doing and pushes on. "The entirety of the Choke ceded over."

Again I have to laugh, tossing back my head. The moisture against my skin, an almost shield, prickles against me. "Useless land," I scoff. "A minefield. You're gifting us with a chore."

The old queen pretends not to hear me. "And a betrothal to Tiberias's heir, a child of Calore and Samos. Twice royal, an heir to two kingdoms."

For appearance sake, I keep laughing. But my stomach churns with revulsion. She's trying to barter with an unborn child. Either mine or Tiora's. Our own flesh and blood. Consent be damned. At the very least, I agreed to my own arrangement. But doing the same to a baby? *Disgusting.*

"And what about your Red dogs?" I ask, leaning forward into her territory. It's my turn to push back. "The Scarlet Guard? The blood freaks of Montfort? Mare Barrow and her kind?"

Julian answers before Anabel can. She doesn't seem pleased—either by his manner or by his intent. "You mean the next step in our evolution?" he says. "It isn't wise to fear the future, Your Majesty. That never ends well."

"Futures can be prevented, Lord Jacos." I think of the other new-blood pet Maven lost, the one who could see too far into the future. I only heard rumors of him, but the rumors were enough. He could see every path as it changed. Even fates that would never come to fruition.

"Not this one." Julian shakes his head. I can't tell if he's happy or regretful. The man is an odd, sad soul. Tormented by a woman, no doubt, as most men like him are. "Not now."

I look between them and do not like what I see. Each could kill me if they wanted, and despite all my training, I would go down easily. But if they were here to murder me, they would have done it already.

"You've lost Piedmont, so you want the Lakelands," I mutter. "You know you can't win without one of us doing your dirty work."

"We do enough dirty work of our own, *Princess*," Anabel replies, her voice low and annoyed. She puts emphasis on my born title. She doesn't recognize Maven as king, so she wouldn't see me as a queen.

"You put so much stock in your Montfort shield," I tell them both. "Are their newbloods really enough to outweigh the might of our three nations?"

Julian folds his hands in his lap, thoughtful. He is more difficult to unsettle. "I think we all know that the full might of the Lakelands will never come to the aid of Maven Calore."

That smarts a little. I was stupid before, signaling what I did to Mare through that newblood in the Piedmont prison. For no reason other than to prove I could. Clearly she passed on the message. Or maybe we're simply that transparent. I bristle, firing back, "Just as *we* all know your Red alliance will not last. That it is another powder keg close to open flame."

This does make Julian uncomfortable. He shifts, thrown off balance, and a slight gray tinge colors his cheeks. Not so with Anabel. She thrives, grinning, as if I've just served her a delicious meal. Even though I don't know how, I feel as if I've misstepped.

The woman puts out her hand and I jerk back, out of her grasp. She seems amused by my fear. "There is something else we can offer."

Julian's blush deepens and he frowns, dropping his gaze. Breaking eye contact with me. Essentially putting down his only weapon. I could move against him right now and get the upper hand. But Anabel is too close, too lethal.

And, I have to admit, I want to know what the last piece of her bargain is.

"Go on," I breathe, almost inaudible.

Her smile is wide, pointed. And while Maven is his mother's son, I see some of him in his grandmother. In the sharp grin, and the scheming mind. "Salin Iral put a knife in your father's back," she says. I flinch at the memory. "I assume you would like to have a conversation with him?"

I respond without thinking. A mistake. "I can think of some things I would like to say, yes," I mutter quickly. The phantom taste of blood fills my mouth.

"I'm sure you know why it was done," she says.

Pain pricks at my edges. My father's death is still an open, oozing wound. "Because this is war. People die."

Her dark eyes, like molten bronze, widen. "Because Salin Iral did as he was commanded to do."

Any sorrow I feel for my loss steadily turns to rage. It licks up my spine, hot and begging.

"Volo," I can't help but hiss. The name of the Samos king sours in my mouth.

But Anabel knows how to push me. "Would you like to speak with him too?" she breathes, almost seductive in her offer. At her side, Julian returns his gaze to me, his lips pressed together. The lines of his face seem to deepen.

I drag a long breath through my teeth.

"Yes, I certainly would," I breathe. "What is your price?"

Grinning, she tells me.

They melt into the city like ghosts. Simply stepping out of the transport at a crowded corner, disappearing into the ranks of Red servants and more common Silvers. My guards don't seem to notice or mind, falling back into our prescheduled route. Julian Jacos did his work well, and when I return to the palace, nothing seems amiss. None of my guards seem to realize they've lost twenty minutes to the abyss of a singer's charm.

I make a quick escape, intending to go to the shrine tucked away in my rooms, needing the familiar and blissfully empty space to collect my thoughts.

Mother must be informed of everything that just transpired, and as soon as possible. But I can't trust that my message won't be intercepted, even through the deepest back channels. Anabel's offer could get me beheaded, burned, mutilated, and murdered. This message can only be passed face-to-face.

I manage to get up to my rooms safely. With a wave of dismissal, I leave my Sentinels at the door to my chambers, as usual. Only when I'm truly alone do I realize what I've done, and what has just happened.

I start to shake, my hands trembling as I step through my receiving salon. My pulse races. I think of Salin Iral and Volo beneath my hands, drowning, dying. Paying the ultimate price for what they did to my father.

"Traffic on the bridge?"

I freeze, eyes wide. His voice always puts a fear in me. Especially when it comes from my bedroom.

My instincts tell me to run. Damn myself. Escape the city somehow, find a way home. An impossible thought. I force myself forward instead, through the double doors leading into my sleeping chamber. Into what could be my coffin.

Maven lazes across the sprawl of my silk blanket, one hand tucked behind his head. The other resting on his chest. His fingers drum in time, bone-white against one of his thousands of black shirts. He seems bored and angry. A bad combination.

"Good afternoon, Wife," he says.

I glance around the room, at the many fountains I keep close. Not for decoration, but my own protection. I feel each as it ripples and chases, more than enough to use should this turn ugly. If he knows what I've done. What I entertained. What I agreed to do.

"What are you doing here?" No use playing the part of doting wife, not while we're alone. He'll know something is wrong, if he doesn't already.

Or, I realize with a cold chill, he could simply be here to fulfill our marital duties, neglected as they've been. I'm not sure what terrifies me more. Even though I agreed to this. Knew this was part of the bargain. Knew *he* was part of our alliance. Perhaps I've overestimated his obsession with Mare, or it has simply worn away.

He turns his head to look at me, one cheek pressed against the silk. A flop of black hair falls across his forehead. He seems younger today. Albeit more manic. His eyes are barely blue, overtaken by wide black pupils.

"I need you to send word to the Lakelands," he says. "To your mother."

Stay still. Don't move. Don't show any relief, I tell myself, even as my knees threaten to give out.

"To say what, exactly?" I reply, donning a mask of indifference.

He moves gracefully, standing with smooth motions. Though Tiberias is the warrior brother, Maven is not without his own physical skill. "Walk with me, Iris," he says, smiling sharply.

I have no choice but to obey. However, I ignore his outstretched arm, keeping a safe distance of a few inches between us.

He doesn't speak, forcing us to walk in silence as we leave my rooms together. I feel dangled on the end of a string, suspended over a pit.

My heart hammers in my chest, and I do everything I can to maintain my mask through long minutes of walking. Only when we reach the throne room, empty at this time of day, does he turn to look at me.

I brace myself for the blow, preparing to fight back.

"Tell your mother to prepare her fleet and her armies," he says, as if remarking on my dress.

Surprise replaces my fear.

He keeps walking, mounting the raised steps to pass behind the throne. I edge around the influence of Silent Stone. Even the brush of it makes me gulp.

"What—*now*?" I sputter, raising a hand to my throat. My mind races as I study Maven, looking for the lie. It's barely been a week since Bracken took back Piedmont. Surely the brother's coalition is still regrouping. "Are we under attack?"

"Not at the moment." He shrugs, indifferent. And still moving. Still drawing me along after him. "But soon enough."

I narrow my eyes, feeling unease deep in my gut.

Maven approaches one of the doors behind the throne, heading for what are supposed to be the queen's public chambers. A library, a study, sitting rooms. I don't use them, preferring my shrine instead.

He passes through and I have to follow.

"How do you know that?" I ask. Dread pools in my stomach.

He shrugs again. The room is dark, the windows heavily curtained. I can barely make out the stripes of white and navy blue, the colors of the last queen to use this place. These rooms have an air of dust and disuse.

"I know my brother," Maven says. "What's more, I know what he needs, and what this country needs from him."

"And that is?"

He smirks at me, opening another door across the sitting area. His teeth flash in the semidarkness. He does all he can to seem a predator.

Something about the next room makes me pause. Makes me *ache*, deep in my marrow.

I keep still, seemingly unaffected. But my heart pounds. "Maven?" I murmur.

"Cal has allies, but not enough. Not in Norta." The young king drums his fingers together, his eyes glazing as he thinks out loud. He remains in the doorway, on the edge. Never stepping through. "He wants to sway more of my subjects to his side, but he isn't a diplomat. Cal is a warrior, and he'll fight to win favor among the High Houses. To show how *worthy* he is of my crown. He has to tip the scales. Make the nobles believe he isn't a hopeless cause."

Maven isn't stupid. Predicting the movements of his opponents is his strong suit, and the only reason he's been able to survive—and win—for this long.

I never take my eyes off the doorway, straining to see what it holds. The room beyond is pitch-black. "So he'll attack another city. Maybe even the capital."

Maven tsks like I'm a stupid child in the classroom. I fight back the urge to stick his head into the nearest fountain.

"My brother and his coalition intend to strike Harbor Bay."

"How can you be sure?"

The king purses his lips. "It's his best option. The fort, the ships in port—not to mention its sentimental value," he adds, spitting out the words with revulsion. "His mother loved that city." His fingers play with the latch on the open door. It's a strong-looking lock. More complicated than it should be.

I swallow hard. If Maven thinks Cal will go for Harbor Bay, I believe him. And I don't want my mother, or our armies, anywhere near the conflict. Excuses spring up in my head, ready to wield.

"Our fleet is still in the Lakes," I offer, sounding apologetic. "It will take time."

Maven doesn't seem surprised, or even concerned, by my words. He passes closer to me, his hands inches from mine. I can feel the sickly heat of his skin. "I expected as much," he says. "So I'll give your royal mother some incentive."

My stomach twists. "Oh?"

His smile flashes. I hate it.

"Have you ever been to Harbor Bay, Iris?"

"No, Maven." If I were a lesser person, untrained, my voice would tremble. Not with the fear he wants from me. But with rage. It ripples through me, furious as a storm.

Maven doesn't seem to notice. Or care. "I certainly hope you enjoy the visit," he says, still grinning.

"So I'm bait," I hiss.

"I would never call you bait. But *incentive*." He heaves a sigh. "Yes, I believe I did call you that."

"How dare you—"

He speaks over me, his voice louder than before. "With you in the city, ready to lead the defense, I'm certain your mother will do all she can to uphold her end of our alliance. Don't you agree?" He doesn't wait for me to answer, and his voice turns ragged. A fist clenches at his side. "I need the armies I was promised. I need reinforcements. I need nymphs in the harbor to drown that city and everyone in it."

Hastily, I nod. If only for the sake of placating him. "I'll tell her. But I can't guarantee—"

Maven closes the distance between us and I tense. His fist closes over my wrist, grip tight, as he pulls me forward. I bite back the instinct to fight. It will only end in pain. "Just as I cannot guarantee your safety there," he says, stopping just short of the dark doorway. His lips twitch, amused. "Or even here."

At some hidden signal, the doorway behind us crowds with a troop of Sentinels. They are all broad, masked and robed, glittering in their black jewels and flaming silks. My guards—and my jailers.

I realize what this is. What the next room, the black place where Maven stands so easily, is supposed to be.

His throne isn't the only thing here made of Silent Stone.

The threat gleams, the edge of a razor pressed against my neck. His grip tightens, fingers cold on my skin. There will be no running from Maven's commands.

"And what about you, my brave and just king?" I snarl, still staring into the black room. I can just feel it, the numbing edge of Stone.

He doesn't rise to the insult. He's too smart for that.

"Don your armor, Iris. Wait for the storm. And hope your mother moves as quickly as my brother can."

EIGHTEEN
Mare

There are no stars this close to New Town. The sky around the slum is permanently choked with a haze of pollution. It smells foul and poisonous, even on the outskirts, where the noxious fog is thinnest. I draw up the kerchief around my neck, breathing through the fabric instead.

The other soldiers around me do the same, pulling faces at the toxic air. But not Cameron. She's used to it.

Relief washes over me every time I look at Cameron, her lean, dark form moving nimbly through the pitch-black forest. She's so tall, easy to pick out among the dozens moving with us. Kilorn keeps close to her side, his silhouette familiar. As I watch the pair of them, my relief quickly melts to shame.

Cameron escaped the Piedmont base, fleeing into the swamps with her brother and a few dozen more survivors. Many died where she did not. Red soldiers of the Dagger Legion, children we swore to keep safe. Newbloods of Montfort. Newbloods of the Notch. Silvers. Reds. So many dead it makes my head spin.

And I'm sending her right back into danger.

"Thanks for doing this, Cam," I murmur, my voice almost inaudible. As if a simple thank-you means anything.

With a grin, she glances over her shoulder at me. Her teeth gleam in the weak light of our lanterns. In spite of the dire circumstances, I've never seen her smile like she does tonight.

"As if you could get this done without me," she whispers back, almost teasing. "But don't thank me, Barrow. I've been dreaming about a day like this since I was a little girl. New Town is *not* going to know what bleeding hit it."

"No, it will not," I mutter to myself, thinking of the morning ahead of us.

Fear and nerves carve me up, as they did on the flight from the Rift. We're about to storm the tech slum she was born in, a place hemmed in by walls and guards and decades of oppression.

And we're not the only assault on the move. Miles to the east, the rest of our coalition is heading toward Harbor Bay

The Rift soldiers will attack from the sea, with the Laris fleet ready on the wing. Tiberias and Farley are in the tunnels by now, ready to lead the main bulk of the army up into the city. I try to picture the three-pronged assault in my mind. It's nothing like any battle I've survived before. Neither is this, separated from the fire prince, from Farley. From so many dear to me. At least I have faithful Kilorn still resolute at my side. There is some symmetry here, I guess. We return to who we were before. Creeping in alleys, clad in dirty clothes. Our faces obscured and unfamiliar. Shadows. Rats.

Rats with sharper teeth and longer claws.

"These trees are rotting," Cameron says aloud, drawing a hand down the black bark of a barrier tree. One of thousands in this cursed forest. Created by greenwardens, the trees were meant to trap and filter out pollution from the slum. They ring all the tech towns, marching up to their walls. "Whoever grew these doesn't care to maintain them. Whatever they're supposed to do, they aren't really doing it anymore.

"They think they're just poisoning us," she continues, her voice seething. "They're poisoning themselves too."

We move under the cover of Haven shadows and the muffling ability of Farrah, one of my old newblood recruits from the Notch. Instead of disguising our fifty troops individually, they mask us as a group, throwing their abilities over us like a blanket. We're invisible and inaudible to anyone outside their circle of influence, able to pass in plain sight. We can see and hear one another, but no one a few yards away can see or hear us.

Premier Davidson steps softly behind me, flanked by his own guards. The vast majority of the Montfort army will assault Harbor Bay, but a few key newbloods are here with him. They don't have their usual uniforms. Even Ella, Tyton, and Rafe have their hair covered, wrapped in scarves or a hat. They all blend in with the rest of us, dressed in discards—rags, hastily patched jackets and threadbare pants. All tech-issue clothing, courtesy of the Whistles network smugglers in Harbor Bay. I wonder if a thief passed them on. A girl with no other choice than to steal. No other way to survive.

The air thickens as we approach, and more than a few of us cough, gagging on the taste of smoke and fumes. The sickly sweet scent of gasoline settles over us, as if the dirt beneath our feet is saturated with it. Overhead, the greasy red leaves of the barrier trees tremble in a slight wind. Even in darkness, they look like blood.

"Mare." Kilorn nudges my arm. "Wall's coming up," he says in warning.

I can only nod in thanks, squinting through the trees. Indeed the squat, thick walls of New Town loom ahead. Not as impressive as the diamondglass of a royal palace, or as intimidating as the high stone walls of a Silver city. But still an obstacle to overcome.

Leadership suits Cameron, though she'll never admit it. She squares her shoulders as we approach, drawing herself up to her towering height. I wonder if she's even turned sixteen yet. No teenager should be as calm, collected, and fearless as she is.

"Watch your feet," she hisses over my head, letting the message pass through our ranks. With a click she switches on her dim, red flashlight. The rest of us follow suit, except for the Haven shadows. They only deepen their focus, masking the hellish glow. "The tunnels come up behind the tree line. Drag your toes. Look for thick undergrowth."

We do as she says, though Kilorn covers far more ground than I do. He kicks his long legs through the dead and rotting leaves, feeling for the telltale hardness of a trapdoor. "Don't suppose you remember exactly where it is, do you?" he grumbles at Cameron.

She looks up from a crouch on the ground, her hands in the leaves. "I've never been in the tunnels before," she huffs. "Not old enough to make the smuggle runs. Besides, that's not my family's way," she adds, her eyes narrowing. "Keep your bleeding head down, that's what we held to. And see where it got us?"

"Digging through the dirt for a hole," Kilorn answers. I hear the smirk in his voice.

"Leading an army," I offer instead. "That's where you got *yourself*, Cameron."

Her expression changes, tightening. But her lips pull into something close to a smile. A sad one. I understand it. She said before, in Corvium, that she was done with the killing. Done with the lethal burden of her ability to silence and suffocate. Her goal now is to protect.

Defend. Though she has more cause than most to feel rage, to seek vengeance, she has the infinite strength to turn away.

I don't.

The tunnels glow with our red light, bathing us all in crimson. Even the Silvers sworn to Cal or the Rift. The Haven shadows, the Iral silks. A dozen of them, scattered into our number. All of them, for a moment, red as the dawn.

I keep an eye on them as we walk, passing beneath the walls of New Town. They have orders from their lords and kings. I don't trust them, not by a long shot, but I trust their allegiances. Silvers are loyal to blood. They do as blood commands.

And we are not helpless either.

Ella and Rafe bring up the rear of our number. Both seem energized by our mission, itching for another fight after our defeat in Piedmont. Tyton walks closer to the middle of our party, letting me take the lead, so that the electricons are evenly dispersed. His eyes seem to glow in the low light.

Cameron taps her hand at her hip. Counting steps. Her keen eyes watch the walls with blistering focus. She slides a finger over the place where the packed dirt fades to concrete. It shifts something in her, shadowing her features.

"I know what it feels like," I whisper to her. "To come back as something else."

Her eyes snap to mine, one brow raised. "What are you talking about?"

"I only went home once after I found out what I was," I explain. *It was only a few hours. But more than enough time to change my life again.*

Remembering that visit to my old village is difficult, if not painful. Shade wasn't dead yet, but I thought he was. And I joined the Scarlet Guard to avenge him. All while Tiberias waited outside, leaning against his rebuilt cycle. Still a prince. *Always a prince.* I try to shake off the memory like a bad dream. "It won't be easy, to look at familiar things and see something you don't recognize."

Cameron only tightens her jaw. "This isn't my home, Barrow. No prison is ever a home," she murmurs. "And that's all these slums are."

"So why not leave?" I want to smack Kilorn for his lack of grace, as well as for the rudeness of the question. He catches my glare and sputters. "I mean, you have these tunnels . . ."

I'm surprised by her answering grin. "You wouldn't understand, Kilorn," she says, shaking her head with a roll of her eyes. "You think you grew up hard, but this is harder. You thought you were tethered to that river village, trapped by what? A little money? A job? Some guards looking at you sideways?" He flushes deeper as she rattles off each word in time. "Well, we had this."

Her hand strays to her collar, pulling it aside to show her tattooed neck in full. Her occupation, her place, her prison stamped in permanent ink. *NT-ARSM-188907.*

"Every one of us is a number up there," Cameron continues, jabbing a finger at the ceiling. "You disappear, the next number in line disappears too. And not well. Whole families have to run. And where do they go? Where *can* they go?"

Her voice trails off, the echo dying in the red shadows.

"I hope that's in the past now," she mumbles, if only to herself.

"I promise it is," Davidson replies from a polite distance. His angled eyes crinkle when he tries to offer a bitter smile. If nothing else, the premier is a firm reminder of what can be. How high someone like us can climb.

Cameron and I exchange glances. We want to believe him.

We have to believe him.

I tie my kerchief tighter into place, blinking harsh tears out of my eyes. The air itself seems to burn, and my skin smarts. It's both dry and damp at the same time, unnatural and just plain *wrong*.

It isn't dawn yet, but the smoky sky is lighter than it was before as the sun begins its approach from the east. A high-pitched, electric whistle blows at the end of the alley, then echoes out over the slum, from one factory to another, signaling the massive migration that is the shift change.

"The dawn walk," Cameron mutters.

The sight makes my breath catch. Hundreds of Red workers flood the streets of New Town. Men and women and children, dark-skinned and pale-faced, old and young, all trudging together through the poisoned air. Like some grim parade. Most look at their feet, exhausted by their work, broken by this place.

It feeds the rage always burning in my heart.

Cameron slips into their midst, with Kilorn and me on her heels. Behind us, the rest of our band melts into the countless dirty faces, blending in with ease. I look back, finding Davidson, who follows at a safe distance. In the growing light, his face tightens, betraying the slight lines of age and care worn into his skin. He fists one hand into his jacket, close to his heart, and gives me a curt nod.

Our steady parade of workers empties onto another street, wider than the rest, lined with stoic block apartments organized like regimented soldiers. Another factory shift hurries toward us from the opposite direction, intent on taking our place.

Gently, Cameron nudges me to the side, moving me in line with the rest of the Red tech workers. They step quickly, in time with one another, creating space for the new shift to pass. As they do, Cameron shoves her fist into her own jacket as Davidson did.

So do I.

Marking ourselves.

The escorts are not Scarlet Guard. Or they weren't, before all this started. Their allegiances are to one another, to their slum. To small resistances, the only kind possible in here.

Ours is a tall, black-skinned man, willowy like Cameron, his hair braided and pulled back into a tight, neat bun streaked with shades of gray. Cameron's foot taps as he approaches, her body almost radiating energy. He reaches us and clasps her arm,

"Daddy," I hear her breathe as he pulls her into an embrace. "Where's Mama?"

He covers her hand with his own. "She's coming off shift. I told her to keep her head down and her eyes open. First bolt of lightning, she's running."

Cameron exhales slowly. She dips her head, nodding to herself. The dark around us continues to lift, fading to lighter shades of blue as dawn approaches. "Good."

"I hope you didn't bring Morrey here," her father adds, his tone light but scolding. And so familiar. It reminds me of my own parents, chiding me for a broken plate.

Cameron's head snaps back to find her father staring, eyes a dark and deep black. "Of course not."

Even though I don't want to interrupt their reunion, I have to. "The power station?" I prod, looking up at the elder Cole.

He glances down at me. He has a kind face, no mean feat in a place like this. "NT has six, one for each sector. But if we cut off the central hub, that will do the job."

Mention of the plan snaps something in Cameron. She straightens, focuses. "This way," she says sharply, beckoning to us.

The shift change is much more crowded than even the worst days in the Stilts market. Silver officers in black uniforms keep watch. Not on the ground, on the filthy streets, but from the overarching walkways and windows of foreboding guard posts. Officers and posts I know well enough. I watch them as I pass, noting their disinterest. It's not the same disinterest Silvers show us at court, their way of making us feel like less than we already are. But a boredom. A disuse. Silvers aren't assigned to slum towns because they're warriors of important bloodlines. This isn't a post anyone would envy.

The guards of New Town are far weaker than any enemy I'm used to. And they have no idea we're already here.

Cameron's father looks her over, thoughtful as we walk. I shiver when his gaze passes over me, then back to his daughter. "So it's true, then. You're something . . . different."

I wonder what he's heard. What the Scarlet Guard told their contacts in New Town. Maven's propaganda and poisoned broadcasts made clear the existence of newbloods. Does he know what his daughter can do?

She holds his stare, his equal. "I am," she says without flinching.

"You walk with the lightning girl."

"I do," she replies.

"And this is . . . ?" he adds, eyeing Kilorn.

With a loopy grin, Kilorn touches his brow and angles himself into a shallow bow. "I'm the muscle."

Mr. Cole almost laughs as he takes in Kilorn's tall but lean form. "Sure, kid."

The buildings around us grow higher, stacked precariously. There are cracks in the walls and windows, and every block needs a fresh coat of paint—or just the good wash of a rainstorm. The workers around us start to peel off, heading into different apartment structures with waves and calls. Nothing seems amiss.

"We're grateful for your help, Mr. Cole," I say under my breath, keeping my focus ahead. A few Silver guards stand on an arch some yards away, and I lower my face as we pass.

"Thank the elders, not me," Mr. Cole answers. He doesn't bother hiding from the guards. He's nothing to them. "They've been ready for this for a long time."

My throat tightens in shame. "Because someone should have done something a long time ago." *Someone like you, Tiberias. You knew these places existed, and for who. For what.*

Cameron grits her teeth. "At least we're doing something now." At her side, she clenches a fist. With her ability, she could kill the two guards above us if she wanted. Drop them right off the arch.

But we pass by without incident, stepping into the shadow of the slouching, gray slum apartment building at the end of the residential street. It looks like the toy blocks of a giant child, piled high against the hazy blue. One section is taller than the rest, dotted with grimy, dim windows.

It's where we need to be.

Mr. Cole glances at me, then at the structure. "Up you go, lightning girl," he says, his voice soft. "Get high, get loud. That's the plan, isn't it?"

"Yes, sir," I mumble. Already I call to the lightning, feeling it respond deep in my bones.

When we reach the base of the building, we're almost alone on the street, joined only by shift stragglers. Cameron turns to her father, eyes wide. "How much time do we have?"

He turns over his wrist and glances at his watch. Then Mr. Cole frowns, the lines cutting deep. "None," he says. "You have to go."

She blinks rapidly, her jaw working. "Okay."

"Sir, I believe this is yours," Kilorn says, reaching into his jacket. He pulls free a small pistol, and extra rounds of ammunition, neat in their case.

Mr. Cole looks at the gun like a snake that might bite. He hesitates, until Cameron takes it from Kilorn and presses it to his chest. She widens her eyes, pleading.

"Point and click, Daddy. Don't hesitate," she says with furious need. "Silvers won't."

Slowly, gingerly, he tucks the gun away into the satchel at his side. As he turns, I catch sight of the tattoo on his neck.

"Fine," he breathes, dazed. I think all this is starting to catch up with him. Then he clears his throat. "The new-shift techs at the hub are informed. They'll power down the city with your first strike, after the signal crosstown. Coordinate the systematic shutoff with your storm. Silvers won't know we're in on it. Buy some time."

This part of the plan was eagerly arranged by both the Scarlet Guard and their contacts within the slum city.

"Everyone knows about the charges?" I ask, if only to be sure. The

Scarlet Guard who slipped in with us are already scattered around the city, planting their bombs. Laying our traps.

Cole's expression darkens and he scowls. "Everyone who can be trusted. We might have our own resistance, but we've got informants all over."

I swallow hard, trying not to think what might happen if the wrong person knew what was about to happen. Maven himself might descend on New Town and crush our insurgency. Bring this poisoned, polluted ground smashing down on us all. And if we fail here, where will that leave the other slum cities? What will it prove?

That nothing can be done. That these people can't be saved.

Kilorn notes my unease and nudges my shoulder, if only to snap me out of it. Cameron is, understandably, more concerned with her father.

"Okay," she says, "just watch where you bleeding step."

Cole clucks his tongue. "Don't curse, Cam."

Without warning, Cameron smiles and throws her long arms around her father's neck, hugging him tightly. "Kiss Mama for me," I hear her murmur.

"You'll kiss her yourself soon enough," he whispers back, lifting her slightly off the ground. Their eyes shut in unison as they hold on to each other. And this fragile, fleeting moment.

I can't help but think of my family, so far away. Safe. Tucked up in the mountains, protected by thousands of miles and another country sworn to fight with us. Living with hope for the first time in too many years. It isn't fair, especially to Cameron, who has survived far worse than I have. But I'm glad I don't have to shoulder the burden of my family's safety alongside everything else. I can barely handle the danger to the people I love who are still fighting.

Cameron pulls away from her father first. It's an act of untold strength. As is letting her go. Mr. Cole steps back, sniffing, looking at his feet. Hiding a sudden redness around his eyes. Tears prick at Cameron too, and she scuffs her boot against the dirty street, kicking up dust in distraction.

"Shall we?" she says, turning to me. Her eyes are wet.

"Let's climb."

We watch the city with hawk focus, each of us at a window looking out in a different direction. I wipe at the glass with my sleeve. It only moves the grime around, leaving brown streaks. The attic space fogs with dust every time we move, kicking up another cloud. Kilorn coughs into his hand, a hoarse sound.

"I see smoke on this side, in between those factories," he says.

At her window, Cameron raises a shoulder. "Autoworks sector," she replies without turning around. "The assembly lines jammed half an hour ago. The shift will be turned out, and they'll idle around the gates asking for the day's wage. Overseers will refuse. Officers will try to keep peace." She grins to herself. "Big mess."

"What color is the smoke, Kilorn?" I ask, still scanning my section of horizon. From this height, New Town seems smaller. But just as depressing. All gray and smoggy, hung with low clouds of brutal haze. It pulses, sluggish, the electricity almost overwhelming.

"Uh, normal?" Kilorn sputters. "Gray."

I huff low in my throat. Eager to get this moving.

"Normal. Just the smokestacks," Cameron drawls. "Not the signal."

He shifts, coughing some more. I wince at the hacking sound. "What are we looking for again?"

"Anything that *isn't* normal," I reply through gritted teeth.

"Right," he grumbles.

On the opposite side of the low room, Cameron taps her knuckles against her greasy window. "You know, maybe this rebellion would be further along if they didn't rely on teenagers so much." She tosses a smirk at Kilorn. "Especially ones who can't read."

He barks out a laugh, rising to the bait. "I *can* read."

"But colors are beyond your bleeding comprehension?" she snaps back with whip quickness.

He shrugs and raises his hands. "I'm just making conversation."

Cameron scoffs, rolling her eyes. "Because we really need distractions right now, Kilorn."

I press my lips together, trying not to giggle at them both. "Is this what Tiberias and I sound like when we argue?" I ask with a raised brow. "Because if so, I sincerely apologize."

Kilorn goes scarlet, flushing, as Cameron quickly turns back to her window, almost pressing her face to the glass.

I missed what was happening with Shade and Farley. Have I missed this too?

"You two are about ten times worse," Kilorn finally says, his voice a low, rumbling grunt.

At the opposite window, Cameron snorts. "You mean a hundred."

Grinning, I glance between the pair of them. Both are on edge, even for the circumstances. I try to read the tightness in Kilorn's shoulders, but the flush still coloring his cheeks is more damning. "I walked into that, didn't I?" I mutter, turning back to my window.

Behind me, he chuffs out a laugh. "Absolutely."

Then Cameron slams a hand to her window, hissing. "Green smoke. Weapons sector. Shit."

Kilorn jumps to her side, drawing his gun. He eyes her, worried. "Why 'shit'?"

"Weapons sector has the most security," she says quickly. With even motions, she peels off her jacket, revealing her own gun and a wicked knife I hope she never has to use. "For obvious reasons."

I exhale slowly. Inside me, the lightning snaps and crackles. "More likely to blow up too."

With a roll of his shoulders, Kilorn dons a scowl. He touches Cameron lightly on the arm, pulling her back from the window. "Let's make sure that doesn't happen," he mutters, kicking out the glass.

Shards explode out and in, shattering with the force of the blow. Still grimacing, he wipes one jacketed sleeve around the frame, knocking loose any jagged edges. He then steps back to let me lean out and brace myself on the ledge. A smoky wind blows against my face, smelling of fumes and distant fire. Without hesitation, I slip one leg out the window, then the other. Kilorn grabs the back of my shirt, keeping a firm grip.

I look skyward, focusing on the blue dawn as it melts to pink. Even though the sky is choked with corrupted clouds, they make for lovely colors. My heartbeat thrums, rising to a steady rhythm. The lightning in me pulses with it, feeding off the electricity below. I clench a fist, trying to remember what Ella taught me.

Storm lightning is the strongest and most destructive kind we can make. It gathers; it grows; it breaks. Overhead, the vibrantly colored clouds begin to darken and swirl, condensing with my power. Before my eyes, identical shadows bloom over two other parts of the city. Ella and Rafe. The three of us make a triangle, with the electricity hub at our center. The city spread out before us like a killing ground. And Tyton is somewhere down there, more dangerous than any of us, ready to loose his pulse lightning on anyone who might get too close.

Blue lightning flashes first, illuminating the curls of a rising thunderhead to my left. The roar of close thunder cracks over us and I feel

Kilorn flinch, the motion tugging my shirt. I stand firm, keeping my grip on the window frame.

Purple and green join the fray as our storms collide, raining bolts down on our target. The hub, a domed building near the center of the city, is easily distinguished by the tangle of wires reaching in every direction. Connecting power stations all over the city, and feeding back electricity into the factories. The lifeblood of any slum town. Even from this distance, I can feel the low hum of it.

"Make it rain," Kilorn snarls.

I bite back a sigh. "That's not how it works," I hiss back, throwing a bolt across the sky. The other electricons do as well, their blue and green racing toward my purple.

Our strikes hit directly above the hub, birthing a blinding flash. On cue, the hum disappears as our allies inside take the hub system offline. They shut it down more quickly than even we could, and with far fewer casualties.

All over the city, smokestacks stop belching out their poison. Assembly lines grind to a halt. Even transports on the streets, isolated with their own energy sources, slow or pull over, surprised by the sudden shutdown. The storm continues, a three-headed monster, sending cracks of lightning across the sky in all directions. I keep my bolts away from the ground for now. I can't aim them well at this distance and don't want to risk innocent lives. Not to mention the Scarlet Guard explosives, which are now set all over the city. One spark from me could set off a chain of bursting death.

"All stop," Cameron murmurs next to me. She looks out on her city with marvel in her eyes. "No power means no work. Shifts turned out all over. Workers baying for their wages. Officers distracted, overseers overrun."

Blind to the cutthroats, criminals, and soldiers now in their midst. Blind to the bombs beneath their feet.

"How long until—"

The first detonation cuts Kilorn off, rumbling a little too close for comfort. An explosion rises to our left, two streets away. At one of the city gates. Rock and smoke streak through the air in a dusty, dragging arc. The next bomb obliterates another gate, followed by the other two. Then the interior charges blow. Beneath security posts, guard towers, Silver barracks, the overseers' quarters. Any and all Silver targets. I wince with each strike, trying not to think of how much blood we spill today. On both sides. *Who will be caught in the crossfire?*

We watch in silence, cowed by the sight. More smoke, more dust, and now ash. Cameron's chest rises and falls as her breath turns to panting. Her wide, dark eyes dart back and forth, always returning to the factories marking the weapons sector. Nothing explodes there.

"The Scarlet Guard isn't stupid enough to put bombs beneath a munitions depot," I tell her, hoping to comfort her a little.

Then it explodes.

The resulting force knocks us all backward, sending us sprawling over broken glass and the dusty attic. Cameron scrambles up first, bleeding from a cut on the forehead. "Then that wasn't the Guard," she yelps, pulling me to my feet.

My ears ring, dulling all sound. I shake my head from side to side, trying to get my bearings. Cameron takes my wrists and I instantly jump, flinching out of her grasp. "No," I snarl, unable to stand the feeling.

She doesn't react and instead focuses on getting Kilorn up, putting one of his arms over her shoulder to hoist him. His lip is busted and one of his hands has a gash from the glass, but the rest of him seems whole.

"I think we might want to get our feet on the ground," he says, focusing on the cracked ceiling above us.

"Agreed." My voice sounds oddly strangled as we bolt for the door.

The stairs are little more than a tight spiral, reaching down and down and down. A chore to climb, and even worse to descend, each step a jolt through my knees. I pull my lightning to my fingertips, letting the purple sparks gather and spit, ready to run through anyone in our way.

Kilorn overtakes me easily, moving down the stairs two at a time. I hate it when he does that, and he knows it. The boy even has the spine to smirk back at me, winking.

In that moment, Cameron screams, seeing the Silver guard before we do.

He waves an arm, sending Kilorn sideways over the railing with the force of telekinetic ability. My vision slows as Kilorn topples, body sprawled in the air, and I feel like someone is digging a knife into my gut. The ringing in my ears threatens to split my head, rising to a shriek. All down the stairwell, lightbulbs pop and hiss with my fear, spreading darkness.

The guard drops before he can turn his wrath on us. He clutches at his throat, eyes rolling as he lands hard on his knee. Cameron curls her hand, fingers clawlike, as she smothers him with her ability. Slowing his heart, darkening his vision. Killing him.

The crack and thud of Kilorn hitting the railing below makes me sick. We sprint as fast as we can, directly into two other Silver guards working their way up to us. A shiver freezes the steps beneath our feet and my boots slide, almost taking me down. I slice him apart with a rocketing bolt, while his partner, a stoneskin, topples under Cameron's wrath. We cut them apart, knives through paper.

I reach Kilorn first. He rolls to a stop two floors down, landing sprawled across several rows of steps. The first thing I see is his chest, rising and falling. Shallow, but moving. Breathing. He's choking on blood. Red and crimson, scarlet, ruby. The color so bright I want to shut my eyes. He coughs violently, flecking both Cameron and me. The hot droplets pepper my face.

"Get him up—we have to get him up," I mumble, scrambling over him. Cameron follows, deathly quiet. I want to scream.

He can't speak but tries to rise on his own. I almost slap him. "Let us," I bark, throwing his arm around me. "Cam, the other side."

She's already there, heaving. He's an anchor, a deadweight.

Kilorn jolts and hacks, painting the steps with his own blood. I don't bother trying to assess the damage. I just know I have to get him out, get him down, get him to any one of the healers all over the city. *I need Davidson, I need someone.* My chest tightens, but I refuse to feel the agony or the strain of him. My legs burn with every new step. Down, down, down, down.

"Mare—" Cameron sobs.

"STOP IT."

He's still warm, still breathing, still retching blood all over himself. That's enough for me. Probably broken ribs, cracked bone, sharp and digging into his organs. Stomach, lungs, liver. *Stay away from the heart,* I beg. We don't have time to survive a pierced heart.

I taste salt and realize I'm crying, washing my face of his blood with my tears.

The floors pass in a blur, sliding by. Kilorn sucks down a wet, rattling breath; his face and hands are paler by the second. All we can do is run.

More guards charge up the stairs, baying like hounds on a scent. I barely see them, barely feel their nerves as they shred beneath my lightning. Some fall quickly, bleeding from the eyes and mouth and ears as Cameron hammers her ability through their bodies. But there are so many, too many, flooding up to meet us.

"This way!" Cameron barks, her voice still tear-filled as she slams her body through a door on the next landing.

I follow without thought, crossing through a cramped and meager apartment. Where Cameron is taking us, I can't say. All I can do is keep hold of Kilorn and my lightning, the only two things in my world.

"Hold on," I hear myself whisper to Kilorn, too low for anyone to hear.

Cameron leads us to the closest window, another square of grimy glass. But this one opens onto an adjoining rooftop. She knocks out the window, using one long leg to kick the pane free. My lightning holds our backs from pursuing Silvers, allowing us enough time to clamber out and onto the roof.

The officers follow, squeezing their larger and broader bodies through the broken window and onto the ashy roof behind us. Beneath the torturous, thundering sky.

Once there's enough distance between us and the guards, I gently lower Kilorn, laying him down against the concrete. His lashes flutter, eyes glassy, as Cameron stands over him, her stance wide and defensive.

I put my back to her, facing down the Silvers struggling onto the roof. I count six already on the roof, with more squeezing through. What their abilities might be, if they belong to any family I recognize, I don't know. And I don't care.

As soon as the last Silver's feet hit the concrete, I unleash.

The storm opens above me, purple and violent, blinding with my fury. I'm screaming, but the force absorbs all sound, all thought. The lightning swallows the bodies, killing them so quickly I don't even feel them. Not their nerves, not their skeletons. Nothing.

When the lightning clears, it's the smell that brings me back. Kilorn's blood, ash, burned hair, and cooked flesh. Behind me, Cameron makes a gulping sound, like she's trying not to vomit. I have to look away from the charred remains. Only their buttons and guns remain intact, smoking with heat.

I barely heave a breath before a deafening crack splits the singed air, and the roof shudders beneath our feet. Cameron drops, covering Kilorn with her body as the entire building lurches. Starts to lean. Slowly at first, then faster and faster.

I fall to my knees, reaching for Cameron and Kilorn as the structure buckles. My storm was too strong, the apartment building too poorly made. The walls are crumbling on one side, making us tip. All I can do is hang on as the roof snaps and falls, sliding forward at a steady incline. I slide with it, scrabbling, fingers grasping for anything to hold on to. My fist closes on the collar of Kilorn's jacket, sticky with hot, wet blood. His breath rattles, weaker than ever, as we move with the collapsing roof.

The ground rises up to meet us, a fist of concrete. Silver officers wait below, ready to kill us if the collapse doesn't. I clench my teeth, bracing for impact. I've never felt so helpless and afraid.

At first I can only blink at the sudden, translucent blue glow in front of me. It hovers, holding up the edge of the tipping roof, stopping the falling slab. But not us. We slide along the angle, dragged through the ash until we smack against the shield. Bullets sound below, and out of instinct I squeeze my eyes shut, curling up.

They ping harmlessly off the shield, sending ripples of force dancing beneath us.

Davidson.

One eye opens to see a massacre below us, a smoky haze of blue
and green and white lightning as it branches among the Silvers. Tyton's
white darts fell four of them in an instant, while Ella and Rafe batter
the rest with their whipping electricity. The shield moves as they fight,
letting the roof down gently. We hit the ground with a low thud, sending up a curtain of gray dust.

Kilorn is tall, lean but heavy. My adrenaline makes him almost
weightless. I barely notice the strain as I lift him again, throwing one of
his arms over my shoulder. *Still breathing, still breathing.* Cameron takes
his other side and we charge through the ash, without thought for the
lightning or the Silvers still fighting.

"Healers!" I roar, screaming as loudly as I can to be heard over the
din. "We need healers!"

Cameron echoes my cries, her voice carrying. She's stronger and
taller than I am, taking the brunt of Kilorn's weight. He doesn't slow
her down.

The premier meets us head-on, his personal guard fanned out
around him. There's a smear of blood on his cheek. Red blood. I don't
have time to wonder who it belongs to.

"We need—" I gasp out, but Kilorn shudders, doubling over on
himself. He almost tumbles out of our grasp and forces us to stop.
Another wave of blood spatters the ground, painting my boots.

I almost faint with relief when the healer charges forward from
Davidson's soldiers. The red-haired newblood has a familiar face, but I
don't have enough energy to remember his name.

"Lay him down," the man barks, and we gratefully obey.

The only thing I can do is hold Kilorn's hand, his skin cold against the flame of my own. He's still alive. We made it in time. We were enough.

Cameron kneels over him, silent and staring, hands knitted in her lap. Afraid to touch him.

"Internal bleeding," the healer mutters, ripping open Kilorn's shirt. His abdomen is almost black with bruises. As the healer dances his fingers, pressing and prodding, they begin to recede. Kilorn grimaces, teeth gritted against the strange sensation. "It's like someone took a hammer to your ribs."

"Feels like it," he grinds out.

His voice is strained but alive. I squeeze my eyes shut, and I wish I had gods to thank for his life. His grip tightens on my hand, squeezing my fingers. Forcing me to look at him.

Bottle-green eyes meet mine. Eyes that have followed me my entire life. Eyes almost shut forever.

"It's okay, Mare. I'm fine," he whispers. "I'm not going anywhere."

We stay by him, silent guardians, as the healer works. I flinch in time with the distant rumble of explosions and artillery. Some of it far away, beyond New Town, muffled by the miles. The assault of Harbor Bay has begun, a three-pronged attack to take the city. *Will they win the day? Will we?*

The electricons close in on us, picking their way back through the dozen Silver corpses littering the road. Tyton idles, turning over a few with his foot, while Rafe looks on.

Ella gives me the smallest wave as she approaches. Her scarf is gone and ash colors her blue hair in streaks of gray, aging her. One hand twists idly at her side, and the thunderheads above, silent for now, spin with the motion. She winks at me, trying to put on a brave face.

Rafe and Tyton are more blatant in their grimness. Both keep their hands free, ready to push back any assault.

But no one seems to be coming. Either the fighting is concentrated elsewhere, or it's already over.

"Thank you," I murmur, my voice cracking.

Tyton's reply is swift. "We protect our own."

"Still more to go, but out of the woods."

I look back to see the healer ease Kilorn into a sitting position. Cameron helps gingerly, putting a hand to the bare skin on his back. Suddenly I feel like I'm intruding on something I shouldn't. With the back of my hand, I quickly swipe away the blood, sweat, and tears dirtying my face.

"I'm going to find out what's going on," I mumble, getting to my feet before anyone can protest.

My boots crunch through the debris as I beeline for the electricons. Rafe offers a weak grin. He rips the covering off his head and runs a hand over his closely cropped green hair.

"Looks like he'll be okay?" he says, jutting his chin back at Kilorn.

I exhale slowly. "Looks like it. What about you all?"

Ella puts an arm around me, lithe as a sapphire cat. "Had less trouble than you, that's for sure. I think we brought a bit more firepower than anyone might expect for a place like this."

"The Nortans here were outnumbered and unprepared." Tyton spits at the street. "Silver kings don't expect anyone to care, let alone fight, for a Red slum."

I blink at the implication, surprised. "So we won?"

"They're certainly acting like we did," Tyton replies. He gestures with a hand, pointing to the Montfort and Guard soldiers now holding the street. They could be Red techies, if not for the machine guns hanging off them. A few seem to be laughing, exchanging pleasantries with the premier as he walks among them.

"Wonder how they're doing in Harbor Bay," Ella says, kicking up a puff of dust.

I lower my eyes. My heart still thunders in my chest, pumping adrenaline through my veins. It makes it hard to think about anything beyond the street. Let alone the people I love, fighting and perhaps dying a few miles away. For a second, I try to forget. Collect myself. Breathe deep and easy. It doesn't work.

"Premier," I bark, crossing to him with force.

He looks back, smiling, and even waves a hand to motion me over. Like I need an invitation. "Barrow," he says. "Congratulations on a job well done."

It's hard to feel celebratory with Kilorn lying a few feet away, even with a healer patching him up. That was far too close.

"What about the city? Any word from Farley?"

His smile freezes in place. "Some."

Something tightens in my chest. "What's that supposed to mean?" I demand. "Is she alive?"

Davidson indicates one of his soldiers, her pack a mess of wires and radio equipment. "As of a few minutes ago, yes. I spoke to the general myself."

And Tiberias? I bite back the urge to ask about him, at least by name. "Did everything go to plan?" I force out, my mind flying over the many facets of the Harbor Bay invasion.

The premier's face tightens. "Did you expect it to?" he murmurs.

I almost snarl in frustration. Another round of artillery thunders miles away.

As the adrenaline in me ebbs, a cold takes over, threatening to numb my body. I look back for a moment, watching Cameron as she kneels with Kilorn. They aren't talking. Both of them are wide-eyed, nearly pinned down by exhaustion and the aftertaste of fear. Then I glance to the electricons. All three of them stare back, resolute.

Ready to follow. Ready to protect their own.

My decision only takes a split second.

"Get me a transport."

NINETEEN
Evangeline

I've never liked Harbor Bay. It stinks of fish and salt water, even in the Silver districts. Soon it will smell only of blood.

The two weeks of rest in the Rift flew by, each minute passing faster than the last. Only last night I was home, nestled against Elane, whispering my good-byes. I wasn't afraid then. I believed Father wouldn't let his heirs anywhere close to true danger. Ptolemus and I would be safe, held in reserve to watch the siege and wade in when the fighting ebbed.

I was wrong.

His hunger is deeper than I ever imagined.

He put us on the front lines without a thought.

Now our boats race over the ocean waves, skimming along the stormy blue, cresting with each flash of white foam. I narrow my eyes against the spray, even behind my goggles. The wind tears at my hair with the damp chill of seawater. It would knock me over if my boots weren't fused to the steel deck below my feet. My ability courses, a low pulse in time with my boat skipping over the water.

We ride with the fog, hidden for now. Montfort's storm soldiers are talented and powerful. I note ours at the corner of my eye, tall and willowy in her green uniform tightened by ballistic armor. She is helmeted too, only her hands bare, fingers splayed at her sides to drag the fog. No more coveralls or training outfits for anyone. This is real.

House Samos leads the assault from the water, pushing on our metal crafts at high speed. Father is willing to risk our house for victory. Three cousins form the diamond wedge of our frontal assault, their crafts slicing ahead of us. Behind me in my boat, Ptolemus stands firm, his body weighed down with mirrored armor and weaponry. Gun belts crisscross my hips, snug against my muscles. I have a pistol, though I prefer to throw the bullets myself if need be. My cousins of House Samos vary, carrying rifles as well as shard explosives. I picture the seawalls of Fort Patriot, high against the waves. Our first obstacle. My focus sharpens as we approach, narrowing to this place and our objective.

Win the city.

Survive.

Go home.

They will see us coming. Or at least they'll see the fog rolling off the water. It's early morning, though, when the air is still heavy and gray. A natural fog wouldn't seem out of place. It could give us cover longer than anything else. And when Cal strikes from the land, and House Laris from the air, the city guards and the Patriot garrison won't know where to turn. Which front to fight.

Everything is well coordinated, from the grander assault to each individual boat. Our ranks are well organized. Two magnetrons, one storm, one gravitron at least to each craft, supplemented by trained Red soldiers or other newbloods of Montfort. As well as a few healers sprinkled through each battalion.

Everyone has their job, and if we're all going to survive, we're going to do them well.

Fort Patriot looms, a hazy shadow darkening as our fog pushes on. The seawall rises from a breaking rush of white waves. No land below. No foothold. No matter.

For all my anger and rage, I wish my father were here. There is no safer place than his side.

My concentration breaks for a moment as my focus shifts to my brother. I can sense him behind me, and easily trace the shape of his armor. We each carry a small but solid disk of copper tucked into our belts. An odd metal for an attack. Easy to distinguish and feel. Easy to track. I hold on to the sensation of his and mine, memorizing it. If things go wrong, I want to be able to find Tolly as quickly as I can.

The fog outstrips us, easing against the fast-approaching seawall. Whatever clock ticks inside me grows louder, more insistent. It's time.

Shivering, I turn with a jolt and wrap my arms around Tolly's shoulders. The hug is quick, sharp, and not gentle. The clang of metal on metal as our armor meets is swallowed by the roaring waves and the rising thunder of my heartbeat.

"Stay alive," he whispers. I can only nod as I turn back around.

No movement on the seawall, either above or below. Just the waves. Maybe the fog has worked.

"Ready?" I hiss over the din, looking to the barrel-chested Mont-fort gravitron.

He dips his chin in assertion before crouching against the boat, putting his hand to each side. His palms go flat. Ready to lift.

In the other boats, the other gravitons do the same.

The soldiers behind me kneel. The storm, our two oblivions of

Lerolan, and Ptolemus brace for the leap. No Reds in my boat. I want to survive this, and do it without relying on the weakness of red blood, no matter how trained they might be.

I bend down with the rest, my muscles tensing, dreading the chance of impact, if the gravitron isn't up to snuff. At this speed, I might not be able to stop the boat from slamming into the seawall.

Waves break along the base of the wall, steel gray beneath the fog. They lap high, higher than the crusted saltwater line worn against the wall. Higher than any high tide.

My heart drops in my chest.

"Nymph strike!" I manage to scream as another towering wave crashes—*backward*.

So begins the battle of Harbor Bay.

The sudden, furious wall of water tosses the lead boats like toys, spilling soldiers of the Rift and Montfort across the churning ocean break. Only the gravitons escape, bouncing up and out of the water's grasp. I spot the Samos cousins utilizing control of their armor to stay afloat or skim the waves, but they're weighed down, and not strong enough to pull themselves out of harm's way. I don't know about the rest.

We have nymphs of our own, Montfort-born Silvers. But far fewer and far weaker than whoever must be on the Patriot walls. Whatever we do to calm the boiling waves isn't enough.

Another wave rises, half as high as the wall, blocking out the graying light, casting a shadow across our line of craft. It will flatten us, drown us, slam us against the seabed.

"Push through!" I command, clenching my fists on the prow of our boat. Pouring myself and my ability into the hull. I hope the gravitron can hear me. I know Ptolemus does.

The craft ripples under our touch, narrowing, fluting, the prow sharpening to a knife's edge. Gaining speed. I flatten myself as much as I can. We angle at the wave, a bullet with passengers.

The water is a cold slap, and all I can do is keep my mouth shut as it blasts over us. We rocket through the wave, bursting into midair on the other side. Sailing up and over, toward the seawall.

"Brace!" Ptolemus roars as we hurtle for the stone at high speed.

I grit my teeth, fingers digging into the metal hull. Pulling, pushing. Hoping we don't fall, hoping we don't crash.

The gravitron gives us the extra bounce we need, keeping us airborne. We hit hard, hull against the seawall. Sliding up, against gravity.

Other crafts slam in alongside us, racing up in tangled formation.

Most of our assault made it.

Metal screams along stone, outpacing the waves below, even as they reach higher and higher, casting spray like rain. I spit seawater and blink, glad for my goggles as we push up and over.

Nymphs line the ramparts, marked by blue stripes on clouded gray or black uniforms. Trained Silver soldiers and guards. The garrison of Fort Patriot, bolstered by Lakelander uniforms.

We spill from our boats with little grace, sliding onto the walkway crowning the wall. I use my own armor to stop me from toppling over the edge, while Ptolemus shreds the boat with abandon, sending razor edges spiraling in all directions. The gravitrons fling enemy soldiers into the sea. Fog crawls over the walls and into the fort, obscuring our soldiers. Somewhere, a few of our storms break off. Their job is to call up thunder. Cultivate lightning. Shock and awe the garrison, send them running. Make them think Barrow is here.

Blooms of fire and smoke dot the walls. Oblivions weave, leaving burning corpses in their wake. One shrieks as he's caught off guard and hurled over the wall into the angry waters.

Fort Patriot crawls with enemy strongarms. Blood of House Rhambos, or their Greco and Carros cousins. One of them, a woman muscled like a mountain, tears a Montfort storm apart before my eyes, ripping flesh and bone like paper.

I keep my head. I've seen worse. *I think.*

Gunfire peppers the air. Bullets and abilities are a deadly combination.

I raise an arm, fist clenched, shielding myself from the assault. Bullets bounce off my ability, flattened or sheered. I catch a few and send them hurtling back into the fog, hunting after the flashes of turret fire.

We have to open the gates. Win the fort.

Our objective, our job, is straightforward but not simple. Fort Patriot bisects the famed harbor of the city, dividing the waters into the civilian Aquarian Port and the War Port. Right now, I only care about one.

The low thunder of heavy guns, the kind found on battleships, beats like a drum. I try to trace the missiles, reaching across the distance to decipher their trajectory. It's too far, but I can guess. I'm Silver. I know how we think.

"Form a shield!" I shout to the Samos magnetrons, pulling upon the metal from our boats and weapons.

Ptolemus follows my lead, knitting together a steel wall as quickly as he can. The whistle of artillery grows closer and I look up, squinting through the haze. With a snap, I rip the goggles off my face to see an arc of smoke looping overhead.

The first missile explodes fifty yards ahead, pulverizing a section of the seawall, turning friend and foe to gray or pink mist in equal measure. Only the oblivions survive, some naked, their armor and uniforms charred right off their bodies. We cower behind our steel, weathering the blast as it pulses forward.

The smoke stings, acrid and poisoned with bone dust.

We won't survive a direct hit like that. Not with what we have here. We can deflect the missiles as best we can, but it's only a matter of time before one of them catches us. "Get off the wall," I force out, tasting blood. "Into the fort."

All to plan.

Get the battleships to open up, pummel their own walls. Keep the heavy fire on the fort, not the city or the Air Fleet.

That's what Cal said they would do, and somehow the idiots are doing it.

Another round hits, cracking stone, as we grapple down the seawall, our ranks bleeding into Patriot. I look back, counting as quickly as I can. Maybe sixty of us made it in, down from our original strike group of seventy-five souls. Seventy-five deadly Silvers and battle-hardened Reds, their guns lethal and precise.

But their fire is reserved for Silvers. I notice they don't bother with the soldiers in rusty red uniforms, the many conscripted assigned to the Patriot garrison. Some of those Reds follow their officers, running out to fight our ranks as we push on. Fewer than expected, though. As General Farley assured us, the word went out through her channels. The Reds of the city have been warned. *When the assault comes, turn. Run. Or fight with us if you can.*

Many do, joining our train of death.

Thunderheads pulse above, turning the sky black. Their lightning is unpredictable, less powerful than Mare's. But a symbol all the same.

Enemy soldiers look up as we approach, the Silvers eyeing what can only be the work of the lightning girl.

She isn't here, you idiots, I sneer in my head. *Cowards, afraid of a bit of flashing light.*

The interior fort is an experiment in chaos. By now Cal will have begun his own assault, marching his battalion up and out of the tunnel system Harbor Bay is built on. It is an old city, well preserved through the ages, with deep and twisting roots. The Scarlet Guard knows them all.

We make it to the central byway of the fort, moving quickly and without pattern. Leading the battleship fire, letting it follow and destroy. Keeping the worst weaponry from the city itself. Cal is so preoccupied with protecting innocents, probably just to show Mare he can. *Hanging me out to dry in the process.*

I cut through another wave of combatants, using a combination of bullets and blades to level the men and women in front of me. Their faces are shadows to me, inhuman. Unworthy of memory. It's the only way to do this properly.

The whine and thrum of artillery become a familiar rhythm. I duck for cover as easily as I fight, moving in time with the noise. Smoke and ash swirl with the fog, leaving everyone blind. The Patriot garrison is hopelessly adrift. They don't have a plan for this kind of attack. We certainly do.

My first burst of fear comes when I realize Ptolemus is no longer at my side, hemmed in by our protective circle of cousins. I glance at each of them, searching familiar faces of pale skin and silver hair. He isn't here.

"Tolly!" I hear myself scream as another missile blasts, closer this time.

I crouch and brace, letting the concussive wave pass over me. Rubble breaks against my armor, coating my left side with dust. Blinking,

I stand before the rest, whirling around. On the hunt. Terror claws up my spine, leaving icy, open wounds.

"PTOLEMUS!"

Whatever focus I had before slips through my grasp and everything splinters. The world spins. *Where is my brother, where is he, did we leave him behind, did he push on, is he hurt, is he dying, is he dead—*

The pop of gunfire snaps too close, a grim reminder. I whirl against our tide of soldiers. One of them knocks into me, her shoulder slamming mine, and I stumble. Gasping, I throw out my senses, reaching with my ability. Trying to locate that disk of copper. That tiny nub of pale orange metal, a different weight, a different feel. I come back empty. Nothing.

I told him we would be safe, even on the front lines of battle. *Father would not waste us. Father would not let us go anywhere that might jeopardize his legacy.* I suck down a poisoned breath, still scanning the silhouettes around me as the ash falls like summer snow. It coats our uniforms, no matter the color. We all start to look the same.

Even if Father doesn't love us the way he should, he still values us. He wouldn't trade our lives like this. Wouldn't let us die for his crown.

But here we are.

Tears prick my eyes. *From the ash,* I tell myself. *The sting of smoke.*

Suddenly the copper rings on the edge of my perception, so small I almost miss it. My neck snaps with force as I turn, hunting for my brother. Without thought, I shove a few soldiers out of my way, vaulting through the swarm of battle. I duck under the arm of an approaching strongarm, tossing a bullet his way as I go. I feel it punch through his neck, a clean through-and-through. He drops behind me, clawing at his open jugular.

Every step brings new shapes into focus. The streets of Fort Patriot, meticulously organized in a grid, are easy to navigate. I hang my closest right, a hound sniffing out a bone.

Above me, walkways connect the various buildings. Soldiers in rusty uniforms charge back and forth, guns at the ready. I raise my forearm, shielding myself from the accompanying volley of gunfire. Red soldiers all, attacking from a safe distance. I let the bullets drop, flattened and useless. No use wasting my energy trying to kill them.

Ptolemus comes into view around the corner, sprinting, blissfully whole. I almost drop in relief. Smoke spirals behind him, evidence of more artillery fire. Missiles whistle overhead again, before exploding with resounding rumbles.

"What were you doing, you idiot?" I shout, skidding to a halt.

"Don't stop—*run!*" he screams, catching me under the arm. I'm almost yanked off my feet by the force.

I know better than to argue when my brother is so incredibly terrified. All I can do is get my feet under myself, reorient, and sprint as fast as I can, keeping pace at his side.

"The seawall," he forces out between pants of exertion.

It isn't difficult to connect the dots.

I make the terrible mistake of looking back over my shoulder. Through the smoke, the fog, the thunder breaking overhead. To the cracks in the wall as they spread, pieces of stone as they crumble. The wall of water forcing itself up and over and *in*.

Standing over it, poised on a balcony, is the person controlling it all, her arms wide, her armor so deeply blue it could be black.

Iris Cygnet watches us run.

A swoop of panic nearly roots me to the spot, but Tolly drags me on, his hand wrapped around my bicep in a painfully tight grip. We skid out, back into the main street, chasing after our battalion only to find the lower levels of the fort deserted. Our soldiers are forward, and the rest, the enemies—they are *up*. Climbing into the buildings, standing on rooftops, clinging to the high ground with their weapons ready. No use trying to get to high ground of our own. All there is now is to get *out*.

We charge through errant gunfire, coming from all directions. Most we can deflect easily enough. Some I throw back with force but no aim.

I curse through gritted teeth, blaming Cal, blaming Davidson, Farley, my father, even myself. Our plan accounted for nymphs, but not someone as powerful as Iris. I can't think of anyone else besides a few nymph lords who could be strong enough to loose the ocean on the fort. And none of them would destroy Patriot so willingly. But Iris, a princess of another nation, a woman with no loyalty to Norta? She could rip this place apart and feel nothing. Still call it victory.

The seawall crashes behind us, echoing loudly even at a distance. Followed by the roar of pummeling waves as they break and swell, rushing through the streets, foaming around the buildings and walls of Fort Patriot. I imagine it in my head, a wall like blue fire, consuming everything in its path.

We sprint on, catching up to our battalion. Ptolemus barks at them to run, and they obey. Even the Montfort newbloods. There isn't time for posturing.

The interior gates of Fort Patriot don't open onto the city, but onto a long bridge crossing the harbor, connecting the artificial island of the fort to the mainland. Meaning we'll have to run the half mile on a bridge over water, with enemy nymphs behind us, not to mention a rising ocean. Not exactly a winning combination if your goal is *don't drown*.

Our oblivions make quick work of the first set of gates, blowing the massive doors out onto the bridge. Iron reinforcements go flying, splashing violently into the water. I barely hear it over the approaching roar of the flood. Iris must still be standing over it all, triumphant, smiling as she watches us scramble like rats caught in a rainstorm.

We hurry through the gate as the first swell hits, bringing with it a swirl of debris. Splintered wood, floating transports, guns, corpses. I run as fast as my legs will allow, wishing I were strong enough to lift us out of harm's way. But neither of us has ever mastered the art of magnetron flight. Only Father can truly do that for any real amount of time.

The gravitrons guard our backs, using their abilities to push against the wave. They buy us time, but this swell is small. Barely higher than the arch of the gate.

Then the second wave, the true wave, hits, cresting over the walls themselves, smashing through the stone and concrete protecting the fort. The gravitrons are no use against such force and can only save themselves, flying up and over. At least one gets caught in the spray, tangled up in a swirl of water. He never resurfaces.

I don't spare him another thought. I can't.

The bridge is meant to be a defense for the fort, a long choke point to prevent any army from storming Patriot by land. It funnels us through a series of locks and gates, each slowing us down. The oblivions do what they can, leading us through a rhythm of explosions as we tear through one obstacle after another. Ptolemus and I split apart hinges and reinforcements, ripping steel and iron in our desperation.

We pass the halfway point, the city of Harbor Bay rising before our eyes, so close and yet so infinitely far. In a glance, I realize that the still, calm waters on either side of us are rising too. Bulging. Surging. Growing like the crashing wave still hunting after us with the inexorable force of a hurricane. Salty spray blasts across my vision, drenching my face, stinging my eyes. I reach blindly, clinging to the collar of Tolly's armor. With a roar of frustration, I launch us both, using my ability to drag us up and over the next gate. Our battalion be damned. They'll follow if they can. And if they can't, they were bound to be left behind anyway.

How much does this armor weigh? a useless voice wonders in my head. *Will I sink before I can shed it? End up at the bottom of the Bay?*

Or worse, will I have to watch Ptolemus go into the waves and never come back up?

Water laps at my ankles. My boots slide over the paved bridge and I almost lose my footing. Only Ptolemus keeps me from plunging into the cloying depths, his arm now wrapped around my waist, holding me close. If we drown, we drown together.

I can almost feel Iris's hunger as her waves pursue. She would love nothing more than to kill us. Kneecap the Rift, one more enemy to her people. Kill us the way our army killed her father.

I refuse to die like this.

But I see no plan, no attack I can make alone. The nymphs controlling the waves will kill us without even showing their faces. Unless we can somehow kill them first.

I need a gravitron.

I need a newblood.

I need Mare and her storms to light these bastards up.

Behind us, the thunder rumbles again, following the flash of random lightning. It isn't enough.

All we can do is run, and hope that someone else will save us.

Such helplessness makes me sick.

Another wave crashes, from our right this time. Smaller than the tidal force at our backs, but still strong. It breaks Tolly's grip on me, splitting us apart. My hands grasp at thin air and then stinging water as I fall headfirst, plunging into the port.

Some fire blooms on the surface, explosions. From oblivions or artillery fire, I can't tell. All I can do is run my hands over myself, shedding armor before it drags me deeper. I try to keep my mental grip on Ptolemus's copper as it moves, struggling through the water with me. He's drowning too.

I kick furiously, trying to surface. As I do, another wave hits me head-on, sending me spiraling into the deep again without a single gasp of air.

The salt water stings my eyes and my lungs burn, but I try to swim, try to outrun the nymphs on the surface. The longer I stay down, the more dead I seem. The farther away I can get.

It's Tolly's turn to find me.

A fist closes on the scruff of my undershirt, dragging me along. Through the murky water, I see his silhouette alongside mine, his other hand clenching something metallic. Steel, shaped like a large bullet. Smooth. It drags us along, pushed by Tolly's own ability. Like a motor.

Clenching my teeth, I grab hold. My lungs scream for relief until I can't stand it any longer, letting loose a stream of bubbles. I gasp reflexively, choking down water.

With a mighty kick and another burst of strength, Tolly angles us to the surface even as my vision spots and darkens. He throws me forward, onto wet and shady sand.

On hands and knees, I sputter and choke, trying to spit up the water as quietly as possible. He thumps a fist on my back.

I can barely think, but I glance around anyway, eager to get my bearings. Even a second off guard could get us killed.

We're under one of the docks of the Aquarian Port, in about six inches of lapping water. Boats hide us on either side, hemming us in with nothing but rotting seaweed, discarded rope, and barnacles.

Ptolemus looks beyond the dock into the few feet of space allowing us a prime view of the bridge and Fort Patriot beyond. The harbor is a surging cauldron, battered by dueling tides as the ocean itself rises and falls. Some wake crashes toward the shore, rapidly pushing water up to our necks. I sputter, grabbing at the rotted wood above my head, and for a moment I think we might find ourselves drowned onshore. But the water recedes, pulling back out again with unnatural force.

We move with it, clambering to the supports holding up the end of the dock. I only have my knives and bullets now, my armor discarded somewhere at the bottom of the port. Not that I care. I can find metal anywhere I want on land.

Ahead of us, waves assault the bridge again and again, tossing soldiers. Our battalion is a ruin, if not completely destroyed. House Samos will pay in blood today. The assault from the sea has failed.

A jet screams through the clouds, circling the thunderheads dissipating over the fort. Two more give chase, their wings tipped in Laris yellow. As I watch, the hunted plane bursts into flame, shearing apart before crashing into the distant waves. A strong wind tears across the harbor as other Laris jets dot the sky, flying low over the city. The sound of them threatens to rip my head open, but I would cheer them on if I could. The fleet is our real advantage.

Especially with Patriot half underwater.

Most of the fort is flooded, including the jetways. Only the navy ships survived intact, still operational. They turn their guns on the Laris jets as they pass, spitting hot iron. One of the jets falls, a wing obliterated, before two more follow.

"We have to disable the battleships," I mutter flatly, already exhausted by the prospect.

Tolly looks at me like I'm crazy.

I very well may be.

We sprint the edge of the harbor as fast as we can, moving in and out of a full-blown battle. Cal's land assault was the biggest of the three planned, utilizing hundreds of soldiers from our entire coalition, not to mention agents of the Scarlet Guard and their contacts already in the city. Trained soldiers grapple alongside thieves and criminals as guerrilla warfare overwhelms Harbor Bay from every gutter and alley. A city of white stone and blue roofs turns black and red, smoke and fire. *Calore colors,* I think bitterly. *But for which brother?*

The Nortan Silvers and conscripted Reds find themselves bogged down in the streets, restricted by their own regimented training. Bottlenecked, their numbers neutralized, but still dangerous. Tolly and I risk our lives as we run, re-forming our armor from whatever we can salvage. Rusty bits and all. If I had the time, I would feel disgusted with my own poor work.

Out on the water, maybe a mile out to sea, the Laris jets meet Nortan and Piedmont jets. Cal's orders again. Keep the worst of their weapons and our own from the city. Even from this distance, I can hear the roar as they dance through the air at blinding speed. Bursts of fire and smoke spread across the aerial battle, sandwiched between the clouds and the horizon. I don't envy the pilots, especially the ones who must contend with Laris windweavers. It's difficult enough flying a jet without fighting the wind itself.

Iris must still be near the War Port, protecting the battleships from rough waves. As we approach, I can see that the water around the four massive steel hulls is still and smooth. The rest of the port boils and tosses, throwing back any attempts to take the ships from the mainland. Soon the Lakelander princess will turn the big guns on the jets out at sea, or the city itself. Destroy Harbor Bay the way she broke the fort. Leave nothing but a ruin, useless to either Calore brother.

Bright red slashes across my vision, jumping out onto the road from an alley. I never thought I'd be so relieved to find an armed squadron of Scarlet Guard. Especially one led by General Farley.

Her band of criminals rounds on us, guns raised. Reluctant but quick, I raise my hands, meeting her eyes. "Just us," I pant, gesturing for Ptolemus to do the same.

She looks between us, eyes ticking like a pendulum. A scale settling on balance. My relief melts in an instant as I realize exactly what she could be weighing.

My brother's life.

She could try to kill him, kill us, right here, and no one would know. We could just be casualties of the battle. And she would have her revenge.

It's what I would do, if someone took Tolly from me.

The blond woman's hand strays, finding the gun at her hip, fastened to a half-empty ammunition belt. She's been busy. I hold her shivering blue gaze, saying nothing, barely daring to breathe. Trying not to tip her in the wrong direction.

I set my teeth on edge, reaching out with every piece of my exhausted ability I can muster. Grabbing for her gun, her remaining bullets, the knives hidden all over her body. To stop her if she decides to strike.

"Cal's this way," she finally says, snapping the string of tension between us. "We need to get those ships out of their hands."

"Of course," Ptolemus replies, and I almost punch him in the teeth. *Be quiet,* I want to hiss.

Instead I step in front of him slightly, shielding his body from her wrath. Farley only twitches, staring at him for another blistering second. "Fall in, soldiers," she sneers, before turning her back on us.

Soldiers. Not Your Highness, not our titles.

If that's the worst she's going to do, I'll take it gladly.

We do as commanded, sliding into formation with the rest of her band. I don't recognize any of them, and her Guard are distinguished only by red sashes tied around arms or waists or wrists. The Guard look ragtag, hastily thrown together, their clothes common. They could be servants or laborers, dockworkers, low traders, cooks, drivers. But they share her steely disposition and determination. And they're armed to the teeth. I wonder how many Silvers kept such wolves in their own houses.

I wonder how many there still are in mine.

Our coalition holds a stretch of the Port Road as it curves around the harbor, looking out on the battleships blocking up the War Port. Behind us are more barracks and military outbuildings, all overtaken. Many of our soldiers take up defensive positions, poking out of windows and doorways, and others form up at the port side, waiting for orders.

Have we won the city?

Cal stalks among his lieutenants and guards, more disheveled than I've ever seen him, his hair slick with sweat, the rest of him striped with ash and blood. I can barely discern the armor beneath, shimmering a deep ruby red between the dirty patches. He paces at the edge of the water, harried and frustrated. And careful to keep out of reach of the surging waves.

Calore princes hold no love for water. It makes them uncomfortable.

Right now, Cal looks like he might crawl out of his own skin.

His grandmother watches as he paces, her silks and gowns discarded for a simple uniform with no insignia to mark her rank. Not even her colors. She could be just an old woman who wandered into the wrong crowd, but anyone with eyes knows better. Anabel Lerolan is not to be underestimated. At her side, Julian Jacos keeps silent, his lips pursed together, eyes fixed on the battleships. Waiting to be of some use.

My brother and I shoulder through the fray, entering Cal's line of vision. His brow rises at the sight of us. He might be as relieved as I am, and just as surprised by the sensation.

"Good to see you standing," he says, offering us both nods. "What about your battalion?"

I put my hands on my hips. "I don't know. Iris tossed us both into the port while our team was crossing the bridge. We had to swim out or drown." He watches me as I speak, intent and sharp. Almost accusatory. As if I should feel shame for staying alive when others couldn't. I push past it. "Did any make it to the city?"

"Hard to say. I sent out the word as best I could to regroup here. We'll see who gets the message and who can get back." He frowns at his hands, then back at the battleships. Out on the water, they steer clear of their docks, idling instead of heading out to sea. Setting their sights on us. "You're the only magnetrons we have right now."

No Samos cousins left. None but us.

Next to me, Ptolemus scowls. "We'll do what we can with the missiles."

Cal looks back to my brother, his dark hair flicking with the motion. "I'm not wasting either of you catching missiles. We have enough

Montfort bombers to destroy what can be destroyed." He points with a single finger, gesturing to the harbor. "I want you on those ships."

I know we have to stop the battleships, but getting *on* them? I pale so quickly I can feel it, an icy cold spreading across my cheeks despite the heat of flame and ash and my own sweat.

"I don't fancy killing myself this late in the day, Calore," I snap. With a sneer, I angle my chin toward the battleships, safe on the water. "Iris will sink us like stones before we even get close. Even gravit-rons—"

Cal just hisses to himself, frustrated. "When we win the city, remind me to give every Silver officer a crash course in newblood abil-ities. Arezzo," he adds, barking out the strange word over his shoulder.

A woman shoulders forward in reply, her uniform the dark green of Montfort, covered in foreign insignia. "Sir," she says, ducking her chin.

"Get your teleporters ready," Cal commands. He seems almost amused, watching as I seethe, angry with him. And with myself for forgetting exactly what kind of army we're working with. *Is there no end to these newblood peculiars?* "Prepare to jump to those ships."

"Yes, sir," she says brusquely. With a wave, she draws forward other Montfort soldiers. Other teleporters, I assume.

I glance at my brother sidelong, to gauge his reaction. Tolly seems more preoccupied with the Red general. He keeps his eyes on her, never wavering. As if she might kill him if he drops his guard. It isn't entirely an irrational fear.

"And when we're on board?" I step forward, putting myself toe-to-toe with my wretched betrothed. "You'll need more than two magnetrons to take apart a battleship. And more than a few minutes. We're good but we're not *that* good."

Jerking, Cal steps back from a particularly exuberant wave, keeping his toes dry. He blinks rapidly, swallowing. "You don't need to take it apart. I want those ships. I *need* those ships. Especially because Iris is here." He licks his lips, a brush of terror flashing in his eyes. "Her mother won't leave her out to dry."

Ugh. Does he try to make such awful puns?

"If the Lakelander fleet gets here before we have real artillery protecting the harbor, we're done for," Cal adds, looking over my head to the water.

I raise a hand, pointing out past the flooded fort to the ocean hazed by smoke and the still-dancing forms of airjets. "You think four ships can hold back a Lakelander armada?"

"They'll have to."

"Well, they won't. You know that."

Only a muscle in his cheek twitches, jumping as he tightens his jaw. *You're going to have to get your hands dirty, Calore. Dirtier than they already are.*

I move again, planting myself in his eye line. "You said yourself, the queen of the Lakelands won't abandon her daughter. So we trade her."

Cal pales like I did, all color draining from his face in shock.

"For the city," I push on. He must understand. "Ptolemus and I can lock the guns in position, make them fire on her. Pin her down. Keep her cornered. Shouldn't be difficult for a fire king to subdue her, should it?"

Again, nothing. Cal doesn't even blink, his face stubborn in its stillness. *Coward,* I sneer in my head. *He doesn't want to face her. The Flame of the North is afraid of a bit of rain.*

"When we have Iris, we bargain. Her life for the Bay."

That snaps his restraint in half. "I don't do that," he barks, his voice rough, all edges. In spite of myself, I take a step back, almost cowed by his sudden fury. "I'm not *him*, Evangeline."

At that, I have to scoff. "Well, *he's* winning."

"I'm not doing it," he says again, the words shaking with anger. Princes aren't used to repeating themselves. "I'm not taking hostages."

I'm not giving Maven a reason, you mean, I think to myself, a bitter echo in my head. *A reason to take her back. To bend all his resources on one particular person.*

He has the unthinkable gall to put a finger in my face. "Get the ships, get the guns. And get Iris out of the Bay. That's an order."

"I'm not your soldier and I'm not your wife yet, Calore. You don't get to order me around," I snarl, feeling as if I could take a bite out of him. "Her mother will drown this city and us if you let her."

He stares at me, furious, his hand trembling. So angry he doesn't notice when a wave hits his ankles. When he jumps, cursing, I want to laugh in his ridiculous face.

"Her mother will let this city be, if her daughter is able to escape," a voice pipes up behind him. *Granny to the rescue, Calore?*

The prince frowns, forehead wrinkling in confusion.

"She's right," his uncle says, his voice far softer than Anabel's.

Cal's eyebrows almost disappear into his hairline. "Julian?" he asks, almost inaudible.

Jacos just shrugs, crossing his hands over his thin chest. "I have little talent on the battlefield, but that doesn't make me talentless. It's a good plan, Cal. Drive Iris out to sea." Then his eyes fall on me. "Get to a ship, Evangeline," he says slowly, his voice empty of his ability.

I realize the threat all the same. I have no choice in this, not with the loaded gun of a singer staring me down. I do this of my own volition or I do it of his.

"Fine."

For all his shortcomings, Cal certainly is noble to a fault. Usually it makes me hate him all the more. Except now. As he pledged before in Montfort, he won't let anyone fight for him unless he's fighting for himself. He won't make anyone do what he isn't willing to do with them. So when the teleporters gather, hands outstretched, he is next to me, armed and ready to storm a battleship.

"The first time isn't pleasant," my teleporter says to me, his face grim and lined with age. A veteran of many battles.

I can only grit my teeth at him and take his hand.

It feels like being squeezed down to my marrow, all my organs twisting, my balance thrown off, my perception turned on its head. I try to gasp and find I can't breathe, can't see, can't think, can't exist— until it disappears, as fast as it came. I gulp down air, knees to the steel-plated deck of a battleship, while the teleporter stands over me. He reaches to cover my mouth but I swat him away, shooting him a murderous glare at the same time.

We're behind the forward gun turret, crouched alongside cold steel and smooth, cylindrical gun barrels. They're red hot and still smoking from their barrage on the fort, and now trained on the city. My ability rushes their length, feeling out the rivets and bolts, jumping from one barrel to another, into the powder magazine—*almost full*—and the artillery shells waiting—*more than a dozen ready*. I assume the same for the two other turrets fore and aft, dotting the length of the ship.

"There's enough ammunition to turn Harbor Bay to ash," I mutter, if only to myself.

The teleporter responds only with a fuming glare. He reminds me of my father. Flint-eyed, focused.

I do as I must. With a grimace, I put my hands to the turret and pull.

It strains against me, already locked and aimed elsewhere. But once I get the gears moving in their track, it goes easily, shifting at my touch. Turning, facing another target.

Iris's own battleship.

She paces the deck of the boat farthest out to sea, a silhouette in dark blue. Her own Lakelanders flank her, their uniforms easy to pick out. Farther down the ship, at the prow, a figure in red blinks into existence, a teleporter and his own soldiers at his back.

"Almost," I hiss, sliding the turret into place, its barrels now aimed at Iris's broadside. With a clenching fist, I fuse the steel and iron plate together, locking the turret into position. No one but a magnetron, or someone with a blowtorch, could aim this gun now. "Next gun."

With another sickening jump, we land alongside the second turret. I do the same again, shifting the guns. This time, a pair of Red conscripts find us. They rush at me, but the teleporter grabs them both and disappears. He flashes at the corner of my eye, out over the water. Both Reds plummet into the Bay. The teleporter returns before I hear their splashes.

The third turret fights worse than the others, straining against my ability, refusing to move as smoothly as the others. "They figured us out," I growl, breaking a sweat. "The gunner is trying to keep the turret in place."

"Are you a magnetron or not?" the teleporter sneers at me.

I hope Ptolemus got someone less mouthy, I think, wincing. With a burst of force, I get the turret turning, and I crush it into position with more fervor than necessary. The base crumples inward, stuck on its track.

"It's done. Give the signal."

It's easier to trip the gun mechanism than I thought it would be. Like pulling a gigantic trigger.

The resulting boom of a single artillery shell sends me sideways, clutching my ears. Everything rings and dulls in succession. I fight to my feet, watching as the round hits home, exploding on the deck of Iris's battleship.

Fire races its length, a vicious snake coiling with hissing fury. Larger than a blow from a single shell. A few soldiers jump into the Bay to escape its wrath.

Cal's wrath.

The Lakelanders are less deterred, drawing an arcing wave up and over the ship. Letting it crash and consume, dousing the fire.

Only for another shell to hit them dead-on, this time from Ptolemus's ship on their opposite side. I can't help but grin, almost cheering him on.

Again Cal runs flame across the battleship. More flee, more jump. Another wave. Another shell. Another flame. The rhythm pulls back and forth.

My teleporter jumps us between the turrets, and each time we find more soldiers to fight off. Reds, mostly. Silvers don't work ships in great numbers, only as officers. They're easy to deflect, between my ability and the Montfortan's.

If I could, I would have him jump me to Cal. He doesn't have the stomach to kill Iris, but I certainly do. The Lakelands are already furious with us after their king's death. It won't matter if she dies too. In fact, it might send them scurrying back to their lakes and farms, to rethink standing against the might of Samos and Calore.

But my job is to man the guns. Hold the ship.

With Cal battling Iris, her attention is off the Bay, and our soldiers begin the crossing. During our third pass down the ship, more teleporters jump onto the deck, bringing with them six soldiers each. And more soldiers arrive in the boats below, fast on the approach.

I squint at the far battleship, watching as I land another round. This one hits hard, punching a smoking hole in the hull a few yards above the waterline. On deck, the sight is terrifying. The clouds darken overhead, thick with lightning. Fire and water collide over the battleship, inferno and tidal wave. The ship tips with the force of such a battle, one royal Silver against another. Warriors equally matched and unevenly set.

For the first time in my life, I truly wonder what will happen if Tiberias Calore dies.

I think Iris is going to kill him.

TWENTY
Mare

The miles are few, but they feel endless. I keep my grip on the door handle, ready to spring out the second we roll onto the Port Road, wheels spinning beneath us. It's just me, the electricons, and our driver. Even Ella is silent, staring out the window at the darkening sky. The smoke of New Town gives way to black, acrid clouds the closer we get to Harbor Bay. At first I'm grateful that I don't have to speak to anyone. But as the minutes wear on, the silence grows thicker, heavier, pressing down on me. It makes it difficult to think of anything beyond the city ahead and the battle raging there. In the distance, the horizon seems to burn.

My mind spins out, filling in the blanks of what we might find. Each scenario is worse than the last. Surrender. Defeat. Farley dying. Tiberias pale and bleeding, his blood a silver halo.

The last time I was in Harbor Bay, I traveled through tunnels and alleyways. I didn't tear through the streets in a military transport, escorted like some kind of dignitary or noble. I barely recognize the place.

I expect opposition as we roll into the city, but the battle lines are farther in than I thought. The streets are largely empty of everything but soldiers. All ours, marching to their posts or working their patrols. Once or twice, I spot a contingent of coalition soldiers flanking prisoners. Silvers handcuffed in iron, being led away to wherever we might be keeping them. Davidson's orders, I assume. He knows how to leverage prisoners best.

The transport angles beneath me, beginning the gentle descent to the harbor.

"The coalition is forming up on the waterfront, fortifying our position before they try to push back into the fort," our driver calls back to us. A radio in his console blares mostly static, but a few jumbled words get through. He relays what he can. "Sounds like the Air Fleet is holding the Nortan jets out at sea, and we're doing what we can to win the warships in the harbor, but there's Lakelander ships on the horizon."

Across from me, Rafe curses under his breath. "Well out of range," he mutters.

"Let me be the judge of that," Ella replies sternly, still at the window.

Tyton leans back in his seat, his lips pursed. "So we hold the city. For now."

"Seems like it," I reply, still wary as ever.

The transport rolls on, passing larger buildings and more important-looking places. My body is tight as a coiled wire, ready to react if this calm is just a trap. A feint to lure Tiberias and the others into a false sense of security. I keep my teeth gritted together and the feel of lightning close. My fellow electricons do the same, each of them stern and ready to fight.

The churning waters of the harbor flash at the end of the street, beyond a scurrying crowd of soldiers. It looks like a storm has just passed through. Every surface is wet, and dark gray clouds are breaking up overhead, blown off by a furious gale. Waves lap at the curved shoreline, still foaming white like the surface of a boiling pot. I can see now that out in the harbor, Fort Patriot is a ruin, one half flooded, the other half burning. I can smell it, even across the water. The bridge to the fort is just as obliterated, parts of it overtaken by the sea.

My forehead touches the glass of the window as I strain to see more. Our soldiers busy themselves clearing debris, building makeshift walls, or setting machine guns. I search their ranks, looking for familiar faces as we drive onto the paved plaza lining the waterfront. They all look the same, even in their differing uniforms. Dirty-faced, bleeding both colors, exhausted and ready to drop. But alive.

Their ranks part for the transport as we round the water, heading toward the center of the waterfront and the now-smashed gates of the fort bridge. Ella and I bunch up at the right-hand window, craning for a better view. Across from us, Rafe does the same. Only Tyton remains still, glaring at his dirty boots.

"The ships are firing on each other," Ella breathes, pointing out the battleships still in the harbor. "Look, three to one."

I bite my lip, confused for only a moment. In the distance, the gray hulks bob in the water, rocking with the force of their own heavy guns. Indeed, three of them seem to be shooting at the fourth. I wonder which side has the upper hand. Our coalition—or Maven's. Smaller boats venture into the choppy waters, carrying soldiers toward the battleships.

The transport barely halts before my boots hit the wet pavement, each step slick and precarious. I keep my balance, shoving through the crowd of soldiers. The other electricons follow. We make for the knot of officers near the waterline, watching over the boats moving across the harbor. In the distance, the fourth battleship rides the waves, tipping back and forth beneath the force of bombardment. I barely glance at it, hunting for familiar faces among the soldiers.

I see Farley first, her golden hair gleaming against the gray of battle. Binoculars dangle around her neck, forgotten for a moment. She barks orders in steady rhythm, gesturing between her officers. She doesn't seem to notice the men stacking up crates, building a meager wall to protect their general. Some of the tension in my chest releases, and I breathe a bit easier.

Julian is here as well, to my relief. He and Queen Anabel hang close, both of them transfixed by the battleships in the harbor. Their stare is unwavering, and Anabel clutches Julian's arm, her knuckles white against his sleeve.

The sight unsettles me, but I can't say why.

"Where do you need us?" I clip, entering their circle as calmly as I can.

Farley rounds on me, sputtering, and I brace for the inevitable rebuke. "What are you doing here?" she snaps. "Is something wrong in New Town—"

"New Town is won," Ella offers, crossing her arms at my side.

Rafe nods. "Put us to work here, General."

"It's Iris Cygnet out there," Farley snarls, gesturing to the ships. Then she hesitates, teeth on edge. It makes me uneasy.

I put a hand to her arm. Maven's queen is formidable, but not unbeatable. "Iris doesn't scare me. Farley, let us help—"

Out in the harbor, a burst of red flame runs the length of the fourth ship, moving strangely. A massive, unnatural wave rises up to meet it, breaking across the deck. Another curl of fire erupts, spiraling in the air as more tongues of water twist and spray. They move together, an elemental dance that could only be the work of two very specific people.

My heart drops in my chest, frozen with fear. And fury.

The sky turns black above the harbor, clouds re-forming in an instant. Purple flashes deep within, matching the rhythm of my beating heart.

"What is he *doing*?" I snarl to no one, taking a step toward the water. Something snaps apart inside me. Any objective I might have had, all thoughts of the city, disappear in an instant.

"Easy, Mare," I hear Ella say, trying to catch my arm, but I shove her off. *I have to get to that ship. I have to stop him.* "You don't have the aim to help him from here!" she shouts, her voice fading. I'm faster in a crowd, more agile. They can't keep up.

I work my way to the water's edge. Desperation might swallow me whole. Cal is fighting a nymph, a powerful nymph. His greatest weakness. It terrifies me.

Boats shuttle back and forth across the harbor, the empty ones returning to load more soldiers. I watch with my teeth gritted so tightly they might shatter. *Too slow.*

"Teleporters!" I shout, desperate and in vain. The sound of the guns all but drowns me out. "Teleporters!" I scream again. No one comes running.

The boats might be slow-moving, but they're my best chance. I have a foot in one when Farley catches up to me, seizing me by the shoulders. She all but drags me backward, my boots splashing through the shallow water of the docks.

I shrug her off, twisting with motions I learned a long time ago in the alleys of the Stilts. She stumbles but catches herself, hands outstretched. Her face flushes scarlet.

"Get me on that ship, Farley." My voice shakes with anger. I feel like I might explode. "I'm not asking for your permission."

"Okay," she concedes, her eyes wide with a fear of her own. "Okay—"

A flash out on the water stills us both, and Farley's words die on her lips. We watch in stunned silence as a succession of explosive rounds pummel into Iris's ship, rocking the craft. Waves rise up to stabilize it, even as the explosions spread, red and angry, each an inferno reaching skyward. Smoke billows, black and reeking, as another wave pulls over the ship. Soldiers fall from the deck, splashing into the harbor below. From this distance, I can't distinguish their uniforms. Red, green, or blue, I can't tell.

But his armor flashes brightly against the fire, impossible to miss.

Without thinking, I rip the binoculars off Farley's neck and press them to my eyes.

I feel frozen by what I see, rooted, unable to move.

Iris dodges a fireball, dipping with liquid motion, faster than Tiberias ever was. She dances out of his reach, circling even as the ship beneath them moves, churning its way toward the mouth of the harbor and the open ocean. The valiant, stupid Calore pursues.

Another wave hits him head-on, crashing blue and white with the full force of Iris Cygnet's power. My heart stops in my chest as I imagine him crushed against the metal ship, drowning before my eyes.

He falls, his armor broken, splintered by battle, his scarlet cape torn to pieces. For such a large man, Tiberias makes such a tiny splash.

My vision spots, hazy with every emotion as my own brain overloads. Everything narrows, edged with black, until I can't hear the crowd around me. Even Farley's voice fades, her barking orders disappearing. I want to scream but find my teeth welded together. If I move, if I speak, all my restraint will disappear too. The lightning will have no mercy. All I can do is stare, stand, and pray to whoever might be listening.

Warm hands hold my shoulders as the electricons surround me, close enough to react if I lose control. Blue, green, white. Ella, Rafe, Tyton.

Cal, Cal, Cal.

Survive.

Nothing matters but the water, blue-and-white waves foaming with battle. Most of the soldiers who fell from the ships are still alive, bobbing up and down. *But they aren't wearing armor. They aren't terrified of water. They didn't face Iris Cygnet and lose.* The glare from the sun makes it impossible to see much, but I squint anyway, until I can't stand it anymore. Until I can't open my eyes. The binoculars drop from my hands and smash.

The chaos on the water's edge grows, until every soldier stands in wait, breathless to see the fate of the Calore prince. When they gasp as one, I force my eyes open and turn. Tyton's grip on me turns viselike, his fingers pressed against my neck. He'll knock me out if he has to, to protect everyone else from my sorrow.

I don't know who dragged Tiberias out of the water, or which teleporter brought him to the shore. I don't watch the healer as she bends, terrified, trying to save his life. I don't care about Iris, still out in the harbor, making her escape. I can only look at him, even though I never want to see him like this. Each passing second is a ruin. I've been shot; I've been stabbed; I've been hollowed out. This is a thousand times worse.

Silver skin is a colder color than our own, as if drained of warmth.

But I've never seen a Silver look like he does. His lips are blue, his cheeks like glowing moonlight, every inch of him soaking or bleeding. His eyes are shut. He isn't breathing. Tiberias looks like a corpse. He could *be* a corpse.

Time stretches. I live in this cursed second, trapped, doomed to watch little pieces of his life ebb away. Kilorn survived in New Town. Will I lose Tiberias in Harbor Bay?

The healer puts her palms to his chest, sweat beading on her brow.

I pray to any god who might exist. To anyone who might listen.

Then I beg.

Water sprays from his mouth as he coughs violently, his eyes flying open at the same time. I almost collapse, and only the electricons keep me standing against the sudden rush. Gasping, I put a hand to my mouth to stifle the sound, only to feel tears on both my cheeks.

The crowd of people around him surges, Anabel moving to kneel at his side. Julian is there too. They croon over their boy, smoothing his hair, bidding him to lie still as the healer continues her work.

He nods weakly, still getting his bearings.

I turn away before he sees me and realizes how much I want to stay.

Ocean Hill was a favorite of Coriane, the dead queen I never knew. It's a favorite of her son as well.

The palace is polished white stone with blue domed roofs crowned in silver flames, still magnificent even through the trailing smoke and falling ash. We circle the plaza in front of the palace gates, usually a mess of traffic. The only activity seems to be at the neighboring Security Center, now overrun with coalition soldiers. As we pass, they rip down the red, black, and silver banners, as well as the hung images of

Maven Calore. One by one, they set fire to the symbols. I watch his face burn, blue eyes locked on mine through a devouring tangle of red flame.

The streets themselves are empty, and the fountain I remember, beautiful beneath a dome of crystal, is dry. War walks the stones of Harbor Bay.

The palace gates are already open, yawning wide for Farley and me. We've been here before, as intruders. Fugitives. Not today.

When the transport slows, Farley is quick to clamber out, gesturing for me to follow. But I hesitate, still haunted by the events of the morning. It's only been a few hours since I watched Tiberias almost die. I can't get the sight out of my head.

"Mare," she prods, her voice low. It's enough to snap me into action.

The cerulean doors of the palace swing open on silent hinges, revealing two members of the Scarlet Guard keeping watch. Their ripped scarves are ruby bright, hopelessly out of place, and a sharp, unmistakable sign.

We have returned here as conquerors.

Ocean Hill still reeks of disuse and abandonment. I don't think Maven ever set foot inside once he became king. Coriane's faded golden colors hang from the walls and vaulted ceiling. It remains a tomb to a forgotten queen, empty but for her memory and perhaps even her ghost.

I see an odd reversal as I walk, noting the faces around me. A few Reds of the Scarlet Guard keep watch, their weapons openly displayed, but most seem without purpose. Recovering in the wake of battle, dozing against opulent columns or lazily exploring the many salons and chambers branching off the central gallery. It's the Silvers who busy themselves with more menial work, probably on Anabel's orders. They have to prepare Tiberias's new seat, his palace, to mark him as a legitimate ruler and king. They open windows, pull the covers from furniture, even dust off sills and statues. I blink at the sight, overwhelmed. *Silvers doing housework. What a concept.* The Red servants must have fled, and the Reds still here certainly won't do it for them.

I don't recognize anyone in passing. No Julian. Not even Anabel supervising as her sworn soldiers prepare the palace. It worries me, because there's only one other place they could be. And clearly they have to be there.

I'm almost sprinting when Evangeline catches me, springing out from around a corner. Her armor is gone, discarded for lighter underclothes. If the battle was difficult for her, she certainly doesn't look it. While everyone else is dirty, if not still bloody, Evangeline Samos looks fresh from a cold bath.

"Get out of my way" is all I can manage, trying to step around her. Farley halts, looking on with a glare.

"Let her go, Samos," she snarls.

Evangeline ignores her. Instead she seizes my shoulders, forcing me to look her in the eye. I resist the familiar urge to deck her and instead let her look. To my surprise, she searches me over, eyes lingering on my many cuts and bruises.

"You should see a healer first; we have plenty," she says. "You look horrible."

"Evangeline—"

She sharpens. "He's fine. I promise you that."

My eyes snap to hers. "I know that," I hiss. "I saw him with my own eyes." Even so, I clench my teeth at the memory, too fresh and still too painful.

He's alive; he survived her, the nymph princess, I remind myself. *His brother's deadly queen.* I could wring his neck for doing it, challenging a nymph *in the middle of the Bay.* I've seen Tiberias Calore balk at swimming across a stream. He hates water, fears it like nothing else. It's the worst and easiest way for him to die.

Evangeline bites her lip, watching me. She likes something in what she sees. When she speaks again, her voice is changed, softened. A featherlight whisper. "I can't forget it. How he sank like a stone, armor and all," she says, moving close enough to speak in my ear. The words twist around me, prickling on my skin. "How long was it until the healers got him breathing again?"

I squeeze my eyes shut, trying not to remember. *I know what you're doing, Evangeline. And it's working.* Tiberias, pale and dead, his body soaked through. Mouth parted, eyes open and empty. Unseeing. Shade's body was the same, and it haunts me still. When I open my eyes again, Tiberias's corpse is still there, hovering in my mind. I can't shake the sight.

"That's *enough,*" Farley says, stepping bodily between us. She all but hauls me away, with Evangeline smirking.

She falls into step behind us, prodding me in the right direction like I'm a cow being led to pasture. Or slaughter.

I don't know Ocean Hill, but I know palaces well enough to know what I'm looking for. We climb a garish, winding stairwell to the residences, a floor dotted with royal chambers and apartments. Up here, away from the more public levels, the dust is worse than ever. It puffs up from the carpet in clouds. Coriane's colors are all over. Gold and yellow, pale and worn. Forgotten everywhere but here. I wonder if they bring her son pain. Her son who almost joined her in death.

The king's chambers are vast, opening off a guarded entry lined with Lerolan soldiers. They share Anabel's colors and her coloring.

Black hair and bronze eyes. Tiberias's eyes. No one stops us as we pass, stepping into the sunken room now serving as a receiving chamber. A very crowded one.

I see Julian first, his back to the arched windows looking out on the now-sparkling Bay. It gleams blue in the afternoon sun. He angles his face to me, features pulling into an expression I can't name. Sara Skonos stands at his side, her posture violently straight with her hands clasped in front of her. Though her hands are clean, the sleeves of her simple uniform are crusted to the elbows in both red and silver blood. I shudder at it. She doesn't notice me at first, focused on the mountainous man in the center of the room. He sinks to his knees.

Farley quietly takes a seat, maneuvering herself in between a pair of Scarlet Guard lieutenants. She gestures for me to join her, but I stay put. I prefer the edges of this particular crowd.

I've never officially met the ruling lord of House Rhambos, but I recognize his bulk, even kneeling. His robes are unmistakable, resplendent in rich chocolate and crimson edged with precious stones. He is their leader, and the ruling governor of this city and region. His hair is dirty blond giving over to gray, braided back from his face in once-intricate rows. They're coming undone, either from the battle or from the great lord pulling at his hair in desperation. I suppose both.

Silvers are not accustomed to surrendering.

I exhale, and will myself to look up from Rhambos's shoulders to the true king standing above him. Sword in hand. The sight of him erases the corpse from my mind.

His fingers hold firm, unwavering, his grip tight on the adorned hilt of the ceremonial blade. Where it came from, I don't know. It isn't the sword Elara made him kill his father with, but it looks close enough. And I'm sure he remembers it now, as he stands above another man begging for his life. It must pain him, to do this to someone else. And of his own volition this time.

Tiberias looks paler than usual, cheeks drained of color. But in shame or fear, I can't tell. Maybe it's exhaustion. Or pain. In spite of it, he is every inch a king. His armor cleaned, his crown donned. The angled lines of his jaw and cheekbones look sharper somehow, honed by the sudden weight on his shoulders. It's a mask, all of it. A brave face he must wear. His other hand is empty, fingers bare without flame. No fire but the one burning in his eyes.

"The city is yours," Rhambos says, his head bowed and hands raised.

Queen Anabel steps close to her grandson's shoulder, fingers curled like talons. She might be the only person on earth who can seem royal without her finery. "You will address him properly, Lord Rhambos."

He is quick to acquiesce, dipping further, almost kissing his lips to the carpeted floor. "Your Majesty, King Tiberias," he offers without hesitation. He spreads his hands wide in open faith. "The city of Harbor Bay, and the entirety of the Beacon region, is rightfully yours. Returned to the true king of Norta."

Tiberias looks down his straight nose, turning the blade. The edge catches the light. The lord flinches, squinting against the sudden glare. "And what of House Rhambos?" he asks.

Next to me, Evangeline snorts into her hand. "What a performance."

"We are yours as well, to do with as you wish," the lord murmurs, his voice broken. For all he knows, Tiberias could execute his entire family. Pull them out at the root. Wipe their name and their blood from the face of the earth. Silver kings have done worse for less. "Our soldiers, our money, our resources are at your disposal," he adds, listing off all his house can give. All his *living* house can give.

A beat of silence stretches, taut as a pulled wire. Threatening to snap apart. Tiberias surveys Lord Rhambos without blinking, without feeling, his face blank and unreadable. Then he bears a smile. It bleeds warmth and understanding. I can't tell if it's real.

"I thank you for it," he says, inclining his head a fraction. Beneath him, Lord Rhambos all but shudders in relief. "Just as I will thank every member of your house when they follow your example and pledge an oath of loyalty to me. Forsaking the false king who sits on my father's throne."

At his side, Anabel beams. If she coached him, she did it well.

"Yes—yes, of course," Rhambos stammers. He all but falls over himself to agree. I notice Tiberias edging his toes away, lest the fallen lord try to kiss them. "That will be arranged as soon as possible. Our strength is yours."

Tiberias's face tightens. "By tomorrow, my lord." Leaving no room for argument.

"By tomorrow, Your Majesty," Rhambos replies, bobbing his head. Still kneeling, he clenches both meaty fists. "All hail Tiberias the Seventh, King of Norta and true Flame of the North!" he shouts, his voice stronger by the second.

The crowd of advisers and soldiers, both Silver and Red, responds in kind, repeating the obnoxious titles. A bit of color returns to Tiberias's cheeks as he flushes. His eyes dart back and forth, trying to note who cries his name and who doesn't. His eyes land on me and my unmoving lips. I hold his gaze, feeling a thrill as I keep my mouth resolutely shut.

Farley does too, examining her nails instead of the unfolding pageantry.

Anabel basks in it, one hand on her grandson's shoulder. Her left hand, laid just so to display an old wedding ring set with a black gemstone. The only jewelry on her, and the only one she ever needs.

"All hail," she murmurs, her eyes shining as she looks up at Tiberias. At some flicker in his face, she springs into action, moving in front of him. She clasps her lethal hands together, ring still exposed. "The king thanks you for your loyalty, as do I. We have much to discuss in the coming hours."

It's as good as a dismissal. Tiberias turns, putting his back to the room, and I realize what an admission it is. He's tired. He's wounded. Maybe not in body, but somewhere deep, where no one can see. The rigid set of his shoulders, his familiar posture, slumps beneath the ruby-red pauldrons of his armor. Releasing some weight. Or giving in to it.

Somehow, all thoughts of his corpse come rushing back. Dread pools in me, threatening to fill me up and drag me down.

I step forward, meaning to stay, but the crowd works against me. As does Evangeline. She takes me under my arm, her decorative claws still donned and digging into soft flesh. I grit my teeth, letting her lead me out of his chambers, not wanting to cause a fuss or a scene. Julian passes by us with a single raised eyebrow, surprised to see us in such close confidence. I try to communicate with my eyes. Try to ask for some help or guidance. But he turns away before he knows what I want. Or he simply doesn't want to give it.

We pass the guards again, the Lerolans looking like Sentinels in their colors of red and orange. Perhaps that's where the robes first came from. I look back, over the heads of Silver lords and Red officers. Farley's blond hair glints somewhere, with Ptolemus Samos keeping a safe distance from her. I see Anabel, watching like a hawk. She plants herself in front of the door to Tiberias's bedchamber. He slips behind it, out of sight without so much as a backward glance.

"Don't argue," Evangeline hisses in my ear.

On instinct, I open my mouth to do just that. But I cut myself off as she drags me sideways, out of the crowd and into the corridor.

Even though we're as safe as possible for the circumstances, my heart beats a ragged rhythm in my chest. "You said yourself, locking us in a closet together wouldn't work."

"I'm not locking anyone anywhere," she whispers back. "I'm just showing you the door."

We turn and turn, taking the side stairs and servants' passages far too slowly and too quickly for my liking. My inner compass spins, and I think we're almost where we started when she halts within a dimly lit passage, almost too narrow for us to squeeze through.

With a ripple of unease, I think of my earring. The one I'm not wearing. A bloodred stone, tucked away in a box in Montfort, hidden from the world.

On my right, Evangeline lays her palm against an old door, rusted over from disuse. The hinges and lock have gone dark red, crusting like dried blood. With a flick of her fingers, the metal spins, shedding the rust like droplets of water.

"This will take you—"

"I know where it's going to take me," I reply, almost too fast. I suddenly feel like I've run a mile.

Her grin sets me on edge, and almost makes me turn around. Almost.

"Very well," she says, taking a step back. Her hand brushes through the air, gesturing to the door like it's a priceless gift. Instead of the naked manipulation it is. "Do what you want, lightning girl. Go where you please. No one will stop you."

I have no clever response for her. All I can do is watch her slink away, eager to be rid of me. Elane must be on her way to the city to help celebrate this victory. I find myself envying them. They're on the same side, at least, allied despite the impossibilities stacked against them. Both Silver, both raised noble. They know each other in a way Tiberias and I could never. They are the same, equals. He and I are not.

I should turn around.

But I'm already through the door, pushing through the semidarkness of a forgotten passage, my fingertips brushing along cool stone. A light bleeds ahead, closer than I thought it would be. Outlining another door.

Turn around.

My hands flatten against the wood, a smooth cut, uniquely carved. I trace the panels for a moment, on edge. I know where this path leads, and who waits on the other side. Footsteps sound inside the room, making me jump as they pass. Then a chair creaks as a heavy weight sits. Two thumps announce his boots as he kicks them up on a desk or table. And then a long, lingering sigh. Not the satisfied kind. Full of frustration. Full of pain.

Turn around.

The knob moves in my hand, as if of its own volition, and I step out blinking into the soft light of afternoon. Tiberias's bedchamber here is large and airy, with vaulted ceilings painted blue and white, almost like clouds. The windows look out on the Bay, and a sunnier day than it should be. The ocean breeze blows the last of the smoke away.

It looks like the king is doing his best to fill the place with his usual mess, despite only having been here a few hours. He sits at a desk haphazardly dragged to the center of the room, angled away from a bed I refuse to even glance at. Papers and books pile around him. One in particular lies open, the text inside handwritten in a tight, looping scrawl.

When I finally get the courage to look at him, Tiberias is already standing. He has a fist raised and flaming, his entire body coiled like a snake, ready to spring.

His eyes rove over me, hand still ablaze even though I'm not a threat. After a long moment, he brushes away the fire, letting it flicker and die.

"You got here in a hurry," Tiberias blurts out, almost breathless.

It takes us both off guard, and he looks away, easing back into his desk chair. He puts his back to me and quickly shuts the book with one hand. It spits dust. The cover is worn, a faded gold, with no writing on it and a broken binding. He shoves it away, tucking it into a drawer with little regard.

Then he pretends to busy himself with some reports. He even bends over them with a very obvious squint. I smirk to myself and take a step toward him.

Turn around.

Another step into the room. The air seems to vibrate on my skin.

"After the . . . " I stumble. There's no easy way to say it. *"After,* I had to see for myself," I reply, watching the side of his mouth lift. His eyes don't move, burning a hole into the page in front of him.

"And?"

Shrugging, I rest my hands on my hips. "You're fine. I shouldn't have bothered."

At the desk, he barks out a harsh but genuine laugh. Tiberias leans backward, putting an arm over his chair, twisting to look at me fully. In the daylight, his bronze eyes gleam like molten metal. They run over me, snagging on the exposed cuts and bruises. His gaze feels like fingers. "What about you?" he asks, his voice lower.

I hesitate a little. My own injuries seem small compared to what he suffered, and to the memory of Kilorn choking on his own blood. "Nothing that can't be mended."

He purses his lips. "That's not what I asked."

"Nothing to compare, I mean," I tell him, circling to the front of his desk. He moves with me, tracking like a hunter. It feels similar to a dance or a pursuit. "Not all of us can say we almost died today."

"Oh, that," he mutters, and runs a hand through his hair. The short locks stand on end, mussing an otherwise kingly appearance. "Everything went to plan."

I scowl, showing my teeth. "Funny, I don't remember fighting a killer nymph in the middle of the ocean being part of the *plan*."

He adjusts in his chair, uncomfortable. Slowly, he starts discarding his armor, revealing the thin, tight shirt and trimmer form beneath. It's a dare, but I hold my ground. Each piece hits the floor with a resounding clatter. "We needed the ships. We needed the harbor."

I keep circling, and he keeps tossing pieces of armor away. He unfastens his gauntlets with his teeth, never taking his eyes off me.

"And we needed you to go toe-to-toe with her? Who had the *advantage* there, Tiberias?"

The king smirks against red steel.

"I'm still alive."

"That isn't funny." Something tightens in my chest. I run a finger down the adorned edge of his desk, swiping at the dusty surface. My skin comes away gray, leached of warmth. Like it was when I masqueraded as a Silver, suffering through painted-on makeup just to keep breathing. "We almost lost Kilorn today."

Tiberias's smirk drops instantly, wiped away, and he forgets the armor for a moment. Darkness clouds his eyes, dulling their gleam. "I thought New Town fell easily. They didn't expect—" He cuts himself off, clenching his teeth. I look away as his gaze lands on me. I don't want to see his pity. "What happened?"

My breath feels ragged in my throat. It feels too close to relive, the danger still near. "Silver guards," I mumble. "A telky. Tossed him down a stairwell. Tore up his insides." The words hitch as the memory reigns. My oldest friend, his skin going pale, dying faster by the second. Red blood on his chin, his chest, his clothes. All over my hands.

The king doesn't say anything, holding his tongue. With a great burst of will, I look back at his face to find him staring, eyes wide, lips pressed into a grim, thin line. The concern is clearly written on him, in his furrowed brow and tight jaw.

I force myself to move again, my path taking me back around. Closer to his chair, into the circle of familiar heat.

"We got him to a healer in time," I say as I walk. "He'll be all right, same as you."

When I pass behind him, I bite back the urge to touch his shoulders. To put one hand on either side of his neck and lean forward, bracing myself against him. Letting him hold me up. Now more than ever, the need to let go and rest, to allow someone else to carry my burdens, is difficult to resist.

"But you're here with me," he whispers so low I almost don't catch it.

Instead the words linger, smoke between us.

I have no answer for him. None I'm willing to give or admit. I'm no stranger to shame. I certainly feel it now, as I stand in his bedchamber, with Kilorn recovering miles away. Kilorn, who wouldn't be here if not for me.

"It isn't your fault," Tiberias pushes on. He knows me well enough to guess my thoughts. "What happens to him isn't on your shoulders.

He makes his own choices. And without you, what you did for him . . ." His voice trails off. "You know where he would have ended up."

Conscripted. Doomed to a trench, or a barracks. Probably dead in the final gasps of the Lakelander War. Another name on a list, another Red lost to Silver greed. Another person forgotten. *Because of people like you,* I think, forcing a deep breath. The bedroom smells like salt air, fresh from the open windows.

I try to take some comfort in what he says. But I can't. It doesn't excuse anything I've done, or what Kilorn has become because of me.

Though I suppose we've all changed since last year. Since that day when his master died and he stood in the dark beneath my house, trying not to mourn his life as it was snatched away. I swallow hard, remembering what I said. *Leave everything to me.*

I wonder if we changed into who we were supposed to become, or if those people are gone forever. I guess only Jon would know, and the seer is long gone, far out of reach.

Clearing my throat, I change the subject with little tact. "I hear there's a Lakelander fleet on the horizon." I put my back to him, turning to face the exterior door, the one leading back into his receiving chamber. I could walk out right now if I wanted. He wouldn't stop me.

I'm just stopping myself with every single breath.

"I hear that too," Tiberias replies. Then his voice drops, deepening. It wavers in fear. "I remember darkness. Emptiness. Nothing."

Reluctantly, I look over my shoulder to watch him stand, shedding the last of his armor. Avoiding my gaze. He's still tall, still broad, but lesser without the weight of the battle-worn steel. Younger-looking too, just twenty years old. Tipping on the edge of manhood, parts of him still clinging to youth. Holding on to something as it disappears, just like the rest of us.

"I went into the water and I couldn't get back up." He kicks the pile of steel on the floor. "Couldn't swim, couldn't breathe, couldn't think."

I feel like I can't breathe either.

Tiberias shudders as I watch, a tremor that starts in his fingers. His fear is terrifying. Then he forces himself to look back at me. With his feet planted and his hands firmly settled on his hips, he is rooted. The king won't move unless I do. He's going to make me surrender first. It's what any good soldier would do. Or he is simply letting me choose. Letting me decide for both of us. He probably thinks it's the honorable thing to do.

"I thought of you before the end," he says. "I saw your face in the water."

And I see his corpse again, suspended before me, dappled by the shifting light of a churning sea. Afloat, at the mercy of a foreign tide.

Neither of us moves.

"I can't," I bite out, looking anywhere but his face.

He responds quickly, with force. "Neither can I."

"But I also can't—"

Stay away. Keep doing this. Denying ourselves in the face of always-looming death.

Tiberias hisses out a breath.

"Neither can I."

When we take the step forward together, from opposite directions, both of us laugh. It almost breaks the spell. But we keep walking, equal in motion and intention. Slow and methodic, measuring. He watches me, I watch him, as the space closes between us. I touch him first, putting my palm flat over his thudding heart. He inhales slowly, his chest rising beneath my fingers. A warm hand slips around my back, splaying wide over the base of my spine. I know he can feel my old scars through my shirt, the knobbled skin familiar to us both. I answer by curling my other hand at the nape of his neck, gently digging my nails into the lock of black hair.

"This doesn't change anything," I say against his collarbone, a firm line against my cheek.

I feel his answer in my rib cage. "No."

"We aren't making different decisions."

His arms tighten around me. "No."

"So what is this, Cal?"

The name has an effect on us both. He shivers, and I move closer, flattening against him. It feels like giving in, for both of us, though we have nothing left to surrender.

"We're choosing not to choose."

"That doesn't sound real."

"Maybe it isn't."

But he's wrong. I can't think of anything more real than the feel of him. The heat, the smell, the taste. It's the only real thing in my world.

"This is the last time," I whisper before I cover his mouth with mine.

Over the next few hours, I say that so many times I lose count.

TWENTY-ONE
Maven

I hate the waves. They offend me.

Every heave of blue against the hull of the boat makes my stomach toss, and it is entirely too difficult to remain still, silent, the image of reserved strength I need to be, Perhaps Iris or her mother is roiling the sea on purpose. In punishment for my risking Iris's life in Harbor Bay. *Even though she survived and escaped easily enough. Survived, escaped, and* lost *the city to my perfect brother.* I wouldn't put it past the Lakelander queen. She's even more powerful than her daughter. Certainly she can control the rise and fall of the ocean around us. I spot her ships ahead, six of them. Small but formidable warships. Less of her armada than we expected.

I snarl to myself, lip curling. *Can no one simply do as they're told?* Even with her daughter in the balance, leading the failed defense of the city, Queen Cenra hasn't brought her full strength. A trickle of heat bursts through me, a tongue of angry fire down my spine. I restrain it quickly.

The constant motion makes it more difficult to keep my grip on the rail of the deck. It drains my focus. And when I lose focus, my head becomes less . . . quiet.

Harbor Bay is gone.

Another thing lost to Cal, the familiar voice whispers. *Another failure, Maven.*

Mother's voice has grown fainter as time passes, but she never truly recedes. Sometimes I wonder if she planted a seed in me, leaving it to bloom only after her death. I don't know if whispers can even do that. But it's an easy explanation for the murmurs and the mutters that rattle around in my skull.

Sometimes I'm glad for her voice. Her guidance from beyond the grave. The advice is always small; sometimes it's something she used to say before she died. Sometimes it could be just memories. But I wake up far too often from uneasy sleep, her words ringing in my ears, for her voice to simply be a product of my own mind. She's here with me still, whether I want her to be or not. I call it a comfort, even when she is anything but.

All that matters is the throne, she whispers again, as she whispered over the years. Her voice is almost lost to the swell of the ocean. Part of me strains to hear, and part of me tries not to listen. *And what you have given to get it.*

That is today's refrain. It repeats as my flagship sails toward the waiting armada, cutting through the waves as the sun sets low and red against the distant coast. Harbor Bay still trails smoke, teasing me on the horizon.

At least her voice is gentle today. When I falter, when I slow down, it turns sharp, a fraying, splintering shriek, steel on steel. Glass popping in the heat of flame. Sometimes it's so awful I check to make sure my eyes and ears aren't bleeding. They never do. Her words never exist beyond the cage of my head.

I stare at the waves ahead, each one a white crest of foam, and think of the path laid out. Not before, but behind. How I came to stand on the prow of a ship, a crown low across my forehead, with the spray of salt water drying on my skin. What I gave to be here. The people I left behind, willingly or not. Dead or abandoned or betrayed. The terrible things I've done and let be done in my name. How much will have been in vain if I fail. And now I race toward a Lakelander fleet. Enemies turned allies, through my own careful maneuvering.

Like the rest of my country, I was taught to hate the Lakelands, to curse their greed. Perhaps more than anyone else, I learned to despise them. After all, my own father and his father spent their lives locked in a stalemate war on the northern border. They saw thousands wasted against the blue uniforms, drowned in the lakes, obliterated by mine-field and missile. Of course, they knew what the war was truly for. I don't know if Cal, the poor, simple brute, ever connected such easily traced dots, but I certainly did.

Our war with the Lakelands served a purpose. Reds outnumber us. Reds can overthrow us. But not if they die in greater numbers than we do. And not if they fear something else more than they fear the Silvers standing over them. Be it dying in war, or just the Lakelanders. Any-one can be manipulated against their own interests, if given the right circumstance. My ancestors knew that well enough, in their deepest hearts. To maintain power, they lied, they manipulated, they spilled blood. Just not their own. They sacrificed life, but not the lives closest to them.

I can't say the same.

Mother is never far from my thoughts. Not just because of her voice running through my mind, but simply because I miss her. The ache is permanent, I think, a dull pain that dogs my every step. Like a missing finger or a shortness of breath. Nothing has ever been the same since she died. I remember it, the sight of her brutalized corpse in that Red girl's hands. The memory is a punch in the gut.

It isn't the same with Father. I saw his corpse too, but felt nothing for it. Not anger, not sadness. Just emptiness. If I ever loved him, I have no memory of it. And searching for one only gives me a headache. Of course, Mother removed it. To protect me, she said, from a man who did not love me as he loved her rival's son, my older brother. The perfect boy in all things.

That love for Cal is gone too, but sometimes I feel its ghost. Moments return at the oddest times, drawn out by a smell or a sound or a word spoken a certain way. Cal loved me—I know that, of course. He proved it many times, over many years. Mother had to be more careful with him, but in the end, it wasn't she who severed the last thread between us.

It was Mare Barrow.

My brilliant fool of a brother couldn't keep sight on all that was his, and what little was mine.

I remember the first time I watched the security footage of them together, dancing in a forgotten room tucked away in the summer palace. It was Cal's idea, their meetings. Their *dance lessons.* Mother sat by my side, near enough if I needed her. I reacted as she trained me to. Without feeling, without even blinking. He kissed her like he didn't know or didn't care what she meant to anyone but himself.

Because Cal is selfish, Mother croons in the memory and in my mind, her voice like silk and like a razor. The words are familiar, another old refrain. *Cal sees only what he can win and what he can take. He thinks he owns the world. And one day, if you let him, he will. What will that leave for you,*

Maven Calore? The scraps, the leftovers? Or nothing at all?

My brother and I have something in common, at least. We both want the crown and we're both willing to sacrifice anything to have it. At least I, in my worst moments, when the wretchedness threatens to overwhelm me, can blame such wanting on my mother.

But who can he blame?

And somehow everyone calls me the monster.

I'm not surprised by it. Cal walks in a light I'll never find.

Iris is always going on and on about her gods, and sometimes I believe they must be real. How else is my brother still living, still smiling, still a constant threat to me? He must be blessed, by someone or something. My only consolation is knowing I'm right about him, and always will be. Right about Mare too. I poisoned her enough, tainted her enough. She'll never tolerate another king, not for any amount of love. And Cal has discovered that firsthand, another gift of mine across the miles between us.

I only wish I'd figured out a way to keep that strange newblood, the one who bridged a connection between Mare and me. But the risk was too great, the reward too small. An obliterated base for the chance to speak with her again? It was a foolish trade, and even for her, I wouldn't make it.

But I wish I could.

She's out there across the waves, somewhere in the city along the distant, crimson coast. Alive, obviously. Or else we would know it. Even though it's only been a few hours, the death of the lightning girl would not be a secret for long. The same goes for my brother. They survived. The thought makes my head pound.

Harbor Bay was a logical choice for Cal, but the Red tech slum was obviously Mare's own brainchild. She is so married to her cause, and all her red-blooded pride. I should have predicted she would go after New Town. It's sad, really, to know that her cause relies on people like Cal, his sneering grandmother, and the Samos traitors. None of them will give her what she wants. It will only end in bloodshed. And probably her own death, when all is done.

If only I had kept her closer. A better guard, a tighter leash. Where would we be now? And where would I be if Mother could have removed her from me, as she removed Father and Cal? I can't say. I don't know. It hurts my head to wonder.

I look down the deck, at the soldiers manning the ship. She might have been beside me, if not for a few missteps. The wind in her hair, her eyes shadowed and sunken, wasted by the manacles keeping her tethered to me. An ugly sight, but still beautiful.

At the very least, she is still alive. Her heart still beats.

Not like Thomas.

I wince as his name crosses my thoughts. Mother couldn't remove him either. Not the agony of his loss, nor the memory of his love.

That future is gone, killed, chased out of existence.

A dead future, that horrible newblood seer used to call it. I think Jon was my tormentor more than I was his jailer. Clearly he could have left whenever he wanted, and whatever he accomplished in my palace is still budding fruit. Again I look out to the water, to the east this time, over a vast and endless ocean. The emptiness should calm me, but two early stars hang above the waves. The bright, cheerful lights offend me too.

Queen Cenra's ship is easy to spot as we sail closer. The waves beside it are calm, almost still, a flat quelling of water. Her ship hardly rocks, even this far from land.

The Lakelander ships aren't as sleek as ours. Our manufacturing capabilities are better than those in the Lakelands, thanks in very large part to the tech slums that Mare is intent on destroying.

Even with her ships and my own, our guns are few, and anything we might use against the city will certainly meet resistance from magnetrons and newbloods, if not my foul brother himself. Only the Harbor Bay battleship, Iris's for now, has any kind of artillery that could be of use this far out.

I glare at it, the steel craft anchored alongside Cenra's ship. It casts a long, jagged shadow, planted firmly between the Lakelander queen and the coast. My scheming queen is using it as a shield. A very expensive shield.

I growl to myself as I board her ship, careful to keep my feet when I step from one deck to the next. My own Sentinels flank me as we walk, too close for comfort. I keep my hands at my sides, ungloved, fingers bare in threat.

"This way, Your Majesty," a single Lakelander says, beckoning from an open door bolted with rivets and a wheel lock. "The queens are waiting."

"Tell them the king waits on deck," I reply, turning aside to walk the edge of the ship.

This isn't a pleasure cruise, and there aren't many places to stand, let alone congregate. But I'd rather stay on deck than go below, to be trapped behind steel with a pair of nymphs. My Sentinels walk ahead of me, careful to keep in formation, as we climb a set of stairs to a landing overlooking the prow.

It doesn't take the queens long to appear, moving in tandem.

Cenra wears a flowing uniform, dark blue with silver and gold chasing. A black sash divides her body from shoulder to hip, clasped in precious sapphire. *In mourning still.* I don't think Mother wore her mourning clothes for more than a few days. Perhaps the Lakelander queen cared for her husband. How strange. She watches me, storm-eyed, her skin a cold bronze washed gold by the setting sun.

I feel as if I can read the battle on Iris. Her blue sleeves are charred to the elbow, the threads stained in two kinds of blood. And her long black hair is undone, still wet, brushed over one shoulder. A healer trails her, tentatively working on Iris's arms as she walks, smoothing away burns and cuts.

Keeping her at an arm's length has been a wise decision. I want little to do with my wife, who would probably prefer to kill me. But like Reds, she can be controlled by fear. And need. She has both in equal measure.

So does Cenra. It's why she dared to leave her borders. She knows I hold her daughter in the palm of my hand. I don't doubt she wants to extricate Iris from our marriage. But she needs this alliance as much as I do. Without me, she faces Cal and his band of traitors and criminals. A united front against her. I'm her shield, as she is mine.

"My queens," I say, bowing slightly to them both as they approach.

Her daughter looks more like a soldier than a queen made and princess born.

The queen of the Lakelands dips into a shallow curtsy. Her sleeves brush the deck. "Your Majesty," she replies.

I turn my face to the horizon. "Harbor Bay has fallen."

"For now," Cenra says, her voice offensively calm.

"Oh?" I sneer, raising an eyebrow "You think we can win it back? Tonight, perhaps."

Again, she dips her head. "In time."

I finish for her. "When the rest of your armada arrives."

Queen Cenra grits her teeth. "Yes, of course," she reluctantly grinds out. "But—"

"But?" I ask. The sea air feels cold on my bared teeth.

"We do have our own shores to guard," she says. At her side, Iris looks smug, glad to let her mother fight this battle. "The Lakes must remain defended, especially from Montfort. They can cross Prairie and strike our western border easily. As can the Kingdom of the Rift on our east."

I have to laugh. Sneering, I wave a hand at the horizon. Full of Samos traitors and Montfort usurpers, all beneath my brother's idiot command. "Strike your border with what army? The one currently occupying my city?"

Cenra flares her nostrils and a flush heats her face, dusting over her cliff-like cheekbones. "Samos has the Nortan Air Fleet, one of the biggest on the continent. Not to mention Montfort's own capabilities, whatever they are. Your brother has the advantage from the air, and he has the speed. Anywhere could be at risk of attack." She speaks slowly, as if I am a child who needs his hand held through war. It tingles my fingers. "That cannot be ignored, Your Majesty."

As if on wretched cue, a battalion of airjets races over the coast in formation. The distant scream of them reaches us slowly, a dull and stretching roar. I fold my arms over my chest, tucking away my hands lest they ignite.

"Bracken's Air Fleet should be enough to hold them off," I mutter, keeping my eyes on the jets as they move. Circling the city. Protective maneuvers.

Iris finally finds her voice. "The bulk of his fleet was cannibalized by the Montfort occupation. They can't match what we're up against."

She clearly delights in correcting me. I let her take this small comfort instead of losing my temper.

To look powerful is to be powerful. Mother said that too many times to count. *Look calm, still, strong. Assured of yourself and your victory.*

"Which is why we have to return to a place of strength," Cenra says. "We're no good out here on the waves, waiting to be picked off from the sky. Even the nymphs of Cygnet Line are not invincible."

Of course they aren't, you proud nit.

Instead I blink at her, trying to burn through her with my eyes. "You suggest a retreat?"

"We've already retreated," Iris snaps. The healer at her side steps back a little, cowed by her anger. "Harbor Bay is one city—"

I clench a fist and a burst of heat ripples on the air. "Harbor Bay is not the only piece of my country lost to my brother," I say quietly, slowly. Low enough that they must strain to hear. "The south is his, the Rift and Delphie. He took Corvium from me. And now he has Fort Patriot too."

My sneering queen doesn't quail against my checked fury. "Fort Patriot will be of little use to them for a long time," she says, looking like a satisfied cat after a particularly big dinner.

"Oh?" I reply. "And why is that?"

She glances sidelong at her mother, sharing a look I cannot decipher. "When it became clear the city was lost, and that Tiberias would win the day, I flooded the fort as much as I could," Iris explains, proud and still. "The seawall came down. Half of it is underwater, and the rest is cut off from land. I would have sunk the battleships if I could, but the escape took too much out of me. Still, the repairs will slow them down, and I've taken valuable resources from their effort."

And from me. Even if we win back the city now, the fort is destroyed. What a waste. Jets, the War Port docks, arms and ammunition, simple infrastructure.

I hold her gaze, letting a bit of my mask slip. Letting her know that I realize what she's doing. Iris and her mother will incapacitate me little by little, cutting me off from my own resources.

The nymph queens are cunning. They don't have to put me in the water to drown me.

It's simply a question of how long that will take, and how to balance their actions against my own. They're letting Cal and me waste ourselves on each other, hoping to face the wounded victor in later days.

Iris stares back at me, her eyes tipping like a scale. She is cold and calculating, still water hiding a riptide.

"So we return to Archeon," she replies. "Gather the full mass of our strength, everyone that can be spared. Bring the full fury of this war to bear on their heads."

I lean back against the rail of the ship, exuding an appearance of calm detachment. Sighing, I glance at the waves as they stain red with sunset. "We'll move tomorrow."

"Tomorrow?" Cenra balks. "We should go now."

Slowly, I grin, careful to show my canines. The kind of smile that sets people off balance. "I have a feeling my brother will be sending us a message soon."

"What are you talking about?" Cenra murmurs.

I offer no explanation and look out to the east instead. On the darkening horizon, smudges stand out against the stark line of the sea. "The islands will be neutral ground," I muse.

"Neutral ground," Cenra repeats, turning the words over in her mouth.

Iris says nothing, but her eyes narrow to slits.

I drum my fingers against my chest, huffing out a low breath.

"What a joyous reunion this will be."

I can only imagine it. A rainbow of scowling backstabbers and betrayers seated across from us, ready to preach and preen. Evangeline, with her claws and her put-upon arrogance. That Red general, Farley, who will bleed for all she's done to my kingdom. Moping, methodic Julian, trailing my brother like a forgotten ghost. Our own grandmother, Anabel, another person who was supposed to love me and never did. The Montfort leader, still a mystery and a danger.

Of course, Mare will be there, a storm in her skin.

And my brother too.

It's been a long time since I've looked into Cal's eyes. I wonder if they've changed.

For I certainly have.

Will we make terms? I very much doubt it. But I want to see them again, both of them. At least once more before this war is done, ended in whatever fate. Their deaths or mine.

Neither future frightens me.

My only fear now is losing the throne, the crown, the reason for all this misery and torment. I won't destroy myself in vain. I won't let this all be for nothing.

TWENTY-TWO

Iris

When Maven returns to his own ship, I fear he might force me to go with him and deny me a few more hours with my mother. To my surprise, his petty rage and his political cunning do not extend so far. We are left alone on Mother's flagship once more, given over to our own devices. With room to talk at length, and time to plan. Either he doesn't see us as a threat, or he doesn't care to fear us. I would venture the latter. He has more immediate enemies right now, and can spare little thought for his own wife.

The *Swan* is a warship, built for battle and speed. What pass for staterooms are spare and rigid, barely suited to Red servants. Still, Mother looks at home in them, equally at ease upon a bolted-down, narrow bed as on a jeweled throne. She isn't a vain woman and carries none of the flawed, materialistic pride most Silvers have. That was Father's domain. He preferred his finery, even on the battlefield. The thought sends a sharp stab of pain through me as I remember the last time I saw him alive. He was dashing in his armor, blue steel studded with sapphires, gray hair pulled back from his face. I suppose Salin Iral found some flaw, and exploited it well.

I pace to settle myself, moving back and forth before my mother, stopping occasionally to glare out the small porthole window. The sea outside has turned bloodred. A bad omen. I feel a familiar itch and make a mental note to pray later on, in the *Swan*'s small shrine. It might bring me a bit of peace.

"Be still. Conserve your strength," Mother says, her Lakelander melodic and fluid. She sits with her legs drawn up under herself, and her long-sleeved coat is tossed aside, making her seem smaller than usual. It has little effect on her bearing, and I feel the weight of her eyes as I walk.

I am a queen too, and hesitate to follow her commands, if only to be contrarian. But she's right. I eventually concede and take a seat on the bench on the opposite wall, an uncomfortable thing with thin padding and rivets fixed to the metal floor. My fingers curl around the edge of it, gripping tight. It vibrates with the reverberations of the ship engines, low and humming. I fixate on the sensation, reclaiming a bit of my calm.

"In your communications, you said there was something you couldn't tell me," Mother says. "Not until we were face-to-face."

Steeling myself, I look up at her. "Yes."

"Well." She spreads her hands wide. "Here we are."

My expression doesn't change, but I feel my heartbeat quicken with nerves. I have to get up again and cross to the window, look out on the crimson waters. Even though my mother's room is the safest place for me, it still feels dangerous to repeat what I know. Anyone could be listening, waiting to report back to Maven.

I put my back to her and force out the words. "We're operating on the assumption that Maven will win."

She scoffs behind me. "Win *this* war, you mean. But not the next."

Our war for this country.

"Yes," I reply. "But I think we're on the losing side now. His brother's coalition, that Montfort army . . ."

Her voice is level, devoid of judgment. "They frighten you."

I spin around, scowling. "Of course they frighten me. And the Scarlet Guard too."

"Reds?" Mother scoffs. She even rolls her eyes. I grit my teeth against a sigh of frustration. "They're of little importance."

"That kind of thinking will be our ruin, Mother," I tell her as sternly as I can. One queen to another. *Listen to me.*

But she dismisses me with a dancing wave. As if I'm still a child pulling at her skirts. "I doubt that," she says. "Silvers war, not Reds. They can't possible hope to win against us."

"And yet they keep doing it," I answer flatly. I fought in Harbor Bay, against the Samos heirs and their battalion. Populated by Silvers and newbloods, mostly, but Reds too. Skilled snipers, trained fighters. Not to mention Norta's own Red soldiers who turned. One of Maven's great strengths lies in the loyalty of his people, but if it wanes? His Silvers will run and leave him empty.

Mother just clucks her tongue. My teeth clench with the sound. "The Reds keep winning because of a Silver *alliance*," she says. "It will quickly crumble when one or both of the Calore brothers die."

Wincing, I try another tactic. Instead of standing tall, I drop to my knees in front of my mother, taking her hands in mine. The pleading image of a child is sure to stir her. "I know Mare Barrow, Mother," I tell her, hoping she hears me. "Reds are made of stronger stuff than we realize. Yes, we make them think themselves inferior, insignificant, to keep them controlled. But we risk falling into our own trap if we forget to fear them too."

My words fall on deaf ears. She pulls one hand away, using it to smooth my hair away from my face. "Mare Barrow isn't Red, Iris."

Her blood certainly is, I think, keeping the retort to myself.

Mother continues to run her fingers through my hair, combing out the strands. "All will be well. All will be taken care of," she croons, as if to soothe a baby. "We'll drown our enemies and return to our peace, safe at home. The glory of the Lakelands will wash forth to this very coast. Across Prairie, into those infernal mountains. To the borders of Ciron and Tiraxes, and Piedmont too. Your sister will rule an empire, with you at her side."

I try to imagine what she dreams of. A map awash in blue, our dynasty secure in power. I think of Tiora, tall against a new dawn, an empress's crown upon her head. Resplendent in sapphire and diamond, the most powerful person from shore to shore, the world kneeling at her feet. I want that future for her. I want that sanctuary so much my heart aches.

But will it ever come to pass?

"Anabel Lerolan and Julian Jacos have given me a message," I whisper, moving my head close to Mother's. If someone is listening at the door, they won't hear much.

"What?" she hisses back, surprised. Her soothing hand drops. The other tightens its grip on me.

"They came to me in Archeon."

"The capital? How?"

"Like I said, Mother," I murmur, "I think Maven will lose this war, and lose quicker than we can imagine. They are a formidable alliance, stronger than our own. Even with Piedmont on our side."

Her eyes widen, and I finally see a flash of fear. As much as it terrifies me, I'm glad for it. We all need to be afraid if we want to stay alive.

"What did they want?" she asks.

"They offered a deal."

Mother's expression sours a little. Her lips twist. "We don't have time for dramatics, Iris. Tell me what happened."

"They were waiting in my transport," I say. "The Jacos singer is a talented one, and he bewitched my guards well. And the Lerolan queen is as dangerous as any."

Her voice climbs an octave, panicked. "Does anyone know? Does Maven—"

I put a hand to her face, forcing her to quiet. The words die on her lips.

"I'd be dead if he knew." Her skin is warm beneath my hand, soft and more wrinkled than ever before. These days have aged her. "Anabel and Julian did their work well. They need me alive and they took no chances."

Mother sighs in relief, her breath washing over my face.

"Salin Iral," I spit, almost unable to say the name of my father's killer. It cuts us both like a dagger. Mother recoils, disgust marring her features. "They'll hand him over. Let us do with him what we wish."

Her eyes go blank and dark. After a moment, she pushes away my hand gently. "Iral is no one. A disgraced lord, stripped of his power. Alone in whatever wilderness he chooses."

Electric anger screams down my spine. I feel myself flush, heat burning my cheeks.

"He killed Father."

"Thank you for the clarification," Mother replies, her voice icy.

Still, that blankness in her. A shield against the agony of my father's loss. "I was not aware."

"I only meant—"

"He killed your father for another king," she says slowly. "He is no one, Iris."

"Maybe." On shaky limbs, I force myself to my feet. I loom over her, and she has to look up to see my face. An odd position, an odd sensation. To have this power over my mother, even a power so small. I suck in another breath. "Anabel offered up Volo Samos as well."

Below me, she blinks. Eyelids closing and opening, revealing a very different pair of eyes. They spark, alight.

"Now, that is something interesting. And perhaps impossible."

I remember Anabel as she leaned forward, bronze eyes gleaming in the light of afternoon. There was no lie in her, only hunger. Only need. "I don't think so."

"What do they want in return?"

Shaking, I tell her. Let her make this decision for me, because I cannot make it myself.

"'Tiberias the Seventh, rightful King of Norta, Flame of the North, alongside his allies the Free Republic of Montfort, the Scarlet Guard, and the independent Kingdom of the Rift, sends word from his temporary capital of Harbor Bay.'" The Sentinel reads from the neatly typed communication, his voice a bit muffled behind his jeweled mask. The floodlights of the ship deck illuminate him in blinding red and orange. Behind him there is only darkness. No stars, no moon. The whole world could be empty.

"*Temporary*, that's presumptuous," Mother sniffs, turning her face in to the cool wind blowing off the black ocean. We exchange glances, annoyed by the pageantry. *Flame of the North.* What nonsense.

"That's Cal," Maven replies from his place among his guards. He called us to hear the message ourselves, summoning us to his ship. "He is a creature of want."

With a raised finger, he indicates for the stocky Sentinel to continue. I recognize his voice and the eyes peering out from his mask. A vibrant blue, made electric by the sharp light overhead. *Haven,* I know, remembering the guard who accompanied me on my journey into Montfort.

"'I control the city behind you,'" he reads. I think of the older brother, the warrior, wreathed in flame. "'I control the southern borders, from Delphie to our allies in the Rift. I control hundreds of miles of coastline. The entirety of the Beacon region, led by Governor Rhambos and his house, has pledged loyalty to the true king. I have this kingdom in my fist, Maven, and you within my grasp.'"

Did we know about Rhambos? I glance across the deck, looking to my twisted husband. Maven's deep scowl is confirmation enough. That betrayal is a surprise. Maven barely responds to the Sentinel's words, only hissing out a breath. "Traitor," I think I hear him mutter.

Sentinel Haven forges on.

"'You have allies beyond your borders, Maven, but few within them. None who will not abandon you as my victories mount. The winds are blowing, the tide is changing. Norta cannot exist as she did beneath our ancestors, and I will not rest until I reclaim the birthright you stole from me, at the cost of our father's life.'"

The guards rustle a little, but none of them speak. To them, this could be the wild accusation of a traitor, as Maven has painted his brother to be. Seduced by a Red freak, manipulated into corruption and murder. But it's probably more likely a confirmation of what we all know to be true. Tiberias Calore did not kill his father. Not willingly. Not the way Maven has said.

Next to me, Mother fixes her eyes on my husband. They gleam, catching the harsh light.

He doesn't react, still and smooth as glass. In his black uniform, his body seems to blend into the darkness, invisible but for his white face and long-fingered hands. Despite his brother's best attempts, Maven stays collected, reluctant to give over to a fiery temper.

"'We are prepared to offer terms to all members of your alliance.'" Sentinel Haven rustles the page as he reads. "'To Her Majesty Queen Cenra of the Lakelands and His Highness Prince Bracken of Piedmont. To you, Maven, usurper and murderer though you may be. No more blood need be spilled in this war of ours. Let us preserve what we can of the kingdom we were born to serve.'"

Such charming words. I wonder if it was written by committee. Anabel, at least, had a controlling hand in the communication. Her fingerprints are all over the statement.

"'We will meet upon the island of your choosing.'"

Sentinel Haven clears his throat, his eyes flicking to me first. Then to his king, a person living on borrowed time upon a stolen throne.

"'At dawn.'"

We wait in silence, watching Maven as he weighs his options. He knew this was coming, and is hardly surprised. Still, he snaps, slowly at first, then faster and faster. A clenching fist, the flamemaker bracelet spinning on a fine-boned wrist. It spits a spark that blooms, growing, a fireball burning white hot and icy blue at its core. With a manic smile, Maven tosses it out onto the water. It trails, a near comet, reflecting with a hellish glow in the choppy water, before he lets it hiss into the nothing among the waves.

"Dawn, then," he repeats.

I can tell by the set of his shoulders that he has no intention of negotiating. I can only guess as to his motive, but I think it rests solely on one Silver prince and one Red lightning girl.

TWENTY-THREE
Cal

I shift, uncomfortable as the minutes wear on. Midnight comes and goes. Only her eyes move, skimming the page with blurring speed. She might have it memorized by now. Mare wanted no part of the message to Maven, remaining in my rooms while the rest of us crafted it. I expected her to be gone when I came back. But she stayed.

I still can't believe what happened. And I still can't believe she's sitting here, on my bed, in the middle of the night. After all that's passed between us.

She stayed.

I've given up focusing on the papers in front of me. Counts, mostly. Of soldiers, civilians, casualties, resources. Enough to make my head spin. Julian is better at deciphering all this, reducing everything to the most important details so I can see the larger picture. But I need the distraction, if only to keep me from the haunting little book in the desk drawer. I almost want to tell Julian to take it back. Keep his so-called gift until this war is won and I actually have the capacity to face what he wants me to face.

Norta's situation requires my attention, not the book. And our situation is dire. Harbor Bay is ours, but it's a poor capital. The city is too old, and vulnerable from all sides, and with Fort Patriot under repair, we'll have to build up new defenses for the time being. At least the city is with us, if only in name. Rhambos surrendered, and the Reds of the Bay willingly follow their own leaders, the Red Watch, who are firmly allied to the Scarlet Guard. I tick off each group in my head, running down the endless list always racing through my brain. At this point, I think I even see it in my sleep.

With a sigh, I try to clear my mind. I focus on her instead. Strange that she is both the anchor against the storm and the storm itself.

Mare sits cross-legged on my bed, her head bent so her hair obscures half her face. The gray ends are creeping through the chocolate brown, dusting up against her collarbone. She keeps my night robe pulled tight around herself, the collar high enough to hide the brand on her skin. I shudder every time I see the mark burned into her and remember that my brother put it there. In the shifting candlelight, she looks like flame. Gold and red, with black shadows dancing at her edges. I watch quietly from my desk, one bare foot planted on the floor, the other on the desktop. My calf twinges, still aching from the battle, and I flex my toes, trying to work out some of the pain. I wish I hadn't sent the healer away earlier, but it's too late in the evening to call anyone back. I'll just have to bear it until morning, along with the other small pains still cropping up whenever I move.

"How long has it been?" she murmurs again, still not looking away from the page.

I lean back in my chair a little and huff at the ornate ceiling. The electric chandelier above me is dark, unlit. It sparked out about an hour ago, when Mare decided to furiously pace the room. Her moods have a trembling effect.

"Twenty minutes since you last asked," I reply. "I told you, Maven's taking his time with a response. He wants to make us sweat."

"But it won't be much longer," she says, unmoving. "He doesn't have that kind of restraint. Not with us. He won't be able to resist the chance of meeting us face-to-face."

"Especially you," I growl.

"And *you*," she replies with equal fervor. "His mother poisoned him toward us both. Made the obsession he carries now." Annoyed, she sighs. "The meeting will be pointless. A waste."

I blink slowly. Her knowledge of my brother and how he thinks unsettles me. Mostly because I know what a high price she paid for it. And, if I'm being honest, because I know it's rooted in emotions I don't want to trace. But who am to judge what she feels? I still love Maven too, or at least I love the person I thought my brother was.

What a mess, both of us.

My knee cracks as I draw back my leg, an echoing snap. Wincing, I massage the joint, letting my hands warm to a soothing temperature. The heat sinks in, relaxing the muscles beneath.

Mare finally looks up, smirking as she tosses her hair back. "You sound like a creaky door."

I hiss out a pained laugh. "Feel like one."

"See a healer in the morning." Despite the playful twist of her lips, I hear her concern all the same. Her eyes narrow, looking darker in the dim light. "Or send for Sara. She'll come now if you want. I don't think she or Julian will sleep until we get an answer."

I shake my head and heave myself out of the chair. "I'll bother them tomorrow," I say, taking even steps toward the bed. Every foot closer seems to tighten my muscles with a different kind of ache.

She tracks me like a cat as I ease down next to her, lying back on my elbows. An ocean breeze rolls in at the window, billowing the golden curtains with an invisible hand. We both shudder. Slowly, I take the letter from her hand, put it to the side without breaking our stare.

I dread these quiet moments, and I think she does too. The silence, the empty waiting, makes it impossible to ignore exactly what we're doing. Or not doing, rather.

No change has been made on either side, in her heart or in mine. No choice reversed. But every passing second makes my decision more difficult as I'm reminded of what I'm going to lose when the time comes. What I lost for so many weeks. Not just her love, but her voice. Her sharpness. The push and pull of a person who has no regard for my blood or my crown. Someone who sees me, and no one else in my place.

Someone who calls me Cal, and not Tiberias.

Mare puts a hand to my cheek, splaying her fingers behind my ear. She is more tentative than before, more clinical. Like a healer examining a wound. I lean into the touch a little, chasing the cooling feel of her skin.

"Are you going to tell me this is the last time?" I ask, looking up at her.

Her expression melts a bit, as if wiped clean. But her eyes don't waver. "Again?"

I nod against her hand.

"This is the last time," she says flatly.

I feel a hum deep in my chest. My fire roars in response, begging to burn free. "Are you lying?"

"Again?"

Her lips twitch as I run a hand the length of her leg, from ankle to hip. The fingers on my face trace a gentle path as I bob my head, feeling my own blood heat.

Mare's response is quiet, barely more than a gasp. "I hope so."

She stops me before I can say anything else.

Her kiss devours.

No choices made.

Again.

Mare is dressed, perched precariously in the open window, when someone knocks on the bedroom door, waking me. I half expect her to duck out and disappear into the night air, but instead she pulls back inside. Her face flushes and she tosses me my robe. I get a faceful of silk.

"Staying put?" I ask, low enough so the person in the adjoining chamber won't hear. "You don't have to."

She just glares at me. "What's the point? Everyone will know soon enough."

Know what, exactly? I want to ask, but I hold my tongue. Stretching, I stand from the bed and pull the robe tight, knotting it at my waist. She watches as I move, eyes trailing. "What?" I whisper, sporting a half grin.

Instead her lips press into a thin line. "You had some scars removed."

I can only shrug. It's been weeks since I had a healer erase the older scars across my back and ribs, wiping away the raised edges of white, knotted flesh. Wounds unbecoming of a king. I'm a bit flattered she remembered enough to know. "Some things don't have to be held on to."

Her eyes narrow. "And some things do, Cal."

I can only nod in silent agreement, unwilling to follow her over the precipice of *that* particular conversation. It won't lead us anywhere productive.

Mare settles against my desk, leaning a bit, squaring herself to the door. Her countenance changes, her eyes sharpening as the rest of her seems to harden into a different person. A bit of Mareena, the Silver she pretended to be. A bit of the lightning girl, all sparks and merciless fury. With herself in between, the girl I'm still figuring out. She ducks her chin, nodding at me.

As I open the door, I can just hear her suck in a fortifying breath.

"Julian," I say, moving aside to let my uncle into the room.

He takes a step forward, already talking, a faded sweater tossed over his nightclothes. The page in his hand has very little writing on it. "We've received Maven's reply," he says. He falters only a little at the sight of Mare, doing his best not to let her break his momentum. He clears his throat a little and forces a casual smile. "Good evening, Mare."

"Good morning would be more appropriate, Julian," she says, dipping her head in greeting. Unwilling to give anything more or anything less. But our appearance says enough. Her with still-disheveled hair, and me in nothing but a robe. Julian reads us as easily as he does his books. At least he has the good sense not to comment, or even smirk.

I prod him farther into the room. "What did Maven say?"

"As we suspected," he replies, recovering, "he agreed. Dawn."

Already I curse my decision to meet so early. I'd much rather do this on a full night's rest. But it's best to get it over with as soon as possible.

"Where?" Mare's voice is ragged.

Julian looks between us. "They've chosen Province Island. Not exactly neutral, but most of the islanders have gone, fleeing the war."

I fold my arms across my chest and try to picture the island in question. It comes to me quickly. Province is the northernmost point of land in the Bahrn Islands, sprinkled in a hook off the coast. It's a little like Tuck, the Scarlet Guard base. Home to little more than disappearing dunes and sea grass. "It's Rhambos territory. And small enough. If anything, this is in our favor."

At the desk, Mare scoffs. She surveys Julian and me like children. "Unless House Rhambos decides to betray you."

"I'd be inclined to agree, if his family didn't hang in the balance. Or his own life. Lord Rhambos won't risk either," I tell her. "Province Island will do."

She doesn't look convinced, but nods anyway. Her eyes pass to Julian, then to the single paper in his hand. The copy of Maven's response. "Did he have any other demands?"

Julian shakes his head. "None."

"May I see it?" She holds out a hand in gentle request, palm turned upward. Julian is happy to oblige.

For a second, she hesitates, gripping the paper between her thumb and forefinger like something unclean. He used to write her letters, back when we were operating from the Notch, collecting newbloods. He used to leave them on the corpses of the ones he got to first. Each one begged her to return, promising to stop the bloodshed if she went back. Eventually, he got his wish. I would take the paper from her, protect her from the pain his words bring, but she doesn't need me to shield her. She's faced worse without me.

Finally, she blinks, steeling herself to read Maven's response. Her frown only deepens as her eyes scan the words, over and over again.

I glance at Julian. "Has Nanabel been informed?"

"She has," he says.

"Does she have thoughts?"

"When doesn't she?"

I offer him a wry smile. "True." Julian and my grandmother aren't exactly the closest of friends, but they're certainly allies, at least where I am concerned. Their shared history, my mother, is enough for them both. At the thought, I feel a sudden cold, and I can't help but look at my desk drawer. It's firmly shut, the book out of sight.

But never far from my mind.

Ocean Hill was my mother's favorite palace, and I see her everywhere, even though I have no memory of her face. Only what I've seen in pictures or paintings. I've asked for some of her portraits to be rehung, at least in the salon outside my bedroom. Her colors were gold, more vibrant than the yellows Julian wears now. Fitting a queen born of a High House, though she was far from the norm.

She slept in this room. She breathed this air. She was alive here.

Julian's voice snaps me out of the quicksand of my mother's memory. "Queen Anabel thinks you should send someone in your stead," he says.

A corner of my mouth tugs into a half smile. "I'm sure she suggested herself."

His face mirrors mine. "She did."

"I'll thank her for the suggestion and politely decline. If anyone is going to face him, it should be me. I'll present our terms—"

"Maven won't bargain." Mare's fist closes, crumpling a bit of the communication. Her gaze feels like her kiss. Devouring.

"He agreed to the meeting—" Julian begins, but she cuts him off.

"And that's all he'll agree to. This isn't to discuss terms. He isn't anywhere close to surrender." I hold her livid stare, watching the storm in her eyes. I almost expect a peal of thunder overhead. "He just wants to see us. It's his way."

To my surprise, Julian takes a harried step toward her. His face pales, draining of color. "We should still try," he pleads, exasperated.

She just blinks at him. "And torture ourselves? Give him the satisfaction?"

I respond before Julian can. "Of course we're going to meet with him." My voice deepens, heavier than before. "And of course he isn't going to bargain."

"So why do this?" Mare spits. I'm reminded of one of Larentia Viper's snakes.

"Because," I mutter, trying not to growl. To keep some semblance of control and dignity. "I want to see him too. I want to look into his eyes and know that my brother is gone forever."

Neither Julian nor Mare, two of the most talkative people I know, has any response to give. She looks at her feet, brows knitting together, while a red bloom rises in her cheeks. It could be shame or frustration or both. Julian only goes paler, white as a sheet. He avoids my eyes.

"I have to know that whatever his mother did to him cannot be reversed. I need to be sure," I murmur, moving closer to Mare. If only to calm myself. I'm suddenly aware of the cloying heat in the room, rising with my own temper. "Thank you, Julian," I add, trying to dismiss him as gently as I can.

He takes the hint well. "Of course," he replies, bowing his head. Even though I've repeatedly asked him never to bow to me. "Have you . . . ," he adds, stumbling over the question. "Have you read what I gave you?"

The pain of another person lost flares in my chest. My eyes dart to the desk drawer again. Mare follows my line of sight, even though she doesn't know what we're talking about.

I'll tell her later. At a better time.

"Some," I manage to say.

Julian looks almost disappointed. "It isn't easy."

"No, it isn't, Julian." *I'm done talking about this.* "And if you could . . . ," I mumble, gesturing feebly between myself and Mare to change the subject. "You know."

Mare snickers slightly, but Julian is happy to comply. "I don't know what you're talking about," he says with an easy grin.

As he goes, stepping back out into the salon, I follow his retreating figure. When he passes the painting, propped up against a chair for now, he slows. But he doesn't stop. He only trails a hand along the frame, unable to spare a glance for his sister.

They have a similar look, based on the portrait. The thin chestnut hair and inquisitive eyes. She was simple, an easy beauty. The kind most overlook. I don't have much of her in me, if anything at all.

I wish I did.

The door swings shut, removing her and my uncle from sight.

Slowly, smooth fingers weave into mine, taking my hand.

"He can't be fixed," Mare breathes, resting her chin against my shoulder. Not quite on top of it—she can't reach—but now isn't the time to tease her. Instead I lean down into her grasp, making it easier on us both.

"I need to see for myself. If I'm going to give up on him—"

Her grip tightens sharply. "There's no giving up against the impossible."

The impossible. Part of me still refuses to believe that. My brother is not a lost cause. He can't be. I won't allow it. "Davidson tried," I whisper. Reluctant to say the words out loud. But I have to. I have to make them real. "He searched. There are no newblood whispers."

She takes a long, trailing breath. "And that's probably for the best," she says after a moment. "In the grand scheme of the world."

It stings to know she's right.

Methodic, she puts her hands on my shoulders, steering me away from the desk. Away from the memory sitting in a drawer. "You should sleep," she says firmly, pushing at the bed. "Maven wears exhaustion better than you do."

I stifle a yawn, eager to follow her commands. With a sigh, I slip between the blankets. When my head hits the pillow, I almost drop asleep instantly. "Will you stay?" I mumble, watching her through slitted eyes.

She crawls over to me in reply, kicking off her boots as she goes. She worms her way under the silk. I watch her, smirking, and she shrugs. "Everyone will know anyway."

Without thought, I take her hand, knitting our fingers at the hem of the blanket. "Julian can keep a secret."

Mare barks out a laugh. "Evangeline can't, not with her agenda."

I have to chuckle too, halfhearted in my exhaustion. "Whoever thought she'd be the one pushing us at each other?"

Next to me, she shifts, trying to get comfortable. Eventually she settles on curling up at my side, one leg kicked free. "Even though Maven can't change, other people can," she mumbles against my chest. The vibrations of her voice make me shiver.

It takes little concentration to douse the candles burning all over the room, plunging us both into a gentle blue darkness.

"I don't want to marry her."

"That's never been my issue."

"I know that," I whisper.

It isn't in me to give her what she wants. Not when it means betraying my father, my birthright, and any chance I may have at making some kind of difference. She might not agree, but I can do more on a throne, with a crown, than I can without them.

"After the parlay," I breathe, hesitant, "once Harbor Bay is secure, I think we hit Gray Town next. Full strength. We won't catch another tech slum off guard, not after New Town."

In the darkness, the brush of her lips on mine takes me off guard. I jump at the sensation. I feel her smile against my skin.

"Thank you," she whispers, shifting back into place.

"It's the right thing to do."

But am I doing it for the wrong reason? For her?

Does that even matter?

"What did Julian give you?" she mumbles, half asleep. Mare is just as tired as I am, if not more. The day has been too long and too bloody.

I blink in the darkness, staring at nothing. Her breathing slows and evens as she drifts away.

She is asleep when I finally answer.

"A copy of my mother's diary."

TWENTY-FOUR
Mare

It's still dark outside when I wake, roused by shuffling across the room. I tense on instinct, ready to fight. For a second, I'm puzzled by the sight of Cal in the same chamber as me. Then I remember the events of yesterday. His near death, and the way it broke us both, shattering whatever resolve we'd had before.

He's already dressed, looking regal in the soft light of a few candles. I watch for a second, seeing him without any kind of mask or shield. Despite his broad, tall form, he looks younger in his fine clothing. His jacket is a deep bloodred, trimmed in black, with silver buttons at the cuffs. The pants match, tucked into oiled leather boots. He hasn't donned a cape or a crown yet, leaving both discarded on his desk. He moves slowly, fastening the buttons up his throat. Shadows ring his eyes. He looks more exhausted than he did last night, if that's possible. I wonder if he slept at all, or if he spent the night tortured by the prospect of seeing Maven again.

When he realizes I'm awake, he straightens, shoulders squaring toward me. He fills the kingly mold quickly. The transformation is small but unmistakable. He puts up his guard, puts on a mask, even with me. I wish he wouldn't, but I understand why. I do it too.

"We leave in an hour," he says, finishing with his buttons. "I've had some clothes brought into the salon for you. Choose whatever you like. Or . . ." He stumbles, as if he's said something wrong. "Whatever you want from your own wardrobe."

"I didn't exactly bring my wardrobe to a battle, and I don't think I can fit into one of your uniforms," I reply, chuckling a little. With a reluctant groan, I stretch out of the blankets and shudder at the touch of cold air. I sit up, intensely aware of the tangled braid over my shoulder. "I'll find something. Should I look a certain way?"

A muscle feathers in his cheek. "However you wish," he says, his voice oddly strained.

"Should I be distracting?" I ask, gingerly trying to work the knots out of my hair. He looks at my fingers, not at me.

"I think you'll be distracting no matter what you wear."

My chest tightens with warmth. "Flattery will get you nowhere, Cal."

But he isn't wrong. It's been months since I last saw Maven in the flesh, his form retreating through the surge of a panicked crowd. Iris ran with him, defending her new husband from the attack on their wedding in the capital. It was a rescue mission, not just for me, but for dozens of newbloods manipulated into his service.

I could wear a potato sack and Maven would still devour me with his eyes.

Yawning, I pad across the room and into the bathroom for a quick, blistering-hot shower. Part of me wishes Cal would join in, but he stays behind, and I scrub the last of my aches away alone. After, I enter the salon to find a rainbow in the semidarkness. With a slight burst of concentration, I make the electric lights flicker to life overhead, illuminating the chamber full of various garments. I'm glad for the wide choice of clothing, but even more grateful for the emptiness of the salon. No maids to attend to my hair and face, no healers to work away the gnawing exhaustion or liven up my body. I'm given only what I need, and exactly what I want.

If only Cal could do that in all things.

I try not to think beyond this morning. He still hasn't turned away from the crown, and I am still just as dedicated to my cause, if not more so. I can't still be in love with a king, when everything I'm doing is to destroy his throne. Destroy all notions of kings and queens and the kingdoms at the mercy of their will. But the love just won't go away, and neither will the need.

I wonder who laid out the variety of clothing, draping chairs and couches with a selection of gowns, suits, blouses, skirts, and pants, with no fewer than six different pairs of shoes on the floor beside them. Many of them are gold, either patterned in dusty yellow or trimmed with the colors of Cal's mother. She was a thin woman, judging by the narrow waistlines of her dresses. Smaller than I would expect for the mother of the man in the room behind me. I avoid her clothing as best I can and search for something that doesn't carry the weight of a dead woman.

I settle for a flowing dress belted at the waist, dyed a deep, rich navy blue. *The colors of someone else's mother.* It's velvet, and I'll certainly sweat out of it later on, but the neckline, a gentle swoop below my collarbone, puts my brand on full display. Let Maven see what he's done to me and never forget what kind of monster he is. I feel stronger as I pull it on, as if the dress is some kind of armor.

I can only imagine what kind of elegant monstrosity Evangeline will pull together for the meeting. Perhaps a gown of razor blades. I hope she does. Evangeline Samos excels in moments such as these, and I can't wait to unleash her on her former betrothed, unbridled by any kind of etiquette or scheme.

When I finish, I comb out my drying hair, letting it fall loose about my shoulders. The gray ends gleam in the lamplight, sharp in contrast to the brown. I am a strange-looking person, I think as I examine myself in a mirror. A Red girl in Silver finery never ceases to surprise me. My skin glows golden with the low light, stubbornly alive and stubbornly Red. I'm less haggard than I thought, my brown eyes luminous with both fear and determination.

I draw some comfort from knowing that Cal's mother, though she was Silver, wasn't fitted to this life either. It's written so clearly in the portrait of her, which lies against the far wall, nestled next to a pair of ornate chairs.

I wonder where Cal will hang her. Out of sight, or always in reach?

Coriane Jacos had soft blue eyes, if the painting is a good likeness. Like a sky before dawn, the haze of blue upon a horizon. Almost colorless, drained of a deeper shade. She looks more like Julian than like her son. Both have the same chestnut hair, hers curling artfully over one shoulder, well dressed with creamy pearls and gold chain. Their faces are similar too. Drawn, older than their years. But while Julian's strain has always seemed pleasant, the accepted frustration of a scholar constantly working a puzzle, Coriane's looks bone-deep. She was a sad woman, I'm told, and it shows even in her portrait.

"Elara killed her," Cal says from the doorway to his bedchamber. He adjusts the cape draped over one shoulder, clasped in silver and glinting chips of black gemstones. In his other hand, he holds a black crown, half hidden like an afterthought. A sword hangs from the belt at his waist, tucked into a sheath jeweled in ruby and jet. It's for fashion at best. No one would choose a sword to fight. "She drove my mother deeper into her sorrows, whispered in her head until she had no other escape. I know that now."

His lips curve downward, frowning, while his eyes go far away. In his sadness, I see a bit of his mother. The only resemblance I can draw between the two of them.

"I wish I could have known her." I say.

"So do I."

We leave Cal's rooms together, walking the halls of Ocean Hill down to the grander, more public receiving chambers in equal step. Last night, I brushed off any worry of gossip, feeling brazen and bold. The discomfort catches up to me now. I wonder if we'll enter to a rash of murmurs—smirks from the Silvers, judgment from the Reds and new-bloods. Will Farley sneer at me for wavering? Will she turn her back entirely?

I can't stand the thought.

Cal senses my unease. His fingers brush the inside of my arm, careful to stay away from the sensitive points of my wrists.

"We don't have to enter together," he murmurs as we descend a flight of stairs, growing closer and closer to the point of no return.

"It doesn't matter now," I answer.

Up ahead, his guards await. Members of House Lerolan, cousins of his grandmother's blood. They stand unmasked, unlike Sentinels, but just as dangerous and silent.

Anabel stands with them, hands clasped at her waist, belted with flaming jewels: rubies and yellow citrine. She proudly wears her rose-gold crown, the simple band fitted across her brow and smooth, gray hair. Her eyes land on me first.

"Good morning," she says, drawing Cal into a quick embrace. He accepts it quickly and dwarfs her.

"Morning," he replies. "Is everyone ready?"

"They should be," she says, waving a wrinkled hand. "But I assume we'll have to wait for the Rift princess to don every piece of metal she can get her hands on. Remind me to make sure she hasn't stolen the doorknobs."

All nerves, Cal doesn't smile, but a corner of his mouth lifts. "I'm sure we can spare them," he says.

"You look well, Miss Barrow," Anabel adds, her eyes flicking to mine.

I don't feel it, I think to myself. "As well as can be expected, for the circumstance." I'm careful not to use any kind of title, but she doesn't seem to notice or care.

Judging by the way her face changes, softening, I must have said the right thing. To my surprise, Anabel has no enmity for me this morning. She draws a slow breath. "Ready or not," she mutters, spinning around, "here we come, Maven."

The receiving hall at the bottom of the grand stairs is vast, feeding into various ballrooms and the throne room of Ocean Hill, as well as the banquet hall and a smaller, less official version of the council chambers in Whitefire. Built to suit a working court of Silvers, and house the moving government of Norta. Now Reds scatter among the rooms, busy as servants, but noticeably *not* servants. The green of Montfort uniforms contrasts harshly with the white marble, ocean-blue trimmings, and many gold banners still hung from the walls and ceilings. I note red among them, the crimson of Cal's uniform. Marking his position as the rightful king, and conqueror of nearly half of Norta.

As in Ascendant, before we addressed the Gallery, Davidson wears his fine suit of dark green. Farley has her dress uniform as well, and is still just as uncomfortable in it. I'm glad I don't have to wear one. The gown is soft against my skin as I walk, my feet tight inside fine blue boots.

Anabel leaves us to stand next to Julian, while Farley watches us approach. She looks between me and Cal as we move closer to the center of the room. Her brow furrows and I brace myself for a scowl, if not a snarl. Instead she blinks, her expression thoughtful. Almost accepting.

"Calore," she says, dipping her head to the king.

He grins at her deliberate use of such an informal greeting. "General Farley," he replies, all propriety. "I'm glad you agreed to join us."

She adjusts her stiff collar, forcing it to lie flat. "The Scarlet Guard is a valuable part of this coalition, and Command should be represented when we negotiate for Maven's surrender."

While Cal nods his head in gentle agreement, I sigh to myself. "I wouldn't be so sure of any deal," I warn her, voice low. I'm getting sick of repeating myself.

Farley only scoffs. "Of course, nothing in this life is that easy. But a woman can dream, can't she?"

I glance over her shoulder, at her various officers hanging back. None of their faces are familiar. "How's Kilorn?" I ask, frowning as shame claws up my spine. I wring my hands together, trying to hide their twitching. At my side, Cal flinches, one hand hanging free. I wish I could take it, but we both refrain from such a naked display of affection.

She looks on me with pity. "Fully healed yesterday, but he's taking some time," she says. I try to picture him whole and healthy, not dancing at the brink of death as he was before I left. It doesn't work. "We've commandeered the barracks at the Security Center, and he's there with the rest of the wounded."

"Good," I push out, unable to say anything more. Farley doesn't prod. Still, I feel the embarrassment of my choices as sharply as a knife wound. Kilorn almost died. Cal almost died. *And you ran to Cal.*

Next to me, the true king looks away, his own face flushed with implication. Even though we both decided not to make choices, we know that choices were made all the same.

"And Cameron?" I add, if only to stem the bleeding of such thoughts.

Farley scratches her chin. "Organizing in New Town. She's a valuable asset there, as is her father. The tech towns have their own underground networks, and word is going out to the rest. Maven's Silvers might be preparing for more attacks, but so are they."

That swells me with pride, as well as trepidation. Certainly Maven will retaliate for what we did in New Town and try to prevent the same from happening again. But if the Red slums rise up, if the tech towns go dark, his war effort will all but grind to a halt. No more resources. No more fuel. We can effectively starve him into surrender.

"I notice we're waiting for Princess Evangeline again," Davidson says as he joins us. His own contingent of advisers hangs back, giving us space.

I tip my head back and sigh. "The only constant in this world."

The premier crosses his arms. If he's nervous, he certainly doesn't show it. "A peacock needs time to groom its feathers, even steel ones."

"We lost a lot of magnetrons yesterday," Cal says, his voice low and stern. Almost reprimanding. "House Samos paid a high price for Harbor Bay."

Farley stiffens, setting her jaw. "I doubt they'll let us forget it. Or fail to make us repay their sacrifice."

"That's a bridge to be crossed," Cal replies.

Despite our history, I feel the strange need to . . . defend Evangeline. "If it *has* to be crossed," I say. "But we can discuss that later," I add, nodding to the far archway, where Evangeline has just appeared with Ptolemus at her side.

The pair of them wear matching clothes of pearly white and bright silver. He has a jacket, tightly fitted and buttoned up to his throat, pants, and black boots similar to Cal's, and a gray sash fastened across his chest from shoulder to hip. The pattern on it is strange, but as he approaches, I realize that the black diamond shapes dotting the sash aren't a pattern at all, but knives fixed directly into the fabric. Weapons, should he need them.

His sister is equally outfitted, the folds of her long gown slashed to show fine white leather leggings beneath. Should this meeting end in blood, she won't find herself restricted by a skirt. I wish I'd thought of that. Her hair is tightly braided back, the silver strands studded with starry glints of pearl metal. Razor-edged. Good for cutting flesh. Her arms are bare, no sleeves to impede her movement or catch on the jewelry on her hands. A ring winks on every finger, white stones and black, and fine strands of chain wrap around each wrist. Garrotes for strangling or slicing. Even her *earrings* look deadly, long and tapering to a wicked point.

I find myself glad Evangeline took so much time. She's wearing an arsenal.

"Shall I have the clocks adjusted in your rooms, Your Highnesses?" Anabel crows from where she stands next to Julian.

Evangeline answers with a smile as sharp as her knives. "Our clocks are exactly on time, Your Majesty." Her skirt billows around her legs as she passes the old queen, making for us. I shudder as she turns that smile on me. "Good morning, Mare. You seem well rested," she says. Then she runs her eyes over Cal, teeth still bared. "And you don't."

"Thank you," I say stiffly, through gritted teeth. I quickly regret any kind feeling I ever had toward her.

She revels in my sharp reply, and in the flush spotting Cal's cheeks. Behind her, Ptolemus crosses his arms behind his back, puffing out his chest. Displaying the daggers proudly. Farley notes each one, her eyes wide and angry.

"A pity this meeting could not be held in the evening," Ptolemus murmurs. His voice is deeper than Cal's and infinitely less kind. He's brave to speak here, especially to Farley and me.

I wonder if she sees Shade, as I do, speared by a blow from Ptolemus Samos. Even standing in his presence feels like a betrayal.

Farley has more restraint than me. While I can only keep my mouth firmly shut, she tosses her head with a sneer. "So your sister could have more time to paint her face?" she snaps, gesturing to the intricate makeup sculpting Evangeline.

The Samos princess shifts, if only a little, putting herself between her brother and us. Protective to the last. I almost expect her to shoo him off and out of our reach.

"So my father could attend," she explains with a proud toss of her head. "King Volo will be here by sunset."

Cal narrows his eyes. He sees the threat as clearly as I do. "With reinforcements?"

"More Samos-sworn to die for you? Hardly," Evangeline sneers. "He's come to oversee the final push against Maven."

Oversee. Her storm-gray eyes darken, if only for a moment, shadowed by meaning. It isn't hard to puzzle out the spaces between her words, what she means against what she says.

He's coming to clean up our mess.

I shiver. The Samos children are formidable, violent, and dangerous, but they are tools at the end of it all. Weapons wielded by an even more powerful man.

"Good, saves me the time of summoning him here," Cal says, resting a hand on the hilt of his bejeweled sword. He grins easily, as if the prospect of Volo Samos were his own idea. "I'm sure you'll give him a happy welcome, Evangeline."

The look she throws at him could poison rivers.

"Let's get this nonsense over with," she snarls under her breath.

Dawn streaks along the waves, bleeding from the horizon in shimmers of pink and paling blue. I keep my forehead braced against the cool glass of the dropjet window to watch our descent. As each second passes, my body tightens, my pulse a rising thrum, until I fear I might explode. It takes all my energy to keep my lightning at bay and the jet safe from my electric fits. Across from me, Farley stares at me, her hands ready at the buckles of her safety belts. To unfasten them and jump out the door if I happen to lose control.

Cal has more faith. He puts on a show of casual disregard, one leg stretched out in front of him, with the left side of his body braced against my side. He radiates soothing warmth, and his fingers brush mine every few seconds, a firm reminder of his presence.

If his grandmother is disgruntled or surprised by our closeness, she doesn't show it. She sits quietly with Julian, his face shadowed like never before.

Davidson rounds out the rest of our jet, and thankfully, Evangeline and her brother are in the other craft, following along. I can see the reflection in the water, their small, whirring jet a blurring shadow among the waves. Dropjets are loud, horrendously so, and for once I'm glad for it. No one can talk right now, or scheme, or snipe. I try to lose myself in the constant hum.

Province Island comes too soon, a circle of green edged in a pale ribbon of sand. From above, it seems like one of Julian's maps. Simply drawn, the village at the edge of the water a small grid of a few streets. The harbor is empty, but almost a dozen warships anchor about a half mile from shore. *Maven could shoot us out of the air if he wanted,* I think, imagining the distant rumble of artillery fire.

But we land without incident. The turning, tightening sensation in my chest grows, moving far beyond my tolerance. I grate my teeth together, feeling as if my jaw might shatter from the force of it, and hop out of the jet as quickly as I can, if only to suck down the fresh air.

And perhaps run right into the sea.

Instead I move away from the circling engines of the dropjet, one hand raised to keep my hair from the worst of the roaring wind. Farley follows, shoulders hunched.

"You okay?" she says over the noise, so only I can hear.

Mouth tight, I shake my head slightly. *No.*

I search the tall grass covering the dunes of the beach, half expecting a contingent of Sentinels to spring out and surround us. Force our surrender, force me back into manacles. Bile rises in my throat, the taste almost making me retch. The sensation of Silent Stone against my skin returns with smirking vengeance. *I can't go back there.* I turn my face away, hiding in my whipping hair. Trying to breathe and take the precious seconds I need to stabilize.

Farley's hand clasps my shoulder, her grip firm but soft. "I'm not going to tell you to get over it," she whispers in my ear. "But you have to get through it. Just for now."

Get through it.

I grit my teeth and turn back to her, my eyes mercifully clear. "Just for now," I echo. I'll fall apart later. After all this is done.

Behind her, Cal hangs back, watchful but hesitant to interrupt. I hold his gaze over her shoulder and give him the slightest nod. I can do this. I have to do this.

We look strange, a contingent of Silver royals, a Red general, and two newbloods, all flanked by guards in our varying colors. While no one is willing to trust Maven to obey the rules of war, we know that the Lakelander queen probably will. Still, I keep close to Farley and her two Scarlet Guard officers. I trust their guns and their loyalty.

Evangeline and Ptolemus step down from their own jet, looking merely inconvenienced by the meeting. As if they have something more important to do. It's an act, of course. Evangeline wants to see Maven as much as I don't. She would never pass up the chance to sneer in his face. The dropjet engines rustle her hair as she stands, eyes sharp and keen on the grass around us.

We agreed to meet at the interior of the island. A chance for the Lakelander nymphs to show good faith. It is a short but silent walk through the dunes toward a sparse forest of gnarled, stubborn trees. I'm reminded of Tuck, now abandoned to the waves. Shade is buried there, with no one to watch over him.

Cal leads us, with Davidson at one shoulder and Farley at the other. To present a united front of our coalition. Red blood allied with Silver. Evangeline and Ptolemus follow at his heels, surprisingly unbothered by their secondary position.

I'm glad so many walk in front of me, giving me a few extra seconds to gather every ounce of bravery I can find. My best comfort is my lightning, webbing beneath my skin, known only to me. I imagine it behind my eyes, the forked, blinding lines of purple and white. It isn't going away and no one can take it from me, not even him. I'll kill him if he tries.

Months ago, I watched Maven make peace with the Lakelanders in a similar fashion. Even though the scenery was vastly different, the endless minefields of the Choke instead of a grassy island between a brightening sky and a calm blue sea, it feels the same. We march toward the unknown, toward people of great and terrible power. At least now I won't be sitting on Maven's side of the table. I'm not his pet anymore.

As in the meeting with the Lakelanders, a platform has been constructed in the middle of a field. Wooden planks, smoothly fit together. There's a circle of chairs on it, half of them occupied. I almost vomit into the grass at my feet.

The person closest to me touches my hand. *Julian.*

I glance up at him, quietly begging. For what, I don't know. I can't turn around. I can't run away. I can't do anything my body is screaming at me to do. All he offers is a kind look and a nod of understanding.

Get through it.

Two Sentinels plant themselves in our path, their faces inscrutable behind their masks. The sea breeze plays through their flaming robes.

"We request that you discard your weapons before approaching His Majesty, the king of Norta," one says, gesturing to Farley and her officers. None of them move. Farley doesn't even blink.

Queen Anabel tosses her head back with a sneer. She peers around Cal, barely taller than his shoulder. "The king of Norta is standing right here, and he doesn't fear Red weapons."

At that, Farley laughs outright, her disdain directed at the Senti-nels. "Why do you care about our guns?" she crows. "These people are more dangerous than anything we might have." With one hand, she gestures around at us, the newbloods and the Silvers. Armed with abil-ities much more destructive than any guns. "Don't tell me your little king is afraid of a few Reds with pistols?"

Next to her, the two Scarlet Guard officers shift a little, as if they can somehow distract from the automatic machine guns clasped in their hands.

But Cal doesn't laugh, or even smile. He senses something amiss and it chills me. "I assume," he says slowly, deliberately, "that we're going to enter a Silent Circle. Is that right, Sentinel Blonos?"

My blood seems to freeze and the air goes clean out of me. *No.*

Julian slowly puts an arm out, giving me something to grab.

The Sentinel flinches, reacting to Cal's use of his house name. I focus on him, if only to keep myself from spiraling out. It's no use. My heart rams a thundering beat and air catches in my throat. *A Silent Circle.* I want to tear my skin off. My fingers twitch on Julian's arm as I tighten my grip past the point of comfort. The whites of my knuckles stand out sharply.

He covers my hand with his own, trying to stem some of my fear.

In front of us, Cal doesn't turn around, but he does angle his chin, eyes flashing. As if he wants to look at me. With pity? With frustra-tion? Or with understanding?

"That's correct," the Sentinel replies, his voice muffled. "King Maven has provided Silent Stone to ensure the meeting is without any harsher disagreements."

A muscle twitches in Cal's cheek as he tightens his jaw. "That isn't protocol," he grinds out. The growl in him seems to ripple on the air, like the warning of a beast. Part of me wants him to snap and burn these two, burn the island, burn Maven and Iris and her mother. Remove every obstacle in our way with a destructive, devouring fire.

The Sentinel straightens and fists both hands in his robes. He's taller than Cal, but nowhere near as imposing. His partner does the same, standing shoulder to shoulder to block our path. "That is the king's wish. It is not a request. Sir," he adds, sounding awkward and stilted. They used to protect Cal, as they protected his father and protect Maven now. I suppose confronting their former charge is one of the few things they aren't trained for.

Cal looks back and forth, searching both Farley and Davidson. My teeth grit together, bone on bone, as I suck in tiny gasps of air through my nose. I can almost feel the Silent Stone again, threatening to drown me. *Not if we refuse. If we turn around. Or if Maven bows, allowing us to pass without suffering.*

Of course he won't. Because that's why he brought the Stone in the first place. Not to protect himself. The rules of war are protection enough, especially with his horribly noble brother leading one side. He did this to hurt us. To hurt me. He knows what kind of prison he trapped me in for six months of my life. How I spent every day wasting, dying so slowly, cut off from half of myself. Trapped behind glass that would never break, no matter how hard I fought.

My stomach sinks when Farley nods begrudgingly. At least she won't feel it. Silent Stone has no effect on her or any other Reds without abilities.

Davidson is decidedly less keen, his spine straight and shoulders tight when he looks at Cal. But he nods with a jarring motion, agreeing to the terms.

"Very well." I barely hear Cal say it, as a roaring rises in my ears.

The ground beneath me spins in a dizzying circle. Only my grip on Julian's arm keeps me steady. At the front of the line, Farley and her officers loudly discard their weapons, making a show of their guns and knives. I flinch as each one drops, useless, disappearing into the dune grass.

"Come on," Julian whispers so only I can hear, as we move.

He forces me to take a step. My limbs tremble, threatening to give out. And I lean on him as surreptitiously as I can, letting him guide me forward.

Get through it.

I raise my eyes as best I can, trying not to shake or fall or run away.

Iris stands out brightly, her armored gown a glowing, radiant blue like cornflower. It spreads around her, artfully draped over her seat. She is the perfect balance between warrior and queen, even in comparison to Evangeline. Her gray eyes track us as we approach, narrowed to predatory slits. She was never unkind to me, by Silver standards. Still, I feel hatred for her, and for what she's done. With the Stone looming close, I have to fill myself with rage. It's the only thing to block out the fear.

I step into the circle of Silent Stone, the unnatural sensation falling over me like a curtain. I bite my lip closed to keep from screaming. My gut turns again when the old, aching weight lands hard on my shoulders. I falter in my step, my eyelids flickering, the only outward show of my intense pain. Inside, my body screams, every nerve alight. Instinct tells me to run, to leave this circle of torture. Sweat trickles down my spine as I force one footstep after another, trying to keep pace with everyone else. If not for the Stone, I would explode in a burst of electric fury to set all my storms to shame. *Lightning has no mercy. Neither do I.*

I glare, eyes narrowed against the need to weep.

I look at anyone but Maven. Iris's mother, Queen Cenra, is more subdued, a smaller woman than her daughter, with the same coloring but a plain face. Like Iris's, her armored dress is deep blue, banded with gold to match the crown on her own brow. They lean together, tucked close, in each other's confidence as only mother and daughter can be. I want to rip them apart.

The fourth royal isn't someone I've seen before, but I can guess his identity easily enough. Prince Bracken towers in his chair, his skin the polished, flawless blue-black of a precious gemstone. His robes are amethyst-edged purple, artfully draped across a breastplate of solid gold. His dark eyes rest not on Cal or me, but on Davidson. The prince looks as if he might turn the premier inside out, clearly craving revenge for his children.

Along with Iris, he flanks Maven.

I try not to look at him at first, but he is impossible to ignore. Even though the sight of him sends hot knives along my skin, so sharp I expect to start bleeding.

Get through it. Hold on to the anger.

My heart stops when I glance to him and find him already staring, a familiar, cursed smirk twisting on his pale lips.

Maven bobs his head as we take our seats, his eyes sweeping between me and Cal, as if no one else exists. Premier Davidson sits between us, a firm divide. Maven seems to enjoy that immensely, grinning at the buffer between his brother and me. The sea breeze ruffles his hair, still longer than Cal's and curling softly beneath the weight of his wretched black-iron crown.

I want to kill him.

His uniform is familiar, raven black, hung with the usual ill-gotten medals of state. He smirks at Cal's jacket, noting the reversed colors with glee. Probably happy to have chased his brother out of their symbols. He regards us with cool and open delight, eager to make this as painful as possible. The mask of the cruel king is firmly set in place.

I must loosen it.

Leaning toward Davidson, I put my elbow on the arm of my chair and jut my collarbone forward. The brand is clear for all to see, burned into my skin. *M* for *Maven*. *M* for *monster*. His gaze snags on the ruined flesh, faltering for a moment. Those ice eyes go blank and faraway. It's like pushing him off a path, or sending him down a long, dark, hallway.

He recovers, blinking at the rest of our coalition, but it's a good start.

Our seating was arranged, so everyone falls in without incident. To my surprise and discomfort, Farley has Cal on one side and none other than Ptolemus on the other. I grimace. If she doesn't fly across the platform to strangle Maven, she might just kill one of her own allies instead.

Farley's glare burns as much as any Calore as she stares down the boy king. They've met before, long ago in the summer palace, when Maven fooled us all with an easy lie, the one we all wanted to believe. He tricked her as much as he tricked me.

"It's truly fascinating to see how high you can rise, *General* Farley," Maven says, addressing her first. I know what he's trying to do. Put cracks in us before we've barely even sat down. "I wonder where you thought you would be now, if I were to ask you a year ago. What a journey." His eyes tick between Farley and Ptolemus, the implication clear.

When I was his prisoner, he cracked my head open, looking through my memories with the help of a Merandus cousin. He saw Shade die at Ptolemus's hands, and he knows what he meant to Farley. How much my brother left behind. It isn't difficult for him to poke and prod at that open wound.

Farley bares her teeth, a predator even without her claws, but Cal answers before she can toss back acid. "I think all of us find ourselves in strange places," he says, his voice stern and even. Diplomatic to the bone. I can't imagine the effort it must require. "It isn't often a Nortan king sits next to Lakelander queens."

Maven only sneers. He's far better at this than Cal will ever be. "It isn't often firstborn sons sit anywhere but the throne. Eh, Brother?" he shoots back, and Cal shuts his mouth with an audible click. "What do you think of all this, Grandmother?" Maven adds, glaring daggers at Anabel. "Your own flesh and blood, warring with each other."

She responds with equal venom. "You're no blood of mine, boy. You lost the right when you helped kill my son."

Maven just clucks, as if pitying her. "Cal raised that sword, not me," he says, tipping his chin at the similar sword at Cal's hip. "Such an imagination. Old women are so prone to their fancies."

At his side, Queen Cenra arches a single, smooth eyebrow. She says nothing, letting Maven spin his web—or knot his own noose.

"Well," he says, clapping his hands together. "I did not request this meeting. I believe that means you present whatever terms you came to offer. Surrender, perhaps?"

Cal shakes his head. "Yes. Yours."

Laughter from Maven is an odd sound. Forced. The air pushed out, the sound calculated and formed, an imitation of what he thinks a laugh should sound like. It rankles his brother, and Cal shifts in his seat, uncomfortable.

Bracken doesn't smile either. His lips tug into a scowl. He rests his chin on one balled fist. I don't know his ability, but I assume it is a powerful one, restrained only by the Stone slowly choking all of us. "I did not come all this way, at such haste, to entertain nonsense, Tiberias Calore," the prince says.

"It isn't nonsense, Your Highness," Cal replies, with a shallow dip of his head. Showing deference and respect.

In his seat, Maven scoffs low and deep. "You see my allies here." He spreads his white hands wide. "Both Silver royals, with the might of their entire nations sworn to our cause. I hold the capital, the wealthiest lands of Norta—"

"You don't hold the Rift," Evangeline snaps, cutting him off. Despite the Stone, her metals are all in place. They're truly made, locked into form, not held together by her ability alone. She prepared for this. *As I should have.* "You don't hold Delphie. You lost Harbor Bay yesterday. You lose more, until all you have left are the people sitting next to you, with no way to repay what they give." Her smile spreads, showing teeth capped with pointed silver. I think she would feast on his heart if she could. "You'll be a king without a crown or a throne before long, Maven. Best give up while you still have something to bargain."

Maven raises his nose. It makes him look like a petulant child. "I will bargain for nothing."

"Not even your own life?" I mutter, my voice small but firm enough to carry. I keep still as he turns his eyes on me, letting the ice pour over my flesh. *No flinching, no blinking. Get through it.*

He just laughs again. "Your bluff is entertaining, to say the least," he chuckles. "I see what you have, who you've swayed to your side. State your terms, Cal. Or go back to Harbor Bay and force us to kill you all."

"Very well," Cal replies. His fist clenches. If not for the Stone, he would probably burst into flame. "Step down, Maven. Step down, and I'll let you live."

"This is ridiculous," Maven sighs, rolling his eyes at Iris. She doesn't return the gesture.

Cal forges on, undeterred. "The alliance with the Lakelands and Piedmont will stand. We'll have peace on our coast, from the frozen shores to the islands of the south. Time to rebuild, regrow what this war has destroyed. Heal wounds and right wrongs that have plagued us for centuries."

"You speak of Red equality?" Iris says. Her voice is as I remember it. Calm, measured. She is a creature of self-control.

"I do," Cal says steadily.

Bracken laughs deep and long, one hand pressed against the sculpted gold on his stomach. If not for the circumstance, I would think the sound comforting and warm. Cenra and Iris remain quiet, unwilling to betray their intentions or thoughts so easily.

"You're ambitious, I'll give you that," Bracken says, pointing a finger at Cal. "And young. And distracted." His dark eyes dart to mine, making his point clear. I squirm under his gaze. "You don't know what you're asking us to do."

Farley isn't so easily cowed. She claws her hands on the arms of her chair, almost rising out of her seat. A flush tinges her cheeks. "Are you so threatened by the people you spit on that you can't allow them simple freedom?" she sneers, looking from Bracken to Cenra and Iris. "Is that how tenuous your grip on power truly is?"

The queen of the Lakelands widens her eyes, the whites a livid contrast to the bronze of her skin and the dark brown of her irises. She looks truly surprised. I doubt a Red has ever addressed her in such a way, and it shows. "How dare you speak to us—" she blurts out.

Dear Julian is the quickest, evenly speaking over her before she can bait Farley into something more drastic. "History favors the underfoot and the oppressed, Your Majesty," he says. He sounds enchanting and methodic, wise, even beneath the weight of Silent Stone. The queen is reluctant, but shuts her mouth slowly to listen. "The years are long, but eventually, *always*, fortunes shift. The people rise. Such is the way of things. Either let change come willingly, help it along, or face the wrath of such force. It might not be you, or even your children. But the day will come when Reds storm the gates of your castles, break your crowns, and slit the throats of your descendants as they beg for the mercy you will not show now."

His words echo long after he is done speaking, as if dancing on the wind. They have a sobering effect on the Lakelander queens and Bracken, who exchange uneasy glances.

Maven is not subdued in the slightest. He leers at the Jacos lord, eyes alight. He has always despised Julian. "Did you rehearse that, Julian? I always wondered why you spent so much time alone in your library."

It's too easy to throw the barb back in his face. "I doubt anyone spends more time alone than you do," I say, again moving forward to display my brand.

The combination makes him go pale, his mouth slightly open. Breath whistles between his exposed teeth. He looks like he wants to kiss me or rip my throat out. I doubt he knows which.

"Careful, Maven," I push on, pressing him closer to the edge of his tolerance. "That mask of yours might slip."

Cold fear flashes in his eyes. Then his face melts, brows creasing and lips pulling down, curling back to show more of his teeth. With the shadows under his eyes and beneath his cheekbones, he looks like a skull, white as moonlight. "I could kill you, Red," he snarls, brazen in the empty threat.

"Funny, you had the chance for six long months." I pat my hands over my arms and chest, letting my fingers brush the brand. "But here I am."

I look away before he can say more, addressing the allies at his side. "Maven Calore is unstable at best." As I speak, I'm intensely aware of their attention, the weight of three crowns staring me down. As well as the weight of Silent Stone, a constant, squeezing pressure. I wish I could feel my lightning and draw a little strength from my ability. Instead I have only my wasted self. And that must be enough.

"You all know it. Whatever the benefits of his rule, you know they don't outweigh the risks. He will be overthrown, either by us directly or by the crumbling of his country. Look around. How many High Houses sit with him? Where are they?" I gesture to the Sentinels, their own guards, but no one else of Norta. Not House Welle or House Osanos or any other. I don't know where they are, but their absence speaks volumes.

"You are his shields. He's using you and your countries. He'll turn on you one day, when he has the strength to cast you both off. He has no loyalties, and no love in his heart. The boy who calls himself king is a shell, empty, a danger to everyone and everything." In his seat, Maven examines his hands, adjusting the cuffs of his jacket. Anything to seem unaffected and unperturbed. It's a terrible act, especially for someone as talented as he is.

I hold my head high. "Why entertain this madness any longer? For what?"

To my left, Farley shifts, her chair creaking. She stares with all the fire the Calores can't muster. "Because they'd rather bleed themselves than be equal to any blood that isn't the right color," she hisses.

"Farley," Cal mutters.

To my surprise, Evangeline takes on that mess, drawing attention to herself instead. She purses her lips and smooths her dress conspicuously.

"It's infinitely clear what's happening here. You say Maven's using them as shields?" she says, almost cackling. "Where are your armies, Queen Cenra? And yours, Prince Bracken? Who really bleeds in this war? If anyone is a shield here, it's Maven. They're using the little boy against his big brother, to play them off each other until they're confident they can destroy what's left. Isn't that it?"

They don't deny it, or don't want to give oxygen to such a claim. Iris tries another tactic, leaning forward toward the Samos princess with an easy, tight-lipped smile. "I must assume the same of you, Evangeline. Or is Tiberias Calore not a weapon of the Rift?"

Maven waves her back. He looks from Cal to Farley. She is the weak spot here, or at least he thinks she is. *Good luck.* "No, not Cal," he says, purring. "The Reds. The Montfort mongrels. I know Volo and the other Silvers in open rebellion. They won't tolerate any kind of Red acceptance beyond what they need. Will you, *Anabel*?" he adds, tossing a grin at his grandmother.

She merely turns away, refusing to so much as look at him. Despite all his posturing, Maven's smile falls a little.

Farley doesn't rise to the bait this time. She keeps still, and Davidson slowly claps his hands, inclining his head toward the false king. "I have to applaud you, Maven," he says. The blank calm of the premier is a welcome respite from so much bile. "I admit, I didn't expect such deft manipulations from someone so young. But I assume that's how your mother built you, didn't she?" he adds, looking to me.

That incenses Maven more than anything. He knows that it means I've told them all I could about him, about what his mother did.

"Yes, he is what she made him," I murmur. It feels like twisting a knife in his gut. "No matter who he was meant to be. That person is completely gone."

Cal's voice is soft in response, landing the final blow. "And he is never coming back."

If not for the Stone, Maven would burn. He slams a fist down, knuckles like exposed bone. "This conversation is pointless," he snaps. "If you don't have real terms, then leave. Fortify your city, gather your dead, prepare for a true war."

His brother doesn't flinch. He has nothing else to fear from Maven. A transformation, a tragic one, has come over Cal, and he slides into the role he's best at. A general, a warrior. Facing an opponent he can defeat. Not a brother he wants to save. There is no blood left between them, only the blood Maven made him spill.

"True war is here," he replies, his calm manner sharply contrasts with Maven's sudden temper. "The storm has broken, Maven, whether you want to admit it or not."

I try to do as Cal has done. Try to let go. The false masquerade of the kind, forgotten boy is already gone. Not even his ghost remains. There is only the person in front of me, with his hatred and his obsession and his twisted love. *Get through it,* I hiss in my head. Maven is a monster. He branded me, imprisoned me, tortured me in the worst way. To keep me at his side, to feed whatever beast prowls around inside his skull. But as much as I try, I can't help but see some of myself reflected in him. Trapped by a storm, unable to break free, unable to walk away from what I've already done and will continue to do.

This world is a storm I helped create. We all did, in ways big and small. With steps we could not fathom, paths we never thought to walk.

Jon saw it all. I wonder which second put this in motion. Which choice. Was it Elara, looking into my head for an opportunity to strike the Scarlet Guard? Was it Evangeline, making me fall into the arena of Queenstrial? Was it Cal, his hand closing on mine when I was just a Red thief? Or Kilorn, his master dead, his fate decided, the doom of conscription looming before him? Maybe this didn't even start with any of us. It could be Farley's mother and sister, drowned by the Lakeland king, their deaths sparking her father, the Colonel, to action. Or Davidson fleeing death in the legions, escaping to Montfort to build a new kind of future? Perhaps someone even further away, a hundred years ago, a thousand. Someone cursed or chosen by a distant god, doomed and blessed to make this all real.

I suppose I'll never know.

TWENTY-FIVE
Evangeline

The Silent Stone grates against me, and my skin itches with the constant pressure. It isn't easy to ignore, even with my extensive years of Training. I fight back the searing urge to rip my nails down my arms, if only to feel a different kind of pain instead of this foul, decaying weight. I wonder where the Stones are buried. Beneath the meeting platform? Under our seats? They feel so close I could choke on them.

Everyone else looks undisturbed by the unnatural sensation of our deepest parts repressed. Even Mare, despite her history. She keeps her head high, her body still. No sign of discomfort or pain. Meaning I have to hide it as well as she does. *Ugh.*

Bracken's lip curls in distaste, hating the feel of the Silent Stone as much as the rest of us. Perhaps it will make him more amenable to our cause. Yes, he despises Montfort, and he has reason to. But I think he hates losing more. And if Cal's blustering works, he certainly won't have faith in Maven much longer.

Maven glares at Cal, as if he can somehow measure up to his warrior brother. Whatever compassion he counted on exploiting seems to disappear as Cal holds firm, unmoved in his seat.

"Those are my terms, Maven," he says, sounding more kingly than his father ever did. "Surrender, and live."

Maven deserves little more than a bullet to the brain or a knife to the gut. He's a danger none of us can afford to leave breathing.

His reply is guttural, coming from the deepest parts of him. "Get off my island."

No one is surprised. Ptolemus lets loose a low breath. His fingers twitch, itching for the knives strapped across his chest. At least the Sentinels didn't think, or didn't care, to disarm us. They must think magnetrons defenseless without ability. *They are wrong.* My brother could put that knife into Maven's gut if the circumstances allowed.

My betrothed leans forward in his seat, rising slowly. "Very well," he says, pained. "Remember this day, Maven, when you are abandoned and alone, with no one to blame but yourself."

Maven has no response but a smirk and a chuff of laughter. He acts well, relying on the carefully crafted image of beleaguered boy called to greatness. The second son never meant to rule. It has no use here. All of us know who he is.

Still in her seat, Queen Cenra angles her face to him, leaning past her daughter. "Our terms, Your Majesty?"

He doesn't reply, too distracted by Cal and Mare to know she's even speaking. Iris nudges him.

"None but surrender," he says quickly. "No pardons, no quarter," he adds, eyes flying to Mare's face. She recoils under his attention. "For any of you."

On Cal's far side, Anabel stands. She wipes her hands, as if ridding herself of this situation and her poisoned grandson. "That's settles it, I suppose," she sighs. "We're all in agreement."

Strangely, her eyes are on Iris. Not on Maven, or even Cenra or Bracken. On the young queen with little to say and even less power in this circle.

The young woman bows her head, gray eyes flashing with some meaning. "Yes, we are," she says. Next to her, Queen Cenra does the same. A Lakelander tradition, probably. As silly and useless as their do-nothing gods.

The two queens rise first on Maven's side of the platform, followed quickly by Bracken. He offers a low bow in my direction and I incline my head. But his eyes darken as they sweep past me, fixing on Davidson. No amount of my posturing can distract him fully from his hatred of that newblood.

It doesn't bother the premier. He remains inscrutable, standing with smooth grace. "This was interesting, to say the least," he mutters with an empty smile.

"Indeed," I hear myself answer.

The rest of us rustle out of our chairs in a swirl of bright color and gleaming armor, until only Maven remains, firmly planted in his seat. Staring.

Mare artfully avoids his gaze, weaving around Farley to take Cal's arm. The sight enrages the false king, who fumes. I almost expect smoke to rise off him. If not for the Silent Stone, it very well might.

"Until we meet again," Cal says over his shoulder.

Something about the words sets Maven off, and he slams his hands down on the arms of his chair before storming away, turning on us all. His cloak, ink black, streams out behind him. I'm reminded of a toddler kicking up a tantrum. A very dangerous toddler.

The Lakelander queens and the Piedmont prince follow him almost reluctantly. Cal's right. They'll abandon Maven's cause if the scales tip against him, if it becomes clear he can't win the war. But will they shift to our side? I don't think so. They'll sit back and wait to strike. I find myself almost envying the Scarlet Guard and Montfort. Their alliance, at least, seems rooted in true loyalty and a common goal. Not like us Silvers. We might speak of peace, but peace isn't what we're built for. We fight always, in throne rooms or battlefields or even across the table of a family dinner. It's what we are cursed to do.

I'm eager to get out of the circle of Silent Stone and breathe free air again. With a tug, I pull Ptolemus along with me, toward the winding path back to our dropjets. I'm careful to keep him close with General Farley so nearby, haunting his steps. A rat stalking a wolf, waiting for the sliver of opportunity.

As we get free of the Silent Stone, the cool relief of my ability comes rushing back. The pieces of metal in my jewelry, my hair, my teeth, tucked away all over my body, tingle against my perception. I reach for the medals on Maven, feeling them as they fade away. He's truly leaving. Escaping the island as we are.

The war is far from won, and if my guesses are correct, both sides are evenly matched at present. Perfectly balanced. This could drag on for years. Leaving me unwed, a princess only, still free of a queen's leash. *I could go home for a few weeks, leave when Father gets here. Let him handle the chaos. Maybe steal away with Elane to some quiet place.* The thought curls my toes.

It almost distracts me from the water seeping up beneath my feet, bleeding through the shallow soil.

At the edge of my perception, Maven's medals stop moving.

"Tolly," I whisper, reaching out to grab his arm.

His eyes widen as he looks over the flooding ground.

So does the rest of our party, lifting their feet, sloshing toward each other. Farley and her officers quickly reclaim their discarded guns, some of them now dripping wet. They react quickly, taking defensive positions, training their sights on the tree line and the platform in the distance.

Mare shifts, putting herself in front of Cal. He looks around, terrified, momentarily stunned by the water slowly rising around us. One of her hands sparks.

"Careful," I bark, jumping backward, dragging Tolly along with me onto drier ground. "You'll fry us all."

She regards me coldly. "Only if I want to."

"The nymphs?" Farley growls, gun against her cheek, one eye pressed to the sight. "I see movement from their direction. Their blue dresses, the Sentinels . . ." She trails off.

I draw a knife from Tolly's sash, letting it spin in my hand. "And?"

"And it's nothing to trouble ourselves with," Anabel says, her voice light and dismissive. "Come, let's return to our jets?"

I'm not the only one who stares at her, jaw gaping open.

Farley speaks first, still in position. "Either this entire island is *sinking* or we're about to face an attack—"

"Nonsense," Anabel sniffs. "It's nothing of the sort."

"Then what is it?" Cal grits out. "What have you done?"

Somehow Anabel gives way to Julian Jacos. The older man offers a thin, empty smile. "We've ended it," he says simply.

Mare finds her voice first. "Wha—"

Something that sounds like a crashing wave echoes beyond the trees, in the opposite direction from the beach. On her knees, Farley jumps, double-checking her sights, while her officers recoil.

I find myself climbing the sandy hill, desperate to get to higher ground and a better vantage point.

As I move, gunfire peppers the air, loud across the grassy field. Below me, Mare flinches. I clench a fist, counting the bullets as they dance on the edge of sensation. They rocket in opposite directions, one volley to answer another.

"They're fighting . . . something," I report.

On the ground, Cal sloshes forward, kicking up the water as his fists ignite. "Maven," I think he snarls, low and under his breath. Mare stays in front of him, trying to hold him back without shocking him— or being burned. His grandmother doesn't move at all.

As I climb, the water ebbs like a small tide, receding and flowing in as someone pulls it. From my spot, I can see color through the knobbled trees. Blue armor, red flame, the fiery robes of Sentinel guards. Someone screams, the sound echoing in a howl. The air turns to mist, as if someone is drawing a gray curtain across the world.

Quickly, my jewelry spreads, forming armor along my hands and wrists, skittering up to my shoulders. "Give me a gun, Farley," I bark.

She doesn't look at me, spitting on the ground instead.

"I have better aim and better range," I snarl.

Her grip tightens on her long gun. "If you think I'm giving you *anything*—"

"If you think I'm *asking*," I snap back, flicking my fingers. Her weapon jumps out of her hands, soaring up to mine.

"Really, ladies, there's no need for that," Anabel says, still oddly unaffected. "See now, it's over." She steps between us and points with a wrinkled finger, indicating the tree line.

The water rushes across the field again, moving with the figures that are approaching in the distance, barely shadows in the mist.

The corpses come first, floating along in the ankle-deep water, their Sentinel robes splayed wide and wet. Their masks are gone or broken, showing the faces beneath. Some I know; some I don't.

The shadowy figures solidify and one raises a hand, waving the mist away. It condenses and drops, passing over us like a sudden rainstorm, revealing Cenra and Iris, their own guards fanned out behind them. Bracken follows, his chest flashing gold while his purple cape drags in the water. They position themselves strangely, obstructing the blue-uniformed guards from view for as long as possible. Then they halt, ten yards away, the risen waters gathered around their feet.

We stare, perplexed, puzzled at the sight before us. Even the premier, his brow furrowed.

Only Anabel and Julian remain unaffected.

"Be a dear and prepare the trade," Anabel murmurs, turning over her shoulder to address the Jacos uncle. He looks oddly pale, as if sick, but nods to her request and turns away, taking two Lerolan guards with him.

Trade, she said.

I glance at Mare. She feels my gaze and turns, eyes wide in fear as well as confusion.

Trade for what? I want to ask.

Or who?

Something struggles in the circle of Lakelander guards, restrained. I see him through the gap between Cenra and Iris, fighting a losing battle against men much stronger than he is.

Maven bleeds from the lip, his crown askew on his mop of mussed black hair. He kicks fruitlessly, forcing the Lakelander guards to drag him by the arms. Water coils the length of his body, ready to strike. Next to him, Iris whistles, spinning his bracelets between her hands. *The flamemakers, key to his ability,* I realize with a swoop of shock. He's defenseless, at the mercy of those he would never show mercy to.

The Lakelander princess grins sharply, a chilling sight in an otherwise measured persona. He spits at her, missing wide.

"Nymph *bitch*," he snarls, kicking again. "You've made a mistake today."

Cenra's lip curls in a scowl, but she lets her daughter handle herself.

"Have I?" Iris replies, unperturbed. Slowly, she pulls the crown from his head and casts it into the water. "Or have you? Many, many mistakes, not the least of which was letting me into your kingdom."

I can't believe my eyes. Maven, the betrayer betrayed. The trickster tricked.

The war.

Over.

I might be sick.

My breathing turns shallow and I wrench my eyes away from Maven to watch his brother. Cal has gone deathly pale. It's clear he didn't know anything about this, whatever Anabel and Julian did. Whatever *trade* they're about to make in his name.

Who will they give over in return?

I need to run. Grab Tolly. Charge right into the sea.

Quickly, I clamber back down the hill to stand by my brother. The false king should be distraction enough. *Don't make it easy for the nymphs. Get to the jet. Get home.*

"Oh, don't flatter yourself, Evangeline!" Maven crows, contorting himself so he can smooth back his hair. It keeps falling back into his eyes. "You're not worth me, no matter how highly you think of yourself."

At his call, the others turn to look at me as I edge away, Ptolemus tight in my grip. I search for a single friendly face, and find that Mare Barrow comes closest. Her eyes dart between me and my hand on Tolly's arm. Something like pity wells up in her, and I want to cut it out with a knife.

"Then who?" I lift my chin, relying on pride as armor. "You trading yourself again, Barrow?"

She blinks, her pity melting into fury. I prefer it.

"No," Julian says, returning with the guards. Like the Lakelanders, they're dragging a prisoner from their jet.

The last time I saw Salin Iral, he was stripped of his titles, nearly choked to death at my father's hand for his foolishness and pride. He killed the Lakelander king outside the walls of Corvium, against orders, for nothing more than a pat on the head. He was too short-sighted to see that that would only strengthen the Lakelander alliance with Maven, and the resolve of both their queens. Now he'll pay for that mistake with his life.

Salin hangs loose, his eyes oddly empty. He stares at his feet, and despite the weak grip from either guard, he doesn't try to run. With Julian Jacos standing close, I can see why. I doubt he's been given *permission* to run.

"What is this—I didn't authorize *any*—" Cal sputters, looming over his grandmother. Gently, she puts a hand to his chest, pushing her king backward.

"But you'll do it. Won't you, Cal?" she says sweetly. With only the tenderness a mother can give, she reaches up to cup his face. "We can end this war today, right now. This is the cost. One life, instead of thousands."

It isn't a difficult choice to make.

"That's right, Cal. You're doing this to save lives, aren't you?" Maven says, his voice dripping with sarcasm. Words are the only weapon he has left. "Noble to the last."

Slowly, Cal raises his eyes to stare at his brother. Even Maven falls silent, letting the moment stretch and burn. Neither blinks. Neither falters. The younger Calore continues to sneer, daring his brother to react. Cal's face never changes and he doesn't say a word. But he speaks volumes as he tips his shoulder, stepping out of his grandmother's path.

Julian puts a finger to Salin's face, lifting his head so their eyes meet. "Walk to the queens," he says, and I hear the melodious ability of a talented singer. The kind who could bewitch us all if he wanted, and sing his way to a throne. Luckily for all of us, Julian Jacos has no interest in power.

Despite his haze, Salin Iral is a silk, and his footsteps are graceful. He crosses the meager distance between our party and Maven. The Lakelander queens look like women starved, watching a meal approach. Iris grabs Salin by the neck, kicks the backs of his legs, and forces him to kneel in the water, hands submerged.

"Send him across," Cenra says quietly, waving a hand toward Maven.

All of this seems wrong, as if filtered through smoked glass, too slow to be real. But it is. The Lakelander guards shove Maven ahead, making him stumble toward his brother. He still grins, spitting blood, but tears gleam in his eyes. He's losing control, and the tight grip he keeps on himself is coming undone.

He knows this is the end. Maven Calore has lost.

The guards keep shoving, never letting him catch his balance. It's a pitiful sight. He starts whispering to himself, harried words between peals of sharp laughter.

"I did as you said," he mutters to no one. "I did as you said."

Before he can fall at his brother's feet, Anabel steps forward, planting herself firmly between the pair of them. Protective as a tiger.

"Not a step closer to the true king," she growls. The woman is smart not to trust him, even now, with nothing left.

Maven sinks to a knee and runs a hand through his hair, mussing the dark, wet curls. He glares at his brother with all the fire he can no longer possess. "Afraid of a boy, Cal? I thought you were the warrior."

At Cal's side, Mare tenses, putting a hand to his arm. To stop him or push him on, I don't know. His throat bobs as he swallows, deciding what to do.

With aching slowness, the last king standing puts a hand on the hilt of his sword. "You'd kill me if our places were exchanged."

Breath whistles between Maven's teeth. He hesitates just long enough, leaving space for a lie. Or the hope of a lie. There is no predicting the mind of Maven Calore, or what face he allows anyone to see.

"Yes, I would," he mutters. He spits blood once more. "Are you proud?"

Cal doesn't reply.

The ice-blue eyes shift, jumping to the girl at his brother's side. Mare hardens under his gaze, firm as tempered steel. She has every reason to fear him, but hides it all.

"Are you happy?" Maven asks, almost a whisper. I'm not sure who the question is for.

Neither says a word.

A gurgling sound draws my attention, and I look up from Maven to see the queens circling their prey. They move in a kind of circle. Not a dance, not a ritual. There is no pattern to it. Only cold, collected rage. Even Bracken looks unsettled by them. He takes a few steps back, allowing them room to do what they must. Still on his knees, Salin sways between them, his mouth foaming with seawater.

They take turns pouring water over his face with torturous

efficiency. Just enough to keep him breathing. Little by little, drop by drop, his face pales, then purples, then blackens. And he falls, twitching, drowning in half a foot of water, unable to sit up. Unable to save himself. They bend over his body, putting their hands to his shoulders. Making sure they are the last thing he sees as he dies.

I've seen torture before, from people who delight in it. It always unsettles. But this brutality is too measured for me to understand. It terrifies me.

Iris catches me watching, and I look away, unable to stand it.

She was certainly right. Maven made a mistake letting her into his kingdom and his palace.

"Are you happy?" Maven asks again, more desperate and ferocious, his teeth like white fangs.

"Be silent, Maven," Julian sings, forcing the boy to look at him. For the first time in his twisted life, Maven Calore shuts his weasel mouth.

I look over my shoulder, only to find Ptolemus as white-faced as I feel. The world has shifted beneath our feet. Alliances broken and remade, leaving borders to be redrawn, betrothals to be carried out.

And, I realize with a sinking sensation, one more piece of the bargain. There must be.

I lean into my brother, whispering so only he can hear.

"This can't just be for Salin."

Iral is a disgraced lord without title or land or any kind of power, in either the Rift or Norta. He isn't worth anything beyond what he did. And even the Lakelander queens wouldn't trade Maven to feed their vengeance. They're strange, not stupid. Anabel said this was the price, but that can't be true. There must be more. Someone else.

I keep my face blank as the realization churns through me. No one can see behind my mask of stillness.

I wasn't far off the mark, when I feared we were the trade.

But Maven's right. A prince and princess for a king? Idiotic. We aren't worth him.

Our father certainly is.

Volo Samos, king of the Rift. Salin stuck a knife in the Lakelander king to please my father and win his favor. It's his fault as much as anyone. It was done in his name.

And he is a rival to the Lakelands as much as he is a rival to Cal.

It would be easy for Anabel to bargain him. A logical move to trade my father's life.

I keep my fingers tightly knit to hide their shaking. I weigh the options as best I can, my expression empty and devoid of any emotion.

If Father dies, the Rift dissolves. It won't stand without him, not with the way things are. I won't be a princess anymore. I won't be his subject, his hand-raised pet, his toy to trade, his sword to use as he pleases.

I won't have to marry anyone I don't love, or live my days as a lie.

But even against all things, I love my father. I can't help it. I can't bear it.

I don't know what to do.

TWENTY-SIX
Mare

I refuse to fly in the same dropjet as Maven. So does Cal. Even bewitched as he is, we still can't look at him. Julian, Davidson, and Anabel fall on that sword for us, escorting Maven in the second jet to give the rest of us some space.

Still, we can't speak to each other. The flight back to Harbor Bay passes in stunned silence. Even Evangeline and Ptolemus are shocked and quiet. The trade has thrown everyone off balance. I still can't believe it. Julian and Anabel, back-channeling with the Lakelanders? Under our noses? Without Cal's blessing or Davidson's involvement? It doesn't make sense. Even Farley, with her vast network of spies, never saw this coming. But she's the only one of us who seems pleased. She smiles in her seat, almost vibrating out of her skin with excitement.

It shouldn't feel like this. The war is won. No more battle, no more death. Maven lost his crown back on Province. No one even bothered to pick it up, abandoning the circle of cold iron to the island. Iris took his bracelets. He couldn't fight us if he wanted. It's all over. The boy king is no more. He can't hurt me for one second longer.

So why do I feel so terrible? Dread settles in the pit of my stomach, heavy as a stone and just as difficult to ignore. *What happens now?*

At first I try to blame it on Iris, her mother, and Bracken too. Despite Cal's pledge to honor the alliance, I doubt they will. They lost too much, and none of them seem like the kind to go home empty-handed. All have personal reasons to seek vengeance, and Norta is still crippled, divided by civil war. Easy pickings for stronger beasts. Whatever peace we find today exists on borrowed time. I can almost hear the tick of the clock against us.

That isn't why you're afraid, Mare Barrow.

Last night, Cal and I agreed not to make any choices, or change decisions already made. Certain things could be ignored while the war hung in the balance. But I thought we would have more time. I didn't think everything would be finished so quickly. I didn't know our toes were already edging over the precipice.

With Maven cast down, Cal is truly the king of Norta. He'll crown himself and take his birthright. He'll marry Evangeline. Nothing before will matter.

And we'll be enemies again.

Montfort and the Scarlet Guard will not stand for another king ruling Norta.

Neither can I, no matter how much he pledges to bring change. The pattern will simply repeat, in his children, or his grandchildren, down the line of kings and queens. Cal refuses to see what must be done. He doesn't have the stomach for the sacrifice required to make a better world.

I steal a glance at him, looking up through my lashes. Cal doesn't notice me staring, his focus elsewhere and inward. Thinking about his brother. The price Maven Calore must pay for the bloodshed he caused, and the wounds he tore across us all.

Before we raided Corros Prison, when Cal thought we might find Maven waiting, he said he would lose control. Go after Maven with everything he had. It frightened him, to have such a tenuous grip on himself. I told him I would kill Maven if he couldn't. It felt easy to pledge then, but when given the opportunity, when Maven looked up at me from a bathtub, vulnerable as a newborn, I turned away.

I want him dead. For what he did to me. For all the pain, all the heartache. For Shade. For the Reds used as pawns in his twisted game. Still, I don't know if I could kill him myself, just to remove the torment of him. And I'm not sure Cal can either.

But he will, and he must. It's the only place this road leads.

The journey back to Harbor Bay seems shorter than before, and we touch down on the edge of the Aquarian Port, the jets crowding what was once a market square at the edge of the water. Soldiers of the coalition ring the pavement, and my stomach flips. So many eyes.

For once it isn't me being put on parade. Though he did it to me so many times, I take little satisfaction in watching Maven forced down from a dropjet. He stumbles over himself, limbs heavy with Julian's ability, looking more like a boy than ever before. Someone binds his hands in manacles. He says nothing, still unable to speak.

Farley looms, close at his shoulder, grinning proudly, one hand raised in triumph. She seizes him by the scruff of his collar.

"Rise, red as the dawn!" she shouts. With one foot, she kicks the back of Maven's leg as Iris did. He falls to his knees, a king brought low. "Victory!"

The stunned quiet of the square quickly dissipates as the crowd realizes what this means. And the jeers rise, howling in a storm, until shrieks of joy and venom echo so loudly I think the entire city must know.

Cal's warmth radiates at my side as he watches the display, his face empty of expression. He doesn't enjoy this.

"Get him to the palace," he murmurs to Anabel when she approaches. "As quickly as we can."

She eyes him with an annoyed sigh. "The people must see, Cal. Let them enjoy your victory. Let them love you for it."

He flinches. "This isn't love," he replies, gesturing at the crowd with his chin. Reds and newbloods greatly outnumber his own Silvers, but all look on Maven with snarls and raised fists. Fury rules the square. "This is hatred. Get him to the palace, and out of the crowd."

It's the right choice. And the easy one. I nod at him, touching his arm with a gentle squeeze. Offering whatever comfort I can, while I still can. Like the alliance, we are on borrowed time.

Anabel sharpens. "We could march him—"

"No," Cal snaps, voice low and snarling. He glances between his grandmother and me. I tighten under his gaze. "I'm not making his mistakes."

"Fine," she spits through gritted teeth. At the edge of the square, transports roll into position, waiting to take us back up to the palace. Cal beelines for the closest one, and I follow, careful to keep a respectful distance.

"We still have to send out reports and broadcasts," Anabel continues as we walk. "Let the people of Norta know their true king has returned. Assemble the High Houses, collect oaths of allegiance. Punish those who won't swear to your crown—"

"I know," he bites out.

Behind us, I hear scuffling and stumbling. Farley pushes Maven along, with Julian flanking them. A few soldiers throw red scarves at her feet, celebrating our triumph. They cheer and shriek in equal measure.

The sound is horrible, even from my own people. It brings me back to Archeon, when I was forced to walk the city in chains. A prisoner, a trophy. Maven made me kneel in front of the world. I wanted to vomit then and I want to vomit now. *Shouldn't we be better than they were?*

Even so, I feel the same ugly hunger in me. The desire for revenge and justice. It begs to be fed. I push it away, trying to ignore the monster I carry with me, born of all my wrongs and all the wrongs done to me.

Anabel jabbers until we reach the transports, and Cal dismisses her with a glare. I don't bother to look back before climbing into our own vehicle, unable to watch another person face one fraction of what I suffered in Archeon. Even Maven.

Cal closes the door behind him, slumping into the semidarkness. The divider is raised, separating us from our driver. Leaving us alone together, with no need to perform. It's almost silent, the sound of jeering muffled to a low drone.

Cal bends forward, elbows braced on his knees, and buries his face in his hands. The emotions of this moment are simply too much to bear. Fear, regret, shame, and so much relief. All undercut by the churning sense of dread, knowing what is to come. I press back against the seat, putting my palms to my eyes.

"It's over," I hear myself say, tasting the lie. He breathes hard against his hands, as if he's just returned from a Training session.

"It isn't over," he says. "Not by a long shot."

★ ★ ★

My rooms in Ocean Hill are on the other side of the residence floors from Cal's rooms, separate from his at my own request. They're finely appointed, bright and airy, but the bathroom is far too small, and currently much too crowded. I shudder against the warm water, letting the soapy bubbles drift around my body. The temperature is soothing, working out the aches and tension in my muscles. Farley leans up against the tub, her back to me, while Davidson does the same at the door, looking shockingly informal for a national leader. His fine suit from the meeting is unbuttoned, open to show a white undershirt and a bobbing throat. He rubs his eyes and yawns, already exhausted though the morning is barely over.

I scrub a hand over my face again, wishing I could wipe away my frustration as easily as sweat and grime. *Impossible to get even one second to myself.*

"And when he refuses?" I grumble to them both. Our plan, one last chance to keep things together, has too many holes to count.

Davidson knits his fingers on a bent knee. "*If* he refuses—"

"He will," Farley and I say in bleak unison.

"Then we do as we say," the premier says plainly, his shoulders rising and falling in an easy shrug. His angled eyes watch me with weary attention. "We're finished if we don't hold to our word. And I have promises to keep to my own country."

Farley nods in agreement. She turns to me over her shoulder, her face inches away from mine. Up close, I can count the freckles across her nose, spreading as the summer wears on. They contrast with her scarred mouth. "So do I," she says. "The other Command generals have made themselves clear."

"I'd like to meet them," Davidson mutters idly.

She offers a bitter smirk. "If this goes as we think it will, they'll be waiting for us when we return."

"Good," he replies.

I spread my fingers across the surface, dragging lines through the milky, perfumed water. "How long will we have?" I say, asking what we're all dancing around. "Before the Lakelands come back?"

Next to me, Farley turns back around to rest her chin on her bent knee. She clacks her teeth together, nervous. An odd emotion for her. "Intelligence in Piedmont and the Lakelands reports movement at their forts and citadels. Armies being assembled." Her voice changes, growing heavy. "It won't be long."

"They'll target the capital," I say flatly. It isn't a question.

"Probably," Davidson says. He taps his lip, thoughtful. "A symbolic victory at the very least. And at best, if the other cities and regions kneel, a quick conquest of the entire country."

Farley tightens at the suggestion. "If Cal dies in the attack . . ." She trails off, stopping herself. In spite of the warm bath, my body runs cold with the thought. I look away from her silhouette, to the window instead. Puffy white clouds move lazily across a friendly blue sky. Too bright and cheerful for such talk.

Whether he knows it or not, Davidson twists the knife that's constantly stuck in my gut, picking up Farley's train of thought. "With no Calore heirs. No king. Chaos will reign across the country."

He says it like that's some kind of option. I shift quickly in the water and glare at him. I put one hand on the porcelain rim of the tub, running a threatening spark down one finger. He draws back, just a little. "It will result in more Red bloodshed, Mare," he explains. It sounds like an apology. "I have no interest in such things. We *must* win Archeon before they can."

Nodding, Farley clenches a fist. Resolute. "And force Cal to step down. Make him see there is no other choice."

I don't move, still staring at the premier. "What about the Rift?"

His eyes narrow to slits. "Volo Samos will never tolerate a world he cannot rule, but Evangeline . . ." He turns her name over in his mouth. "She might be persuaded. Or, at the very least, bribed."

"With what?" I scoff. I know Evangeline would do anything to stop her marriage to Cal, but betray her family, throw away her crown? I can't imagine it. She'd rather suffer. "She's richer than all of us. And too proud."

Davidson raises his chin, looking superior. Like he knows something we don't. "With her own future," he says. "With freedom."

I wrinkle my nose, unconvinced. "I'm not sure what you could ask from her. She's not going to get rid of her own father."

The premier dips his head in agreement. "No, but she can destroy an alliance. Refuse to marry. Cut the Rift from Norta. Give Cal nowhere else to turn. Help force his hand. He can't survive without allies."

He isn't wrong, but the secondary plan is too precarious. Letting it depend on Evangeline's shared motive is one thing, but her loyalty to her blood? Her family? It seems impossible. She said herself, she can't refuse the betrothal, and she can't go against her father's wishes when all is done.

Steam rises in the silence, spiraling through the air.

On the other side of the door, an exasperated voice sounds. "What are the odds any of this actually goes to plan?" Kilorn calls from my bedroom.

I have to laugh. "Has it ever?"

He responds with a long, frustrated groan. The door shudders as his head clunks against it.

★ ★ ★

Kilorn and Davidson are good enough to leave me to dress in peace, but Farley stays put, sprawled across the sea-green covers of my bed. At first I want to chase her out so I can have a bit of time alone, but as the minutes wear on, I'm glad for her presence. If I'm alone, I might lose it entirely and never open the door again. With Farley here, I have no excuse but to get ready as quickly as I can. Hopefully the momentum carries me through the rest of what promises to be an *interesting* day.

She snickers slightly as I force myself into a formal Scarlet Guard uniform. Freshly cleaned and tailored, just for me. I've been oathed to the Guard for almost a year, but it's never felt official. The uniform is supposed to be symbolic, to properly divide me from Cal and his Silver allies, but I really think Farley just wanted someone else to suffer with her. The bright, bloodred outfit is tight and stiff, buttoned too high up my throat. I fuss with it, trying to loosen the stranglehold a little.

"Not fun, is it?" Farley chuckles. Her own collar is open, folded over for now.

I glance at myself in the mirror, noting the way the special-made garment outlines my form. It's boxy on top, with straight-legged pants tucked into boots, giving me a rather rectangular silhouette. This is no ball gown, that's for sure.

While the buttons are polished and gleaming, I have no other decoration on my uniform. No badges, no insignia. I run a hand over my chest, the fabric bare.

"Do I finally get a rank?" I ask, glancing over to Farley. As in the People's Gallery, she has her three general's squares on her collar, but most of the false medals and ribbons have been abandoned. No use standing on ceremony in front of Cal, who will know better.

She lies back, looking at the ceiling. One leg crosses over the other,

her foot dangling free. "Private has a nice ring to it."

I put a hand to my heart, pretending to be insulted. "I've been with you a year."

"Maybe I can pull some strings," she says. "Put in a good word. Get you bumped up to corporal."

"How generous."

"You report to Kilorn."

In spite of the nervous fear tearing up my insides, I laugh out loud. "Whatever you do, don't tell him that." I can only imagine the hell he would give me. The teasing, the fake orders. I'd never live it down.

Farley laughs with me, her short blond hair splayed around her face in a halo of gold. She isn't exactly sparse with her smiles or laughter, but this is different. Not tainted by a smirk or any sharpness. A small burst of real happiness. It's a rarity these days, in all of us.

Slowly, she catches herself, the echoes of her laughter dying in her throat. I look away quickly, as if I've seen something I shouldn't.

"You stayed with him last night." Her voice is certain. She knows, as I'm sure everyone does. Cal and I weren't exactly discreet.

I answer bluntly, without shame. "Yes."

Her smile fades, and she sits up on the bed. In the mirror's reflection, I watch her expression shift. The corners of her mouth turn downward and her eyes soften, taking on an air of sadness, if not pity. And perhaps a glint of suspicion as well.

"It doesn't change things," I force out, bristling as I turn around. "For either of us."

Farley is quick to respond, one hand raised. "I know that," she says, as if calming an animal. Her throat bobs and she licks her lip, choosing her words very carefully. "I miss Shade. I'd do terrible things to bring him back. To get one more day with him. To let Clara meet her father."

My hands ball at my sides and I look at my feet, feeling my cheeks flush. With shame, because she doesn't trust me. And with anger, deep sorrow, regret, for my brother lost to all of us. "I won't—"

She pushes up to her feet and closes the distance between us in firm strides. Her hands grip my shoulders, forcing me to look up into her scarred face. "I'm saying you're stronger than I am, Mare," she breathes, eyes shining. It takes a long moment for the words to sink in. "When it comes to him. Not anything else," she adds quickly, breaking the tension.

"Nothing else," I say, agreeing with a small, forced chuckle. "Except electrocuting people."

Farley just shrugs her broad shoulders. "Well, who knows? I haven't tried that yet."

The throne room of Ocean Hill looks out over the city, across blue rooftops and white walls, all the way down to the harbor. Grand windows arch over the king's seat, flooding the chamber with the golden light of late afternoon. It gives everything an almost dreamlike quality, as if this moment isn't real. Part of me thinks I might wake up to the darkness of this morning, before we set out for Province. Before the war was so easily won, and a life so easily traded.

Cal didn't say anything about Salin Iral afterward, but he didn't have to. I know him well enough to understand how much the memory weighs on him. A disgraced lord, but a lord all the same, drowned and murdered in payment for Cal's brother. It hasn't gone easy for Cal. But looking at King Tiberias the Seventh, no one would be able to tell.

He sits on his father's throne, tall against the diamondglass chair, looking like flame itself in his crimson and black. The windows make his silhouette glow, and I wonder if one of his guards is a Haven shadow, manipulating the light to create an image of power and strength. It's certainly working. He seems a king, like his father. Like Maven never was.

I despise the sight. The shimmering throne, the simple crown on his head. Rose gold, like his grandmother's. Finer than iron. More elegant. Less violent. A crown for peace, not war.

Farley and I sit side by side, to the left of the throne with Davidson and his Montfort attendants. On the right, at Cal's hand, is Anabel, her seat closer to the throne than any other. House Samos sits near her, clustered around another king.

I wonder how long Volo Samos spent constructing his own throne of steel and pearly metal. The materials weave in intricate braids of silver and white, studded with the occasional flash of black jet. My lips twitch at the thought of the Samos king wasting hours of his day to make a chair. As always, the pageantry of Silvers never ceases to amaze.

Evangeline seems oddly nervous next to her father. Usually she delights in these things, content to watch and be watched. Instead she can't sit still, her fingers twitching and one foot tapping slightly beneath the folds of her gown. I wonder what she knows, or suspects. It can't be Davidson's offer. He hasn't extended it yet, not until he's sure we'll need her. Still, her dark gray eyes flash back and forth, searching the hall. And always returning to the tall doors thrown wide at the far end of the chamber, open to the receiving halls of the palace. A crowd idles outside them, Silver and Red, hoping to catch a glimpse inside. I feel myself coil with fear. Evangeline is not one to scare easily.

But I quickly forget all that when Julian enters the hall, his hand on a familiar arm as he guides the royal prisoner toward the throne. Bold murmurs follow, silenced only when the chamber doors swing shut with an echoing thud, separating us from the rest of the palace. Cal isn't the kind to require an audience, and he's smart enough to know we shouldn't have one while he decides his brother's fate.

Maven doesn't stumble this time. He holds his head high, even with his wrists bound. I'm remind of a bird of prey, a falcon or an eagle, surveying us all with sharp eyes and sharper talons. But he isn't a threat. Not without his bracelets. Not without anyone here to follow his command. The guards flanking him are Lerolan, loyal to Cal and Anabel. Not Maven.

I see no way out of this, even for him.

They stop a few yards from Cal's feet, and Anabel stands, her body casting a long shadow. She draws her eyes over Maven slowly, as if they are knives skinning him alive. "Kneel to your king, Maven," she says, her voice echoing around the deathly silent chamber.

He tips his head. "No, I don't think so."

Suddenly I'm back in another palace, staring at a different Calore king. On my knees next to Maven, my hands shackled behind my back as he stands. When he betrayed us all and revealed who his heart truly belonged to.

Maven, help me up.

No, I don't think so.

Maven Calore chooses his words carefully, and he does so now. Even when they have no meaning, when he has no power left, he can still cause us pain.

On the throne, Cal darkens, one hand curling into a fist. I feel the monster rise up inside me, begging to tear Maven into pieces. Obliterate him. I can't deny the desire, but I have to. For my sanity. For my humanity.

"Stand if you wish," Cal finally says, some tension in him releasing again. He waves a hand like he doesn't care at all. "It doesn't change *where* you're standing. And where I currently sit."

"*Currently*, yes," Maven replies, careful to emphasize his meaning. His eyes glint, cold as ice, hot as blue flame. "I doubt you'll sit there long."

"That's not your concern," Cal says. "You have committed treason and murder, Maven Calore. Crimes too numerous to name, so I won't even try."

Maven just scoffs, rolling his eyes. "Low effort."

His older brother knows better than to take the easy bait, and he lets the insult slide off. Instead he angles his body, turning toward Davidson as if consulting an adviser, or even a friend.

"Premier, what would his punishment be in your country?" he asks, his face open and inviting. It's a brilliant show of solidarity, all part of the image Cal is trying to build for himself. A king who unites, rather than destroys. A Silver who looks to Reds for counsel, disdaining the divisions of blood.

It already has consequences.

On his throne, Volo curls his lip, rustling in his robe like an annoyed bird puffing up his feathers. Maven is quick to notice.

"You're going to allow that, Volo?" he croons. "Standing second to a Red?" His laughter echoes, a sharp sound to cut glass. "How far the House of Samos has fallen."

Like Cal, Volo has little desire to sink to Maven's taunting. He stills, crossing his chrome-covered arms over his chest. "I still have a crown, Maven. Do you?"

Maven only sneers in response, one corner of his mouth twitching.

"Execution," Premier Davidson says firmly, leaning forward. He plants his elbows on the arms of his chair as he shifts for a better view of the fallen, false king. "We punish treason with execution."

Cal's eyelids barely flicker. He turns again, leaning to Volo. "Your Majesty, how would you deal with him in the Rift?"

Volo is quick to respond, teeth clicking. Like Evangeline's, his eyeteeth are capped in pointed silver. "Execution."

Cal nods. "General Farley?"

"Execution," she replies, raising her chin.

On the floor below, Maven doesn't seem bothered by the sentence. Or even surprised. He spares little attention for the premier, or Farley, or Volo. Or even me. Whatever snake coils in his brain has eyes for one person. He stares up at his brother, unblinking, his chest rising and falling in tiny puffs of breath. I forgot how similar they are, even as half brothers. Not just in coloring, but in their fire. Determined, driven. Constructions of their parents. Cal is built from his father's dreams, and Maven from his mother's nightmares.

"And what will you do, Cal?" he asks, his voice so low and quiet I almost can't hear him.

Cal doesn't hesitate. "Exactly what you tried to do to me."

Maven almost laughs again. Instead he chuffs out a short breath. "So I'll die in the arena?"

"No," the king replies, shaking his head. "I don't intend to watch you spend your last moments embarrassing yourself." It isn't a joke. Maven isn't a fighter. He would barely last a minute in the arena. But he doesn't deserve what Cal is offering, a little piece of mercy in otherwise iron judgment. "It will be quick. I can give you that."

"How noble of you, *Tiberias*." Maven scowls. Then he thinks better of it, his face clearing. He widens his eyes, and I'm reminded of a dog begging for scraps. A puppy who knows exactly what he's doing. "Can I make a request?"

At that Cal nearly rolls his eyes. He fixes Maven with a look of pure derision. "You can try."

"Bury me with my mother."

The request drives a hole through me.

I think I hear someone on the other side of the council gasp, perhaps Anabel. When I glance at her, she has a hand over her mouth, but her eyes are stoically dry. Cal has gone bone white, both hands clawed to the arms of his throne. His gaze wavers, falling for a moment, before he forces himself to look back at his brother.

I don't know where Elara's body ended up. Last I knew, it was with the Guard on Tuck Island, the island we abandoned.

An island of corpses. My brother's, and hers.

"That can be arranged," Cal finally murmurs.

But Maven isn't finished. He takes a step, not forward but to the side. In my direction. The full force of his gaze almost knocks me out of my seat. "And I want to die the way my mother did," he says plainly, as if asking for an extra blanket.

Again I feel too stunned to think. All I can do is keep my jaw locked in place so my mouth won't gape open in shock.

"Ripped apart by your fury," he pushes on, his eyes horrible, unforgettable, searing into me. The brand on my collarbone seems to burn. "And your hatred."

Inside me, the monster roars. *I'll do it right now. I helped start this. It's only fair I get to end it.* Like Cal's, my fingers curl on my chair, nails digging into wood. I try to anchor myself, pull inward, keep the lightning at bay, but I feel as if I could spark a storm in a single heartbeat. I won't give him the satisfaction of his last seduction. That's what this is. One more drop of poison, a last curl of rot, his final corruption of who I was before he got his claws into me. He knows some piece of me, a large piece, wants this. And he knows it will ruin whatever I managed to salvage from his prison and the torture of his love.

Kill him, Mare Barrow. Be done with him for good.

He stares up at me, waiting for my decision. So do the others. Even Cal, a king, won't say a word. As before, he's letting me choose which path I want to take.

For some reason, I think of Jon. The seer who told my fate. *To rise, and rise alone.* I wonder if that fate has already changed, or if this is how I change it.

Slowly, I shake my head.

"I won't be your ending, Maven. And you won't be mine."

On the floor, Maven seems to tighten. His eyes flicker back and forth, searching my face from eyes to lips. He stays quiet for a long minute, as if waiting for me to change my mind. I stand firm, teeth clenched to stop myself from wavering. *Lightning has no mercy,* I said once. But lightning is only one part of me. It doesn't rule me.

I rule it.

"Fine," Maven forces out, angry to be denied. I feel a tiny bloom of triumph, a counterbalance to the monster in me. He turns away, spinning on his heels to face Cal again. "Then a bullet. A sword. Cut my head off if you want. I have little interest in what you choose."

Cal is steadily losing his grip, the mask of a king sliding as the ordeal wears on him. I half expect him to get up and walk out of the room. But that isn't like him. No surrender, no show of weakness. That has been drilled into his bones since childhood. "It will be quick" is all he says again, hesitant.

"You already said that," Maven snaps like a petulant child. Silver flushes high on his cheeks, twin spots of darkening color.

Anabel clasps her hands. She looks at the brothers, weighing them against each other. The tension between them jumps and crackles like a live wire, and I wonder if Maven is simply trying to goad Cal into killing him outright. Since he couldn't do it to me.

"Guards, we're finished with the traitor," she says, looking imperious.

Taking the decision out of Cal's hands entirely.

In spite of myself, I glance at Maven, and he's already looking at me. *Cal can't make choices.*

He told me that so many times, and I learned the truth of it in many painful ways. Even with Maven removed, Cal is still reluctant, unable to make up his mind. Maven told me Cal would make a poor king because of it. Or at the very least another king on a leash, reliant on someone else to help him along. I have to agree. The younger Calore might be a beast, but he isn't a fool.

The Lerolan guards turn him forcibly, seizing his shoulders to push him out of the chamber. I expect Julian to go with him, but he stays, instead taking a place behind the throne. He folds his hands, thoughtful and silent. Footsteps are the only sound in the room, echoing with such finality as Maven is led away. I wonder if I'll ever see him again. If I'll have the stomach to watch him die.

When the massive doors swing shut behind his form, I slump a little in my seat, exhaling a long breath. I want nothing more than to go upstairs and take a nap.

I think Cal feels the same. He shifts on his throne, making to stand. "I believe that concludes any business we might have," he says, his voice strained with fatigue. The king makes a show of looking back and forth among us, as if consulting a loyal council instead of a room of precarious allies. Maybe he thinks he can make it so, if he just acts the part.

Good luck.

Queen Anabel is quick but gentle, laying a hand on his arm to stop his movement. He stills under her touch, perturbed. "We have to decide on your coronation," she reminds him with a placid smile. Cal seems annoyed by the prospect, or just by his grandmother nannying him. "It must be as soon as possible—tomorrow, even. No need for a fuss, just something official."

Not to be outdone, Volo braces his bearded chin on one hand. The slightest motion, and a clear signal for attention. "And there's the issue of New Town to be settled, not to mention your wedding." He looks between Cal and Evangeline. If not for their well-trained restraint, I think both might squirm or even gag. "It will take some weeks to prepare—"

I latch on to something else instead. "Would you mind explaining the issue of New Town?" I ask, adjusting myself to look at Volo fully. He stares back at me, his gray eyes almost black with disgust. At my side, Farley's lips twitch, but she quickly schools her expression into neutral blankness.

Anabel answers before Volo can say anything, or bluster at my rudeness. "We don't need to discuss that now," she says, hand still on Cal's arm.

Cal looks at me, wary of what I might do and what it could trigger in the Samos king. He purses his lips and furrows his brow, as if to warn me off the subject.

No chance, Calore.

"I think we should," I tell them all. My voice is strong, clear, a cold echo of Mareena Titanos, the weapon the Silvers gave me. "Among other things."

Cal raises an eyebrow. "Such as?"

The premier clears his throat, taking up his piece of our hastily planned and barely rehearsed conversation. But Davidson is a skilled politician and diplomat. Nothing about his words sounds premeditated. He acts well, and speaks with great skill.

"It's clear the Lakelands and Prince Bracken, not to mention his allies in Piedmont, have little intention of leaving Norta alone," he says, directing his speech at all the Silver royals. Especially Cal, who must be won over. "She is united again, but your country has been weakened by a bitter war. Two of your largest forts are either destroyed or neutralized. You're still waiting for the rest of your noble families to pledge allegiance, betting on their support. Queen Cenra doesn't seem like the kind to let such an opportunity pass by."

Cal relaxes a little, shoulders dropping their infinite tension. The Lakelands are an easier subject than Red oppression. He glances at me, almost winking, as if this is just a playful game, a way to flirt. Instead of three hunters pushing a wolf into a corner.

"Yes, I agree," he says with a grateful nod. "And with our own alliances strong, we can defend Norta from any invaders, north or south."

Davidson doesn't drop his serene expression. He only tips a finger. "About that."

I brace myself, toes curling in my shoes. Heat rises in my chest. I tell myself to expect nothing. I know Cal well enough to predict what he will say. Still, there's the slim chance that he's changed, that I've changed him. Or that he is simply too tired of fighting, sick of the bloodshed, fed up with the evils his kind have made.

Cal doesn't follow where the premier hopes to lead, but Anabel sees right through him. Her eyes narrow to slits, snakelike. Behind her, Volo looks like he might run us all through with a few well-placed spikes.

On the side closest to me, hidden from the rest, Davidson lowers a hand. It glows vaguely blue, ready to shield us from any attack. His face remains unchanged, his voice still even and firm. "Now that your brother is deposed, and you stand to rule as king, I'd like to propose another option."

"Premier?" Cal asks, still unable, or unwilling, to understand.

The naked fury in Volo and Anabel gives me pause. Like Davidson, I lower a hand, and call sparks to my skin.

Davidson pushes on, despite the Silver king and queen scowling openly at him. "Years ago, the Free Republic of Montfort was not as it stands today. We were a collection of kingdoms and lordships, Silver-ruled, as you are now. Civil war roamed the mountains." Even though I've heard what he's about to say before, I still get a chill. "Peace was unheard of. Reds died for Silver wars, Silver pride, Silver power."

"Sounds familiar," I murmur, my eyes on Cal. I try to weigh his reaction, noting the slight ticks of motion in his face. Lips pressing together, dark brows curving. A tightening of the jaw, the release of breath. It's like trying to read a picture, or smell a song. Frustrating and impossible.

The premier gains momentum. He enjoys this, and excels in the effort. "It was only through an uprising," he says, "an alliance of Reds, bolstered by the growing ranks of Ardents, as well as Silvers sympathetic to our plight, that we were able to re-form ourselves into the democratic nation we are today. It took sacrifice. It took many lives. But more than a decade later, we are better for it. And growing better by the day." Satisfied, he leans back, still ignoring the positively murderous looks from Anabel and Volo. "I hope you would endeavor to do the same, Cal."

Cal.

The use of the name here, while he sits a throne with a crown on his head, has clear meaning. Even Cal seems to get it. He blinks once, twice, gathering himself.

Before he can say anything, Farley squares herself to Cal, eager to play her part in this.

Her general's squares glint, gleaming sharply, reflecting points of light onto Cal's face. "We have an opportunity right now that will not come again. Norta is in shambles, begging to be rebuilt," she says. Farley isn't as good a speaker as Davidson, but she isn't an amateur. The Scarlet Guard picked her to be their voice all those months ago, and they picked her for a reason. She has enough fire and enough belief to stir even the coldest hearts. "Let us rebuild her together, into something new."

Anabel speaks before her grandson can say anything. Almost hissing, she says, "Into something like *your* country, Premier? And, let me guess, you'll offer your services in helping make this glorious new nation?" she adds, tossing the barb with deadly accuracy. Planting the seed of suspicion she needs. I see it land, shadowing Cal's eyes. *Will it take root?* "Perhaps you might even offer to help rule her?"

A bit of Davidson's restraint flickers. He almost smirks. "I have a country of my own to serve, Your Majesty, while I am *allowed* to serve."

Volo barks an empty laugh. It's almost worse than Maven's. "You want us to give up our thrones, everything we worked for. Throw away our lineage and betray our houses, our fathers and grandfathers?"

Anabel scowls. "And grandmothers," I think she growls under her breath.

Even though I want to jump up, I keep my seat. It isn't wise to escalate this into a more physical display.

"And what have *we* worked for, Volo?" I say. Volo barely deigns to look at me. It only feeds the anger in me, making it useful. "What have we bled for? The right to be ruled again? To be shuttered into slum towns, bound into conscription, returned to the lives we escaped? How is this right? How is that fair?"

My grip on myself begins to loosen, and I try to hold back, ignoring the telltale tightening in my throat as I speak. Saying all of this out loud, to people who have made this world cruel, or kept it that way, has a strange effect. I feel as if I could cry or explode, and I don't know which way I might tip. I want to take Anabel by the shoulders or grab Volo by the neck, force them to listen and see what they've done and what they want to continue doing. But if they keep their eyes shut? Or if they look and see nothing wrong? What more can I do?

The Samos king scoffs at me, disgusted. "This world is neither right nor fair, *girl*. I would think anyone born Red would know that," he sniffs. Next to him, Evangeline keeps still, her eyes on the floor, her mouth pursed shut. "You're not our equals, no matter how much you try to be. That is nature."

Cal finally breaks his silence, his eyes flaring. "Volo, quiet," he says sharply. No title, no niceties. But no denial either. Whatever line he walks is growing thinner by the minute. "What exactly are you asking, Premier?" he adds. He's going to make us spell it out.

"It's not just my request," Davidson replies, looking to me.

Cal looks at me, too, his bronze stare fully trained on my face. In spite of myself, my gaze runs over him, from his hands to the crown on his forehead. Everything he is.

I don't hesitate. I've survived too much and too long. After all we've been through, Cal shouldn't be surprised.

"Step down," I tell him. "Or we step back."

His voice flattens, hollow of emotion. No shock.

He saw this coming.

"You'll end the alliance."

Davidson nods once. "The Free Republic of Montfort has no interest in creating a kingdom like the one we escaped."

Proud, Farley speaks up too. "The Scarlet Guard won't stand for it either."

I feel a low tremor of heat, a small ripple from Cal's direction. A bad sign. With a sigh, I let go of any hope that he might finally see reason. It draws his attention, if only for a second. I see hurt in him, enough to evoke the same in me. Just a tiny pinprick, dull compared to all the wounds I have from the Calore brothers.

Cal looks back to Davidson, directing his rising anger to someone else. "So you'll leave us to the Lakelanders and Piedmont. Kingdoms and princes worse than I will ever be?" he says, exasperated, almost stumbling over the words. It's clear he's trying to salvage this, and doing all he can to keep us here. "Like you said, we're weak right now. Easy prey. Without your armies—"

"Red armies," the premier reminds him coolly. "Newblood armies."

"It can't be done," Cal replies, his voice blunt. He puts his hands out, palms up, empty. With nothing to offer. "It just can't be done. Not now. In time, maybe, but the High Houses won't kneel if there isn't a king. We'll splinter. Norta won't exist anymore. We don't have time to change our *entire form of government* while preparing for an inevitable invasion—"

Farley cuts him off. "Make the time."

Despite his height, his broad form, the crown, the uniform, all the trappings of a warrior and a king, Cal has never seemed more like a child. He looks between us, glancing from me to his grandmother to Volo. The latter offer no respite, their faces carved into matching scowls. If he bends to us, they will refuse. And the other side of his alliance will be broken.

Behind Cal, unseen, Julian lowers his head. He says nothing to anyone, and keeps his mouth shut.

Volo runs one deadly hand through his silver beard. His eyes flash. "The Silver lords of Norta will not give up their birthrights."

Fast as lightning, Farley jumps out of her seat. She spits impressively at Volo's feet. "That's what I think of your birthright."

The Samos king is, to my infinite surprise, stunned into silence. He gawks at her, mouth agape. I've never known a Samos to be at a loss for words.

"Rats don't change," Anabel snarls. She taps one hand against the arm of her chair, the threat clear as day. Not that it affects Farley much.

Cal only repeats himself, his voice barely more than a mumble. The hunters have pushed him into a corner. "It can't be done," he says.

Slowly, with finality, Davidson stands from his seat, and I follow suit. "Then we're sorry to leave you like this," he says. "Truly. I consider you a friend."

Cal glances between us, eyes running back and forth. I see sadness in him, the same I feel in myself. We share an acceptance too. This was always the path we chose to walk.

"I know that," Cal replies. His voice shifts, deepening. "And you should know I don't respond well to ultimatums, friendly or otherwise."

A warning.

And not just to us.

We step down together, Reds aligned in our beliefs and our goals.

Red uniforms and green, our skin kissed by the same undertones of rose and scarlet. We leave behind the Silvers, as cold and unmoving as if they were carved from stones, statues with living eyes and dead hearts.

"Good luck," I manage to say over my shoulder, stealing one last glance.

Cal responds in kind, watching me go. "Good luck."

In Corvium, when he chose the crown, I thought the world had been snatched away, leaving me to fall through an abyss. This isn't the same. My heart has already been broken, and one night did not sew it back together. This wound isn't new; this ache isn't unfamiliar. Cal is the person he told me he was. Nothing and no one will ever change him. I can love him, and perhaps always will, but I can't make him move when he decides to stay still. The same could be said of me.

Farley nudges my hand, a sharp reminder as we walk. Our last request is yet to be made.

I turn again, angling my face to him. I try to look as I must. Determined, deadly, an inevitable downfall for the Silver king. But still Mare, still the girl he loves. The Red who tried to turn his heart. "Will you let Reds leave the slums, at the very least?"

Next to me, Farley barks out the rest. "And end conscription?"

We expect nothing in return. Perhaps a pantomime of sadness, or another tragic explanation of how *impossible* such things would be. Maybe even Anabel chasing us from the room.

Instead Cal speaks without looking at the Silvers on his right. Deciding without their input. I didn't know he had it in him. "I can promise fair wages."

I almost scoff out loud, but he keeps speaking.

"Fair wages," he continues. Volo blanches, looking disgusted. "No restrictions on movement. They're free to live and work where they please. Same for the armies. Fair wages, fair enlistment terms. No conscription."

It's my turn to be caught off guard. I have to blink and bow my head. He returns the gesture. "Thank you for that," I force out.

His grandmother slaps the arm of his throne, indignant. "We're about to fight another war," she sneers, as if anyone needs reminding of the Lakelander danger.

I turn back around to hide my smile. Next to me, Farley does the same. We exchange glances, pleasantly surprised by the acquiescence. It means little in the grand scheme; it could be an empty promise, and it probably won't last. But it serves one purpose, at least.

Driving a wedge between the Silvers, putting cracks in an already precarious alliance. The only one Cal has left.

Behind me, Cal's voice takes on a dangerous edge as he talks his grandmother down. "I am king. Those are my orders," he says to her.

Her response is a whisper I cannot hear, muffled by the groaning noise of the doors as they swing open again and then shut. The receiving hall in front of us is as crowded as before, full of rubbernecking nobles and soldiers, eager to glimpse the new king and his patchwork council. We pass through in silence, our faces blank and unreadable. Farley and Davidson mutter to their officers, relaying our decision. It's time for us to leave Harbor Bay and Norta behind. I unbutton my uniform collar, letting the jacket fall open so I can breathe more easily, unfettered by stiff fabric.

Kilorn is the only person waiting for me, and he is quick to reach my side. He doesn't bother to ask how the meeting went. Our exit, along with our silence, is answer enough.

"Damn it," he growls as we walk, our pace brisk and determined.

I don't have anything to pack. All my clothes are borrowed or easily replaced, even the ones I came to Harbor Bay in. I have nothing in the way of personal belongings, except the piercings in my ear. And the earring back in Montfort, tucked away in a box. The red stone, the one I couldn't bear to part with. Until now.

I wish I had it here. To leave it in his room, on the pillow I slept on.

That would be a fitting good-bye. And easier than the one I have to make now.

I break off from Farley and Davidson, who are heading for their own rooms at the bottom of the grand staircase. "I'll meet you outside in a few minutes," I tell them both. Neither questions my decision, or my purpose, letting me go with a wave and a nod.

Kilorn hesitates on the first step, waiting for an invitation to follow. He'll never get one.

"You too," I mutter. "This won't take long."

His green eyes narrow, hard as chips of emerald. "Don't let him ruin you."

"He's already done what he can to me, Kilorn," I say. "Maven can't break anything else."

The lie soothes him, enough for him to turn away, satisfied with my safety.

But there's always something left to be broken.

His door guards step aside, letting me turn the knob of his room. I do it quickly, so I can't lose my nerve or change my mind. His cell is not a cell, but a fine sitting room tucked away on an upper floor, facing the ocean. No bed, just a few chairs and a long couch. Either he'll die this afternoon, and he has no use for sleeping arrangements, or a bed hasn't been prepared yet.

He stands at the window, one hand on the curtains, as if to pull them shut.

"No use," he mutters, his back to me as I shut the door again. "They don't block the light."

"I thought that's what you wanted," I reply. "To stay in the light?"

I echo words he said to me months ago, when I was his prisoner, chained to a room like this one, doomed to stare out windows and waste.

"We have an odd symmetry, don't we?" he says, gesturing to the room with a lazy smile. I almost laugh at the circumstances. Instead I sink into one of the armchairs, careful to keep my hands free and my sparks close.

I watch him, still at the window. He doesn't move.

"Or maybe Calore kings just have similar taste in jail cells."

"Doubtful," he replies. "But fine prisons, it seems, are how we show affection. Small mercies for prisoners we can't help but love."

His declarations mean nothing to me anymore. I barely feel a twinge, easy to ignore, deep in my heart.

"What Cal feels for you and what you feel for me are very different."

Maven laughs darkly. "I would hope so," he says, running the curtain through his hands again. He glances at my jacket, then at my collarbone, now covered by an undershirt. My brand is hidden away. "When will it be?" he adds, his voice going soft.

The execution. "I don't know."

Another tainted laugh. He starts to pace, hands folded behind his back. "You mean that grand council couldn't make a decision? How predictable. But then, I suppose I'll die of old age before your lot agrees on something. Especially with Samos close by."

"Your grandmother too."

"I have no grandmother," he says sharply. "You heard her yourself: she's no blood of mine." The memory sours Maven. He quickens his step, crossing the floor in a few even strides before turning back again. Despite his calm exterior, he seems manic in these moments, dangling by a thinning thread. I try not to look at his eyes as they glint, alight with a fire close enough to burn. "What are you doing here? I have to say, I didn't enjoy taunting you half as much when you were *my* prisoner."

I shrug, watching him with ticking eyes. "You're not my prisoner."

"Cal's, yours." He waves a hand. "What difference does it make?"

A great deal of difference. I feel the frown tug at my face, the familiar sadness welling up inside me. He sees it behind my own mask of indifference.

"Oh," he murmurs, stopping in the center of the room. He peers at me intensely, as if he can stare through my skull and into my brain. The way his mother did. But he doesn't need to read my mind to know what I'm thinking, or know what his brother has done. "So a decision has been made."

"Just one," I whisper.

Maven takes a single step forward. I'm the danger here, not him, and he's careful to stay out of my reach. "Let me guess, you Reds gave him a choice? The same choice you gave him months ago?"

"Something like that."

His lips curl, showing teeth. But not in a smile. No matter what else, he doesn't enjoy seeing me in pain, physical or otherwise. "He didn't surprise you, did he?"

"No."

"Good. I told you just as much. Cal follows orders. He'll be following his father's wishes until the day he dies." Maven looks almost apologetic as he speaks—regretful, even. Sorry for what his brother became. *I'm sure Cal shares the feeling.* "He'll never change. Not for you, not for anyone."

Like Maven, I don't need weapons to hurt. Just words.

"That isn't true," I tell him, looking him in the eye fully.

He tips his head, clucking his tongue like I'm a child to be scolded. "I thought you had learned by now, Mare. Anyone can betray anyone. And he's betrayed you once again." He takes one more daring step forward, a few feet away now. I can hear the breath hissing through his teeth, like he's trying to taste the air in my lungs. "Can't you admit what he is?" he murmurs. It sounds like begging. The last request of a dead man.

I raise my chin, holding his gaze. "Flawed, just like the rest of us."

His snarl reverberates deep in my chest. "He's a Silver king. A brute, a coward. A stone who will never move and can never change."

That isn't true, I repeat in my head. All these months have proven that, but nothing more so than a few minutes ago. When he chose, even with his grandmother hanging at his shoulder. Fair wages, no conscription. Steps that seem small but are also gigantic. *Inches for miles.*

"But he is changing," I say, my voice steady, drawing this out. I'm taunting him. Maven pales as I speak, unable to move. "Slower than we need, but I see it. A glimmer of who he could be. He's making himself into someone else." Finally, I lower my eyes, as the cracks in Maven's mask begin to show. "I don't expect you to understand that."

He grits his teeth, furious. And a bit confused. "Why?"

"Because every change in you was not your own." The razor-edged words tumble, cutting as they go. He flinches, blinking quickly.

"Thank you for the reminder," he replies. "I so needed it."

I draw my last blade, ready to drive it deep into his heart. And perhaps make him feel one piece of what he lost, if only a fleeting sensation. "You know Cal hunted for someone who could fix you?" I tell him.

Maven's mouth flaps open and closed, searching for something cunning or at least clever to say. He only manages a stammering "Wh-what?"

"In Montfort," I explain. "He had the premier search for a newblood, an Ardent, some kind of whisper powerful enough to undo whatever your mother did." It almost hurts to see the flickers in him, tiny flashes of emotion beyond rage or hunger. They fight to the surface, but whatever Elara did holds fast. His face goes still, slack as he listens. "But no one like that exists. And even if they did, there's no changing what you are. I realized that a long time ago, when I was your prisoner. But your brother—he didn't believe you were truly gone until today. When he looked into your eyes."

Slowly, the fallen king sits down in the chair opposite mine. His legs stretch out before him and he slumps, letting go of his steel spine. Numb, he runs a hand through his hair, fingering the curling black locks. So like Cal's hair, like his father's hair. He stares at the ceiling, wordless, unable to speak. I imagine Maven in quicksand, fighting to climb out. Fighting the impossible nature his mother gave him. It's no use. His face turns to stone again, his eyes narrowed and icy, doing all they can to ignore what his heart wants to feel.

"There's no way to complete a puzzle with missing pieces, or put together shattered glass," I mumble, only to myself, repeating what Julian told me weeks ago.

Maven sits up, drawing his back straight. One hand circles his wrist, touching the skin where his bracelet used to be. Without it, he's power-less, useless. He doesn't even need Arven guards.

"Cenra and Iris are going to drown you all," he hisses. "At least I'll be dead before they get their hands on me."

"What a consolation."

"I would not have liked to watch you die." The admission is small and matter-of-fact. There is no agenda to it, only the ugly, naked truth. "Will you enjoy watching me?"

At least I can respond with some truth of my own. "Part of me will."

"And the rest?"

"No," I whisper. "I won't enjoy it."

He smiles. "That's enough for me. A better good-bye than I deserve."

"And what do I deserve, Maven?"

"Better than we ever gave you."

The door bangs open before I can ask what he means. I start to rise, expecting guards to usher me out now that I'm no longer part of the coalition. Instead I find Farley and Davidson standing over us. She glares at Maven with more fire than even Cal could muster, and I expect her to skin him alive in front of us.

"General Farley," Maven drawls. He might be trying to goad her into doing the deed before his brother can. She only snarls in reply, like a beast.

Davidson is more polite, ushering someone else into the room. I notice that the hall behind him is empty, the door guards gone. "So sorry to interrupt," the premier says. He gestures, and his companion, the Montfort newblood Arezzo, steps into the chamber. I blink at her, confused, but only for a second.

She's a teleporter. Like Shade. And her hands are reaching.

"It's time we all go," Davidson sighs, looking between us.

I jolt as Arezzo grabs my wrist, but I'm not the only one she's taking.

Before the room disappears, squeezing to nothing, I see Maven. His white face, paler by the second. His blue eyes, wide with rare shock. And Arezzo's hand on his own.

TWENTY-SEVEN
Evangeline

The throne room feels empty without the Reds, colder somehow.

Anabel is stupid if she thinks we can coronate Cal tomorrow. Foolish, eager woman. No king of Norta can be crowned anywhere but the capital, and it will take a few days at least to stabilize Harbor Bay before anyone can leave for Archeon. There's also the High Houses who were loyal to Maven. They'll need to kneel, pledge themselves to Cal, and be present at any coronation, if the country is to pull itself back together. I say none of this, of course. Let them figure it out for themselves. An unstable King Tiberias will hardly have time for marriage.

Unfortunately, he has Julian Jacos, and the singer lord is more adept at politics than he has ever let on. He overrides Anabel and suggests they wait a week before the coronation. Cal is happy to take his advice in this and other matters too.

Even now, Cal slumps on his throne, looking drained by the battle and the aftermath. Mostly the aftermath. He keeps stealing glances at the door too, willing Mare to return. But it's been almost an hour. She and her companions are probably long gone by now, fleeing to the distant mountains of Montfort. Her family is there, waiting. She'll be happy to go back to them. I wish I could do the same, and escape back to the Rift.

Or to Montfort, a voice whispers. Figures flash in my head, the premier and his husband presiding over our dinner. Hands clasped, relaxed and self-assured. Allowed to be who they are. I touch a finger to my temple, trying to massage away the low, dull ache in my skull. Everything seems impossible right now.

Elane isn't in the throne room, but she is close by. She suffered the journey with my parents, arriving this afternoon. I'm itching to be free of this council, if only to steal a few hours with her. I don't know how many I have left.

"I'll send out the word," Julian says, hands folded as he stands at Cal's side. Without the Reds, the raised dais of the throne room is hilariously lopsided. "The lords and ladies of the High Houses will be summoned to the capital in a week's time, and you'll be waiting, happy to receive them. Afterward, we can crown you as king." He sounds less than thrilled.

Cal barely nods. He wants to be done with all this. He doesn't notice Anabel and her bronze eyes, now fixed on Julian. Both hope to win the ear of a king, seeking to be highest in his favor, like children vying for a parent's attention. I'd bet on Anabel. She has the stomach for court. And the spine to eliminate anyone who might threaten her grasp on her grandson.

I sigh to myself, already exhausted by the thought of a life chained to him. It excited me once, the lure of a queen's power. I like to think Elane changed me, but I loved her long before, even when I told myself she was just a pawn like Sonya Iral, a Silver lady to do my bidding and back my machinations. I think the war has done something to me.

Put a fear in me I never had before. Not for myself, but for Ptolemus and Elane. The ones I love most, and would kill to protect. Sacrifice everything to keep safe and close. I've tasted a crown now, and I know it doesn't compare.

Father does not share the sentiment, nor will he let me abandon my duties.

I haven't mentioned my suspicions about the last piece of Anabel and Julian's deal, not to him. I could be wrong. Maybe Queen Cenra and Iris were satisfied with Salin Iral, eager to hand over a king for a single drop of vengeance.

You know that isn't true.

Neither of them is a fool. They wouldn't pay such a high price for such a small prize.

Because the true prize is your father.

I glance at him sidelong, noting the set of his shoulders, proud and straight beneath the curves of his chromium armor, polished so well I can see my reflection in it. I look afraid, my eyes wide and darting, ringed with dark makeup to hide the circles beneath my eyes. I fought well yesterday, enough to keep myself and my brother alive while so many of our kin died. Father hasn't said a word about it. Nothing to indicate he's happy that his children, his legacy, survived. Volo Samos is as hard as the steel we come from, all sharp edges. Even his beard is manicured and pruned to mathematic perfection. I have his coloring, his disposition, and his hunger. But now we yearn for different things. He wants power, as much of it as he can consume. I want freedom. I want my own fate.

I want the impossible.

"Now, as for the royal wedding—" Anabel begins, but I can't stand it any longer.

"Excuse me," I snap, not bothering to look at any of them as I go. It feels like a surrender. But no one stops me, not even Father. No one says a word.

I'm barely up the grand staircase before my mother cuts across my path. She almost hisses in anger, imitating one of her snakes. How such a small woman can take up an entire hallway, I'll never understand.

"Hello, Mother. Don't worry, I'm all right. Not a scratch on me," I mutter.

She waves off the greeting. Like Father, she doesn't seem to care, or mind, that I faced death yesterday.

"Really, Evangeline," she scolds, planting her jeweled hands on her hips. Today she favors pale green clothing. Her nose twitches slightly, and I can tell I don't have her undivided attention. The rest is in a mouse still watching the council. "You can climb the walls of Fort Patriot, but a simple meeting is too much for you?"

I shudder, trying not to think about the battle. With some effort, I push the memory away. "I hardly enjoy wasting my time," I tell her with a sneer.

She rolls her eyes as only a mother can. "Discussing your own wedding?"

"There's no discussion to it," I scoff. "I have no say, so why does it matter if I'm there? Besides, Tolly will tell me everything later. All of Father's *commands*," I add, spitting out the last word like a bad taste.

Mother seems to coil, taut and dangerous. "You act like this is some kind of punishment."

I raise my chin. All over my body, the steel threads of my gown tighten with my anger. "Isn't it?"

She reacts like I've slapped her and insulted her entire bloodline. "I don't understand you!" she says, throwing up her hands. "This is what you want, what you've worked for your entire life."

I have to laugh at her blindness. No matter how many eyes my mother sees through, she will never see through mine. My laughter unsettles her at least. I glance at her brow, tracing her braid blooming with gemstones. Let no one say Larentia Viper does not play the part of a queen well. *All this for that.* "A crown suits you, Mother," I sigh.

"Don't change the subject, Eve," she says, exasperated, as she closes the distance between us. With all the warmth she can muster, she puts both hands to my arms as if to pull me into an embrace. I keep still, rooted. Slowly, her fingers run up and down my arms, rubbing my bare skin. The image is almost maternal, far more than I'm used to. "It's almost over, darling."

No, it is not.

Deliberate, I step out of her grasp. The air is warmer than her hands, so cold they could be reptilian. She looks pained by the sudden distance, but holds her own ground. "I'm going to have a bath," I tell her. "Keep your ears and eyes away from me while I do."

Mother purses her lips. She makes no promises. "Everything we do is for your own good."

I turn to go, my dress swishing in my wake as I walk from her. "Keep telling yourself that."

By the time I get back to my rooms, I feel like breaking something, smashing a vase or a window or a mirror. Glass, not metal. I want to shatter something I cannot put back together. I resist the urge, mostly because I don't want to clean up the ensuing mess. There are Red servants left in Ocean Hill, but few. Only those who wish to continue their profession, at better compensation, will still serve in the palace here, or in any Silver employ.

I wonder how far the ripples of Cal's decision will travel. How much will change? Red equality will have far-reaching consequences, and not just for the tidiness of my bedroom.

I step deeper into my chamber, throwing open the windows as I go. Late afternoon in the Bay is a beautiful time, filled with golden light and a fragrant sea breeze. I try to find some comfort in it, but it just makes me angrier. The high keening of the gulls seems to taunt me. I think about skewering one, just for target practice. Instead I throw back the soft blankets of the bed and start to crawl in. A nap is better than a bath. I just want this day to end.

I freeze when my hand slides over paper amid the silk.

The note is short and small, written in tight, looping script. Nothing like Elane's elegant, ostentatious cursive. I don't recognize the penmanship, but I don't have to. Very few people would leave me secret notes, and even fewer could actually get access to my bed. My heartbeat quickens in my chest, breath catching.

We're right to call the Scarlet Guard rats. I think they might actually live in the walls.

> *I apologize I could not give you this invitation in person, but the circumstances allow little else. Leave Norta. Leave the Rift. Come to Montfort. Allowances will be made for you, and for Lady Elane. You will be welcome in the mountains, free to be as you wish. Abandon this empty shell of a life. Don't subject yourself to that fate. The choice is in your own hands, and no one else's. We ask nothing in return.*

I almost crumple Davidson's note at such naked dishonesty. *Nothing in return.* My simple presence is a gift in itself. Without me, Cal's alliance to the Rift will be in jeopardy. His only remaining ally might waver. It's a way for Davidson and the Scarlet Guard to pull him back into their grasp.

If you agree, order a cup of tea to your room. We'll take care of the rest.

—D

The words burn, branding themselves into my mind. I stare at them for what feels like hours, but only a few minutes pass.

The choice is in your own hands. Nothing could be further from the truth. Father will chase me to the ends of the earth, no matter who stands in his way. I'm his investment, part of his legacy.

"What will you do?" a familiar voice asks, sweeter than a song.

Elane blooms into existence across the room, silhouetted against a window. Still beautiful, but with none of her glow. The sight makes me ache.

I glance at the note in hand. "There's nothing I can do," I mutter. "If . . ." I can't even say the words aloud, even to her. "It will only make things worse. For me, and for you."

She doesn't move, no matter how much I want her to cross the room. Her eyes remain far away, fixed on the city and the ocean. "You really think things aren't already worse for me?"

Her whisper, fragile and soft, breaks my heart.

"My father would kill you, Elane. He would kill you if he thought—if he knew how tempted we are by *this*," I say, tightening my grip on the note.

And what about Tolly? I can't leave him alone, the only heir to the throne of a small and precariously positioned kingdom. The letters of the note seem to blur and swirl.

I'm crying, I realize with a sick jolt.

Fat tears land on the paper, one by one. The ink bleeds, blue and wet.

"Evangeline, I don't know how much longer I can live like this." The admission is small, matter-of-fact. Her face crumples and I have to turn away. Slowly, I rise from the bed and walk past her. Red hair flashes at the edge of my vision. She doesn't follow me into the bathroom, leaving me to think.

Hands shaking, tears endless, I do as I told my mother I would. I draw myself a bath and sink the note in the water. Letting the words, the offer, and our future drown.

As I lie back into the warmth, I feel sick with myself, with my cowardice, with everything in my rotted life. I dip my head back and submerge myself, letting the bathwater replace any tears still fresh on my cheeks. Underwater, I open my eyes to the strange, rippling world beneath the surface. I exhale slowly, watching the bubbles drift and burst. I decide I can do one thing, and one thing alone, about all of this.

I can keep my mouth shut.

And let Julian and Anabel play their games.

My hair is still wet at dinner, coiled into a neat spiral at the base of my neck. My face is bare too. No makeup, no war paint. No use for any of my usual trappings among family, though Mother doesn't seem to realize that. She's dressed for a state dinner, even though it's just the five of us dining in the grand salon of my father's chambers. Mother glitters as always, poured into a long-sleeved and high-necked gown of black material that glistens purple and green like oil. Her crown is still there too, woven into her braided hair. Father has no use for a crown of his own right now. He's intimidating no matter what he does or doesn't wear. Like Ptolemus, he is simple in unadorned clothing, our silver and black. Elane looks serene next to him, her eyes dry and empty.

I pick at my food, silent as I have been through the last two courses. My parents speak enough for all of us, though Ptolemus edges words in now and then. As before, I still feel sick, my belly roiling with unease. Because of my parents and what they want from me, because of how much I'm hurting Elane, and because of what I've done as well. I could be dooming my own father with my silence. His kingdom too. But I just can't say the words aloud.

"I think Ocean Hill's kitchens are taking the brunt of the young king's new proclamations," Mother observes, pushing the food around on her plate. Usually delicious courses have been replaced with bland, simple fare. Plain chicken, lightly seasoned, with greens, boiled potatoes, and some kind of watery sauce. An easy meal for anyone to prepare. Even *me*. I suppose the Red cooks of the palace have taken their leave.

Father slices a piece of chicken in two, the motion vicious and cutthroat. "It won't last" is all he says, the words carefully chosen.

"What makes you think that?" Tolly, the treasured heir, gets the rare privilege of questioning Father without any threat of consequence.

That doesn't mean Father will answer. He says nothing, continuing to chew the tasteless meat with a grimace.

I respond instead, trying to make my brother see what I do. "He'll force Cal however he can." I gesture at our father. "Prove that the country needs Red labor somehow."

Dear Tolly furrows his brow, thoughtful. "It will still have Red labor. Reds need to eat too. With fair wages—"

"And who pays those wages?" Mother snaps, looking at Tolly like he's some kind of imbecile. Odd for her. She dotes on him most of the time, more than she does on me. "Certainly not us." She goes on and on, spearing her dinner with tight, jerking motions. The twitchy speed of a rabbit, maybe. "It isn't right. It isn't *natural.*"

I run the meager proclamations over in my head. Announced and effective immediately. Fair wages, freedom of movement, equal punishment and protection under Silver law, and— "What about conscription?" I ask aloud.

Our mother slaps her hand on the table. "Another folly. Conscription is a good incentive. Work or serve. Without the latter, why would anyone choose the former?"

It's a circular conversation, and I breathe heavily through my nose. Across the table, Elane shoots me a warning glance. Obviously I don't care for our lack of servants either, and the new world Cal wants to build will result in great upheaval, mostly for Silvers accustomed to our traditional place. It won't last. It can't last. Silvers won't allow it. *But they do in Montfort. Just like Davidson said. Their country was built from one like ours.*

I remember something else he said, only to me, back in the mountains. He stood too close, whispered too quickly. But the shock of his words hit home. *You are denied what you want because of what you are. A choice you never made, a piece of yourself you cannot change—and do not want to change.*

I've never thought myself akin to Reds in any way. I'm a Silver-born lady, a princess made by the accomplishments of a powerful father. I was meant to be a queen. And but for the longing in my heart, the odd changes to my nature I've only begun to understand, I would be one. Davidson was right in Montfort. Like Reds, I am different from what my world demands I be. And I am not worse for it.

Under the table, Ptolemus grabs my hand, his touch kind but fleeting. I feel a burst of love for my brother, as well as another burst of shame.

One last chance, then.

"I assume Elane will come with us to Archeon," I say aloud, looking between my parents. They exchange a pointed glance, one I know well and do not like. Elane drops her gaze, staring at her hands beneath the table. "She'll have to stand with the rest of her house, pledge loyalty with Haven," I explain coolly, my reasoning sound enough.

But not for Mother, apparently. She puts down her fork with a clang of metal on porcelain. "Princess Elane is *your brother's wife*," she says, emphasizing the words. They sound like nails on glass. She speaks like Elane isn't even here. It sets my teeth on edge. "And your brother, as well as our family, has already proven himself loyal to King Tiberias. There's no need for her to make the journey. She will return home to Ridge House."

A flush colors the tops of Elane's cheeks. Still, she bites her tongue, knowing better than to fight this battle herself.

I push out an exasperated breath. *Long journey. What a load of—*

"Well, as a princess of the Rift, she should be at the coronation. To show the kingdom who we are. The pictures and recordings will go out all over the Rift as well as Norta. Our kingdom should know its future queen, shouldn't they?" My argument is shaky at best, and it sounds as desperate as I feel. I hate reminding anyone, most of all myself, of Elane's title, because it comes from my brother. Not from me.

"It is not your decision."

Father's glare used to shut me up, stop me cold, when I was a child. Sometimes I would run from him, but that landed me worse punishments. So I learned to stare back, in spite of my own fear. To meet what terrifies me head-on.

"She doesn't belong to him, or to you," I hear myself growl, sounding like one of my mother's great cats.

I don't know how much longer I can live like this, she said before.

And neither do I.

Her jaw works furiously as she grinds her teeth together, unable to speak.

Tolly leans forward, as if he can defend me from our parents. "Eve . . . ," he murmurs, if only to end this before things take an even worse turn.

Mother throws back her head and laughs, the noise horrendous and sharp. I feel dismissed, spit upon, diminished by someone who is supposed to love me. "Does she belong to you, Evangeline?" she croons, still smirking. I want to slap her.

The fear in me melts to anger, iron turning to steel.

"We belong to each other," I reply, forcing down a sip of wine.

Elane's eyes snap to mine. They burn me through.

"I've never heard anything so ridiculous in my life," Mother scoffs, shoving her plate away. "This is inedible."

Again, Father glares at me. "It won't last," he says again, and I think it's an answer to us both.

Mirroring my mother's actions, I push away my plate of untouched food. "We'll see," I mutter to myself. I've had enough of this. All of this.

Before I can leave the table, storm away for a second time, Anabel Lerolan enters the room, her guards on her heels. Even she isn't presumptuous enough to face down a Samos brood without protection.

"My apologies," she says quickly, nodding her head. Her own crown gleams, reflecting the fading light with a warm flash. "For the interruption."

When confronted with Queen Anabel, Mother quickly takes on the mantle of Queen Larentia. She improves her already flawless posture, drawing up her spine and dropping her shoulders. With an imperious gaze, she turns to look at Cal's grandmother. "I assume you have a reason."

The Lerolan queen nods. "Maven Calore is gone."

Next to me, Ptolemus exhales. He almost smiles. So do my parents, both of them glad to finally be rid of Maven. I only wish I could have seen it done, to know it is finally over for the monstrous boy who plagued us all for so long.

My brother speaks first, shifting to look at Anabel head-on. "Did Cal do it himself?"

Her expression turns stony. "I mean he isn't here."

I feel a slight pressure, the slow squeeze of my bracelets tightening at my wrists. On the table, the silverware starts to tremble. Not with my own anger, or Ptolemus's, but with our father's. Volo curls one fist on the table, and the knives and forks curl with it.

Father narrows his eyes. "He escaped?"

Improbable, but not impossible. Many Silvers are still loyal. Some of House Haven. They could sneak into the palace easily, stow him away, pull him out. My mind spins through the possibilities. Haven interference would be the worst. Because it could blow back on Elane.

Anabel shakes her head, her scowl deepening with every passing second. "It doesn't seem to be so," she hisses.

Mother sucks in a sharp breath. "Then—"

I finish the thought for her. "He was taken."

The old queen curls her lip. "Yes."

"By the Reds," I murmur.

For a quivering moment, I think Anabel might explode. She bares her teeth.

"Yes."

The sun has fully set by the time we reach Cal's quarters, crowding into the large salon where he met us all yesterday. He paces furiously, still dressed in his court regalia, including the rose-gold crown. He stalks around his uncle Julian, seated primly in one of the seats with his legs crossed and arms folded. A woman leans up behind him, pale hands planted on Julian's narrow shoulders. Sara Skonos, the skin healer. She says nothing, letting the pair talk, as she weighs their words.

"The intent is quite obvious—" Julian stops himself as we troop in. "Two council meetings in one day, what a treat," he says dryly. "Queen Larentia, interesting to see you."

Instead of glaring at the singer lord, Mother dons the falsest smile she can muster. It has the same effect. "Lord Jacos," she purrs, careful to keep her distance.

I'm quietly glad Elane isn't with us, having returned to my chambers. Her presence would simply put too much strain on an already stressful situation.

Father wastes no time, swooping into a chair like a bird of prey finding a perch. He stares at Cal as he continues pacing. "So, your brother is in enemy hands."

Across the floor, Julian purses his lips. "*Enemy* is a strong word."

"They aren't with us any longer," Father replies, not bothering to check his tone against anyone. "They stole a valuable hostage. That makes Montfort and the Scarlet Guard our enemies."

Still circling, Cal puts a hand to his chin. He meets Father's gaze. "And what do you propose we do about it, King Volo?" he asks. "You want me to take our still-recovering armies, gather the fleet, and assault a distant nation to win back one useless, broken teenager? I don't think so."

I can almost see the hairs on Father's neck rise. He sets his jaw. "As long as Maven breathes, he's a threat to Norta."

Cal is quick to nod, gesturing with an open palm. "On that we can agree."

Usually any destabilization of Cal's fledgling reign would be cause for celebration, but I find little to cheer here. Instead I take a seat of my own, leaning back with a huff. "Most of the High Houses will still swear their loyalty to you," I say aloud, speaking mostly to myself. "They know he's finished."

Above me, Cal clucks his tongue in a very annoying fashion. I imagine cutting it out of his head. "That isn't good enough. We need a united country if we're going to fight off the Lakelands and Piedmont."

Behind us, Anabel shuts the door and crosses the room to stand at her grandson's side. Her constant posturing is becoming tedious. "Those bloody rats can't wait for us all to kill each other so they can feed on our corpses."

I sneer up at her, remembering when she first came to the Rift. Then, she pledged that any Red alliance would be fleeting and Norta as we knew it would return to its traditions. "If I'm not mistaken," I say as innocently as I can, "didn't we plan to do the same?"

She looks at me with disgust, as Cal continues his walk. He passes between us, shielding me for a moment. I meet his eyes, locking our gaze for a second. I can't speak, but I try to communicate what I can. He doesn't trust me, doesn't care for me, and I feel the same. But we need each other right now, no matter how much we might despise the thought.

He turns away, moving to face my parents again. "We can't lose sight of the true danger right now. The Lakelands will return, in full force, with Piedmont backing their play."

"Who knows what they promised Bracken for his help," Anabel curses.

On her couch, my mother can't help but sneer. "Well, *they* didn't ally with the people who kidnapped his children," she says coolly, inspecting her nails. "For a start."

I almost expect the Lerolan queen to lay hands on my mother, but she doesn't move.

Father maneuvers, his voice smooth. "We're quite able to do two things at once, King Tiberias."

Cal responds with his usual fire. "I'm not fighting two wars, Volo. And neither are you."

The command lingers, shocking us all. Even Mother draws back, looking to Father with fear in her eyes. For what he might do, how he could respond to such impudence.

They stare each other down, one king against another. The contrast is jarring. Cal is young, a tested warrior but a floundering politician. Driven by love, passion, some kind of fire that's always burning inside him. My father is deadly in many ways, with weapons or words. And he is infinitely cold, a calculating statue, his heart nothing but an empty hole.

This could end everything. Cut the Rift from Norta, and me with it. But no, Father would never do that. He has plans of his own, plans I cannot fathom. And they hinge on Cal keeping his throne.

Father speaks slowly, as if restraining himself. "I'm not talking about a war with Montfort, or the Red criminals they conspire with." He lays his hands flat on his knees, displaying many rings and bracelets. All deadly under his command. "Hit them where it hurts. Take back whatever victory they thought they won here. Be a Silver king, a king for your own people."

The singer lord speaks first. I brace myself for his voice, always afraid of the sound. "What are you suggesting?"

Father doesn't condescend to look at Julian. "Your proclamations will cripple this country," he says to Cal. "Erase them."

To my surprise, Julian laughs openly. The sound is oddly kind, a gentle sort of laughter. I'm not familiar with it. "I'm sorry, Your Majesty, but my nephew can't very well reverse what he did today. That isn't strength. That isn't kingly at all."

Now my father turns, fixing Julian with the full weight of his stare. "It's a fitting punishment for their Red betrayal."

That strikes a chord in Cal. "I rule in Norta, not you," he says, careful to speak as clearly as possible. "Or anyone else," he adds, shooting a meaningful look at both his uncle and his grandmother. "The proclamations remain."

Father's response is quick. "Not in my kingdom."

Like Mother, I feel myself pull back as Cal steps forward, closing the distance between himself and my father. It almost looks like a challenge. "Fine," he grinds out, glaring at the king of the Rift.

Again, they hold each other's gaze, never blinking, never breaking. I wish I could give both of them a shove. Destroy all this for good.

Anabel intervenes before either side of the scale can tip. She cuts neatly between the kings, putting a hand to Cal's shoulder. "We'll pick this up in the morning, when we have clearer heads and a better view of the situation."

Behind them, Julian rises to his feet. He adjusts his robes. "I agree, Your Majesty."

Mother sees reason too, and she gestures for Ptolemus to follow. I stand with them, exhausted. Only Father remains sitting. He won't break first.

Cal is less inclined to play such games. He turns away, dismissing all of us with a disinterested wave of one hand. "Very well, I'll see you all in the morning." Then he pauses, looking back. Not at Father. But at me. "Actually, Evangeline, could I have a word?" I blink at him, feeling very sly indeed. The rest of the room could not look more confused. "In private."

Slowly, I sit back down as the rest go. Even Father, who prowls away with the rest of my family in tow. Only Ptolemus looks back, locking eyes with me for a moment. I wave him off. I'll be fine; there's nothing for him to worry about here.

Julian is quick to acquiesce to his nephew's wishes, but Anabel lingers. "Is this something I can help with?" she asks, glancing between us.

"No, Nanabel," Cal replies. He walks with her, deftly herding her toward the door. She notes his intention with a sour twist of her lips, but bows her head. He is her king, and she is bound to obey.

When the door shuts behind her, I relax a little, my posture drooping. Cal hesitates, his back to me, and I hear him take a shuddering breath.

"Crowns are heavy, aren't they?" I say to him.

"Indeed." Reluctant, he turns around. Without the pressure to perform for the council and his family, Cal slumps as I do. Exhausted by the days, ready to drop.

I raise an eyebrow. "Worth the price?"

Cal doesn't respond, walking silently to the chair across from mine. He leans backward, one leg bent, the other stretched. As he moves, I think I hear a click in his knee. "Is yours?" he finally says, gesturing to my empty brow. There isn't any animosity to his words, not like I expect. He's too tired to fight me.

And I see no use now in fighting him.

"No, I don't think so," I mumble back.

The admission surprises him. "Are you planning to do anything about it?" he says, voice colored by what could be hope.

My plan is to do nothing, I think to myself.

"There isn't much I can do," I say aloud. "Not with *him* holding my leash." He knows who I mean.

"Evangeline Samos on a leash," Cal replies, forcing a false smirk. "Seems impossible."

I don't have the energy to correct him properly. "I wish that were so" is all I can manage.

He runs a hand over his face, squeezing his eyes shut for a moment. "Me too."

I have to scoff. The whining of men never ceases to amaze. "What leash could there be on the king of Norta?" I sneer at him.

"More than a few."

"You backed yourself into this corner." I shrug, unable to summon any real sympathy for the young man before me. "They gave you a choice, one last chance to change things before they left."

He bristles, leaning forward on his elbows. "And what would have happened if I'd done what they wanted? Thrown this infernal thing away?" To illustrate his point, he reaches up and grabs his own crown. He discards it with a thunk. *How dramatic.* "Chaos. Riots. Maybe another civil war. And certainly war with your father. Maybe my own grandmother too."

"Maybe."

"Oh, don't preach to me, Evangeline," he snaps, really starting to lose his temper. "You can sit here and blame me for all your problems if you want, but don't act like you don't have a hand in them."

I feel warmth rise in my cheeks as I flush. "Excuse me?"

"You've got a choice too, and you keep choosing to stay right here."

"Because I'm afraid, Cal," I try to snarl, but it comes out like a whisper.

That stills him, just a little. A cool compress over a fresh burn. "So am I," he says, his voice echoing the pain in mine.

Without thinking, I say what I really mean. "I miss her."

He responds in kind. "So do I."

We're talking about two different people, but the sentiment is the same. He looks down at his hands, as if ashamed of the love he feels for someone he cannot have. I know what that agony is like. What an anchor it is. How it will eventually drown us both.

"If I tell you something, will you promise to keep it a secret?" I murmur. Like him, I lean forward, until I could take his hands if I wanted. "Even from Julian and Anabel. *Especially* from them."

Cal glances up again. He searches my eyes, looking for the trick in me. Waiting for whatever Samos trap he thinks I'm about to spring. "Yes."

I lick my lips and speak before my brain can tell me to stop. "I think they're going to kill my father."

He blinks, confused. "That doesn't make any sense."

"Well, *they* won't do it, but . . ." For the first time in my life, I take

Tiberias Calore's hand and do not hate the sensation. I grip his fingers tightly, trying to make him understand. "Do you really think Cenra and Iris would trade Maven for someone like Salin Iral?"

"No, I don't," Cal breathes. He squeezes my hand, his grasp stronger than mine. "And with your father dead . . ."

I nod as he follows my train of thought. "The Rift dies with him. Returns to Norta," I say. "Ptolemus won't have the spine to fight a war with Father dead. No matter how good he is at fighting, he isn't meant for it."

"I find that hard to believe," Cal scoffs, his tone changing. Then his eyes shift, brows knitting together, before releasing like a weight cut loose. Realization washes over him. "You haven't told your parents this, have you?"

I shake my head.

His mouth hangs open. "Evangeline, if you're right—"

"I'm going to let him die. I know," I hiss to myself, at myself. I snatch my hand away, unable to touch or look at him. Fuming, I stare at the carpeted floor, tracing the fine patterns of Red-made artistry. "You've always thought me terrible. Is it nice to know you're right?"

His fingers are hot beneath my chin, tipping my face up to look him. *"Evangeline,"* he murmurs, but I don't want his pity. I push him away.

"I hope the gods of Iris Cygnet aren't real. I can't imagine what punishments they have in store for me."

Cal rests his mouth against his knuckles, idly running his hand back and forth over his lips. Eyes far away, he nods in agreement.

"For all of us."

TWENTY-EIGHT
Iris

Citadel of the Lakes is the safest place I could ever be, and yet I'm on edge, nervous, constantly looking over my shoulder. I see only familiar guards in their blues, almost blending into the mist of a rainy summer morning. Jidansa is here too, the old telky trailing my mother and me as we walk the pathways arching over the vast training grounds. She has a calming presence, much like my mother, and I try to relax with them so close. Below us, regiments of the Lakelander army prepare for war. Those who have already fought, legions ceded to Maven while we were allied, have earned some well-needed rest. The soldiers here are fresh, ready to fight. Eager to win a country for the glory of the Lakelands. The hills and rivers, the beaches of Norta. Their powerful tech towns, bursting with electricity and economic value. The Kingdom of Norta is a gold mine just waiting to be claimed.

Thousands upon thousands of soldiers drill in the rain, unbothered by the wet weather. The same will be true across our kingdom. From Citadel of the Snows to Citadel of the Rivers, the call has gone out. We are mobilizing all we can gather, Silver and Red. The army of the

Lakelands is assembled and ready to strike. We have the numbers; we have the abilities. Our enemy is already crippled, and we need only put it out of its misery.

So why do I feel so unsettled, deep in my heart?

Reviewing troops doesn't require royal finery, and both of us are dressed like the soldiers we support, in blue uniforms edged with glinting silver and gold. Even Mother has stopped wearing her mourning blacks. But we haven't forgotten Father, or our vengeance. It weighs on us all like a heavy stone. I feel it with every step.

We cross the last bridge, stepping onto one of the many balconies ringing the central structure of the citadel. The windows glow, beckoning with warmth. Despite the calming effect of the rain, I'm eager to get out of the weather. My mother moves quickly, setting our pace, and leads us inside. We're supposed to meet Tiora for lunch, but by the time we reach the room prepared for our meal, she still isn't there.

It isn't like my sister to be late.

I glance at my mother for some kind of explanation, but she merely takes her seat at the head of the table. If Queen Cenra isn't bothered by Tiora's absence, then I won't be either.

Like Mother, I take my seat, ready to wait for Tiora to arrive. The guards hang back at the door, taking up flanking positions, but Jidansa sits. She is a noble of the Merin Line, an ancient and distinguished family here in the Lakelands, and she has served us for many years. While the queen helps herself to some fluffy bread, I inspect the vast array of silverware. Forks, spoons—knives especially. I count the possible weapons on the table out of habit, careful to include the filled water glasses. More deadly than any knife in my hands.

I stare at the water, letting it fill my perception as it fills each glass. The sense is as familiar as my own face. But somehow different now.

After what I helped my mother do.

It's been days since we made our trade, and I can't get it out of my head. The sound especially. How the Iral lord choked on his last breaths, unable to fight us off. The Calore king's uncle, someone named Jacos, is a singer, and he removed any fight from the man before we could get our hands on him. Maybe if he could have fought back, I wouldn't feel so strange. He deserved to die. Deserved worse punishment than we gave. But the memory still fills me with the strange, foreign sense of shame. As if I have betrayed the gods in some way. Gone against their will and their nature.

I'll pray some more tonight, and hope to find an answer in their wisdom.

"Eat before the food gets cold," Mother says, gesturing to the plates before us. "Tiora will be with us in a moment."

I nod and move mechanically, serving myself. Precautions have to be taken. No Red servants, not while we discuss the path ahead. The Scarlet Guard has ears and eyes everywhere. We must be vigilant.

Most of the meal is fish. Butterflied trout, sliced open and fried with butter and lemon. Yellow perch, crusted with pepper and salt. A warming stew of lamprey eel, the heads removed and proudly displayed at the center of the table. Their rows of spiraling teeth gleam in the soft light of the dining room. The other plates hold ears of golden corn, greens tossed in spiced oil, braided breads—the usual bounty from Lakelander crops. Our farms are far-flung and prosperous, able to feed our country twice over. Lakelanders never want for food, not even the lowest Red.

I help myself to a little of each, careful to leave the lamprey for Tiora. It's an acquired taste, not to mention her favorite.

Another minute goes by in silence, marked only by the kindly ticking of a clock on the wall. Outside, the rain picks up, lashing the windows in merciless sheets.

"The army should break until this clears," I mutter. "No use letting our soldiers get sick, and feed an epidemic of colds."

"True," Mother replies around bites of food. She tips a hand at Jidansa, who stands quickly.

She ducks into a curt bow. "I'll make it so, Your Majesty," she says before setting off to deliver the order.

"The rest of you, wait outside," my mother continues, glancing at each of our guards in turn. They don't hesitate, almost leaping to follow her commands.

I watch the room empty, my nerves prickling. Whatever Mother wants to say to me isn't meant for an audience. When the door shuts again, leaving us alone, she steeples her fingers together and leans forward.

"It isn't the rain that bothers you, *monamora*."

For a second, I debate denying it. Pasting on a smile, forcing a laugh and a dismissal. But I don't like to wear masks with my mother. It's dishonest. And besides, she sees right through them.

I sigh, setting aside my fork. "I keep seeing his face."

She softens, wavering from queen to mother. "I miss your father too."

"No." The word stumbles out, too quick, startling my mother. Her eyes widen a little, darker than usual in the dim light. "I do think about him, all the time but . . ." I search for the proper way to say this. Instead I put it bluntly. "I'm talking about the man who killed him."

"Who we then killed," Mother says, her voice even. It isn't an accusation, but a simple statement of fact. "At *your* suggestion."

Once more, I feel rare shame. A flush creeps over my cheeks. Yes, it was my idea to take up Queen Anabel's offer. To trade Maven for the man who killed my father. And later on, the man he killed my father for. But that part of the bargain has yet to be paid.

"I'd do it again," I mutter, playing with my food for some distraction. I feel exposed beneath my mother's gaze. "He deserves to die a hundred times, but—"

She tightens, as if in pain. "You've killed before. In defense of your own life." I open my mouth to try to explain, only to find her still speaking. "But not like that," she adds, laying one hand on mine. Her eyes shine, full of understanding.

"No," I admit, bitter and disappointed in myself. This was a righteous kill, payment for the death of my father. It shouldn't be this way.

Mother's fingers grip mine. "Of course it would feel different. Feel wrong somehow."

My breath catches in my throat as I stare at our joined hands. "Will it go away?" I murmur, forcing myself to look back up at her.

But Mother isn't looking at me. She glances out the window, into the obscuring rain. Her eyes dance with the lashing water. *How many people has she killed?* I wonder. I have no way of knowing, and no way of finding out. "Sometimes," she finally says. "Sometimes not."

Before I can tug on that thread to unravel exactly what she means, Tiora enters the room, her own guards left behind in the hallway, like ours. While Mother came to Norta briefly, against all traditions of the Lakelands, Tiora stayed behind to keep our nation's borders safe. And our armies ready for the next step in our journey. She was well suited to the job, and it seems to cheer her, even as we leap between wars.

The heiress to the Lakelander throne looks like just another soldier, her uniform wrinkled, without any livery or insignia to it. She could be a simple messenger, if not for the Cygnet look. High cheekbones and a higher opinion of oneself.

She sits with our father's grace, folding her long limbs into the chair across from mine.

"Lovely, I'm famished," she says, picking at the spread with both hands. I nudge the stew in her direction, along with the display of lamprey heads. As children, we used to throw them at each other. Tiora remembers, and she offers a tiny grin in reply.

Then she gets down to business, facing our mother with the gravity of a general. "We have word from Snows, Hills, Trees, Rivers, and Plains," she says, rattling off the other citadels dotting the vast expanse of the Lakelands. "All are ready."

Queen Cenra nods, pleased by the news. "As they should be. The time to strike is coming, and coming soon."

The time to strike. We've spoken of nothing else since I returned to my homeland. I haven't even had time to enjoy my freedom beyond the bounds of Maven's kingdom or his marriage. Mother has me in endless meetings and reviews. After all, I'm the only one of us to have faced Tiberias and his contingent of unknown Red soldiers, not to mention his Rift allies.

We have Bracken and Piedmont on our side, yes, but is he a better ally than Maven was? A better shield against the Calore brother now on the throne? Is it even any use to wonder? Our decision is long since made. Maven is a card we've already played and traded off.

Tiora forges on. "More importantly, it seems Tiberias Calore's newly made kingdom is splintering again."

I blink at her, forgetting the food on my plate. "How so?"

"The Reds are no longer with him," she replies. I feel myself twitch in surprise. "According to our intelligence reports, the Scarlet Guard, that strange newblood, and the Montfort armies, have all disappeared. Returned to the mountains, we think. Or gone underground."

At the head of the table, Mother sighs aloud. She raises one hand, massaging her temple. "When is anyone going to learn that young kings are fools?"

Tiora smirks in amusement, enjoying Mother's show of female frustration.

I'm more interested in the implication of Red desertion. Without Montfort, the newbloods, the spies of the Scarlet Guard, without Mare Barrow, the scales have certainly tipped against Tiberias Calore. And it isn't difficult to understand why.

"The Reds won't support him on the throne," I say. I didn't know Mare well, but I saw enough of her to guess. She fought Maven at every turn, even as a prisoner. Surely she wouldn't stomach another king. "They must have had an agreement, to win the country back and build anew. Tiberias refused his end of the bargain. Silvers still rule in Norta."

After a bite of lamprey, Tiora shakes her head. "Not entirely. There have been proclamations. More rights for the Reds of Norta. Better wages. The end of forced labor. They've stopped conscription too."

My eyes widen. Mostly out of shock, but also from unease. If Reds across the border are offered such boons, what will happen to Reds in the Lakelands? It will be an exodus, a mad dash.

"We have to close our borders," I say quickly. "Stop any Reds from crossing into Norta."

Again, Mother sighs. "He's truly an idiot," she mutters. "Of course, we'll double our watch at the Nortan border. Leave it to a Calore to cause us more headaches."

Tiora hums low in her throat. "He's causing himself headaches as well. Their tech towns are draining as we speak. I assume any economic might they have now will soon follow."

At that, our mother almost laughs to herself. I would join her if I could. All I can think about is the magnificent stupidity of Tiberias Calore. He's only just won back his throne, and now he seeks to strip his country of its greatest strengths? For who? Some red-blooded nobodies? For the myth of equality, justice, honor, or whatever other foolish ideal he hopes to achieve? I scoff to myself. I wonder if the Calore king, left to his own devices, will simply drown under the weight of his crown. Or be devoured by the Rift king, scheming to leech what he can from the so-called Flame of the North.

He won't be the only Silver in the Nortan territories to chafe under the proclamations. I feel a smirk curl on my lips, twisting to one side as I think. "I doubt the Silvers of Norta will like that," I say, waving a finger over my water glass. Inside, the liquid swirls with my motions.

Mother eyes me, trying to follow my train of thought. "Indeed."

"I could reach out to a few of them," I continue, the plan coming as quickly as I speak it. "Offer condolences. Or *incentives*."

"If some could be swayed, just a few key regions . . . ," Mother says, seeming to light up.

I nod. "Then this war will be over in a single battle. Archeon falls, and Norta with it."

Across from me, Tiora pushes her favored stew away. "What about the Reds?"

I gesture to her with an open hand. "You said it yourself: They've gone to ground. Retreated. Left Norta open for the taking." Grinning, I glance between my mother and sister. All thoughts of the Iral lord and his death seem to evaporate from my mind. We have more important things to worry about. "And we have to take it."

"For the gods," Tiora breathes, gently hitting her fist against the table.

I stifle the urge to correct her. Instead I dip my head to my older sister. "For our own protection."

She blinks, confused. "Our protection?"

"We sit here, serving our own lunch, for fear of the Scarlet Guard. Reds surround us, in our nation and outside it. If their rebellion continues to spread, hungry as a cancer, where will that leave us?" I brush my fingers over the plates and cups, then gesture to the empty room and windows. The rain has lessened, easing to a steady pattern of drips. In the distance, to the west, the sun breaks through the gray clouds in tiny spatters of light. "And what about Montfort? An entire country of Reds and those strange newbloods set against us? We have to defend ourselves. Make ourselves too big and too strong to challenge."

Neither of you has been there. You haven't seen their city, high in the mountains. Red and Silver and newblood, joined together. And stronger for the joining. It was easy to sneak into Ascendant, to rescue Bracken's children, but I can't imagine an army doing the same. Any war with Montfort will be bloody, for both sides. It must be prevented, made impossible, before it can even begin.

I steel myself. "Give them no chance to rise up or stand against us."

Mother is quick to respond. "Agreed."

"Agreed," Tiora offers with the same speed. She even raises her glass, the clear liquid turning in the faceted cup.

Outside, as the rain ebbs to nothing, I feel a bit calmer. Still anxious about what is to come, but satisfied by the plan taking shape. If Maven's houses can be made loyal to us, then Tiberias will be severely hobbled. Losing allies left and right. Alone on the throne is no place for anyone to be.

Maven was alone too, no matter how many advisers and nobles surrounded him. I'm glad he never tried to make me share his empty hours, at least not more than was necessary. He frightened me, when he was alive. He was an impossible person to predict. I never knew what he might say or do, and it forced me to live on edge. I've only just begun to catch up on all the sleep lost in his palace, too close to the monstrous king for comfort.

"I'm surprised they didn't execute him publicly," I muse aloud, my voice low. "I wonder how they did it."

I see Maven in my head, struggling weakly against our guards. He didn't see it coming. *I'm impossible to predict too.*

My sister dips her spoon in the lamprey stew, not eating, but pushing the liquid back and forth. It sloshes, filling the silence.

"What is it, Tiora?" Mother prods, seeing right through her display.

Tiora hesitates, but not for long. "There's been some speculation about that," she says. "He hasn't been seen or heard from since he was taken to the palace in Harbor Bay."

I shrug. "Because he's dead."

Tiora doesn't look at me. Can't look at me. "Our spies don't think so."

Despite the warmth of the room and the food, I feel a sudden chill deep in my chest. I swallow hard, trying to understand—and ignore the fear threatening to return. *Don't be a coward. He's far away, imprisoned if not dead. He's not your problem anymore.*

Mother shares none of my terror. She just blusters. "Why keep him alive? I swear, these Calore brothers are trying to out-idiot each other."

I try to be more thoughtful. I speak if only to mask my unease. "Perhaps the older brother can't do it. He seemed softhearted." *He must be, to allow himself to be so manipulated by a Red girl.*

Tiora is just as observant as our mother, and she tries to be gentle as she explains. "There are rumors that Maven isn't there anymore."

The queen of the Lakelands blanches. "Well, where could he be?"

There are few options, and I run through them quickly. Of course, one is more obvious than the rest. And woefully awful for that lightning girl. At least I escaped Maven Calore. She, it seems, cannot. "I suspect Montfort," I say. "He's with the newbloods and the Scarlet Guard. With Mare Barrow."

Tiora bobs her head, thinking as she nods. "So when the Reds left . . ."

"He's a valuable hostage, yes," I tell her. "If Maven is still alive, Tiberias is vulnerable. Nobles might still be loyal to his brother."

Mother surveys me like an adviser, not a daughter. It thrills me, and I feel my spine straighten, flattening my back against my seat as I draw up to my full height. "Do you think that's possible?" she asks.

I chew on the answer for a moment, weighing what I know of Norta and its Silvers. "I think those Silver houses just want a reason not to back Tiberias. To hold on to their country as it was." Both my mother and Tiora, a queen and a queen to be, watch me silently. I raise my chin.

"I say we give them a reason."

TWENTY-NINE
Mare

It's nightfall when we reach Ascendant, gliding through the mountains in almost pitch darkness. I try not to think about being smashed against the black slopes. But the pilots are skilled, landing our airjet on the alpine runway with ease. The rest of Montfort's Air Fleet, as well as the transport convoys carrying the bulk of their army, is down on the plain. They'll have to climb the Hawkway to get to the city, or disperse along other roads and travel routes throughout Montfort to return to their posts. The country will then take up defensive positions, guarding its own borders, on the off chance the Lakelanders decide to try their might against the mountains. Or prod the raiders and Prairie into doing their work for them.

Farley, Davidson, their attendants, and I make the trek into the city in silence, walking the steps beneath an arc of glittering starlight. I watch the sky as we go, trying to name the constellations. I refuse to think about either Calore brother. Not the one we left in Norta, nor the one marching with us, bound in chains, held at gunpoint. He chatters occasionally, asking questions about Montfort. No one answers, and his voice dies slowly, left to echo into nothing. Before we reach the premier's home, Maven is taken away, down another flight of steps, where more guards appear to flank him. Montfort won't risk losing another prisoner. Maven won't get the gentle treatment given to Bracken's children. He will be being taken deep into the city, to the prison below the Ascendant main barracks. I try not to watch his silhouette as it grows smaller and smaller. He never looks back.

Farley outpaces everyone, even Kilorn and his long strides. I don't have to be a mind reader to guess her thoughts are of her daughter, left behind with the rest of our family.

Davidson was good enough to send word on ahead, so his palatial home is ablaze when we approach, the many windows and balconies lit by warm candles and lights. Familiar figures cast shadows across the stones, and we beeline for them. My mother hands off Clara, the baby girl sleepy but smiling as Farley lifts her up. Out of the corner of my eye, I see Davidson embrace his husband, Carmadon, before my mom does the same to me. Her arms squeeze my shoulders tightly, and she hugs me to her chest with a deep sigh. I relax as I only can with the rest of my family, letting them usher us inside and up to our rooms.

The reunion is sentimental as ever, even though it's become a habit. I leave, face death, and, against all odds, return in one piece. I know my parents would tie me down to stop me from repeating the cycle, if they thought it might work. But they trust me to make my own choices, and besides, I'm a newblood. The lightning girl. There are very few bonds that can hold me back. No matter how much I might want to stay, the need to move on, to keep fighting, is always stronger.

Farley disappears into her own bedroom, Clara on her hip, with an exhausted smile. No one stops her. She needs time alone with her daughter, and we're all happy to give it.

Instead my family filters onto the tiled terrace, which is bursting with more flowers than I remember. Tramy has been busy. "They're beautiful," I tell him, gesturing to a lovely array of white blooms curling up and over the railing. He heaves himself into a chair with a bashful grin, and Gisa perches on the arm of the seat. I plop down next to them both, content to sit on a flat, squashy cushion set on the tile.

"Mom helped," Tramy says, gesturing across to her.

At the edge of the terrace, she waves a hand. Her hair is down tonight. I'm used to long years of my mother in twisted braids and neat buns, always keeping her hair out of her face. Despite the gray, she looks younger like this. "I just followed you around with a watering can," she says.

I've never considered Ruth Barrow beautiful. How could anyone, let alone a poor Red woman, be considered beautiful next to Silvers? But Montfort brings a glow to her, a healthiness in her golden skin that makes it gleam. Even her wrinkles seem lessened, softened by the gentle lamplight. Of course, Dad looks better than ever, heartier than he was in the Stilts. He's gained weight where he needs to, arms and legs filling out, while his waist looks trimmer. I chalk it up to nutrition, and of course his replaced leg and lung. After he greets me, he settles into his usual gruff silence, claiming a seat of his own next to Bree. The weeks have been good to all of them. Especially Gisa. Her dark red hair glints like oil in the dim light. I take in her clothing, a repurposed Montfort uniform. But the cuffs and collar are heavily embroidered in swirls of colored thread, pricking out a pattern of flowers and purple-bright zags of lightning. I reach out to her, running my fingers over her careful handiwork.

"I can make you one, if you like," she says, eyeing my own

uniform. The offensively bright red of the Scarlet Guard outfit makes her wrinkle her nose. "Maybe downplay all this," she mutters, waving her hands a little. "Give you something a little better than medals."

Kilorn eases himself down next to me, leaning back on his hands with his legs crossed. "Do I get one too?"

"If I feel like it," Gisa replies with her usual sniff. She eyes him up and down, as if assessing a customer. "Fish instead of flowers, I think."

I can't help but chuckle into my hand, grinning at Kilorn's exaggerated pout.

"So how long will you be here this time?" My father's voice is still a low grunt, full of accusation. I glance at him, meeting his dark brown eyes. The same eyes as Bree and Tramy, darker than my own.

Mom puts a hand on his shoulder, as if she can push him off the subject. "Daniel, she just got back."

He doesn't look at her. "That's my point."

"It's fine," I murmur, glancing between them. It's an honest question, and a good one, especially based on recent circumstances. "To tell you the truth, I don't know. It could be days. Could be weeks. Could be months." My family seems to brighten with each larger measurement of time. It pains me to give them what could be false hope, even though I want it to be true. "We still don't know how things will proceed."

Dad purses his lips. "With Norta."

I shake my head. "With the Lakelands, mostly." The others look on, silent as I explain. Except for Kilorn. His brow furrows slowly, creasing his forehead with deep, angry lines. "They hold all the power right now. Cal is still consolidating a torn country, and we're waiting to see how everything shakes out. If the Lakelands strike—"

My oldest brother draws an angry breath before pushing it out in an exasperated sigh. He glares at me because there's simply no one else to glare at. "You'll help fight them off?" As with Dad, I hear an accusation in him.

I can only shrug. It isn't me he's frustrated with, but the situation I keep finding myself in. Pulled toward danger, torn between Silver kings, a weapon to be wielded, a face to be used. "I don't know," I mutter. "We aren't allied to him anymore."

At my side, Kilorn shifts, uncomfortable on the tile. Or the subject. "And what about the other one?"

Around the cluster of chairs, my family blanches in varying levels of confusion. Mom crosses her arms over her chest, fixing me with a piercing stare I know all too well. "Who?" she asks, even though she knows. She just wants to make me say it.

Gritting my teeth, I force an answer. "He means Maven."

My father's voice turns deadly, like I've never heard it before. "He should be dead by now."

"He's not, and he's here," Kilorn snarls before I can stop him.

A pulse of fury thrums through my family, every face turning red, every lip curling, all eyes sharpening with glints of rage.

"Kilorn, don't start trouble," I hiss, squeezing his wrist. But the damage is already done. The silence around our circle runs heavy with scarlet anger, so strong I can almost taste it.

Finally, Gisa speaks, her tone as feral as my father's. "We should kill him."

My sister is not a violent girl, better suited to a needle than a knife. But she looks like she could claw Maven's eyes out if given the opportunity. I would feel guilty for bringing this anger out in her, but I can't get beyond the sudden swell of love, appreciation, and pride.

My brothers nod slowly, agreeing with her sentiment. They might even be cooking up some harebrained attempt to get into Maven's cell right now.

"He's valuable alive," I say quickly, if only to stop them short.

"I don't give a shit about his *value*," Bree snaps.

I expect our mother to scold him for his language, but she isn't bothered by the curse. In fact, she looks positively murderous herself, and for an instant I see the violent love of Queen Anabel, Larentia Viper, and even Elara Merandus in her eyes. "That creature took my son from me, and he took you."

"I'm right here, Mom," I murmur, swallowing around the sudden, painful memory of Shade.

"You know what I mean," she says. "I'll slit his throat myself."

Most shocking of all is Dad's silence. He's a naturally quiet man, but not when it comes to despising Silvers. When I glance at him, I realize why he won't say anything. Because he can't. His face is a furious red, boiling with a steady, rising hatred. If he opens his mouth, who knows what might tumble out.

"Can we talk about something else?" I have to ask, looking around at the rest of my family.

"Please do," Dad barely manages through gritted teeth.

"You all look well," I say quickly. "Is Montfort—"

Mom seems annoyed, but dips her head in acceptance. She answers for all of them, cutting me off. "It's a dream, Mare."

My natural suspicion flares, in spite of all I know about Davidson. But I don't know his country or his city. I don't know the politicians he serves or the people they represent.

"Is it too good, though?" I ask. "Do you think we'll wake up to find ourselves in trouble? To find something gone horribly wrong?"

She heaves a heavy sigh, looking out at the sparkling lights of

Ascendant. "I suppose we should always be wary but—"

"I don't think so," Dad offers, neatly finishing her thought. His words are few but expressive. "This place is different."

Gisa nods along with them. "I've never seen Reds and Silvers together like this. Back in Norta, when I went to sell with my mistress, Silvers wouldn't even look at us. Wouldn't touch us." Her brown eyes, the same as mine, glaze a little as she remembers her life as it was so long ago, before a Silver officer smashed apart her sewing hand. "Not here."

In his seat, Tramy settles back, some of his ire melting away. Like a cat smoothing his fur after a scare. "We feel like equals."

I can't help but wonder if it's because of me. They're family to the lightning girl, a valuable asset to the Montfort premier. Of course they'd be treated well. But I don't say any of that out loud, if only to maintain some kind of peace on an otherwise tumultuous night. After that, the conversation becomes far more pleasant.

Servants, kindly and smiling, bring up a sizable spread for dinner. The food is simple, but rich and tasty, ranging from fried chicken to sugary, dark purple berries spread over toast. The food is mostly for my benefit and Kilorn's, but Bree and Tramy help themselves to full portions. Gisa favors a tray of fruits and cheeses, while Dad fixes himself a plate of cold meats and crackers to share with Mom. We eat slowly, talking more than chewing. I mostly listen, letting my siblings regale me with stories of their explorations throughout Ascendant. Bree swims in the lake every morning. Sometimes he wakes up Tramy with it too, dumping a bottle of icy water on his head. Gisa has an almost scientific knowledge of the shops and markets, as well as the grounds of the premier's compound. She likes to walk the high meadows with Tramy, while Mom prefers the gardens in the city, terraced down the slopes. Dad has been honing his walking abilities, going deeper and deeper into the valley every day, strengthening his new muscles and relearning two legs with every step down and every step back up.

Kilorn fills in as well as he can, detailing our exploits since we left Montfort last. It's a sparse recollection, and he is gracious enough to leave out the more embarrassing or upsetting details. Including any mention of Cameron Cole. For Gisa's sake, but judging by the way she spoke about a young girl and the jeweler's shop she worked in, I think her old crush on my best friend has passed.

Eventually my eyelids begin to droop. It's been a long, difficult day. I try not to remember how I woke up this morning, in the dark of Cal's royal bedchamber, his blankets over my body. Tonight I'll sleep in a bed by myself. Not alone, though. Gisa will be just across the room. I still can't sleep without someone else there. Or, at least, I haven't tried since I escaped Maven's imprisonment.

Don't think about him.

I chant it to myself as I prepare for bed, repeating the words over and over.

Cal's face seems burned against my eyelids, while Maven haunts even my fleeting, distant dreams. Those stupid boys. They never leave me alone.

In the morning, my nerves twitch with energy. It's a constant pull, a tug behind my stomach, like someone has a hook around my spine. I know where it wants me to go. Down into the city, toward the central barracks of Ascendant. The structure squats over the city prison, drilled into the bedrock of the mountainside. I try not to picture him, alone behind bars, pacing like a dying animal. Why I want to see him, I can hardly understand. Maybe some part of me knows he's still useful. Or wants to understand him a little more, before time runs out. We're alike in some ways, too many ways. I've tasted darkness, and he lives in it. He represents what I could become, without my family, without an anchor, if I'm pushed into the abyss.

But Maven *is* the abyss. I can't face him. Not yet. I'm not strong enough to do it. He'll just laugh in my face, taunt and torture, turning the screws embedded too deeply. I need to heal a bit, before he can pick open my wounds again.

So instead of walking down into the city, I go up. And up. And *up*.

At first I follow the road we took over the mountain, when the raiders struck down on the plain. We know now that it was a planned attack, meant to distract us while the Lakelanders rescued Prince Bracken's children. The raiders were paid to do it, and paid well. I kick at stones as I go, replaying the battle in my mind. The silence clawed at my body, like something alive and unnatural beneath my skin. Replacing my lightning with emptiness. Cursing, I push the thought away and turn off the road, into the rocks and trees.

The hours pass, and the air seems to burn in my lungs, searing down my throat. It's matched only by the fire in my muscles. They scream with each new step, every foot forward and upward over the rocks. Snow puddles in the shadows, white and pure even in the late summer. It turns ever colder as I climb, my feet sliding over dirt and pine needles, gravel and naked rock. In spite of the pain, I push on.

Streams trickle past, running down the mountainside to pool in the lake far below. I look back through the gaps in the pines, into the valley. The mountains dwarf Ascendant, and the foreign capital looks like a child's toy from this distance. White blocks strewn around ribbon-thin roads and winding stairs. The mountain range seems endless, a jagged wall of stone and snow dividing the world in half. Above, the clear blue sky beckons me to continue the climb. I do my best, stopping at the streams to drink and splash my red, sweaty face.

Occasionally I fish out crackers from my pack or strips of salted meat. I wonder if the smell might lure a bear or a wolf across my path.

I have my lightning, of course, close as the breath in my lungs. But no predator ever comes near. I think they know I'm as dangerous as they are.

All except for one.

At first I mistake him for an outcropping of rock, silhouetted against the perfect blue, still in gray clothing. The pines are sparser at this high altitude, offering little shade from the noon sun. I have to blink, rubbing my eyes, before I realize what I'm looking at.

Who I'm looking at.

My lightning splits the granite boulder beneath him in two. He moves before it strikes, sliding off into the rocks.

"You bastard," I snarl, advancing with speed, the adrenaline sudden and surging in my blood. It drives me, as does frustration. Because I know, no matter how fast I am, no matter how strong my lightning, I'll never catch him.

Jon will always see me coming.

His laughter echoes over the slope, coming from higher up. I snarl to myself and follow the sound, letting him lead me. He laughs and laughs, and I climb and climb. By the time we're out of the trees, over earth too high for anything to grow, the air has turned harsh and cold. I choke down a gasp of anger, letting the temperature shock my lungs. And I slump, unable to go any farther. Unwilling to let Jon, or anyone, control where I go and what I do.

But mostly I'm just exhausted.

I lean back, bumping against a large boulder smoothed by centuries of unforgiving wind and snow.

My breathing comes hard and heavy. I think I might never catch my breath, just as I'll never catch the damned seer.

"The altitude," his voice says. "It makes everything difficult if you aren't used to it. Even your fire prince would have a hard time climbing his first mountain."

I'm too tired to do much more than glance at him, eyes half lidded. He perches above me, legs dangling. Jon is dressed for the mountain weather, in a thick coat, with well-worn boots on his feet. I wonder how long he's been walking, or how long he had to wait up here for me.

"You know as well as I do he isn't a prince anymore," I answer, choosing my words very carefully. Maybe I can get him to reveal something, just a sniff of the future ahead of us all. "Just like you know how long he'll be a king."

"Yes," he replies, smirking slightly. Of course he knows what I'm doing, and he says only what he intends to say.

I heave another heavy breath, sucking air into my starved lungs. "What are you doing here?"

"Taking in the view."

He still hasn't looked at me, his red eyes trained on the horizon. The sight before us is amazing, more splendid than it was a thousand feet below. I really do feel small, and large, everything and nothing, sitting here on the rim of the world. My breath fogs before my eyes, a testament to the chill. I can't stay long. Not if I want to get down before nightfall.

I wish I could take Jon's head with me.

"I told you this would happen," he murmurs.

Snarling, I bare my teeth at him. "You didn't tell me anything. My brother might be alive if you did. Thousands of people—"

"Have you considered the alternative?" he snaps. "That what I did, what I said and didn't say, did and didn't do, saved *more*?"

I ball a fist and kick my foot, sending a shower of gravel skittering down the slope. "Have you considered just *keeping your nose out of everything?*"

Jon barks a laugh. "Many times. But whether I involve myself or not, I see the path. I see the destination. And sometimes I just can't let it happen."

"So nice you get to decide," I sneer, bitter as I always am with the wretched newblood.

"Would you like the burden, Mare Barrow?" Jon replies, lowering himself down so we sit side by side. He smiles sadly. "I didn't think so."

I shudder beneath his crimson attention. "You told me I would rise, and rise alone," I mutter, repeating the words he spoke so long ago, in an abandoned coal town half shrouded by the rain. That was my fate. And I've watched it become truer with every passing day. When I lost Shade. When I lost Cal. But also in the steady detachment, the cold hand that seems to worm itself between me and everyone else I love. No matter how hard I try to ignore it, I can't help but feel different, broken and angry, and therefore alone. With only one person left who truly understands. And he is a monster.

I lost Maven too. The person he pretended to be, the friend I loved and needed when I was so alone and so afraid. *I've lost so many people.*

But I've gained many. Farley, Clara. My family is still with me, safe but for Shade. Kilorn, never wavering in his loyalty and friendship. I have the electricons, newbloods like me, who prove I am not alone. Premier Davidson and all he hopes to do. They outnumber everyone I've lost.

"I don't think you were right," I mumble, half believing the words. Next to me, Jon jolts, his neck cracking as he looks at me sharply. "Or has that path changed too?"

Even though I hate his eyes, I force myself to stare into them. To look for a lie or the truth.

"Did I change it?"

He blinks slowly. "You changed nothing."

I feel like elbowing him in the throat, or the gut, or the skull. Instead I slump backward, tipping my head to glare at the sky. Jon watches, chuckling a little.

"What?" I snarl, eyeing him.

"Rise," he murmurs, pointing to the valley thousands of feet below. Then he points to my chest. "And rise alone."

This time I bat his arm weakly, wishing I could inflict more hurt on the seer. "I know you weren't talking about climbing a mountain," I growl. "'No longer the lightning, but the storm. The storm that will swallow the world entire.'"

He just rolls his shoulders and looks out to the range again, his breath steaming in the cold air. "Who knows what I was talking about."

"*You* do."

"And I'll keep that weight to myself, thank you very much. No one else needs it."

I scoff. "You act as if you enjoy lording our fates over us." Chewing my lip, I weigh my chances again. A hint from him could be infinitely valuable, or damning, throwing me onto a path of his choosing. I simply have to take the chance, and consider what he says with a mountain of salt. "Any more choice words, little nudges, you might condescend to give?"

The corner of his mouth lifts, but his eyes waver, almost sad. "Your friend is better at fishing than you."

Cold air whistles down my throat as I inhale sharply. "What do you know about Kilorn?" I ask, my voice climbing an octave. Kilorn is no one to Jon, no one to grand movements of kingdoms and fate. He shouldn't take up an inch of space in Jon's head, not in comparison to the thousands of dangerous and horrible things he does keep in there. I move to grab his arm, but he shifts neatly from my touch.

His red eyes stare, like twin drops of blood. "He's the catalyst for all this, isn't he? For your part in it, at least," he says. "The poor friend doomed to conscription, with only you to save him."

Jon's words are slow, methodic. Deliberate. Giving me time to put together the pieces of this part of the puzzle. I try not to know, try not to accept what is staring me in the face. I want to kill him. Smash his head against the rock. But I can't move.

"Because he lost his apprenticeship," I say, trembling. "Because Kilorn's master died."

"Because Kilorn's master fell." It isn't a question. Jon knows exactly what happened to Old Cully, the fisherman my best friend used to serve. A simple man, gray before his years, just like the rest of us.

Tears fill my eyes. I've been a puppet for too long, even longer than I thought possible. "You pushed him."

"I push many people, in many different ways."

"Did you push an innocent man to his death?" I seethe.

Something switches in him, like a lamp turning off or on. Shifting his focus. He gathers himself and sniffs, his voice suddenly clear, more forceful. As if he is addressing a crowd of soldiers, rather than just me. "The Lakelands will strike Archeon soon," he says. "Within a few weeks. They're preparing as we speak, drilling their armies past the point of perfection. Tiberias Calore is weak and they know it." I don't have the heart or stomach to argue. He's right, and I'm still reeling. "If they take the city, Tiberias will never win Norta. Not this year. Not the next. Not even a *hundred* years from now."

I clench my teeth. "You could be lying."

He ignores me, forging on. "If the capital falls to the queen of the Lakelands, the road becomes long and bloody, worse than anything you've experienced before." In his lap, he knits his fingers together, knuckles going white against the gray of his clothes. "Even I can barely see the ending of that path. But I know it's terrible."

"I don't like being your chess piece."

"Everyone is someone else's pawn, Mare, whether we know it or not."

"Whose pawn are you?"

He doesn't respond, only raising his eyes to the clear, cold sky. With a final sigh, he pushes himself to his feet, dislodging rocks with the motion. "You should get moving," he says, gesturing down the mountain.

"So I can pass on your message?" I snap, sounding bitter. Taking Jon's orders is the last thing I want to do right now, even if he's right. I think I'd rather freeze than give him the satisfaction.

"So you can avoid *that*," he replies. With his chin, he points off to the north, where a band of clouds gathers across the peaks. "Storms move quickly up here."

"I can handle storms."

"Do as you wish," Jon replies, shrugging. He pulls his coat tighter around himself. "We will not see each other again, Mare Barrow."

Still on the ground, I sneer up at him. "Good."

He doesn't respond and turns around to continue his climb.

I watch his figure grow smaller, a gray man against gray stone, until he disappears.

To rise, and rise alone.

The storm breaks on the summit as soon as I step into the protection of the tree line, escaping a howl of wind and freezing rain. It hurts almost as much as going up, my knees jarring with the hard impact of every step. I have to be careful and focus on where I put my feet, lest I break an ankle on the loose stones and pine needles piled over the trail. Above me, back up the mountain, a low thrum of thunder peals, alive as my own beating heart.

I reach Ascendant as the sun first sinks beneath the peaks across the valley. Even though I'm sore from the climb and aching from the conversation, my pace quickens as I enter the premier's palace. I pass Montfort soldiers and officers, as well as politicians from his government, marked by their fine suits, all milling around the lower level of the building, leaving meetings or going to them. They watch me pass with scrutiny, but not fear. I'm not a freak here.

Two heads of shocking hair, one blue, one bone white, stand out in the crowd of dark green suits and uniforms. Ella and Tyton. My fellow electricons idle in one of the windowed alcoves, taking up enough space that they can be left alone.

"Waiting for me? You shouldn't have," I say with a smile, my breath still uneven and ragged from the climb.

Tyton looks me up and down, a lock of white hair falling into his face. He leans back calmly, one long leg planted against the seat across from him. "You shouldn't climb mountains alone," he says. "Especially when you're not good at it."

"You should spend more time with my brothers, Tyton," I reply with little bite. "They're better at teasing me than you are."

His grin comes easily, but it doesn't reach his dark eyes. Ella huffs at him. "Everyone's in Davidson's library. General Farley and the rest," she offers, gesturing down the hall.

My stomach swoops at the prospect of facing yet another council. I grit my teeth. "How do I look?"

The woman licks her lips, her eyes running over me.

Tyton is less diplomatic. "Her hesitation should be answer enough. But you don't exactly have time to put on your war paint, Barrow."

"Right, great," I grumble, leaving them both behind.

Quickly, I smooth my hair back, trying to hide the wind-tangled knots with a hasty braid. *The rest.* Who else could be with Farley and the premier?

The library isn't difficult to find. It's one floor up, occupying a large expanse of the eastern side of the palace. Guards flank the double doors, but they don't stop me as I approach, letting me pass in silence. Like the rest of the compound, the library is bright and cheerful, wood-paneled in lacquered, gleaming oak. The chamber is lined with double rows of shelving, the second story ringed by a narrow landing railed in bronze. Currently, soldiers of the Scarlet Guard perch there, blazing in their red uniforms, guns hanging bare. They note me as I enter, tense but ready to protect their charges should I pose a threat.

The Red generals of Command.

Farley sits with them in the center of the room, on green leather couches arranged in a half circle. Ada is with them too, having returned after long weeks with Command. She stands to the side with her arms crossed. Silent, observing everything. She offers me a shadow of a smile as I approach.

The Scarlet Guard faces a corresponding arrangement of chairs, all occupied by Montfort officers and politicians, with Davidson himself in the center. They murmur in low voices, undisturbed by my presence. Or perhaps expecting it.

Again, I feel too dirty to be here, stinking of the cold and the mountain. But I really shouldn't worry. The Command generals are as disheveled as I feel, if not more so. They just arrived from wherever their roving headquarters were. They look like Farley, not in appearance but in attitude. If Farley had thirty or more years under her belt, a lifetime of hard-lived and hard-won survival. The three men and three women are all gray-haired, with short haircuts like Farley's own. I wonder if she wanted to imitate them. Because, despite their similarities, Farley sits in harsh contrast to them all. She is still young, still blooming. Their firebrand.

Her father stands among the many officers lining the landing above, leaning against the railing, hands knit together. If he's jealous of his daughter and her position, he doesn't show it. He glances at me as I enter, and even dips his head in greeting, his red eye glowering.

The low conversation continues as I move closer. Farley shifts a little, making room for me next to her. But I'm not a general. I'm not Command. I haven't earned the right to sit. I fall in behind her, close as a guardian, and cross my arms over my chest.

"Good to meet you, Miss Barrow," a curly-haired general says, turning to look at me over her shoulder with the stern eye of a teacher. As if I've just disturbed a particularly important lesson. I nod in return, not wanting to interrupt the meeting any further. Though the subject matter does not seem dire. Many advisers talk among themselves, and conversation buzzes among the soldiers above.

"We've only just finished introductions," Ada offers kindly, sidling up next to me.

Farley watches with a glint in her eye. She leans, whispering in my direction. "Don't mind Swan," she adds, nudging the female general. "She's just giving you a hard time."

To my surprise, the older woman smirks a little. They have a familiar way about them, like old friends or even family. But they share very little resemblance. Swan is short and slim, with sandy skin dusted in dark freckles. They give her an almost childish look, despite her lines of age.

"General Swan," I murmur, ducking my head again in an attempt to be polite. She returns in kind, smiling this time.

Under her breath, Ada rattles off the other generals seated on the remaining couches. After her time at their headquarters, she knows them well. The remaining women are Horizon and Sentry, and the men are Drummer, Crimson, and Southern. Code names, clearly. Still in use, even here.

"General Palace is still in Norta, keeping our operations moving," Ada says. "She'll relay whatever we can dig up, in Norta and on the borders."

"What about the Lakelands?" I ask. "Iris is going to invade, and we'll need to know when." *A few weeks,* Jon said. Not nearly specific enough.

Swan clears her throat. "The Lakelanders closed the borders. I wasn't sure I would be able to get myself out, let alone my staff, and we went as quickly as we could." Her eyes darken. "Took some doing, if you catch my meaning."

Grimly, I nod and try not to think about how many dead friends she left behind.

My eyes skitter across the assembled soldiers and politicians, almost all of them Red. A few Silvers of Montfort sit with Davidson, but they are greatly outnumbered. I recognize Radis, the blond representative from the Gallery, among them. He nods his head in the smallest acknowledgment.

Davidson does the same, meeting my gaze.

With a flush, I clear my throat loudly, stepping out a little. Only the nearby generals turn to look at me. Their soldiers are more difficult to silence, and I have to try again, with more force. Slowly but surely, quiet ripples through them, until every eye in the library lands on me. I swallow hard against the familiar but still unsettling sensation. *Don't flinch. Don't blush. Don't hesitate.*

"My name is Mare Barrow," I say to the assembled crowd. Someone on the landing scoffs quietly. I suppose I need no introduction at this point. "Thank you for coming here." I push on, searching for the right way to say what I have to. *A man who can see the entire future passed along some tips* just doesn't sound right. "I'm sorry I'm late, but I was . . . climbing. And I met a man on the mountain."

"Is that a metaphor?" General Crimson mutters gruffly, only to be hushed by the aptly named Drummer, a fantastically round man.

I glance at Ada, then down at Farley. "Jon," I explain, and her eyes widen. The shock on her face speaks volumes to the room. "He's a newblood seer, and we've dealt with him before."

Davidson raises his chin. "So has Maven. If I'm not mistaken, that man was instrumental in your capture."

"Yes," I mutter, almost ashamed.

The premier purses his lips. "And he served Maven for a time."

I nod again. "He did. For his own reasons."

Even though several of his compatriots look dismissive, Davidson leans forward on his elbows, fixing me with his intense, unreadable gaze. "What did he say, Mare?"

"That we can't let the Nortan capital fall to the Lakelands," I reply. "If we do, the road will be 'long and bloody.' Worse than anything before. If they win Archeon, the Lakelands will control Norta for a hundred years."

Radis huffs, inspecting his polished nails. He isn't the only one to roll their eyes at such a statement. "I don't need a seer to know that," he mutters.

A few of the generals bob their heads in agreement. Swan speaks for them. "We know an invasion is coming; it's just a matter of when."

"A few weeks." I can already feel the clock ticking against us. "That's what Jon told me."

Swan narrows her eyes, not with unkindness or suspicion, but with pity. "And you believe him? After all he did to you?"

Images flash in my head, memories of my captivity. The prison Jon bought me with whatever scheme of fate he put in motion. I told him before that I didn't like being his pawn, and it's exactly what I'm doing now.

"Somehow, I think I do," I reply, fighting to keep my voice firm.

The words set off another round of murmurs and even a bit of shouting. From the generals, the representatives, even the soldiers above us.

Only three of us remain silent, trading glances.

Farley, Davidson, and myself.

As I look between them, jumping from golden eyes to blue, I see the same resolve in both of them, and feel it in myself.

We'll fight again. We just need to figure out how.

As usual, Farley jumps in first.

She stands up, hands outstretched, motioning for quiet. It works a little, silencing her soldiers as well as the generals. Some of the Montfort diplomats still whisper among themselves.

"We need a plan," she barks. "Regardless of what the seer says, we all know this road leads to Archeon. Montfort and the Scarlet Guard have to be able to overthrow the Nortan capital if we want any chance of freeing the country. No matter who sits on the throne."

Swan nods. "I was stationed in the Lakelands before we fled here. I've seen more of their strength than anyone here. If the Cygnet queens gain the city before we can, it will be almost impossible to take it back. It's in our best interest to fight the weaker enemy."

Cal. Never have I thought of him as the weaker half of anything, but it's certainly true. His position is precarious at best. I try not to picture him alone in his palace, trying to balance the world his father and brother broke.

"You still have Scarlet Guard in Archeon, yes?" Davidson asks, and his voice is enough to quiet the rest of his people.

"Palace is stationed just outside," Farley says. "With her own teams still in place through as much of the country as can be managed. Harbor Bay, Delphie, the Archeon outskirts."

Drummer, the portly general, jumps in. "Palace has orders to move into the city—quietly, of course. The new king is not his brother, and his regime is not yet openly hostile to the Scarlet Guard. We can risk it."

"So we'll have eyes in the city, at least," Davidson muses. "Yours as well as our own. We'll make sure they coordinate."

"The Scarlet Guard has infiltrated Archeon before." Drummer

puffs out his impressive chest. "It can be done again."

The premier's lips press into a thin, grim line. "But not in the same way," he says. "Too dangerous from the air, now that Cal has the full force of the Air Fleet behind him. We can't match their aerial strength for a landing, and we can't rely on surprise like we did at Maven's wedding."

"And the tunnels," Farley mutters, thinking of a coup that failed before it even began. "King Maven closed up everything beneath the city."

"Not everything," I blurt out. The others blink at me, hard-eyed and eager. "I've seen Maven's train, his escape plan. It runs straight under the Treasury, and there are more entrances below the palace. He used it to leave the city unseen. I'm willing to bet he left some tunnels intact, if only for his own use."

With a will, Drummer rolls to his feet. He's surprisingly agile for his age and size. "I can relay to Palace, have her start sniffing it out. Ada, you've got city plans in your head, yes?"

"I do, sir," she anwers quickly. I can't imagine what Ada *doesn't* have preserved in her perfect mind.

Drummer ducks his chin. "Get on the comms with Palace. Help her run her operatives."

Without hestitation, Ada nods. "Yes, sir," she says, already walking from the library.

Farley clenches her jaw and watches our friend go, disappearing from the room. Then she glances sidelong at me, weighing my response. "Do we have time for that?"

"Probably not," I mutter. If only Jon had been more precise in his damned warning. But I suppose that's too easy. It isn't his way.

"So what can we do?" she prods.

A sudden headache throbs at my temples and I pinch the bridge of my nose. Earlier today, I climbed a mountain to keep away from Maven.

Of course my efforts only prolonged the inevitable. And the necessary.

"Well, I guess we can just ask."

Without Julian to sing a confession out of him, or any whispers, newblood or otherwise, an interrogation of Maven Calore will be a two-sided battle of wills and deception. Though Montfort has Silvers to spare, none can draw truth through ability alone.

But they can draw it through pain.

Before Maven is brought in, one of the officers returns with Tyton in tow, the white-haired electricon looking dour as he enters the room. He settles into his seat on Davidson's side of the room and drums his fingers, the movement quick and twitching, like the lightning he may have to use on Maven. His ability is far more precise than my own, able to push a body to its limit without destroying what cannot be repaired.

The room is deathly silent, empty of the soldiers above, as well as most of the Montfort representatives. Davidson and the Guard generals are smart enough not to give Maven an audience. He's too good a performer, too good a liar.

I can sit now, sandwiched between Farley and the armrest of her couch. She's broader than I am, but I'm glad for her close presence. The thought of Maven still chills my blood. At least in Archeon there was Cal to split his attention, his obsession, and his fury. Now there's just me.

His guards are many, a half dozen at least. Montfort soldiers and Scarlet Guard alike, armed to the teeth with weapons and abilities.

He revels in the attention and the need for such precautions, smiling slightly as they lead him into the library.

His icy eyes sweep over the chamber quickly, noting the windows, the books, and the people waiting for him. I hold his gaze.

"I must admit, I never expected to see you again, Premier," he says, breaking his stare to look at Davidson. The unflappable man doesn't react, his face still and neutral. "Nor did I ever think I would set foot in the mysterious wilds of Montfort. But this isn't so wild, is it? Not as much as you would have us believe."

It's wild enough, I think, remembering our battle with a herd of bison.

"I was taught your country was a land of Silvers as much as my own, albeit divided by many kings and lords. How wrong my instructors were." Maven keeps on, turning slightly as he speaks. He could be counting us. The seven generals of Command, matched by Davidson and the representatives from his government and military. He stops when he spots Radis, plainly silver-blooded with his cold-hued skin. "How interesting," he murmurs. "I don't believe we've had the pleasure, sir?"

The older Silver flexes a hand, the waning sunlight flashing on his long nails. A soft brush of wind rustles through Maven's hair. A warning. "Save your breath, princeling. There are things to discuss."

Maven only grins. "I just didn't expect to see Silvers here, in the midst of such . . . crimson company."

I huff, already bored with his stalling tactics. "You said yourself, you don't know anything about this place." Maven turns back to me, glaring, but I wave him off. "And you don't need to."

He bares his teeth. "Because you'll execute me before long? Is that the threat you're trying to make, Mare?" I set my jaw, electing not to answer. "It's an empty one. If you were going to kill me, you would have done it already. I'm worth more alive. To you and your cause."

The room remains silent in reply.

"Oh, don't play coy," Maven sneers. "As long as I breathe, I'm a threat to my brother. Same as he was to me. I assume he's collecting loyalties now, recalling the High Houses of Norta. Trying to win over those who pledged allegiance to me. And some will, but all?" Slowly, he ticks his head back and forth, clucking his tongue like a scolding mother. "No, they'll sit back and wait. Or they'll fight him."

"For you?" I snap back. "I doubt that."

He makes a noise low in his throat, a growl more suited to an animal.

"What exactly do you need from me?" he says, wrenching his eyes away. He moves gracefully, swiveling on his toes to face the rest of the chamber. The fallen king has no cage, but he is obviously trapped. For some reason, his eyes waver on Tyton, looking over the electricon, with his white hair and calmly murderous disposition. "And who is he?"

To my surprise, I hear fear in Maven Calore.

Farley pounces, smelling blood in the water. "You're going to tell us what you did to the Archeon tunnels. Which ones are closed, which ones are open. Which ones you built after you took the throne."

In spite of his predicament, Maven rolls his eyes and laughs. "You people and your tunnels."

The young general is not deterred. "Well?"

"And what do I get out of this?" He leers at her. "A better view from my cell? Not that it would be difficult. I currently have no windows." With oddly twitching hands, he counts off on his fingers. "Better food? Visitors, perhaps?" Maven wavers a little, teeth on edge. His body seems to shiver. Whatever control he maintains is beginning to slip. "A painless death?"

I fight the urge to grab him, if only to keep him still. He reminds me of a rat in a trap, squirming for his life.

"You get the satisfaction, Maven," I force out.

I should be used to the sensation of his eyes running through me. I'm not, and I shudder, his gaze a featherweight on my skin. "Of what?" he murmurs.

Despite the yards between us, Maven feels much too close.

The words taste sour in my mouth. "You know what."

His grin widens, a white knife to taunt us. "If I can't have the throne, neither can he," he says plainly. "Well, that's something, at least." His voice drops, as does his grin. "But not enough."

Behind him, Davidson looks to his side, exchanging a stern glance with Tyton. After a long moment, the white-haired electricon unfolds from his chair. He rises slowly, deliberately, hands loose at each side. Maven turns at the sound, sharp in his motions. His eyes widen.

"Who is he?" Maven asks again. I try to ignore the tremor in his voice.

I raise my chin. "Someone like me."

Tyton drums a hand against his leg, running a single, blinding white spark down his finger.

"But stronger."

Dark lashes flutter against pale cheeks, and Maven's throat bobs.

His next words are reluctant, stumbling. Low, almost inaudible. "I need something in exchange," he hisses.

My teeth clench in frustration. "Maven, I already told you—"

The fallen king cuts me off, wrenching his eyes from Tyton to look back at me with all his black fire. "When you invade, which you're planning to do," he sneers, baring his teeth, "I'll lead you where you need to go. Which tunnels, which paths. I'll bring your whole army into the city myself, and set you loose on my wretched brother."

Farley scoffs from her seat. "Into a trap, no doubt. Into the teeth of your Cygnet bride—"

"Oh, she'll be there, no doubt," Maven replies, waving a finger at her. Her face flushes with anger. "That snake and her mother have been planning to take Norta since the moment she set foot in my kingdom."

"The moment you let her in," I mutter.

Maven barely flinches. "A calculated risk. And so is this."

Hardly convincing, even to those who don't know him. The Command generals look more disgusted than when he walked in, no mean feat, while the newbloods of Montfort seem more inclined to skin Maven alive. The premier, usually so levelheaded, curls his lips into the rare, obvious scowl. Again he nods to Tyton, and the electricon takes one shuddering step forward.

It sets something off in Maven. He jumps out of reach, keeping his distance from all of us. The twitching returns in force, but his eyes blaze, all fire. No fear.

"You think I can't lie through pain," he snarls, his voice thundering through the room. "You think I haven't done it a thousand times?"

No one has an answer for him, especially not me. I try not to react, not to give him the satisfaction of seeing an emotion from me. I fail horribly, unable to keep my eyes open. For a brief, empty moment I see nothing but darkness, and I try not to think of Maven. His words. What his life was and continues to be.

And how we've all suffered because of it.

I expect the others to give him no quarter. To torture what we need from him. Draw it out with lightning and pain. Will I be strong enough to watch?

Even Farley falters.

She stares at Maven, trying to read him. To weigh the risk and the cost. He meets her eyes without quailing.

She swears under her breath.

For once, he's telling the truth.

Maven Calore is our only chance.

THIRTY
Cal

A coronation has always been in my future. The ceremonial crown is not a surprise. I turn it over in my hands, feeling the formidable weight of iron, silver, and gold. In less than an hour, my grandmother will put the monstrosity on my head. My father wore it too. He was already a king when I was born, with a different queen from the only one I recall.

I wish I could remember her. I wish the memories I had of my mother were my own, and not stories from Julian. Not the brush of oil paint instead of living flesh.

The diary copy is still locked away, hidden in a drawer at my bedside in my Archeon chambers. I'll have to move it soon, once the king's rooms are prepared, washed clean of Maven's presence. I shudder at the thought. I don't know why I'm so hesitant to lay hands on such a small and terrible thing. It's just a book. Just a jumble of scrawled letters pieced together. I've faced down execution squads and armies. Fought lightning and storm. Dodged bullets. Fallen through the sky more than once.

And, somehow, my mother's diary scares me more than anything else. I could barely get through a few pages, and even those I had to read with my flamemaker bracelet far away. Her words set me so on edge, I didn't want to risk turning the pages to ash in my hands. The last pieces of Coriane Jacos, carefully preserved by my uncle. The original is long gone, but he was able to save this much of her.

I don't know what her voice sounded like. I could find out, if I really wanted to. There are many recordings of her, and photographs too. But like my father did, I stay away from them. From a ghost I never knew.

Part of me doesn't want to get up from the table here in this room. It's quiet, peaceful, the inside of a bubble about to burst. I feel as if I'm standing on a threshold. The windows look out on Caesar's Square, offering a full view of the chaos to come. Silvers in their house colors stream back and forth over the plaza, most of them heading for the Royal Court. I can barely look at the structure, one of many ringing the Square.

My father was crowned there, beneath a glittering dome. And Maven was married in the court some months ago.

Mare was with him then.

She won't be here now.

The loss of her still hurts, a deep wound, but it's missing the same edge as before. We both knew what we were doing, what our choices would be when the time came to choose. I only wish we'd had a few more days, a few more hours.

Now she's gone. With Maven again.

I should be angry. It's a betrayal by any other name. She stole a valuable prisoner from me. His execution would have been an easy and almost bloodless way to reunite my kingdom. But somehow I can't feel anything but annoyance. Partly because I'm not surprised. And mostly because Maven is far beyond my reach.

He's her problem now.

At least I won't have to be the one to kill him.

It's the thought of a coward, something I was never allowed to be. I think it anyway.

I hope he dies without pain.

The knock at the door gets me up faster than I want, my legs unfolding beneath me. I wrench it open before Julian or Nanabel steps inside, hoping to do just one last thing on my own. I'm not a fool. I know what they are to me, besides my last remaining family. Advisers, mentors. Rivals to each other. I only hope they haven't come together, to poison my peace with their competition.

It's just Julian waiting, to my relief.

He offers a twitch of a smile and spreads his arms wide, showing off his new clothing, specially made for the coronation. His colors dominate, the dusty yellow-gold of House Jacos forming the base of his trim jacket and pants. But his lapels are bloodred, my own color. Displaying his allegiance not just to House Calore, but to me.

It forces me to think of what he's done in my name. Traded a man's life for my brother, and maybe another life too. I haven't forgotten. His scheming, as well as my grandmother's, is never far from my mind. It makes me wary, even of him.

Is this what being king is? Trusting no one?

I force a laugh to disguise my unease. "You look good," I tell him. It isn't like Julian to be so put together, nearly handsome in his lean form.

My uncle steps inside. "This old thing?" he offers with a dry smile. "What about you? Are you ready?"

I gesture to my own clothes. The now-familiar bloodred suit edged in black, with silver adornments and enough medals to sink a

Lakelander ship. I haven't donned the matching cape yet. It's too heavy, and kind of stupid-looking.

"I'm not talking about the clothes, Cal," Julian says.

My cheeks flush. I turn quickly, trying to hide any sign of weakness or trepidation. "I figured you weren't."

"Well?" he asks, taking a step closer.

I do as I've always been taught. I hold my ground. "Father told me once there's no such thing as being ready. If you think you are, you aren't."

"Then I guess it's a good thing you look like you might escape out a window."

"Comforting."

"Your father was nervous too," Julian says softly. Tentative, he puts a hand on my shoulder, his touch a soft weight.

My tongue sticks in my mouth, unable to form the words I want to say.

But Julian is smart enough to know what I want to ask. "Your mother told me," my uncle explains. "She said he'd wished he had more time."

More time.

I feel like Julian just hit me in the chest with a hammer.

"Don't we all?"

He shrugs in his usual, frustrating way. Like he knows more than I do, which I suspect he does. "For different reasons, I think," he says. "Strange, isn't it? No matter how different we might be, we all end up wanting the same thing." I avoid his eyes when they rise to mine. They look far too much like the eyes in my mother's painting. "But for all the wanting, all the hoping, all the dreaming we might do—"

All I can do is nod, cutting him off. "I don't have the luxury of that anymore."

"Dreaming?" He blinks, perplexed. But also intrigued. My uncle Julian delights in puzzles, and he looks on me as one. "You're about to be a king, Cal. You could dream with your eyes open, and build what you wish."

Again I feel the hammer blow. My chest aches with the force of his words, as well as the judgment behind them. And of course because I've heard that same damned sentiment *so many times*. "I'm tired of telling people that isn't true."

Julian narrows his eyes and I cross my arms instinctively, shielding myself. "Are you sure?" he asks.

"If you're talking about Mare . . . she's already halfway across the continent. And she won't—"

Almost smiling, Julian holds up a hand, showing long, thin fingers. Soft hands, better suited to book pages. Never used in war. Never needed in battle. I envy those hands.

"Cal, I'm a romantic, but I'm sorry to say, I'm not talking about her or your broken heart. That is . . . incredibly low on my list of worries. You have my sympathy, but there are many, many other things to be considered right now."

Again heat flares on my cheeks, and even the tops of my ears. Julian takes it in stride and, thankfully, looks away.

"When you're ready to go, I'll be outside the door."

But time is up. I can't hide any longer.

"Like Father said," I murmur. With a will, I sling the cape around my shoulders, fastening it in place. "I'll never be ready."

I walk around him and pull open the door. Stepping out of the protection of my private chambers feels like running a mile. Sweat prickles down my back, rolling along my spine. With every fiber, I fight the urge to run away, to go back, to stand still.

Julian keeps pace at my side, like a crutch.

"Chin up," he warns. "Your grandmother is around the corner."

I shoot him the best grin I can muster. It feels weak and false. Like so many things these days.

The crystal dome of the Royal Court is a masterwork of Silver craftsmanship. As a boy, I thought it was made of stars stolen from the night sky, each one molded to glittering perfection. It still gleams today, but not as brightly as it should. Red servants are few, many having elected to leave their posts rather than accept better pay and treatment. They aren't around to make the capital gleam and shine the way it should for a coronation. *I can't even look the part,* I think bitterly. My reign begins in ashes.

Such is the way across the capital, and across my new kingdom. Reds pursuing a new place in the world, and Silvers scrambling to understand what it means for the rest of us. The tech towns are almost empty, and rolling power outages plague many cities, Archeon included. Our manufacturing capabilities will follow quickly, with stores and supplies already strained. I can barely fathom the effect this will have on our war effort, and our military might. I expected this, of course. I knew this would happen.

At least the Lakelander War is over. Or, I should say, the first Lakelander war. Another is certainly about to start. It's only a matter of time before Iris and her mother return, their armies in tow.

Murmurs follow me down the long aisle of the court, until I reach the center of the floor beneath the dome. The massive hall echoes, as if filled with hissing ghosts, all sneering about my failure, my betrayal, my *weakness*.

I try not to think about such things as I kneel before the eyes of dozens, my neck bare and vulnerable. We attacked Maven after a ceremony in this very place. Who's to say someone else wouldn't repay the favor?

Try not to think about that either.

I focus instead on the floor beneath my knees, bone-white marble swirled with charcoal gray. The absence of color in the room is supposed to look striking next to a crowd of the multicolored High Houses. White and black against the rainbow. The court seats a thousand comfortably, but less than a hundred are here today. Many houses were decimated by the civil war, lost in battle on both sides, for both sons of House Calore. My grandmother's house stands out proudly in their flaming colors, as do the surviving members of Evangeline's family, Samos and Viper both. Allies like House Laris and Iral are easy to pick out. There are others too, families who were loyal to Maven before, but no longer. Rhambos, Welle, Macanthos sit in their colors. Red-brown, green and gold, silvery blue. But others are missing entirely. The Osanos nymphs are nowhere to be seen. The same can be said of Eagrie, Provos, and, to my chagrin, many Skonos skin healers and every Arven silent. They aren't the only ones. I'm sure Julian and Nanabel are taking stock of who refused to come, carefully noting who is an ally—and who is still an enemy.

Not enough of one, too many of the other.

Above me, Nanabel is careful not to look bothered by the obvious absences in the court. Her face is still and proud, her bronze eyes nearly aflame as she holds my father's crown.

"Long live the true king, Tiberias the Seventh!" she says firmly, her voice echoing around the chamber.

Even though the circle of iron is cold on my brow, I don't startle or flinch. I'm trained not to bat an eye at gunshots or flame. But when the Silver nobles around me repeat her words, I start to shiver. They say it again and again. *The true king.* It resounds like a heartbeat. It's real. This is happening.

I am a king, *the* king. Finally, I'm where I was born to be.

On the one hand, I feel the same as I did this morning. I'm still Cal. Still plagued by aches old and new, bruises seen and unseen. Still terrified of what is to come, and what I might have to do in order to protect my weak kingdom. Terrified of who this crown will turn me into.

Has the transformation already begun?

Perhaps. In small parts of me, forgotten corners, I may be changing. I already feel apart, alone. Even with Julian and my grandmother looming close, my own flesh and blood. But too many people are missing.

My mother.

My father.

Mare.

And Maven too. The brother I thought I had, the person who barely existed.

Never existed.

We grew up knowing I would be king and he would stand at my side. My strongest ally, my most fervent supporter. My best adviser, a shield and a crutch. A second opinion. A sanctuary. Not once did I question the arrangement, and I never thought he did either. How wrong I was.

The loss of him hurt before, but now, with a crown on my head, with no one to take his place?

Suddenly it's very difficult to breathe.

I have to look at Nanabel, to hopefully find whatever solace I can in my grandmother.

She smiles just for me, bracing her hands on my shoulders. I try to see my father in her. A flawed king, a flawed parent. And I miss him terribly, especially right now.

I would hug her if she'd let me, but she keeps me at a distance, her elbows locked. Forcing me to stand up straight, on display. On parade. A vision for the nobles, a message.

Tiberias Calore is king, and he will never kneel again.

Not even to Volo Samos.

We approach him first, Nanabel on my arm, one king to another. I bow my head and so does Volo.

He looks me over slowly, his expression stony but vague.

"Congratulations, Your Majesty," he says, eyeing my crown.

I do the same, nodding at the naked steel across his forehead. "Thank you, Your Majesty."

At his side, the Viper queen stiffens, one hand firm on her husband's arm. As if to hold him back. But Volo does nothing, and neither do I. My grandmother and I manage to pass without incident, nodding in turn to the Samos royals.

Evangeline catches my eye, looking small at her brother's side. She is more subdued than usual, her gown and jewelry dull in comparison to the rest of her family. Silver silk so dark it might be black, better suited to attending a funeral instead of a coronation. After what she said a week ago, she very well could be. If her suspicions are correct, her father is living on borrowed time, and she won't raise a finger to stop it.

The moment shudders between us, born of a mutual secret and an understanding that neither of us wants what comes next.

Now that I'm officially the king of Norta, there's nothing standing in the way of my marriage to Evangeline. It's been a long time coming, and yet somehow nowhere near long enough.

We have no more illusions where this betrothal is concerned. Evangeline's face falls, melting from detached apathy to disgust. She turns away, using the bulk of her brother's body to hide her face.

The next few hours blur together in a swirl of color and pleasantries. I'm no stranger to royal celebrations. It's easy to slip back into the rhythm, playing an easy game of conversation. Saying much and still saying nothing at all. Nanabel and Julian stay with me through it, and we make a formidable team. If only the two of them weren't so obvious at their game. With Maven defeated and a war momentarily ended, their alliance is shaky at best. There's nothing to unite them besides me, and I feel like little more than a bone tugged between two hounds. My grandmother is more vicious, more daring, a queen of many years who knows how to navigate both a court and a battlefield.

But Julian knows my heart better than she does.

I do my best to enjoy the food at dinner. It's edible, but nothing compared to the feasts we used to have. Somehow I find myself missing Carmadon and Premier Davidson's dinner. While this is infinitely less awkward, what they prepared was delicious.

I'm not the only one who notices the quality. Evangeline doesn't touch a single course, and her mother doesn't even condescend to feed her meat to the panther curled around her ankles.

Like the electricity, like the servants, like the factories grinding to a halt all over Norta, good food seems to be growing scarce. In the fields, the deliveries, the preparation. I'd wager most of the palace chefs are gone too.

Nanabel cleans her plate like nothing is amiss.

"We're going to lose this war," I can't help but murmur, leaning to my left so only Julian can hear me.

A muscle flexes in his cheek and he drains his glass of wine. "Not here, Cal," he replies, hiding his mouth with the rim of his glass. "Would the king like to retire?"

"The king would."

"Very well," my uncle mutters, putting his glass back down.

For a second, I don't know what to do. I realize I'm waiting to be dismissed, but no one here can do such a thing. This is my throne and my palace. I need only stand.

I do so quickly, clearing my throat to excuse myself. Nanabel is quick to recognize the signal. I need to be done with this.

"Our thanks for your presence today, and your loyalty," she says, her hands spread wide to better command the attention of the chamber. The nobles in front of us fall silent, their murmurs and conversations sliding to a graceful halt. "We have all journeyed through the storm, as it were, and I speak for the royal family when I say how grateful we are to have you with us. And to have Norta made whole again."

It's a naked lie, plain as the food forgotten on so many plates. Norta is far from whole. The half-empty banquet hall is proof of that. And while I don't want to be a king like Maven, building my throne on deceit and dishonesty, I see no other option now. We need to be strong, even if it is only an illusion.

I put a hand to Nanabel's shoulder, a careful gesture. She obliges, angling back to let me speak. "One storm has passed, yes. But I would be a fool to pretend another is not gathering on the horizon," I say, speaking as clearly as I can. So many eyes look back at me. Their clothes and colors vary, but not their blood. Everyone seated here is Silver, and

I shudder at the implication. Our Red allies are gone for good. When war comes again, we will be fighting alone. "The Lakelands will not be satisfied behind their borders. Not when they came so close to ruling Maven through their princess."

Some of the nobles murmur, their heads drawn together. Volo doesn't move, staring at me from his seat farther down the high table. I feel pierced by his glare.

"When the storm breaks, I'll be ready. I promise you that."

Ready to fight. To lose. And probably die.

"Strength and power!" someone shouts from the crowd, cheering the old refrain of my father and his father before him. An emblem of Silver Norta. Others echo the call. I should too.

But I can't. I know what those words mean. Who exactly we have strength and power over. My jaw remains firmly shut.

Julian stays close on my heels as I escape the banquet hall, utilizing the serving passages instead of the main halls. My grandmother trails us, with her Lerolan soldiers bringing up the rear of our patchwork parade. I still don't have Sentinels, as a king should, as I did when I was a prince and things still worked properly. We're rightfully wary of the guards once oathed to protect Maven, even if many of them have pledged their loyalty with their houses. Finding guards of my own, people I can trust, is simply another item on an increasingly long list of things to be accomplished. Just the thought exhausts me.

I'm yawning by the time I reach the door to my temporary quarters, even though it's barely past nightfall. At least I have a good excuse to be tired. It isn't every day one becomes king. The crown is an infinite reminder.

Both Nanabel and Julian follow me into the adjoining salon, leaving the guards in the hall. I stop my grandmother with a look.

"If it's all right, I'd like to speak to Julian." I try to make it sound like an order. I shouldn't be asking permission to talk with one of my closest advisers alone. Still, I feel tentative, and sound worse.

Her face falls, pulling into an affronted frown. Wounded, even. Like I've hurt her.

"Briefly," I add, trying to undo the harm. Next to her, Julian clasps his hands together, his expression blank.

She stiffens. "Of course, Your Majesty," she murmurs, ducking her head. Her iron-gray hair reflects the lamps like a flash of steel. "I'll leave you to it."

With a rushing whirl of flame-colored clothing, my grandmother turns on her heel without another word. My fist clenches, keeping me from reaching out. It's difficult balancing the love of family with the needs of a kingdom.

The door shuts behind her, sharper than it needs to. I wince with the sound.

Julian wastes no time, opening his mouth before he manages to take a seat on the plump sofa. I brace myself for the inevitable lecture.

"You shouldn't speak that way in public, Cal."

We're going to lose this war.

He isn't wrong. I grimace anyway, crossing to the arched windows overlooking the Bridge of Archeon, the river, and the star-dappled horizon beyond. From this distance, the ships on the water look like stars too. As with the crowd at the coronation, there are fewer ships than there should be. Less trade, less travel. I've been king for a day and my kingdom is already living on borrowed time. I can only guess what might happen to the people in it, should the rest collapse.

I lay a hand against the window glass. It steams beneath my touch. "We don't have the manpower to turn back an invasion."

"Your decree puts our armies at forty-percent strength, if the current reports are accurate. Most Red soldiers have left the military or are leaving. New recruits, mostly. Those left behind are battle-hardened, at least," he says.

"But spread too thin," I mutter. "The Lakelander border is hostile again, not to mention Piedmont to the south. We're surrounded and outnumbered. And with fall coming, what harvest can we expect with no farmers? How can we shoot the guns if no one is making the bullets?"

My uncle brushes a hand under his chin, studying me. "You regret making your decrees."

He is one of only two people I would ever admit it to. "I do."

"It was the right decision."

"For how long?" I can't help but snap. Flaring with heat, I turn away from the window, undoing the top buttons of my jacket as I move. The colder air hits my fevered skin, chilling and soothing. "When the Lakelands return, they'll wipe away whatever I've tried to do."

"This is the way of things, Cal." Julian's calm tone only serves to rankle me further. "In the histories, great moments of upheaval, whole shifts in societies, they take time to rebalance. Reds will return to work, albeit with better pay and treatment. They need to feed and protect their families too."

"We don't have that kind of time, Julian," I mutter, exasperated. "I think someone will have to redraw your maps very soon. The Kingdom of Norta will fall."

He tracks me as I pace, never moving from his seat. "I suppose I should have asked this days ago, but is there a reason you're so married to the idea of this kingdom? And that crown?"

Instead of spinning out, my mind slows. My tongue feels heavy in my mouth, a stone weighing down whatever I might struggle to say. Julian continues on through my silence.

"You say now that you think we'll lose, *you'll* lose, because of the decrees and changes you've chosen to make. Because you have no allies." On the sofa, he stretches, gesturing with one hand. He casts his fingers toward the window, meaning all things. "You did almost everything the Scarlet Guard and Montfort asked. Gave up everything they wanted. Except *that*." He points at the crown still nestled on my head "Why? If you knew you would never be able to keep it?"

My answer sounds foolish, like it comes from a child. I say it anyway. "This is my father's crown."

"But the crown is not your father," he says quickly, rising to his feet. In two strides he has me by the shoulder, and his voice softens. "It isn't your mother either. And it won't bring either of them back."

I can't bear to look at him. He is too much like her, like the shadow of my mother I carry in my head. A wish and a dream, probably, not a real reflection of her. An impossibility. Maven was tortured by his mother who lived and breathed, but I am tortured too. Tortured by a woman taken away from me.

"This is who I am, Julian." I try to keep my breathing even, try to sound like a king. The words make sense as I think them, but they come out wrong. Stumbling, unsure. "It's everything I've ever known, the only path I've ever wanted or been made to want."

My uncle tightens his grip on my shoulders. "Your brother could say the same, and where did that lead him?"

I bristle at that, glaring at him. "We're not the same."

"No, you aren't," he replies hastily. Then his attitude changes, a strange look coming over him. Julian narrows his eyes, lips pressing into a thin, grim line. "You haven't read the diary, have you?"

Again I drop my gaze. Ashamed of how afraid I am of a simple, small book. "I don't think I can," I whisper, barely audible.

Julian offers no quarter, no comfort. He stands back, crossing his arms. He doesn't need many words to scold me.

"Well, you need to," he says simply, taking on the air of a teacher again. "Not just for yourself. But for the rest of us. *All* of us."

"I don't see how the diary of a dead woman can be any help right now."

"Well, hopefully you summon the courage to find out."

Reading it feels like pushing a stone through mud. Sluggish, difficult, foolish. The words pull at me with inky fingers, trying to hold me back. Each page is heavier than the last. Until they aren't. Until the stone is rolling down a hill, and the voice I give my mother rings in my head, speaking as quickly as my mind allows. Sometimes my eyes blur. I don't stop to wipe the tears from the pages, letting them mark the hours as the night passes. Sometimes I find myself smiling. My mother liked to tinker with things. Repair and build. Just like me.

Sometimes I even laugh. The way she talks about Julian, their kind rivalry, how he gave her books she would never read. I can almost trick myself into thinking she's alive. Sitting next to me instead of trapped in a book.

But mostly I feel a deep ache. Hunger for her. Sorrow. Regret. My mother had her demons, just like the rest of us. Her own pains that began long before she became a queen. Before my father married her and put a target on her back.

Her entries grow scarcer as time wears on. As her life changes.

There are only a few pages dedicated to me.

He will not be a soldier. I owe him that much. Too long the sons and daughters of House Calore have been fighting, too long has this country had a warrior king. Too long have we been at war, on the front and—and also within. It might be a crime to write such things, but I am a queen. I am the queen. I can say and write what I think.

The Calores are children of fire, as strong and destructive as their flame, but Cal will not be like the others before. Fire can destroy, fire can kill, but it can also create. Forest burned in the summer will be green by spring, better and stronger than before. Cal's flame will build and bring roots from the ashes of war. The guns will quiet, the smoke will clear, and the soldiers, Red and Silver both, will come home. One hundred years of war, and my son will bring peace. He will not die fighting. He will not. HE WILL NOT.

I run a finger over the letters, feeling the press of a faraway pen. This isn't her handwriting but Julian's. Her real diaries were destroyed by Elara Merandus, but Julian had the wherewithal to preserve something before they disappeared. He painstakingly copied each letter, even these. He nearly put a hole in the page writing those words.

They certainly put a hole through me.

Coriane Jacos wanted a different life for her son, entirely separate from how I was raised, and who my father made me into.

I have to wonder if there is some fate in between what each of my parents wanted for me, a path that is truly my own to choose.

Or is it simply too late?

THIRTY-ONE
Maven

I am not even afforded a window. At least I gave Mare one, when she was my prisoner. Of course, that was a torture as much as anything else. Letting her see the world pass, the seasons change, from behind the bars of her opulent cage. I don't think this is quite as personal an affront. Clearly, they will take no chances with me. My flamemaker bracelets are long gone, probably destroyed. There's Silent Stone set in the floor, dulling any ability I have left. I'm watched night and day by no less than twelve guards, each one alert and ready on the other side of cell bars.

I'm the only person being held here. No one speaks to me, not even the guards.

Only Mother whispers to me still, and those words are ever fleeting, growing dim. Leaving me with my thoughts. It's the only benefit of Silent Stone. While it weakens the rest of me, it weakens her voice as well. I felt the same thing on my old throne. It was a shield as much as an anchor, making me ache, but also keeping me insulated from influence, both within and without. Any choice I made in that seat was mine alone.

It's the same here.

I choose to sleep, mostly.

Even the Stone won't allow me to dream. It can't undo whatever she did. Mother took that ability away long ago, and it never came back.

Sometimes I stare at the walls. They're cool to the touch, and I suspect we're partially underground. I was blindfolded when I was led into the city and brought to speak before that strange council. I must spend hours tracing the lines of mortar and cement holding the slabs together, running my fingers over rough and smooth textures. Normally, I'd talk out my thoughts to myself, but the guards are always there, always listening. It would be more than stupid to give them any glimpse, however small, into my mind.

Cal is alone, cut off from his strongest allies. He did it to himself, the fool. Iris and her mother won't waste much time, or give him the opportunity to try to stabilize the kingdom. He got that crown he wanted so much, but he won't keep it long.

I smile to think of my perfect brother perfectly ruining things for himself. All he had to do was say no. Turn aside the throne. He'd have his armies; he'd have a chance; he'd have Mare. But even she wasn't enough for him.

I guess I understand that.

She wasn't enough for me either. Enough to make me change, to pull me back from what I've willingly become.

I wonder if Thomas would have been enough.

As usual, the splitting headache comes whenever I think his name, or remember his face, or feel his touch on my hands. I lie back against the cot in the corner, pressing my fists against my eyes. Trying to relieve the pressure of the memory and this place.

I know less than I should about Montfort, let alone its capital, Ascendant. Even trying to plan an escape from here would be a waste of my time and limited energy. Of course, I'll take my chances in Archeon. Lose them in the tunnels after setting another army on my brother. The last revenge of Maven Calore, before I disappear. To where, I don't know. It's just another waste to try to plan beyond Archeon. I'll cross that bridge when it comes.

Certainly Mare will suspect. She knows me well enough by now. I might have to kill her, at the end of this.

Her life or mine.

A difficult choice, but I'll choose myself.

I do it every time.

"We need to know where to enter the tunnels."

At first, I wonder if I'm actually dreaming. If that piece of my mother has finally been washed away.

But that's impossible.

I open my eyes to see Mare standing on the other side of the bars, far enough to be out of reach. The guards are gone, or at least out of sight. Probably gathered at either end of the corridor, ready to be called upon if necessary.

It's been two days since I was summoned to the premier's council, and she doesn't look like she's slept since. The lightning girl is worn, with shadows beneath her eyes and cheekbones. Still, she looks better than she did when she was my prisoner, in spite of the gowns and jewels I kept her in. Her eyes spark here. She isn't hollowed out, aching to the bone. I know that sensation intimately. I feel it here now, and I felt it when I was a king, shielded by a silent throne.

Slowly, I rise up on my elbows, peering at her over the toes of my shoes.

"Two days to agree to my terms," I say, counting off on my fingers. "Must have been quite the argument."

"Careful, Maven." She barks out the warning, all rough edges. "Any difficulty and I'll be happy to call Tyton down here."

The other newblood who shares her ability is a stranger, with his white hair and inscrutable eyes. *Stronger than me,* she said back in the council. And I have seen such strength from Mare Barrow. Certainly his lightning will shred me, nerve from nerve. Not that it will help them. I can withstand torture. I know how to keep my mouth shut, even if it means dying.

Still, I don't fancy being turned into a lightbulb this early in the day.

"No, I'd rather you didn't," I answer her. "I do so enjoy our time alone."

Her eyes narrow, dancing over me. Even at a distance, I can hear her sharp intake of breath. I smirk a little, satisfied that I can still draw such a reaction from her. Even if her response is firmly rooted in fear. That's something, at least. Better than apathy. Better than nothing at all.

"I suppose this is the end of that," I continue, swinging my legs out and onto the floor. The metal is cool against my forehead as I lean, bracing myself against the bars. "No more whispers between Maven and Mare."

She sneers, and I brace myself for the inevitable spray of spit. It never comes.

"I'm done trying to understand you," she hisses, still out reach. But she doesn't flinch when I look her over. Doesn't tremble when I raise a hand, stretching out my fingers to brush within an inch of her face.

Because it isn't me she fears, not really.

Her eyes flicker, looking down at the floor of my cell. At the Stone set neatly in cement.

I laugh, deep in my throat. It echoes off the walls.

"I really did break something in you, didn't I?"

Mare recoils like I've struck her. I can almost see the bruise forming on her heart. She grits her teeth, straightening her spine. "Nothing that I can't fix," she grinds out.

I can feel the smile on my face turn bitter, tainted, corrupted. Like the rest of me. "If only I could say the same."

My words echo, soften, and die.

She crosses her arms and looks at her feet. I watch her keenly, trying to commit every piece of her to memory. "The tunnels, Maven."

"You heard my terms," I reply. "I go with you, I lead your armies . . ."

Her head snaps up. If not for the Stone beneath my feet, I might feel the hum of static. "That isn't good enough," she says.

Time to call her bluff. "Then electrocute me. Call your torturer and risk your war on the words bought with my blood. Trust that they're the truth. Are you willing to do that?"

She throws up her hands, exasperated. Like I'm a child instead of a king. It rankles, sandpaper on my skin. "We need a compromise, at least. Where the tunnels *start*."

I raise an eyebrow coolly. "And where they end?"

"That's your piece of the puzzle to keep. Until we need it."

"Hmm," I hum out, tapping a finger to my chin. I even start to pace, putting on a grand show for my rapturous audience. Her eyes track my movements, and I'm reminded of the panther Evangeline's mother keeps so close. "I assume you'll be coming along?"

She barely scoffs. Her mouth curves into a delicious scowl. "It isn't like you to ask empty, stupid questions."

I just shrug. "Whatever keeps you standing here."

To that she has no retort. Whatever words she wants to say die on her lips. If only I could touch them. Feel the skin beneath my fingers, smooth and full and pulsing with hot, red blood. Part of me wonders why she is still so transfixing, even though I know she's my sworn enemy. That I would kill her, and she would kill me. Another mystery of my mind that will never be unraveled.

She stands firm, letting me look. Never wavering beneath my gaze. Letting me see past the mask I helped her make. There is exhaustion, and hope, and sadness, of course. A sorrow for so many things.

My brother among them.

"He broke your heart, didn't he?"

Mare only exhales, her chest falling.

"What a fool," I whisper, speaking the familiar thought aloud.

It doesn't bother her. She tosses her head, letting brown and gray hair flip over her shoulder. Revealing the bare skin beneath, and the brand still clear as day. *M* for *Maven. M* for *mine. M* for *monster. M* for *Mare*.

"So did you."

A sour taste floods my mouth. I expected her to quail, but I'm the one who has to look away. "At least I had a good reason," I mutter.

Her laugh is sharp and harsh, a single bark that snaps like a whip-crack.

"He did it for the crown," I hiss.

Mare leers at me, but never moves her feet. Never gets close enough to touch. "And you didn't, Maven?"

"I did it for her, of course." I try to sound detached, matter-of-fact. The cold, broken, doomed Maven. "And what she made me into."

"You keep blaming your mother. I suppose that's easy." My heart leaps in my chest when her feet slide. Moving sideways. Not closer, not farther. Now it's her turn to prowl. "You think Cal's father didn't make him into something too? You think we all aren't made or unmade by someone else?" Even though she's only walking, it feels like a dance. I mirror her movements, stepping with her. She's more graceful than I am, a lithe thief born of many years and many twists of fate. "But we all still have the ability to choose, in the end. And you chose to keep the blood on your hands."

My fist clenches, and I wish for a spark. For flame. For *something* to burn. She knows what I want, and grins to herself. On the other side of the bars, her fingers tap against the air, alight with purple and white. The electric energy is a tease at best. Beyond my reach, beyond the sphere of Silent Stone. I ache for my ability the way I ache for Mare, for Thomas, for who I was supposed to be.

"At least I can admit when I'm wrong," she continues. "When I make a mistake. When the horrible things I've done and will do are my own fault." The sparks reflect in her eyes. They shudder from brown to purple, giving her an unearthly look, like her gaze might run me through. Part of me wishes she would. "I suppose you taught me that."

Instead I grin again. "Then you should thank me properly."

She responds in kind, spitting at my feet. At least some things in this world are still predictable.

"You never disappoint," I hiss, scraping my shoe against the cement floor.

She doesn't waver. "The tunnels."

Heaving a breath, I pretend to be so desperately put-upon. I make her wait, letting the silence stretch for several long, blistering moments. I take the time to look at her. To see Mare Barrow for who she is right now. Not who I remember. And not who I wish she could be.

Mine.

But she doesn't belong to anyone, not even my brother. I take comfort in such a small consolation. We're alone together, she and I. Our paths may be horrible, but they're the paths we made for ourselves.

The golden glow of her skin is warm, even down here, illuminated by the harsh light of fluorescence. She is so stubbornly alive, still burning like a candle fighting against rain.

"Fine."

I give her what she wants.

I think it's what I want too.

Their plan was always to kill me. After I ceased to be useful. I'm not surprised. It's what I'd do. Still, when the cloth is pulled off my head, revealing the mountains bowled around us, I can't help but feel afraid. If I'm allowed to see this place, see Montfort and its capital, then I am well and truly dead. It's only a matter of time.

The air is cold, biting at my exposed face. My shivers of fear are more than warranted. I blink up at the purple sky, hazed before dawn, streaked with the light of a distant sunrise creeping over the mountain peaks. Snow clings to the heights, even in summer. Quickly, I try to get my bearings.

The city of Ascendant reaches into the valley below, sweeping over the slopes to an alpine lake. It doesn't remind me of any city I've seen, not in Norta or even the Lakelands. This place is too new, but somehow old at the same time. Grown among the trees and the rocks, a part of this strange land as much as a human-built place. But the city doesn't matter. I'll never come back here. Not if I escape, nor if they execute me. There is simply no reality where I return to Montfort.

We're standing near a runway, cut evenly between two mountains. The smell of jet fuel is sharp on the otherwise fresh air. Several airjets line up on the paved straightaway, ready to take flight. I squint over the heads of the guards around me, glimpsing a white palace in the distance, looking down at the capital. That must be where I was taken before, when I was dragged before that strange council of Reds, Silvers, and newbloods.

The faces hemming me in are unfamiliar, their uniforms equally split between Montfort green and the hellish red of the Scarlet Guard. They keep me locked in place, unable to do much more than stand on my toes for a craning look at the crowd.

For this is certainly a crowd. Dozens of soldiers and their commanders, organized into neat lines, wait patiently for the jets. But far fewer than I expected. *Do they really think this is enough to assault Archeon?* Even if they have newbloods of strange and terrible abilities, this is foolish. Suicide. *How did I lose to such rampant idiots?*

Someone chuckles nearby, and I'm seized by the familiar sense that they're laughing at me. I turn sharply, only to see the premier of Montfort himself staring between the shoulders of my guards.

With a gesture of his hand, the two soldiers move, allowing him to approach. To my surprise, he's dressed like a soldier, unremarkable in a dark green uniform. No medals or honors on his breast, nothing to mark him as the leader of an entire country. *No wonder he and Cal got along so well. They're both stupid enough to fight on the front lines.*

"Something funny?" I sneer, looking up at him.

The premier merely shakes his head. As in the council, the man keeps his face still and almost empty, showing only enough emotion to allow an audience to project their own assumptions.

I would congratulate him on the talent if I felt so inclined.

Like me, Davidson is a skilled actor. But his performance is wasted. I see through him.

"What happens when this is over, and the time comes to divide the spoils?" I smile, the air freezing against my teeth. "Who picks up my brother's crown, Davidson?"

The man doesn't flinch, seemingly unaffected. But I catch the minuscule twitch as his eyes narrow. "Look around, Calore. No one wears crowns in my country."

"So clever," I muse. "Not all crowns are worn where people can see."

He smirks, refusing to rise to the bait. Either his temper is extraordinary, or somehow this man is truly without a lust for power. It's the former, of course. No person on earth can ignore the lure of a throne.

"Uphold your end of the bargain, and it will be quick," the older man says, backing away. "Board him," he adds, his voice harder in command.

The guards move as one, well trained, and if I shut my eyes, I could pretend they were Sentinels. My own Silver protectors, oathed to keep me safe, instead of these rats and blood traitors bent on keeping me chained.

At least they don't bother with manacles. My wrists remain unbound, albeit bare.

No bracelets, no flame.

No sparks that I can make.

Lucky, then, that we're traveling with a lightning girl.

I manage to catch a glimpse of her as I'm marched forward, over the runway to the airjet idling ahead. She clusters with her friend, the Farley woman who was so easily misled a year ago, as well as her fellow electricon, the white-haired man. Odd hair must be a style in Mont-fort, because there's a woman with blue locks and a man with closely cut green hair as well.

Mare smiles at them, a true grin. When she moves, I realize her hair is different too. The gray ends are gone, replaced by a beautiful, familiar purple. I love it.

I feel a tug deep in my chest. She's on my jet. Probably to keep an eye on me. To let her torturer friend stand over me for the entire flight. That's fine. I'll suffer it.

A few hours of fear are worth the dwindling time we have left.

Our jet has dark green wings, a symbol of the Montfort fleet. I'm led up and into a military craft lined with seats, plus a lower compart-ment running the length of the fuselage. For more passengers or arms. Maybe both. My mouth turns sour as I realize this jet is Montfort-made, and certainly not the only one. The strange mountain country is better equipped than we realized, even after Corvium, after Harbor Bay. And they are mobilizing.

As I'm strapped into my seat, the buckles fastened just a hair too tight, I realize why Davidson was laughing.

The jets on the runway, the soldiers assembled outside—they're just the beginning.

"How many thousands are you leading into Archeon?" I ask aloud, letting my voice carry over the bustle of the filling compartment.

I'm ignored, and that's answer enough.

Across the jet, Mare takes her own seat, with Farley at her side. The pair of them glance at me, eyes hard as flint, and just as easy to spark. I fight the urge to wag my fingers at them.

Then a body crosses my vision, blocking the two women out.

I heave a sigh, and look up slowly.

So predictable.

"Try something," the white-haired electricon says.

Instead I shut my eyes and lean back. "Shan't," I reply, doing my best to hide how difficult it is to breathe against these infernal belts.

He doesn't move, even when the jet roars into the air.

So I keep my eyes shut, and I run through my precarious plan.

Again, and again, and again.

THIRTY-TWO
Evangeline

It's been at least two weeks since Barrow left, a week since my betrothed was crowned king, and a few days since I saw Elane last. I can still feel her, though, her pale skin smooth and cool beneath my fingers. But she is far, far beyond my reach. Dispatched back to the Ridge, away from the danger.

Cal would have let me keep her here, if my father had allowed it. In spite of everything, an understanding is falling into place between us. Funny, I used to dream of such a thing. A king who left me to my own devices and my own crown. Now it's the best I can hope for, and a prison all the same. It traps us both, locking us away from the ones we care about most. He can't bring back Mare, and I won't bring Elane back. Not with the Lakelander queens on the horizon and an invasion imminent. I won't risk her life for a few days of my own comfort.

My new rooms in Whitefire Palace are meant for the queen, and they still echo with the presence of Iris Cygnet. Everything is blue, blue, *blue*, from the curtains to the plush carpets, even down to the

flowers wilting in an obscene amount of crystal vases. With fewer servants, the process of clearing the rooms is slow going. I end up ripping
down most of the curtains myself. They're still in the salon outside my
bedroom, collecting dust in a pile of cobalt-blue silk.

The long balcony overlooking the river is the only respite from her,
the distant princess who will return to kill us all. And even here, standing with my face to the sun, I can't escape the thought of the Cygnet
nymph. The Capital River courses below, splitting the city of Archeon
in two as it winds toward the sea. I try to ignore the rush of water, calm
as it is. I focus on braiding my hair instead, pulling the silver strands
back from my face. The simple act is a good distraction. The tighter the
braids, the more severe, the more determined I feel.

I plan to train a little this morning, go through the motions. Run
the barracks track, maybe spar with Ptolemus if he wants. I find myself
wishing Barrow were here. She's a good workout and a good challenge.
And easier to deal with than my mother.

I'm surprised she hasn't breezed in yet, as she often does these days.
Trying to prod me toward more queenly activities, as she puts it. But I
don't have the stomach to charm or intimidate nobles today, especially
for her benefit. My parents want me to sway more Silvers, earn the
loyalty they pledged to Cal. To pull allies away from him, like saving
rats from a sinking ship.

Mother and Father want me to be his queen the way Iris was
Maven's. A snake in his bed, a wolf at his side. Gathering strength and
waiting for an opportunity to strike. Even though I do not care for Cal,
and never could, somehow it feels wrong.

But if Anabel and Julian play out their scheme . . .

I have no idea where that leaves me.

Suspended on a bridge, trapped in the middle, with both ends on fire.

The Bridge.

My hands drop, leaving half my hair undone, and I squint at the massive structure spanning the river. The other side of Archeon gleams beneath the rising sun, its many buildings crowned with steel and bronze birds of prey. Nothing seems amiss. It's still busy with transports and a roving populace. So is the Bridge, all three levels of it bustling with traffic. Less than usual, but that's to be expected.

It's the supports below that worry me, and the water breaking around them. Still steady, moving at the same speed. But the current, the wash of white breakwater at each base . . .

The river is flowing the wrong way.

And it's rising.

I fly through my bedchamber and the adjoining rooms, seeing nothing until I reach Ptolemus's quarters. The locked door unlatches without a thought, blowing back on twisted hinges as I sprint through. I barely hear myself shout his name. The buzzing in my head is far too loud, overwhelming everything but the cold, acid rush of adrenaline.

He stumbles out into the sitting room toward me, half dressed. I catch a glimpse of rumpled bedsheets through the door behind him, as well as a blue-black arm. It moves, pulling out of sight, as Wren Skonos busies herself with her clothes.

"What is it?" my brother asks, his eyes wide with panic.

I want to run; I want to scream; I want to fight.

"The invasion."

"How could they do this? Move their army without us knowing?"

Ptolemus dogs at my heels, barely keeping pace as we stalk through the palace halls. Galleries, salons, receiving chambers, and even ball-rooms blur at the edge of my vision. In a few hours it could all be destroyed. Burned or drowned or simply erased. For a moment, I see my brother's corpse, broken and sprawled across the intricate marble floor, his blood like a mirror. I blink, fighting off the thought. Bile rises in my mouth anyway.

I glance back at him—alive and breathing, towering in his armor—if only to convince myself he's still here. Wren follows, her healer's uniform clearly marked. I hope they stay together over the next few hours. I would tie her to him if I could.

"We had eyes on their citadels," I mutter, speaking to keep myself focused. "We knew the Lakelands were gathering for something, but not when."

Wren's voice is slow and steady, but not soothing. "They must have gone north. Moved overland."

"Without the Scarlet Guard, we don't have many eyes left in the Lakelands," Ptolemus curses as we round another corner, angling for the throne room.

Our parents haven't found us yet, and that can only mean they're with the king and his advisers. They must already know.

Lerolan guards open the doors for us, putting their lethal hands to the tall, lacquered panels. We march past together, the three of us keep-ing a tight formation on the off chance the Lakelanders have already infiltrated the city. My ability buzzes, flung wide to catch any errant bullets. I count the rounds in the guards' guns, letting them hang at the edge of my perception as we cross the floor.

At the raised platform containing Cal's throne, as well as the seats for his uncle and grandmother, the royals collect. Mother and Father are here, with the latter armored as usual. Sunlight flashes off him with every small movement, and he is almost blinding to look at. Mother is more subdued, without armor but not without weapons. Larentia Viper has abandoned her beloved panther for now, despite its prowess as a hunter. Instead she has two shaggy wolves sitting at her heels, their eyes, ears, and snouts all twitching. Both are fearsome to behold, but just as skilled at detection as they are at fighting. No one will catch my mother unawares with them at her disposal.

Julian Jacos and Queen Anabel flank Cal. She is more prepared for battle than the singer uncle, her small, thick form belted into a flame-orange uniform, sculpted by snug body armor. Her hands are bare, even of her wedding ring. Julian is not so protected. His eyes are ringed by dark shadows, hinting at a night with no sleep. He remains close to his nephew, standing only a few inches away. I'm not sure who is more protective of who.

The king of Norta himself has burnished red-and-silver armor, not to mention a gun on one hip and a gleaming sword buckled to the other. No cloak or cape drapes across his shoulders. It would only get in the way. Cal is barely a man, but he seems to have aged overnight. And not from the impending battle. He is no stranger to war or bloodshed. Something else hangs on his heart, something even an invasion can't distract from. He raises his shadowed face, watching me as I approach.

"How long do we have?" I ask aloud, not bothering with pleasantries.

Cal is quick to answer. "The Air Fleet is on the wing," he says, casting his gaze to the south. "There's a storm out to sea, moving too quickly. I'd wager there's a Lakelander armada inside it."

It's a tactic we used ourselves in the battle of Harbor Bay, but in far fewer numbers and with much less strength. I shudder to think of what a nymph-born assault might look like with the queen of the Lakelands herself leading the charge. As before, I picture myself swathed in my steel, sinking quickly through deep and dark water, never to surface again.

I try not to let that fear bleed into my voice. "Their objective?" It's the best way to fight, and fight back. Identify what your opponent is trying to do, and calculate how best to stop them.

Behind Cal, his uncle shifts uncomfortably. He lowers his eyes, touching his nephew on the shoulder. "That would be you, my boy. They get to you, and all this is finished before we have even begun."

My father remains silent, weighing the outcomes. What it means for him if Cal is captured or dies. We still aren't married. The Kingdom of the Rift is not so irrevocably tied to Norta, just as we weren't tied to Maven. The last time enemy forces attacked Archeon, House Samos was prepared, and we fled. Will he do the same again?

I grit my teeth, already feeling a headache form on top of everything else.

"Maven's escape train is still in use," Julian continues. In reply, Cal shifts smoothly out of his grasp. "We can get you out of the city, at least."

The young king pales, his skin turning the color of old bone. The suggestion makes him sick. "And surrender the capital?"

Julian responds quickly. "Of course not. We'll defend her, and you'll be well out of danger, far beyond their grasp."

Cal's retort is just as quick, and twice as resolute. Not to mention predictable. "I'm not running."

His uncle doesn't seem surprised. Still, he tries to argue valiantly. And in vain. "Cal—"

"I'm not going to let others fight while I hide."

The old queen is more forceful, seizing him by the wrist. I despair of this family bickering but have little recourse. Even as the clock ticks against us. "You're not a prince anymore, or a general," Anabel pleads. "You are the king, and your well-being is integral to—"

As with his uncle, Cal gently extricates himself from her grip, peeling off her fingers and removing her hand. His eyes smolder and burn. "If I abandon this city, I abandon any hope of ever being a king. Don't let your fear blind you to that."

Sick of this nonsense, I cluck my tongue and say the obvious, if only to save precious time. "The remaining High Houses will never swear to a king who flees." I lift my chin, utilizing all my court training to project the image of strength I need. "And the ones who have will never respect him."

"Thank you," Cal says slowly.

I point one finger at the windows, toward the cliffs. "The river has changed course, and it's rising. High enough to allow their largest ships to come this far upriver."

Cal nods, grateful for the return to the subject. He shifts, putting some distance between himself and his relatives. Crossing to my side.

"They intend to split the city in two," he says, looking between my still-silent father and his own grandmother. "I've already given orders to even the guards on either side of the city, and supplement with the soldiers still in our service."

Ptolemus wrinkles his nose. "Wouldn't it be better to gather our strength, fortify the Square and the palace? Keep our ourselves united?"

My brother is a warrior as much as Cal is, but no strategist. He is all brutal strength. And Cal is quick to point out his error.

"The Cygnet queens will feel out which side is weakest," he says. "If both sides are balanced, they won't find a weaker side to prey on. And we can pin them in the river."

"Concentrate the Air Fleet over the city." It isn't a suggestion, but an order. And no one shoots me down. Despite our impending doom, I feel a surge of pride. "Use their weapons on the ships. If we can sink one downriver, we'll slow their pace." A dark grin plays on my lips. "Even nymphs can't keep a ship full of holes afloat."

There is no joy in Tiberias Calore when he speaks next, his eyes flickering with some inner torment. "Turn the river into a graveyard."

A graveyard for both kinds of blood, Silver and Red. Lakelanders, soldiers of Piedmont. Enemies. That's all they are. Faceless, nameless. Sent to kill us. It's an easy equation to balance, with the people I love on one side. Still, my stomach turns a little, though I'll never admit it to anyone. Not even Elane. What color will the river be when all this is over?

"We'll be outnumbered on the ground." Cal begins to pace, his words taking on a manic quality. He's almost talking to himself, puzzling out a battle plan before our eyes. "And whatever their storms cook up will keep most of the Air Fleet busy."

My father still hasn't spoken a word.

"They'll have Red soldiers among the Silvers," Julian says. He sounds almost apologetic. Again my stomach churns, and Cal seems to feel the same trepidation. He falters a little in his steps.

Anabel merely scoffs. "That's one advantage, at least. Their numbers are more vulnerable. And less dangerous."

The rift between Cal's closest advisers yawns like a canyon. Julian almost sneers at her, his usually calm manner fading a little. "That's not what I meant."

More vulnerable. Less dangerous. Anabel isn't wrong, but not for the reason she thinks. "The Lakelands haven't eased their treatment of Reds," I say. "Norta has."

The withered stare from the old queen is a thing of lethal beauty. "So?"

I speak slowly, like I'm explaining battle theory to a child. It rankles her delightfully. "So the Lakelander Reds might be less willing to fight. They might even want to surrender to a country where they'll be given better treatment."

Her eyes narrow. "As if we can rely on that."

I shrug with a practiced smirk, raising the steel pauldrons on both shoulders. "They did in Harbor Bay. It's worth keeping in mind."

The bug-eyed looks of the Silvers around me are not difficult to interpret. Even Ptolemus is perplexed by what I'm saying. Only Cal and Julian seem open to the idea, their expressions measured but oddly thoughtful. My gaze lingers on Cal, and he meets my eyes firmly, inclining his head in a small, almost invisible nod.

He licks his lips, vaulting into another round of planning. "We don't have any newblood teleporters, but if we can somehow get you two"—he gestures to Ptolemus and me—"onto the battleships again, neutralize their guns—"

"My children will do no such thing."

Volo's voice is low but resounding, almost vibrating on the air. I feel it in my chest, and suddenly I'm a little girl again, cowering before a commanding father. Willing to do whatever I must to keep him happy, to win a rare smile or show of affection, however small.

Don't, Evangeline. Don't let him do that.

My fist clenches at my side, nails digging into the flesh of my palm. It grounds me somehow. The sharp pain brings me back to who I am, and the cliff we all stand upon.

Cal glares openly at my father, the two of them locked in a silent battle of wills. Mother remains quiet, one hand resting on the head of a wolf. Its yellow eyes stare up at the young king, never wavering from his face.

My parents don't intend to fight at all, or let us do it either. In Harbor Bay, they were willing to send us into the fighting. Risk us both. For victory.

They think this battle is already lost.

They're going to run.

Father speaks again, breaking the tense silence. "My own soldiers and guards, my surviving cousins of House Samos, are yours, Tiberias. But my heirs are not yours to gamble with."

Cal grits his teeth. He plants his hands on his hips, thumbs drumming. "And what about you, King Volo? Will you sit back as well?"

I blink, stunned. He all but called the king of the Rift a coward. A shudder runs through my mother's wolf, mirroring her anger.

My father has his own schemes already working. He must. Or else he wouldn't let the slight pass so easily. With a wave of his hand, he brushes off the accusation. "I don't have to buy loyalty with my own blood," he says simply, jabbing back. "We'll be here, defending the Square. If the Lakelanders strike the palace, they'll find quite the opposition."

Cal grinds his teeth, gnashing them together. A habit he'll have to break if he ever hopes to hold a throne. Kings shouldn't be so easily read.

His uncle looms close at his shoulder, his own watery eyes alight as he stares.

At Father.

Almost smiling, Julian opens his mouth, lips parting to draw in a long, threatening breath. I expect my father to drop his gaze. Break eye contact. Take away the singer's weapon. But then that would be an admission of fear. He would never do that, even to protect his own mind.

It's a standoff.

"Is that wise, Jacos?" my mother purrs, and the wolves at her knees growl in response.

Julian merely smiles. The sharp thread of tension snaps. "I don't know what you mean, Your Majesty," he says, his voice blissfully normal. No haunting melody, no aura of power. "But Cal, if I can get to the Lakelander queen, I could be of some use," he adds softly. Not for some part of the pageantry. It isn't an act to send a message. It's an actual proposition.

True pain cross Cal's face. He turns, forgetting my parents.

"That's little more than suicide, Julian," he hisses. "You won't even get close to her."

The old singer just raises an eyebrow. "And if do? I could end this."

"*Nothing* will end." Cal slices a hand in dismissal, and I swear I can almost hear the air singe. His eyes are wide, desperate, all masks of propriety sliding away. "You can't sing both Cenra and Iris out of this war. Even if you manage to make them both drown themselves, or turn their entire army around, they'll just come back. Another Cygnet waits in the Lakelands."

"It could buy us valuable time."

The uncle isn't wrong, but Cal won't hear of it. "And it will lose us a valuable person."

Julian lowers his eyes, stepping back. "Very well."

"This is all very touching," I can't help but mutter.

My dear brother mirrors my sentiment. I'm surprised his eyes don't roll out of his head. "That aside, do we know what we're going to be facing out there?"

Our mother scoffs in reply. Like Father, she thinks this battle is already hopeless. The city already lost. "Besides the full might of the Lakelands? Red legions with all the Silvers they can muster, not to mention powerful nymphs with a river to wield?"

"And perhaps some might of Norta too." I tap a finger against my lip. I'm not the only one who thinks this. I can't be. It's too obvious. Judging by the flushes on the faces around me, the others realize what I'm saying, and they've had the same suspicions. "The High Houses missing from your coronation. None have come to pledge loyalty. None have responded to your commands."

Cal's throat bobs. A silver blush blooms high on his cheeks. "Not while Maven lives. They still kneel to another king."

"They knelt to another queen," I muse.

His face falls, dark brows pulling together. "You think Iris has Nortans on her side?"

"I think she'd be stupid not to try." I shrug my shoulders. "And Iris Cygnet is anything but stupid."

The implication hangs over us, thick as a fog, and just as difficult to ignore. Even Father seems unsettled by the possibility of another split within the Nortan kingdom, cleaving apart a land he one day hopes to control.

Anabel shifts, uneasy down to her toes. She runs a hand across the tight pull of her gray hair, smoothing down an already severe style. The old woman mutters under her breath.

"I didn't think it was possible, but I think I miss those grubby Reds."

"A bit late for that," Cal snarls, his voice like furious thunder.

My father's lip twitches, the closest he's ever come to flinching.

★ ★ ★

Of course, there are plans in place. Tactics and strategies for defending the capital against an invasion. After a century of war with the Lakelanders, it would be foolish to think otherwise. But whatever the Calore kings cooked up to fight the Cygnet nymphs relied on things that no longer exist. A Nortan army at full strength. A country united. Tech towns operating at full capacity, churning out electricity and ammunition. Cal can't count on any of it.

The barracks and military facilities adjoining the Square are the safest place outside the spiraling vaults of the Treasury, but I don't fancy burying myself belowground with only a rickety train to rely on. My parents take up refuge in the nerve center of War Command, overseeing the many reports flooding in from the circling Air Fleet. I suspect King Volo enjoys standing in a place of such power, especially while Cal is readying himself to lead a battalion into the fray.

I'm less inclined to stare at printouts and grainy footage, watching battle from afar. I'd rather trust my own eyes. And I can't be close to my parents right now. Somehow the approaching army, the ships hidden on a cloudy horizon, make my choices very clear.

Ptolemus sits with me, perched on the steps of War Command. His armor ripples slightly, still taking shape across the planes of his muscles. Trying to find the perfect fit. He inclines his head skyward, eyes roving over the gathering gray clouds overhead. They thicken with every passing minute. Wren is close by too, hovering at his shoulder, her hands bare and ready to heal.

"It's going to rain," he says with a sniff. "Any second now."

Wren looks past us, toward the Bridge of Archeon on the far side of the Square gates. Its many arches and supports seem faded, as the oncoming mist bleeds into the city. "I wonder how high the river is now," she murmurs.

I reach out with my ability, trying to distinguish the armada rapidly closing the miles. But the ships are still too far out. Or I'm too distracted.

Father is going to run again. House Samos will run. Leave Norta to crumble, with only the Rift remaining, an island against the lapping Cygnet sea.

Eventually we'll be overrun too.

Queen Cenra has no sons. No one to sell me to. Volo Samos has no more bargains left to make. He'll have to surrender.

And die at her hands, probably. The way Salin did.

If he even survives today.

So where does that leave me?

If my father faces defeat as much as my betrothed does?

I think . . . it leaves me free.

"Tolly, do you love me?"

Both Wren and my brother snap to attention, their faces whirling to mine. Ptolemus almost sputters, his lips flapping with surprise. "Of course," he says, almost too quickly to be understood. His silver brows furrow, and something like anger crosses his features. "How can you even ask that?"

Just the simple question offends him, wounds him. It would do the same to me.

I take his hand, squeezing tight. Feeling the bones in the newly grown appendage he lost some months ago. "I sent Elane away from the Ridge. When you get home, she won't be there."

Red hair, a mountain breeze. It seems like a dream. *Could it be real? Is this my chance?*

"Eve, what are you talking about? Where—"

"I'm not going to tell you, so you won't have to lie."

Slowly, I force myself to stand on oddly shaking limbs. A baby learning to walk, taking steps for the first time. I quiver all over, toes to fingertips.

Ptolemus jumps up with me, bending so we're eye to eye, inches away from each other. His hands are tight on my shoulders, but not enough to keep me in place if I choose to move.

"I'm going inside. I need to ask him a question," I murmur. "But I think I already know the answer."

"Eve—"

I look into his eyes, the same eyes as mine. As our father's. I would ask for his help, but splitting him apart like that, asking him to choose a side? I love my brother, and he loves me, but he loves our parents too. He is a better heir than I ever was.

"Don't follow me."

Still trembling, I pull him into a crushing hug. He returns the gesture reflexively, but he stumbles over his words, unable to understand what I'm saying.

I don't look back for what could be my last glimpse of my brother's face. It's too difficult. He could die today, or tomorrow, or a month from now, when the Cygnet queens storm my home to lay my family bare. I want to remember his smile, not a confused frown.

War Command is a mess, a study in chaos. Silver officers buzz through passages and chambers, calling out developments and army movements. The Lakelander boats, the Piedmont airjets. It all passes in a blur.

My parents are easy to find. My mother's wolves guard the door to one of the communications chambers, flanking each side with bright, keen eyes. The beasts turn to me in unison, neither hostile nor friendly as I pass.

Static-filled screens fill the command room with a crackling glow of shifting light. Only a few are still operational. Not a good sign. The Air Fleet must be well into the storm. If it even still exists.

Volo and Larentia stand firm, mirror images of each other. Postures violently straight, unblinking as they take in such dire circumstances. On one of the screens, the first armada ship takes shape, a hulking shadow obscured by mist. Others slowly come into focus. At least a dozen, and still more.

I've seen this room before, but never so empty. A skeleton crew of Silver officers mans the screens and radios, trying to keep up with the flood of information. Runners bustle in and out, taking the newest items with them. Probably to Cal, wherever he is now.

"Father?" I sound like a child.

And he dismisses me like one. "Evangeline, not now."

"What happens when we go home?"

With a sneer, he looks over his shoulder. Father cut his hair shorter than usual, cropping the silver close to his scalp. It gives him a skullish look. "When this war is won."

I let him parrot the lie, feeling myself tighten as he spouts nonsense. *You'll be queen. Peace will reign. Life will return to what it was.* Lies, all of it.

"What happens to me? What plans do you have in store?" I ask, remaining in the doorway. I'll have to be quick. "Who will you make me become next?"

Both of them know what I'm asking, but neither can answer. Not with Nortan officers close by, few as they may be. They must maintain the illusion of this alliance until the last second.

"If you're going to run, so will I," I murmur.

The king of the Rift clenches a fist, and the metal throughout the room responds in kind. A few screens crack, their casings twisted by his rage. "We're not going anywhere, Evangeline," he lies.

Mother tries another tactic, closing the distance between us. Her dark, angled eyes go wide and pleading. Imitating a puppy or a cub. She puts a hand to my face, ever the image of the doting mother. "We need you," she whispers. "Our family needs you, your brother—"

I step out of her grasp, toward the hallway again. Luring them both with me. *Two rights, out the front, into the Square—*

"Let me go."

Father shoulders past my mother, almost knocking her out of the way so he can stand over me. The chromium armor gleams harshly in the fluorescent light.

He knows what I'm saying, what I'm really asking for.

"I will not," he hisses. "You are mine, Evangeline. My own daughter. You belong with us. You have a duty to *us.*"

Another step backward. At the door, the wolves rise to their feet.

"I don't."

Like a shadow, like a giant, Father moves with me, matching my steps. "What are you, if not a Samos?" he snarls. "Nothing."

I knew this would be his answer, and the last thread, already thin and fraying, snaps apart. In spite of myself, tears bite at the corners of my eyes. If they fall, I don't know. I feel nothing but the burn of my own anger.

"You don't need me anymore. Not for power, not for greed," I spit back in his face. "And you still won't let me go free."

He blinks, and for a brief second the rage in him dissipates. The trick almost works. He's my father, and I can't help but love him. Even though he treats me this way. Even though he wants to use that love to keep me locked up, a prisoner to my own blood.

I was raised to value family above all else. *Loyalty to your own.*

And that's who Elane is. My family, my own.

"I'm done asking for your permission," I whisper, clenching a fist.

The lights overhead rip free, smashing down, a crashing blow that takes even my father off guard. A rush of silver blood gushes from cuts on his head as he stumbles, dazed. But not dead. Not even incapacitated. I can't find the stomach for that.

I've never run so fast, never sprinted like this in all my life, not even in battle. Because I've never been so afraid.

The wolves are faster than me. They snarl at my heels, trying to trip me. I strike at them with the metal on my arms, drawing armor into knives. One howls, whimpering when I cut a ruby-red wound across its belly. The other is stronger, bigger, leaping to knock me over.

I try to dodge, and end up falling flat on my back, with a wolf lunging for my throat. It lands hard, almost two hundred pounds of muscle crashing into my chest. I gasp, feeling the air rush from my lungs.

Teeth clamp around my neck, but they don't bite down. The points dig in, enough to bruise. Enough to pin me in place.

Overhead, all around, the lights quiver in their metal holdings, and hinges shudder on doors.

I can't move, can barely breathe.

I made it ten whole yards.

"Don't lift a finger," my mother crows, stepping into my very limited line of vision. Above me, the wolf trembles, yellow eyes boring into mine.

My father shudders at her side, a storm cloud of rage. He keeps one hand to his head, stemming the flow of blood. His eyes are worse than the wolf's.

"You stupid girl," he breathes. "After all we've done for you. All we made you."

"But for one flaw," my mother replies. She tsks, clucking her tongue over me. Like I'm one of her prize animals, bred for her personal use. I suppose that's not incorrect. "One deep, unnatural flaw."

I try to gasp against the wolf's grip, if only to choke back a sob. My stomach coils and churns. *Let me go,* I want to beg.

But he never will. He doesn't know how.

And perhaps that's the fault of his own father, and his father before.

I don't know why, but I think of Mare Barrow. Of her parents, holding her close, saying good-bye as we left Montfort. They are nothing, insignificant people, of no great beauty, intellect, or power. I envy them so deeply it makes me sick.

"Please," I manage to force out.

The wolf holds firm.

Father takes a step closer, his fingers painted in liquid silver. With a flick of his hand, he sprays me with his blood. With what I did.

"I'll drag you back to the Rift myself."

I don't doubt it.

I stare up at him, struggling to breathe, fingers scrabbling over the floor. Even my own armor betrays me, melting off my body under his command. Leaving me bare and without weapons. Vulnerable. A prisoner still and always.

Then my father flies away from me, crashing backward, his face pulled into unfamiliar surprise. He's being *dragged* by the chromium painted up and down his body. He slams into the nearest wall, head cracking backward. My mother screams as he slumps forward, eyes rolling in his skull.

The wolf above me meets a different fate.

A blade cuts through its neck, and the severed head flies, landing with a sick squelch a few feet away. A hot spray of fresh, scarlet blood coats my face.

I don't flinch. A familiar, cool hand closes around my wrist, giving me a tug.

"You trained us too well," Ptolemus says, helping me to my feet.

We run together, and this time, I look back.

Mother bends over Father, her hands running over him. He tries to rise, but the blow makes him stagger. He's still alive.

"Good-bye, Evangeline," another man says.

Julian Jacos steps out from an adjoining corridor, and Anabel is with him, her fingers drumming together. She doesn't spare a glance for me as she approaches, hands raised. Such lethal power in so small a woman.

"Run away, Larentia." I fight the urge to cover my ears, even though Julian's melodic voice is not directed at me. Still, the singer's power shudders on the air, palpable as a sugary taste. "Forget your children."

Her footsteps are quick and scurrying, like one of her spying rats.

"Larentia!" my father gurgles, barely able to speak in his dazed state.

But he can certainly scream.

I leave him to Anabel and Julian. To whatever fate they have in store for the king of the Rift.

Outside, the fog has truly fallen, coating the Square in a gray haze too thick to be born of nature. Wren stands silhouetted, waiting for us, her trim form a sharp outline against the other shadows slouching into formation. Cal's forces, maybe even an entire legion, judging by the many shapes.

At the sight of us, Wren waves a hand. "This way," she calls, before turning to the fog and the soldiers.

Something weighs at the edge of my perception, heavy enough to register even from a great distance. *The Lakelander ships.* They have to be. Overhead, unseen, jets scream back and forth. Somewhere, missiles whine and bloom, spouting bursts of flame where the armada must be. I feel trapped by the fog, blinded. All I can do is focus on Wren and Ptolemus, staying close enough to their silhouettes as we barrel through the legions marching into place. A few soldiers stare as we pass, but none try to stop us. And soon War Command fades into the distance, swallowed by the fog.

We angle across the Square, making for the Treasury. A strange, familiar feeling comes over me as I remember Maven's wedding. The Square was a battleground then as well, and he fled for his train, his precious escape. I never liked the contraption, but I push aside any discomfort. It's the fastest way out. The safest. We'll be far beyond the city before the battle is even finished.

And then . . .

I don't have the time or energy to follow that thought.

Rain follows the fog, slamming down with a sudden hiss. I'm soaked in seconds, and the deluge turns the Square slick, forcing us to slow our pace or risk broken ankles. Down in the river, a boom like a drum sounds, rhythmic and shuddering. It shakes the ground beneath my feet.

The ships are firing on the city, their heavy rounds peppering both East and West Archeon.

I reach for Ptolemus, my fingers sliding over his wet armor as I try to find some grip on him. The rest of me braces for the inevitable impact as the Lakelander fire reaches this part of the city.

My instincts aren't wrong.

The first missile howls over the Square gates, barely visible as it arcs in and out of the fog cover. I don't see where it lands, but judging by the concussive blast behind us, I'd guess Whitefire just suffered a direct hit. The force knocks a few soldiers off their feet and sends us scrambling. Ptolemus and I ground ourselves in our armor, and Tolly catches Wren before she falls, holding her tightly.

"Keep moving!" I shout over the shriek of another round, this one exploding somewhere near War Command.

Someone else is shouting too, barking barely audible orders over the din. A streak of flame accompanies his voice, whirling through the fog near the head of the gathered legion. Whatever stirring speech Cal cooked up will be of little use now. It's too loud, too wet, and his soldiers are too distracted by the armada currently choking the river. Still, they begin to march, lurching forward to follow whatever his orders might be. Probably to line the cliffs. Concentrate their attack on the river below.

We're suddenly caught in their motion.

The legion surges like a tide, carrying us with them. I try to shove against the uniformed bodies, searching the Silver faces for Ptolemus and Wren. Still close, but the distance between us is steadily growing. I feel for the copper in my brother's belt, holding on to the sensation of the metal.

"Move," I snarl, trying to tear my way through the crowd. Using my armor to propel me, using Ptolemus's as a beacon. "Move!"

The next blow is closer, dead on target, dropping out of the sky like a hammer. A shell, not a missile. Smaller, unguided, but still deadly. In unison, separated though we are, Ptolemus and I raise our hands, throwing out our ability with a mighty burst of energy.

I grab on to the steel casing, gritting my teeth against the strain of stopping a fast-moving projectile. But we manage and, with equal grunts, fling the shell back into the fog, spiraling off to hopefully explode somewhere in the Lakelander fleet. A few telkies among Cal's legion do the same, banding together to throw back shells and missiles. But there are too many rounds rocketing out of the fog, almost on top of us before we even know it.

The Air Fleet races among the clouds, still weaving through the sky, peppering the armada as best they can with all they can. They aren't the only jets up there. The Lakelanders have aerial battalions of their own, as does Piedmont in fewer numbers. Between the thunder of the ships and the scream of the jets, I can barely hear myself think. And the Nortan guns only add to the chaotic din. The turrets up ahead spit sparks and hot iron, flashing with gunfire. They're usually disguised as part of the walls around the Square, or supports to the Bridge, but not now. A few telkies stand at the turrets, using their abilities to fling explosives with deadly aim.

This city was built to survive, and that's what it's trying to do.

A wind picks up, probably born of our own windweavers. House Laris is still allied to Cal, and they use their ability to its full extent. A howling gale streaks over the Square, blowing from somewhere behind us. It knocks some of the shells and missiles off course, and a few land harmlessly in the river while others spiral off into the fog. I squint against the slapping wind, keeping Ptolemus and Wren in sight, but the hurricane force makes the soldiers tighten their ranks, squashing us in with them.

Gritting my teeth, I painstakingly shove my way through, slipping under arms, pressing past guns and torsos. Every step is an ordeal, made more difficult by the lashing wind, the rain, the press of the legion. The crowd tosses like the river below, now whitecapped with rising waves.

My hands close on Tolly's wrist, his armor cold against my fingers. He heaves, pulling me to him over the last yard, until I'm tucked safely into his side. My brother holds Wren in the same manner, his arms braced across both our shoulders.

What now?

We have to get the edge of the crowd, but the walls and buildings of the Square keep the legion hemmed in, funneling all of us toward the Bridge. Even from a distance, I can see Cal elevated above the rest, his red armor like blood against the howling storm. He stands to the side of the open gates, perched on a stone turret.

Like some idiotic target.

A good sniper could pick him off from a thousand yards if they cared to try.

But he risks it for the morale of his troops, shouting encouragement as they charge onto the Bridge. More shells hurtle toward him, but he flicks a hand, exploding the rounds in midair before they can do any harm.

On the Bridge itself, Silver soldiers disappear into the fog. I can guess their destination. Even now, the rhythmic, haunting drum of the armada's guns breaks its pattern. I try not to picture Nortan soldiers fighting on the ship decks, facing the full might of Queen Cenra's and Prince Bracken's forces.

If we can get you two onto the ships . . . Cal's voice echoes in my head. I grit my teeth against the curl of shame licking through me. I'm not wading into this battle, not on another river. Not with *them* down there.

This is our chance, and we have to take it.

"Keep pushing!" I shout, hoping Tolly can hear me over the din. The Treasury is behind us now, the distance growing with every passing step. It's suffocating, being shoved like this, prodded forward against my will.

I don't have much armor left—my father stripped most of it away—but what little I have re-forms along my arm, flattening into a round shield. Ptolemus mirrors my action, creating a smooth disk over his arm. We use them like battering rams, pushing against the human tide with our abilities and our own strength. It works slowly but steadily, creating enough space for us to move.

Until red armor blocks our path, a fireball hovering over one hand.

Cal stares between us, and I expect accusation. His flame gutters against the rain, refusing to surrender. His soldiers form a protective cocoon around him.

Rainwater drips down his face, steaming on his exposed skin.

"How many are you taking with you?" he says, barely audible.

I blink water out of my eyes and gesture blankly at Wren and Ptolemus.

"Your father, Evangeline. How many will he manage to flee with?" Cal takes a long step forward, never breaking eye contact. "I need to know who I still have left."

Something releases in my chest. I shake my head, slow at first, then faster and faster.

"I wouldn't know," I murmur.

Cal's expression doesn't change, but for a moment I think the flame in his hand burns a bit brighter. Again his gaze bounds between my brother and me, weighing us both. I let it wash over me like the rain and the fog and the rising smoke. Tiberias Calore is not my future anymore.

Without another word, he stands aside, and his soldiers move with him. Clearing a path over the slick tiles of the Square.

As I move past him, I feel a ghost of warmth bleeding from his hand as it hovers near my arm. I think he almost hugs me. Cal has always been an odd sort, different from other Silvers. Strange and soft in his inclinations, while the rest of us were raised to razors and hard edges.

Instead of embracing him, I grab his arm, just for a moment. Pull him close enough for one last whisper, one last barb from Evangeline Samos before she disappears. Without her crown, without her house, without her colors. To become a new person entirely.

"If it isn't too late for me, it isn't too late for you."

When we sit down on the train, its lights flickering and engine lumbering to life, only then do I dimly wonder where the tracks end.

It will be a long walk to Montfort.

THIRTY-THREE
Mare

I'm still not used to the purple hair.

It isn't as garish as Ella's, at least. I only let Gisa dye the gray ends, leaving the roots untouched. I twist a spare lock around my finger, staring at the odd color as I walk. Strange as it looks, it gives me a small burst of pride. I'm an electricon, and I'm not alone.

After the first attack on Archeon, Maven and his loyal advisers took up a campaign of collapsing or flooding the immense tunnel system beneath the city. They concentrated heavily on the southern edges, where the tunnels were more numerous, all of them leading to the ruins of Naercey at the mouth of the Capital River. Davidson originally suggested striking out from the abandoned city, but Farley and I knew better. Maven destroyed that too, rooting out the Scarlet Guard's stronghold while obliterating whatever remained. He was inspired by the Guard as well, constructing tunnels of his own in addition to an escape train. I can't be certain, not this deep or after this long underground, but I think we'll link up with the train line eventually.

My inner compass spins, searching for true north in vain. We have to rely on Guard intelligence, what they know of the tunnels. And we have to rely on Maven. Stupid as it is, he is our best hope for getting as far into the city as we can. The combined force of Montfort and the Scarlet Guard is too big to simply strike from the air, or the river, or the ground. We have to do all three.

Of course I'm stuck scrabbling in the darkness, walking for hours beneath several tons of rock and soil.

Maven cuts a harsh silhouette, backlit by our lanterns. He's still wearing the simple uniform the Montfortans gave him when they locked him up. Washed-out gray pants and shirt, the fabric too thin and the cut too big on his frame. It makes him look younger than he is, more gaunt and drawn than ever before.

I hang back, using Farley as a human shield between us. His own guards are close at hand as well, an even mix of Reds and newbloods. None of them falter, hands resting on their holstered guns. Tyton walks close by, never breaking his concentration on Maven. They're prepared for the first sign of trouble.

So am I. My body buzzes, a live wire, not from my own electricity but from sheer nerves. I've felt it for hours, since Maven brought us down here, leading us through a service hatch a few miles north of the city limits.

Our army lumbers along with us. Thousands winding through the darkness, marching at an even, steady pace that echoes off the tunnel walls. It sounds like a heartbeat, rhythmic and pulsing, vibrating in my rib cage.

On my right, Kilorn shuffles along, his steps a bit stilted to keep pace with mine. He notices me staring and pulls a tight smile.

I try to return the gesture. He almost died in New Town. I remember the feel of his blood spraying across my lips. The memory fills me with a numb fear.

My old friend reads my face, even in the dim light. He nudges my arm. "You have to admit, I have a talent for survival."

"Let's hope it holds," I mutter back.

I'm just as concerned for Farley, in spite of all her skills and wiles. Not that I'd ever say it out loud.

Farley has command of half the ground forces—all the Scarlet Guard soldiers as well as the Red Nortan defectors collected over the months of rebellion. Davidson leads the other half, though he is content to walk in line with the rest of us, letting her take precedence.

Up ahead, the tunnel splits. One side narrows but angles sharply upward, the path scrambling over a few ancient steps punctuated by gentle slopes of packed dirt. The other carries on like this one, wide and flat, with the slightest incline.

Maven slows before the fork, resting both hands on his hips. He seems amused by the guards flanking him, all six of them moving in lockstep.

"Which way?" Farley barks.

Maven glances over at her, wearing a familiar smirk. The shadows cut deep along his cheekbones and make his blue eyes stand out, vivid in their icy coldness. He doesn't answer.

She doesn't hesitate, striking him across the jaw. Silver blood spatters the tunnel floor, winking in the lantern light.

At my side, I clench a fist. I would let Farley grind Maven into a pulp under any other circumstances, but we need him right now.

"Farley," I hiss, wishing I could call back the word as soon as I speak.

She frowns at me, even as Maven grins, showing silvered teeth.

"Up," he says simply, pointing to the steeper way.

I'm not the only one to curse under their breath.

The narrower path isn't difficult, but it does slow us down. Maven seems to delight in the prospect, looking back with a haunting sneer every few minutes or so. We have to walk three abreast, instead of twelve as before, making for a cramped ascent. The tunnel quickly grows hot with the presence of so many bodies, all of them nervous and agitated. A bead of sweat rolls down my neck. I would prefer to storm the capital at full strength, but I guess this will have to do.

Some of the steps are uneven and too high, forcing me to scramble. Kilorn watches me go, almost laughing. I can call forth a lightning storm, but tall steps are apparently beyond me.

The climb doesn't take longer than a half hour, but it feels like days spent in the dim light, scuffling in relative silence. Even Kilorn keeps his mouth shut. The circumstances settle over the long train of soldiers like a cloud, sobering us all. What will we find when we finally reach the surface?

I try not to look at Maven, but find myself focusing on the outline of his body. It's instinctual. I don't trust him in any capacity. I expect him to dart into a crevice, disappear, and escape. But he keeps an even pace, never faltering in his steps.

The path flattens again, joining a wider tunnel with rounded walls and stone supports. The air is colder, sending a chill over my fevered skin.

"I think you know where we are," Maven says, his voice echoing down to me. With one hand, he gestures to the center of the tunnel floor.

A pair of new tracks gleams, reflecting our lanterns.

We've reached the escape train.

I swallow hard, feeling a swell of fear rise in my throat. Not long now. Everyone else knows it too, judging by the thrum of activity rising through our ranks. From here, Farley's half of our forces can easily get up to Whitefire, Caesar's Square, and the cliffs that make up West Archeon. The rest, following Premier Davidson and General Swan, will cross under the river and link up with General Palace, the last member of Command still operating in the city. If all goes to plan, we'll be able to overrun both sides of Archeon before anyone knows we're here. And the Lakelanders will be caught in the middle.

But will Cal fight with us?

He has to, I tell myself. *He has no other choice.*

The official objective is to keep the city out of Lakelander hands. We can do that, at the very least. *We can do that.*

Next to me, Kilorn brushes my arm, sensing my discomfort. The burst of warmth makes me shiver again.

At the edge of my perception, something tinges. It hums and buzzes, the whine of distant electricity. Not above us, strangely, but ahead. And steadily approaching.

"Something's coming," I bark aloud.

Tyton reacts in the same manner, his body tensing. "Stand back!" he shouts, pushing Maven against the wall. The rest of us follow suit, moving quickly as the sound reaches us.

An engine screeches far ahead, closing the distance as it gains speed over the tracks. The lights round a gentle curve, blinding in comparison to our lanterns, and I have to turn my head to shield my eyes.

I end up looking at Maven, who doesn't flinch. He doesn't even blink.

The familiar train speeds by in a blur of gray metal, too fast for us to glimpse who may be inside. Still, Maven searches the windows as they fly by, his blue eyes big as dinner plates. He pales, going whiter than Tyton's hair, and his throat works furiously, lips pressing into a disappearing line. All this passes in an instant as he quickly wrestles his emotions under control, but the moment is enough for me.

I know what fear looks like in Maven Calore, and he is terrified now. For very good reason.

Whatever plan he had, whatever hope there was for escape, just disappeared with that train.

He catches me staring, reading the fading expression on his face. His jaw tightens just a little and his eyes run over me, slow as a caress.

You can't run from what you've done, I want to say aloud.

He gets the message.

As the train fades to nothing again, beyond my perception, his eyes flutter shut.

I think he's saying good-bye.

Like the lights of the train, the spiraling white of the Treasury vaults is blinding.

Tyton has Maven by the neck. He uses the leverage to increase our pace, forcing Maven to march faster and faster as we ascend the vault levels. The air fills with the sound of weapons and body armor being checked. Guns loaded, blades drawn, buttons fastened, buckles clicked into place. The pistol on my own hip is still an unusual weight, and I lean a little to compensate. I doubt I'll fire a bullet up there. Not like Farley. She sheds her jacket, tossing it to the side to be trampled by the hundreds behind us. Without the red overcoat, I can see the many belts and holsters crossing her back and hips, slung with half a dozen different guns and corresponding ammunition, as well as her radio. She has her knives as well, now in plain sight. Diana Farley is ready for war.

Somewhere behind us, one of the Scarlet Guard shouts, her voice echoing oddly. I can't decipher it, but others repeat her words. The cheer reverberates off the walls, the sound rising like thunder, until I realize what they're chanting.

"Rise, red as the dawn."

In spite of my fear, I feel a wicked, wild grin rise to my lips.

"Rise, red as the dawn."

The spiraling passage choruses with the battle cry.

We're almost running, Maven struggling to keep up with Tyton's pace. Farley matches his speed, her long strides eating up the white marble beneath our feet.

"Rise, red as the dawn."

Kilorn's voice joins the din.

"Rise, red as the dawn."

The lights overhead flicker in time with my heartbeat.

I look back, searching through the ranks of red and green, Scarlet Guard and Montfort. The range of faces, skin every shade, blood both colors, all speaking in shuddering unison. Some raise their fists or weapons or both, but no one is silent. Our voices are so loud I can barely hear my own.

"Rise, red as the dawn."

I call to lightning, call to thunder, call to all the strength left in my body. I'm not a general or commander. The only things I have to worry about topside are myself, Kilorn, and Farley, if she'll let me. That's all I have the capacity for.

And Cal, wherever he might be. Leading his army, fighting in vain against a greater force. Defending a city from almost inevitable ruin.

Tyton is first through the great doors of the Treasury, vaulting out into the spiraling rain with Maven in tow. The younger prince skids, his shoes sliding over the wet tiles of Caesar's Square, but Tyton keeps his grip. I follow, half expecting Tyton to kill Maven on the spot, already shivering in the rain. We never planned on letting Maven survive the battle. And we don't need him anymore, not really.

It could be over right now.

I feel tugged by both ends of the decision. As if it's really my decision to make.

The other electricon never loosens his grasp, almost holding Maven down. Tyton isn't as temperamental as the rest of us. He is slow to fury, even now, with Maven in hand. He's a good jailer for someone the rest of us despise so much.

"Do it," I hear Maven grit out, head still bowed. He extends his white hands and I watch his fingers tremble in the rain. Like me, he knows where this road leads.

Behind us, more and more of Farley's forces flood into the Square, still cheering the words of the Scarlet Guard. They fill the space with color, uniforms of red and green standing out starkly even in the wet fog. I focus on the fallen king, now shuddering a hundred yards from his own palace. Even the rhythmic thud of gunfire and explosions barely penetrates my awareness.

"I said, do it," Maven snarls again. Trying to goad Tyton.

Or me.

Above us, the storm clouds churn. I feel the flash of lightning before it crackles across the sky, purple and white, an emblem of our presence. *Let Cal know we're here.*

"You don't have any more use for me." Rainwater drips down his face, tracing familiar paths. "Be done with it."

Slowly, he raises his eyes to mine. I expect sorrow, or defeat.

Not icy anger.

"Ty—" I start, but the word is hardly out of my mouth when a shell strikes true, exploding over the columned walls of the Treasury.

The force of it blows us sideways, falling over already slippery ground. My skull cracks against the tile and I see dizzy stars for a second. I try to stand and fall again, colliding with an equally disoriented Tyton. He holds me down, pushing me flat against the Square as a leaping tongue of flame passes over us, singing the air directly above our heads.

"Maven!" I scream, my voice lost in the surge of battle. Against the guns, the missiles, the mortar shells, the wind and the rain, I might as well whisper.

Beneath me, Tyton tenses, pushing up on his elbows. His head whips back and forth, searching the crowd around us for a gray form and black hair.

I roll to my knees, cursing, the twists of my hair already coming undone. Purple strands drift, unfamiliar. Kilorn skids to a stop at my shoulder, his face already sweaty and flush with exertion.

"Is he gone?" he pants, trying to help me up.

As my head clears, I manage to get my feet underneath me. My muscles tighten, ready to dodge another flaming blow. *Not that I need to. That isn't his way. Maven isn't a warrior.*

"He's gone," I hear myself hiss.

I can choose to hunt him down. Or I can make sure we finish what we've started. I can keep my friends alive.

With a burst of determination, I force myself to turn, face the gates of the Square, and the Bridge beyond. "We have work to do."

Though it's still shrouded in fog, I can just make out hundreds of soldiers spanning the Bridge, with the looming hulks of Lakelander ships below. In the sky, airjets give chase, with wings of yellow, purple, red, blue, and green swooping like deadly birds of prey. I can't make out anything beyond the river. The other half of the city is entirely obscured. At least Farley and the officers have their radios. They should be able to communicate with Davidson on the far side.

Extending a hand, I take Tyton by the wrist, hoisting him to his feet. His face darkens as he scowls, disgusted with himself.

"I'm sorry," I think I hear him whisper. "I should have killed him when I had the chance."

Spinning on my heel, I make for Farley. "Join the club," I mutter, sending another angry bolt across the sky.

In the fog, flashes of blue and green pulse, as if in reply.

"They made it across," Kilorn muses, pointing out the distant lights. "Rafe and Ella. Davidson's army."

In spite of Maven's escape, my lips twitch, wanting to smile. A small burst of triumph blooms in my chest. "Well, that's something."

More than something.

Caesar's Square contains the center of Nortan government—the palace, the courts, the Treasury, and War Command—but the bulk of the capital is on the other side of the river. Our side might be more valuable, but East Archeon is larger, with a greater population. Red *and* Silver. They won't be left to fend for themselves against the Lakelander assault while Cal's army concentrates on the armada.

Farley stares down the gullet of the Bridge, standing tall and stoic, a statue against the soldiers moving around her. Her lieutenants bark orders, organizing their troops into predetermined formation. Half form a shield wall of bodies facing Whitefire and War Command, where some of Cal's own Silvers could still be. The others face out, looking down the cliffs to the river or blocking this end of the Bridge.

Essentially trapping Cal between this side of the water and the other, suspended over the armada below.

We reach her without delay, the Scarlet Guard and Montfort soldiers parting to let us pass. Tyton is quick to get to work, hurling his blinding-white darts of electricity at the ships below. The steel leviathans seem impenetrable, even for magnetrons. Blue rumbles in the clouds, before one of Ella's storm bolts hits the prow of a battleship with the keening scream of tearing metal. I squint over the walls of the cliff edge, searching the river. It should be hundreds of feet below, but it seems closer than I remember. My mouth goes dry when I realize the Lakelanders must have raised the river to allow their largest ships to sail this far.

"It's still rising," Farley says over her shoulder, making room for me on her perch. "We won't be able to escape the way we came."

I bite my lip, thinking of the tunnels beneath us. "Flooded?"

She nods. "More than likely." Her eyes waver, looking between the river and the silhouettes on the bridge. Smoke spirals with the fog, black against the white and gray. "We made it through just in time."

Kilorn settles in next to us. His attention is on the Bridge, not the water. From this vantage point, I can see that Cal's forces aren't defending the Bridge, but striking from it. Through the fog, swifts blur along the decks of the boats below, alongside strongarms, Anabel's oblivions, and other Silvers best suited to close combat. Shivers of House Gliacon seem to be making the most headway. They use their abilities to freeze. One of the smaller battleships is completely iced in, frozen against the supports of the Bridge.

I sigh in relief when I don't see fire dancing among the ships. Nothing but the usual explosive blasts. Cal isn't down there fighting the armada himself. *Yet.*

"Do you think he knows we're here?" Kilorn wonders, still looking at the Bridge.

Farley clenches her jaw. She rests her hand at her side, not on her gun but on the radio strapped high on her hip. "Cal seems a bit preoccupied."

"He knows," I mutter, another peal of purple lightning streaking across the sky. The air is thick, like the clouds have come down to obscure the battle raging before us. I flinch as another round strikes the Square, missiles crashing through a wing of the palace.

"I don't see Maven," Farley says, shifting closer to me. I find myself facing the full weight of her cerulean stare, clear and bright even in the haze. "Is it done?"

I bite my lip, almost drawing blood. The sharp pain is better than shame. She reads my hesitation, and her face purples quicker than I thought possible.

"Mare Barrow—"

The crackle of the radio at her side cuts her off, saving me from her rage. She rips it free, snarling into the receiver. "This is General Farley."

The voice on the other end does not belong to a Command general or a Montfort officer. It isn't Davidson either.

I would know that voice anywhere, even punctuated by gunfire.

"I thought you weren't coming back," Cal says, sounding tinny and far away, distorted by static. The electricity in the air must not be very good for radio waves.

Breathless, I look from Farley toward the Bridge. Sure enough, one of the shadows in the fog seems to be solidifying. Broad shoulders and a familiar, determined stride move closer and closer. I keep still, my feet rooted in place on our perch above the fray.

Farley smirks down at her radio. "So nice of you to make time for us."

"It's only polite," he replies.

With a sigh, Farley angles herself toward the form on the Bridge, now less than fifty yards away. Cal is surrounded by his guards, and he halts, stopping the group. The Silvers seem tense, their guns ready, waiting for an order. He acknowledges us with a tip of his head. Farley furrows her brow a little, hesitant.

"I'm guessing you know where things stand, Cal," she says.

His response is almost too quick. "I do."

Farley bites her lip. "And?"

A long rush of static drones, before he speaks again. "Mare?"

The radio is in my hand before I can even think to ask for it.

"I'm here," I say, locking eyes with him across a canyon.

"Is it too late?"

The question has too many implications to count.

Purple, white, green, and blue flash through the clouds, enough to penetrate the mist and blind us all for a moment. Shutting my eyes, I smile with the burst of energy as it thrums through me.

When the lightning passes, I answer him, and everything he means.

"No, it isn't," I tell him, before returning the radio to Farley.

She doesn't stop me as I clamber down the steps, and Cal's guards stand aside when I approach, walking through the broken gates of the ruinous Square.

He waits at the edge of the Archeon Bridge, unmoving. As before, he lets me come to him. He lets me set the pace, choose the direction, make the decision. He puts it all in my hands.

I keep an even step, in spite of the rumblings far below. Something smashes, wailing and roaring. One of the ships, maybe, colliding into another. I hardly notice.

The embrace is short, far too short, but enough. I steady myself against him, holding tightly for as long as I dare, feeling the warm, hard lines of his body pressed against me. He smells like smoke and blood and sweat. His arms cross my back, holding me around the shoulders to pull me into his chest.

"I'm done with crowns," he murmurs to the top of my head.

"Finally," I whisper.

We push back in unison, turning to the situation at hand. We don't have time for anything else, and I certainly don't have the capacity to think about much more.

He raises the radio again, one hand still resting on my shoulder. "General, I believe Volo Samos and some of his own soldiers are still in War Command," he says. Through the mist, I glance at the hulking building on the edge of the Square. "You'll want to keep an eye on your backs."

"Got it, will do," she answers. "Anything else?"

She's on the move, barking orders to her lieutenants, as she relays the advice. Kilorn and Tyton flank her like guards.

"We're working on blocking up the river. If the ships can't turn around . . ."

"They can't escape," I finish for him, glancing out at the destruction on both sides of the city. Missiles spiral overhead, trailing smoke like black ink over paper as they arc and explode.

In spite of Cal's soldiers, as well as the jets overhead, the Lakelander armada doesn't seem to be taking much damage. As I watch, another one of Ella's storm bolts cracks, but a wave rises with blinding speed, taking the brunt of the blow to save a battleship. It lights up with the eerie glow of electricity before fading and falling harmlessly back into the river. It must be Queen Cenra's doing, maybe with her daughter's help. I've never seen such a display of power, even from people who delight in that sort of thing.

Cal watches with me, his face still and grim. "We have to start sinking the ships, but with the river, they have all the shields they'll ever need. Right now it's all we can do to minimize the damage to the city." He curses as a wave knocks back another volley of gunfire. "They have to run out of ammunition eventually, right?" he says dryly.

I glare at the offending ships, eyes running over their steel hides. "Call up some teleporters. Let's get Lerolan oblivions and Evangeline onto a ship. Have them tear some holes."

"Evangeline is gone."

"But you said her father . . ."

Somehow, Cal looks oddly *proud.* "She had an opportunity and she took it."

An opportunity to run and put all this behind her. I don't need much of an imagination to guess where she might be running. Or who she's running with. Like Cal, I feel a strange mix of pride and surprise.

"The train," I say, almost smirking to myself. *Well done,* I can't help but think.

He quirks an eyebrow. "What?"

"In the tunnels, we saw Maven's escape train on the move. It must have been her," I answer. It stings to say his name, and I grimace. A sour taste fills my mouth. "He's here, by the way," I blurt out.

The temperature around us rises a few degrees. Cal's lips drop open in shock. *"Maven?"*

I nod. Heat flares up in my cheeks. "He led us back into the city. To spite you."

Still sputtering, Cal runs a hand over his face. "Well, too bad I can't thank him," he finally mumbles, attempting a smirk. I don't laugh, unable to do much more than bite my lip. "What's that look for?"

It's no use lying. "He slipped us."

He blinks at me. Another missile whines past. "This is a very odd time for a very odd joke, Mare."

I waver, dropping my gaze. *I'm not joking.*

The flamemaker bracelet on his wrist sparks, and he turns the spark to a ball of flame. Angry, surprised, exasperated, he tosses the fiery orb over the edge of the Bridge, letting it singe the fog as it fades.

"So he's somewhere in the city," he snaps. "Fantastic."

"You keep an eye on Kilorn and Farley. I'll find him," I say quickly, putting a hand to his arm. The plates of steel beneath my touch feel like they've been sitting in an oven.

Cal brushes me away gently. He glances back toward the Square again, teeth gritted. "No, I will."

I've always been faster than he is. I dodge his hands with ease, planting myself firmly between him and the Square. Putting my palm on his chest, I hold him at arm's length. "You're a little busy," I say, jerking my chin toward the armada below us.

"A little," he grinds out.

"I can finish this."

"I know you can."

His armor warms beneath my hand, and he covers my fingers with his own.

Then the Bridge buckles beneath us as something slams into it, a dozen times, from all angles. Above, below. Missiles, shells. A crashing wave sends spray up the supports and onto the level where we stand. Heavier in his armor, Cal loses his balance, falling flat while I fight to stay upright.

Except there is no such thing as upright.

The three-tiered Bridge of Archeon, massive stone and steel, bows toward its center, drooping downward. It isn't difficult to guess why. Another explosion shudders, and a spray of debris plummets outward, falling with the central supports of the Bridge.

Cal scrambles, trying to get his feet, and I seize him beneath the arm. I would drag him if I could, but the armor is too heavy.

"Help!" I shout, looking for his guards.

The Lerolan soldiers, his grandmother's own kin, waste no time dragging Cal to his feet. But the Bridge fights us, falling faster and faster, roaring against its own demise.

I scream when the pavement under our feet gives way, slamming into the next tier thirty feet below. I land hard on my side and something cracks in my ribs, sending spiderwebs of pain over me. Hissing, I try to roll and get my bearings. *Get off the Bridge, get off the Bridge* drums in my head.

Cal is already on his knees, a hand outstretched. Not to grab me.

To stop me.

"Don't move!" he screams, fingers splayed.

I freeze midstep, my arm wrapped around my rib cage.

His eyes stand out sharply, so afraid, his pupils blown wide and dark.

Instead of the armada, their guns raining concussive hell upon us, I can only hear one thing. Like a whisper, but worse.

Cracking. Crumbling.

"Cal—"

Everything collapses beneath us.

THIRTY-FOUR
Cal

I fall like a stone.

The useless, patronizing armor that never did anything but slow me down won't protect me from a hundred-foot drop into raging water. It can't save me, and I can't save her. My hands claw through open air, reaching for anything to grab, but the fog just whistles through my fingers. I can't even shout.

Debris tumbles with us, and I brace for the impact of solid concrete. Maybe it'll crush me before I get the chance to drown. What a small mercy that would be.

I try to see her, even as the river rises up to meet me.

Someone grabs me around my middle, arms squeezing so tightly the breath is crushed from my lungs. My vision spots. I might be passing out.

Or not.

I howl as the river and the fog and the crumbling bridge disappear, swallowed up by a blackness. My entire body tightens, tensing up, and when I hit something solid, I expect all my bones to shatter into dust.

But nothing breaks.

"I didn't know kings could scream like that."

My eyes fly open to see Kilorn Warren standing over me, his face pale behind a friendly smile. He offers a hand and I take it gladly, letting him pull me up.

The Montfort teleporter looks on, panting slightly in her green uniform. She's small, almost as small as Mare, and gives me a curt nod.

"Thanks," I gasp, still trying to wrap my brain around surviving.

She shrugs. "Just following orders, sir."

"Will we ever get used to that?" Mare says from a few feet away, still on her knees. She spits a little, looking a green in the face.

Her teleporter, the Montfort officer Arezzo, looks down at her with a smirk. "Would you prefer the alternative?"

Mare just rolls her eyes. She glances at me and sticks out her hand, gesturing for help. Kilorn takes one side, with me on the other, and we pull her to her feet. She pats dirt from her own uniform, the bloodred color of the Scarlet Guard, if only to do something for a moment. She's just as unsettled as I am, though she is loath to show it. I suppose you never get used to being plucked from the jaws of death, no matter how many times it happens.

"How many fell?" she asks, still not looking up.

I bite my lip and glance around, spotting a few Lerolan guards recovering alongside us. But teleporters can only do so much, and I had hundreds of soldiers on the Bridge, with even more below. My stomach churns with the implication. Gritting my teeth, I get my bearings and realize we're back at the edge of the Square, embedded within Farley's troops now rapidly fortifying the cliff. Beyond, a skeleton of the Archeon Bridge remains, collapsed in the middle, with the river boiling below. One of the Lakelander ships is pinned, sinking beneath the weight of a bridge support that fell like a tree in a storm, crashing down on the steel hull. Too heavy, even for the Lakelander queens.

Through the fog, I can't see the far end of the Bridge, but I can only hope the bulk of my forces made it to one of the surviving edges. We didn't have much of an army to begin with, but every life lost is another weight on my shoulders. I feel as if the burden might crush me already, and this battle is far from over.

Mare shifts to stand at my side, looking out as I do. Her fingers lace with mine for a second before she reluctantly pulls away. "I need to find him," she whispers.

As much as I want to help her in such an endeavor, I simply can't. Not unless I want to leave Nanabel in command or, by my colors, *Julian*. Neither is equipped to defend Archeon properly, especially in conjunction with Diana Farley.

"Go," I tell Mare, putting my hand on the small of her back. With a heavy sigh, I give her the slightest push. *Toward my brother. To kill him.* "Be rid of him."

I should be the one to do it. I should have the spine for that.

But I can't bear it. I can't bear the weight of killing him. Not Mavey.

As she goes, Kilorn tagging along with her, I shut my eyes and draw in a long, rattling breath.

How many times do I have to say good-bye to him?

How many times have I lost him?

"The river!" someone barks.

I snap to attention, letting instinct take hold. I trained for years to be a warrior and a general, to see battle inches in front of me and from miles away. Immediately I try to picture the city in my head, split down the middle by the Capital River, now choked with the Lakelander armada. We're cut off from the other side of Archeon, isolated here, with only teleporters for transport. How many, I don't know. But it certainly isn't enough if the Lakelanders decide to turn their attention on the cliffs and the people there.

Farley still holds her perch, a long gun slung over one shoulder. She presses her eyes to a pair of binoculars, looking downward, unmoving. Like a statue, silhouetted by mist and smoke.

"Is it still rising?" I ask, stepping up next to her for a better look. She passes me the binoculars without breaking her stare.

"And rising faster. Look downriver," she adds, jerking her thumb to the south.

It isn't hard to spot what she means. Whitecaps approach, waves breaking in choppy motion, as the Lakelanders pull in more and more water from the ocean. The river surges forward at a steady pace, solidifying into a wall of water like a single, unbroken ripple twenty feet high. I'd bet the river here has risen at least thirty feet so far, and it's about to rise a lot more.

In spite of the Scarlet Guard fortifications, the cliffs take a beating, pieces of rock shearing away as another volley of missiles hits home. I duck, raising an arm to block the debris as it sprays over us. Farley simply turns her head.

"Julian's running the infirmary at the barracks with Sara Skonos. Better get some runners ready," I instruct, watching as a few soldiers turn away from the cliffs, their faces bloody.

"And Anabel?" she replies. Her tone is forcibly neutral.

"War Command."

"With Samos?"

I hesitate, thinking about what Evangeline told me before my coronation. That Julian and Anabel were scheming to kill him. Remove the

Rift from the equation. And maybe buy us some peace with his corpse. If that's the price, I won't stop her.

"Perhaps" is all I can manage before I try to change the subject. "What's your plan?" I ask her. I've never known Diana Farley to strike without some kind of idea, maybe even an outright trick up her sleeve. Especially not with someone like Davidson backing her, not to mention the entire Scarlet Guard. "You've got one, right?"

"We might," she replies. "And you?"

"We were trying to clog up the armada, trap them maybe, force a cease-fire, but those nymph queens are unbeatable on the water."

"Are they?" Farley narrows her eyes at me. "I think that Iris gave you a good scare back in Harbor Bay."

I try not to think about it. The crushing weight of water, pulling me down faster than I thought possible. "Perhaps."

"Well then, we should return the favor."

"Fine. I'll take some oblivions, some teleporters, see if we can—"

To my surprise, she waves me off. I flush, taken aback by her dismissal. "There's no need for that," Farley says, turning away from me. She raises her radio and twists the knob to some corresponding channel. "Premier, how's your side of things?"

Davidson's voice filters back in reply, and I hear echoes of gunfire on his end. "Holding steady for now. Some Piedmontese tried the cliffs, but they didn't expect to run into us. Sent them back."

I imagine Piedmont soldiers in purple and gold, falling from the bank. Split apart by newblood troops.

"What about your end, General?" Davidson presses.

Farley grins. "I've got the more reasonable Calore with me here, and Barrow is going after the other one."

"Premier," I say into the radio, "I have a few hundred Silvers of my own spread between the Bridge ruins and still fighting down on the ships. Can you give them cover?"

"I can do you one better. They need to get off the water, and I'll send my teleporters in now," he replies.

"Mine as well," Farley clips back. "Grab as many as we can before things really heat up."

I glance at her, brow furrowed. "Another wave of ships?"

Her smile spreads. "Something like that."

"Now isn't really the time for surprises."

"Honestly, it's like you've forgotten what we're capable of," she chuckles. It's an odd sight, to see her laughing against the backdrop of war and destruction. "We had to wait until the water was high enough. And luckily for us, those nymph queens were happy to oblige."

I look at the water again, along with the surge now breaking against the ships, raising their hulls until they're level with the lower cliffs. A few more surges and we'll be staring right into their teeth, with every missile and shell pointed our way. *Somehow I don't see how that's a desirable position to be in.*

Farley looks amused by my confusion. "I'm glad you decided to see things our way, Cal."

"The *right* way," I reply. "The way it should be."

Her smile fades, but not in displeasure. Surprise, maybe. For the first time, her touch is gentle, driven by compassion. Her finger graze my shoulder.

"No more kings, Calore."

"No more kings," I echo.

Instead of Farley, the missiles, the ships, the water, the scream of wounded soldiers, I hear my mother's voice. The voice I think she had.

Cal will not be like the others.

She wanted a certain path for me, just like my father. She wanted me to be different, but she still wanted me to be a king.

I hope my choice would make her proud.

"Speaking of kings," Farley mutters; her demeanor changes in an instant. She straightens and points at a figure crossing the Square. "Is that—"

His black cape flutters in the fog, snapping back to reveal limbs coated in perfect, mirrored armor. His steps are sure and quick as he moves through the crowd, soldiers jumping out of his way to let him pass. Without breaking pace, he steps onto the crumbling Bridge.

"Volo Samos," I breathe, gritting my teeth. Whatever he's about to do won't end well for us.

But he doesn't slow, even as the Bridge beneath him becomes more and more precarious. The ships, rising on the forced tide, are almost directly beneath him. And still he doesn't stop.

Not even at the edge.

Farley gasps when he plummets, his body falling slowly, his cape and armor unmistakable through a gap in the fog.

I turn away, unable to watch him break himself on the steel below.

Across the Square, I spy my grandmother, standing resolute, her battle uniform aglow in red and orange. She stares at me through the fray of soldiers.

At her side, Julian hangs his head.

I don't think he's ever killed someone before.

THIRTY-FIVE
Iris

"Another tidal pull and we can off-load directly from the ships," Mother mutters, stepping out of the ship's bridge to stand in the open air. Rain pelts down, beading on her exposed face. I follow her closely, as do her guards. She's armored to the throat, swathed in black and cobalt-blue plate. We won't take any chances. A stray bullet could catch her at any moment and bring our invasion crashing down around our ears.

"Be patient, Mother," I murmur, almost glued to her side. "They won't be able to hold us off for much longer."

I can't help but hope. Tiberias Calore crippled his country so perfectly, betraying his own people as well as the Reds. Casting aside any chance he had to keep the throne he won from his wretched brother.

Archeon will fall, and fall soon.

I glance up at the cliffs on either side of the river, both edges wreathed in smoke and mist. Lightning streaks across the sky, oddly colored, and I'm reminded of my own wedding. The freak Reds and blood traitors of the mountains attacked the city that day, albeit with less success than we are having. The waters of the river thrum around us, caressing the hulls of our armada. I feel it keenly, every curve of the waves, as far as my ability can reach.

The broken Archeon Bridge juts out above us, still crumbling. Debris splashes into the river harmlessly. I raise a hand, batting away a particularly large chunk of concrete with a rising swell of water. Another tumbles after it, falling oddly. It flashes, metallic, as it turns, end over end, hurtling right for the deck of the ship.

My fingers brush against the air, raising another wave, but my mother grabs my wrist.

"Let him fall," she says, her eyes locked on the figure.

I don't realize it's a body until it lands on the deck a few yards in front of us, limbs mangled and skull split open like a melon, spewing silver and white across the deck. His mirrored armor shatters like his bones, some of it splintering into dust at the impact. The wrecked corpse is a tall man, older, judging by the remains of a beard beneath his crumpled face. A fold of his black cape splays over the rest of his body. The fabric is edged in silver.

Familiar colors.

Suddenly the battle seems far away, distant as a dream, and the world at the edge of my vision goes hazy. Everything narrows to this man, destroyed in front of us. No crown on his brow. He doesn't even have a face anymore.

"So ends Volo Samos, and the Kingdom of the Rift," Mother says, stepping neatly to stand over his broken bones. She toes aside his cape and turns the ruined remains of his skull without flinching.

I glance away, unable to look. My stomach flips queasily. "Queen Anabel's trade is complete."

Still examining the corpse, Mother tuts loudly. Her dark eyes run over the dead king, drinking him in. "She thinks this will save her city and her grandson."

Steeling myself, I force my gaze back to Samos. I'm no stranger to blood. Another corpse shouldn't frighten me. *This man is the reason my father is dead, and our country is without its king, my mother without her husband.* He deserves every inch of this ending. And what a brutal ending it was.

"Foolish woman," I seethe, my thoughts turning to Anabel Lerolan and her weak attempt to stop an invasion. *You will not succeed. The price is already paid.*

Satisfied, Mother steps back over the body. She gestures with one hand, and two of our guards begin the gruesome process of removing Samos from the deck. Silver blood streaks like paint as they drag him away.

"We're all fools for the people we love, dear," Mother says airily, clasping her hands in front of her. Without breaking stride, she glances at one of our lieutenants. "Even concentration on both sides of the city, focused on the massing troops."

With a nod, the officer ducks back into the command bridge, and her orders are relayed across the armada. Both Lakelander and Piedmontese ships respond in kind, their guns erupting with a volley of fire. Explosions and smoke crackle along the riverbanks, shearing off cliff rock as well as city structures. After a moment, our enemies on both sides return fire, but weakly. Most bullets ping off steel or sink in the water.

Mother watches with a grim smile. "Break their lines and we'll have an easy way of it, once the river is high enough." She's thinking about the thousands of soldiers belowdecks, waiting to spring from our ships and overrun whoever waits above.

A harsh wind blows up, carrying with it the sound of jets screaming far overhead. I grit my teeth. The Nortan Air Fleet is their only measure of superiority, with Piedmont's fleet diminished and our own sorely lacking in comparison. All we can do is hold them at bay with the storm, using our own meager jets to distract them from the armada. It seems to be working, for now, at least.

As for the Nortan soldiers Tiberias foolishly sent down among us, the deck troops aren't having a difficult time holding them off. Even with strongarms and swifts leading the charge, the many nymphs of House Osanos use the river to their advantage. *Our* advantage.

Even now, I can see their numbers dwindling. "Teleporters," I snarl, watching as the Montfort oddities blink in and out of existence. They snatch away the last of the Nortans, returning them to the relative safety of the city cliffs.

"They're retreating from the ships." I turn to Mother, torn between pride and disappointment. The Nortans fear us enough to run. "What's left of them, at least."

The queen of the Lakelands raises her chin, looking imperious and regal. "Recalling to make a last stand. Good."

I'm quickly struck by the image of my mother striding boldly through Caesar's Square, up the steps of the palace that was once my glorified prison, to sit the throne the Calores have finally lost. Will my mother be an empress when all this is done? Master of all between the lakes and the sea, from the frozen tundra to the radiated borders of the Wash? *Don't get ahead of yourself, Iris. The battle is not yet won.*

I try to center myself in the moment. The sharp tang of smoke and Samos's blood is a good anchor. I inhale sharply, letting the smell overwhelm my senses. It's funny, I expected this anger inside me to waste away and die with the Samos king. But I still feel it, deep in my chest, gnawing at my heart. My father is dead, and no throne, no crown, can bring him back. No amount of vengeance paid can push away this pain.

I draw another breath, focusing on the waters below us. The envoy of our gods, it carries every blessing and curse. Normally, the sensation would calm me down. Being so close to such power has a way of humbling even me. Right now, I sense no gods that I recognize.

But I do sense something.

"Do you feel that?" I whirl to my mother. The armor all over my body seems to tighten, threatening to smother me as every one of my nerve endings lights up with fear. *What is that—that* thing *in the water?*

Mother blinks at me, reading my unease. Her eyes glaze for a moment as she reaches out with her own considerable ability, hunting through the waves for what has me so on edge. I watch, breathless, waiting for her to tell me it's nothing. My imagination. Confusion. A mistake.

She sharpens, her eyes narrowing to slits, and the rain suddenly feels like icicles down my spine.

"Another current?" she hisses, snapping her fingers at one of the officers nearby. A Nortan betrayer, he is quick to oblige, his face drawn and pale. He still seems uncomfortable in the blue uniform of the Lakelands. "Osanos," she barks at him, "are your nymphs pulling another tide—"

He shakes, bowing low. Osanos and his extended family aren't as talented as us, but they're formidable in their own right. Not to mention integral to our efforts. "Not by my orders, Your Majesty."

I bite my lip, my sensation still edging around the gargantuan *thing* moving through the water. I try to push it off course, but the object is just too heavy. "A whale?" I mutter, hardly believing my own suggestion.

Mother shakes her head, teeth on edge. "Bigger, heavier," she says. "And more than one."

Behind us, the ship officers scramble in the command bridge, reacting to a sudden dozen blinking lights and alarms. The sound hits me like knives.

"Brace for impact!" one of them shouts, gesturing for us to take cover.

Mother grabs me, her arm sliding around my waist to hold me close. We watch in horror, feeling the currents below us as the many somethings move through the armada. They must be mechanical, weapons of war we have no knowledge of.

The first strike comes in the middle of the fleet, a battleship suddenly leaning with a groan of tearing metal. An explosion erupts below the waterline, blowing out in an arc of foam and shrapnel. A Piedmont ship catches fire, its powder magazine obliterating the front half of the hull. The blast of heat feels like a burn, but I can't turn away, watching in horrified awe as the ship sinks in less than a minute, drowning gods know how many within its belly.

Our flagship shudders under us, clanking as something rams the hull beneath the surface.

"Push, Iris, push," Mother commands, letting go of me to rush to the edge of the deck. She leans forward, arms outstretched, and the waters below obey her will, rushing backward in waves.

I join her, letting my ability take hold. I press and push, trying to dislodge whatever is ramming the ship. But it's so heavy, so big, with an engine of its own.

We're so focused on protecting the flagship, I hardly notice the rest of the armada floundering all around us. Without orders, a few of the ships painstakingly try to turn, navigating the foaming river among the growing steel hulks bobbing and sinking. Sweat breaks out across my brow, joining with the hurtling rain, and I taste salt on my lips. It stings, forcing me to blink and lose focus.

"Mother," I force out.

She doesn't answer, her hands clawed into the mist, as if she can lift the new weaponry directly out of the water. She snarls a little, the sound lost in the howling wind.

Lightning flashes again, another blue bolt striking down. I'm not fast enough to deflect it and it hits home on the ship next to us, striking the deck with the sizzle of water and flesh. Soldiers scream, leaping off the ship entirely to escape the glowing hell of electrocution. They're quickly swallowed by the churning waters.

"Mother!" I say again, shouting this time.

She curses through gritted teeth. "Those Red bastards have boats below the water. Boats and weapons."

"We can't stop them, can we?"

Her eyes shine, bright even against the storm and the sudden shift in our fortunes. Without warning, she drops her hands. "Not without great loss. And not with any guarantees," she murmurs, as if dazed.

I try to shake her out of it. "We have to get up to the cliffs, get on land. We can still overwhelm their forces—"

Behind us, our guards close in, tense and ready to spring. Waiting for my mother's command.

She ignores them, staring at me instead. "Can we?" she says, her voice oddly soft and detached. Like she's been sleeping, and now she is awake.

Mother pats me on the cheek, her touch cold and wet. She looks past me, fixating on the deck. I turn to follow her gaze, only to see the last of Samos's blood darkening against the steel. The last piece of our revenge. Even the rain can't wash it away. Even the gods can't heal this pain.

I flinch as another ship succumbs to attack, keeling over into the river. "Is this finally ended?" I wonder aloud.

Her fingers lace with mine.

"Ended?" she breathes, squeezing my hand. "Never, not truly. But for now, I'm getting my daughter out of here alive."

For the first time today, I look backward, downriver. Toward retreat. I swallow hard, dazed by the sudden turn in the battle. It feels like being cut open.

But there is only one choice between death and defeat.

"Let's go home."

THIRTY-SIX
Maven

After so many days in captivity, smothered by Silent Stone and separated from my bracelets, the burst of flame is more quenching than water to a thirsty man. I let it lick up inside me, trailing like a lover's kiss, and explode along my skin, powerful and furious enough to throw back that wretched electricon. He falls and Mare falls too, both of them slamming backward onto the hard tile of Caesar's Square.

I don't spare a glance for her as I run, leaving fire in my wake, a wall to defend my escape. I keep another burst of flame close, coiling in my fist, using all my energy to keep it burning. My feet carry me over the Square and I sprint like never before. I'm not Cal, I'm not particularly fast or strong, but fear keeps me alert and daring. The chaos of Archeon works to my advantage, not to mention my intimate knowledge of the palace. Whitefire was my home, and I have not forgotten it.

The sudden arrival of hundreds of Scarlet Guard soldiers is more than enough to distract Cal's troops, still trying to organize themselves against the Lakelander assault. Nevertheless, I keep my head down, black hair falling forward to obscure my all-too-recognizable face.

These soldiers were mine. Should still be mine.

The voice in my head shifts from my own to hers.

Fools, all of them, my mother sneers. I can almost feel her hands ghosting along my shoulders, keeping me upright as I run. *Replacing you with that wretched, spineless boy. He will be the end of a dynasty. The end of an age.*

She isn't wrong. She was never truly wrong.

If only Father could see you now, Cal. See what you've become, and what you've done to his kingdom.

Of all my many wishes and regrets, that one cuts deepest. My father is dead, but he died loving Cal, trusting Cal, believing in Cal's greatness and perfection. I wonder if I should have let things run their course. If somehow I could have simply made him see how flawed the perfect son was.

But Mother had her reasons. She knew best.

And that is simply another path untaken. A dead future, as Jon would say.

Another missile explodes nearby, and as before, I use the resulting explosion to my advantage. It breaks around me, harmless, allowing me to escape through a bloom of smoke and fire. I can't return to the Treasury tunnels, not with those Red rats still crawling around. But there are other ways down to the tracks, other ways to get out of Archeon undetected. The ways I know best are in Whitefire itself, and I beat a path to the palace as quickly as I can.

That damn train. I curse whoever stole it, whatever sniveling weasel is now riding along, safe and sound. At least I can still walk the track. I'm well accustomed to darkness by now. What's a few more miles?

Nothing at all. I've always felt darkness all over me, stubborn as a stain. It follows wherever I go.

And where will *I* go? Where *can* I go?

I'm a fallen king, a murderer, a betrayer. A monster to anyone with eyes and a modicum of sense. They'll kill me in the Lakelands, in Montfort, in my own country. *I deserve it,* I think as I run. *I should be dead a thousand times, executed in a hundred different ways, each one more painful than the last.*

I think of Mare behind me, sprawled across the tiles of the Square. Picking herself up again, ready to give chase. My brother too, leading some stupidly valiant effort to defend the city and his ill-gotten throne. I scoff at the thought as I vault up the steps of Whitefire, flying over familiar stone. The flame in my palm gutters, reducing to a flicker before I push it back to life, letting it envelop my hand.

The interior is just as empty as the Square is full. Whatever nobles and courtiers aren't out fighting must be deep within the palace, barricaded in their rooms, or perhaps they've fled too. Either way, my footsteps are the only sound as I cross the entrance hall, my path familiar as my own heartbeat.

Even though it's midday, the halls are dark and cold, with the windows clouded by fog and smoke. Electricity flickers as the power grid reacts to the battle outside, turning the lights on and off in patternless bursts. *Good,* I think. In my gray clothing, I can blend into the shadows of Whitefire. I used to do it as a boy, hide in alcoves or behind curtains. Spying and listening, not for my mother then, but for my own curiosity.

Cal used to spy with me, when he had the time. Or cover for me at Lessons, telling tutors I was sick or otherwise detained. Odd, that I can remember all that, but that the emotion behind it, the connection we must have had, is almost entirely gone. Severed or surgically removed by my mother. And no one can ever make it grow back.

Even though he tried. He searched. He wanted to save you. The thought almost makes me vomit, and I push it away.

The doors of the throne room are heavier than I expected. Funny to think I've never opened them myself. There's always been a guard or a Sentinel, usually a telky. I feel weak as I drive my shoulder into one, pushing it ajar enough to slip through.

My throne is gone, the Silent Stone dragged away to only Cal knows where. Our father's seat is returned, the inferno carved from diamondglass. I sneer at the sparkling monstrosity, a symbol of our father, his crown, and everything he lacked. Other chairs flank Cal's throne, one for Julian Jacos and one for our grandmother. The thought of both makes my lip curl. Without them, Cal would never have made it this far. And that snake Iris would have never handed me over.

I hope she drowns on the river, suffocated by her own ability.

No, better yet, I hope she *burns*. Isn't that the punishment of her gods, to suffer forever beneath an opposing element? Maybe Iris and Cal will manage to kill each other. They came so close last time.

A boy can certainly hope.

The door to the left of the throne is smaller, leading to the king's private rooms, including a study, meeting areas, and the council chamber. As I step into the long room lined with shelving, the lights switch off again, plunging me into semidarkness. The windows in here are tall, looking out on a gray, empty courtyard. I pass them quickly, counting. *One, two, three . . .*

After the fourth window, I stop and count shelves. *Three up . . .*

Thankfully, Cal hasn't had time to rearrange the books in here. Or else he would have discovered the mechanism attached to a leather-bound tome regarding economic fluctuations during the last decade.

It glides forward with the lightest pull, activating rotating gears behind the lacquered wood. The entire shelf swings forward, revealing a narrow stairwell cut into the exterior wall.

Using my still-burning flame as a torch, I plunge downward, letting the shelf swing into place behind me.

The darkness is thick with damp and the air is stale. I suck it down anyway, careful on the steps as I descend. This is an old servants' stair, long out of use, but it still connects to the other passages beneath the palace. From there I can get to the Treasury, War Command, the courts, or any other place of value around Caesar's Square. My ancestors built these passages for use during war and siege. I'm glad for their foresight, as well as my own.

The steps empty out into a wider hall lined with rough stone, the floor beneath sloping at a gentle decline. I plod along, daring to breathe a bit deeper and slower. There's a battle raging above my head, but I'm long gone. The only people who know about these tunnels are otherwise preoccupied.

I might actually survive this.

Then something flickers ahead, a reflection of fire, but distorted somehow, rippling. I slow my pace, shuffling my feet to muffle the sound of my steps. Another deep breath, and I smell water.

Those fucking Lakelanders.

The path ahead of me slopes into black water, its surface reflecting my flaming hand. I feel like punching a wall. Instead I curse against gritted teeth. In spite of the wet, I take a few steps forward, until the water laps over my ankles, chilling me to the bone. It only gets deeper. Furious, I trudge back out, kicking at the dirt floor. A few bits skitter, plopping into the inscrutable flood. I bite back another curse and turn, hurrying back the way I came.

My body burns with frustration, and heat spreads over my cheeks.

Another stair, another tunnel, I tell myself, even though I know exactly where that will lead.

Another flooded passage. Another barred escape.

The walls suddenly feel too close, pressing down from every side. I quicken my pace, the fire in my hand waning as I begin to stumble. My fingers graze the stone within reach, brushing over the uneven surface as I reach the steps again. I'm almost sprinting when I reach the top and spill out again into the fresh air of the adjoining chamber.

If I can't get into the tunnels, I'll have to go over the walls. Somehow get up and down, and head west, avoiding the slums upriver, the vast estates ringing the land around the capital. *I'll need to disguise my face somehow.* Instead of focusing, my mind spirals out, paralyzed by fear. I need to stay on the task at hand—get out of the city—but everything blurs. I need food, a map, supplies. Every step aboveground is a step toward danger. They'll hunt me down and kill me. Mare and my brother, if they manage to survive.

I raid the study first, searching in vain for anything that might be of use. Bracelets especially. Flamemakers. Cal might keep a spare somewhere, but there's nothing in the many drawers and compartments of the fine desk that was once mine. I contemplate a particularly sharp letter opener for a moment, holding the daggerlike piece of metal up to a ray of weak light. With a swipe of my hand, I draw a slice across a painting of my father. Even mangled, his face still taunts me, eyes burning from the ripped canvas. I tighten my grip on the letter opener as I turn away, unable to face his stare for very long.

The royal bedchamber is next. I blink and I'm there, nearly kicking the doors off their hinges. But I stop short, perplexed. Instead of a luxurious suite fit only for the king of Norta, I find empty rooms stripped of furnishings and even paint. No curtains, no rugs. Nothing but a haphazard collection of cleaning supplies.

Cal isn't sleeping here. Not while bits of me still linger. *Coward.*

This time I really do punch a wall, leaving my knuckles raw and smarting.

I have no way of knowing which room might be his. The residence wings are home to dozens of bedrooms, and I hardly have time to search them all. I'll have to settle for stealing what I can outside the city. Flint and steel make sparks as easily as any bracelet. I can acquire that. *Somehow.*

My vision blurs at the edges, an odd haze that pulses in time with my rapidly increasing heartbeat. I shake my head, trying to make the sensation dissipate, but it stays put. A pain springs up in my skull, digging into the bone. I suck down another breath, forcing myself to take big gasps of air in an attempt to calm down. As in the tunnel, the walls feel too close and like they're getting closer by the second. I wonder if the windows are about to shatter all over me, cutting my flesh to ribbons.

I trip on the stairs as I make my way back down to the throne room. *No choice, Maven,* Mother croons to me as I slip in again. That's all I get. She was never one to advise retreat or surrender. Elara Merandus gave no ground in life, and she instilled the same instinct in me. My headache spreads, arcing across my skull in a web of sharp pain.

Above me, the lights kick on again, so brightly they whine in their bulbs. The electricity surge is too strong.

One by one, they pop, raining smashed glass along the polished floor behind me. I manage to dodge as the bulb directly above me shrieks apart.

The filaments continue to burn, sparking white.

And purple.

Stoic, calm and deadly, Mare Barrow stands firm, silhouetted in the narrow opening. Without blinking, she slides through and shuts the door behind her. Locking us both in. Together.

"It's over, Maven," she whispers.

This time, I sprint for the other side of the throne and burst into another set of rooms usually reserved for the queen. I made my own modifications to them. Modifications that would disagree with most.

Mare is faster than I am, but she follows at a languid pace. Haunting me. Teasing me. She could run me down at any second. Electrocute me with one well-aimed bolt of lightning.

Good, I think. *Keep on coming, Barrow.*

I feel the telltale twinge up ahead. The empty ache that plagues all Silvers and newbloods. One more door to push open. One last chance to survive where so many others would die.

I will not fail, Mother.

Grinning, I turn around, letting her watch me as I back farther into the dark chamber. The single window is small, and a weak light fills the space. Illuminating the dark walls, patterned like a checkerboard of gray and black. The gray bits gleam dully, showing ribbons of liquid silver. *Arven blood, Silence blood.*

She hesitates at the threshold, feeling the press of Silent Stone. I watch it ruin her.

The color drains from her face, and she almost looks Silver in the cold, gray light. I keep walking, back and back. To the next door. The next passage. My chance.

She doesn't stop me.

Her throat bobs as she swallows around the fear clawing at her. I gave her this wound. I locked her away in chains, drained her ability, made her live like a wasting ghost. If she steps forward, she'll have no weapons at all. No shield. No guarantee.

The letter opener in my hand feels suddenly heavy.

I could drop it. Leave the blade and run.

I could let her live.

Or I could kill her.

The choice is easy. And so very difficult.

I hold my ground.

My grip tightens on the iron.

THIRTY-SEVEN
Mare

The room is a coffin. A maw of stone that will swallow me whole. I feel dead, even on the threshold, hesitating to fully succumb to this place and the person who built it.

My heart pounds so loudly I know Maven can hear it.

His eyes trace over me in a way that is too familiar and too close, despite the yards between us. He focuses on my throat, on the vein pulsing with all my fear. I expect him to lick his lips. My hand flexes in vain, attempting to call up a bolt of lightning. All I get are weak sparks, darkly purple, dying quickly against the might of so much Silent Stone.

Something gleams in his hand, flashing in the dim light. A knife, I think, thin and small but sharp enough.

My hand strays to my hip, for the pistol Tyton harangued me into wearing. But the holster is gone entirely, probably lost in the Bridge collapse. I gulp again. I have no weapons at all.

And Maven knows it.

He grins, teeth white and wicked. "Aren't you going to try to stop me?" he says, tipping his head like some curious puppy.

My mouth feels dry when I speak. "Don't make me do this, Maven." It comes out raspy.

Maven just shrugs. Somehow he manages to make his simple gray clothing look like silk and fur and steel. He isn't a king anymore, but no one seems to have told him.

"I'm not making you do anything," he says imperiously. "You don't have to suffer this. You can stand right there, or even turn around. It makes no difference to me."

I force another breath, stronger than before. The too-familiar memory of Silent Stone claws up my spine. "Don't make me kill you like this," I growl, sounding dangerous and lethal.

"What are you going to do, stare at me?" he shoots back dryly. "I'm terrified."

It's a brash show, his forced nonchalance. I know Maven well enough to see the truth in his words, the real fear weaving through his practiced arrogance. His eyes dart, quicker than before, not over my face, but my feet. So he can move when I move. Run when I lunge.

In spite of the dagger, he's without his weapons too.

I don't tremble when I take the first, slow step, sliding into the prison of Silent Stone.

"You should be."

Maven stumbles back, surprised, almost tripping over himself. But he recovers quickly, the dagger tight in his hand as I continue forward. He mirrors my movements, stepping backward. The lethal dance is achingly slow, and we never break our stare. We don't even blink. I feel as if I'm walking a tightrope over a pit of wolves, barely keeping balance. One wrong move and I'll fall to their fangs.

Or maybe I'm the wolf.

I see myself in his eyes. And his mother. And Cal. All we did to get here, in the middle of the end of his world. I lied and was lied to. Betrayed and was betrayed. I hurt people, and so many people hurt me. I wonder what Maven sees in my eyes.

"It won't end here," he murmurs, his voice low and smooth. I'm reminded of Julian and his melodic ability. "You can drag my corpse across the world, and it won't end any of this."

"Likewise," I reply, showing my teeth. The inches close between us, in spite of his best efforts. I'm more agile than he is. "The Red dawn won't stop with me."

He offers a twisting smirk. "Then it seems we're both dispensable. We don't matter anymore."

I bark out a laugh. I've never mattered the way he still does. "I'm used to it."

"I like the hair," Maven murmurs, filling the empty space. His eyes run over the tangle of brown and purple spilling over one shoulder. I don't reply.

The last card he plays is obvious, but it still stings. Not because I want what he offers, but because I remember a girl who would have accepted it. She knows better now.

"We can still run." His voice deepens, letting the offer hang in the air. "Together."

I should laugh at him. Twist the knife. Make him suffer as much as I can in these last moments we have. Instead I feel some piece of my heart break for someone so irrevocably lost. And I feel true sorrow for the other brother in the midst of all this, who tried and failed. Who never deserved what's happening now.

"Maven," I sigh, shaking my head at his blindness. "The last person who loves you isn't standing in this room. He's out there. And you burned that bridge to ashes."

He goes deathly still, face white as bone. Not even his icy eyes move. When I take another step, coming within arm's length, he doesn't seem to notice. I ball a fist at my side, bracing myself.

Slowly, he blinks. And I see nothing in him.

Maven Calore is empty.

"Very well."

The dagger cuts at my throat, swiping with vicious and blistering speed. I lean backward, dodging the blow without thought. He keeps coming, keeps slicing, saying nothing. My body reacts before my brain, all instinct as I deflect his strikes. I'm faster than he is, and my arms swing in time with his movements, catching his wrists before he can do any damage with the tiny, wicked gleam of sharp iron.

I have nothing except my own fists and feet. My focus is on keeping the dagger away from my skin, and I barely land any blows of my own. I twist, trying to trip him with a hooked ankle, but he steps neatly over the attempt. My first mistake, leaving my back exposed. I move as he does, and a stab for my lungs becomes a long but shallow gash across my side. Hot, red blood wells up, filling the air with a copper tang.

I almost expect him to apologize. Maven has never truly delighted in my pain. But he gives no quarter. And neither do I.

Ignoring the spreading pain, I jab at his throat with a closed fist, hitting hard. He wheezes and stumbles, dropping to a knee. I strike again, kicking him across the jaw. The momentum sends him sideways, his eyes wide and dazed as he spits silver blood in all directions. If not for the dagger, I would use the opportunity to get my arms around his throat and squeeze until his body is cold.

Instead I leap, using my weight to keep him pinned as I fight the fingers still clawed around the dagger hilt. He growls beneath me, in spite of the jaw, trying to force me off.

I have to use my teeth.

The taste of silver blood poisons my mouth when I clamp down on his fingers, cutting through flesh straight to the bone. His growls turn to wailing screams. The sound rips into me, made worse by the effect of Silent Stone. Everything hurts more than it should.

I push through it and pry his fingers off, biting where I must, until the dagger is mine. It's slick with his blood and mine, silver and red, darker by the second.

Suddenly his other hand is around my throat, squeezing without any restraint, crushing the air from my windpipe. He's heavier than me and uses his weight to fling me onto my back. One of his knees digs into my shoulder, keeping my dagger arm pinned. The other presses into my collarbone, right over the brand he gave me. It shrieks and stings beneath the pressure, and I feel the bone crack with an agonizing slowness.

It's my turn to scream.

"I tried, Mare," he hisses, his cold breath washing over my face. Still struggling for air, I can't do much more than gasp and choke. My vision splits and spots, leaving only his eyes above me. Too blue, too frozen, inhuman in their blankness. They are not the eyes of a fire prince. This is not Maven Calore. That boy is gone, lost. Whoever he was born as will not be buried with him.

My neck aches, bruising beneath his fingers as blood vessels burst. I can barely think, my mind narrowing to the dagger still clenched in my fist. I try to raise my arm again, but Maven's weight makes it impossible.

Tears prick at my eyes when I realize this is how it ends. No lightning, no thunder. I'll die a Red girl, one of thousands crushed beneath a Silver crown.

Maven's grip on my throat never loosens. If anything, it becomes tighter, crushing the muscles in my neck until I feel like my spine might snap clean. The world dims, the spots across my vision spreading like black rot.

But Maven leans. Slightly, in the smallest way. Putting more pressure on my broken collarbone. And less on my shoulder.

Enough to free my arm.

I don't think. I just swing wildly, blade ready, as his eyes fade. They seem sad and . . .

Satisfied.

Before I open my eyes, I'm intensely aware of how big my tongue feels in my mouth. An odd thing to fixate on, against everything else. I try to swallow, which only exacerbates the pain in my throat. It flares up, angry, as the muscles in my neck scream in protest. I tense against the pain, limbs shifting beneath the blanket of the bed . . . wherever I am.

"Give Sara a second," I hear Kilorn say, his voice close at my ear. He stinks of sweat and smoke. "Don't move if you can help it."

"Okay," I rasp, and that hurts worse than anything before.

He laughs a bit. "Don't speak either. Might be a bit difficult for you."

Normally, I'd hit him, or tell him how wretched he smells. But feeling rather restrained, I elect to keep my eyes shut and jaw clenched against the ache. Sara shuffles around the bed, her touch lingering as she weaves around to my left side.

She puts her blissful hands to my neck, and I realize that the gash on my ribs must be gone. I can't feel it anymore.

She tips my head just so, forcing me to lift my chin in spite of the pain. I wince, hissing a little, and Kilorn puts a steadying hand on my wrist. Sara's healing ability quickly mitigates my discomfort, pooling over the bruises and swelling.

"Your vocal cords aren't as bad as I expected," she muses. Sara Skonos has a lovely voice, light like a bell. After so many years without a tongue, one might think she would make up for lost time, but she still speaks sparingly, her words chosen with careful intention. "They won't be difficult."

"Take your time, Sara. No rush," Kilorn mutters.

I snap my eyes open, glaring at him as he grins.

The lights above are bright, but not harsh, hardly the fluorescent sharpness one might expect from an infirmary. I blink, trying to place myself. With a jolt, I realize I'm not in the infirmary of the barracks at all, but in one of the palace bedrooms. No wonder the bed is so soft and the room is so quiet.

Kilorn lets me look around, giving me the space I need. I shift, turning my wrist so I can take his hand in mine. "So you're still kicking around." Already my throat hurts less, only twinging. Hardly enough to keep me quiet.

"In spite of my best efforts," he replies, giving me a reassuring squeeze. I can see where he tried to wipe his face, leaving streaks of clean skin edged by dirt and blood. The rest of him is just as filthy, which makes him stand out like a sore thumb against the elegant trappings of the palatial bedroom. "Mostly, I just stayed out of the way."

"Finally," I mutter. Sara's fingers continue their dance across my neck, spreading a soothing warmth. "Someone beat some sense into you."

He chuckles. "It certainly took long enough."

The smile, the easy manner on him, even the way he holds his shoulders without weight or tension—it can only mean one thing. "So

I'm guessing we won," I sigh, too surprised to even comprehend what that means. I have no idea what a real victory would even look like.

"Not entirely." Kilorn rubs a hand over his dirty cheek, smearing the grime across the clean parts of him. *Idiot,* I think kindly. "The mersives were enough to scare off the armada, and the Lakelanders managed to limp back out to sea. I think the big shots are still negotiating a cease-fire now."

I try to sit up a little, only to have Sara press me back down gently. "But not surrender?" I ask, forced to watch Kilorn from the corner of my eye.

He shrugs. "It could become one. But no one tells me much of anything," he adds with a good-natured wink.

"A cease-fire isn't permanent." I grit my teeth, thinking of the Lakelanders returning a year from now. "They won't let this last—"

"Could you just enjoy being alive for one damn second?" Kilorn chuckles, shaking his head at me. "You'll at least be pleased to know there's a joint effort under way to start cleanup of the city. Silver and Red." He puffs out his chest, very proud of his report. "Cameron and her father are on their way down too. They're coordinating with Cal for worker compensation."

Worker compensation. Fair pay. A symbolic gesture, at the very least. Even if Cal is no longer a king, and whatever control he had over the country is gone. I doubt he has much, if any, say in what happens to the Treasury. And frankly, I'm not concerned with that right now.

Kilorn knows it. But he dances around the information I want, trying to lead me away.

Slowly, I shift my gaze to Sara as she works. Up close, she smells as soothing as her touch, carrying a fresh scent like clean linens. Her steel-gray eyes focus on my neck, finishing up the last of my bruises.

"Sara, do we have a casualty count?" I ask quietly.

Kilorn shifts uncomfortably in the chair next to my bed, coughing a little. He shouldn't be surprised by the question.

Sara certainly isn't. She doesn't break her rhythm. "Don't worry yourself with that," the skin healer answers.

"Everyone's alive," Kilorn offers quickly. "Farley, Davidson. Cal."

I already knew as much. He wouldn't be smiling, and I would have woken up to a great deal more chaos, if any of them had died. No, he knows exactly what I'm asking. Who I'm asking about.

"All done," Sara says, ignoring my question fully. Instead she offers a tight-lipped smile as she steps back from my bedside. "You should rest now. You need it, Mare Barrow."

Nodding, I watch her go, seeing herself out of the bedroom with a sweep of her silvery clothing. Unlike the other healers I remember, she has no uniform to speak of anymore. Probably ruined in the battle, when she attended to so many dead or dying. The door closes softly behind her, leaving Kilorn and me to weather the heavy silence.

"Kilorn," I finally mutter, prodding at him with tentative fingers.

He glances at me, watching with a pained expression as I draw myself up against the pillows. Ashamed, his eyes flicker to my healed side. Even though the wound is gone, his expression darkens.

So does his voice. "You were bleeding to death when we found you," he whispers, as if even the memory is too horrible to recall at a normal volume. "We didn't know if you would . . . if Sara could . . ." His voice trails away, laced with a pain I know all too well.

I've seen Kilorn bleeding to death too, when he nearly lost his life in New Town. I guess I repaid the favor. Swallowing hard, I touch my ribs, feeling nothing but unbroken skin beneath the folds of a fresh shirt. I guess the gash was worse than I thought. Not that it matters anymore.

"And . . . Maven?" I can barely say his name.

Kilorn holds my gaze, his expression unchanging. Giving no indication of an answer for an agonizing moment. Long enough for me to wonder what answer I'm hoping to get. Which future I want to live in.

When he drops his eyes, focusing on my hands, my blankets, anywhere but my face, I realize what he's saying. A muscle twitches in his cheek as he clenches his jaw.

Something in me unwinds, a coil finally springing loose. I sigh and lie back, shutting my eyes as a storm of emotions rolls over me. All I can do is bear it as the world spins.

Maven is dead.

Shame and pride battle in equal measure, as well as sorrow and relief. For a second, I think I might actually throw up. But the nausea passes and I open my eyes again to find everything in its place.

Kilorn waits silently. It's odd for him to be so patient. Or it would have been, a year ago. When he was just the fish boy, another kid from the Stilts with no future but whatever tomorrow held. I was the same.

"Where is the body?"

"I don't know," he says, and I see no lie in him. He has no reason to lie about this.

As with Elara, I'll need to see the corpse. To know it's well and truly finished. But his body frightens me more than hers, for obvious reason. Death is a mirror, and to look at him like that . . . I'm afraid I'll see myself. Or worse, see *him* as I thought he was.

"Does Cal know what I did?" My voice breaks as I speak, suddenly fraught with emotion. I press a hand to my mouth, trying to calm myself. I refuse to cry over him. I refuse.

Kilorn merely watches. I wish he would hug me, or hold my hand, or maybe bring me something sweet to stuff in my mouth. Instead he pulls away to stand up. He looks on me with such pity, it makes me wince. I don't expect him to understand and I don't want him to.

Like Sara, he crosses to the door, and I feel suddenly abandoned.

"Kilorn—" I protest, until he turns the knob.

And someone else steps into the room.

Cal fills the chamber with warmth, as if someone just lit a crackling fire. His gleaming red armor is gone, replaced by simple clothing. He wears a mismatch of colors, without a stitch of black or scarlet. Because they aren't his colors anymore. Kilorn slips out behind him, leaving us alone.

Before I can even wonder if Cal heard my question, he answers it.

"You only did what you had to do," he says, slowly taking Kilorn's chair. But he keeps his distance, letting the inches stretch between us in a gaping rift.

It isn't difficult to guess why.

"I'm sorry." He goes watery before me as tears rise in my eyes. *I killed his brother. I took him away.* I killed a murderer, a torturer. An evil person, twisted and broken. A man who would have killed me if I hadn't stopped him. Killed everyone I love. A boy, made into a monster. A boy with no chance and no hope. "Cal, I'm so sorry."

He leans forward, one hand on my blanket. Careful to keep out of reach. The silk beneath our fingers is smooth and cold, a long road of blue-gray embroidery. He stares at the pattern on the blanket, tracing the thread without speaking. I fight the urge to sit up and touch his cheek, to make him look me in the eye and say what he wants to say.

We both knew this would happen. We both knew Maven was

beyond our help. It doesn't stop the pain, though. And his is so much deeper than mine.

"What now?" he whispers, as if to himself.

Or maybe we were wrong. Maybe he could have been saved somehow. The thought cuts me apart, and the first tear falls. *Maybe I'm just a murderer too.*

Only one thing is certain. We will never know.

"What now," I reply, turning away.

I stare at the window, the sky spotted with haze and weak starlight.

Minutes stretch and pass. We don't speak. No one comes to see me, or find Cal to pull him away. I almost wish someone would.

Until his fingers move, brushing against mine. Barely touching.

But it's enough.

EPILOGUE

Mare

"Are you sure you don't want to go back and see it?"

I stare at Kilorn like he's just grown a second head. The suggestion is so absurd, I almost don't answer. But he looks at me, expectant, innocent as a child. Or at least as innocent as he can be. Kilorn was never particularly innocent, even when we were children.

He shoves his hands in the pockets of his Montfort uniform, waiting for my response.

"See what?" I scoff, shrugging my shoulders as we walk across the Archeon airfield. Clouds hang low on the horizon, obscuring the setting sun, as well as the smoke still trailing from parts of the city. It's been a week, and they're still putting out fires. "A house on rickety sticks? It's probably ransacked, if someone else isn't living there," I mutter, thinking of my old home in the Stilts. I haven't been back and I have little desire to ever return. I wouldn't be surprised if the stilt house were no longer standing. I can easily imagine Maven destroying it out of spite. When he was alive. I don't care to find out either way.

"Why, do *you* want to go back to the Stilts?"

Kilorn shakes his head, almost bouncing in his steps. "Nope. Anything I cared about isn't there anymore."

"Flattery will get you nowhere," I reply. He seems oddly eager to return to Montfort. "What about Cameron?" I add, careful to keep my voice low. Currently, Cameron and her parents are helping everyone else coordinate with the tech towns. Obviously, they know the former slums best, and how to repurpose them.

"What about her?" Kilorn smirks down at me, offering a shrug of his own. He's trying to throw me off. A hint of a flush dusts his cheeks with color. "She'll be coming out to Montfort in a month or so, with the Red Nortan contingent and some newbloods. Once things are a bit more settled."

"To train?"

His blush spreads. "Sure."

I can't help but grin. *Must remember to tease him later,* I think, as Farley approaches with a few Command generals in tow. Swan nods in greeting, bowing her head.

I extend a hand to her, nodding. "Thank you, General Swan."

"Call me Addison," she replies. The older woman matches my smile. "I think we might be able to do away with code names for a while."

Farley just glances between us, pretending to be annoyed.

"If only this jet were powered by hot air. We'd never have to charge up between the two of you," she says sharply, her eyes betraying one of her rare good moods.

Smiling, I take her arm. She leans into the embrace. Hardly like her at all. "You act like I can't actually charge a jet, Farley."

She only rolls her eyes. Like Kilorn and me, she's ready to go back to Montfort. I can only imagine how excited she must be to leave Norta behind, and return to her daughter. Clara is growing bigger in leaps and bounds, happy and safe. With no memory of what came before her.

Not even her father.

The thought of Shade always darkens even the brightest of days, and now is no different. But the pain is less somehow. Still an ache, still bone-deep, but not so sharp. It doesn't take my breath away anymore.

"Come on," Farley urges, forcing me to match her quicker pace. "The faster we board, the faster we're airborne."

"Is that how it works?" I can't help but retort.

A cluster of people stands by the jet idling on the runway, waiting for us and the rest of the group departing for Montfort today. Davidson is already gone, having returned to his nation a few days ago. Some of his officials have been left behind to coordinate, and I spot Tahir among them. He's probably relaying all this to his brothers right now, allowing the Montfort premier to track the rebuilding process in real time.

Julian stands out from the pack, wearing new clothes for what is possibly the first time in his life. They gleam, golden like his house colors once were, flashing brightly in the late afternoon sun. Sara waits at his side, as does Anabel. The old woman looks incomplete without her crown, and she regards me with naked disinterest.

"Make it quick, Barrow," Farley says, gesturing for Kilorn to follow her onto the jet. The pair of them nod at the Silvers as they pass, giving me the space I need for my own farewells.

I don't see Cal with his uncle or grandmother, but I don't expect him to stand in line. He waits farther down the jetway, separated from the rest of them.

Julian extends his arms to me and I embrace him tightly, inhaling the warm scent of old paper that still seems to cling to him through everything.

After a long minute, he pushes me back gently. "Oh, come on, I'll see you in a month or so."

Like Cameron, Julian is scheduled to visit Montfort in a few weeks. Officially, he's an envoy of the Nortan Silvers. But I expect he'll spend more time combing through whatever archives Davidson puts at his disposal, utilizing the time to investigate the emergence of newbloods.

I grin up at my old teacher, patting him on the shoulder. "I doubt you'll be able to tear yourself out of the Montfort vaults long enough to say hello."

At his side, Sara raises her head. "I'll make sure he does," she says quietly, taking Julian's arm.

Anabel is not so understanding. She glares at me one last time before scoffing aloud, disgusted by my presence, and walking off at a brisk pace. I don't blame her. After all, in her eyes, I'm still the reason her grandson denied a dynasty, cast away a crown for something as stupid as the love of a Red girl.

She hates me for that. Even if it isn't true.

"Anabel Lerolan may not see reason, but she does see logic. You've opened a door that can't be closed," Julian says quietly, watching the old queen clamber into a waiting transport. "She couldn't put Cal back on the throne now, even if he wanted it."

"What about the Rift? The Lakelands? Piedmont?"

Julian cuts me off with a gentle shake of his head. "I think you've earned the right to not worry about such things for a while." He pats my hand kindly. "There's rioting; there's movement, Reds crossing our borders by the thousands. Know the stone is truly rolling, my dear."

For a second, I feel overcome. Equal parts happy and afraid. *This can't last,* I think again, knowing the words to be true. Sighing, I let go of them. This isn't over, but it is for me. For now.

I have to hug Julian one more time. "Thank you," I whisper.

Again he pushes me back, his eyes shiny. "Yes, well—enough of that. My ego's already bigger than it should be," he stammers out. "You've wasted enough time with me," he adds, giving me another push. In the direction of his nephew. "Go on."

I don't need any more prodding than that, in spite of the nerves currently wreaking havoc on me. Gulping a little, I pass the rest of the dignitaries from our reforged alliance, smiling as I go. No one stops me, allowing me to approach the former king unimpeded.

Cal feels me coming. "Let's walk," he says, already moving. I follow him under one of the wings of our jet, stepping into shadow. Farther down the runway, an engine roars to life, close enough to shield us from anyone who might bother to eavesdrop.

"I'd come with you if I could," he says suddenly, turning around to watch me with burning eyes of bronze.

"I'm not asking you to do that," I reply. The words are familiar. We've had the same discussion about a dozen times by now. "You have to be here, to pick up the pieces. And there's work to be done in the west. Ciron, Tiraxes—if we can do something . . ." I trail off, imagining those far-off countries, vast and strange. "It's better this way, I think."

"*Better?*" Cal snaps, and the air warms around him. Gently, I put a hand on his wrist. "You think walking away is *better*? Why? I'm not a king anymore. I'm not even royal. I'm—"

"Don't say 'nothing,' Cal. You're not nothing."

I see accusation in his eyes, his skin hot beneath my fingers. It hurts to look at him, to see the pain I'm causing.

"I'm what you want me to be," he forces out, his voice a little stran-gled.

I'm seized by the realization that I don't know when I'll see him again. But I can't look back up. It will just make this more difficult.

"Don't pretend like you gave all this up because I asked you to. We both know that isn't what happened." *For your mother, for what is right. For yourself.* "And I'm glad for it," I mutter, still staring at his hand in mine.

He tries to pull me closer, but I stand my ground.

"I need time, Cal. So do you."

His voice drops so low he could be growling. It makes me shiver. "I decide what I want and need."

"Then give me the same courtesy." Without thinking, I look back up sharply, surprising him. Even though I feel anything but strong, I play the part well. "Let me figure out who I am now."

Not Mareena, not the lightning girl. Not even Mare Barrow. But whoever came out on the other side of all this. He needs space too, whether he can admit it or not. *We* need to heal. Rebuild. Just like this country, and the rest that might follow.

Worst of all, best of all—we have to do it without each other.

There's still a gap between us, a rift. Even in death, Maven is good at keeping us apart. Cal will never admit it, but I saw the resentment in his eyes that day. The sorrow and accusation. I killed his brother, and that weighs on him still. I know it weighs on me.

Cal searches my eyes, his own flashing as the sunlight above us turns red. His eyes could be made of flame.

Whatever he's looking for, a weakness, a crack in my resolve—he doesn't find it.

One blazing hand trails up my neck, until it stills at the side of my jaw, fingers resting behind my ear. His skin isn't hot enough to burn, not like Maven's, which marked me forever. Cal wouldn't do that, even if I asked him to.

"How long?" he whispers.

"I don't know." It's the truth, easy to admit. I have no idea how long it will take to feel like myself again, or whoever I am now. But I am only eighteen. I have time.

The next part is far more difficult, and my breath hitches. "I won't ask you to wait for me."

When his lips brush mine, the touch is fleeting, a farewell.

For however long it takes.

The Paradise Valley is well named. It stretches for miles, a rolling plain in the bowl of the mountains. The rivers and lakes are pristine and strange, unlike any place I've ever seen before. Not to mention the wildlife. No wonder Davidson sent us here for a little peace and quiet. It seems untouched, removed from the rest of the world.

We walk the path at dawn, careful to keep away from the red-hot geyser fields running the length of the clearing. Most of the watery pools are still and flat, but they spiral in a rainbow of colors. Beautiful but deadly, able to cook a person in a matter of seconds. Or so I've been told. In the distance, one of them spits boiling water and clouds of steam high into the hazy purple sky. The stars fade one by one. It's cold, and I pull the heavy wool shawl tighter around my shoulders. Our footsteps echo against the wooden walkway beneath us, built up and over the rust-colored basin floor.

I glance at Gisa sidelong, watching her keep stride. She's more willowy these days, and her dark red hair hangs in a long braid. The breakfast basket dangles in her hand, swinging idly. She wanted to watch the sun rise over the big spring, and who am I to deny my little sister anything?

"Look at the colors," she murmurs as we reach our destination. Indeed, the big hot spring looks like something out of a dream. Ringed in red, then yellow, then bright green, and finally the deepest, purest blue, it doesn't seem real.

We were well warned, and in spite of the urge, neither of us dips a finger in the waters below. I don't fancy boiling the skin off my bones. Instead Gisa sits down on the walkway, her legs folded beneath herself. She pulls out a tiny notebook and starts to sketch, occasionally scribbling notes.

I wonder what this place might inspire in her.

I'm more inclined to eat, and I fish through the basket, pulling out a pair of still-warm breakfast rolls. Mom made sure we were well provisioned before we set off for the morning.

"Do you miss him?" she says suddenly, not looking up.

The question catches me off guard, especially the vagueness. She could be talking about anybody. "Kilorn is fine. He's back in Ascendant, and Cameron will be there in a few days."

Gisa doesn't mind the thought of someone else with Kilorn. She cares more for the pretty shopgirl back in the city, these days.

"I don't mean Kilorn," she says pointedly, annoyed with my dodging.

"Oh?" I ask, raising an eyebrow dramatically.

She doesn't seem amused.

"Of course I miss him."

I mean Cal. I mean Shade. I mean Maven, even in the smallest of pieces.

Gisa doesn't press me further.

The silence feeds me as much as the breakfast. It's easy to forget out here. To feel lost in another time. I relish the detachment, even with the usual worries clinging to the corners of my mind. *What happens now?* I still haven't figured that out.

And, for a little while, I don't have to.

"Bison," Gisa says softly, raising a hand to point across the geyser basin.

I tense up, ready to spring. If one of those beasts gets too close, it'll be my responsibility to get Gisa out of here safely. My lightning prickles beneath my skin, ready to unleash. It feels almost unfamiliar these days. I haven't been training or sparring, not since we returned to Montfort. I keep telling myself I need the rest. Bree and Tramy keep telling me I'm lazy.

The bison are far off, fifty yards at least, and lumbering slowly in the opposite direction. The herd is small but impressive, a dozen at least, all shaggy and dark brown, moving with surprising grace for things so big and heavy. I remember my last encounter with a bison. It wasn't exactly peaceful.

Gisa returns to her sketch, thoughtful. "Davidson's guide told me something interesting." The premier was good enough to send an escort with us into the valley.

"Oh, what's that?" I ask, not taking my eyes off the herd. If they bolt, I'll be ready.

My sister continues to chatter, oblivious to the possible threat currently picking its way across the basin. I'm quietly happy that she doesn't know enough to be afraid. "She said that once, the bison were almost gone. Thousands upon thousands hunted and killed, maybe millions, until only a few were left on the entire continent."

"That's impossible," I scoff. "They're all over Paradise, and the plains."

"Well, that's what the guide said," Gisa replies, sounding annoyed by my dismissal. "And it's her job to know what goes on up here."

"Fine," I sigh. "So what happened?"

"They came back. Slowly, but they came back."

My brow furrows, confused by the simplicity of her answer. "How?"

"People," she says bluntly.

"I thought the people killed them—"

"They did, but something changed," she replied, her voice sharpening. Now I think she despairs of my comprehension. "Something big enough to . . . change course."

I don't know why, but I'm reminded of something Julian taught me once, long ago.

We destroy. It's the constant of our kind.

I've seen that firsthand. In Archeon, in Harbor Bay, on every battlefield. In the way Reds were treated and are still treated across the continent.

But that world is changing.

We destroy, but we also rebuild.

The bison move off, slowly disappearing into the trees on the horizon. Seeking new grasslands, oblivious to two small girls sitting at the edge of the water.

They returned from slaughter. So will we.

As we make our way back to the cabin, now sweating beneath the heat of the rising sun, Gisa chatters on about everything she's learned in the past week. She likes the guide, and I think Bree does too, in more ways than one.

My mind wanders, as it usually does in these small moments. Drifting back through memory, and forward too. We'll return to the Montfort capital in a few weeks. I wonder how different the world will be by then. It was already unrecognizable when we left. *Evangeline Samos*, of all people, was living in Ascendant, last I heard, as an honored guest of the premier. Part of me still hates her, and her family, for all they took from us. But I'm learning to live with the anger, to keep it close without letting it eat me alive.

Slowly, I touch the stones pierced along my ear, naming each one in turn. They ground me. Pink, red, purple, green. Bree, Tramy, Shade, Kilorn.

I couldn't stay, I think again, for the thousandth time. I still don't know if he'll wait for me.

But maybe, when I go back . . .

My fingers brush the last earring, the newest. It's another red gem, red as fire, red as my blood.

I will go back.

ACKNOWLEDGMENTS

People keep asking what it feels like to finish a book series, and I keep telling people that I'm waiting to feel something. I thought the experience left me numb, but the sensations of *something* are creeping up. Relief, of course. Anxiety. Fear. But most of all, gratitude. So much gratitude I can barely even make sense of it.

My deepest and most sincere thanks go to my family, for making the beginning, middle, and end of all this possible. It's easy to look back and see the moments where my life changed, and you were integral to each. Thank you to Mom, Dad, and Andy, to the Aveyards and the Coyles, for everything you've done for me, and will continue to do.

I refuse to get sappy or emotional while thanking my friends, largely because they won't tolerate it. Thank you to Morgan, Jen, and Tori for making sure I never get in too deep. Thank you to Bayan and Angela, to Natalie, to Lauren, to Alex. Thank you to all the rest, too many to name. We've been going to the same party for seven years and that is in no way depressing.

Indy is a dog, so this is kind of useless, but thank you. You're the best girl. I love you more than is socially acceptable or psychologically healthy.

This series has occupied almost six years of my life, and landed me a career I used to dream about. And the books themselves would not exist without some tremendous people who pushed us both along. Thank you to Christopher Cosmos, Pouya Shahbazian, and Suzie Townsend for sparking everything, no pun intended, and keeping this train rolling as smoothly as it can. Thank you to Jo Volpe, Kathleen Ortiz, Veronica Grijalva, Sara Stricker, Mia Roman, Danielle Barthel, Jackie Lindert, Cassandra Baim, Hilary Pecheone, and the rest of the dynamite team at New Leaf Literary. Thank you to Sara Scott, Max Handelman, Elizabeth Banks, Alison Small, and all the heroes of Universal Pictures and Brownstone Productions. Thank you for loving these books as much as we do. All my love to the army at HarperCollins and HarperTeen, doing battle for Red Queen for so long. Thank you to my fearless, ferociously talented editors, Kristen Pettit and Alice Jerman, as well as Jen Klonsky, Kate Morgan Jackson, Erica Sussman, and every person who ever put a fingerprint on an Aveyard manuscript. You've made these books what they are. Thank you to Gina Rizzo, who has now successfully guided me through four years of festivals, tours, interviews, and too many airports to count. Thank you to Elizabeth Ward, Margot Wood, Elena Yip, the Epic Reads crew, and all the geniuses behind the Red Queen campaigns over the years. Never thought I'd have a foam sword with my book on it, but here I am. And of course, thank you to Sarah Kaufman for turning what I saw in my head into the most beautiful and iconic covers any author could ask for.

I've been lucky enough to gain some friends out of my excellent colleagues. You've all been wonderful support in what is a truly weird career. Love and thanks to my Patties, Susan Dennard, Alex Bracken, and Leigh Bardugo, for sharing their friendship, talent, and advice. To Renee Ahdieh and Sabaa Tahir, stars from the start. To Veronica Roth, a beacon. To Brendan Reichs and Soman Chainani, for putting up with me. To Jenny Han, fearlessly leading the way. To Emma Theriault, who helped will this series into being. To Adam Silvera, for suffering four hours of mimosas and not running away from me. To Nicola Yoon, for your steadfast kindness. To Sarah Enni and Maurene Goo, my bright lights east of the 405. To Morgan Matson, for 'bux. To Margaret Stohl and Melissa de la Cruz, dear YALL moms to us all. And to everyone I've left out entirely by accident, but I love and thank you just the same.

I would not be here without my teachers. Quite literally, because my parents are teachers. Thank you to the public school system that launched me out of a small town and into the big city. Thank you to the University of Southern California and the professors in the Writing for Screen & Television division of the School of Cinematic Arts, who saw something in a seventeen-year-old nobody from nowhere. One of my favorite professors once told me that good luck is an opportunity you are prepared for, and bad luck is an opportunity you aren't. Thank you for giving me so much good luck.

Outside my small sphere of great people, I have others I'd like to thank as well. Thank you to my senators, Kamala Harris and Dianne Feinstein, as well as my congressional representative, Ted Lieu. You fight more than any warrior in my books, and you fight for all of us. Thank you to President Barack Obama and Michelle Obama, for their grace and strength. Thank you to Hillary Rodham Clinton, a pinnacle. Thank you to the Sierra Club and the indigenous tribes standing up to protect the beautiful, sacred, and wild lands of the United States. Thank you to the members of our government working to serve your constituents over corporations. Thank you to those in uniform and your families for their unfathomable sacrifice and dedication to our country. Thank you to all speaking truth to power.

Thank you to the student survivors of Marjory Stoneman Douglas High School. Your voices and your convictions are doing more than anyone ever imagined.

Once more, thank you to Morgan, Jen, and Tori. To Suzie Townsend. To Mom and Dad. I love you all so much and would not be here without you.

To my readers, there is very little I can say to explain the depth of my awe and gratitude. To quote a much greater writer than me, no story lives unless someone wants to listen. Thank you for listening. Thank you for making sure this journey has not yet ended.

A thank you from Victoria Aveyard

I can't express how much it means to have readers at all,
let alone readers all around the world. The United Kingdom has a
very special place in my heart. I love your country and all of you so
much. It's fantastic to feel that love in return from you. Thank you
from the bottom of my heart for following my little tale of blood,
rebellion, and the storm that resides in all of us. I hope you
enjoyed the ending, and I hope you continue to listen
to the stories I can't wait to tell.